Fairy Tales

Hans Christian Andersen

Reprint 2023

FiNGERPRINT! CLASSICS
An imprint of Prakash Books India Pvt. Ltd.

113/A, Darya Ganj,
New Delhi-110 002
Tel: (011) 2324 7062 – 65, Fax: (011) 2324 6975
Email: info@prakashbooks.com/sales@prakashbooks.com

www.facebook.com/fingerprintpublishing
www.twitter.com/FingerprintP
www.fingerprintpublishing.com

ISBN: 978 93 8836 972 5

Processed & printed in India

Hans Christian Andersen was born on April 2, 1805, in Odense, Denmark. He was introduced to literature by his father who read *Arabian Nights* to him. Andersen's fantasies and imaginations began taking shape when he visited a theatre in Odense at the age of seven.

He received his education from a local school for poor children and worked as a weaver's, and later as a tailor's, apprentice to support himself. In 1819, the fourteen-year-old Andersen travelled to Copenhagen to find work at The Royal Theatre. For the next couple of years, he tried to obtain a position and be successful as a soprano, an actor or dancer, and also began writing.

The director of the theatre arranged for him to be formally educated. Andersen published his first story, 'The Ghost at Palnatoke's Grave', in 1822. In 1827, his poems were published in *Kjøbenhavns flyvende Post*, a famous literary journal. His short story 'A Journey on Foot from Holmen's Canal to the East Point of Amager', his first play—*Love on St. Nicholas Church Tower*, and a volume of poems, all brought him considerable success in 1829.

At twenty-eight, Andersen was given a travel grant by the king and he travelled to Europe. His journeys through Switzerland and Italy inspired his works. He published his first novel, *The Improvisatore*, in 1835. Andersen began writing fairy tales, which were based on the folk tales he had heard as a child. *Fairy Tales Told for Children. First Collection. (Eventyr, fortalte for Børn. Første Samling.)*, a collection of nine tales, was published in three instalments in Copenhagen, Denmark, between 1835 and 1837. It included 'The Tinder-box', 'The Princess and the Pea', 'Little Claus and Big Claus', 'Thumbelina', and 'The Emperor's New Clothes' among other stories. These were not very successful initially.

Andersen's novels *O.T.* (1836) and *Only a Fiddler* (1837) were extremely well-received and translated into various languages including German, English, and Swedish. He received the standard royal literary scholarship in 1838. The same year, he began writing the second series of fairy tales. Andersen published the *Picture Book without Pictures* in 1840. By now, he had become well known throughout Europe. Another series of fairy tales was published in 1844, and in 1845, translations of his fairy tales appeared. Andersen never ceased writing fairy tales.

In Sweden (1851), *Shadow Pictures of a Journey to the Harz, A Poet's Bazaar,* and *A Visit to Portugal in 1866* are some of Andersen's travelogues which were widely acclaimed. He visited England in 1847 and met Charles Dickens there. They read and respected each other's work, which had in common the depictions of the lives of the poor and underclass who were affected by the Industrial Revolution and poverty.

Andersen's last fairy tales were published in 1872. He died on August 4, 1875. Admired and respected throughout the world, his fairy tales have continued to be a part of every child's growing up years. They have been adapted into numerous animated films time and again and have also been an inspiration for several children's classics. Andersen's unrestrained imagination continues to inspire and fire the imagination of young and old alike.

Contents

The Tinder-Box	11
Little Claus and Big Claus	19
The Princess and the Pea	30
Little Ida's Flowers	33
Thumbelina	41
The Naughty Boy	51
The Travelling Companion	54
The Little Mermaid	72
The Emperor's New Clothes	95
The Goloshes of Fortune	101
The Daisy	130
The Steadfast Tin Soldier	134
The Wild Swans	139
The Elf of the Rose	154

The Garden of Paradise	159
The Flying Trunk	173
The Storks	180
What the Moon Saw	186
The Wicked Prince	227
The Sandman	230
The Swineherd	242
The Buckwheat	248
The Metal Pig	250
The Shepherd's Story of the Bond of Friendship	260
A Rose from Homer's Grave	268
The Angel	270
The Nightingale	273
The Top and Ball	282
The Ugly Duckling	285
The Fir Tree	295
The Snow Queen	304
The Little Elder-Tree Mother	335
The Elfin Hill	343
The Red Shoes	350
The Jumper	357
The Shepherdess and the Chimney-Sweep	360
Holger Danske	366
The Bell	372
Grandmother	377

The Darning-Needle	380
The Little Match Girl	384
By the Almshouse Window	388
The Old Street Lamp	391
Little Tuk	398
The Shadow	404
The Old House	416
The Drop of Water	424
The Happy Family	426
The Story of a Mother	430
The Shirt Collar	437
The Phœnix Bird	440
The Loveliest Rose in the World	442
In a Thousand Years	445
The Swan's Nest	448
The Old Grave-Stone	450
The Goblin and The Huckster	454
Under the Willow Tree	458
Jack the Dullard	474
The Last Pearl	480
A Leaf from the Sky	483
Two Maidens	486
Ib and Little Christine	489
The Thorny Road of Honour	502
The Bell Deep	507

The Bottle Neck	511
The Old Bachelor's Nightcap	521
The Last Dream of the Old Oak Tree: A Christmas Tale	536
The Marsh King's Daughter	542
The Girl who Trod on the Loaf	579
Ole The Tower-Keeper	588
Anne Lisbeth	598
Children's Prattle	611
The Pen and the Inkstand	614
The Farm-Yard Cock and the Weathercock	617
A Story from the Sand-Dunes	620
The Butterfly	652
The Bishop of Börglum and His Warriors	655
What the Old Man does is Always Right	662
The Snow Man	668
In the Duck-Yard	674
The Ice Maiden	681
The Snail and the Rose-Tree	732
The Old Church Bell	735
The Silver Shilling	741
The Snowdrop	746
The Teapot	750
"The Will-o'-the-Wisp is in the Town," says the Moor-Woman	752
The Windmill	764

Our Aunt	767
The Toad	773
The Dryad	781
The Court Cards	801
Good Luck Can Lie in a Pin	806
Sunshine Stories	809
The Thistle's Experiences	813
The Candles	818
Danish Popular Legends	821
The Great Sea-Serpent	829
The Gardener and the Manor	838
The Gate Key	845
The Flea and the Professor	856
The Pea Blossom	861

The Tinder-Box

Translated by Mrs. H. P. Paull

A soldier came marching along the high road: "Left, right—left, right." He had his knapsack on his back, and a sword at his side; he had been to the wars, and was now returning home.

As he walked on, he met a very frightful-looking old witch in the road. Her under-lip hung quite down on her breast, and she stopped and said, "Good evening, soldier; you have a very fine sword, and a large knapsack, and you are a real soldier; so you shall have as much money as ever you like."

"Thank you, old witch," said the soldier.

"Do you see that large tree," said the witch, pointing to a tree which stood beside them. "Well, it is quite hollow inside, and you must climb to the top, when you will see a hole, through which you can let yourself down into the tree to a great depth. I will tie a rope round your body, so that I can pull you up again when you call out to me."

"But what am I to do, down there in the tree?" asked the soldier.

"Get money," she replied; "for you must know that when you reach the ground under the tree, you will find yourself in a large hall, lighted up by three hundred lamps; you will then see three doors, which can be easily opened, for the keys are in all the locks. On entering the first of the chambers, to which these doors lead, you will see a large chest, standing in the middle of the floor, and upon it a dog seated, with a pair of eyes as large as teacups. But you need not be at all afraid of him; I will give you my blue checked apron, which you must spread upon the floor, and then boldly seize hold of the dog, and place him upon it. You can then open the chest, and take from it as many pence as you please, they are only copper pence; but if you would rather have silver money, you must go into the second chamber. Here you will find another dog, with eyes as big as mill-wheels; but do not let that trouble you. Place him upon my apron, and then take what money you please. If, however, you like gold best, enter the third chamber, where there is another chest full of it. The dog who sits on this chest is very dreadful; his eyes are as big as a tower, but do not mind him. If he also is placed upon my apron, he cannot hurt you, and you may take from the chest what gold you will."

"This is not a bad story," said the soldier; "but what am I to give you, you old witch? for, of course, you do not mean to tell me all this for nothing."

"No," said the witch; "but I do not ask for a single penny. Only promise to bring me an old tinder-box, which my grandmother left behind the last time she went down there."

"Very well; I promise. Now tie the rope round my body."

"Here it is," replied the witch; "and here is my blue checked apron."

As soon as the rope was tied, the soldier climbed up the tree, and let himself down through the hollow to the ground beneath; and here he found, as the witch had told him, a large hall, in which many hundred lamps were all burning. Then he opened the first door. "Ah!" there sat the dog, with the eyes as large as teacups, staring at him.

"You're a pretty fellow," said the soldier, seizing him, and placing him on the witch's apron, while he filled his pockets from the chest with as many pieces as they would hold. Then he closed the lid, seated the dog upon it again, and walked into another chamber. And, sure enough, there sat the dog with eyes as big as mill-wheels.

"You had better not look at me in that way," said the soldier; "you will make your eyes water;" and then he seated him also upon the apron, and opened the chest. But when he saw what a quantity of silver money it contained, he very quickly threw away all the coppers he had taken, and filled his pockets and his knapsack with nothing but silver.

Then he went into the third room, and there the dog was really hideous; his eyes were, truly, as big as towers, and they turned round and round in his head like wheels.

"Good morning," said the soldier, touching his cap, for he had never seen such a dog in his life. But after looking at him more closely, he thought he had been civil enough, so he placed him on the floor, and opened the chest. Good gracious, what a quantity of gold there was! enough to buy all the sugar-sticks of the sweet-stuff women; all the tin soldiers, whips, and rocking-horses in the world, or even the whole town itself. There was, indeed, an immense quantity. So the soldier now threw away all the silver money he had taken, and filled his pockets and his knapsack with gold instead; and not only his pockets and his knapsack, but even his cap and boots, so that he could scarcely walk.

He was really rich now; so he replaced the dog on the chest, closed the door, and called up through the tree, "Now pull me out, you old witch."

"Have you got the tinder-box?" asked the witch.

"No; I declare I quite forgot it." So he went back and fetched the Tinder-box, and then the witch drew him up out of the tree, and he stood again in the high road, with his pockets, his knapsack, his cap, and his boots full of gold.

"What are you going to do with the tinder-box?" asked the soldier.

"That is nothing to you," replied the witch; "you have the money, now give me the tinder-box."

"I tell you what," said the soldier, "if you don't tell me what you are going to do with it, I will draw my sword and cut off your head."

"No," said the witch.

The soldier immediately cut off her head, and there she lay on the ground. Then he tied up all his money in her apron, and slung it on his back like a bundle, put the Tinder-box in his pocket, and walked off to the nearest town. It was a very nice town, and he put up at the best inn, and ordered a dinner of all his favourite dishes, for now he was rich and had plenty of money.

The servant, who cleaned his boots, thought they certainly were a shabby pair to be worn by such a rich gentleman, for he had not yet bought any new ones. The next day, however, he procured some good clothes and proper boots, so that our soldier soon became known as a fine gentleman, and the people visited him, and told him all the wonders that were to be seen in the town, and of the king's beautiful daughter, the princess.

"Where can I see her?" asked the soldier.

"She is not to be seen at all," they said; "she lives in a large copper castle, surrounded by walls and towers. No one but the king himself can pass in or out, for there has been a prophecy that she will marry a common soldier, and the king cannot bear to think of such a marriage."

"I should like very much to see her," thought the soldier; but he could not obtain permission to do so. However, he passed a very pleasant time; went to the theatre, drove in the king's garden, and gave a great deal of money to the poor, which was very good of him; he remembered what it had been in olden times to be without a shilling. Now he was rich, had fine clothes, and many friends, who all declared he was a fine fellow and a real gentleman, and all this gratified him exceedingly. But his money would not last forever; and as he spent and gave away a great deal daily, and received none, he found himself at last with only two shillings left. So he was obliged to leave his elegant rooms, and live in a little garret under the roof, where he had to clean his own boots, and even mend them with a large needle. None of his friends came to see him, there were too many stairs to mount up. One dark evening, he had not even a penny to buy a candle; then all at once he remembered that there was a piece of candle stuck in the tinder-box, which he had brought from the old tree, into which the witch had helped him.

He found the tinder-box, but no sooner had he struck a few sparks from the flint and steel, than the door flew open and the dog with eyes as big as teacups, whom he had seen while down in the tree, stood before him, and said, "What orders, master?"

"Hallo," said the soldier; "well this is a pleasant Tinder-box, if it brings me all I wish for."

"Bring me some money," said he to the dog.

He was gone in a moment, and presently returned, carrying a large bag of coppers in his mouth. The soldier very soon discovered after this the value of the tinder-box. If he struck the flint once, the dog who sat on the chest of copper money made his appearance; if twice, the dog came from the chest of silver; and if three times, the dog with eyes like towers, who watched over the gold. The soldier had now plenty of money; he returned to his elegant rooms, and reappeared in his fine clothes, so that his friends knew him again directly, and made as much of him as before.

After a while he began to think it was very strange that no one could get a look at the princess. "Every one says she is very beautiful," thought he to himself; "but what is the use of that if she is to be shut up in a copper castle surrounded by so many towers. Can I by any means get to see her. Stop! where is my tinder-box?" Then he struck a light, and in a moment the dog, with eyes as big as teacups, stood before him.

"It is midnight," said the soldier, "yet I should very much like to see the princess, if only for a moment."

The dog disappeared instantly, and before the soldier could even look round, he returned with the princess. She was lying on the dog's back asleep, and looked so lovely, that every one who saw her would know she was a real princess. The soldier could not help kissing her, true soldier as he was. Then the dog ran back with the princess; but in the morning, while at breakfast with the king and queen, she told them what a singular dream she had had during the night, of a dog and a soldier, that she had ridden on the dog's back, and been kissed by the soldier.

"That is a very pretty story, indeed," said the queen. So the next night one of the old ladies of the court was set to watch by the princess's bed, to discover whether it really was a dream, or what else it might be.

The soldier longed very much to see the princess once more, so he sent for the dog again in the night to fetch her, and to run with her as fast as ever he could. But the old lady put on water boots, and ran after him as quickly as he did, and found that he carried the princess into a large house. She thought it would help her to remember the place if she made a large cross on the door with a piece of chalk. Then she went home to bed, and the dog presently returned with the princess. But when he saw that a cross had been made on the door of the house, where the soldier lived, he took another piece of chalk and made crosses on all the doors in the town, so that the lady-in-waiting might not be able to find out the right door.

Early the next morning the king and queen accompanied the lady and all the officers of the household, to see where the princess had been.

"Here it is," said the king, when they came to the first door with a cross on it.

No, my dear husband, it must be that one," said the queen, pointing to a second door having a cross also.

"And here is one, and there is another!" they all exclaimed; for there were crosses on all the doors in every direction.

The Tinder-Box

So they felt it would be useless to search any farther. But the queen was a very clever woman; she could do a great deal more than merely ride in a carriage. She took her large gold scissors, cut a piece of silk into squares, and made a neat little bag. This bag she filled with buckwheat flour, and tied it round the princess's neck; and then she cut a small hole in the bag, so that the flour might be scattered on the ground as the princess went along. During the night, the dog came again and carried the princess on his back, and ran with her to the soldier, who loved her very much, and wished that he had been a prince, so that he might have her for a wife. The dog did not observe how the flour ran out of the bag all the way from the castle wall to the soldier's house, and even up to the window, where he had climbed with the princess. Therefore in the morning the king and queen found out where their daughter had been, and the soldier was taken up and put in prison. Oh, how dark and disagreeable it was as he sat there, and the people said to him, "Tomorrow you will be hanged." It was not very pleasant news, and besides, he had left the tinder-box at the inn. In the morning he could see through the iron grating of the little window how the people were hastening out of the town to see him hanged; he heard the drums beating, and saw the soldiers marching. Every one ran out to look at them. and a shoemaker's boy, with a leather apron and slippers on, galloped by so fast, that one of his slippers flew off and struck against the wall where the soldier sat looking through the iron grating. "Hallo, you shoemaker's boy, you need not be in such a hurry," cried the soldier to him. "There will be nothing to see till I come; but if you will run to the house where I have been living, and bring me my tinder-box, you shall have four shillings, but you must put your best foot foremost."

The shoemaker's boy liked the idea of getting the four shillings, so he ran very fast and fetched the tinder-box, and gave it to the soldier. And now we shall see what happened. Outside the town a large gibbet had been erected, round which stood the soldiers and several thousands of people. The king and the queen sat on splendid thrones opposite to the judges and the whole council. The soldier already stood on the ladder; but as they were about to place the rope around his neck, he said that an innocent request was often granted to a poor criminal before he suffered death. He wished very much to smoke a pipe, as it would be the last pipe he should ever smoke in the world. The king could not refuse this request, so the soldier took his tinder-box, and struck fire, once, twice, thrice—and there in a moment stood all the dogs—the one with eyes as big as teacups, the one with eyes as large as mill-wheels, and the third, whose eyes were like towers. "Help me now, that I may not be hanged," cried the soldier.

And the dogs fell upon the judges and all the councillors; seized one by the legs, and another by the nose, and tossed them many feet high in the air, so that they fell down and were dashed to pieces.

"I will not be touched," said the king. But the largest dog seized him, as well as the queen, and threw them after the others. Then the soldiers and all the people were afraid, and cried, "Good soldier, you shall be our king, and you shall marry the beautiful princess."

So they placed the soldier in the king's carriage, and the three dogs ran on in front and cried "Hurrah!" and the little boys whistled through their fingers, and the soldiers presented arms. The princess came out of the copper castle, and became queen, which was very pleasing to her. The wedding festivities lasted a whole week, and the dogs sat at the table, and stared with all their eyes.

Little Claus and Big Claus

Translated by Mrs. H. P. Paull

In a village there once lived two men who had the same name. They were both called Claus. One of them had four horses, but the other had only one; so to distinguish them, people called the owner of the four horses, "Great Claus," and he who had only one, "Little Claus." Now we shall hear what happened to them, for this is a true story.

Through the whole week, Little Claus was obliged to plough for Great Claus, and lend him his one horse; and once a week, on a Sunday, Great Claus lent him all his four horses. Then how Little Claus would smack his whip over all five horses, they were as good as his own on that one day. The sun shone brightly, and the church bells were ringing merrily as the people passed by, dressed in their best clothes, with their prayer-books under their arms. They were going to hear the clergyman preach. They looked at Little Claus ploughing with his five horses, and he was so proud that he smacked his whip, and said, "Gee-up, my five horses."

"You must not say that," said Big Claus; "for only one of them belongs to you." But Little Claus soon forgot what he ought to say, and when any one passed he would call out, "Gee-up, my five horses!"

"Now I must beg you not to say that again," said Big Claus; "for if you do, I shall hit your horse on the head, so that he will drop dead on the spot, and there will be an end of him."

"I promise you I will not say it any more," said the other; but as soon as people came by, nodding to him, and wishing him "Good day," he became so pleased, and thought how grand it looked to have five horses ploughing in his field, that he cried out again, "Gee-up, all my horses!"

"I'll Gee-up your horses for you," said Big Claus; and seizing a hammer, he struck the one horse of Little Claus on the head, and he fell dead instantly.

"Oh, now I have no horse at all," said Little Claus, weeping. But after a while he took off the dead horse's skin, and hung the hide to dry in the wind. Then he put the dry skin into a bag, and, placing it over his shoulder, went out into the next town to sell the horse's skin. He had a very long way to go, and had to pass through a dark, gloomy forest. Presently a storm arose, and he lost his way, and before he discovered the right path, evening came on, and it was still a long way to the town, and too far to return home before night. Near the road stood a large farmhouse. The shutters outside the windows were closed, but lights shone through the crevices at the top. "I might get permission to stay here for the night," thought Little Claus; so he went up to the door and knocked. The farmer's wife opened the door; but when she heard what he wanted, she told him to go away, as her husband would not allow her to admit strangers. "Then I shall be obliged to lie out here," said Little Claus to himself, as the farmer's wife shut the door in his face. Near to the farmhouse stood a large haystack, and between it and the house was a small shed, with a thatched roof. "I can lie up there," said Little Claus, as he saw the roof; "it will make a famous bed, but I hope the stork will not fly down and bite my legs;" for on it stood a living stork, whose nest was in the roof. So Little Claus climbed to the roof of the shed, and while he turned himself to get comfortable, he discovered that the wooden shutters, which were closed, did not reach to the tops of the windows of the farmhouse, so that he could see into a room, in which a large table was laid out with wine, roast meat, and a splendid fish. The farmer's wife and the sexton were sitting at the table together; and she filled his glass, and helped him plenteously to fish, which appeared to be his favourite dish. "If I could only get some, too," thought Little Claus; and then, as he stretched his neck towards the window he spied a large, beautiful pie—indeed they had a glorious feast before them.

At this moment he heard some one riding down the road, towards the farmhouse. It was the farmer returning home. He was a good man, but still he had a very strange prejudice—he could not bear the sight of a sexton. If one appeared before him, he would put himself in a terrible rage. In consequence of this dislike, the sexton had gone to visit the farmer's wife during her husband's absence from home, and the good woman had placed before him the best she had in the house to eat. When she heard the farmer coming she was frightened, and begged the sexton to hide himself in a large empty chest that stood in the room. He did so, for he knew her husband could not endure the sight of a sexton. The woman then quickly put away the wine, and hid all the rest of the nice things in the oven; for if her husband had seen them he would have asked what they were brought out for.

"Oh, dear," sighed Little Claus from the top of the shed, as he saw all the good things disappear.

"Is any one up there?" asked the farmer, looking up and discovering Little Claus. "Why are you lying up there? Come down, and come into the house with me." So Little Claus came down and told the farmer how he had lost his way and begged for a night's lodging.

"All right," said the farmer; "but we must have something to eat first."

The woman received them both very kindly, laid the cloth on a large table, and placed before them a dish of porridge. The farmer was very hungry, and ate his porridge with a good appetite, but Little Claus could not help thinking of the nice roast meat, fish and pies, which he knew were in the oven. Under the table, at his feet, lay the sack containing the horse's skin, which he intended to sell at the next town. Now Little Claus did not relish the porridge at all, so he trod with his foot on the sack under the table, and the dry skin squeaked quite loud. "Hush!" said Little Claus to his sack, at the same time treading upon it again, till it squeaked louder than before.

"Hallo! what have you got in your sack!" asked the farmer.

"Oh, it is a conjuror," said Little Claus; "and he says we need not eat porridge, for he has conjured the oven full of roast meat, fish, and pie."

"Wonderful!" cried the farmer, starting up and opening the oven door; and there lay all the nice things hidden by the farmer's wife, but which he supposed had been conjured there by the wizard under the table. The woman dared not say anything; so she placed the things before them, and they both ate of the fish, the meat, and the pastry.

Then Little Claus trod again upon his sack, and it squeaked as before. "What does he say now?" asked the farmer.

"He says," replied Little Claus, "that there are three bottles of wine for us, standing in the corner, by the oven."

So the woman was obliged to bring out the wine also, which she had hidden, and the farmer drank it till he became quite merry. He would have liked such a conjuror as Little Claus carried in his sack. "Could he conjure up the evil one?" asked the farmer. "I should like to see him now, while I am so merry."

"Oh, yes!" replied Little Claus, "my conjuror can do anything I ask him—can you not?" he asked, treading at the same time on the sack till it squeaked. "Do you hear? he answers 'Yes,' but he fears that we shall not like to look at him."

"Oh, I am not afraid. What will he be like?"

"Well, he is very much like a sexton."

"Ha!" said the farmer, "then he must be ugly. Do you know I cannot endure the sight of a sexton. However, that doesn't matter, I shall know who it is; so I shall not mind. Now then, I have got up my courage, but don't let him come too near me."

"Stop, I must ask the conjuror," said Little Claus; so he trod on the bag, and stooped his ear down to listen.

"What does he say?"

"He says that you must go and open that large chest which stands in the corner, and you will see the evil one crouching down inside; but you must hold the lid firmly, that he may not slip out."

"Will you come and help me hold it?" said the farmer, going towards the chest in which his wife had hidden the sexton, who now lay inside, very much frightened. The farmer opened the lid a very little way, and peeped in.

"Oh," cried he, springing backwards, "I saw him, and he is exactly like our sexton. How dreadful it is!" So after that he was obliged to drink again, and they sat and drank till far into the night.

"You must sell your conjuror to me," said the farmer; "ask as much as you like, I will pay it; indeed I would give you directly a whole bushel of gold."

"No, indeed, I cannot," said Little Claus; "only think how much profit I could make out of this conjuror."

"But I should like to have him," said the fanner, still continuing his entreaties.

"Well," said Little Claus at length, "you have been so good as to give me a night's lodging, I will not refuse you; you shall have the conjuror for a bushel of money, but I will have quite full measure."

"So you shall," said the farmer; "but you must take away the chest as well. I would not have it in the house another hour; there is no knowing if he may not be still there."

So Little Claus gave the farmer the sack containing the dried horse's skin, and received in exchange a bushel of money—full measure. The farmer also gave him a wheelbarrow on which to carry away the chest and the gold.

"Farewell," said Little Claus, as he went off with his money and the great chest, in which the sexton lay still concealed. On one side of the forest was a broad, deep river, the water flowed so rapidly that very few were able to swim against the stream. A new bridge had lately been built across it, and in the middle of this bridge Little Claus stopped, and said, loud enough to be heard by the sexton, "Now what shall I do with this stupid chest; it is as heavy as if it were full of stones: I shall be tired if I roll it any farther, so I may as well throw it in the river; if it swims after me to my house, well and good, and if not, it will not much matter."

So he seized the chest in his hand and lifted it up a little, as if he were going to throw it into the water.

"No, leave it alone," cried the sexton from within the chest; "let me out first."

"Oh," exclaimed Little Claus, pretending to be frightened, "he is in there still, is he? I must throw him into the river, that he may be drowned."

"Oh, no; oh, no," cried the sexton; "I will give you a whole bushel full of money if you will let me go."

"Why, that is another matter," said Little Claus, opening the chest. The sexton crept out, pushed the empty chest into the water, and went to his house, then he measured out a whole bushel full of gold for Little Claus, who had already received one from the farmer, so that now he had a barrow full.

"I have been well paid for my horse," said he to himself when he reached home, entered his own room, and emptied all his money into a heap on the floor. "How vexed Great Claus will be when he finds out how rich I have become all through my one horse; but I shall not tell him exactly how it all happened." Then he sent a boy to Great Claus to borrow a bushel measure.

"What can he want it for?" thought Great Claus; so he smeared the bottom of the measure with tar, that some of whatever was put into it might stick there and remain. And so it happened; for when the measure returned, three new silver florins were sticking to it.

"What does this mean?" said Great Claus; so he ran off directly to Little Claus, and asked, "Where did you get so much money?"

"Oh, for my horse's skin, I sold it yesterday."

"It was certainly well paid for then," said Great Claus; and he ran home to his house, seized a hatchet, and knocked all his four horses on the head, flayed off their skins, and took them to the town to sell. "Skins, skins, who'll buy skins?" he cried, as he went through the streets. All the shoemakers and tanners came running, and asked how much he wanted for them.

"A bushel of money, for each," replied Great Claus.

"Are you mad?" they all cried; "do you think we have money to spend by the bushel?"

"Skins, skins," he cried again, "who'll buy skins?" but to all who inquired the price, his answer was, "a bushel of money."

"He is making fools of us," said they all; then the shoemakers took their straps, and the tanners their leather aprons, and began to beat Great Claus.

"Skins, skins!" they cried, mocking him; "yes, we'll mark your skin for you, till it is black and blue."

"Out of the town with him," said they. And Great Claus was obliged to run as fast as he could, he had never before been so thoroughly beaten.

"Ah," said he, as he came to his house; "Little Claus shall pay me for this; I will beat him to death."

Meanwhile the old grandmother of Little Claus died. She had been cross, unkind, and really spiteful to him; but he was very sorry, and took the dead woman and laid her in his warm bed to see if he could bring her to life again. There he determined that she should lie the whole night, while he seated himself in a chair in a corner of the room as he had often done before. During the night, as he sat there, the door opened, and in came Great Claus with a hatchet. He knew well where Little Claus's bed stood; so he went right up to it, and struck the old grandmother on the head. thinking it must be Little Claus.

"There," cried he, "now you cannot make a fool of me again;" and then he went home.

"That is a very wicked man," thought Little Claus; "he meant to kill me. It is a good thing for my old grandmother that she was already dead, or he would have taken her life." Then he dressed his old grandmother in her best clothes, borrowed a horse of his neighbour, and harnessed it to a cart. Then he placed the old woman on the back seat, so that she might not fall out as he drove, and rode away through the wood. By sunrise they reached a large inn, where Little Claus stopped and went to get something to eat. The landlord was a rich man, and a good man too; but as passionate as if he had been made of pepper and snuff.

"Good morning," said he to Little Claus; "you are come betimes today."

"Yes," said Little Claus; "I am going to the town with my old grandmother; she is sitting at the back of the wagon, but I cannot bring her into the room. Will you take her a glass of mead? but you must speak very loud, for she cannot hear well."

"Yes, certainly I will," replied the landlord; and, pouring out a glass of mead, he carried it out to the dead grandmother, who sat upright in the cart. "Here is a glass of mead from your grandson," said the landlord. The dead woman did not answer a word, but sat quite still. "Do you not hear?" cried the landlord as loud as he could; "here is a glass of mead from your grandson."

Again and again he bawled it out, but as she did not stir he flew into a passion, and threw the glass of mead in her face; it struck her on the nose, and she fell backwards out of the cart, for she was only seated there, not tied in.

"Hallo!" cried Little Claus, rushing out of the door, and seizing hold of the landlord by the throat; "you have killed my grandmother; see, here is a great hole in her forehead."

"Oh, how unfortunate," said the landlord, wringing his hands. "This all comes of my fiery temper. Dear Little Claus, I will give you a bushel of money; I will bury your grandmother as if she were my own; only keep silent, or else they will cut off my head, and that would be disagreeable."

So it happened that Little Claus received another bushel of money, and the landlord buried his old grandmother as if she had been his own. When Little Claus reached home again, he immediately sent a boy to Great Claus, requesting him to lend him a bushel measure. "How is this?" thought Great Claus; "did I not kill him? I must go and see for myself." So he went to Little Claus, and took the bushel measure with him. "How did you get all this money?" asked Great Claus, staring with wide open eyes at his neighbour's treasures.

"You killed my grandmother instead of me," said Little Claus; "so I have sold her for a bushel of money."

"That is a good price at all events," said Great Claus. So he went home, took a hatchet, and killed his old grandmother with one blow. Then he placed her on a cart, and drove into the town to the apothecary, and asked him if he would buy a dead body.

"Whose is it, and where did you get it?" asked the apothecary.

"It is my grandmother," he replied; "I killed her with a blow, that I might get a bushel of money for her."

"Heaven preserve us!" cried the apothecary, "you are out of your mind. Don't say such things, or you will lose your head." And then he talked to him seriously about the wicked deed he had done, and told him that such a wicked man would surely be punished. Great Claus got so frightened that he rushed out of the surgery, jumped into the cart, whipped up his horses, and drove home quickly. The apothecary and all the people thought him mad, and let him drive where he liked.

"You shall pay for this," said Great Claus, as soon as he got into the highroad, "that you shall, Little Claus." So as soon as he reached home he took the largest sack he could find and went over to Little Claus. "You have played me another trick," said he. "First, I killed all my horses, and then my old grandmother, and it is all your fault; but you shall not make a fool of me any more." So he laid hold of Little Claus round the body, and pushed him into the sack, which he took on his shoulders, saying, "Now I'm going to drown you in the river."

He had a long way to go before he reached the river, and Little Claus was not a very light weight to carry. The road led by the church, and as they passed he could hear the organ playing and the people singing beautifully. Great Claus put down the sack close to the church-door, and thought he might as well go in and hear a psalm before he went any farther. Little Claus could not possibly get out of the sack, and all the people were in church; so in he went.

"Oh dear, oh dear," sighed Little Claus in the sack, as he turned and twisted about; but he found he could not loosen the string with which it was tied. Presently an old cattle driver, with snowy hair, passed by, carrying a large staff in his hand, with which he drove a large herd of cows and oxen before him. They stumbled against the sack in which lay Little Claus, and turned it over. "Oh dear," sighed Little Claus, "I am very young, yet I am soon going to heaven."

"And I, poor fellow," said the drover, "I who am so old already, cannot get there."

"Open the sack," cried Little Claus; "creep into it instead of me, and you will soon be there."

"With all my heart," replied the drover, opening the sack, from which sprung Little Claus as quickly as possible. "Will you take care of my cattle?" said the old man, as he crept into the bag.

"Yes," said Little Claus, and he tied up the sack, and then walked off with all the cows and oxen.

When Great Claus came out of church, he took up the sack, and placed it on his shoulders. It appeared to have become lighter, for the old drover was not half so heavy as Little Claus.

"How light he seems now," said he. "Ah, it is because I have been to a church." So he walked on to the river, which was deep and broad, and threw the sack containing the old drover into the water, believing it to be Little Claus. "There you may lie!" he exclaimed; "you will play me no more tricks now." Then he turned to go home, but when he came to a place where two roads crossed, there was Little Claus driving the cattle. "How is this?" said Great Claus. "Did I not drown you just now?"

"Yes," said Little Claus; "you threw me into the river about half an hour ago."

"But wherever did you get all these fine beasts?" asked Great Claus.

"These beasts are sea-cattle," replied Little Claus. "I'll tell you the whole story, and thank you for drowning me; I am above you now, I am really very rich. I was frightened, to be sure, while I lay tied up in the sack, and the wind whistled in my ears when you threw me into the river from the bridge, and I sank to the bottom immediately; but I did not hurt myself, for I fell upon beautifully soft grass which grows down there; and in a moment, the sack opened, and the sweetest little maiden came towards me. She had snow-white robes, and a wreath of green leaves on her wet hair. She took me by the hand, and said, 'So you are come, Little Claus, and here are some cattle for you to begin with. About a mile farther on the road, there is another herd for you.' Then I saw that the river formed a great highway for the people who live in the sea. They were walking and driving here and there from the sea to the land at the, spot where the river terminates. The bed of the river was covered with the loveliest flowers and sweet fresh grass. The fish swam past me as rapidly as the birds do here in the air. How handsome all the people were, and what fine cattle were grazing on the hills and in the valleys!"

"But why did you come up again," said Great Claus, "if it was all so beautiful down there? I should not have done so?"

"Well," said Little Claus, "it was good policy on my part; you heard me say just now that I was told by the sea-maiden to go a mile farther on the road, and I should find a whole herd of cattle. By the road she meant the river, for she could not travel any other way; but I knew the winding of the river, and how it bends, sometimes to the right and sometimes to the left, and it seemed a long way, so I chose a shorter one; and, by coming up to the land, and then driving across the fields back again to the river, I shall save half a mile, and get all my cattle more quickly."

"What a lucky fellow you are!" exclaimed Great Claus. "Do you think I should get any sea-cattle if I went down to the bottom of the river?"

"Yes, I think so," said Little Claus; "but I cannot carry you there in a sack, you are too heavy. However if you will go there first, and then creep into a sack, I will throw you in with the greatest pleasure."

"Thank you," said Great Claus; "but remember, if I do not get any sea-cattle down there I shall come up again and give you a good thrashing."

"No, now, don't be too fierce about it!" said Little Claus, as they walked on towards the river. When they approached it, the cattle, who were very thirsty, saw the stream, and ran down to drink.

"See what a hurry they are in," said Little Claus, "they are longing to get down again,"

"Come, help me, make haste," said Great Claus; "or you'll get beaten." So he crept into a large sack, which had been lying across the back of one of the oxen.

"Put in a stone," said Great Claus, "or I may not sink."

"Oh, there's not much fear of that," he replied; still he put a large stone into the bag, and then tied it tightly, and gave it a push.

"*Plump!*" In went Great Claus, and immediately sank to the bottom of the river.

"I'm afraid he will not find any cattle," said Little Claus, and then he drove his own beasts homewards.

The Princess and the Pea

Translated by Mrs. H. P. Paull

Once upon a time there was a Prince who wanted to marry a princess; but she would have to be a *real* princess. He travelled all over the world to find one, but nowhere could he get what he wanted. There were princesses enough, but it was difficult to find out whether they were real ones. There was always something about them that was not as it should be. So he came home again and was sad, for he would have liked very much to have a real princess.

One evening a terrible storm came on; there was thunder and lightning, and the rain poured down in torrents. Suddenly a knocking was heard at the city gate, and the old king went to open it.

It was a Princess standing out there in front of the gate. But, good gracious! what a sight the rain and the wind had made her look. The water ran down from her hair and clothes; it ran down into the toes of her shoes and out again at the heels. And yet she said that she was a real princess.

"Well, we'll soon find that out," thought the old queen. But

The Princess and the Pea

31

she said nothing, went into the bedroom, took all the bedding off the bedstead, and laid a pea on the bottom; then she took twenty mattresses and laid them on the pea, and then twenty eider-down beds on top of the mattresses.

On this the Princess had to lie all night. In the morning she was asked how she had slept.

"Oh, very badly!" said she. "I have scarcely closed my eyes all night. Heaven only knows what was in the bed, but I was lying on something hard, so that I am black and blue all over my body. It's horrible!"

Now they knew that she was a real princess because she had felt the pea right through the twenty mattresses and the twenty eider-down beds.

Nobody but a real princess could be as sensitive as that.

So the Prince took her for his wife, for now he knew that he had a real princess; and the pea was put in the museum, where it may still be seen, if no one has stolen it.

There, that is a true story.

Little Ida's Flowers

Translated by W. A. & J. K. Craigie

"My poor flowers are quite dead!" said little Ida. "They were so pretty yesterday evening, and now all the leaves hang withered. Why do they do that?" she asked the student, who sat on the sofa; for she liked him very much. He knew the prettiest stories, and could cut out the most amusing pictures—hearts, with little ladies in them who danced, flowers, and great castles in which one could open the doors: he was a merry student. "Why do the flowers look so faded today?" she asked again, and showed him a whole bouquet, which was quite withered.

"Do you know what's the matter with them?" said the student. "The flowers have been at a ball last night, and that's why they hang their heads."

"But flowers cannot dance!" cried little Ida.

"Oh, yes," said the student, "when it grows dark, and we are asleep, they jump about merrily. Almost every night they have a ball."

"Can no children go to this ball?"

"Yes," said the student, "quite little daisies, and lilies of the valley."

"Where do the most beautiful flowers dance?" asked little Ida.

"Have you not often been outside the town gate, by the great castle, where the king lives in summer, and where the beautiful garden is, with all the flowers? You have seen the swans, which swim up to you when you want to give them bread crumbs? There are capital balls there, believe me."

"I was out there in the garden yesterday, with my mother," said Ida; "but all the leaves were off the trees, and there was not one flower left. Where are they? In the summer I saw so many."

"They are within, in the castle," replied the student. "You must know, as soon as the king and all the court go to town, the flowers run out of the garden into the castle, and are merry You should see that. The two most beautiful roses seat themselves on the throne, and then they are king and queen; all the red coxcombs range themselves on either side, and stand and bow; they are the chamberlains. Then all the pretty flowers come, and there is a great ball. The blue violets represent little naval cadets: they dance with hyacinths and crocuses, which they call young ladies; the tulips and the great tiger-lilies are old ladies who keep watch that the dancing is well done, and that everything goes on with propriety."

"But," asked little Ida, "does nobody do anything to the flowers, for dancing in the king's castle?"

"There is nobody who really knows about it," answered the student. "Sometimes, certainly, the old steward of the castle comes at night, and he has to watch there. He has a great bunch of keys with him; but as soon as the flowers hear the keys rattle they are quite quiet, hide behind the long curtains, and only poke their heads out. Then the old steward says, 'I smell that there are flowers here,' but he cannot see them."

"That is famous!" cried little Ida, clapping her hands. "But should not I be able to see the flowers?"

"Yes," said the student; "only remember, when you go out again, to peep through the window; then you will see them. That is what I did today. There was a long yellow lily lying on the sofa and stretching herself. She imagined herself to be a court lady."

"Can the flowers out of the Botanical Garden get there? Can they go the long distance?"

"Yes, certainly," replied the student; "if they like they can fly. Have you not seen the beautiful butterflies, red, yellow, and white? They almost look like flowers; and that is what they have been. They have flown off their stalks high into the air, and have beaten it with their leaves, as if these leaves were little wings, and thus they flew. And because they behaved themselves well, they got leave to fly about in the daytime too, and were not obliged to go home again and to sit still upon their stalks; and thus at last the leaves became real wings. That you have seen yourself. It may be, however, that the flowers in the Botanical Garden have never been in the king's castle, or that they don't know of the merry proceedings there at night. Therefore I will tell you something: he will be very much surprised, the botanical professor, who lives close by here. You know him, do you not? When you come into his garden, you must tell one of the flowers that there is a great ball yonder in the castle. Then that flower will tell it to all the rest, and then they will fly away: if the professor then comes out into the garden, there will not be a single flower left, and he won't be able to make out where they are gone."

"But how can one flower tell it to another? For, you know, flowers cannot speak."

"That they cannot, certainly," replied the student; "but then they make signs. Have you not noticed that when the wind blows a little, the flowers nod at one another, and move all their green leaves? They can understand that just as well as if they talked."

"Can the professor understand these signs?" asked Ida.

"Yes, certainly. He came one morning into his garden, and saw a great stinging-nettle standing there, and making signs to a beautiful red carnation with its leaves. It was saying, 'You are so pretty, and I love you so much.' But the professor does not like that kind of thing, and he directly slapped the stinging-nettle upon its leaves, for those are its fingers; but he stung himself, and since that time he has not dared to touch a stinging-nettle."

"That was funny," cried little Ida; and she laughed.

"How can any one put such notions into a child's head?" said the tiresome privy councillor, who had come to pay a visit, and was sitting on the sofa. He did not like the student, and always grumbled when he saw him cutting out the comical funny pictures—sometimes a man hanging on a gibbet and holding a heart in his hand, to show that he stole hearts; sometimes an old witch riding on a broom, and carrying her husband on her nose. The councillor could not bear this, and then he said, just as he did now, "How can any one put such notions into a child's head? Those are stupid fancies!"

But to little Ida, what the student told about her flowers seemed very entertaining; and she thought much about it. The flowers hung their heads, for they were tired because they had danced all night; they were certainly ill. Then she went with them to all her other toys, which stood on a pretty little table, and the whole drawer was full of beautiful things. In the doll's bed lay her doll Sophy, asleep; but little Ida said to her,

"You must really get up, Sophy, and manage to lie in the drawer for tonight. The poor flowers are ill, and they must lie in your bed; perhaps they will then get well again."

And she at once took the doll out; but the doll looked cross, and did not say a single word; for she was angry because she could not keep her own bed.

Then Ida laid the flowers in the doll's bed, pulled the little coverlet quite up over them, and said they were to lie still and be good, and she would make them some tea, so that they might get well again, and be able to get up tomorrow. And she drew the curtains closely round the little bed, so that the sun should not shine in their eyes. The whole evening through she could not help thinking of what the student had told her. And when she was going to bed herself, she was obliged first to look behind the curtain which hung before the windows where her mother's beautiful flowers stood—hyacinths as well as tulips; then she whispered quite softly, "I know you're going to the ball tonight!" But the flowers made as if they did not understand a word, and did not stir a leaf; but still little Ida knew what she knew.

When she was in bed she lay for a long time thinking how pretty it must be to see the beautiful flowers dancing out in the king's castle. "I wonder if my flowers have really been there?" And then she fell asleep. In the night she awoke again: she had dreamed of the flowers, and of the student with whom the councillor found fault. It was quite quiet in the bedroom where Ida lay; the night-lamp burned on the table, and father and mother were asleep.

Little Ida's Flowers

"I wonder if my flowers are still hang in Sophy's bed?" she thought to herself. "How I should like to know it!" She raised herself a little, and looked at the door, which stood ajar; within lay the flowers and all her playthings. She listened, and then it seemed to her as if she heard some one playing on the piano in the next room, but quite softly and prettily, as she had never heard it before.

"Now all the flowers are certainly dancing in there!" thought she. "Oh, how much I should like to see it!" But she dared not get up, for she would have disturbed her father and mother.

"If they would only come in!" thought she. But the flowers did not come, and the music continued to play beautifully; then she could not bear it any longer, for it was too pretty; she crept out of her little bed, and went quietly to the door, and looked into the room. Oh, how splendid it was, what she saw!

There was no night-lamp burning, but still it was quite light: the moon shone through the window into the middle of the floor; it was almost like day. All the hyacinths and tulips stood in two long rows on the floor; there were none at all left at the window. There stood the empty flowerpots. On the floor all the flowers were dancing very gracefully round each other, making a perfect chain, and holding each other by the long green leaves as they swung round. But at the piano sat a great yellow lily, which little Ida had certainly seen in summer, for she remembered how the student had said, "How like that one is to Miss Lina." Then he had been laughed at by all; but now it seemed really to little Ida as if the long yellow flower looked like the young lady; and it had just her manners in playing—sometimes bending its long yellow face to one side, sometimes to the other, and nodding in tune to the charming music! No one noticed little Ida. Then she saw a great blue crocus hop into the middle of the table, where the toys stood, and go to the doll's bed and pull the curtains aside; there lay the sick flowers, but they got up directly, and nodded to the others, to say that they wanted to dance too. The old chimney-sweep doll, whose under lip was broken off, stood up and bowed to the pretty flowers: these did not look at all ill now; they jumped down among the others, and were very merry.

Then it seemed as if something fell down from the table. Ida looked that way. It was the Shrovetide birch rod which was jumping down! it seemed almost as if it belonged to the flowers. At any rate it was very neat; and a little wax doll, with just such a broad hat on its head as the councillor wore, sat upon it. The birch rod hopped about among the flowers on its three red legs, and stamped quite loud, for it was dancing the mazurka; and the other flowers could not manage that dance, because they were too light, and unable to stamp like that.

The wax doll on the birch rod all at once became quite great and long, turned itself over the paper flowers, and said, "How can one put such things in a child's head? Those are stupid fancies!" and then the wax doll was exactly like the councillor with the broad hat, and looked just as yellow and cross as he. But the paper flowers hit him on his thin legs, and then he shrank up again, and became quite a little wax doll. That was very amusing to see; and little Ida could not restrain her laughter. The birch rod went on dancing, and the councillor was obliged to dance too; it was no use whether he might make himself great and long, or remained the little yellow wax doll with the big black hat. Then the other flowers put in a good word for him, especially those who had lain in the doll's bed, and then the birch rod gave over. At the same moment there was a loud knocking at the drawer, inside where Ida's doll, Sophy, lay with many other toys. The chimney-sweep ran to the edge of the table, lay flat down on his stomach, and began to pull the drawer out a little. Then Sophy raised herself, and looked round quite astonished.

"There must be a ball here," said she; "why did nobody tell me?"

"Will you dance with me?" asked the chimney-sweep.

"You are a nice sort of fellow to dance!" she replied, and turned her back upon him.

Then she seated herself upon the drawer, and thought that one of the flowers would come and ask her; but not one of them came. Then she coughed, "Hem! hem! hem!" but for all that not one came. The chimney-sweep now danced all alone, and that was not at all so bad.

As none of the flowers seemed to notice Sophy, she let herself fall down from the drawer straight upon the floor, so that there was a great noise. The flowers now all came running up, to ask if she had not hurt herself; and they were all very polite to her, especially the flowers that had lain in her bed. But she had not hurt herself at all;

and Ida's flowers all thanked her for the nice bed, and were kind to her, took her into the middle of the floor, where the moon shone in, and danced with her; and all the other flowers formed a circle round her. Now Sophy was glad, and said they might keep her bed; she did not at all mind lying in the drawer.

But the flowers said, "We thank you heartily, but we cannot live so long. Tomorrow we shall be quite dead. But tell little Ida she is to bury us out in the garden, where the canary lies; then we shall wake up again in summer, and be far more beautiful."

"No, you must not die," said Sophy; and she kissed the flowers.

At that moment the door opened, and a great number of splendid flowers came dancing in. Ida could not imagine whence they had come; these must certainly all be flowers from the king's castle yonder. First of all came two glorious roses, and they had little gold crowns on; they were a king and a queen. Then came the prettiest stocks and carnations; and they bowed in all directions. They had music with them. Great poppies and peonies blew upon pea-pods till they were quite red in the face. The blue hyacinths and the little white snowdrops rang just as if they had bells on them. That was wonderful music! Then came many other flowers, and danced all together; the blue violets and the pink primroses, daisies and the lilies of the valley. And all the flowers kissed one another. It was beautiful to look at!

At last the flowers wished one another good night; then little Ida, too, crept to bed, where she dreamed of all she had seen.

When she rose next morning, she went quickly to the little table, to see if the flowers were still there. She drew aside the curtains of the little bed; there were they all, but they were quite faded, far more than yesterday. Sophy was lying in the drawer where Ida had laid her; she looked very sleepy.

"Do you remember what you were to say to me!" asked little Ida.

But Sophy looked quite stupid, and did not say a single word.

"You are not good at all!" said Ida. "And yet they all danced with you."

Then she took a little paper box, on which were painted beautiful birds, and opened it, and laid the dead flowers in it.

"That shall be your pretty coffin," said she, "and when my Norwegian cousins come to visit me by and by, they shall help me to bury you outside in the garden, so that you may grow again in summer, and become more beautiful than ever."

The Norwegian cousins were two smart boys. Their names were Jonas and Adolphe; their father had given them two new crossbows, and they had brought these with them to show to Ida. She told them about the poor flowers which had died, and then they got leave to bury them. The two boys went first, with their crossbows on their shoulders, and little Ida followed with the dead flowers in the pretty box. Out in the garden a little grave was dug. Ida first kissed the flowers, and then laid them in the earth in the box, and Adolphe and Jonas shot with their crossbows over the grave, for they had neither guns nor cannons.

Thumbelina

Translated by Mrs. H. P. Paull

There was once a woman who wished very much to have a little child, but she could not obtain her wish. At last she went to a fairy, and said, "I should so very much like to have a little child; can you tell me where I can find one?"

"Oh, that can be easily managed," said the fairy. "Here is a barleycorn of a different kind to those which grow in the farmer's fields, and which the chickens eat; put it into a flowerpot, and see what will happen."

"Thank you," said the woman, and she gave the fairy twelve shillings, which was the price of the barleycorn. Then she went home and planted it, and immediately there grew up a large handsome flower, something like a tulip in appearance, but with its leaves tightly closed as if it were still a bud. "It is a beautiful flower," said the woman, and she kissed the red and golden-coloured leaves, and while she did so the flower opened, and she could see that it was a real tulip. Within the flower, upon the green velvet stamens, sat a very delicate and graceful little maiden. She was scarcely half as long as a thumb, and they gave her the name of "Thumbelina," or Tiny, because she was so small. A walnut-shell, elegantly polished, served her for a cradle; her bed was formed of blue violet-leaves, with a rose-leaf for a counterpane. Here she slept at night, but during the day she amused herself on a table, where the woman had placed a plateful of water. Round this plate were wreaths of flowers with their stems in the water, and upon it floated a large tulip-leaf, which served Tiny for a boat. Here the little maiden sat and rowed herself from side to side, with two oars made of white horse-hair. It really was a very pretty sight. Tiny could, also, sing so softly and sweetly that nothing like her singing had ever before been heard. One night, while she lay in her pretty bed, a large, ugly, wet toad crept through a broken pane of glass in the window, and leaped right upon the table where Tiny lay sleeping under her rose-leaf quilt. "What a pretty little wife this would make for my son", said the toad, and she took up the walnut-shell in which little Tiny lay asleep, and jumped through the window with it into the garden.

In the swampy margin of a broad stream in the garden lived the toad, with her son. He was uglier even than his mother, and when he saw the pretty little maiden in her elegant bed, he could only cry, "Croak, croak, croak."

"Don't speak so loud, or she will wake," said the toad, "and then she might run away, for she is as light as swan's down. We will place her on one of the water lily leaves out in the stream; it will be like an island to her, she is so light and small, and then she cannot escape; and, while she is away, we will make haste and prepare the state-room under the marsh, in which you are to live when you are married."

Far out in the stream grew a number of water lilies, with broad green leaves, which seemed to float on the top of the water. The largest of these leaves appeared farther off than the rest, and the old toad swam out to it with the walnut-shell, in which little Tiny lay still asleep. The tiny little creature woke very early in the morning, and began to cry bitterly when she found where she was, for she could see nothing but water on every side of the large green leaf, and no way of reaching the land. Meanwhile the old toad was very busy under the marsh, decking her room with rushes and wild yellow flowers, to make it look pretty for her new daughter-in-law. Then she swam out with her ugly son to the leaf on which she had placed poor little Tiny.

Thumbelina

She wanted to fetch the pretty bed, that she might put it in the bridal chamber to be ready for her. The old toad bowed low to her in the water, and said, "Here is my son, he will be your husband, and you will live happily in the marsh by the stream."

"Croak, croak, croak," was all her son could say for himself; so the toad took up the elegant little bed, and swam away with it, leaving Tiny all alone on the green leaf, where she sat and wept. She could not bear to think of living with the old toad, and having her ugly son for a husband. The little fishes, who swam about in the water beneath, had seen the toad, and heard what she said, so they lifted their heads above the water to look at the little maiden. As soon as they caught sight of her, they saw she was very pretty, and it made them very sorry to think that she must go and live with the ugly toads. "No, it must never be!" so they assembled together in the water, round the green stalk which held the leaf on which the little maiden stood, and gnawed it away at the root with their teeth. Then the leaf floated down the stream, carrying Tiny far away out of reach of land.

Tiny sailed past many towns, and the little birds in the bushes saw her, and sang, "What a lovely little creature;" so the leaf swam away with her farther and farther, till it brought her to other lands. A graceful little white butterfly constantly fluttered round her, and at last alighted on the leaf. Tiny pleased him, and she was glad of it, for now the toad could not possibly reach her, and the country through which she sailed was beautiful, and the sun shone upon the water, till it glittered like liquid gold. She took off her girdle and tied one end of it round the butterfly, and the other end of the ribbon she fastened to the leaf, which now glided on much faster than ever, taking little Tiny with it as she stood. Presently a large cockchafer flew by; the moment he caught sight of her, he seized her round her delicate waist with his claws, and flew with her into a tree. The green leaf floated away on the brook, and the butterfly flew with it, for he was fastened to it, and could not get away.

Oh, how frightened little Tiny felt when the cockchafer flew with her to the tree! But especially was she sorry for the beautiful white butterfly which she had fastened to the leaf, for if he could not free himself he would die of hunger. But the cockchafer did not trouble himself at all about the matter. He seated himself by her side on a large green leaf, gave her some honey from the flowers to eat, and told her she was very pretty, though not in the least like a cockchafer. After a time, all the cockchafers turned up their feelers, and said, "She has only two legs! how ugly that looks." "She has no feelers," said another. "Her waist is quite slim. Pooh! she is like a human being."

"Oh! she is ugly," said all the lady cockchafers, although Tiny was very pretty. Then the cockchafer who had run away with her, believed all the others when they said she was ugly, and would have nothing more to say to her, and told her she might go where she liked. Then he flew down with her from the tree, and placed her on a daisy, and she wept at the thought that she was so ugly that even the cockchafers would have nothing to say to her. And all the while she was really the loveliest creature that one could imagine, and as tender and delicate as a beautiful rose-leaf. During the whole summer poor little Tiny lived quite alone in the wide forest. She wove herself a bed with blades of grass, and hung it up under a broad leaf, to protect herself from the rain. She sucked the honey from the flowers for food, and drank the dew from their leaves every morning. So passed away the summer and the autumn, and then came the winter—the long, cold winter. All the birds who had sung to her so sweetly were flown away, and the trees and the flowers had withered. The large clover leaf under the shelter of which she had lived, was now rolled together and shrivelled up, nothing remained but a yellow withered stalk. She felt dreadfully cold, for her clothes were torn, and she was herself so frail and delicate, that poor little Tiny was nearly frozen to death. It began to snow too; and the snowflakes, as they fell upon her, were like a whole shovelful falling upon one of us, for we are tall, but she was only an inch high. Then she wrapped herself up in a dry leaf, but it cracked in the middle and could not keep her warm, and she shivered with cold. Near the wood in which she had been living lay a corn-field, but the corn had been cut a long time; nothing remained but the bare dry stubble standing up out of the frozen ground. It was to her like struggling through a large wood. Oh! how she shivered with the cold. She came at last to the door of a field-mouse, who had a little den under the corn-stubble. There dwelt the field-mouse in warmth and comfort, with a whole roomful of corn, a kitchen, and a beautiful dining room. Poor little Tiny stood before the door just

Thumbelina

like a little beggar-girl, and begged for a small piece of barley-corn, for she had been without a morsel to eat for two days.

"You poor little creature," said the field-mouse, who was really a good old field-mouse, "come into my warm room and dine with me." She was very pleased with Tiny, so she said, "You are quite welcome to stay with me all the winter, if you like; but you must keep my rooms clean and neat, and tell me stories, for I shall like to hear them very much." And Tiny did all the field-mouse asked her, and found herself very comfortable.

"We shall have a visitor soon," said the field-mouse one day; "my neighbour pays me a visit once a week. He is better off than I am; he has large rooms, and wears a beautiful black velvet coat. If you could only have him for a husband, you would be well provided for indeed. But he is blind, so you must tell him some of your prettiest stories".

But Tiny did not feel at all interested about this neighbour, for he was a mole. However, he came and paid his visit dressed in his black velvet coat.

"He is very rich and learned, and his house is twenty times larger than mine," said the field-mouse.

He was rich and learned, no doubt, but he always spoke slightingly of the sun and the pretty flowers, because he had never seen them. Tiny was obliged to sing to him, "Lady-bird, lady-bird, fly away home," and many other pretty songs. And the mole fell in love with her because she had such a sweet voice; but he said nothing yet, for he was very cautious. A short time before, the mole had dug a long passage under the earth, which led from the dwelling of the field-mouse to his own, and here she had permission to walk with Tiny whenever she liked. But he warned them not to be alarmed at the sight of a dead bird which lay in the passage. It was a perfect bird, with a beak and feathers, and could not have been dead long, and was lying just where the mole had made his passage. The mole took a piece of phosphorescent wood in his mouth, and it glittered like fire in the dark; then he went before them to light them through the long, dark passage. When they came to the spot where lay the dead bird, the mole pushed his broad nose through the ceiling, the earth gave way, so that there was a large hole, and the daylight shone into the passage. In the middle of the floor lay a dead swallow, his beautiful wings pulled close to his sides, his feet and his head drawn up under his feathers; the poor bird had evidently died of the cold. It made little Tiny very sad to see it, she did so love the little birds; all the summer they had sung and twittered for her so beautifully. But the mole pushed it aside with his crooked legs, and said, "He will sing no more now. How miserable it must be to be born a little bird! I am thankful that none of my children will ever be birds, for they can do nothing but cry, 'Tweet, tweet,' and always die of hunger in the winter."

"Yes, you may well say that, as a clever man!" exclaimed the field-mouse, "What is the use of his twittering, for when winter comes he must either starve or be frozen to death. Still birds are very high bred."

Tiny said nothing; but when the two others had turned their backs on the bird, she stooped down and stroked aside the soft feathers which covered the head, and kissed the closed eyelids. "Perhaps this was the one who sang to me so sweetly in the summer," she said; "and how much pleasure it gave me, you dear, pretty bird."

The mole now stopped up the hole through which the daylight shone, and then accompanied the lady home. But during the night Tiny could not sleep; so she got out of bed and wove a large, beautiful carpet of hay; then she carried it to the dead bird, and spread it over him; with some down from the flowers which she had found in the field-mouse's room. It was as soft as wool, and she spread some of it on each side of the bird, so that he might lie warmly in the cold earth. "Farewell, you pretty little bird," said she, "farewell; thank you for your delightful singing during the summer, when all the trees were green, and the warm sun shone upon us. Then she laid her head on the bird's breast, but she was alarmed immediately, for it seemed as if something inside the bird went "thump, thump." It was the bird's heart; he was not really dead, only benumbed with the cold, and the warmth had restored him to life. In autumn, all the swallows fly away into warm countries, but if one happens to linger, the cold seizes it, it becomes frozen, and falls down as if dead; it remains where it fell, and the cold snow covers it. Tiny trembled very much; she was quite frightened, for the bird was large, a great deal larger than herself—she was only an inch high. But she took courage, laid the wool more thickly over the poor swallow, and then took a leaf which she had used for her own counterpane, and laid it over the head of the poor bird. The next morning she again stole out to see him. He was alive but very weak; he could only open his eyes for a moment to look at Tiny, who stood by holding a piece of decayed wood in her hand, for she had no other lantern. "Thank you, pretty little maiden," said the sick swallow; "I have been so nicely warmed, that I shall soon regain my strength, and be able to fly about again in the warm sunshine."

"Oh," said she, "it is cold out of doors now; it snows and freezes. Stay in your warm bed; I will take care of you."

Then she brought the swallow some water in a flower-leaf, and after he had drank, he told her that he had wounded one of his wings in a thorn-bush, and could not fly as fast as the others, who were soon far away on their journey to warm countries. Then at last he had fallen to the earth, and could remember no more, nor how he came to be where she had found him. The whole winter the swallow remained underground, and Tiny nursed him with care and love. Neither the mole nor the field-mouse knew anything about it, for they did not like swallows. Very soon the spring time came, and the sun warmed the earth. Then the swallow bade farewell to Tiny, and she opened the hole in the ceiling which the mole had made. The sun shone in upon them so beautifully, that the swallow asked her if she would go with him; she could sit on his back, he said, and he would fly away with her into the green woods. But Tiny knew it would make the field-mouse very grieved if she left her in that manner, so she said, "No, I cannot."

"Farewell, then, farewell, you good, pretty little maiden," said the swallow; and he flew out into the sunshine.

Tiny looked after him, and the tears rose in her eyes. She was very fond of the poor swallow.

"Tweet, tweet," sang the bird, as he flew out into the green woods, and Tiny felt very sad. She was not allowed to go out into the warm sunshine. The corn which had been sown in the field over the house of the field-mouse had grown up high into the air, and formed a thick wood to Tiny, who was only an inch in height.

"You are going to be married, Tiny," said the field-mouse. "My neighbour has asked for you. What good fortune for a poor child like you. Now we will prepare your wedding clothes. They must be both woollen and linen. Nothing must be wanting when you are the mole's wife."

Tiny had to turn the spindle, and the field-mouse hired four spiders, who were to weave day and night. Every evening the mole visited her, and was continually speaking of the time when the summer would be over. Then he would keep his wedding-day with Tiny; but now the heat of the sun was so great that it burned the earth, and made it quite hard, like a stone. As soon, as the summer was over, the wedding should take place. But Tiny was not at all pleased; for she did not like the tiresome mole. Every morning when the sun rose, and every evening when it went down, she would creep out at the door, and as the wind blew aside the ears of corn, so that she could see the blue sky, she thought how beautiful and bright it seemed out there, and wished so much to see her dear swallow again. But he never returned; for by this time he had flown far away into the lovely green forest.

When autumn arrived, Tiny had her outfit quite ready; and the field-mouse said to her, "In four weeks the wedding must take place."

Then Tiny wept, and said she would not marry the disagreeable mole.

"Nonsense," replied the field-mouse. "Now don't be obstinate, or I shall bite you with my white teeth. He is a very handsome mole; the queen herself does not wear more beautiful velvets and furs. His kitchen and cellars are quite full. You ought to be very thankful for such good fortune."

So the wedding-day was fixed, on which the mole was to fetch Tiny away to live with him, deep under the earth, and never again to see the warm sun, because he did not like it. The poor child was very unhappy at the thought of saying farewell to the beautiful sun, and as the field-mouse had given her permission to stand at the door, she went to look at it once more.

"Farewell bright sun," she cried, stretching out her arm towards it; and then she walked a short distance from the house; for the corn had been cut, and only the dry stubble remained in the fields. "Farewell, farewell," she repeated, twining her arm round a little red flower that grew just by her side. "Greet the little swallow from me, if you should see him again."

"Tweet, tweet," sounded over her head suddenly. She looked up, and there was the swallow himself flying close by. As soon as he spied Tiny, he was delighted; and then she told him how unwilling she felt to marry the ugly mole, and to live always beneath the earth, and never to see the bright sun any more. And as she told him she wept.

"Cold winter is coming," said the swallow, "and I am going to fly away into warmer countries. Will you go with me? You can sit on my back, and fasten yourself on with your sash. Then we can fly away from the ugly mole and his gloomy rooms—far away, over the mountains, into warmer countries, where the sun shines more brightly—than here; where it is always summer, and the flowers bloom in greater beauty. Fly now with me, dear little Tiny; you saved my life when I lay frozen in that dark passage."

"Yes, I will go with you," said Tiny; and she seated herself on the bird's back, with her feet on his outstretched wings, and tied her girdle to one of his strongest feathers.

Then the swallow rose in the air, and flew over forest and over sea, high above the highest mountains, covered with eternal snow. Tiny would have been frozen in the cold air, but she crept under the bird's warm feathers, keeping her little head uncovered, so that she might admire the beautiful lands over which they passed. At length they reached the warm countries, where the sun shines brightly, and the sky seems so much higher above the earth. Here, on the hedges, and by the wayside, grew purple, green, and white grapes; lemons and oranges hung from trees in the woods; and the air was fragrant with myrtles and orange blossoms. Beautiful children ran along the country lanes, playing with large gay butterflies; and as the swallow flew farther and farther, every place appeared still more lovely.

At last they came to a blue lake, and by the side of it, shaded by trees of the deepest green, stood a palace of dazzling white marble, built in the olden times. Vines clustered round its lofty pillars, and at the top were many swallows' nests, and one of these was the home of the swallow who carried Tiny.

"This is my house," said the swallow; "but it would not do for you to live there—you would not be comfortable. You must choose for yourself one of those lovely flowers, and I will put you down upon it, and then you shall have everything that you can wish to make you happy."

"That will be delightful," she said, and clapped her little hands for joy.

A large marble pillar lay on the ground, which, in falling, had been broken into three pieces. Between these pieces grew the most beautiful large white flowers; so the swallow flew down with Tiny, and placed her on one of the broad leaves. But how surprised she was to see in the middle of the flower, a tiny little man, as white and transparent as if he had been made of crystal! He had a gold crown on his head, and delicate wings at his shoulders, and was not much larger than Tiny herself. He was the angel of the flower; for a tiny man and a tiny woman dwell in every flower; and this was the king of them all.

"Oh, how beautiful he is!" whispered Tiny to the swallow.

The little prince was at first quite frightened at the bird, who was like a giant, compared to such a delicate little creature as himself; but when he saw Tiny, he was delighted, and thought her the prettiest little maiden he had ever seen. He took the gold crown from his head, and placed it on hers, and asked her name, and if she would be his wife, and queen over all the flowers.

This certainly was a very different sort of husband to the son of a toad, or the mole, with my black velvet and fur; so she said, "Yes," to the handsome prince. Then all the flowers opened, and out of each came a little lady or a tiny lord, all so pretty it was quite a pleasure to look at them. Each of them brought Tiny a present; but the best gift was a pair of beautiful wings, which had belonged to a large white fly and they fastened them to Tiny's shoulders, so that she might fly from flower to flower. Then there was much rejoicing, and the little swallow who sat above them, in his nest, was asked to sing a wedding song, which he did as well as he could; but in his heart he felt sad for he was very fond of Tiny, and would have liked never to part from her again.

"You must not be called Tiny any more," said the spirit of the flowers to her. "It is an ugly name, and you are so very pretty. We will call you Maia."

"Farewell, farewell," said the swallow, with a heavy heart as he left the warm countries to fly back into Denmark. There he had a nest over the window of a house in which dwelt the writer of fairy tales. The swallow sang, "Tweet, tweet," and from his song came the whole story.

The Naughty Boy

Translated by Caroline Peachey

There was once an old poet, such a good, honest old poet! He was sitting alone in his own little room on a very stormy evening; the wind was roaring without, and the rain poured down in torrents. But the old man sat cosily by his warm stove, the fire was blazing brightly, and some apples were roasting in front of it.

"Those poor people who have no roof to shelter them tonight will, most assuredly, not have a dry thread left on their skin," said the kind-hearted old man.

"Oh, open the door! open the door! I am so cold, and quite wet through besides open the door!" cried a voice from without. The voice was like a child's, and seemed half-choked with sobs. "Rap, rap, rap!" it went on knocking at the door, whilst the rain still kept streaming down from the clouds, and the wind rattled among the window-panes.

"Poor thing!" said the old Poet; and he arose and opened the door. There stood a little boy, almost naked; the water trickled down from his long flaxen hair; he was shivering with cold, and had he been left much longer out in the street, he must certainly have perished in the storm.

"Poor boy!" said the old poet again, taking him by the hand, and leading him into his room. "Come to me, and we'll soon make thee warm again, and I will give thee some wine, and some roasted apples for thy supper, my pretty child!"

And, of a truth, the boy was exceedingly pretty. His eyes shone as bright as stars, and his hair, although dripping with water, curled in beautiful ringlets. He looked quite like a little cherub, but he was very pale, and trembled in every limb with cold. In his hand he held a pretty little cross-bow, but it seemed entirely spoilt by the rain, and the colours painted on the arrows all ran one into another.

The old Poet sat down again beside the stove, and took the little boy in his lap; he wrung the water out of his streaming hair, warmed the child's hands within his own, and gave him mulled wine to drink. The boy soon became himself again, the rosy colour returned to his cheeks, he jumped down from the old man's lap, and danced around him on the floor.

"Thou art a merry fellow!" said the Poet. "Thou must tell me thy name."

"They call me Cupid," replied the boy. "Don't you know me? There lies my bow; ah, you can't think how capitally I can shoot! See, the weather is fine again now; the moon is shining bright."

"But thy bow is spoilt," said the old man.

"That would be a sad disaster, indeed," remarked the boy, as he took the bow in his hand and examined it closely. "Oh, it is quite dry by this time, and it is not a bit damaged; the string, too, is quite strong enough, I think. However, I may as well try it!" He then drew his bow, placed an arrow before the string, took his aim, and shot direct into the old poet's heart. "Now you may be sure that my cross-bow is not spoilt!" cried he, as, with a loud laugh, he ran away.

The naughty boy! This was, indeed, ungrateful of him, to shoot to the heart the good old man who had so kindly taken him in, warmed him, and dried his clothes, given him sweet wine, and nice roasted apples for supper!

The poor Poet lay groaning on the ground, for the arrow had wounded him sorely. "Fie, for shame, Cupid!" cried he, "thou art a wicked boy! I will tell all good children how thou hast treated me, and bid them take heed and never play with thee, for thou wilt assuredly do them a mischief, as thou hast done to me."

All the good boys and girls to whom he related this story were on their guard against the wicked boy, Cupid; but, notwithstanding, he made fools of them again and again, he is so terribly cunning! When the students are returning home from lecture, he walks by their side, dressed in a black gown, and with a book under his arm. They take him to be a fellow-student, and so they suffer him to walk arm-in-arm with them, just as if he were one of their intimate friends. But whilst they are thus familiar with him, all of a sudden he thrusts his arrows into their bosoms. Even when young girls are going to church, he will follow and watch for his opportunity: he is always waylaying people. In the theatre, he sits in the great chandelier, and kindles such a bright, hot flame, men fancy it a lamp, but they are soon undeceived. He wanders about in the Royal Gardens and all the public walks, making mischief everywhere; nay, once he even shot thy father and mother to the heart! Only ask them, dear child, and they will certainly tell thee all about it. In fine, this fellow, this Cupid, is a very wicked boy! Do not play with him! He waylays everybody, boys and girls, youths and maidens, men and women, rich and poor, old and young. Only think of this: he once shot an arrow into thy good old grandmother's heart! It happened a long time ago, and she has recovered from the wound, but she will never forget him, depend upon it.

Fie, for shame! wicked Cupid! Is he not a mischievous boy?

Beware of him, beware of him, dear child!

The Travelling Companion

Translated by Mrs. H. P. Paull

Poor John was very sad; for his father was so ill, he had no hope of his recovery. John sat alone with the sick man in the little room, and the lamp had nearly burnt out; for it was late in the night.

"You have been a good son, John," said the sick father, "and God will help you on in the world." He looked at him, as he spoke, with mild, earnest eyes, drew a deep sigh, and died; yet it appeared as if he still slept.

John wept bitterly. He had no one in the wide world now; neither father, mother, brother, nor sister. Poor John! he knelt down by the bed, kissed his dead father's hand, and wept many, many bitter tears. But at last his eyes closed, and he fell asleep with his head resting against the hard bedpost. Then he dreamed a strange dream; he thought he saw the sun shining upon him, and his father alive and well, and even heard him laughing as he used to do when he was very happy. A beautiful girl, with a golden crown on her head, and long, shining hair, gave him her hand; and his father said, "See what a bride you have won. She is the loveliest maiden on the whole earth." Then he awoke, and all the beautiful things vanished before his eyes, his father lay dead on the bed, and he was all alone. Poor John!

During the following week the dead man was buried. The son walked behind the coffin which contained his father, whom he so dearly loved, and would never again behold. He heard the earth fall on the coffin-lid, and watched it till only a corner remained in sight, and at last that also disappeared. He felt as if his heart would break with its weight of sorrow, till those who stood round the grave sang a psalm, and the sweet, holy tones brought tears into his eyes, which relieved him. The sun shone brightly down on the green trees, as if it would say, "You must not be so sorrowful, John. Do you see the beautiful blue sky above you? Your father is up there, and he prays to the loving Father of all, that you may do well in the future."

"I will always be good," said John, "and then I shall go to be with my father in heaven. What joy it will be when we see each other again! How much I shall have to relate to him, and how many things he will be able to explain to me of the delights of heaven, and teach me as he once did on earth. Oh, what joy it will be!"

He pictured it all so plainly to himself, that he smiled even while the tears ran down his cheeks.

The little birds in the chestnut-trees twittered, "Tweet, tweet;" they were so happy, although they had seen the funeral; but they seemed as if they knew that the dead man was now in heaven, and that he had wings much larger and more beautiful than their own; and he was happy now, because he had been good here on earth, and they were glad of it. John saw them fly away out of the green trees into the wide world, and he longed to fly with them; but first he cut out a large wooden cross, to place on his father's grave; and when he brought it there in the evening, he found the grave decked out with gravel and flowers. Strangers had done this; they who had known the good old father who was now dead, and who had loved him very much.

Early the next morning, John packed up his little bundle of clothes, and placed all his money, which consisted of fifty dollars and a few shillings, in his girdle; with this he determined to try his fortune in the world. But first he went into the churchyard; and, by his father's grave, he offered up a prayer, and said, "Farewell."

As he passed through the fields, all the flowers looked fresh and beautiful in the warm sunshine, and nodded in the wind, as if they wished to say, "Welcome to the green wood, where all is fresh and bright."

Then John turned to have one more look at the old church, in which he had been christened in his infancy, and where his father had taken him every Sunday to hear the service and join in singing the psalms. As he looked at the old tower, he espied the ringer standing at one of the narrow openings, with his little pointed red cap on his head, and shading his eyes from the sun with his bent arm. John nodded farewell to him, and the little ringer waved his red cap, laid his hand on his heart, and kissed his hand to him a great many times, to show that he felt kindly towards him, and wished him a prosperous journey.

John continued his journey, and thought of all the wonderful things he should see in the large, beautiful world, till he found himself farther away from home than ever he had been before. He did not even know the names of the places he passed through, and could scarcely understand the language of the people he met, for he was far away, in a strange land. The first night he slept on a haystack, out in the fields, for there was no other bed for him; but it seemed to him so nice and comfortable that even a king need not wish for a better. The field, the brook, the haystack, with the blue sky above, formed a beautiful sleeping-room. The green grass, with the little red and white flowers, was the carpet; the elder-bushes and the hedges of wild roses looked like garlands on the walls; and for a bath he could have the clear, fresh water of the brook; while the rushes bowed their heads to him, to wish him good morning and good evening. The moon, like a large lamp, hung high up in the blue ceiling, and he had no fear of its setting fire to his curtains. John slept here quite safely all night; and when he awoke, the sun was up, and all the little birds were singing round him, "Good morning, good morning. Are you not up yet?"

It was Sunday, and the bells were ringing for church. As the people went in, John followed them; he heard God's word, joined in singing the psalms, and listened to the preacher. It seemed to him just as if he were in his own church, where he had been christened, and had sung the psalms with his father. Out in the churchyard were several graves, and on some of them the grass had grown very high. John thought of his father's grave, which he knew at last would look like these, as he was not there to weed and attend to it. Then he set to work, pulled up the high grass, raised the wooden crosses which had fallen down, and replaced the wreaths which had been blown away from their places by the wind, thinking all the time, "Perhaps some one is doing the same for my father's grave, as I am not there to do it "

Outside the church door stood an old beggar, leaning on his crutch. John gave him his silver shillings, and then he continued his journey, feeling lighter and happier than ever. Towards evening, the weather became very stormy, and he hastened on as quickly as he could, to get shelter; but it was quite dark by the time he reached a little lonely church which stood on a hill. "I will go in here," he said, "and sit down in a corner; for I am quite tired, and want rest."

So he went in, and seated himself; then he folded his hands, and offered up his evening prayer, and was soon fast asleep and dreaming, while the thunder rolled and the lightning flashed without. When he awoke, it was still night; but the storm had ceased, and the moon shone in upon him through the windows. Then he saw an open coffin standing in the centre of the church, which contained a dead man, waiting for burial. John was not at all timid; he had a good conscience, and he knew also that the dead can never injure any one. It is living wicked men who do harm to others. Two such wicked persons stood now by the dead man, who had been brought to the church to be buried. Their evil intentions were to throw the poor dead body outside the church door, and not leave him to rest in his coffin.

"Why do you do this?" asked John, when he saw what they were going to do; "it is very wicked. Leave him to rest in peace, in Christ's name."

"Nonsense," replied the two dreadful men. "He has cheated us; he owed us money which he could not pay, and now he is dead we shall not get a penny; so we mean to have our revenge, and let him lie like a dog outside the church door."

"I have only fifty dollars," said John, "it is all I possess in the world, but I will give it to you if you will promise me faithfully to leave the dead man in peace. I shall be able to get on without the money; I have strong and healthy limbs, and God will always help me."

"Why, of course," said the horrid men, "if you will pay his debt we will both promise not to touch him. You may depend upon that;" and then they took the money he offered them, laughed at him for his good nature, and went their way.

Then he laid the dead body back in the coffin, folded the hands, and took leave of it; and went away contentedly through the great forest. All around him he could see the prettiest little elves dancing in the moonlight, which shone through the trees. They were not disturbed by his appearance, for they knew he was good and harmless among men. They are wicked people only who can never obtain a glimpse of fairies. Some of them were not taller than the breadth of a finger, and they wore golden combs in their long, yellow hair. They were rocking themselves two together on the large dew-drops with which the leaves and the high grass were sprinkled. Sometimes the dew-drops would roll away, and then they fell down between the stems of the long grass, and caused a great deal of laughing and noise among the other little people. It was quite charming to watch them at play. Then they sang songs, and John remembered that he had learnt those pretty songs when he was a little boy. Large speckled spiders, with silver crowns on their heads, were employed to spin suspension bridges and palaces from one hedge to another, and when the tiny drops fell upon them, they glittered in the moonlight like shining glass. This continued till sunrise. Then the little elves crept into the flower-buds, and the wind seized the bridges and palaces, and fluttered them in the air like cobwebs.

As John left the wood, a strong man's voice called after him, "Hallo, comrade, where are you travelling?"

"Into the wide world," he replied; "I am only a poor lad, I have neither father nor mother, but God will help me."

"I am going into the wide world also," replied the stranger; "shall we keep each other company?"

"With all my heart," he said, and so they went on together. Soon they began to like each other very much, for they were both good; but John found out that the stranger was much more clever than himself. He had travelled all over the world, and could describe almost everything. The sun was high in the heavens when they seated themselves under a large tree to eat their breakfast, and at the same moment an old woman came towards them. She was very old and almost bent double. She leaned upon a stick and carried on her back a bundle of firewood, which she had collected in the forest; her apron was tied round it, and John saw three great stems of fern and some willow twigs peeping out. just as she came close up to them, her foot slipped and she fell to the ground screaming loudly; poor old woman, she had broken her leg! John proposed directly that they should carry the old woman home to her cottage; but the stranger opened his knapsack and took out a box, in which he said he had a salve that would quickly make her leg well and strong again, so that she would be able to walk home herself, as if her leg had never been broken. And all that he would ask in return was the three fern stems which she carried in her apron.

"That is rather too high a price," said the old woman, nodding her head quite strangely. She did not seem at all inclined to part with the fern stems. However, it was not very agreeable to lie there with a broken leg, so she gave them to him; and such was the power of the ointment, that no sooner had he rubbed her leg with it than the old mother rose up and walked even better than she had done before. But then this wonderful ointment could not be bought at a chemist's.

"What can you want with those three fern rods?" asked John of his fellow-traveller.

"Oh, they will make capital brooms," said he; "and I like them because I have strange whims sometimes." Then they walked on together for a long distance.

"How dark the sky is becoming," said John; "and look at those thick, heavy clouds."

"Those are not clouds," replied his fellow-traveller; "they are mountains—large lofty mountains—on the tops of which we should be above the clouds, in the pure, free air. Believe me, it is delightful to ascend so high, tomorrow we shall be there." But the mountains were not so near as they appeared; they had to travel a whole day before they reached them, and pass through black forests and piles of rock as large as a town. The journey had been so fatiguing that

John and his fellow-traveller stopped to rest at a roadside inn, so that they might gain strength for their journey on the morrow. In the large public room of the inn a great many persons were assembled to see a comedy performed by dolls. The showman had just erected his little theatre, and the people were sitting round the room to witness the performance. Right in front, in the very best place, sat a stout butcher, with a great bull-dog by his side who seemed very much inclined to bite. He sat staring with all his eyes, and so indeed did every one else in the room. And then the play began. It was a pretty piece, with a king and a queen in it, who sat on a beautiful throne, and had gold crowns on their heads. The trains to their dresses were very long, according to the fashion; while the prettiest of wooden dolls, with glass eyes and large mustaches, stood at the doors, and opened and shut them, that the fresh air might come into the room. It was a very pleasant play, not at all mournful; but just as the queen stood up and walked across the stage, the great bull-dog, who should have been held back by his master, made a spring forward, and caught the queen in the teeth by the slender wrist, so that it snapped in two. This was a very dreadful disaster. The poor man, who was exhibiting the dolls, was much annoyed, and quite sad about his queen; she was the prettiest doll he had, and the bull-dog had broken her head and shoulders off. But after all the people were gone away, the stranger, who came with John, said that he could soon set her to rights. And then he brought out his box and rubbed the doll with some of the salve with which he had cured the old woman when she broke her leg. As soon as this was done the doll's back became quite right again; her head and shoulders were fixed on, and she could even move her limbs herself: there was now no occasion to pull the wires, for the doll acted just like a living creature, excepting that she could not speak. The man to whom the show belonged was quite delighted at having a doll who could dance of herself without being pulled by the wires; none of the other dolls could do this.

During the night, when all the people at the inn were gone to bed, some one was heard to sigh so deeply and painfully, and the sighing continued for so long a time, that every one got up to see what could be the matter. The showman went at once to his little theatre and found that it proceeded from the dolls, who all lay on the floor sighing piteously, and staring with their glass eyes; they all wanted to be rubbed with the ointment, so that, like the queen, they might be able to move of themselves. The queen threw herself on her knees, took off her beautiful crown, and, holding it in her hand, cried, "Take this from me, but do rub my husband and his courtiers."

The poor man who owned the theatre could scarcely refrain from weeping; he was so sorry that he could not help them. Then he immediately spoke to John's comrade, and promised him all the money he might receive at the next evening's performance, if he would only rub the ointment on four or five of his dolls. But the fellow-traveller said he did not require anything in return, excepting the sword which the showman wore by his side. As soon as he received the sword he anointed six of the dolls with the ointment, and they were able immediately to dance so gracefully that all the living girls in the room could not help joining in the dance. The coachman danced with the cook, and the waiters with the chambermaids, and all the strangers joined; even the tongs and the fire-shovel made an attempt, but they fell down after the first jump. So after all it was a very merry night. The next morning John and his companion left the inn to continue their journey through the great pine-forests and over the high mountains. They arrived at last at such a great height that towns and villages lay beneath them, and the church steeples looked like little specks between the green trees. They could see for miles round, far away to places they had never visited, and John saw more of the beautiful world than he had ever known before. The sun shone brightly in the blue firmament above, and through the clear mountain air came the sound of the huntsman's horn, and the soft, sweet notes brought tears into his eyes, and he could not help exclaiming, "How good and loving God is to give us all this beauty and loveliness in the world to make us happy!"

His fellow-traveller stood by with folded hands, gazing on the dark wood and the towns bathed in the warm sunshine. At this moment there sounded over their heads sweet music. They looked up, and discovered a large white swan hovering in the air, and singing as never bird sang before. But the song soon became weaker and weaker, the bird's head drooped, and he sunk slowly down, and lay dead at their feet.

"It is a beautiful bird," said the traveller, "and these large white wings are worth a great deal of money. I will take them with me. You see now that a sword will be very useful."

So he cut off the wings of the dead swan with one blow, and carried them away with him.

They now continued their journey over the mountains for many miles, till they at length reached a large city, containing hundreds of towers, that shone in the sunshine like silver. In the midst of the city stood a splendid marble palace, roofed with pure red gold, in which dwelt the king. John and his companion would not go into the town immediately; so they stopped at an inn outside the town, to change their clothes; for they wished to appear respectable as they walked through the streets. The landlord told them that the king was a very good man, who never injured any one: but as to his daughter, "Heaven defend us!"

She was indeed a wicked princess. She possessed beauty enough—nobody could be more elegant or prettier than she was; but what of that? for she was a wicked witch; and in consequence of her conduct many noble young princes had lost their lives. Any one was at liberty to make her an offer; were he a prince or a beggar, it mattered not to her. She would ask him to guess three things which she had just thought of, and if he succeed, he was to marry her, and be king over all the land when her father died; but if he could not guess these three things, then she ordered him to be hanged or to have his head cut off. The old king, her father, was very much grieved at her conduct, but he could not prevent her from being so wicked, because he once said he would have nothing more to do with her lovers; she might do as she pleased. Each prince who came and tried the three guesses, so that he might marry the princess, had been unable to find them out, and had been hanged or beheaded. They had all been warned in time, and might have left her alone, if they would. The old king became at last so distressed at all these dreadful circumstances, that for a whole day every year he and his soldiers knelt and prayed that the princess might become good; but she continued as wicked as ever. The old women who drank brandy would colour it quite black before they drank it, to show how they mourned; and what more could they do?

"What a horrible princess!" said John; "she ought to be well flogged. If I were the old king, I would have her punished in some way."

Just then they heard the people outside shouting, "Hurrah!" and, looking out, they saw the princess passing by; and she was really so beautiful that everybody forgot her wickedness, and shouted "Hurrah!" Twelve lovely maidens in white silk dresses, holding golden tulips in their hands, rode by her side on coal-black horses. The princess herself had a snow-white steed, decked with diamonds and rubies. Her dress was of cloth of gold, and the whip she held in her hand looked like a sunbeam. The golden crown on her head glittered like the stars of heaven, and her mantle was formed of thousands of butterflies' wings sewn together. Yet she herself was more beautiful than all.

When John saw her, his face became as red as a drop of blood, and he could scarcely utter a word. The princess looked exactly like the beautiful lady with the golden crown, of whom he had dreamed on the night his father died. She appeared to him so lovely that he could not help loving her.

"It could not be true," he thought, "that she was really a wicked witch, who ordered people to be hanged or beheaded, if they could not guess her thoughts. Every one has permission to go and ask her hand, even the poorest beggar. I shall pay a visit to the palace," he said; "I must go, for I cannot help myself."

Then they all advised him not to attempt it; for he would be sure to share the same fate as the rest. His fellow-traveller also tried to persuade him against it; but John seemed quite sure of success. He brushed his shoes and his coat, washed his face and his hands, combed his soft flaxen hair, and then went out alone into the town, and walked to the palace.

"Come in," said the king, as John knocked at the door. John opened it, and the old king, in a dressing gown and embroidered slippers, came towards him. He had the crown on his head, carried his sceptre in one hand, and the orb in the other. "Wait a bit," said he, and he placed the orb under his arm, so that he could offer the other hand to John; but when he found that John was another suitor, he began to weep so violently, that both the sceptre and the orb fell to the floor, and he was obliged to wipe his eyes with his dressing gown. Poor old king! "Let her alone," he said; "you will fare as badly as all the others. Come, I will show you." Then he led him out into the princess's pleasure gardens, and there he saw a frightful sight. On every tree hung three or four king's sons who had wooed the princess, but had not been able to guess the riddles she gave them. Their skeletons rattled in every breeze, so that the terrified birds never dared to venture into the garden. All the flowers were supported by human bones instead of sticks, and human skulls in the flowerpots grinned horribly. It was really a doleful garden for a princess. "Do you see all this?" said the old king; "your fate will be the same as those who are here, therefore do not attempt it. You really make me very unhappy—I take these things to heart so very much."

John kissed the good old king's hand, and said he was sure it would be all right, for he was quite enchanted with the beautiful princess. Then the princess herself came riding into the palace yard with all her ladies, and he wished her "Good morning." She looked wonderfully fair and lovely when she offered her hand to John, and he loved her more than ever. How could she be a wicked witch, as all the people asserted? He accompanied her into the hall, and the little pages offered them gingerbread nuts and sweetmeats, but the old king was so unhappy he could eat nothing, and besides, gingerbread nuts were too hard for him. It was decided that John should come to the palace the next day, when the judges and the whole of the counsellors would be present, to try if he could guess the first riddle. If he succeeded, he would have to come a second time; but if not, he would lose his life—and no one had ever been able to guess even one. However, John was not at all anxious about the result of his trial; on the contrary, he was very merry. He thought only of the beautiful princess, and believed that in some way he should have help, but how he knew not, and did not like to think about it; so he danced along the high road as he went back to the inn, where he had left his fellow-traveller waiting for him. John could not refrain from telling him how gracious the princess had been, and how beautiful she looked. He longed for the next day so much, that he might go to the palace and try his luck at guessing the riddles. But his comrade shook his head, and looked very mournful. "I do so wish you to do well," said he; "we might have continued together much longer, and now I am likely to lose you; you poor dear John! I could shed tears, but I will not make you unhappy on the last night we may be together. We will be merry, really merry this evening; tomorrow, after you are gone, shall be able to weep undisturbed."

It was very quickly known among the inhabitants of the town that another suitor had arrived for the princess, and there was great sorrow in consequence. The theatre remained closed, the women who sold sweetmeats tied crape round the sugar-sticks, and the king and the priests were on their knees in the church. There was a great lamentation, for no one expected John to succeed better than those who had been suitors before.

In the evening John's comrade prepared a large bowl of punch, and said, "Now let us be merry, and drink to the health of the princess." But after drinking two glasses, John became so sleepy, that he could not keep his eyes open, and fell fast asleep. Then his fellow-traveller lifted him gently out of his chair, and laid him on the bed; and as soon as it was quite dark, he took the two large wings which he had cut from the dead swan, and tied them firmly to his own shoulders. Then he put into his pocket the largest of the three rods which he had obtained from the old woman who had fallen and broken her leg. After this he opened the window, and flew away over the town, straight towards the palace, and seated himself in a corner, under the window which looked into the bedroom of the princess.

The town was perfectly still when the clocks struck a quarter to twelve. Presently the window opened, and the princess, who had large black wings to her shoulders, and a long white mantle, flew away over the city towards a high mountain. The fellow-traveller, who had made himself invisible, so that she could not possibly see him, flew after her through the air, and whipped the princess with his rod, so that the blood came whenever he struck her. Ah, it was a strange flight through the air! The wind caught her mantle, so that it spread out on all sides, like the large sail of a ship, and the moon shone through it. "How it hails, to be sure!" said the princess, at each blow she received from the rod; and it served her right to be whipped.

At last she reached the side of the mountain, and knocked. The mountain opened with a noise like the roll of thunder, and the princess went in. The traveller followed her; no one could see him, as he had made himself invisible. They went through a long, wide passage. A thousand gleaming spiders ran here and there on the walls, causing them to glitter as if they were illuminated with fire. They next entered a large hall built of silver and gold. Large red and blue flowers shone on the walls, looking like sunflowers in size, but no one could dare to pluck them, for the stems were hideous poisonous snakes, and the flowers were flames of fire, darting out of their jaws. Shining glow-worms covered the ceiling, and sky-blue bats flapped their transparent wings. Altogether the place had a frightful appearance. In the middle of the floor stood a throne supported by four skeleton horses, whose harness had been made by fiery-red spiders. The throne itself was made of milk-white glass, and the cushions were little black mice, each biting the other's tail. Over it hung a canopy of rose-coloured spider's webs, spotted with the prettiest little green flies, which sparkled like precious stones. On the throne sat an old magician with a crown on his ugly head, and a sceptre in his hand. He kissed the princess on the forehead, seated her by his side on the splendid throne, and then the music commenced. Great black grasshoppers played the mouth organ, and the owl struck herself on the body instead of a drum. It was altogether a ridiculous concert. Little black goblins with false lights in their caps danced about the hall; but no one could see the traveller, and he had placed himself just behind the throne where he could see and hear everything. The courtiers who came in afterwards looked noble and grand; but any one with common sense could see what they really were, only broomsticks, with cabbages for heads. The magician had given them life, and dressed them in embroidered robes. It answered very well, as they were only wanted for show. After there had been a little dancing, the princess told the magician that she had a new suitor, and asked him what she could think of for the suitor to guess when he came to the castle the next morning.

"Listen to what I say," said the magician, "you must choose something very easy, he is less likely to guess it then. Think of one of your shoes, he will never imagine it is that. Then cut his head off; and mind you do not forget to bring his eyes with you tomorrow night, that I may eat them."

The princess curtsied low, and said she would not forget the eyes.

The magician then opened the mountain and she flew home again, but the traveller followed and flogged her so much with the rod, that she sighed quite deeply about the heavy hailstorm, and made as much haste as she could to get back to her bedroom through the window. The traveller then returned to the inn where John still slept, took off his wings and laid down on the bed, for he was very tired. Early in the morning John awoke, and when his fellow-traveller got up, he said that he had a very wonderful dream about the princess and her shoe, he therefore advised John to ask her if she had not thought of her shoe. Of course the traveller knew this from what the magician in the mountain had said.

"I may as well say that as anything," said John. "Perhaps your dream may come true; still I will say farewell, for if I guess wrong I shall never see you again."

Then they embraced each other, and John went into the town and walked to the palace. The great hall was full of people, and the judges sat in arm-chairs, with eider-down cushions to rest their heads upon, because they had so much to think of. The old king stood near, wiping his eyes with his white pocket-handkerchief. When the princess entered, she looked even more beautiful than she had appeared the day before, and greeted every one present most gracefully; but to John she gave her hand, and said, "Good morning to you."

Now came the time for John to guess what she was thinking of; and oh, how kindly she looked at him as she spoke. But when he uttered the single word shoe, she turned as pale as a ghost; all her wisdom could not help her, for he had guessed rightly. Oh, how pleased the old king was! It was quite amusing to see how he capered about. All the people clapped their hands, both on his account and John's, who had guessed rightly the first time. His fellow-traveller was glad also, when he heard how successful John had been. But John folded his hands, and thanked God, who, he felt quite sure, would help him again; and he knew he had to guess twice more. The evening passed pleasantly like the one preceding. While John slept, his companion flew behind the princess to the mountain, and flogged her even harder than before; this time he had taken two rods with him. No one saw him go in with her, and he heard all that was said. The princess this time was to think of a glove, and he told John as if he had again heard it in a dream. The next day, therefore, he was able to guess correctly the second time, and it caused great rejoicing at the palace. The whole court jumped about as they had seen the king do the day before, but the princess lay on the sofa, and would not say a single word. All now depended upon John. If he only guessed rightly the third time, he would marry the princess, and reign over the kingdom after the death of the old king: but if he failed, he would lose his life, and the magician would have his beautiful blue eyes. That evening John said his prayers and went to bed very early, and soon fell asleep calmly. But his companion tied on his wings to his shoulders, took three rods, and, with his sword at his side, flew to the palace. It was a very dark night, and so stormy that the tiles flew from the roofs of the houses, and the trees in the garden upon which the skeletons hung bent themselves like reeds before the wind. The lightning flashed, and the thunder rolled in one long-continued peal all night. The window of the castle opened, and the princess flew out. She was pale as death, but she laughed at the storm as if it were not bad enough. Her white mantle fluttered in the wind like a large sail, and the traveller flogged her with the three rods till the blood trickled down, and at last she could scarcely fly; she contrived, however, to reach the mountain. "What a hailstorm!" she said, as she entered; "I have never been out in such weather as this."

"Yes, there may be too much of a good thing sometimes," said the magician.

Then the princess told him that John had guessed rightly the second time, and if he succeeded the next morning, he would win, and she could never come to the mountain again, or practice magic as she had done, and therefore she was quite unhappy. "I will find out something for you to think of which he will never guess, unless he is a greater conjuror than myself. But now let us be merry."

Then he took the princess by both hands, and they danced with all the little goblins and Jack-o'-lanterns in the room. The red spiders sprang here and there on the walls quite as merrily, and the flowers of fire appeared as if they were throwing out sparks. The owl beat the drum, the crickets whistled and the grasshoppers played the mouth-organ. It was a very ridiculous ball. After they had danced enough, the princess was obliged to go home, for fear she should be missed at the palace. The magician offered to go with her, that they might be company to each other on the way. Then they flew away through the bad weather, and the traveller followed them, and broke his three rods across their shoulders. The magician had never been out in such a hailstorm as this. Just by the palace the magician stopped to wish the princess farewell, and to whisper in her ear, "Tomorrow think of my head."

But the traveller heard it, and just as the princess slipped through the window into her bedroom, and the magician turned round to fly back to the mountain, he seized him by the long black beard, and with his sabre cut off the wicked conjuror's head just behind the shoulders, so that he could not even see who it was. He threw the body into the sea to the fishes, and after dipping the head into the water, he tied it up in a silk handkerchief, took it with him to the inn, and then went to bed. The next morning he gave John the handkerchief, and told him not to untie it till the princess asked him what she was thinking of. There were so many people in the great hall of the palace that they stood as thick as radishes tied together in a bundle. The council sat in their arm-chairs with the white cushions. The old king wore new robes, and the golden crown and sceptre had been polished up so that he looked quite smart. But the princess was very pale, and wore a black dress as if she were going to a funeral.

"What have I thought of?" asked the princess, of John. He immediately untied the handkerchief, and was himself quite frightened when he saw the head of the ugly magician. Every one shuddered, for it was terrible to look at; but the princess sat like a statue, and could not utter a single word. At length she rose and gave John her hand, for he had guessed rightly.

She looked at no one, but sighed deeply, and said, "You are my master now; this evening our marriage must take place."

"I am very pleased to hear it," said the old king. "It is just what I wish."

Then all the people shouted "Hurrah." The band played music in the streets, the bells rang, and the cake-women took the black crape off the sugar-sticks. There was universal joy. Three oxen, stuffed with ducks and chickens, were roasted whole in the market-place, where every one might help himself to a slice. The fountains spouted forth the most delicious wine, and whoever bought a penny loaf at the baker's received six large buns, full of raisins, as a present. In the evening the whole town was illuminated. The soldiers fired off cannons, and the boys let off crackers. There was eating and drinking, dancing and jumping everywhere. In the palace, the high-born gentlemen and beautiful ladies danced with each other, and they could be heard at a great distance singing the following song:—

> "Here are maidens, young and fair,
> Dancing in the summer air;
> Like two spinning wheels at play,
> Pretty maidens dance away-
> Dance the spring and summer through
> Till the sole falls from your shoe."

But the princess was still a witch, and she could not love John. His fellow-traveller had thought of that, so he gave John three feathers out of the swan's wings, and a little bottle with a few drops in it. He told him to place a large bath full of water by the princess's bed, and put the feathers and the drops into it. Then, at the moment she was about to get into bed, he must give her a little push, so that she might fall into the water, and then dip her three times. This would destroy the power of the magician, and she would love him very much. John did all that his companion told him to do. The princess shrieked aloud when he dipped her under the water the first time, and struggled under his hands in the form of a great black swan with fiery eyes. As she rose the second time from the water, the swan had become white, with a black ring round its neck. John allowed the water to close once more over the bird, and at the same time it changed into a most beautiful princess. She was more lovely even than before, and thanked him, while her eyes sparkled with tears, for having broken the spell of the magician. The next day, the king came with the whole court to offer their congratulations, and stayed till quite late. Last of all came the travelling companion; he had his staff in his hand and his knapsack on his back. John kissed him many times and told him he must not go, he must remain with him, for he was the cause of all his good fortune. But the traveller shook his head, and said gently and kindly, "No: my time is up now; I have only paid my debt to you. Do you remember the dead man whom the bad people wished to throw out of his coffin? You gave all you possessed that he might rest in his grave; I am that man." As he said this, he vanished.

The wedding festivities lasted a whole month. John and his princess loved each other dearly, and the old king lived to see many a happy day, when he took their little children on his knees and let them play with his sceptre. And John became king over the whole country.

The Little Mermaid

Translated by Mrs. H. P. Paull

Far out in the ocean, where the water is as blue as the prettiest cornflower, and as clear as crystal, it is very, very deep; so deep, indeed, that no cable could fathom it: many church steeples, piled one upon another, would not reach from the ground beneath to the surface of the water above. There dwell the Sea King and his subjects. We must not imagine that there is nothing at the bottom of the sea but bare yellow sand. No, indeed; the most singular flowers and plants grow there; the leaves and stems of which are so pliant, that the slightest agitation of the water causes them to stir as if they had life. Fishes, both large and small, glide between the branches, as birds fly among the trees here upon land. In the deepest spot of all, stands the castle of the Sea King. Its walls are built of coral, and the long, gothic windows are of the clearest amber. The roof is formed of shells, that open and close as the water flows over them. Their appearance is very beautiful, for in each lies a glittering pearl, which would be fit for the diadem of a queen.

The Sea King had been a widower for many years, and his

aged mother kept house for him. She was a very wise woman, and exceedingly proud of her high birth; on that account she wore twelve oysters on her tail; while others, also of high rank, were only allowed to wear six. She was, however, deserving of very great praise, especially for her care of the little sea-princesses, her granddaughters. They were six beautiful children; but the youngest was the prettiest of them all; her skin was as clear and delicate as a rose-leaf, and her eyes as blue as the deepest sea; but, like all the others, she had no feet, and her body ended in a fish's tail. All day long they played in the great halls of the castle, or among the living flowers that grew out of the walls. The large amber windows were open, and the fish swam in, just as the swallows fly into our houses when we open the windows, excepting that the fishes swam up to the princesses, ate out of their hands, and allowed themselves to be stroked. Outside the castle there was a beautiful garden, in which grew bright red and dark blue flowers, and blossoms like flames of fire; the fruit glittered like gold, and the leaves and stems waved to and fro continually. The earth itself was the finest sand, but blue as the flame of burning sulphur. Over everything lay a peculiar blue radiance, as if it were surrounded by the air from above, through which the blue sky shone, instead of the dark depths of the sea. In calm weather the sun could be seen, looking like a purple flower, with the light streaming from the calyx. Each of the young princesses had a little plot of ground in the garden, where she might dig and plant as she pleased. One arranged her flower-bed into the form of a whale; another thought it better to make hers like the figure of a little mermaid; but that of the youngest was round like the sun, and contained flowers as red as his rays at sunset. She was a strange child, quiet and thoughtful; and while her sisters would be delighted with the wonderful things which they obtained from the wrecks of vessels, she cared for nothing but her pretty red flowers, like the sun, excepting a beautiful marble statue. It was the representation of a handsome boy, carved out of pure white stone, which had fallen to the bottom of the sea from a wreck. She planted by the statue a rose-coloured weeping willow. It grew splendidly, and very soon hung its fresh branches over the statue, almost down to the blue sands. The shadow had a violet tint, and waved to and fro like the branches; it seemed as if the crown of the tree and the root were at play, and trying to kiss each other. Nothing gave her so much pleasure as to hear about the world above the sea. She made her old grandmother tell her all she knew of the ships and of the towns, the people and the animals. To her it seemed most wonderful and beautiful to hear that the flowers of the land should have fragrance, and not those below the sea; that the trees of the forest should be green; and that the fishes among the trees could sing so sweetly, that it was quite a pleasure to hear them. Her grandmother called the little birds fishes, or she would not have understood her; for she had never seen birds.

"When you have reached your fifteenth year," said the grandmother, "you will have permission to rise up out of the sea, to sit on the rocks in the moonlight, while the great ships are sailing by; and then you will see both forests and towns."

In the following year, one of the sisters would be fifteen: but as each was a year younger than the other, the youngest would have to wait five years before her turn came to rise up from the bottom of the ocean, and see the earth as we do. However, each promised to tell the others what she saw on her first visit, and what she thought the most beautiful; for their grandmother could not tell them enough; there were so many things on which they wanted information. None of them longed so much for her turn to come as the youngest, she who had the longest time to wait, and who was so quiet and thoughtful. Many nights she stood by the open window, looking up through the dark blue water, and watching the fish as they splashed about with their fins and tails. She could see the moon and stars shining faintly; but through the water they looked larger than they do to our eyes. When something like a black cloud passed between her and them, she knew that it was either a whale swimming over her head, or a ship full of human beings, who never imagined that a pretty little mermaid was standing beneath them, holding out her white hands towards the keel of their ship.

As soon as the eldest was fifteen, she was allowed to rise to the surface of the ocean. When she came back, she had hundreds of things to talk about; but the most beautiful, she said, was to lie in the moonlight, on a sandbank, in the quiet sea, near the coast, and to gaze on a large town nearby, where the lights were twinkling like hundreds of stars; to listen to the sounds of the music, the noise of carriages, and the voices of human beings, and then to hear the merry bells peal out from the church steeples; and because she could not go near to all those wonderful things, she longed for them more than ever. Oh, did not the youngest sister listen eagerly to all these descriptions? and afterwards, when she stood at the open window looking up through the dark blue water, she thought of the great city, with all its bustle and noise, and even fancied she could hear the sound of the church bells, down in the depths of the sea.

In another year the second sister received permission to rise to the surface of the water, and to swim about where she pleased. She rose just as the sun was setting, and this, she said, was the most beautiful sight of all. The whole sky looked like gold, while violet and rose-coloured clouds, which she could not describe, floated over her; and, still more rapidly than the clouds, flew a large flock of wild swans towards the setting sun, looking like a long white veil across the sea. She also swam towards the sun; but it sunk into the waves, and the rosy tints faded from the clouds and from the sea.

The third sister's turn followed; she was the boldest of them all, and she swam up a broad river that emptied itself into the sea. On the banks she saw green hills covered with beautiful vines; palaces and castles peeped out from amid the proud trees of the forest; she heard the birds singing, and the rays of the sun were so powerful that she was obliged often to dive down under the water to cool her burning face. In a narrow creek she found a whole troop of little human children, quite naked, and sporting about in the water; she wanted to play with them, but they fled in a great fright; and then a little black animal came to the water; it was a dog, but she did not know that, for she had never before seen one. This animal barked at her so terribly that she became frightened, and rushed back to the open sea. But she said she should never forget the beautiful forest, the green hills, and the pretty little children who could swim in the water, although they had not fish's tails.

The fourth sister was more timid; she remained in the midst of the sea, but she said it was quite as beautiful there as nearer the land. She could see for so many miles around her, and the sky above looked like a bell of glass. She had seen the ships, but at such a great distance that they looked like sea-gulls. The dolphins sported in the waves, and the great whales spouted water from their nostrils till it seemed as if a hundred fountains were playing in every direction.

The fifth sister's birthday occurred in the winter; so when her turn came, she saw what the others had not seen the first time they went up. The sea looked quite green, and large icebergs were floating about, each like a pearl, she said, but larger and loftier than the churches built by men. They were of the most singular shapes, and glittered like diamonds. She had seated herself upon one of the largest, and let the wind play with her long hair, and she remarked that all the ships sailed by rapidly, and steered as far away as they could from the iceberg, as if they were afraid of it. Towards evening, as the sun went down, dark clouds covered the sky, the thunder rolled and the lightning flashed, and the red light glowed on the icebergs as they rocked and tossed on the heaving sea. On all the ships the sails were reefed with fear and trembling, while she sat calmly on the floating iceberg, watching the blue lightning, as it darted its forked flashes into the sea.

When first the sisters had permission to rise to the surface, they were each delighted with the new and beautiful sights they saw; but now, as grown-up girls, they could go when they pleased, and they had become indifferent about it. They wished themselves back again in the water, and after a month had passed they said it was much more beautiful down below, and pleasanter to be at home. Yet often, in the evening hours, the five sisters would twine their arms round each other, and rise to the surface, in a row. They had more beautiful voices than any human being could have; and before the approach of a storm, and when they expected a ship would be lost, they swam before the vessel, and sang sweetly of the delights to be found in the depths of the sea, and begging the sailors not to fear if they sank to the bottom. But the sailors could not understand the song, they took it for the howling of the storm. And these things were never to be beautiful for them; for if the ship sank, the men were drowned, and their dead bodies alone reached the palace of the Sea King.

When the sisters rose, arm-in-arm, through the water in this way, their youngest sister would stand quite alone, looking after them, ready to cry, only that the mermaids have no tears, and therefore they suffer more. "Oh, were I but fifteen years old," said she: "I know that I shall love the world up there, and all the people who live in it."

At last she reached her fifteenth year. "Well, now, you are grown up," said the old dowager, her grandmother; "so you must let me adorn you like your other sisters;" and she placed a wreath of white lilies in her hair, and every flower leaf was half a pearl. Then the old lady ordered eight great oysters to attach themselves to the tail of the princess to show her high rank.

"But they hurt me so," said the little mermaid.

"Pride must suffer pain," replied the old lady. Oh, how gladly she would have shaken off all this grandeur, and laid aside the heavy wreath! The red flowers in her own garden would have suited her much better, but she could not help herself: so she said, "Farewell," and rose as lightly as a bubble to the surface of the water. The sun had just set as she raised her head above the waves; but the clouds were tinted with crimson and gold, and through the glimmering twilight beamed the evening star in all its beauty. The sea was calm, and the air mild and fresh. A large ship, with three masts, lay becalmed on the water, with only one sail set; for not a breeze stiffed, and the sailors sat idle on deck or amongst the rigging. There was music and song on board; and, as darkness came on, a hundred coloured lanterns were lighted, as if the flags of all nations waved in the air. The little mermaid swam close to the cabin windows; and now and then, as the waves lifted her up, she could look in through clear glass windowpanes, and see a number of well-dressed people within. Among them was a young prince, the most beautiful of all, with large black eyes; he was sixteen years of age, and his birthday was being kept with much rejoicing. The sailors were dancing on deck, but when the prince came out of the cabin, more than a hundred rockets rose in the air, making it as bright as day. The little mermaid was so startled that she dived under water; and when she again stretched out her head, it appeared as if all the stars of heaven were falling around her, she had never seen such fireworks before. Great suns spurted fire about, splendid fireflies flew into the blue air, and everything was reflected in the clear, calm sea beneath. The ship itself was so brightly illuminated that all the people, and even the smallest rope, could be distinctly and plainly seen. And how handsome the young prince looked, as he pressed the hands of all present and smiled at them, while the music resounded through the clear night air.

It was very late; yet the little mermaid could not take her eyes from the ship, or from the beautiful prince. The coloured lanterns had been extinguished, no more rockets rose in the air, and the cannon had ceased firing; but the sea became restless, and a moaning, grumbling sound could be heard beneath the waves: still the little mermaid remained by the cabin window, rocking up and down on the water, which enabled her to look in. After a while, the sails were quickly unfurled, and the noble ship continued her passage; but soon the waves rose higher, heavy clouds darkened the sky, and lightning appeared in the distance. A dreadful storm was approaching; once more the sails were reefed, and the great ship pursued her flying course over the raging sea. The waves rose mountains high, as if they would have overtopped the mast; but the ship dived like a swan between them, and then rose again on their lofty, foaming crests. To the little mermaid this appeared pleasant sport; not so to the sailors. At length the ship groaned and creaked; the thick planks gave way under the lashing of the sea as it broke over the deck; the mainmast snapped asunder like a reed; the ship lay over on her side; and the water rushed in. The little mermaid now perceived that the crew were in danger; even she herself was obliged to be careful to avoid the beams and planks of the wreck which lay scattered on the water. At one moment it was so pitch dark that she could not see a single object, but a flash of lightning revealed the whole scene; she could see every one who had been on board excepting the prince; when the ship parted, she had seen him sink into the deep waves, and she was glad, for she thought he would now be with her; and then she remembered that human beings could not live in the water, so that when he got down to her father's palace he would be quite dead. But he must not die. So she swam about among the beams and planks which strewed the surface of the sea, forgetting that they could crush her to pieces. Then she dived deeply under the dark waters, rising and falling with the waves, till at length she managed to reach the young prince, who was fast losing the power of swimming in that stormy sea. His limbs were failing him, his beautiful eyes were closed, and he would have died had not the little mermaid come to his assistance. She held his head above the water, and let the waves drift them where they would.

In the morning the storm had ceased; but of the ship not a single fragment could be seen. The sun rose up red and glowing from the water, and its beams brought back the hue of health to the prince's cheeks; but his eyes remained closed. The mermaid kissed his high, smooth forehead, and stroked back his wet hair; he seemed to her like the marble statue in her little garden, and she kissed him again, and wished that he might live. Presently they came in sight of land; she saw lofty blue mountains, on which the white snow rested as if a flock of swans were lying upon them. Near the coast were beautiful green forests, and close by stood a large building, whether a church or a convent she could not tell. Orange and citron trees grew in the garden, and before the door stood lofty palms. The sea here formed a little bay, in which the water was quite still, but very deep; so she swam with the handsome prince to the beach, which was covered with fine, white sand, and there she laid him in the warm sunshine, taking care to raise his head higher than his body. Then bells sounded in the large white building, and a number of young girls came into the garden. The little mermaid swam out farther from the shore and placed herself between some high rocks that rose out of the water; then she covered her head and neck with the foam of the sea so that her little face might not be seen, and watched to see what would become of the poor prince. She did not wait long before she saw a young girl approach the spot where he lay.

She seemed frightened at first, but only for a moment; then she fetched a number of people, and the mermaid saw that the prince came to life again, and smiled upon those who stood round him. But to her he sent no smile; he knew not that she had saved him. This made her very unhappy, and when he was led away into the great building, she dived down sorrowfully into the water, and returned to her father's castle. She had always been silent and thoughtful, and now she was more so than ever. Her sisters asked her what she had seen during her first visit to the surface of the water; but she would tell them nothing. Many an evening and morning did she rise to the place where she had left the prince. She saw the fruits in the garden ripen till they were gathered, the snow on the tops of the mountains melt away; but she never saw the prince, and therefore she returned home, always more sorrowful than before. It was her only comfort to sit in her own little garden, and fling her arm round the beautiful marble statue which was like the prince; but she gave up tending her flowers, and they grew in wild confusion over the paths, twining their long leaves and stems round the branches of the trees, so that the whole place became dark and gloomy. At length she could bear it no longer, and told one of her sisters all about it. Then the others heard the secret, and very soon it became known to two mermaids whose intimate friend happened to know who the prince was. She had also seen the festival on board ship, and she told them where the prince came from, and where his palace stood.

"Come, little sister," said the other princesses; then they entwined their arms and rose up in a long row to the surface of the water, close by the spot where they knew the prince's palace stood. It was built of bright yellow shining stone, with long flights of marble steps, one of which reached quite down to the sea. Splendid gilded cupolas rose over the roof, and between the pillars that surrounded the whole building stood life-like statues of marble. Through the clear crystal of the lofty windows could be seen noble rooms, with costly silk curtains and hangings of tapestry; while the walls were covered with beautiful paintings which were a pleasure to look at. In the centre of the largest saloon a fountain threw its sparkling jets high up into the glass cupola of the ceiling, through which the sun shone down upon the water and upon the beautiful plants growing round the basin of the fountain. Now that she knew where he lived, she spent many an evening and many a night on the water near the palace. She would swim much nearer the shore than any of the others ventured to do; indeed once she went quite up the narrow channel under the marble balcony, which threw a broad shadow on the water. Here she would sit and watch the young prince, who thought himself quite alone in the bright moonlight. She saw him many times of an evening sailing in a pleasant boat, with music playing and flags waving. She peeped out from among the green rushes, and if the wind caught her long silvery-white veil, those who saw it believed it to be a swan, spreading out its wings. On many a night, too, when the fishermen, with their torches, were out at sea, she heard them relate so many good things about the doings of the young prince, that she was glad she had saved his life when he had been tossed about half-dead on the waves. And she remembered that his head had rested on her bosom, and how heartily she had kissed him; but he knew nothing of all this, and could not even dream of her. She grew more and more fond of human beings, and wished more and more to be able to wander about with those whose world seemed to be so much larger than her own. They could fly over the sea in ships, and mount the high hills which were far above the clouds; and the lands they possessed, their woods and their fields, stretched far away beyond the reach of her sight. There was so much that she wished to know, and her sisters were unable to answer all her questions. Then she applied to her old grandmother, who knew all about the upper world, which she very rightly called the lands above the sea.

"If human beings are not drowned," asked the little mermaid, "can they live forever? Do they never die as we do here in the sea?"

"Yes," replied the old lady, "they must also die, and their term of life is even shorter than ours. We sometimes live to three hundred years, but when we cease to exist here we only become the foam on the surface of the water, and we have not even a grave down here of those we love. We have not immortal souls, we shall never live again; but, like the green sea-weed, when once it has been cut off, we can never flourish more. Human beings, on the contrary, have a soul which lives forever, lives after the body has been turned to dust. It rises up through the clear, pure air beyond the glittering stars. As we rise out of the water, and behold all the land of the earth, so do they rise to unknown and glorious regions which we shall never see."

"Why have not we an immortal soul?" asked the little mermaid mournfully; "I would give gladly all the hundreds of years that I have to live, to be a human being only for one day, and to have the hope of knowing the happiness of that glorious world above the stars."

"You must not think of that," said the old woman; "we feel ourselves to be much happier and much better off than human beings."

"So I shall die," said the little mermaid, "and as the foam of the sea I shall be driven about never again to hear the music of the waves, or to see the pretty flowers nor the red sun. Is there anything I can do to win an immortal soul?"

"No," said the old woman, "unless a man were to love you so much that you were more to him than his father or mother; and if all his thoughts and all his love were fixed upon you, and the priest placed his right hand in yours, and he promised to be true to you here and hereafter, then his soul would glide into your body and you would obtain a share in the future happiness of mankind. He would give a soul to you and retain his own as well; but this can never happen. Your fish's tail, which amongst us is considered so beautiful, is thought on earth to be quite ugly; they do not know any better, and they think it necessary to have two stout props, which they call legs, in order to be handsome."

Then the little mermaid sighed, and looked sorrowfully at her fish's tail.

"Let us be happy," said the old lady, "and dart and spring about during the three hundred years that we have to live, which is really quite long enough; after that we can rest ourselves all the better. This evening we are going to have a court ball."

It is one of those splendid sights which we can never see on earth. The walls and the ceiling of the large ballroom were of thick, but transparent crystal. May hundreds of colossal shells, some of a deep red, others of a grass green, stood on each side in rows, with blue fire in them, which lighted up the whole saloon, and shone through the walls, so that the sea was also illuminated. Innumerable fishes, great and small, swam past the crystal walls; on some of them the scales glowed with a purple brilliancy, and on others they shone like silver and gold. Through the halls flowed a broad stream, and in it danced the mermen and the mermaids to the music of their own sweet singing. No one on earth has such a lovely voice as theirs. The little mermaid sang more sweetly than them all. The whole court applauded her with hands and tails; and for a moment her heart felt quite gay, for she knew she had the loveliest voice of any on earth or in the sea. But she soon thought again of the world above her, for she could not forget the charming prince, nor her sorrow that she had not an immortal soul like his; therefore she crept away silently out of her father's palace, and while everything within was gladness and song, she sat in her own little garden sorrowful and alone. Then she heard the bugle sounding through the water, and thought—"He is certainly sailing above, he on whom my wishes depend, and in whose hands I should like to place the happiness of my life. I will venture all for him, and to win an immortal soul, while my sisters are dancing in my father's palace, I will go to the sea witch, of whom I have always been so much afraid, but she can give me counsel and help."

And then the little mermaid went out from her garden, and took the road to the foaming whirlpools, behind which the sorceress lived. She had never been that way before: neither flowers nor grass grew there; nothing but bare, gray, sandy ground stretched out to the whirlpool, where the water, like foaming mill-wheels, whirled round everything that it seized, and cast it into the fathomless deep. Through the midst of these crushing whirlpools the little mermaid was obliged to pass, to reach the dominions of the sea witch; and also for a long distance the only road lay right across a quantity of warm, bubbling mire, called by the witch her turfmoor. Beyond this stood her house, in the centre of a strange forest, in which all the trees and flowers were polypi, half animals and half plants; they looked like serpents with a hundred heads growing out of the ground. The branches were long slimy arms, with fingers like flexible worms, moving limb after limb from the root to the top. All that could be reached in the sea they seized upon, and held fast, so that it never escaped from their clutches. The little mermaid was so alarmed at what she saw, that she stood still, and her heart beat with fear, and she was very nearly turning back; but she thought of the prince, and of the human soul for which she longed, and her courage returned. She fastened her long flowing hair round her head, so that the polypi might not seize hold of it. She laid her hands together across her bosom, and then she darted forward as a fish shoots through the water, between the supple arms and fingers of the ugly polypi, which were stretched out on each side of her. She saw that each held in its grasp something it had seized with its numerous little arms, as if they were iron bands. The white skeletons of human beings who had perished at sea, and had sunk down into the deep waters, skeletons of land animals, oars, rudders, and chests of ships were lying tightly grasped by their clinging arms; even a little mermaid, whom they had caught and strangled; and this seemed the most shocking of all to the little princess.

She now came to a space of marshy ground in the wood, where large, fat water-snakes were rolling in the mire, and showing their ugly, drab-coloured bodies. In the midst of this spot stood a house, built with the bones of shipwrecked human beings. There sat the sea witch, allowing a toad to eat from her mouth, just as people sometimes feed a canary with a piece of sugar. She called the ugly water-snakes her little chickens, and allowed them to crawl all over her bosom.

"I know what you want," said the sea witch; "it is very stupid of you, but you shall have your way, and it will bring you to sorrow, my pretty princess. You want to get rid of your fish's tail, and to have two supports instead of it, like human beings on earth, so that the young prince may fall in love with you, and that you may have an immortal soul." And then the witch laughed so loud and disgustingly, that the toad and the snakes fell to the ground, and lay there wriggling about. "You are but just in time," said the witch; "for after sunrise tomorrow I should not be able to help you till the end of another year. I will prepare a draught for you, with which you must swim to land tomorrow before sunrise, and sit down on the shore and drink it. Your tail will then disappear, and shrink up into what mankind calls legs, and you will feel great pain, as if a sword were passing through you. But all who see you will say that you are the prettiest little human being they ever saw. You will still have the same floating gracefulness of movement, and no dancer will ever tread so lightly; but at every step you take it will feel as if you were treading upon sharp knives, and that the blood must flow. If you will bear all this, I will help you."

"Yes, I will," said the little princess in a trembling voice, as she thought of the prince and the immortal soul.

"But think again," said the witch; "for when once your shape has become like a human being, you can no more be a mermaid. You will never return through the water to your sisters, or to your father's palace again; and if you do not win the love of the prince, so that he is willing to forget his father and mother for your sake, and to love you with his whole soul, and allow the priest to join your hands that you may be man and wife, then you will never have an immortal soul. The first morning after he marries another your heart will break, and you will become foam on the crest of the waves."

"I will do it," said the little mermaid, and she became pale as death.

"But I must be paid also," said the witch, "and it is not a trifle that I ask. You have the sweetest voice of any who dwell here in the depths of the sea, and you believe that you will be able to charm the prince with it also, but this voice you must give to me; the best thing you possess will I have for the price of my draught. My own blood must be mixed with it, that it may be as sharp as a two-edged sword."

"But if you take away my voice," said the little mermaid, "what is left for me?"

"Your beautiful form, your graceful walk, and your expressive eyes; surely with these you can enchain a man's heart. Well, have you lost your courage? Put out your little tongue that I may cut it off as my payment; then you shall have the powerful draught."

"It shall be," said the little mermaid.

Then the witch placed her cauldron on the fire, to prepare the magic draught.

"Cleanliness is a good thing," said she, scouring the vessel with snakes, which she had tied together in a large knot; then she pricked herself in the breast, and let the black blood drop into it. The steam that rose formed itself into such horrible shapes that no one could look at them without fear. Every moment the witch threw something else into the vessel, and when it began to boil, the sound was like the weeping of a crocodile. When at last the magic draught was ready, it looked like the clearest water. "There it is for you," said the witch. Then she cut off the mermaid's tongue, so that she became dumb, and would never again speak or sing. "If the polypi should seize hold of you as you return through the wood," said the witch, "throw over them a few drops of the potion, and their fingers will be torn into a thousand pieces." But the little mermaid had no occasion to do this, for the polypi sprang back in terror when they caught sight of the glittering draught, which shone in her hand like a twinkling star.

So she passed quickly through the wood and the marsh, and between the rushing whirlpools. She saw that in her father's palace the torches in the ballroom were extinguished, and all within asleep; but she did not venture to go in to them, for now she was dumb and going to leave them forever, she felt as if her heart would break. She stole into the garden, took a flower from the flower-beds of each of her sisters, kissed her hand a thousand times towards the palace, and then rose up through the dark blue waters. The sun had not risen when she came in sight of the prince's palace, and approached the beautiful marble steps, but the moon shone clear and bright. Then the little mermaid drank the magic draught, and it seemed as if a two-edged sword went through her delicate body: she fell into a swoon, and lay like one dead. When the sun arose and shone over the sea, she recovered, and felt a sharp pain; but just before her stood the handsome young prince. He fixed his coal-black eyes upon her so earnestly that she cast down her own, and then became aware that her fish's tail was gone, and that she had as pretty a pair of white legs and tiny feet as any little maiden could have; but she had no clothes, so she wrapped herself in her long, thick hair. The prince asked her who she was, and where she came from, and she looked at him mildly and sorrowfully with her deep blue eyes; but she could not speak. Every step she took was as the witch had said it would be, she felt as if treading upon the points of needles or sharp knives; but she bore it willingly, and stepped as lightly by the prince's side as a soap-bubble, so that he and all who saw her wondered at her graceful-swaying movements. She was very soon arrayed in costly robes of silk and muslin, and was the most beautiful creature in the palace; but she was dumb, and could neither speak nor sing.

Beautiful female slaves, dressed in silk and gold, stepped forward and sang before the prince and his royal parents: one sang better than all the others, and the prince clapped his hands and smiled at her. This was great sorrow to the little mermaid; she knew how much more sweetly she herself could sing once, and she thought, "Oh if he could only know that! I have given away my voice forever, to be with him."

The slaves next performed some pretty fairy-like dances, to the sound of beautiful music. Then the little mermaid raised her lovely white arms, stood on the tips of her toes, and glided over the floor, and danced as no one yet had been able to dance. At each moment her beauty became more revealed, and her expressive eyes appealed more directly to the heart than the songs of the slaves. Every one was enchanted, especially the prince, who called her his little foundling; and she danced again quite readily, to please him, though each time her foot touched the floor it seemed as if she trod on sharp knives."

The prince said she should remain with him always, and she received permission to sleep at his door, on a velvet cushion. He had a page's dress made for her, that she might accompany him on horseback. They rode together through the sweet-scented woods, where the green boughs touched their shoulders, and the little birds sang among the fresh leaves. She climbed with the prince to the tops of high mountains; and although her tender feet bled so that even her steps were marked, she only laughed, and followed him till they could see the clouds beneath them looking like a flock of birds travelling to distant lands. While at the prince's palace, and when all the household were asleep, she would go and sit on the broad marble steps; for it eased her burning feet to bathe them in the cold seawater; and then she thought of all those below in the deep.

Once during the night her sisters came up arm-in-arm, singing sorrowfully, as they floated on the water. She beckoned to them, and then they recognized her, and told her how she had grieved them. After that, they came to the same place every night; and once she saw in the distance her old grandmother, who had not been to the surface of the sea for many years, and the old Sea King, her father, with his crown on his head. They stretched out their hands towards her, but they did not venture so near the land as her sisters did.

As the days passed, she loved the prince more fondly, and he loved her as he would love a little child, but it never came into his head to make her his wife; yet, unless he married her, she could not receive an immortal soul; and, on the morning after his marriage with another, she would dissolve into the foam of the sea.

"Do you not love me the best of them all?" the eyes of the little mermaid seemed to say, when he took her in his arms, and kissed her fair forehead.

"Yes, you are dear to me," said the prince; "for you have the best heart, and you are the most devoted to me; you are like a young maiden whom I once saw, but whom I shall never meet again. I was in a ship that was wrecked, and the waves cast me ashore near a holy temple, where several young maidens performed the service. The youngest of them found me on the shore, and saved my life. I saw her but twice, and she is the only one in the world whom I could love; but you are like her, and you have almost driven her image out of my mind. She belongs to the holy temple, and my good fortune has sent you to me instead of her; and we will never part."

"Ah, he knows not that it was I who saved his life," thought the little mermaid. "I carried him over the sea to the wood where the temple stands: I sat beneath the foam, and watched till the human beings came to help him. I saw the pretty maiden that he loves better than he loves me;" and the mermaid sighed deeply, but she could not shed tears. "He says the maiden belongs to the holy temple, therefore she will never return to the world. They will meet no more: while I am by his side, and see him every day. I will take care of him, and love him, and give up my life for his sake."

Very soon it was said that the prince must marry, and that the beautiful daughter of a neighbouring king would be his wife, for a fine ship was being fitted out. Although the prince gave out that he merely intended to pay a visit to the king, it was generally supposed that he really went to see his daughter. A great company were to go with him. The little mermaid smiled, and shook her head. She knew the prince's thoughts better than any of the others.

"I must travel," he had said to her; "I must see this beautiful princess; my parents desire it; but they will not oblige me to bring her home as my bride. I cannot love her; she is not like the beautiful maiden in the temple, whom you resemble. If I were forced to choose a bride, I would rather choose you, my dumb foundling, with those expressive eyes." And then he kissed her rosy mouth, played with her long waving hair, and laid his head on her heart, while she dreamed of human happiness and an immortal soul. "You are not afraid of the sea, my dumb child," said he, as they stood on the deck of the noble ship which was to carry them to the country of the neighbouring king. And then he told her of storm and of calm, of strange fishes in the deep beneath them, and of what the divers had seen there; and she smiled at his descriptions, for she knew better than any one what wonders were at the bottom of the sea.

In the moonlight, when all on board were asleep, excepting the man at the helm, who was steering, she sat on the deck, gazing down through the clear water. She thought she could distinguish her father's castle, and upon it her aged grandmother, with the silver crown on her head, looking through the rushing tide at the keel of the vessel. Then her sisters came up on the waves, and gazed at her mournfully, wringing their white hands. She beckoned to them, and smiled, and wanted to tell them how happy and well off she was; but the cabin-boy approached, and when her sisters dived down he thought it was only the foam of the sea which he saw.

The next morning the ship sailed into the harbor of a beautiful town belonging to the king whom the prince was going to visit. The church bells were ringing, and from the high towers sounded a flourish of trumpets; and soldiers, with flying colours and glittering bayonets, lined the rocks through which they passed. Every day was a festival; balls and entertainments followed one another.

But the princess had not yet appeared. People said that she was being brought up and educated in a religious house, where she was learning every royal virtue. At last she came. Then the little mermaid, who was very anxious to see whether she was really beautiful, was obliged to acknowledge that she had never seen a more perfect vision of beauty. Her skin was delicately fair, and beneath her long dark eyelashes her laughing blue eyes shone with truth and purity.

"It was you," said the prince, "who saved my life when I lay dead on the beach," and he folded his blushing bride in his arms. "Oh, I am too happy," said he to the little mermaid; "my fondest hopes are all fulfilled. You will rejoice at my happiness; for your devotion to me is great and sincere."

The little mermaid kissed his hand, and felt as if her heart were already broken. His wedding morning would bring death to her, and she would change into the foam of the sea. All the church bells rung, and the heralds rode about the town proclaiming the betrothal. Perfumed oil was burning in costly silver lamps on every altar. The priests waved the censers, while the bride and bridegroom joined their hands and received the blessing of the bishop. The little mermaid, dressed in silk and gold, held up the bride's train; but her ears heard nothing of the festive music, and her eyes saw not the holy ceremony; she thought of the night of death which was coming to her, and of all she had lost in the world. On the same evening the bride and bridegroom went on board ship; cannons were roaring, flags waving, and in the centre of the ship a costly tent of purple and gold had been erected. It contained elegant couches, for the reception of the bridal pair during the night. The ship, with swelling sails and a favourable wind, glided away smoothly and lightly over the calm sea. When it grew dark a number of coloured lamps were lit, and the sailors danced merrily on the deck. The little mermaid could not help thinking of her first rising out of the sea, when she had seen similar festivities and joys; and she joined in the dance, poised herself in the air as a swallow when he pursues his prey, and all present cheered her with wonder. She had never danced so elegantly before. Her tender feet felt as if cut with sharp knives, but she cared not for it; a sharper pang had pierced through her heart. She knew this was the last evening she should ever see the prince, for whom she had forsaken her kindred and her home; she had given up her beautiful voice, and suffered unheard-of pain daily for him, while he knew nothing of it.

This was the last evening that she would breathe the same air with him, or gaze on the starry sky and the deep sea; an eternal night, without a thought or a dream, awaited her: she had no soul and now she could never win one. All was joy and gayety on board ship till long after midnight; she laughed and danced with the rest, while the thoughts of death were in her heart. The prince kissed his beautiful bride, while she played with his raven hair, till they went arm-in-arm to rest in the splendid tent. Then all became still on board the ship; the helmsman, alone awake, stood at the helm. The little mermaid leaned her white arms on the edge of the vessel, and looked towards the east for the first blush of morning, for that first ray of dawn that would bring her death. She saw her sisters rising out of the flood: they were as pale as herself; but their long beautiful hair waved no more in the wind, and had been cut off.

"We have given our hair to the witch," said they, "to obtain help for you, that you may not die tonight. She has given us a knife: here it is, see it is very sharp. Before the sun rises you must plunge it into the heart of the prince; when the warm blood falls upon your feet they will grow together again, and form into a fish's tail, and you will be once more a mermaid, and return to us to live out your three hundred years before you die and change into the salt sea foam. Haste, then; he or you must die before sunrise. Our old grandmother moans so for you, that her white hair is falling off from sorrow, as ours fell under the witch's scissors. Kill the prince and come back; hasten: do you not see the first red streaks in the sky? In a few minutes the sun will rise, and you must die." And then they sighed deeply and mournfully, and sank down beneath the waves.

The little mermaid drew back the crimson curtain of the tent, and beheld the fair bride with her head resting on the prince's breast. She bent down and kissed his fair brow, then looked at the sky on which the rosy dawn grew brighter and brighter; then she glanced at the sharp knife, and again fixed her eyes on the prince, who whispered the name of his bride in his dreams. She was in his thoughts, and the knife trembled in the hand of the little mermaid: then she flung it far away from her into the waves; the water turned red where it fell, and the drops that spurted up looked like blood. She cast one more lingering, half-fainting glance at the prince, and then threw herself from the ship into the sea, and thought her body was dissolving into foam. The sun rose above the waves, and his warm rays fell on the cold foam of the little mermaid, who did not feel as if she were dying. She saw the bright sun, and all around her floated hundreds of transparent beautiful beings; she could see through them the white sails of the ship, and the red clouds in the sky; their speech was melodious, but too ethereal to be heard by mortal ears, as they were also unseen by mortal eyes. The little mermaid perceived that she had a body like theirs, and that she continued to rise higher and higher out of the foam. "Where am I?" asked she, and her voice sounded ethereal, as the voice of those who were with her; no earthly music could imitate it.

"Among the daughters of the air," answered one of them. "A mermaid has not an immortal soul, nor can she obtain one unless she wins the love of a human being. On the power of another hangs her eternal destiny. But the daughters of the air, although they do not possess an immortal soul, can, by their good deeds, procure one for themselves. We fly to warm countries, and cool the sultry air that destroys mankind with the pestilence. We carry the perfume of the flowers to spread health and restoration. After we have striven for three hundred years to all the good in our power, we receive an immortal soul and take part in the happiness of mankind. You, poor little mermaid, have tried with your whole heart to do as we are doing; you have suffered and endured and raised yourself to the spirit-world by your good deeds; and now, by striving for three hundred years in the same way, you may obtain an immortal soul."

The little mermaid lifted her glorified eyes towards the sun, and felt them, for the first time, filling with tears. On the ship, in which she had left the prince, there were life and noise; she saw him and his beautiful bride searching for her; sorrowfully they gazed at the pearly foam, as if they knew she had thrown herself into the waves. Unseen she kissed the forehead of her bride, and fanned the prince, and then mounted with the other children of the air to a rosy cloud that floated through the aether.

"After three hundred years, thus shall we float into the kingdom of heaven," said she. "And we may even get there sooner," whispered one of her companions. "Unseen we can enter the houses of men, where there are children, and for every day on which we find a good child, who is the joy of his parents and deserves their love, our time of probation is shortened. The child does not know, when we fly through the room, that we smile with joy at his good conduct, for we can count one year less of our three hundred years. But when we see a naughty or a wicked child, we shed tears of sorrow, and for every tear a day is added to our time of trial!"

The Emperor's New Clothes

Translated by Mrs. H. P. Paull

Many, many years ago lived an emperor, who thought so much of new clothes that he spent all his money in order to obtain them; his only ambition was to be always well dressed. He did not care for his soldiers, and the theatre did not amuse him; the only thing, in fact, he thought anything of was to drive out and show a new suit of clothes. He had a coat for every hour of the day; and as one would say of a king "He is in his cabinet," so one could say of him, "The emperor is in his dressing-room."

The great city where he resided was very gay; every day many strangers from all parts of the globe arrived. One day two swindlers came to this city; they made people believe that they were weavers, and declared they could manufacture the finest cloth to be imagined. Their colours and patterns, they said, were not only exceptionally beautiful, but the clothes made of their material possessed the wonderful quality of being invisible to any man who was unfit for his office or unpardonably stupid.

"That must be wonderful cloth," thought the emperor. "If I were to be dressed in a suit made of this cloth I should be able to find out which men in my empire were unfit for their places, and I could distinguish the clever from the stupid. I must have this cloth woven for me without delay." And he gave a large sum of money to the swindlers, in advance, that they should set to work without any loss of time. They set up two looms, and pretended to be very hard at work, but they did nothing whatever on the looms. They asked for the finest silk and the most precious gold-cloth; all they got they did away with, and worked at the empty looms till late at night.

"I should very much like to know how they are getting on with the cloth," thought the emperor. But he felt rather uneasy when he remembered that he who was not fit for his office could not see it. Personally, he was of opinion that he had nothing to fear, yet he thought it advisable to send somebody else first to see how matters stood. Everybody in the town knew what a remarkable quality the stuff possessed, and all were anxious to see how bad or stupid their neighbours were.

"I shall send my honest old minister to the weavers," thought the emperor. "He can judge best how the stuff looks, for he is intelligent, and nobody understands his office better than he."

The good old minister went into the room where the swindlers sat before the empty looms. "Heaven preserve us!" he thought, and opened his eyes wide, "I cannot see anything at all," but he did not say so. Both swindlers requested him to come near, and asked him if he did not admire the exquisite pattern and the beautiful colours, pointing to the empty looms. The poor old minister tried his very best, but he could see nothing, for there was nothing to be seen. "Oh dear," he thought, "can I be so stupid? I should never have thought so, and nobody must know it! Is it possible that I am not fit for my office? No, no, I cannot say that I was unable to see the cloth."

"Now, have you got nothing to say?" said one of the swindlers, while he pretended to be busily weaving.

"Oh, it is very pretty, exceedingly beautiful," replied the old minister looking through his glasses. "What a beautiful pattern, what brilliant colours! I shall tell the emperor that I like the cloth very much."

"We are pleased to hear that," said the two weavers, and described to him the colours and explained the curious pattern. The old minister listened attentively, that he might relate to the emperor what they said; and so he did.

Now the swindlers asked for more money, silk and gold-cloth, which they required for weaving. They kept everything for themselves, and not a thread came near the loom, but they continued, as hitherto, to work at the empty looms.

Soon afterwards the emperor sent another honest courtier to the weavers to see how they were getting on, and if the cloth was nearly finished. Like the old minister, he looked and looked but could see nothing, as there was nothing to be seen.

"Is it not a beautiful piece of cloth?" asked the two swindlers, showing and explaining the magnificent pattern, which, however, did not exist.

"I am not stupid," said the man. "It is therefore my good appointment for which I am not fit. It is very strange, but I must not let any one know it;" and he praised the cloth, which he did not see, and expressed his joy at the beautiful colours and the fine pattern. "It is very excellent," he said to the emperor.

Everybody in the whole town talked about the precious cloth. At last the emperor wished to see it himself, while it was still on the loom. With a number of courtiers, including the two who had already been there, he went to the two clever swindlers, who now worked as hard as they could, but without using any thread.

"Is it not magnificent?" said the two old statesmen who had been there before. "Your Majesty must admire the colours and the pattern." And then they pointed to the empty looms, for they imagined the others could see the cloth.

"What is this?" thought the emperor, "I do not see anything at all. That is terrible! Am I stupid? Am I unfit to be emperor? That would indeed be the most dreadful thing that could happen to me."

"Really," he said, turning to the weavers, "your cloth has our most gracious approval;" and nodding contentedly he looked at the empty loom, for he did not like to say that he saw nothing. All his attendants, who were with him, looked and looked, and although they could not see anything more than the others, they said, like the emperor, "It is very beautiful." And all advised him to wear the new magnificent clothes at a great procession which was soon to take place. "It is magnificent, beautiful, excellent," one heard them say; everybody seemed to be delighted, and the emperor appointed the two swindlers "Imperial Court Weavers."

The whole night previous to the day on which the procession was to take place, the swindlers pretended to work, and burned more than sixteen candles. People should see that they were busy to finish the emperor's new suit. They pretended to take the cloth from the loom, and worked about in the air with big scissors, and sewed with needles without thread, and said at last: "The emperor's new suit is ready now."

The emperor and all his barons then came to the hall; the swindlers held their arms up as if they held something in their hands and said: "These are the trousers!" "This is the coat!" and "Here is the cloak!" and so on. "They are all as light as a cobweb, and one must feel as if one had nothing at all upon the body; but that is just the beauty of them."

"Indeed!" said all the courtiers; but they could not see anything, for there was nothing to be seen.

"Does it please your Majesty now to graciously undress," said the swindlers, "that we may assist your Majesty in putting on the new suit before the large looking-glass?"

The emperor undressed, and the swindlers pretended to put the new suit upon him, one piece after another; and the emperor looked at himself in the glass from every side.

"How well they look! How well they fit!" said all. "What a beautiful pattern! What fine colours! That is a magnificent suit of clothes!"

The master of the ceremonies announced that the bearers of the canopy, which was to be carried in the procession, were ready.

"I am ready," said the emperor. "Does not my suit fit me marvellously?" Then he turned once more to the looking-glass, that people should think he admired his garments.

The chamberlains, who were to carry the train, stretched their hands to the ground as if they lifted up a train, and pretended to hold something in their hands; they did not like people to know that they could not see anything.

The emperor marched in the procession under the beautiful canopy, and all who saw him in the street and out of the windows exclaimed: "Indeed, the emperor's new suit is incomparable! What a long train he has! How well it fits him!" Nobody wished to let others know he saw nothing, for then he would have been unfit for his office or too stupid. Never emperor's clothes were more admired.

"But he has nothing on at all," said a little child at last. "Good heavens! listen to the voice of an innocent child," said the father, and one whispered to the other what the child had said. "But he has nothing on at all," cried at last the whole people. That made a deep impression upon the emperor, for it seemed to him that they were right; but he thought to himself, "Now I must bear up to the end." And the chamberlains walked with still greater dignity, as if they carried the train which did not exist.

The Goloshes of Fortune

Translated by Mrs. H. P. Paull

1
A Beginning

In a house in Copenhagen, not far from the King's New Market, a very large party had assembled, the host and his family expecting, no doubt, to receive invitations in return. One half of the company were already seated at the card-tables, the other half seemed to be waiting the result of their hostess's question, "Well, how shall we amuse ourselves?"

Conversation followed, which, after a while, began to prove very entertaining. Among other subjects, it turned upon the events of the Middle Ages, which some persons maintained were more full of interest than our own times. Counsellor Knapp defended this opinion so warmly that the lady of the house immediately went over to his side, and both exclaimed against Oersted's Essays on Ancient and Modern Times, in which the preference is given to our own. The counsellor considered the times of the Danish King, Hans,[*] as the noblest and happiest.

The conversation on this topic was only interrupted for a moment by the arrival of a newspaper, which did not, however, contain much worth reading, and while it is still going on we will pay a visit to the ante-room, in which cloaks, sticks, and goloshes were carefully placed. Here sat two maidens, one young, and the other old, as if they had come and were waiting to accompany their mistresses home; but on looking at them more closely, it could easily be seen that they were no common servants. Their shapes were too graceful, their complexions too delicate, and the cut of their dresses much too elegant. They were two fairies. The younger was not Fortune herself, but the chambermaid of one of Fortune's attendants, who carries about her more trifling gifts. The elder one, who was named Care, looked rather gloomy; she always goes about to perform her own business in person; for then she knows it is properly done. They were telling each other where they had been during the day. The messenger of Fortune had only transacted a few unimportant matters; for instance, she had preserved a new bonnet from a shower of rain, and obtained for an honest man a bow from a titled Nobody, and so on; but she had something extraordinary to relate, after all.

"I must tell you," said she, "that today is my birthday; and in honour of it I have been intrusted with a pair of goloshes, to introduce amongst mankind. These goloshes have the property of making every one who puts them on imagine himself in any place he wishes, or that he exists at any period. Every wish is fulfilled at the moment it is expressed, so that for once mankind have the chance of being happy."

"No," replied Care; "you may depend upon it that whoever puts on those goloshes will be very unhappy, and bless the moment in which he can get rid of them."

"What are you thinking of?" replied the other. "Now see; I will place them by the door; some one will take them instead of his own, and he will be the happy man."

This was the end of their conversation.

---

[*] He died in 1513. He married Christine, daughter of the Electoral Prince Ernest of Saxony.

2
What Happened to the Counsellor

It was late when Counsellor Knapp, lost in thought about the times of King Hans, desired to return home; and fate so ordered it that he put on the goloshes of Fortune instead of his own, and walked out into the East Street. Through the magic power of the goloshes, he was at once carried back three hundred years, to the times of King Hans, for which he had been longing when he put them on. Therefore he immediately set his foot into the mud and mire of the street, which in those days possessed no pavement.

"Why, this is horrible; how dreadfully dirty it is!" said the counsellor; "and the whole pavement has vanished, and the lamps are all out." The moon had not yet risen high enough to penetrate the thick foggy air, and all the objects around him were confused together in the darkness. At the nearest corner, a lamp hung before a picture of the Madonna; but the light it gave was almost useless, for he only perceived it when he came quite close and his eyes fell on the painted figures of the Mother and Child.

"That is most likely a museum of art," thought he, "and they have forgotten to take down the sign."

Two men, in the dress of olden times, passed by him.

"What odd figures!" thought he; "they must be returning from some masquerade."

Suddenly he heard the sound of a drum and fifes, and then a blazing light from torches shone upon him. The counsellor stared with astonishment as he beheld a most strange procession pass before him. First came a whole troop of drummers, beating their drums very cleverly; they were followed by life-guards, with longbows and crossbows. The principal person in the procession was a clerical-looking gentleman. The astonished counsellor asked what it all meant, and who the gentleman might be.

"That is the Bishop of Zealand."

"Good gracious!" he exclaimed; "what in the world has happened to the bishop? what can he be thinking about?" Then he shook his head and said, "It cannot possibly be the bishop himself."

While musing on this strange affair, and without looking to the right or left, he walked on through East Street and over Highbridge Place. The bridge, which he supposed led to Palace Square, was nowhere to be found; but instead, he saw a bank and some shallow water, and two people, who sat in a boat.

"Does the gentleman wish to be ferried over the Holm?" asked one.

"To the Holm!" exclaimed the counsellor, not knowing in what age he was now existing; "I want to go to Christian's Haven, in Little Turf Street." The men stared at him. "Pray tell me where the bridge is!" said he. "It is shameful that the lamps are not lighted here, and it is as muddy as if one were walking in a marsh." But the more he talked with the boatmen the less they could understand each other.

"I don't understand your Outlandish talk," he cried at last, angrily turning his back upon them. He could not, however, find the bridge nor any railings.

"What a scandalous condition this place is in," said he; never, certainly, had he found his own times so miserable as on this evening. "I think it will be better for me to take a coach; but where are they?" There was not one to be seen! "I shall be obliged to go back to the King's New Market," said he, "where there are plenty of carriages standing, or I shall never reach Christian's Haven." Then he went towards East Street, and had nearly passed through it, when the moon burst forth from a cloud.

"Dear me, what have they been erecting here?" he cried, as he caught sight of the East Gate, which in olden times used to stand at the end of East Street. However, he found an opening through which he passed, and came out upon where he expected to find the New Market. Nothing was to be seen but an open meadow, surrounded by a few bushes, through which ran a broad canal or stream. A few miserable-looking wooden booths, for the accommodation of Dutch watermen, stood on the opposite shore.

"Either I behold a *Fata Morgana*, or I must be tipsy," groaned the counsellor. "What can it be? What is the matter with me?" He turned back in the full conviction that he must be ill. In walking through the street this time, he examined the houses more closely; he found that most of them were built of lath and plaster, and many had only a thatched roof.

The Goloshes of Fortune

"I am certainly all wrong," said he, with a sigh; "and yet I only drank one glass of punch. But I cannot bear even that, and it was very foolish to give us punch and hot salmon; I shall speak about it to our hostess, the agent's lady. Suppose I were to go back now and say how ill I feel, I fear it would look so ridiculous, and it is not very likely that I should find any one up." Then he looked for the house, but it was not in existence.

"This is really frightful; I cannot even recognize East Street. Not a shop to be seen; nothing but old, wretched, tumble-down houses, just as if I were at Roeskilde or Ringstedt. Oh, I really must be ill! It is no use to stand upon ceremony. But where in the world is the agent's house. There is a house, but it is not his; and people still up in it, I can hear. Oh dear! I certainly am very queer." As he reached the half-open door, he saw a light and went in. It was a tavern of the olden times, and seemed a kind of beershop. The room had the appearance of a Dutch interior. A number of people, consisting of seamen, Copenhagen citizens, and a few scholars, sat in deep conversation over their mugs, and took very little notice of the new comer.

"Pardon me," said the counsellor, addressing the landlady, "I do not feel quite well, and I should be much obliged if you will send for a fly to take me to Christian's Haven." The woman stared at him and shook her head. Then she spoke to him in German. The counsellor supposed from this that she did not understand Danish; he therefore repeated his request in German. This, as well as his singular dress, convinced the woman that he was a foreigner. She soon understood, however, that he did not find himself quite well, and therefore brought him a mug of water. It had something of the taste of seawater, certainly, although it had been drawn from the well outside. Then the counsellor leaned his head on his hand, drew a deep breath, and pondered over all the strange things that had happened to him.

"Is that today's number of the *Day*?"* he asked, quite mechanically, as he saw the woman putting by a large piece of paper. She did not understand what he meant, but she handed him the sheet; it was a woodcut, representing a meteor, which had appeared in the town of Cologne.

"That is very old," said the counsellor, becoming quite cheerful at the sight of this antique drawing. "Where did you get this singular sheet? It is very interesting, although the whole affair is a fable. Meteors are easily explained in these days; they are northern lights, which are often seen, and are no doubt caused by electricity."

Those who sat near him, and heard what he said, looked at him in great astonishment, and one of them rose, took off his hat respectfully, and said in a very serious manner, "You must certainly be a very learned man, monsieur."

"Oh no," replied the counsellor; "I can only discourse on topics which every one should understand."

"*Modestia* is a beautiful virtue," said the man. "Moreover, I must add to your speech *mihi secus videtur*; yet in this case I would suspend my *judicium*".

"May I ask to whom I have the pleasure of speaking?"

"I am a Bachelor of Divinity," said the man. This answer satisfied the counsellor. The title agreed with the dress.

---

* An evening paper in Copenhagen.

"This is surely," thought he, "an old village schoolmaster, a perfect original, such as one meets with sometimes even in Jutland."

"This is not certainly a *locus docendi*," began the man; "still I must beg you to continue the conversation. You must be well read in ancient lore."

"Oh yes," replied the counsellor; "I am very fond of reading useful old books, and modern ones as well, with the exception of Every-day Stories, of which we really have more than enough."

"Every-day Stories?" asked the bachelor.

"Yes, I mean the new novels that we have at the present day."

"Oh," replied the man, with a smile; "and yet they are very witty, and are much read at Court. The king likes especially the romance of Messeurs Iffven and Gaudian, which describes King Arthur and his knights of the round table. He has joked about it with the gentlemen of his Court."

"Well, I have certainly not read that," replied the counsellor. "I suppose it is quite new, and published by Heiberg."

"No," answered the man, "it is not by Heiberg; Godfred von Gehman brought it out."

"Oh, is he the publisher? That is a very old name," said the counsellor; "was it not the name of the first publisher in Denmark?"

"Yes; and he is our first printer and publisher now," replied the scholar.

So far all had passed off very well; but now one of the citizens began to speak of a terrible pestilence which had been raging a few years before, meaning the plague of 1484. The counsellor thought he referred to the cholera, and they could discuss this without finding out the mistake. The war in 1490 was spoken of as quite recent. The English pirates had taken some ships in the Channel in 1801, and the counsellor, supposing they referred to these, agreed with them in finding fault with the English. The rest of the talk, however, was not so agreeable; every moment one contradicted the other. The good bachelor appeared very ignorant, for the simplest remark of the counsellor seemed to him either too bold or too fantastic. They stared at each other, and when it became worse the bachelor spoke in Latin, in the hope of being better understood; but it was all useless.

"How are you now?" asked the landlady, pulling the counsellor's sleeve.

Then his recollection returned to him. In the course of conversation he had forgotten all that had happened previously.

"Goodness me! where am I?" said he. It bewildered him as he thought of it.

"We will have some claret, or mead, or Bremen beer," said one of the guests; "will you drink with us?"

Two maids came in. One of them had a cap on her head of two colours.* They poured out the wine, bowed their heads, and withdrew.

The counsellor felt a cold shiver run all over him. "What is this? what does it mean?" said he; but he was obliged to drink with them, for they overpowered the good man with their politeness. He became at last desperate; and when one of them said he was tipsy, he did not doubt the man's word in the least—only begged them to get a droschky; and then they thought he was speaking the Muscovite language. Never before had he been in such rough and vulgar company. "One might believe that the country was going back to heathenism," he observed. "This is the most terrible moment of my life."

Just then it came into his mind that he would stoop under the table, and so creep to the door. He tried it; but before he reached the entry, the rest discovered what he was about, and seized him by the feet, when, luckily for him, off came the goloshes, and with them vanished the whole enchantment.

---

* In the time of king Hans, chambermaids were obliged to wear caps of two colours.

The counsellor now saw quite plainly a lamp, and a large building behind it; everything looked familiar and beautiful. He was in East Street, as it now appears; he lay with his legs turned towards a porch, and just by him sat the watchman asleep.

"Is it possible that I have been lying here in the street dreaming?" said he. "Yes, this is East Street; how beautifully bright and gay it looks! It is quite shocking that one glass of punch should have upset me like this."

Two minutes afterwards he sat in a droschky, which was to drive him to Christian's Haven. He thought of all the terror and anxiety which he had undergone, and felt thankful from his heart for the reality and comfort of modern times, which, with all their errors, were far better than those in which he so lately found himself.

3
The Watchman's Adventures

"Well, I declare, there lies a pair of goloshes," said the watchman. "No doubt, they belong to the lieutenant who lives up stairs. They are lying just by his door." Gladly would the honest man have rung, and given them in, for a light was still burning, but he did not wish to disturb the other people in the house; so he let them lie. "These things must keep the feet very warm," said he; "they are of such nice soft leather." Then he tried them on, and they fitted his feet exactly. "Now," said he, "how droll things are in this world! There's that man can lie down in his warm bed, but he does not do so. There he goes pacing up and down the room. He ought to be a happy man. He has neither wife nor children, and he goes out into company every evening. Oh, I wish I were he; then I should be a happy man."

As he uttered this wish, the goloshes which he had put on took effect, and the watchman at once became the lieutenant. There he stood in his room, holding a little piece of pink paper between his fingers, on which was a poem—a poem written by the lieutenant himself. Who has not had, for once in his life, a moment of poetic inspiration? and at such a moment, if the thoughts are written down, they flow in poetry. The following verses were written on the pink paper:—

"OH WERE I RICH!

"Oh were I rich! How oft, in youth's bright hour,
When youthful pleasures banish every care,
I longed for riches but to gain a power,
The sword and plume and uniform to wear!
The riches and the honour came for me;
Yet still my greatest wealth was poverty:
Ah, help and pity me!

"Once in my youthful hours, when gay and free,
A maiden loved me; and her gentle kiss,
Rich in its tender love and purity,
Taught me, alas! too much of earthly bliss.
Dear child! She only thought of youthful glee;
She loved no wealth, but fairy tales and me.
Thou knowest: ah, pity me!

"Oh were I rich! again is all my prayer:
That child is now a woman, fair and free,
As good and beautiful as angels are.
Oh, were I rich in lovers' poetry,
To tell my fairy tale, love's richest lore!
But no; I must be silent—I am poor.
Ah, wilt thou pity me?

"Oh were I rich in truth and peace below,
I need not then my poverty bewail.
To thee I dedicate these lines of woe;
Wilt thou not understand the mournful tale?
A leaf on which my sorrows I relate—
Dark story of a darker night of fate.
Ah, bless and pity me!"

"Well, yes; people write poems when they are in love, but a wise man will not print them. A lieutenant in love, and poor. This is a triangle, or more properly speaking, the half of the broken die of fortune." The lieutenant felt this very keenly, and therefore leaned his head against the window-frame, and sighed deeply. "The poor watchman in the street," said he, "is far happier than I am. He knows not what I call poverty. He has a home, a wife and children, who weep at his sorrow and rejoice at his joy. Oh, how much happier I should be could I change my being and position with him, and pass through life with his humble expectations and hopes! Yes, he is indeed happier than I am."

At this moment the watchman again became a watchman; for having, through the goloshes of Fortune, passed into the existence of the lieutenant, and found himself less contented than he expected, he had preferred his former condition, and wished himself again a watchman. "That was an ugly dream," said he, "but droll enough. It seemed to me as if I were the lieutenant up yonder, but there was no happiness for me. I missed my wife and the little ones, who are always ready to smother me with kisses." He sat down again and nodded, but he could not get the dream out of his thoughts, and he still had the goloshes on his feet. A falling star gleamed across the sky. "There goes one!" cried he. "However, there are quite enough left; I should very much like to examine these a little nearer, especially the moon, for that could not slip away under one's hands. The student, for whom my wife washes, says that when we die we shall fly from one star to another. If that were true, it would be very delightful, but I don't believe it. I wish I could make a little spring up there now; I would willingly let my body lie here on the steps."

There are certain things in the world which should be uttered very cautiously; doubly so when the speaker has on his feet the goloshes of Fortune. Now we shall hear what happened to the watchman.

Nearly every one is acquainted with the great power of steam; we have proved it by the rapidity with which we can travel, both on a railroad or in a steamship across the sea. But this speed is like the movements of the sloth, or the crawling march of the snail, when compared to the swiftness with which light travels; light flies nineteen million times faster than the fleetest race-horse, and electricity is more rapid still. Death is an electric shock which we receive in our hearts, and on the wings of electricity the liberated soul flies away swiftly, the light from the sun travels to our earth ninety-five millions of miles in eight minutes and a few seconds;

but on the wings of electricity, the mind requires only a second to accomplish the same distance. The space between the heavenly bodies is, to thought, no farther than the distance which we may have to walk from one friend's house to another in the same town; yet this electric shock obliges us to use our bodies here below, unless, like the watchman, we have on the goloshes of Fortune.

The Goloshes of Fortune

In a very few seconds the watchman had travelled more than two hundred thousand miles to the moon, which is formed of a lighter material than our earth, and may be said to be as soft as new fallen snow. He found himself on one of the circular range of mountains which we see represented in Dr. Madler's large map of the moon. The interior had the appearance of a large hollow, bowl-shaped, with a depth about half a mile from the brim. Within this hollow stood a large town; we may form some idea of its appearance by pouring the white of an egg into a glass of water. The materials of which it was built seemed just as soft, and pictured forth cloudy turrets and sail-like terraces, quite transparent, and floating in the thin air. Our earth hung over his head like a great dark red ball. Presently he discovered a number of beings, which might certainly be called men, but were very different to ourselves. A more fantastical imagination than Herschel's must have discovered these. Had they been placed in groups, and painted, it might have been said, "What beautiful foliage!" They had also a language of their own. No one could have expected the soul of the watchman to understand it, and yet he did understand it, for our souls have much greater capabilities then we are inclined to believe. Do we not, in our dreams, show a wonderful dramatic talent? each of our acquaintance appears to us then in his own character, and with his own voice; no man could thus imitate them in his waking hours. How clearly, too, we are reminded of persons whom we have not seen for many years; they start up suddenly to the mind's eye with all their peculiarities as living realities. In fact, this memory of the soul is a fearful thing; every sin, every sinful thought it can bring back, and we may well ask how we are to give account of "every idle word" that may have been whispered in the heart or uttered with the lips. The spirit of the watchman therefore understood very well the language of the inhabitants of the moon. They were disputing about our earth, and doubted whether it could be inhabited. The atmosphere, they asserted, must be too dense for any inhabitants of the moon to exist there. They maintained that the moon alone was inhabited, and was really the heavenly body in which the old world people lived. They likewise talked politics.

But now we will descend to East Street, and see what happened to the watchman's body. He sat lifeless on the steps. His staff had fallen out of his hand, and his eyes stared at the moon, about which his honest soul was wandering.

"What is it o'clock, watchman?" inquired a passenger. But there was no answer from the watchman.

The man then pulled his nose gently, which caused him to lose his balance. The body fell forward, and lay at full length on the ground as one dead.

All his comrades were very much frightened, for he seemed quite dead; still they allowed him to remain after they had given notice of what had happened; and at dawn the body was carried to the hospital. We might imagine it to be no jesting matter if the soul of the man should chance to return to him, for most probably it would seek for the body in East Street without being able to find it. We might fancy the soul inquiring of the police, or at the address office, or among the missing parcels, and then at length finding it at the hospital. But we may comfort ourselves by the certainty that the soul, when acting upon its own impulses, is wiser than we are; it is the body that makes it stupid.

As we have said, the watchman's body had been taken to the hospital, and here it was placed in a room to be washed. Naturally, the first thing done here was to take off the goloshes, upon which the soul was instantly obliged to return, and it took the direct road to the body at once, and in a few seconds the man's life returned to him. He declared, when he quite recovered himself, that this had been the most dreadful night he had ever passed; not for a hundred pounds would he go through such feelings again. However, it was all over now.

The same day he was allowed to leave, but the goloshes remained at the hospital.

4
The Eventful Moment –
A Most Unusual Journey

Every inhabitant of Copenhagen knows what the entrance to Frederick's Hospital is like; but as most probably a few of those who read this little tale may not reside in Copenhagen, we will give a short description of it.

The hospital is separated from the street by an iron railing, in which the bars stand so wide apart that, it is said, some very slim patients have squeezed through, and gone to pay little visits in the town. The most difficult part of the body to get through was the head; and in this case, as it often happens in the world, the small heads were the most fortunate. This will serve as sufficient introduction to our tale. One of the young volunteers, of whom, physically speaking, it might be said that he had a great head, was on guard that evening at the hospital. The rain was pouring down, yet, in spite of these two obstacles, he wanted to go out just for a quarter of an hour; it was not worth while, he thought, to make a confidant of the porter, as he could easily slip through the iron railings. There lay the goloshes, which the watchman had forgotten. It never occurred to him that these could be goloshes of Fortune. They would be very serviceable to him in this rainy weather, so he drew them on. Now came the question whether he could squeeze through the palings; he certainly had never tried, so he stood looking at them. "I wish to goodness my head was through," said he, and instantly, though it was so thick and large, it slipped through quite easily. The goloshes answered that purpose very well, but his body had to follow, and this was impossible. "I am too fat," he said; "I thought my head would be the worst, but I cannot get my body through, that is certain." Then he tried to pull his head back again, but without success; he could move his neck about easily enough, and that was all. His first feeling was one of anger, and then his spirits sank below zero. The goloshes of Fortune had placed him in this terrible position, and unfortunately it never occurred to him to wish himself free. No, instead of wishing he kept twisting about, yet did not stir from the spot. The rain poured, and not a creature could be seen in the street. The porter's bell he was unable to reach, and however was he to get loose! He foresaw that he should have to stay there till morning, and then they must send for a smith to file away the iron bars, and that would be a work of time. All the charity children would just be going to school: and all the sailors who inhabited that quarter of the town would be there to see him standing in the pillory. What a crowd there would be. "Ha," he cried, "the blood is rushing to my head, and I shall go mad. I believe I am crazy already; oh, I wish I were free, then all these sensations would pass off." This is just what he ought to have said at first. The moment he had expressed the thought his head was free. He started back, quite bewildered with the fright which the goloshes of Fortune had caused him. But we must not suppose it was all over; no, indeed, there was worse to come yet. The night passed, and the whole of the following day; but no one sent for the goloshes. In the evening a declamatory performance was to take place at the amateur theatre in a distant street. The house was crowded; among the audience was the young volunteer from the hospital, who seemed to have quite forgotten his adventures of the previous evening. He had on the goloshes; they had not been sent for, and as the streets were still very dirty, they were of great service to him. A new poem, entitled *"My Aunt's Spectacles,"* was being recited. It described these spectacles as possessing a wonderful power; if any one put them on in a large assembly the people appeared like cards, and the future events of ensuing years could be easily foretold by them. The idea struck him that he should very much like to have such a pair of spectacles; for, if used rightly, they would perhaps enable him to see into the hearts of people, which he thought would be more interesting than to know what was going to happen next year; for future events would be sure to show themselves, but the hearts of people never. "I can fancy what I should see in the whole row of ladies and gentlemen on the first seat, if I could only look into their hearts; that lady, I imagine, keeps a store for things of all descriptions; how my eyes would wander about in that collection; with many ladies I should no doubt find a large millinery establishment. There is another that is perhaps empty, and would be all the better for cleaning out. There may be some well stored with good articles. Ah, yes," he sighed, "I know one, in which everything is solid, but a servant is there already, and that is the only thing against it. I dare say from many I should hear the words, 'Please to walk in.' I only wish I could slip into the hearts like a little tiny thought." This was the word of command for the goloshes. The volunteer shrunk up together, and commenced a most unusual journey through the hearts of the spectators in the first row. The first heart he entered was that of a lady, but he thought he must have got into one of the rooms of an Orthopedic Institution where plaster casts of deformed limbs were hanging on the walls, with this difference, that the casts in the institution are formed when the patient enters, but here they were formed and preserved after the good people had left. These were casts of the bodily and mental deformities of the lady's female friends carefully preserved. Quickly he passed into another heart, which had the appearance of a spacious, holy church, with the white dove of innocence fluttering over the altar. Gladly would he have fallen on his knees in such a sacred place; but he was carried on to another heart, still, however, listening to the tones of the organ, and feeling himself that he had become another and a better man. The next heart was also a sanctuary, which he felt almost unworthy to enter; it represented a mean garret, in which lay a sick mother; but the warm sunshine streamed through the window, lovely roses bloomed in a little flowerbox on the roof, two blue birds sang of childlike joys, and the sick mother prayed for a blessing on her daughter. Next he crept on his hands and knees through an overfilled butcher's shop; there was meat, nothing but meat, wherever he stepped; this was the heart of a rich, respectable man, whose name is doubtless in the directory. Then he entered the heart of this man's wife; it was an old, tumble-down pigeon-house; the husband's portrait served as a Weathercock; it was connected with all the doors, which opened and shut just as the husband's decision turned. The next heart was a complete cabinet of mirrors, such as can be seen in the Castle of Rosenberg. But these mirrors magnified in an astonishing degree; in the middle of the floor sat, like the Grand Lama, the insignificant I of the owner, astonished at the contemplation of his own features. At his next visit he fancied he must have got into a narrow needlecase, full of sharp needles: "Oh," thought he, "this must be the heart of an old maid;" but such was not the fact; it belonged to a young officer, who wore several orders, and was said to be a man of intellect and heart.

The poor volunteer came out of the last heart in the row quite bewildered. He could not collect his thoughts, and imagined his foolish fancies had carried him away. "Good gracious!" he sighed, "I must have a tendency to softening of the brain, and here it is so exceedingly hot that the blood is rushing to my head." And then suddenly recurred to him the strange event of the evening before, when his head had been fixed between the iron railings in front of the hospital. "That is the cause of it all!" he exclaimed, "I must do something in time. A Russian bath would be a very good thing to begin with. I wish I were lying on one of the highest shelves." Sure enough, there he lay on an upper shelf of a vapor bath, still in his evening costume, with his boots and goloshes on, and the hot drops from the ceiling falling on his face. "Ho!" he cried, jumping down and rushing towards the plunging bath. The attendant stopped him with a loud cry, when he saw a man with all his clothes on. The volunteer had, however, presence of mind enough to whisper, "It is for a wager;" but the first thing he did, when he reached his own room, was to put a large blister on his neck, and another on his back, that his crazy fit might be cured. The next morning his back was very sore, which was all he gained by the goloshes of Fortune.

5
The Clerk's Transformation

The watchman, whom we of course have not forgotten, thought, after a while, of the goloshes which he had found and taken to the hospital; so he went and fetched them. But neither the lieutenant nor any one in the street could recognize them as their own, so he gave them up to the police. "They look exactly like my own goloshes," said one of the clerks, examining the unknown articles, as they stood by the side of his own. "It would require even more than the eye of a shoemaker to know one pair from the other."

"Master Clerk," said a servant who entered with some papers. The clerk turned and spoke to the man; but when he had done with him, he turned to look at the goloshes again, and now he was in greater doubt than ever as to whether the pair on the right or on the left belonged to him. "Those that are wet must be mine," thought he; but he thought wrong, it was just the reverse. The goloshes of Fortune were the wet pair; and, besides, why should not a clerk in a police office be wrong sometimes? So he drew them on, thrust his papers into his pocket, placed a few manuscripts under his arm, which he had to take with him, and to make abstracts from at home. Then, as it was Sunday morning and the weather very fine, he said to himself, "A walk to Fredericksburg will do me good:" so away he went.

There could not be a quieter or more steady young man than this clerk. We will not grudge him this little walk, it was just the thing to do him good after sitting so much. He went on at first like a mere automaton, without thought or wish; therefore the goloshes had no opportunity to display their magic power. In the avenue he met with an acquaintance, one of our young poets, who told him that he intended to start on the following day on a summer excursion. "Are you really going away so soon?" asked the clerk. "What a free, happy man you are. You can roam about where you will, while such as we are tied by the foot."

"But it is fastened to the bread-tree," replied the poet. "You need have no anxiety for the morrow; and when you are old there is a pension for you."

"Ah, yes; but you have the best of it," said the clerk; "it must be so delightful to sit and write poetry. The whole world makes itself agreeable to you, and then you are your own master. You should try how you would like to listen to all the trivial things in a court of justice." The poet shook his head, so also did the clerk; each retained his own opinion, and so they parted. "They are strange people, these poets," thought the clerk. "I should like to try what it is to have a poetic taste, and to become a poet myself. I am sure I should not write such mournful verses as they do. This is a splendid spring day for a poet, the air is so remarkably clear, the clouds are so beautiful, and the green grass has such a sweet smell. For many years I have not felt as I do at this moment."

We perceive, by these remarks, that he had already become a poet. By most poets what he had said would be considered commonplace, or as the Germans call it, "insipid." It is a foolish fancy to look upon poets as different to other men. There are many who are more the poets of nature than those who are professed poets. The difference is this, the poet's intellectual memory is better; he seizes upon an idea or a sentiment, until he can embody it, clearly and plainly in words, which the others cannot do. But the transition from a character of every-day life to one of a more gifted nature is a great transition; and so the clerk became aware of the change after a time. "What a delightful perfume," said he; "it reminds me of the violets at Aunt Lora's. Ah, that was when I was a little boy. Dear me, how long it seems since I thought of those days! She was a good old maiden lady! she lived yonder, behind the Exchange. She always had a sprig or a few blossoms in water, let the winter be ever so severe. I could smell the violets, even while I was placing warm penny pieces against the frozen panes to make peep-holes, and a pretty view it was on which I peeped. Out in the river lay the ships, icebound, and forsaken by their crews; a screaming crow represented the only living creature on board. But when the breezes of spring came, everything started into life. Amidst shouting and cheers the ships were tarred and rigged, and then they sailed to foreign lands."

"I remain here, and always shall remain, sitting at my post at the police office, and letting others take passports to distant lands. Yes, this is my fate," and he sighed deeply. Suddenly he paused. "Good gracious, what has come over me? I never felt before as I do now; it must be the air of spring. It is overpowering, and yet it is delightful."

He felt in his pockets for some of his papers. "These will give me something else to think of," said he. Casting his eyes on the first page of one, he read, "'*Mistress Sigbirth; an original Tragedy, in Five Acts.*' What is this?—in my own handwriting, too! Have I written this tragedy?" He read again, "'*The Intrigue on the Promenade; or, the Fast-Day. A Vaudeville.*' However did I get all this? Some one must have put them into my pocket. And here is a letter!" It was from the manager of a theatre; the pieces were rejected, not at all in polite terms.

"Hem, hem!" said he, sitting down on a bench; his thoughts were very elastic, and his heart softened strangely. Involuntarily he seized one of the nearest flowers; it was a little, simple daisy. All that botanists can say in many lectures was explained in a moment by this little flower. It spoke of the glory of its birth; it told of the strength of the sunlight, which had caused its delicate leaves to expand, and given to it such sweet perfume. The struggles of life which arouse sensations in the bosom have their type in the tiny flowers. Air and light are the lovers of the flowers, but light is the favoured one; towards light it turns, and only when light vanishes does it fold its leaves together, and sleep in the embraces of the air."

"It is light that adorns me," said the flower.

"But the air gives you the breath of life," whispered the poet.

Just by him stood a boy, splashing with his stick in a marshy ditch. The water-drops spurted up among the green twigs, and the clerk thought of the millions of animalculae* which were thrown into the air with every drop of water, at a height which must be the same to them as it would be to us if we were hurled beyond the clouds. As the clerk thought of all these things, and became conscious of the great change in his own feelings, he smiled, and said to himself, "I must be asleep and dreaming; and yet, if so, how wonderful for a dream to be so natural and real, and to know at the same time too that it is but a dream. I hope I shall be able to remember it all when I wake tomorrow. My sensations seem most unaccountable.

---

* Little animal—Ed.

I have a clear perception of everything as if I were wide awake. I am quite sure if I recollect all this tomorrow, it will appear utterly ridiculous and absurd. I have had this happen to me before. It is with the clever or wonderful things we say or hear in dreams, as with the gold which comes from under the earth, it is rich and beautiful when we possess it, but when seen in a true light it is but as stones and withered leaves."

"Ah!" he sighed mournfully, as he gazed at the birds singing merrily, or hopping from branch to branch, "they are much better off than I. Flying is a glorious power. Happy is he who is born with wings. Yes, if I could change myself into anything I would be a little lark." At the same moment his coat-tails and sleeves grew together and formed wings, his clothes changed to feathers, and his goloshes to claws. He felt what was taking place, and laughed to himself. "Well, now it is evident I must be dreaming; but I never had such a wild dream as this." And then he flew up into the green boughs and sang, but there was no poetry in the song, for his poetic nature had left him. The goloshes, like all persons who wish to do a thing thoroughly, could only attend to one thing at a time. He wished to be a poet, and he became one. Then he wanted to be a little bird, and in this change he lost the characteristics of the former one. "Well," thought he, "this is charming; by day I sit in a police-office, amongst the dryest law papers, and at night I can dream that I am a lark, flying about in the Gardens of Fredericksburg. Really a complete comedy could be written about it." Then he flew down into the grass, turned his head about in every direction, and tapped his beak on the bending blades of grass, which, in proportion to his size, seemed to him as long as the palm-leaves in Northern Africa.

In another moment all was darkness around him. It seemed as if something immense had been thrown over him. A sailor boy had flung his large cap over the bird, and a hand came underneath and caught the clerk by the back and wings so roughly, that he squeaked, and then cried out in his alarm, "You impudent rascal, I am a clerk in the police-office!" but it only sounded to the boy like "tweet, tweet;" so he tapped the bird on the beak, and walked away with him. In the avenue he met two school-boys, who appeared to belong to a better class of society, but whose inferior abilities kept them in the lowest class at school. These boys bought the bird for eightpence, and so the clerk returned to Copenhagen. "It is well for me that I am dreaming," he thought; "otherwise I should become really angry. First I was a poet, and now I am a lark. It must have been the poetic nature that changed me into this little creature. It is a miserable story indeed, especially now I have fallen into the hands of boys. I wonder what will be the end of it." The boys carried him into a very elegant room, where a stout, pleasant-looking lady received them, but she was not at all gratified to find that they had brought a lark—a common field-bird as she called it. However, she allowed them for one day to place the bird in an empty cage that hung near the window. "It will please Polly Perhaps," she said, laughing at a large gray parrot, who was swinging himself proudly on a ring in a handsome brass cage. "It is Polly's birthday," she added in a simpering tone, "and the little field-bird has come to offer his congratulations."

Polly did not answer a single word, he continued to swing proudly to and fro; but a beautiful canary, who had been brought from his own warm, fragrant fatherland, the summer previous, began to sing as loud as he could.

"You Screamer!" said the lady, throwing a white handkerchief over the cage.

"Tweet, tweet," sighed he, "what a dreadful snowstorm!" and then he became silent.

The clerk, or as the lady called him the field-bird, was placed in a little cage close to the canary, and not far from the parrot. The only human speech which Polly could utter, and which she sometimes chattered forth most comically, was *"Now let us be men."* All besides was a scream, quite as unintelligible as the warbling of the canary-bird, excepting to the clerk, who being now a bird, could understand his comrades very well.

"I flew beneath green palm-trees, and amidst the blooming almond-trees," sang the canary. "I flew with my brothers and sisters over beautiful flowers, and across the clear, bright sea, which reflected the waving foliage in its glittering depths; and I have seen many gay parrots, who could relate long and delightful stories."

"They were wild birds," answered the parrot, "and totally uneducated. Now let us be men. Why do you not laugh? If the lady and her visitors can laugh at this, surely you can. It is a great failing not to be able to appreciate what is amusing. Now let us be men."

"Do you remember," said the canary, "the pretty maidens who used to dance in the tents that were spread out beneath the sweet blossoms? Do you remember the delicious fruit and the cooling juice from the wild herbs?"

"Oh, yes," said the parrot; "but here I am much better off. I am well fed, and treated politely. I know that I have a clever head; and what more do I want? Let us be men now. You have a soul for poetry. I have deep knowledge and wit. You have genius, but no discretion. You raise your naturally high notes so much, that you get covered over. They never serve me so. Oh, no; I cost them something more than you. I keep them in order with my beak, and fling my wit about me. Now let us be men."

"O my warm, blooming fatherland," sang the canary bird, "I will sing of thy dark-green trees and thy quiet streams, where the bending branches kiss the clear, smooth water. I will sing of the joy of my brothers and sisters, as their shining plumage flits among the dark leaves of the plants which grow wild by the springs."

"Do leave off those dismal strains," said the parrot; "sing something to make us laugh; laughter is the sign of the highest order of intellect. Can a dog or a horse laugh? No, they can cry; but to man alone is the power of laughter given. Ha! ha! ha!" laughed Polly, and repeated his witty saying, "Now let us be men."

"You little gray Danish bird," said the canary, "you also have become a prisoner. It is certainly cold in your forests, but still there is liberty there. Fly out! they have forgotten to close the cage, and the window is open at the top. Fly, fly!"

Instinctively, the clerk obeyed, and left the cage; at the same moment the half-opened door leading into the next room creaked on its hinges, and, stealthily, with green fiery eyes, the cat crept in and chased the lark round the room. The canary-bird fluttered in his cage, and the parrot flapped his wings and cried, "Let us be men;" the poor clerk, in the most deadly terror, flew through the window, over the houses, and through the streets, till at length he was obliged to seek a resting-place. A house opposite to him had a look of home. A window stood open; he flew in, and perched upon the table. It was his own room. "Let us be men now," said he, involuntarily imitating the parrot; and at the same moment he became a clerk again, only that he was sitting on the table. "Heaven preserve us!" said he; "How did I get up here and fall asleep in this way? It was an uneasy dream too that I had. The whole affair appears most absurd."

6
The Best Thing the Goloshes Did

Early on the following morning, while the clerk was still in bed, his neighbour, a young divinity student, who lodged on the same storey, knocked at his door, and then walked in. "Lend me your goloshes," said he; "it is so wet in the garden, but the sun is shining brightly. I should like to go out there and smoke my pipe." He put on the goloshes, and was soon in the garden, which contained only one plum-tree and one apple-tree; yet, in a town, even a small garden like this is a great advantage.

The student wandered up and down the path; it was just six o'clock, and he could hear the sound of the post-horn in the street. "Oh, to travel, to travel!" cried he; "there is no greater happiness in the world: it is the height of my ambition. This restless feeling would be stilled, if I could take a journey far away from this country. I should like to see beautiful Switzerland, to travel through Italy, and,"—It was well for him that the goloshes acted immediately, otherwise he might have been carried too far for himself as well as for us. In a moment he found himself in Switzerland, closely packed with eight others in the diligence. His head ached, his back was stiff, and the blood had ceased to circulate, so that his feet were swelled and pinched by his boots. He wavered in a condition between sleeping and waking. In his right-hand pocket he had a letter of credit; in his left-hand pocket was his passport; and a few louis d'ors were sewn into a little leather bag which he carried in his breast-pocket. Whenever he dozed, he dreamed that he had lost one or another of these possessions; then he would awake with a start, and the first movements of his hand formed a triangle from his right-hand pocket to his breast, and from his breast to his left-hand pocket, to feel whether they were all safe.

Umbrellas, sticks, and hats swung in the net before him, and almost obstructed the prospect, which was really very imposing; and as he glanced at it, his memory recalled the words of one poet at least, who has sung of Switzerland, and whose poems have not yet been printed:—

> "How lovely to my wondering eyes
> Mont Blanc's fair summits gently rise;
> 'Tis sweet to breathe the mountain air—
> If you have gold enough to spare."

Grand, dark, and gloomy appeared the landscape around him. The pine-forests looked like little groups of moss on high rocks, whose summits were lost in clouds of mist. Presently it began to snow, and the wind blew keen and cold. "Ah," he sighed, "if I were only on the other side of the Alps now, it would be summer, and I should be able to get money on my letter of credit. The anxiety I feel on this matter prevents me from enjoying myself in Switzerland. Oh, I wish I was on the other side of the Alps."

And there, in a moment, he found himself, far away in the midst of Italy, between Florence and Rome, where the lake Thrasymene glittered in the evening sunlight like a sheet of molten gold between the dark blue mountains. There, where Hannibal defeated Flaminius, the grape vines clung to each other with the friendly grasp of their green tendril fingers; while, by the wayside, lovely half-naked children were watching a herd of coal-black swine under the blossoms of fragrant laurel. Could we rightly describe this picturesque scene, our readers would exclaim, "Delightful Italy!"

But neither the student nor either of his travelling companions felt the least inclination to think of it in this way. Poisonous flies and gnats flew into the coach by thousands. In vain they drove them away with a myrtle branch, the flies stung them notwithstanding. There was not a man in the coach whose face was not swollen and disfigured with the stings. The poor horses looked wretched; the flies settled on their backs in swarms, and they were only relieved when the coachmen got down and drove the creatures off.

The Goloshes of Fortune

As the sun set, an icy coldness filled all nature, not however of long duration. It produced the feeling which we experience when we enter a vault at a funeral, on a summer's day; while the hills and the clouds put on that singular green hue which we often notice in old paintings, and look upon as unnatural until we have ourselves seen nature's colouring in the south. It was a glorious spectacle; but the stomachs of the travellers were empty, their bodies exhausted with fatigue, and all the longings of their heart turned towards a resting-place for the night; but where to find one they knew not. All the eyes were too eagerly seeking for this resting-place, to notice the beauties of nature.

The road passed through a grove of olive-trees; it reminded the student of the willow trees at home. Here stood a lonely inn, and close by it a number of crippled beggars had placed themselves; the brightest among them looked, to quote the words of Marryat, "like the eldest son of Famine who had just come of age." The others were either blind, or had withered legs, which obliged them to creep about on their hands and knees, or they had shrivelled arms and hands without fingers. It was indeed poverty arrayed in rags. "*Eccellenza, Miserabili!*" they exclaimed, stretching forth their diseased limbs. The hostess received the travellers with bare feet, untidy hair, and a dirty blouse. The doors were fastened together with string; the floors of the rooms were of brick, broken in many places; bats flew about under the roof; and as to the odor within—

"Let us have supper laid in the stable," said one of the travellers; "then we shall know what we are breathing."

The windows were opened to let in a little fresh air, but quicker than air came in the withered arms and the continual whining sounds, "*Miserabili, Eccellenza*". On the walls were inscriptions, half of them against "*La bella Italia.*"

The supper made its appearance at last. It consisted of watery soup, seasoned with pepper and rancid oil. This last delicacy played a principal part in the salad. Musty eggs and roasted cocks' combs were the best dishes on the table; even the wine had a strange taste, it was certainly a mixture. At night, all the boxes were placed against the doors, and one of the travellers watched while the others slept. The student's turn came to watch. How close the air felt in that room; the heat overpowered him. The gnats were buzzing about and stinging, while the *miserabili*, outside, moaned in their dreams.

"Travelling would be all very well," said the student of divinity to himself, "if we had no bodies, or if the body could rest while the soul if flying. Wherever I go I feel a want which oppresses my heart, for something better presents itself at the moment; yes, something better, which shall be the best of all; but where is that to be found? In fact, I know in my heart very well what I want. I wish to attain the greatest of all happiness."

No sooner were the words spoken than he was at home. Long white curtains shaded the windows of his room, and in the middle of the floor stood a black coffin, in which he now lay in the still sleep of death; his wish was fulfilled, his body was at rest, and his spirit travelling.

"Esteem no man happy until he is in his grave," were the words of Solon. Here was a strong fresh proof of their truth. Every corpse is a sphinx of immortality. The sphinx in this sarcophagus might unveil its own mystery in the words which the living had himself written two days before—

> "Stern death, thy chilling silence waketh dread;
>   Yet in thy darkest hour there may be light.
> Earth's garden reaper! from the grave's cold bed
>   The soul on Jacob's ladder takes her flight.
>
> Man's greatest sorrows often are a part
>   Of hidden griefs, concealed from human eyes,
> Which press far heavier on the lonely heart
>   Than now the earth that on his coffin lies."

Two figures were moving about the room; we know them both. One was the Fairy named Care, the other the messenger of Fortune. They bent over the dead.

"Look!" said Care; "what happiness have your goloshes brought to mankind?"

"They have at least brought lasting happiness to him who slumbers here," she said.

"Not so," said Care, "he went away of himself, he was not summoned. His mental powers were not strong enough to discern the treasures which he had been destined to discover. I will do him a favour now." And she drew the goloshes from his feet.

The sleep of death was ended, and the recovered man raised himself. Care vanished, and with her the goloshes; doubtless she looked upon them as her own property.

The Daisy

Translated by Mrs. H. P. Paull

Now listen! In the country, close by the high road, stood a farmhouse; perhaps you have passed by and seen it yourself. There was a little flower garden with painted wooden palings in front of it; close by was a ditch, on its fresh green bank grew a little daisy; the sun shone as warmly and brightly upon it as on the magnificent garden flowers, and therefore it thrived well. One morning it had quite opened, and its little snow-white petals stood round the yellow centre, like the rays of the sun. It did not mind that nobody saw it in the grass, and that it was a poor despised flower; on the contrary, it was quite happy, and turned towards the sun, looking upward and listening to the song of the lark high up in the air.

The little daisy was as happy as if the day had been a great holiday, but it was only Monday. All the children were at school, and while they were sitting on the forms and learning their lessons, it sat on its thin green stalk and learnt from the sun and from its surroundings how kind God is, and it rejoiced that the song of the little lark expressed so sweetly and distinctly its own feelings. With a sort of reverence the daisy looked up to the bird that could fly and sing, but it did not feel envious. "I can see and hear," it thought; "the sun shines upon me, and the forest kisses me. How rich I am!"

In the garden close by grew many large and magnificent flowers, and, strange to say, the less fragrance they had the haughtier and prouder they were. The peonies puffed themselves up in order to be larger than the roses, but size is not everything! The tulips had the finest colours, and they knew it well, too, for they were standing bolt upright like candles, that one might see them the better. In their pride they did not see the little daisy, which looked over to them and thought, "How rich and beautiful they are! I am sure the pretty bird will fly down and call upon them. Thank God, that I stand so near and can at least see all the splendour." And while the daisy was still thinking, the lark came flying down, crying "Tweet," but not to the peonies and tulips—no, into the grass to the poor daisy. Its joy was so great that it did not know what to think. The little bird hopped round it and sang, "How beautifully soft the grass is, and what a lovely little flower with its golden heart and silver dress is growing here." The yellow centre in the daisy did indeed look like gold, while the little petals shone as brightly as silver.

How happy the daisy was! No one has the least idea. The bird kissed it with its beak, sang to it, and then rose again up to the blue sky. It was certainly more than a quarter of an hour before the daisy recovered its senses. Half ashamed, yet glad at heart, it looked over to the other flowers in the garden; surely they had witnessed its pleasure and the honour that had been done to it; they understood its joy. But the tulips stood more stiffly than ever, their faces were pointed and red, because they were vexed. The peonies were sulky; it was well that they could not speak, otherwise they would have given the daisy a good lecture. The little flower could very well see that they were ill at ease, and pitied them sincerely.

Shortly after this a girl came into the garden, with a large sharp knife. She went to the tulips and began cutting them off, one after another. "Ugh!" sighed the daisy, "that is terrible; now they are done for."

The girl carried the tulips away. The daisy was glad that it was outside, and only a small flower—it felt very grateful. At sunset it folded its petals, and fell asleep, and dreamt all night of the sun and the little bird.

On the following morning, when the flower once more stretched forth its tender petals, like little arms, towards the air and light, the daisy recognized the bird's voice, but what it sang sounded so sad. Indeed the poor bird had good reason to be sad, for it had been caught and put into a cage close by the open window. It sang of the happy days when it could merrily fly about, of fresh green corn in the fields, and of the time when it could soar almost up to the clouds. The poor lark was most unhappy as a prisoner in a cage. The little daisy would have liked so much to help it, but what could be done? Indeed, that was very difficult for such a small flower to find out. It entirely forgot how beautiful everything around it was, how warmly the sun was shining, and how splendidly white its own petals were. It could only think of the poor captive bird, for which it could do nothing. Then two little boys came out of the garden; one of them had a large sharp knife, like that with which the girl had cut the tulips. They came straight towards the little daisy, which could not understand what they wanted.

"Here is a fine piece of turf for the lark," said one of the boys, and began to cut out a square round the daisy, so that it remained in the centre of the grass.

"Pluck the flower off" said the other boy, and the daisy trembled for fear, for to be pulled off meant death to it; and it wished so much to live, as it was to go with the square of turf into the poor captive lark's cage.

"No let it stay," said the other boy, "it looks so pretty."

And so it stayed, and was brought into the lark's cage. The poor bird was lamenting its lost liberty, and beating its wings against the wires; and the little daisy could not speak or utter a consoling word, much as it would have liked to do so. So the forenoon passed.

"I have no water," said the captive lark, "they have all gone out, and forgotten to give me anything to drink. My throat is dry and burning. I feel as if I had fire and ice within me, and the air is so oppressive. Alas! I must die, and part with the warm sunshine, the fresh green meadows, and all the beauty that God has created." And it thrust its beak into the piece of grass, to refresh itself a little. Then it noticed the little daisy, and nodded to it, and kissed it with its beak and said: "You must also fade in here, poor little flower. You and the piece of grass are all they have given me in exchange for the whole world, which I enjoyed outside. Each little blade of grass shall be a green tree for me, each of your white petals a fragrant flower. Alas! you only remind me of what I have lost."

"I wish I could console the poor lark," thought the daisy. It could not move one of its leaves, but the fragrance of its delicate petals streamed forth, and was much stronger than such flowers usually have: the bird noticed it, although it was dying with thirst, and in its pain tore up the green blades of grass, but did not touch the flower.

The evening came, and nobody appeared to bring the poor bird a drop of water; it opened its beautiful wings, and fluttered about in its anguish; a faint and mournful "Tweet, tweet," was all it could utter, then it bent its little head towards the flower, and its heart broke for want and longing. The flower could not, as on the previous evening, fold up its petals and sleep; it dropped sorrowfully. The boys only came the next morning; when they saw the dead bird, they began to cry bitterly, dug a nice grave for it, and adorned it with flowers. The bird's body was placed in a pretty red box; they wished to bury it with royal honours. While it was alive and sang they forgot it, and let it suffer want in the cage; now, they cried over it and covered it with flowers. The piece of turf, with the little daisy in it, was thrown out on the dusty highway. Nobody thought of the flower which had felt so much for the bird and had so greatly desired to comfort it.

The Steadfast Tin Soldier

Translated by Mrs. H. P. Paull

There were once five-and-twenty tin soldiers, who were all brothers, for they had been made out of the same old tin spoon. They shouldered arms and looked straight before them, and wore a splendid uniform, red and blue. The first thing in the world they ever heard were the words, "Tin soldiers!" uttered by a little boy, who clapped his hands with delight when the lid of the box, in which they lay, was taken off. They were given him for a birthday present, and he stood at the table to set them up. The soldiers were all exactly alike, excepting one, who had only one leg; he had been left to the last, and then there was not enough of the melted tin to finish him, so they made him to stand firmly on one leg, and this caused him to be very remarkable.

The table on which the tin soldiers stood, was covered with other playthings, but the most attractive to the eye was a pretty little paper castle. Through the small windows the rooms could be seen. In front of the castle a number of little trees surrounded a piece of looking-glass, which was intended to represent a transparent lake.

The Steadfast Tin Soldier

Swans, made of wax, swam on the lake, and were reflected in it. All this was very pretty, but the prettiest of all was a tiny little lady, who stood at the open door of the castle; she, also, was made of paper, and she wore a dress of clear muslin, with a narrow blue ribbon over her shoulders just like a scarf. In front of these was fixed a glittering tinsel rose, as large as her whole face. The little lady was a dancer, and she stretched out both her arms, and raised one of her legs so high, that the tin soldier could not see it at all, and he thought that she, like himself, had only one leg. "That is the wife for me," he thought; "but she is too grand, and lives in a castle, while I have only a box to live in, five-and-twenty of us altogether, that is no place for her. Still I must try and make her acquaintance." Then he laid himself at full length on the table behind a snuff-box that stood upon it, so that he could peep at the little delicate lady, who continued to stand on one leg without losing her balance. When evening came, the other tin soldiers were all placed in the box, and the people of the house went to bed. Then the playthings began to have their own games together, to pay visits, to have sham fights, and to give balls. The tin soldiers rattled in their box; they wanted to get out and join the amusements, but they could not open the lid. The nut-crackers played at leap-frog, and the pencil jumped about the table. There was such a noise that the canary woke up and began to talk, and in poetry too. Only the tin soldier and the dancer remained in their places. She stood on tiptoe, with her legs stretched out, as firmly as he did on his one leg. He never took his eyes from her for even a moment. The clock struck twelve, and, with a bounce, up sprang the lid of the snuff-box; but, instead of snuff, there jumped up a little black goblin; for the snuff-box was a toy puzzle.

"Tin soldier," said the goblin, "don't wish for what does not belong to you."

But the tin soldier pretended not to hear.

"Very well; wait till tomorrow, then," said the goblin.

When the children came in the next morning, they placed the tin soldier in the window. Now, whether it was the goblin who did it, or the draught, is not known, but the window flew open, and out fell the tin soldier, heels over head, from the third story, into the street beneath. It was a terrible fall; for he came head downwards, his helmet and his bayonet stuck in between the flagstones, and his one leg up in the air. The servant maid and the little boy went down stairs directly to look for him; but he was nowhere to be seen, although once they nearly trod upon him. If he had called out, "Here I am," it would have been all right, but he was too proud to cry out for help while he wore a uniform.

Presently it began to rain, and the drops fell faster and faster, till there was a heavy shower. When it was over, two boys happened to pass by, and one of them said, "Look, there is a tin soldier. He ought to have a boat to sail in."

So they made a boat out of a newspaper, and placed the tin soldier in it, and sent him sailing down the gutter, while the two boys ran by the side of it, and clapped their hands. Good gracious, what large waves arose in that gutter! and how fast the stream rolled on! for the rain had been very heavy. The paper boat rocked up and down, and turned itself round sometimes so quickly that the tin soldier trembled; yet he remained firm; his countenance did not change; he looked straight before him, and shouldered his musket. Suddenly the boat shot under a bridge which formed a part of a drain, and then it was as dark as the tin soldier's box.

"Where am I going now?" thought he. "This is the black goblin's fault, I am sure. Ah, well, if the little lady were only here with me in the boat, I should not care for any darkness."

Suddenly there appeared a great water-rat, who lived in the drain.

"Have you a passport?" asked the rat, "give it to me at once." But the tin soldier remained silent and held his musket tighter than ever. The boat sailed on and the rat followed it. How he did gnash his teeth and cry out to the bits of wood and straw, "Stop him, stop him; he has not paid toll, and has not shown his pass." But the stream rushed on stronger and stronger. The tin soldier could already see daylight shining where the arch ended. Then he heard a roaring sound quite terrible enough to frighten the bravest man. At the end of the tunnel the drain fell into a large canal over a steep place, which made it as dangerous for him as a waterfall would be to us. He was too close to it to stop, so the boat rushed on, and the poor tin soldier could only hold himself as stiffly as possible, without moving an eyelid, to show that he was not afraid. The boat whirled round three or four times, and then filled with water to the very edge; nothing could save it from sinking. He now stood up to his neck in water, while deeper and deeper sank the boat, and the paper became soft and loose with the wet, till at last the water closed over the soldier's head. He thought of the elegant little dancer whom he should never see again, and the words of the song sounded in his ears:

> "Farewell, warrior! ever brave,
> Drifting onward to thy grave."

Then the paper boat fell to pieces, and the soldier sank into the water and immediately afterwards was swallowed up by a great fish. Oh how dark it was inside the fish! A great deal darker than in the tunnel, and narrower too, but the tin soldier continued firm, and lay at full length shouldering his musket. The fish swam to and fro, making the most wonderful movements, but at last he became quite still. After a while, a flash of lightning seemed to pass through him, and then the daylight approached, and a voice cried out, "I declare here is the tin soldier." The fish had been caught, taken to the market and sold to the cook, who took him into the kitchen and cut him open with a large knife. She picked up the soldier and held him by the waist between her finger and thumb, and carried him into the room. They were all anxious to see this wonderful soldier who had travelled about inside a fish; but he was not at all proud. They placed him on the table, and—how many curious things do happen in the world!—there he was in the very same room from the window of which he had fallen, there were the same children, the same playthings, standing on the table, and the pretty castle with the elegant little dancer at the door; she still balanced herself on one leg, and held up the other, so she was as firm as himself. It touched the tin soldier so much to see her that he almost wept in tears, but he kept them back. He only looked at her and they both remained silent. Presently one of the little boys took up the tin soldier, and threw him into the stove. He had no reason for doing so, therefore it must have been the fault of the black goblin who lived in the snuff-box. The flames lighted up the tin soldier, as he stood, the heat was very terrible, but whether it proceeded from the real fire or from the fire of love he could not tell. Then he could see that the bright colours were faded from his uniform, but whether they had been washed off during his journey or from the effects of his sorrow, no one could say. He looked at the little lady, and she looked at him. He felt himself melting away, but he still remained firm with his gun on his shoulder. Suddenly the door of the room flew open and the draught of air caught up the little dancer, she fluttered like a sylph right into the stove by the side of the tin soldier, and was instantly in flames and was gone. The tin soldier melted down into a lump, and the next morning, when the maid servant took the ashes out of the stove, she found him in the shape of a little tin heart. But of the little dancer nothing remained but the tinsel rose, which was burnt black as a cinder.

The Wild Swans

Translated by Mrs. H. P. Paull

Far away in the land to which the swallows fly when it is winter, dwelt a king who had eleven sons, and one daughter, named Eliza. The eleven brothers were princes, and each went to school with a star on his breast, and a sword by his side. They wrote with diamond pencils on gold slates, and learnt their lessons so quickly and read so easily that every one might know they were princes. Their sister Eliza sat on a little stool of plate-glass, and had a book full of pictures, which had cost as much as half a kingdom. Oh, these children were indeed happy, but it was not to remain so always. Their father, who was king of the country, married a very wicked queen, who did not love the poor children at all. They knew this from the very first day after the wedding. In the palace there were great festivities, and the children played at receiving company; but instead of having, as usual, all the cakes and apples that were left, she gave them some sand in a tea-cup, and told them to pretend it was cake. The week after, she sent little Eliza into the country to a peasant and his wife, and then she told the king so many untrue things about the young princes, that he gave himself no more trouble respecting them.

"Go out into the world and get your own living," said the queen. "Fly like great birds, who have no voice." But she could not make them ugly as she wished, for they were turned into eleven beautiful wild swans. Then, with a strange cry, they flew through the windows of the palace, over the park, to the forest beyond. It was early morning when they passed the peasant's cottage, where their sister Eliza lay asleep in her room. They hovered over the roof, twisted their long necks and flapped their wings, but no one heard them or saw them, so they were at last obliged to fly away, high up in the clouds; and over the wide world they flew till they came to a thick, dark wood, which stretched far away to the seashore. Poor little Eliza was alone in her room playing with a green leaf, for she had no other playthings, and she pierced a hole through the leaf, and looked through it at the sun, and it was as if she saw her brothers' clear eyes, and when the warm sun shone on her cheeks, she thought of all the kisses they had given her. One day passed just like another; sometimes the winds rustled through the leaves of the rose bush, and would whisper to the roses, "Who can be more beautiful than you!" But the roses would shake their heads, and say, "Eliza is." And when the old woman sat at the cottage door on Sunday, and read her hymn-book, the wind would flutter the leaves, and say to the book, "Who can be more pious than you?" and then the hymn-book would answer "Eliza." And the roses and the hymn-book told the real truth. At fifteen she returned home, but when the queen saw how beautiful she was, she became full of spite and hatred towards her. Willingly would she have turned her into a swan, like her brothers, but she did not dare to do so yet, because the king wished to see his daughter. Early one morning the queen went into the bath-room; it was built of marble, and had soft cushions, trimmed with the most beautiful tapestry. She took three toads with her, and kissed them, and said to one, "When Eliza comes to the bath, seat yourself upon her head, that she may become as stupid as you are." Then she said to another, "Place yourself on her forehead, that she may become as ugly as you are, and that her father may not know her." "Rest on her heart," she whispered to the third, "then she will have evil inclinations, and suffer in consequence." So she put the toads into the clear water, and they turned green immediately. She next called Eliza, and helped her to undress and get into the bath. As Eliza dipped her head under the water, one of the toads sat on her hair, a second on her forehead, and a third on her breast, but she did not seem to notice them, and when she rose out of the water, there were three red poppies floating upon it. Had not the creatures been venomous or been kissed by the witch, they would have been changed into red roses. At all events they became flowers, because they had rested on Eliza's head, and on her heart. She was too good and too innocent for witchcraft to have any power over her. When the wicked queen saw this, she rubbed her face with walnut-juice, so that she was quite brown; then she tangled her beautiful hair and smeared it with disgusting ointment, till it was quite impossible to recognize the beautiful Eliza.

When her father saw her, he was much shocked, and declared she was not his daughter. No one but the watch-dog and the swallows knew her; and they were only poor animals, and could say nothing. Then poor Eliza wept, and thought of her eleven brothers, who were all away. Sorrowfully, she stole away from the palace, and walked, the whole day, over fields and moors, till she came to the great forest. She knew not in what direction to go; but she was so unhappy, and longed so for her brothers, who had been, like herself, driven out into the world, that she was determined to seek them. She had been but a short time in the wood when night came on, and she quite lost the path; so she laid herself down on the soft moss, offered up her evening prayer, and leaned her head against the stump of a tree. All nature was still, and the soft, mild air fanned her forehead. The light of hundreds of glow-worms shone amidst the grass and the moss, like green fire; and if she touched a twig with her hand, ever so lightly, the brilliant insects fell down around her, like shooting-stars.

All night long she dreamt of her brothers. She and they were children again, playing together. She saw them writing with their diamond pencils on golden slates, while she looked at the beautiful picture book which had cost half a kingdom. They were not writing lines and letters, as they used to do; but descriptions of the noble deeds they had performed, and of all they had discovered and seen. In the picture book, too, everything was living. The birds sang, and the people came out of the book, and spoke to Eliza and her brothers; but, as the leaves turned over, they darted back again to their places, that all might be in order.

When she awoke, the sun was high in the heavens; yet she could not see him, for the lofty trees spread their branches thickly over her head; but his beams were glancing through the leaves here and there, like a golden mist. There was a sweet fragrance from the fresh green verdure, and the birds almost perched upon her shoulders. She heard water rippling from a number of springs, all flowing in a lake with golden sands. Bushes grew thickly round the lake, and at one spot an opening had been made by a deer, through which Eliza went down to the water. The lake was so clear that, had not the wind rustled the branches of the trees and the bushes, so that they moved, they would have appeared as if painted in the depths of the lake; for every leaf was reflected in the water, whether it stood in the shade or the sunshine. As soon as Eliza saw her own face, she was quite terrified at finding it so brown and ugly; but when she wetted her little hand, and rubbed her eyes and forehead, the white skin gleamed forth once more; and, after she had undressed, and dipped herself in the fresh water, a more beautiful king's daughter could not be found in the wide world. As soon as she had dressed herself again, and braided her long hair, she went to the bubbling spring, and drank some water out of the hollow of her hand. Then she wandered far into the forest, not knowing whither she went. She thought of her brothers, and felt sure that God would not forsake her. It is God who makes the wild apples grow in the wood, to satisfy the hungry, and He now led her to one of these trees, which was so loaded with fruit, that the boughs bent beneath the weight. Here she held her noonday repast, placed props under the boughs, and then went into the gloomiest depths of the forest. It was so still that she could hear the sound of her own footsteps, as well as the rustling of every withered leaf which she crushed under her feet. Not a bird was to be seen, not a sunbeam could penetrate through the large, dark boughs of the trees. Their lofty trunks stood so close together, that, when she looked before her, it seemed as if she were enclosed within trellis-work. Such solitude she had never known before. The night was very dark. Not a single glow-worm glittered in the moss.

Sorrowfully she laid herself down to sleep; and, after a while, it seemed to her as if the branches of the trees parted over her head, and that the mild eyes of angels looked down upon her from heaven. When she awoke in the morning, she knew not whether she had dreamt this, or if it had really been so. Then she continued her wandering; but she had not gone many steps forward, when she met an old woman with berries in her basket, and she gave her a few to eat. Then Eliza asked her if she had not seen eleven princes riding through the forest.

"No," replied the old woman, "But I saw yesterday eleven swans, with gold crowns on their heads, swimming on the river close by." Then she led Eliza a little distance farther to a sloping bank, and at the foot of it wound a little river. The trees on its banks stretched their long leafy branches across the water towards each other, and where the growth prevented them from meeting naturally, the roots had torn themselves away from the ground, so that the branches might mingle their foliage as they hung over the water. Eliza bade the old woman farewell, and walked by the flowing river, till she reached the shore of the open sea. And there, before the young maiden's eyes, lay the glorious ocean, but not a sail appeared on its surface, not even a boat could be seen. How was she to go farther? She noticed how the countless pebbles on the sea-shore had been smoothed and rounded by the action of the water. Glass, iron, stones, everything that lay there mingled together, had taken its shape from the same power, and felt as smooth, or even smoother than her own delicate hand. "The water rolls on without weariness," she said, till all that is hard becomes smooth; so will I be unwearied in my task. Thanks for your lessons, bright rolling waves; my heart tells me you will lead me to my dear brothers." On the foam-covered sea-weeds, lay eleven white swan feathers, which she gathered up and placed together. Drops of water lay upon them; whether they were dew-drops or tears no one could say. Lonely as it was on the sea-shore, she did not observe it, for the ever-moving sea showed more changes in a few hours than the most varying lake could produce during a whole year. If a black heavy cloud arose, it was as if the sea said, "I can look dark and angry too;" and then the wind blew, and the waves turned to white foam as they rolled. When the wind slept, and the clouds glowed with the red sunlight, then the sea looked like a rose leaf. But however quietly its white glassy surface rested, there was still a motion on the shore, as its waves rose and fell like the breast of a sleeping child. When the sun was about to set, Eliza saw eleven white swans with golden crowns on their heads, flying towards the land, one behind the other, like a long white ribbon. Then Eliza went down the slope from the shore, and hid herself behind the bushes. The swans alighted quite close to her and flapped their great white wings. As soon as the sun had disappeared under the water, the feathers of the swans fell off, and eleven beautiful princes, Eliza's brothers, stood near her. She uttered a loud cry, for, although they were very much changed, she knew them immediately. She sprang into their arms, and called them each by name. Then, how happy the princes were at meeting their little sister again, for they recognized her, although she had grown so tall and beautiful. They laughed, and they wept, and very soon understood how wickedly their mother had acted to them all. "We brothers," said the eldest, "fly about as wild swans, so long as the sun is in the sky; but as soon as it sinks behind the hills, we recover our human shape. Therefore must we always be near a resting place for our feet before sunset; for if we should be flying towards the clouds at the time we recovered our natural shape as men, we should sink deep into the sea. We do not dwell here, but in a land just as fair, that lies beyond the ocean, which we have to cross for a long distance; there is no island in our passage upon which we could pass, the night; nothing but a little rock rising out of the sea, upon which we can scarcely stand with safety, even closely crowded together. If the sea is rough, the foam dashes over us, yet we thank God even for this rock; we have passed whole nights upon it, or we should never have reached our beloved fatherland, for our flight across the sea occupies two of the longest days in the year. We have permission to visit out home once in every year, and to remain eleven days, during which we fly across the forest to look once more at the palace where our father dwells, and where we were born, and at the church, where our mother lies buried. Here it seems as if the very trees and bushes were related to us. The wild horses leap over the plains as we have seen them in our childhood. The charcoal burners sing the old songs, to which we have danced as children. This is our fatherland, to which we are drawn by loving ties; and here we have found you, our dear little sister., Two days longer we can remain here, and then must we fly away to a beautiful land which is not our home; and how can we take you with us? We have neither ship nor boat."

"How can I break this spell?" said their sister. And then she talked about it nearly the whole night, only slumbering for a few hours. Eliza was awakened by the rustling of the swans' wings as they soared above. Her brothers were again changed to swans, and they flew in circles wider and wider, till they were far away; but one of them, the youngest swan, remained behind, and laid his head in his sister's lap, while she stroked his wings; and they remained together the whole day. Towards evening, the rest came back, and as the sun went down they resumed their natural forms. "Tomorrow," said one, "we shall fly away, not to return again till a whole year has passed. But we cannot leave you here. Have you courage to go with us? My arm is strong enough to carry you through the wood; and will not all our wings be strong enough to fly with you over the sea?"

"Yes, take me with you," said Eliza. Then they spent the whole night in weaving a net with the pliant willow and rushes. It was very large and strong. Eliza laid herself down on the net, and when the sun rose, and her brothers again became wild swans, they took up the net with their beaks, and flew up to the clouds with their dear sister, who still slept. The sunbeams fell on her face, therefore one of the swans soared over her head, so that his broad wings might shade her. They were far from the land when Eliza woke. She thought she must still be dreaming, it seemed so strange to her to feel herself being carried so high in the air over the sea. By her side lay a branch full of beautiful ripe berries, and a bundle of sweet roots; the youngest of her brothers had gathered them for her, and placed them by her side. She smiled her thanks to him; she knew it was the same who had hovered over her to shade her with his wings. They were now so high, that a large ship beneath them looked like a white sea-gull skimming the waves. A great cloud floating behind them appeared like a vast mountain, and upon it Eliza saw her own shadow and those of the eleven swans, looking gigantic in size. Altogether it formed a more beautiful picture than she had ever seen; but as the sun rose higher, and the clouds were left behind, the shadowy picture vanished away. Onward the whole day they flew through the air like a winged arrow, yet more slowly than usual, for they had their sister to carry. The weather seemed inclined to be stormy, and Eliza watched the sinking sun with great anxiety, for the little rock in the ocean was not yet in sight. It appeared to her as if the swans were making great efforts with their wings. Alas! she was the cause of their not advancing more quickly. When the sun set, they would change to men, fall into the sea and be drowned. Then she offered a prayer from her inmost heart, but still no appearance of the rock. Dark clouds came nearer, the gusts of wind told of a coming storm, while from a thick, heavy mass of clouds the lightning burst forth flash after flash. The sun had reached the edge of the sea, when the swans darted down so swiftly, that Eliza's head trembled; she believed they were falling, but they again soared onward. Presently she caught sight of the rock just below them, and by this time the sun was half hidden by the waves. The rock did not appear larger than a seal's head thrust out of the water. They sunk so rapidly, that at the moment their feet touched the rock, it shone only like a star, and at last disappeared like the last spark in a piece of burnt paper. Then she saw her brothers standing closely round her with their arms linked together. There was but just room enough for them, and not the smallest space to spare. The sea dashed against the rock, and covered them with spray. The heavens were lighted up with continual flashes, and peal after peal of thunder rolled. But the sister and brothers sat holding each other's hands, and singing hymns, from which they gained hope and courage. In the early dawn the air became calm and still, and at sunrise the swans flew away from the rock with Eliza. The sea was still rough, and from their high position in the air, the white foam on the dark green waves looked like millions of swans swimming on the water. As the sun rose higher, Eliza saw before her, floating on the air, a range of mountains, with shining masses of ice on their summits. In the centre, rose a castle apparently a mile long, with rows of columns, rising one above another, while, around it, palm-trees waved and flowers bloomed as large as mill wheels. She asked if this was the land to which they were hastening. The swans shook their heads, for what she beheld were the beautiful ever-changing cloud palaces of the "Fata Morgana," into which no mortal can enter. Eliza was still gazing at the scene, when mountains, forests, and castles melted away, and twenty stately churches rose in their stead, with high towers and pointed gothic windows. Eliza even fancied she could hear the tones of the organ, but it was the music of the murmuring sea which she heard. As they drew nearer to the churches, they also changed into a fleet of ships, which seemed to be sailing beneath her; but as she looked again, she found it was only a sea mist gliding over the ocean. So there continued to pass before her eyes a constant change of scene, till at last she saw the real land to which they were bound, with its blue mountains, its cedar forests, and its cities and palaces. Long before the sun went down, she sat on a rock, in front of a large cave, on the floor of which the over-grown yet delicate green creeping plants looked like an embroidered carpet. "Now we shall expect to hear what you dream of tonight," said the youngest brother, as he showed his sister her bedroom.

"Heaven grant that I may dream how to save you," she replied. And this thought took such hold upon her mind that she prayed earnestly to God for help, and even in her sleep she continued to pray. Then it appeared to her as if she were flying high in the air, towards the cloudy palace of the "Fata Morgana," and a fairy came out to meet her, radiant and beautiful in appearance, and yet very much like the old woman who had given her berries in the wood, and who had told her of the swans with golden crowns on their heads. "Your brothers can be released," said she, "if you have only courage and perseverance. True, water is softer than your own delicate hands, and yet it polishes stones into shapes; it feels no pain as your fingers would feel, it has no soul, and cannot suffer such agony and torment as you will have to endure. Do you see the stinging nettle which I hold in my hand? Quantities of the same sort grow round the cave in which you sleep, but none will be of any use to you unless they grow upon the graves in a churchyard. These you must gather even while they burn blisters on your hands. Break them to pieces with your hands and feet, and they will become flax, from which you must spin and weave eleven coats with long sleeves; if these are then thrown over the eleven swans, the spell will be broken. But remember, that from the moment you commence your task until it is finished, even should it occupy years of your life, you must not speak. The first word you utter will pierce through the hearts of your brothers like a deadly dagger. Their lives hang upon your tongue. Remember all I have told you." And as she finished speaking, she touched her hand lightly with the nettle, and a pain, as of burning fire, awoke Eliza.

It was broad daylight, and close by where she had been sleeping lay a nettle like the one she had seen in her dream. She fell on her knees and offered her thanks to God. Then she went forth from the cave to begin her work with her delicate hands. She groped in amongst the ugly nettles, which burnt great blisters on her hands and arms, but she determined to bear it gladly if she could only release her dear brothers. So she bruised the nettles with her bare feet and spun the flax. At sunset her brothers returned and were very much frightened when they found her dumb. They believed it to be some new sorcery of their wicked step-mother. But when they saw her hands they understood what she was doing on their behalf, and the youngest brother wept, and where his tears fell the pain ceased, and the burning blisters vanished. She kept to her work all night, for she could not rest till she had released her dear brothers. During the whole of the following day, while her brothers were absent, she sat in solitude, but never before had the time flown so quickly. One coat was already finished and she had begun the second, when she heard the huntsman's horn, and was struck with fear. The sound came nearer and nearer, she heard the dogs barking, and fled with terror into the cave. She hastily bound together the nettles she had gathered into a bundle and sat upon them. Immediately a great dog came bounding towards her out of the ravine, and then another and another; they barked loudly, ran back, and then came again. In a very few minutes all the huntsmen stood before the cave, and the handsomest of them was the king of the country. He advanced towards her, for he had never seen a more beautiful maiden.

"How did you come here, my sweet child?" he asked. But Eliza shook her head. She dared not speak, at the cost of her brothers' lives. And she hid her hands under her apron, so that the king might not see how she must be suffering.

"Come with me," he said; "here you cannot remain. If you are as good as you are beautiful, I will dress you in silk and velvet, I will place a golden crown upon your head, and you shall dwell, and rule,

The Wild Swans

and make your home in my richest castle." And then he lifted her on his horse. She wept and wrung her hands, but the king said, "I wish only for your happiness. A time will come when you will thank me for this." And then he galloped away over the mountains, holding her before him on this horse, and the hunters followed behind them. As the sun went down, they approached a fair royal city, with churches, and cupolas. On arriving at the castle the king led her into marble halls, where large fountains played, and where the walls and the ceilings were covered with rich paintings. But she had no eyes for all these glorious sights, she could only mourn and weep. Patiently she allowed the women to array her in royal robes, to weave pearls in her hair, and draw soft gloves over her blistered fingers. As she stood before them in all her rich dress, she looked so dazzlingly beautiful that the court bowed low in her presence. Then the king declared his intention of making her his bride, but the archbishop shook his head, and whispered that the fair young maiden was only a witch who had blinded the king's eyes and bewitched his heart. But the king would not listen to this; he ordered the music to sound, the daintiest dishes to be served, and the loveliest maidens to dance. After-wards he led her through fragrant gardens and lofty halls, but not a smile appeared on her lips or sparkled in her eyes. She looked the very picture of grief. Then the king opened the door of a little chamber in which she was to sleep; it was adorned with rich green tapestry, and resembled the cave in which he had found her. On the floor lay the bundle of flax which she had spun from the nettles, and under the ceiling hung the coat she had made. These things had been brought away from the cave as curiosities by one of the huntsmen.

"Here you can dream yourself back again in the old home in the cave," said the king; "here is the work with which you employed yourself. It will amuse you now in the midst of all this splendor to think of that time."

When Eliza saw all these things which lay so near her heart, a smile played around her mouth, and the crimson blood rushed to her cheeks. She thought of her brothers, and their release made her so joyful that she kissed the king's hand. Then he pressed her to his heart. Very soon the joyous church bells announced the marriage feast, and that the beautiful dumb girl out of the wood was to be made the queen of the country. Then the archbishop whispered wicked words in the king's ear, but they did not sink into his heart. The marriage was still to take place, and the archbishop himself had to place the crown on the bride's head; in his wicked spite, he pressed the narrow circlet so tightly on her forehead that it caused her pain. But a heavier weight encircled her heart—sorrow for her brothers. She felt not bodily pain. Her mouth was closed; a single word would cost the lives of her brothers. But she loved the kind, handsome king, who did everything to make her happy more and more each day; she loved him with all her heart, and her eyes beamed with the love she dared not speak. Oh! if she had only been able to confide in him and tell him of her grief. But dumb she must remain till her task was finished. Therefore at night she crept away into her little chamber, which had been decked out to look like the cave, and quickly wove one coat after another. But when she began the seventh she found she had no more flax. She knew that the nettles she wanted to use grew in the churchyard, and that she must pluck them herself. How should she get out there? "Oh, what is the pain in my fingers to the torment which my heart endures?" said she. "I must venture, I shall not be denied help from heaven." Then with a trembling heart, as if she were about to perform a wicked deed, she crept into the garden in the broad moonlight, and passed through the narrow walks and the deserted streets, till she reached the churchyard. Then she saw on one of the broad tombstones a group of ghouls. These hideous creatures took off their rags, as if they intended to bathe, and then clawing open the fresh graves with their long, skinny fingers, pulled out the dead bodies and ate the flesh! Eliza had to pass close by them, and they fixed their wicked glances upon her, but she prayed silently, gathered the burning nettles, and carried them home with her to the castle. One person only had seen her, and that was the archbishop—he was awake while everybody was asleep. Now he thought his opinion was evidently correct. All was not right with the queen. She was a witch, and had bewitched the king and all the people. Secretly he told the king what he had seen and what he feared, and as the hard words came from his tongue, the carved images of the saints shook their heads as if they would say. "It is not so. Eliza is innocent."

But the archbishop interpreted it in another way; he believed that they witnessed against her, and were shaking their heads at her wickedness. Two large tears rolled down the king's cheeks, and he went home with doubt in his heart, and at night he pretended to sleep, but there came no real sleep to his eyes, for he saw Eliza get up every night and disappear in her own chamber. From day to day his brow became darker, and Eliza saw it and did not understand the reason, but it alarmed her and made her heart tremble for her brothers. Her hot tears glittered like pearls on the regal velvet and diamonds, while all who saw her were wishing they could be queens. In the meantime she had almost finished her task; only one coat of mail was wanting, but she had no flax left, and not a single nettle. Once more only, and for the last time, must she venture to the churchyard and pluck a few handfuls. She thought with terror of the solitary walk, and of the horrible ghouls, but her will was firm, as well as her trust in Providence. Eliza went, and the king and the archbishop followed her. They saw her vanish through the wicket gate into the churchyard, and when they came nearer they saw the ghouls sitting on the tombstone, as Eliza had seen them, and the king turned away his head, for he thought she was with them—she whose head had rested on his breast that very evening. "The people must condemn her," said he, and she was very quickly condemned by every one to suffer death by fire. Away from the gorgeous regal halls was she led to a dark, dreary cell, where the wind whistled through the iron bars. Instead of the velvet and silk dresses, they gave her the coats of mail which she had woven to cover her, and the bundle of nettles for a pillow; but nothing they could give her would have pleased her more. She continued her task with joy, and prayed for help, while the street-boys sang jeering songs about her, and not a soul comforted her with a kind word. Towards evening, she heard at the grating the flutter of a swan's wing, it was her youngest brother—he had found his sister, and she sobbed for joy, although she knew that very likely this would be the last night she would have to live. But still she could hope, for her task was almost finished, and her brothers were come. Then the archbishop arrived, to be with her during her last hours, as he had promised the king. But she shook her head, and begged him, by looks and gestures, not to stay; for in this night she knew she must finish her task, otherwise all her pain and tears and sleepless nights would have been suffered in vain. The archbishop withdrew, uttering bitter words against her; but poor Eliza knew that she was innocent, and diligently continued her work.

The little mice ran about the floor, they dragged the nettles to her feet, to help as well as they could; and the thrush sat outside the grating of the window, and sang to her the whole night long, as sweetly as possible, to keep up her spirits.

It was still twilight, and at least an hour before sunrise, when the eleven brothers stood at the castle gate, and demanded to be brought before the king. They were told it could not be, it was yet almost night, and as the king slept they dared not disturb him. They threatened, they entreated. Then the guard appeared, and even the king himself, inquiring what all the noise meant. At this moment the sun rose. The eleven brothers were seen no more, but eleven wild swans flew away over the castle.

And now all the people came streaming forth from the gates of the city, to see the witch burnt. An old horse drew the cart on which she sat. They had dressed her in a garment of coarse sackcloth. Her lovely hair hung loose on her shoulders, her cheeks were deadly pale, her lips moved silently, while her fingers still worked at the green flax. Even on the way to death, she would not give up her task. The ten coats of mail lay at her feet, she was working hard at the eleventh, while the mob jeered her and said, "See the witch, how she mutters! She has no hymn-book in her hand. She sits there with her ugly sorcery. Let us tear it in a thousand pieces."

And then they pressed towards her, and would have destroyed the coats of mail, but at the same moment eleven wild swans flew over her, and alighted on the cart. Then they flapped their large wings, and the crowd drew on one side in alarm.

"It is a sign from heaven that she is innocent," whispered many of them; but they ventured not to say it aloud.

As the executioner seized her by the hand, to lift her out of the cart, she hastily threw the eleven coats of mail over the swans, and they immediately became eleven handsome princes; but the youngest had a swan's wing, instead of an arm; for she had not been able to finish the last sleeve of the coat.

"Now I may speak," she exclaimed. "I am innocent."

Then the people, who saw what happened, bowed to her, as before a saint; but she sank lifeless in her brothers' arms, overcome with suspense, anguish, and pain.

"Yes, she is innocent," said the eldest brother; and then he related all that had taken place; and while he spoke there rose in the air a fragrance as from millions of roses. Every piece of faggot in the pile had taken root, and threw out branches, and appeared a thick hedge, large and high, covered with roses; while above all bloomed a white and shining flower, that glittered like a star. This flower the king plucked, and placed in Eliza's bosom, when she awoke from her swoon, with peace and happiness in her heart. And all the church bells rang of themselves, and the birds came in great troops. And a marriage procession returned to the castle, such as no king had ever before seen.

The Elf of the Rose

Translated by Mrs. H. P. Paull

In the midst of a garden grew a rose-tree, in full blossom, and in the prettiest of all the roses lived an elf. He was such a little wee thing, that no human eye could see him. Behind each leaf of the rose he had a sleeping chamber. He was as well formed and as beautiful as a little child could be, and had wings that reached from his shoulders to his feet. Oh, what sweet fragrance there was in his chambers! and how clean and beautiful were the walls! for they were the blushing leaves of the rose.

During the whole day he enjoyed himself in the warm sunshine, flew from flower to flower, and danced on the wings of the flying butterflies. Then he took it into his head to measure how many steps he would have to go through the roads and cross-roads that are on the leaf of a linden-tree. What we call the veins on a leaf, he took for roads; ay, and very long roads they were for him; for before he had half finished his task, the sun went down: he had commenced his work too late. It became very cold, the dew fell, and the wind blew; so he thought the best thing he could do would be to return home. He

The Elf of the Rose

hurried himself as much as he could; but he found the roses all closed up, and he could not get in; not a single rose stood open. The poor little elf was very much frightened. He had never before been out at night, but had always slumbered secretly behind the warm rose-leaves. Oh, this would certainly be his death. At the other end of the garden, he knew there was an arbor, overgrown with beautiful honeysuckles. The blossoms looked like large painted horns; and he thought to himself, he would go and sleep in one of these till the morning. He flew thither; but "hush!" two people were in the arbor—a handsome young man and a beautiful lady. They sat side by side, and wished that they might never be obliged to part. They loved each other much more than the best child can love its father and mother.

"But we must part," said the young man; "your brother does not like our engagement, and therefore he sends me so far away on business, over mountains and seas. Farewell, my sweet bride; for so you are to me."

And then they kissed each other, and the girl wept, and gave him a rose; but before she did so, she pressed a kiss upon it so fervently that the flower opened. Then the little elf flew in, and leaned his head on the delicate, fragrant walls. Here he could plainly hear them say, "Farewell, farewell;" and he felt that the rose had been placed on the young man's breast. Oh, how his heart did beat! The little elf could not go to sleep, it thumped so loudly. The young man took it out as he walked through the dark wood alone, and kissed the flower so often and so violently, that the little elf was almost crushed. He could feel through the leaf how hot the lips of the young man were, and the rose had opened, as if from the heat of the noonday sun.

There came another man, who looked gloomy and wicked. He was the wicked brother of the beautiful maiden. He drew out a sharp knife, and while the other was kissing the rose, the wicked man stabbed him to death; then he cut off his head, and buried it with the body in the soft earth under the linden-tree.

"Now he is gone, and will soon be forgotten," thought the wicked brother; "he will never come back again. He was going on a long journey over mountains and seas; it is easy for a man to lose his life in such a journey. My sister will suppose he is dead; for he cannot come back, and she will not dare to question me about him."

Then he scattered the dry leaves over the light earth with his foot, and went home through the darkness; but he went not alone, as he thought—the little elf accompanied him. He sat in a dry rolled-up linden-leaf, which had fallen from the tree on to the wicked man's head, as he was digging the grave. The hat was on the head now, which made it very dark, and the little elf shuddered with fright and indignation at the wicked deed.

It was the dawn of morning before the wicked man reached home; he took off his hat, and went into his sister's room. There lay the beautiful, blooming girl, dreaming of him whom she loved so, and who was now, she supposed, travelling far away over mountain and sea. Her wicked brother stopped over her, and laughed hideously, as fiends only can laugh. The dry leaf fell out of his hair upon the counterpane; but he did not notice it, and went to get a little sleep during the early morning hours. But the elf slipped out of the withered leaf, placed himself by the ear of the sleeping girl, and told her, as in a dream, of the horrid murder; described the place where her brother had slain her lover, and buried his body; and told her of the linden-tree, in full blossom, that stood close by.

"That you may not think this is only a dream that I have told you," he said, "you will find on your bed a withered leaf."

Then she awoke, and found it there. Oh, what bitter tears she shed! and she could not open her heart to any one for relief.

The window stood open the whole day, and the little elf could easily have reached the roses, or any of the flowers; but he could not find it in his heart to leave one so afflicted. In the window stood a bush bearing monthly roses. He seated himself in one of the flowers, and gazed on the poor girl. Her brother often came into the room, and would be quite cheerful, in spite of his base conduct; so she dare not say a word to him of her heart's grief.

As soon as night came on, she slipped out of the house, and went into the wood, to the spot where the linden-tree stood; and after removing the leaves from the earth, she turned it up, and there found him who had been murdered. Oh, how she wept and prayed that she also might die! Gladly would she have taken the body home with her; but that was impossible; so she took up the poor head with the closed eyes, kissed the cold lips, and shook the mould out of the beautiful hair.

"I will keep this," said she; and as soon as she had covered the body again with the earth and leaves, she took the head and a little sprig of jasmine that bloomed in the wood, near the spot where he was buried, and carried them home with her. As soon as she was in her room, she took the largest flowerpot she could find, and in this she placed the head of the dead man, covered it up with earth, and planted the twig of jasmine in it.

"Farewell, farewell," whispered the little elf. He could not any longer endure to witness all this agony of grief, he therefore flew away to his own rose in the garden. But the rose was faded; only a few dry leaves still clung to the green hedge behind it.

"Alas! how soon all that is good and beautiful passes away," sighed the elf.

After a while he found another rose, which became his home, for among its delicate fragrant leaves he could dwell in safety. Every morning he flew to the window of the poor girl, and always found her weeping by the flowerpot. The bitter tears fell upon the jasmine twig, and each day, as she became paler and paler, the sprig appeared to grow greener and fresher. One shoot after another sprouted forth, and little white buds blossomed, which the poor girl fondly kissed. But her wicked brother scolded her, and asked her if she was going mad. He could not imagine why she was weeping over that flowerpot, and it annoyed him. He did not know whose closed eyes were there, nor what red lips were fading beneath the earth. And one day she sat and leaned her head against the flowerpot, and the little elf of the rose found her asleep. Then he seated himself by her ear, talked to her of that evening in the arbor, of the sweet perfume of the rose, and the loves of the elves. Sweetly she dreamed, and while she dreamt, her life passed away calmly and gently, and her spirit was with him whom she loved, in heaven. And the jasmine opened its large white bells, and spread forth its sweet fragrance; it had no other way of showing its grief for the dead. But the wicked brother considered the beautiful blooming plant as his own property, left to him by his sister, and he placed it in his sleeping room, close by his bed, for it was very lovely in appearance, and the fragrance sweet and delightful. The little elf of the rose followed it, and flew from flower to flower, telling each little spirit that dwelt in them the story of the murdered young man, whose head now formed part of the earth beneath them, and of the wicked brother and the poor sister. "We know it," said each little spirit in the flowers, "we know it, for have we not sprung from the eyes and lips of the murdered one. We know it, we know it," and the flowers nodded with their heads in a peculiar manner. The elf of the rose could not understand how they could rest so quietly in the matter, so he flew to the bees, who were gathering honey, and told them of the wicked brother. And the bees told it to their Queen, who commanded that the next morning they should go and kill the murderer. But during the night, the first after the sister's death, while the brother was sleeping in his bed, close to where he had placed the fragrant jasmine, every flower cup opened, and invisibly the little spirits stole out, armed with poisonous spears. They placed themselves by the ear of the sleeper, told him dreadful dreams and then flew across his lips, and pricked his tongue with their poisoned spears. "Now have we revenged the dead," said they, and flew back into the white bells of the jasmine flowers. When the morning came, and as soon as the window was opened, the rose elf, with the Queen Bee, and the whole swarm of bees, rushed in to kill him. But he was already dead. People were standing round the bed, and saying that the scent of the jasmine had killed him. Then the elf of the rose understood the revenge of the flowers, and explained it to the Queen Bee, and she, with the whole swarm, buzzed about the flowerpot. The bees could not be driven away. Then a man took it up to remove it, and one of the bees stung him in the hand, so that he let the flowerpot fall, and it was broken to pieces. Then every one saw the whitened skull, and they knew the dead man in the bed was a murderer. And the Queen Bee hummed in the air, and sang of the revenge of the flowers, and of the elf of the rose and said that behind the smallest leaf dwells One, who can discover evil deeds, and punish them also.

The Garden of Paradise

Translated by Mrs. H. P. Paull

There was once a King's son who had a larger and more beautiful collection of books than any one else in the world, and full of splendid copper-plate engravings. He could read and obtain information respecting every people of every land; but not a word could he find to explain the situation of the Garden of Paradise, and this was just what he most wished to know. His grandmother had told him when he was quite a little boy, just old enough to go to school, that each flower in the Garden of Paradise was a sweet cake, that the pistils were full of rich wine, that on one flower history was written, on another geography or tables; so those who wished to learn their lessons had only to eat some of the cakes, and the more they ate, the more history, geography, or tables they knew. He believed it all then; but as he grew older, and learnt more and more, he became wise enough to understand that the splendor of the Garden of Paradise must be very different to all this. "Oh, why did Eve pluck the fruit from the tree of knowledge? why did Adam eat the forbidden fruit?" thought the King's son: "if I had been there it would never have happened, and there would have been no sin in the world." The Garden of Paradise occupied all his thoughts till he reached his seventeenth year.

One day he was walking alone in the wood, which was his greatest pleasure, when evening came on. The clouds gathered, and the rain poured down as if the sky had been a waterspout; and it was as dark as the bottom of a well at midnight; sometimes he slipped over the smooth grass, or fell over stones that projected out of the rocky ground. Every thing was dripping with moisture, and the poor prince had not a dry thread about him. He was obliged at last to climb over great blocks of stone, with water spurting from the thick moss. He began to feel quite faint, when he heard a most singular rushing noise, and saw before him a large cave, from which came a blaze of light. In the middle of the cave an immense fire was burning, and a noble stag, with its branching horns, was placed on a spit between the trunks of two pine-trees. It was turning slowly before the fire, and an elderly woman, as large and strong as if she had been a man in disguise, sat by, throwing one piece of wood after another into the flames.

"Come in," she said to the prince; "sit down by the fire and dry yourself."

"There is a great draught here," said the prince, as he seated himself on the ground.

"It will be worse when my sons come home," replied the woman; "you are now in the Cavern of the Winds, and my sons are the four Winds of heaven: can you understand that?"

"Where are your sons?" asked the Prince.

"It is difficult to answer stupid questions," said the woman. "My sons have plenty of business on hand; they are playing at shuttlecock with the clouds up yonder in the king's hall," and she pointed upwards.

"Oh, indeed," said the Prince; "but you speak more roughly and harshly and are not so gentle as the women I am used to."

"Yes, that is because they have nothing else to do; but I am obliged to be harsh, to keep my boys in order, and I can do it, although they are so head-strong. Do you see those four sacks hanging on the wall? Well, they are just as much afraid of those sacks, as you used to be of the rat behind the looking-glass. I can bend the boys together, and put them in the sacks without any resistance on their parts, I can tell you. There they stay, and dare not attempt to come out until I allow them to do so. And here comes one of them."

It was the North Wind who came in, bringing with him a cold, piercing blast; large hailstones rattled on the floor, and snowflakes were scattered around in all directions. He wore a bearskin dress and cloak. His sealskin cap was drawn over his ears, long icicles hung from his beard, and one hailstone after another rolled from the collar of his jacket.

"Don't go too near the fire," said the Prince, "or your hands and face will be frost-bitten."

"Frost-bitten!" said the North Wind, with a loud laugh; "why frost is my greatest delight. What sort of a little snip are you, and how did you find your way to the Cavern of the Winds?"

"He is my guest," said the old woman, "and if you are not satisfied with that explanation you can go into the sack. Do you understand me?"

That settled the matter. So the North Wind began to relate his adventures, whence he came, and where he had been for a whole month. "I come from the Polar Seas," he said; "I have been on the Bear's Island with the Russian walrus-hunters. I sat and slept at the helm of their ship, as they sailed away from North Cape. Sometimes when I woke, the storm-birds would fly about my legs. They are curious birds; they give one flap with their wings, and then on their outstretched pinions soar far away."

"Don't make such a long story of it," said the mother of the Winds; "what sort of a place is Bear's Island?"

"A very beautiful place, with a floor for dancing as smooth and flat as a plate. Half-melted snow, partly covered with moss, sharp stones, and skeletons of walruses and polar-bears, lie all about, their gigantic limbs in a state of green decay. It would seem as if the sun never shone there. I blew gently, to clear away the mist, and then I saw a little hut, which had been built from the wood of a wreck, and was covered with the skins of the walrus, the fleshy side outwards; it looked green and red, and on the roof sat a growling bear. Then I went to the sea shore, to look after birds' nests, and saw the unfledged nestlings opening their mouths and screaming for food. I blew into the thousand little throats, and quickly stopped their screaming. Farther on were the walruses with pig's heads, and teeth a yard long, rolling about like great worms."

"You relate your adventures very well, my son," said the mother, "it makes my mouth water to hear you."

"After that," continued the North Wind, "the hunting commenced. The harpoon was flung into the breast of the walrus, so that a smoking stream of blood spurted forth like a fountain, and besprinkled the ice. Then I thought of my own game; I began to blow, and set my own ships, the great icebergs sailing, so that they might crush the boats. Oh, how the sailors howled and cried out! but I howled louder than they. They were obliged to unload their cargo, and throw their chests and the dead walruses on the ice. Then I sprinkled snow over them, and left them in their crushed boats to drift southward, and to taste salt water. They will never return to Bear's Island."

"So you have done mischief," said the mother of the Winds.

"I shall leave others to tell the good I have done," he replied. "But here comes my brother from the West; I like him best of all, for he has the smell of the sea about him, and brings in a cold, fresh air as he enters."

"Is that the little Zephyr?" asked the Prince.

"Yes, it is the little Zephyr," said the old woman; "but he is not little now. In years gone by he was a beautiful boy; now that is all past."

He came in, looking like a wild man, and he wore a slouched hat to protect his head from injury. In his hand he carried a club, cut from a mahogany tree in the American forests, not a trifle to carry.

"Whence do you come?" asked the mother.

"I come from the wilds of the forests, where the thorny brambles form thick hedges between the trees; where the water-snake lies in the wet grass, and mankind seem to be unknown."

"What were you doing there?"

"I looked into the deep river, and saw it rushing down from the rocks. The water drops mounted to the clouds and glittered in the rainbow. I saw the wild buffalo swimming in the river, but the strong tide carried him away amidst a flock of wild ducks, which flew into the air as the waters dashed onwards, leaving the buffalo to be hurled over the waterfall. This pleased me; so I raised a storm, which rooted up old trees, and sent them floating down the river."

"And what else have you done?" asked the old woman.

"I have rushed wildly across the Savannahs; I have stroked the wild horses, and shaken the cocoa-nuts from the trees. Yes, I have many stories to relate; but I need not tell everything I know. You know it all very well, don't you, old lady?" And he kissed his mother so roughly, that she nearly fell backwards. Oh, he was, indeed, a wild fellow.

Now in came the South Wind, with a turban and a flowing Bedouin cloak.

"How cold it is here!" said he, throwing more wood on the fire. "It is easy to feel that the North Wind has arrived here before me."

"Why it is hot enough here to roast a bear," said the North Wind.

"You are a bear yourself," said the other.

"Do you want to be put in the sack, both of you?" said the old woman. "Sit down, now, on that stone, yonder, and tell me where you have been."

"In Africa, mother. I went out with the Hottentots, who were lion-hunting in the Kaffir land, where the plains are covered with grass the colour of a green olive; and here I ran races with the ostrich, but I soon outstripped him in swiftness. At last I came to the desert, in which lie the golden sands, looking like the bottom of the sea. Here I met a caravan, and the travellers had just killed their last camel, to obtain water; there was very little for them, and they continued their painful journey beneath the burning sun, and over the hot sands, which stretched before them a vast, boundless desert. Then I rolled myself in the loose sand, and whirled it in burning columns over their heads. The dromedarys stood still in terror, while the merchants drew their caftans over their heads, and threw themselves on the ground before me, as they do before Allah, their God. Then I buried them beneath a pyramid of sand, which covers them all. When I blow that away on my next visit, the sun will bleach their bones, and travellers will see that others have been there before them; otherwise, in such a wild desert, they might not believe it possible."

"So you have done nothing but evil," said the mother. "Into the sack with you;" and, before he was aware, she had seized the South Wind round the body, and popped him into the bag. He rolled about on the floor, till she sat herself upon him to keep him still.

"These boys of yours are very lively," said the Prince.

"Yes," she replied, "but I know how to correct them, when necessary; and here comes the fourth." In came the East Wind, dressed like a Chinese.

"Oh, you come from that quarter, do you?" said she; "I thought you had been to the Garden of Paradise."

"I am going there tomorrow," he replied; "I have not been there for a hundred years. I have just come from China, where I danced round the porcelain tower till all the bells jingled again. In the streets an official flogging was taking place, and bamboo canes were being broken on the shoulders of men of every high position, from the first to the ninth grade. They cried, 'Many thanks, my fatherly benefactor;' but I am sure the words did not come from their hearts, so I rang the bells till they sounded, 'Ding, ding-dong.'"

"You are a wild boy," said the old woman; "it is well for you that you are going tomorrow to the Garden of Paradise; you always get improved in your education there. Drink deeply from the fountain of Wisdom while you are there, and bring home a bottleful for me."

"That I will," said the East Wind; "but why have you put my brother South in a bag? Let him out; for I want him to tell me about the Phoenix-bird. The Princess always wants to hear of this bird when I pay her my visit every hundred years. If you will open the sack, sweetest mother, I will give you two pocketfuls of tea, green and fresh as when I gathered it from the spot where it grew."

"Well, for the sake of the tea, and because you are my own boy, I will open the bag."

She did so, and the South Wind crept out, looking quite cast down, because the Prince had seen his disgrace.

"There is a palm-leaf for the Princess," he said. "The old Phoenix, the only one in the world, gave it to me himself. He has scratched on it with his beak the whole of his history during the hundred years he has lived. She can there read how the old Phoenix set fire to his own nest, and sat upon it while it was burning, like a Hindu widow. The dry twigs around the nest crackled and smoked till the flames burst forth and consumed the Phoenix to ashes. Amidst the fire lay an egg, red hot, which presently burst with a loud report, and out flew a young bird. He is the only Phoenix in the world, and the king over all the other birds. He has bitten a hole in the leaf which I give you, and that is his greeting to the Princess."

"Now let us have something to eat," said the mother of the Winds. So they all sat down to feast on the roasted stag; and as the Prince sat by the side of the East Wind, they soon became good friends.

"Pray tell me," said the Prince, "who is that Princess of whom you have been talking! and where lies the Garden of Paradise?"

"Ho! ho!" said the East Wind, "would you like to go there? Well, you can fly off with me tomorrow; but I must tell you one thing—no human being has been there since the time of Adam and Eve. I suppose you have read of them in your Bible."

"Of course I have," said the Prince.

"Well," continued the East Wind, "when they were driven out of the Garden of Paradise, it sunk into the earth; but it retained its warm sunshine, its balmy air, and all its splendor. The fairy queen lives there, in the Island of Happiness, where death never comes, and all is beautiful. I can manage to take you there tomorrow, if you will sit on my back. But now don't talk any more, for I want to go to sleep;" and then they all slept.

When the Prince awoke in the early morning, he was not a little surprised at finding himself high up above the clouds. He was seated on the back of the East Wind, who held him faithfully; and they were so high in the air that woods and fields, rivers and lakes, as they lay beneath them, looked like a painted map.

"Good morning," said the East Wind. "You might have slept on a while; for there is very little to see in the flat country over which we are passing unless you like to count the churches; they look like spots of chalk on a green board." The green board was the name he gave to the green fields and meadows.

"It was very rude of me not to say goodbye to your mother and your brothers," said the Prince.

"They will excuse you, as you were asleep," said the East Wind; and then they flew on faster than ever.

The leaves and branches of the trees rustled as they passed. When they flew over seas and lakes, the waves rose higher, and the large ships dipped into the water like diving swans. As darkness came on, towards evening, the great towns looked charming; lights were sparkling, now seen now hidden, just as the sparks go out one after another on a piece of burnt paper. The Prince clapped his hands with pleasure; but the East Wind advised him not to express his admiration in that manner, or he might fall down, and find himself hanging on a church steeple. The eagle in the dark forests flies swiftly; but faster than he flew the East Wind. The Cossack, on his small horse, rides lightly o'er the plains; but lighter still passed the Prince on the winds of the wind.

"There are the Himalayas, the highest mountains in Asia," said the East Wind. "We shall soon reach the Garden of Paradise now."

Then, they turned southward, and the air became fragrant with the perfume of spices and flowers. Here figs and pomegranates grew wild, and the vines were covered with clusters of blue and purple grapes. Here they both descended to the earth, and stretched themselves on the soft grass, while the flowers bowed to the breath of the wind as if to welcome it. "Are we now in the Garden of Paradise?" asked the Prince.

"No, indeed," replied the East Wind; "but we shall be there very soon. Do you see that wall of rocks, and the cavern beneath it, over which the grape vines hang like a green curtain? Through that cavern we must pass. Wrap your cloak round you; for while the sun scorches you here, a few steps farther it will be icy cold. The bird flying past the entrance to the cavern feels as if one wing were in the region of summer, and the other in the depths of winter."

"So this then is the way to the Garden of Paradise?" asked the Prince, as they entered the cavern. It was indeed cold; but the cold soon passed, for the East Wind spread his wings, and they gleamed like the brightest fire. As they passed on through this wonderful cave, the prince could see Great blocks of stone, from which water trickled, hanging over their heads in fantastic shapes. Sometimes it was so narrow that they had to creep on their hands and knees, while at other times it was lofty and wide, like the free air. It had the appearance of a chapel for the dead, with petrified organs and silent pipes. "We seem to be passing through the valley of death to the Garden of Paradise," said the Prince.

But the East Wind answered not a word, only pointed forwards to a lovely blue light which gleamed in the distance. The blocks of stone assumed a misty appearance, till at last they looked like white clouds in moonlight. The air was fresh and balmy, like a breeze from the mountains perfumed with flowers from a valley of roses. A river, clear as the air itself, sparkled at their feet, while in its clear depths could be seen gold and silver fish sporting in the bright water, and purple eels emitting sparks of fire at every moment, while the broad leaves of the water lilies, that floated on its surface, flickered with all the colours of the rainbow. The flower in its colour of flame seemed to receive its nourishment from the water, as a lamp is sustained by oil. A marble bridge, of such exquisite workmanship that it appeared as if formed of lace and pearls, led to the Island of Happiness, in which bloomed the Garden of Paradise. The East Wind took the Prince in his arms, and carried him over, while the flowers and the leaves sang the sweet songs of his childhood in tones so full and soft that no human voice could venture to imitate. Within the garden grew large trees, full of sap; but whether they were palm-trees or gigantic water-plants, the prince knew not. The climbing plants hung in garlands of green and gold, like the illuminations on the margins of old missals or twined among the initial letters. Birds, flowers, and festoons appeared intermingled in seeming confusion. Close by, on the grass, stood a group of peacocks, with radiant tails outspread to the sun. The Prince touched them, and found, to his surprise, that they were not really birds, but the leaves of the burdock tree, which shone with the colours of a peacock's tail. The lion and the tiger, gentle and tame, were springing about like playful cats among the green bushes, whose perfume was like the fragrant blossom of the olive. The plumage of the wood-pigeon glistened like pearls as it struck the lion's mane with its wings; while the antelope, usually so shy, stood near, nodding its head as if it wished to join in the frolic. The Fairy of Paradise next made her appearance. Her raiment shone like the sun, and her serene countenance beamed with happiness like that of a mother rejoicing over her child. She was young and beautiful, and a train of lovely maidens followed her, each wearing a bright star in her hair. The East Wind gave her the palm-leaf, on which was written the history of the Phoenix; and her eyes sparkled with joy. She then took the prince by the hand, and led him into her palace, the walls of which were richly coloured, like a tulip-leaf when it is turned to the sun. The roof had the appearance of an inverted flower, and the colours grew deeper and brighter to the gazer. The Prince walked to a window, and saw what appeared to be the tree of knowledge of good and evil, with Adam and Eve standing by, and the serpent near them. "I thought they were banished from paradise," he said.

The Princess smiled, and told him that time had engraved each event on a window-pane in the form of a picture; but, unlike other pictures, all that it represented lived and moved—the leaves rustled, and the persons went and came, as in a looking-glass. He looked through another pane, and saw the ladder in Jacob's dream, on which the angels were ascending and descending with outspread wings. All that had ever happened in the world here lived and moved on the panes of glass, in pictures such as time alone could produce. The fairy now led the Prince into a large, lofty room with transparent walls, through which the light shone. Here were portraits, each one appearing more beautiful than the other—millions of happy beings, whose laughter and song mingled in one sweet melody: some of these were in such an elevated position that they appeared smaller than the smallest rosebud, or like pencil dots on paper. In the centre of the hall stood a tree, with drooping branches, from which hung golden apples, both great and small, looking like oranges amid the green leaves. It was the Tree of Knowledge of good and evil, from which Adam and Eve had plucked and eaten the forbidden fruit, and from each leaf trickled a bright red dewdrop, as if the tree were weeping tears of blood for their sin. "Let us now take the boat," said the Fairy: "a sail on the cool waters will refresh us. But we shall not move from the spot, although the boat may rock on the swelling water; the countries of the world will glide before us, but we shall remain still."

It was indeed wonderful to behold. First came the lofty Alps, snow-clad, and covered with clouds and dark pines. The horn resounded, and the shepherds sang merrily in the valleys. The banana-trees bent their drooping branches over the boat, black swans floated on the water, and singular animals and flowers appeared on the distant shore. New Holland, the fifth division of the world, now glided by, with mountains in the background, looking blue in the distance. They heard the song of the priests, and saw the wild dance of the savage to the sound of the drums and trumpets of bone; the pyramids of Egypt rising to the clouds; columns and sphinxes, overthrown and buried in the sand, followed in their turn; while the northern lights flashed out over the extinguished volcanoes of the north, in fireworks none could imitate.

The Prince was delighted, and yet he saw hundreds of other wonderful things more than can be described. "Can I stay here forever?" asked he.

"That depends upon yourself," replied the Fairy. "If you do not, like Adam, long for what is forbidden, you can remain here always."

"I should not touch the fruit on the Tree of Knowledge," said the Prince; there is abundance of fruit equally beautiful."

"Examine your own heart," said the princess, "and if you do not feel sure of its strength, return with the East Wind who brought you. He is about to fly back, and will not return here for a hundred years. The time will not seem to you more than a hundred hours, yet even that is a long time for temptation and resistance. Every evening, when I leave you, I shall be obliged to say, 'Come with me,' and to beckon to you with my hand. But you must not listen, nor move from your place to follow me; for with every step you will find your power to resist weaker. If once you attempted to follow me, you would soon find yourself in the hall, where grows the Tree of Knowledge, for I sleep beneath its perfumed branches. If you stooped over me, I should be forced to smile. If you then kissed my lips, the Garden of Paradise would sink into the earth, and to you it would be lost. A keen wind from the desert would howl around you; cold rain fall on your head, and sorrow and woe be your future lot."

"I will remain," said the Prince.

So the East Wind kissed him on the forehead, and said, "Be firm; then shall we meet again when a hundred years have passed. Farewell, farewell." Then the East Wind spread his broad pinions, which shone like the lightning in harvest, or as the northern lights in a cold winter.

"Farewell, farewell," echoed the trees and the flowers.

Storks and pelicans flew after him in feathery bands, to accompany him to the boundaries of the garden.

"Now we will commence dancing," said the fairy; "and when it is nearly over at sunset, while I am dancing with you, I shall make a sign, and ask you to follow me: but do not obey. I shall be obliged to repeat the same thing for a hundred years; and each time, when the trial is past, if you resist, you will gain strength, till resistance becomes easy, and at last the temptation will be quite overcome. This evening, as it will be the first time, I have warned you."

After this the Fairy led him into a large hall, filled with transparent lilies. The yellow stamina of each flower formed a tiny golden harp, from which came forth strains of music like the mingled tones of flute and lyre. Beautiful maidens, slender and graceful in form, and robed in transparent gauze, floated through the dance, and sang of the happy life in the Garden of Paradise, where death never entered, and where all would bloom forever in immortal youth. As the sun went down, the whole heavens became crimson and gold, and tinted the lilies with the hue of roses. Then the beautiful maidens offered to the Prince sparkling wine; and when he had drank, he felt happiness greater than he had ever known before. Presently the background of the hall opened and the Tree of Knowledge appeared, surrounded by a halo of glory that almost blinded him. Voices, soft and lovely as his mother's sounded in his ears, as if she were singing to him, "My child, my beloved child." Then the Fairy beckoned to him, and said in sweet accents, "Come with me, come with me." Forgetting his promise, forgetting it even on the very first evening, he rushed towards her, while she continued to beckon to him and to smile. The fragrance around him overpowered his senses, the music from the harps sounded more entrancing, while around the tree appeared millions of smiling faces, nodding and singing. "Man should know everything; man is the lord of the earth." The Tree of Knowledge no longer wept tears of blood, for the dewdrops shone like glittering stars.

"Come, come," continued that thrilling voice, and the Prince followed the call. At every step his cheeks glowed, and the blood rushed wildly through his veins. "I must follow," he cried; "it is not a sin, it cannot be, to follow beauty and joy. I only want to see her sleep, and nothing will happen unless I kiss her, and that I will not do, for I have strength to resist, and a determined will."

The Fairy threw off her dazzling attire, bent back the boughs, and in another moment was hidden among them.

"I have not sinned yet," said the Prince, "and I will not;" and then he pushed aside the boughs to follow the Princess. She was lying already asleep, beautiful as only a fairy in the Garden of Paradise could be. She smiled as he bent over her, and he saw tears trembling out of her beautiful eyelashes. "Do you weep for me?" he whispered. "Oh weep not, thou loveliest of women. Now do I begin to understand the happiness of paradise; I feel it to my inmost soul, in every thought. A new life is born within me. One moment of such happiness is worth an eternity of darkness and woe." He stooped and kissed the tears from her eyes, and touched her lips with his.

A clap of thunder, loud and awful, resounded through the trembling air. All around him fell into ruin. The lovely Fairy, the beautiful garden, sunk deeper and deeper. The Prince saw it sinking down in the dark night till it shone only like a star in the distance beneath him. Then he felt a coldness, like death, creeping over him; his eyes closed, and he became insensible.

When he recovered, a chilling rain was beating upon him, and a sharp wind blew on his head. "Alas! what have I done?" he sighed; "I have sinned like Adam, and the Garden of Paradise has sunk into the earth." He opened his eyes, and saw the star in the distance, but it was the morning star in heaven which glittered in the darkness.

Presently he stood up and found himself in the depths of the forest, close to the Cavern of the Winds, and the mother of the Winds sat by his side. She looked angry, and raised her arm in the air as she spoke. "The very first evening!" she said. "Well, I expected it! If you were my son, you should go into the sack."

"And there he will have to go at last," said a strong old man, with large black wings, and a scythe in his hand, whose name was Death. "He shall be laid in his coffin, but not yet. I will allow him to wander about the world for a while, to atone for his sin, and to give him time to become better. But I shall return when he least expects me. I shall lay him in a black coffin, place it on my head, and fly away with it beyond the stars. There also blooms a Garden of Paradise, and if he is good and pious he will be admitted; but if his thoughts are bad, and his heart is full of sin, he will sink with his coffin deeper than the garden of Paradise has sunk. Once in every thousand years I shall go and fetch him, when he will either be condemned to sink still deeper, or be raised to a happier life in the world beyond the stars."

The Flying Trunk

Translated by Mrs. H. P. Paull

There was once a merchant who was so rich that he could have paved the whole street with gold, and would even then have had enough for a small alley. But he did not do so; he knew the value of money better than to use it in this way. So clever was he, that every shilling he put out brought him a crown; and so he continued till he died. His son inherited his wealth, and he lived a merry life with it; he went to a masquerade every night, made kites out of five pound notes, and threw pieces of gold into the sea instead of stones, making ducks and drakes of them. In this manner he soon lost all his money. At last he had nothing left but a pair of slippers, an old dressing-gown, and four shillings. And now all his friends deserted him, they could not walk with him in the streets; but one of them, who was very good-natured, sent him an old trunk with this message, "Pack up!" "Yes," he said, "it is all very well to say 'pack up,'" but he had nothing left to pack up, therefore he seated himself in the trunk. It was a very wonderful trunk; no sooner did any one press on the lock than the trunk could fly. He shut the lid and pressed the lock, when away flew the trunk up the chimney with the merchant's son in it, right up into the clouds. Whenever the bottom of the trunk cracked, he was in a great fright, for if the trunk fell to pieces he would have made a tremendous somerset over the trees. However, he got safely in his trunk to the land of Turkey. He hid the trunk in the wood under some dry leaves, and then went into the town: he could so this very well, for the Turks always go about dressed in dressing-gowns and slippers, as he was himself. He happened to meet a nurse with a little child. "I say, you Turkish nurse," cried he, "what castle is that near the town, with the windows placed so high?"

"The king's daughter lives there," she replied; "it has been prophesied that she will be very unhappy about a lover, and therefore no one is allowed to visit her, unless the king and queen are present."

"Thank you," said the merchant's son. So he went back to the wood, seated himself in his trunk, flew up to the roof of the castle, and crept through the window into the princess's room. She lay on the sofa asleep, and she was so beautiful that the merchant's son could not help kissing her.

Then she awoke, and was very much frightened; but he told her he was a Turkish angel, who had come down through the air to see her, which pleased her very much. He sat down by her side and talked to her: he said her eyes were like beautiful dark lakes, in which the thoughts swam about like little mermaids, and he told her that her forehead was a snowy mountain, which contained splendid halls full of pictures. And then he related to her about the stork who brings the beautiful children from the rivers. These were delightful stories; and when he asked the princess if she would marry him, she consented immediately.

"But you must come on Saturday," she said; "for then the king and queen will take tea with me. They will be very proud when they find that I am going to marry a Turkish angel; but you must think of some very pretty stories to tell them, for my parents like to hear stories better than anything. My mother prefers one that is deep and moral; but my father likes something funny, to make him laugh."

"Very well," he replied; "I shall bring you no other marriage portion than a story," and so they parted. But the princess gave him a sword which was studded with gold coins, and these he could use.

Then he flew away to the town and bought a new dressing-gown, and afterwards returned to the wood, where he composed a story, so as to be ready for Saturday, which was no easy matter. It was ready however by Saturday, when he went to see the princess. The king, and queen, and the whole court, were at tea with the princess; and he was received with great politeness.

"Will you tell us a story?" said the queen, "one that is instructive and full of deep learning."

"Yes, but with something in it to laugh at," said the king.

"Certainly," he replied, and commenced at once, asking them to listen attentively. "There was once a bundle of matches that were exceedingly proud of their high descent. Their genealogical tree, that is, a large pine-tree from which they had been cut, was at one time a large, old tree in the wood. The matches now lay between a tinder-box and an old iron saucepan, and were talking about their youthful days. 'Ah! then we grew on the green boughs, and were as green as they; every morning and evening we were fed with diamond drops of dew. Whenever the sun shone, we felt his warm rays, and the little birds would relate stories to us as they sung. We knew that we were rich, for the other trees only wore their green dress in summer, but our family were able to array themselves in green, summer and winter. But the woodcutter came, like a great revolution, and our family fell under the axe. The head of the house obtained a situation as mainmast in a very fine ship, and can sail round the world when he will. The other branches of the family were taken to different places, and our office now is to kindle a light for common people. This is how such high-born people as we came to be in a kitchen.'

The Flying Trunk

"'Mine has been a very different fate,' said the iron pot, which stood by the matches; 'from my first entrance into the world I have been used to cooking and scouring. I am the first in this house, when anything solid or useful is required. My only pleasure is to be made clean and shining after dinner, and to sit in my place and have a little sensible conversation with my neighbours. All of us, excepting the water-bucket, which is sometimes taken into the courtyard, live here together within these four walls. We get our news from the market-basket, but he sometimes tells us very unpleasant things about the people and the government. Yes, and one day an old pot was so alarmed, that he fell down and was broken to pieces. He was a liberal, I can tell you.'

"'You are talking too much,' said the tinder-box, and the steel struck against the flint till some sparks flew out, crying, 'We want a merry evening, don't we?'

"'Yes, of course,' said the matches, 'let us talk about those who are the highest born.'

"'No, I don't like to be always talking of what we are,' remarked the saucepan; 'let us think of some other amusement; I will begin. We will tell something that has happened to ourselves; that will be very easy, and interesting as well. On the Baltic Sea, near the Danish shore'—

"'What a pretty commencement!' said the plates; 'we shall all like that story, I am sure.'

"'Yes; well in my youth, I lived in a quiet family, where the furniture was polished, the floors scoured, and clean curtains put up every fortnight,'

"'What an interesting way you have of relating a story,' said the carpet-broom; 'it is easy to perceive that you have been a great deal in women's society, there is something so pure runs through what you say.'

"'That is quite true,' said the water-bucket; and he made a spring with joy, and splashed some water on the floor.

"Then the saucepan went on with his story, and the end was as good as the beginning.

"The plates rattled with pleasure, and the carpet-broom brought some green parsley out of the dust-hole and crowned the saucepan, for he knew it would vex the others; and he thought, 'If I crown him today he will crown me tomorrow.'

"'Now, let us have a dance,' said the fire-tongs; and then how they danced and stuck up one leg in the air. The chair-cushion in the corner burst with laughter when she saw it.

"'Shall I be crowned now?' asked the fire-tongs; so the broom found another wreath for the tongs.

"'They were only common people after all,' thought the matches. The tea-urn was now asked to sing, but she said she had a cold, and could not sing without boiling heat. They all thought this was affectation, and because she did not wish to sing excepting in the parlor, when on the table with the grand people.

"In the window sat an old quill-pen, with which the maid generally wrote. There was nothing remarkable about the pen, excepting that it had been dipped too deeply in the ink, but it was proud of that.

"'If the tea-urn won't sing,' said the pen, 'she can leave it alone; there is a nightingale in a cage who can sing; she has not been taught much, certainly, but we need not say anything this evening about that.'

"'I think it highly improper,' said the tea-kettle, who was kitchen singer, and half-brother to the tea-urn, 'that a rich foreign bird should be listened to here. Is it patriotic? Let the market-basket decide what is right.'

"'I certainly am vexed,' said the basket; 'inwardly vexed, more than any one can imagine. Are we spending the evening properly? Would it not be more sensible to put the house in order? If each were in his own place I would lead a game; this would be quite another thing.'

"'Let us act a play,' said they all. At the same moment the door opened, and the maid came in. Then not one stirred; they all remained quite still; yet, at the same time, there was not a single pot amongst them who had not a high opinion of himself, and of what he could do if he chose.

"'Yes, if we had chosen,' they each thought, 'we might have spent a very pleasant evening.'

"The maid took the matches and lighted them; dear me, how they sputtered and blazed up!

"'Now then,' they thought, 'every one will see that we are the first. How we shine; what a light we give!' Even while they spoke their light went out.

"What a capital story," said the queen, "I feel as if I were really in the kitchen, and could see the matches; yes, you shall marry our daughter."

"Certainly," said the king, "thou shalt have our daughter." The king said thou to him because he was going to be one of the family. The wedding-day was fixed, and, on the evening before, the whole city was illuminated. Cakes and sweetmeats were thrown among the people. The street boys stood on tiptoe and shouted "hurrah," and whistled between their fingers; altogether it was a very splendid affair.

"I will give them another treat," said the merchant's son. So he went and bought rockets and crackers, and all sorts of fire-works that could be thought of, packed them in his trunk, and flew up with it into the air. What a whizzing and popping they made as they went off! The Turks, when they saw such a sight in the air, jumped so high that their slippers flew about their ears. It was easy to believe after this that the princess was really going to marry a Turkish angel.

As soon as the merchant's son had come down in his flying trunk to the wood after the fireworks, he thought, "I will go back into the town now, and hear what they think of the entertainment." It was very natural that he should wish to know. And what strange things people did say, to be sure! every one whom he questioned had a different tale to tell, though they all thought it very beautiful.

"I saw the Turkish angel myself," said one; "he had eyes like glittering stars, and a head like foaming water."

"He flew in a mantle of fire," cried another, "and lovely little cherubs peeped out from the folds."

He heard many more fine things about himself, and that the next day he was to be married. After this he went back to the forest to rest himself in his trunk. It had disappeared! A spark from the fireworks which remained had set it on fire; it was burnt to ashes! So the merchant's son could not fly any more, nor go to meet his bride. She stood all day on the roof waiting for him, and most likely she is waiting there still; while he wanders through the world telling fairy tales, but none of them so amusing as the one he related about the matches.

The Storks

Translated by Mrs. H. P. Paull

On the last house in a little village the storks had built a nest, and the mother stork sat in it with her four young ones, who stretched out their necks and pointed their black beaks, which had not yet turned red like those of the parent birds. A little way off, on the edge of the roof, stood the father stork, quite upright and stiff; not liking to be quite idle, he drew up one leg, and stood on the other, so still that it seemed almost as if he were carved in wood. "It must look very grand," thought he, "for my wife to have a sentry guarding her nest. They do not know that I am her husband; they will think I have been commanded to stand here, which is quite aristocratic;" and so he continued standing on one leg.

In the street below were a number of children at play, and when they caught sight of the storks, one of the boldest amongst the boys began to sing a song about them, and very soon he was joined by the rest. These are the words of the song, but each only sang what he could remember of them in his own way.

> "Stork, stork, fly away,
> Stand not on one leg, I pray,
> See your wife is in her nest,
> With her little ones at rest.
> They will hang one,
> And fry another;
> They will shoot a third,
> And roast his brother."

"Just hear what those boys are singing," said the young storks; "they say we shall be hanged and roasted."

"Never mind what they say; you need not listen," said the mother. "They can do no harm."

But the boys went on singing and pointing at the storks, and mocking at them, excepting one of the boys whose name was Peter; he said it was a shame to make fun of animals, and would not join with them at all. The mother stork comforted her young ones, and told them not to mind. "See," she said, "How quiet your father stands, although he is only on one leg."

"But we are very much frightened," said the young storks, and they drew back their heads into the nests.

The next day when the children were playing together, and saw the storks, they sang the song again—

> "They will hang one,
> And roast another."

"Shall we be hanged and roasted?" asked the young storks.

"No, certainly not," said the mother. "I will teach you to fly, and when you have learnt, we will fly into the meadows, and pay a visit to the frogs, who will bow themselves to us in the water, and cry 'Croak, croak,' and then we shall eat them up; that will be fun."

"And what next?" asked the young storks.

"Then," replied the mother, "all the storks in the country will assemble together, and go through their autumn manoeuvres, so that it is very important for every one to know how to fly properly. If they do not, the general will thrust them through with his beak, and kill them. Therefore you must take pains and learn, so as to be ready when the drilling begins."

"Then we may be killed after all, as the boys say; and hark! they are singing again."

"Listen to me, and not to them," said the mother stork. "After the great review is over, we shall fly away to warm countries far from hence, where there are mountains and forests. To Egypt, where we shall see three-cornered houses built of stone, with pointed tops that reach nearly to the clouds. They are called Pyramids, and are older than a stork could imagine; and in that country, there is a river that overflows its banks, and then goes back, leaving nothing but mire; there we can walk about, and eat frogs in abundance."

"Oh, o——h!" cried the young storks.

"Yes, it is a delightful place; there is nothing to do all day long but eat, and while we are so well off out there, in this country there will not be a single green leaf on the trees, and the weather will be so cold that the clouds will freeze, and fall on the earth in little white rags." The stork meant snow, but she could not explain it in any other way.

"Will the naughty boys freeze and fall in pieces?" asked the young storks.

"No, they will not freeze and fall into pieces," said the mother, "but they will be very cold, and be obliged to sit all day in a dark, gloomy room, while we shall be flying about in foreign lands, where there are blooming flowers and warm sunshine."

Time passed on, and the young storks grew so large that they could stand upright in the nest and look about them. The father brought them, every day, beautiful frogs, little snakes, and all kinds of stork-dainties that he could find. And then, how funny it was to see the tricks he would perform to amuse them. He would lay his head quite round over his tail, and clatter with his beak, as if it had been a rattle; and then he would tell them stories all about the marshes and fens.

"Come," said the mother one day, "Now you must learn to fly." And all the four young ones were obliged to come out on the top of the roof. Oh, how they tottered at first, and were obliged to balance themselves with their wings, or they would have fallen to the ground below.

"Look at me," said the mother, "you must hold your heads in this way, and place your feet so. Once, twice, once, twice—that is it. Now you will be able to take care of yourselves in the world."

Then she flew a little distance from them, and the young ones made a spring to follow her; but down they fell plump, for their bodies were still too heavy.

"I don't want to fly," said one of the young storks, creeping back into the nest. "I don't care about going to warm countries."

"Would you like to stay here and freeze when the winter comes?" said the mother, "Or till the boys comes to hang you, or to roast you?—Well then, I'll call them."

"Oh no, no," said the young stork, jumping out on the roof with the others; and now they were all attentive, and by the third day could fly a little. Then they began to fancy they could soar, so they tried to do so, resting on their wings, but they soon found themselves falling, and had to flap their wings as quickly as possible. The boys came again in the street singing their song:—

"Stork, stork, fly away."

"Shall we fly down, and pick their eyes out?" asked the young storks.

"No; leave them alone," said the mother. "Listen to me; that is much more important. Now then. One-two-three. Now to the right. One-two-three. Now to the left, round the chimney. There now, that was very good. That last flap of the wings was so easy and graceful, that I shall give you permission to fly with me tomorrow to the marshes. There will be a number of very superior storks there with their families, and I expect you to show them that my children are the best brought up of any who may be present. You must strut about proudly—it will look well and make you respected."

"But may we not punish those naughty boys?" asked the young storks.

"No; let them scream away as much as they like. You can fly from them now up high amid the clouds, and will be in the land of the pyramids when they are freezing, and have not a green leaf on the trees or an apple to eat."

"We will revenge ourselves," whispered the young storks to each other, as they again joined the exercising.

Of all the boys in the street who sang the mocking song about the storks, not one was so determined to go on with it as he who first began it. Yet he was a little fellow not more than six years old. To the young storks he appeared at least a hundred, for he was so much bigger than their father and mother. To be sure, storks cannot be expected to know how old children and grown-up people are. So they determined to have their revenge on this boy, because he began the song first and would keep on with it. The young storks were very angry, and grew worse as they grew older; so at last their mother was obliged to promise that they should be revenged, but not until the day of their departure.

"We must see first, how you acquit yourselves at the grand review," said she. "If you get on badly there, the general will thrust his beak through you, and you will be killed, as the boys said, though not exactly in the same manner. So we must wait and see."

"You shall see," said the young birds, and then they took such pains and practised so well every day, that at last it was quite a pleasure to see them fly so lightly and prettily. As soon as the autumn arrived, all the storks began to assemble together before taking their departure for warm countries during the winter. Then the review commenced. They flew over forests and villages to show what they could do, for they had a long journey before them. The young storks performed their part so well that they received a mark of honour, with frogs and snakes as a present. These presents were the best part of the affair, for they could eat the frogs and snakes, which they very quickly did.

"Now let us have our revenge," they cried.

"Yes, certainly," cried the mother stork. "I have thought upon the best way to be revenged. I know the pond in which all the little children lie, waiting till the storks come to take them to their parents. The prettiest little babies lie there dreaming more sweetly than they will ever dream in the time to come. All parents are glad to have a little child, and children are so pleased with a little brother or sister. Now we will fly to the pond and fetch a little baby for each of the children who did not sing that naughty song to make game of the storks."

"But the naughty boy, who began the song first, what shall we do to him?" cried the young storks.

"There lies in the pond a little dead baby who has dreamed itself to death," said the mother. "We will take it to the naughty boy, and he will cry because we have brought him a little dead brother. But you have not forgotten the good boy who said it was a shame to laugh at animals: we will take him a little brother and sister too, because he was good. He is called Peter, and you shall all be called Peter in future."

So they all did what their mother had arranged, and from that day, even till now, all the storks have been called Peter.

What the Moon Saw

Translated by H. W. Dulcken

Introduction

It is a strange thing, that when I feel most fervently and most deeply, my hands and my tongue seem alike tied, so that I cannot rightly describe or accurately portray the thoughts that are rising within me; and yet I am a painter: my eye tells me as much as that, and all my friends who have seen my sketches and fancies say the same.

I am a poor lad, and live in one of the narrowest of lanes; but I do not want for light, as my room is high up in the house, with an extensive prospect over the neighbouring roofs. During the first few days I went to live in the town, I felt low-spirited and solitary enough. Instead of the forest and the green hills of former days, I had here only a forest of chimney-pots to look out upon. And then I had not a single friend; not one familiar face greeted me.

So one evening I sat at the window, in a desponding mood; and presently I opened the casement and looked out. Oh, how my heart leaped up with joy! Here was a well-known face at last—a round, friendly countenance, the face of a good friend I had known at home. In, fact it was the MOON that looked in upon me. He was quite unchanged, the dear old Moon, and had the same face exactly that he used to show when he peered down upon me through the willow trees on the moor. I kissed my hand to him over and over again, as he shone far into my little room; and he, for his part, promised me that every evening, when he came abroad, he would look in upon me for a few moments. This promise he has faithfully kept. It is a pity that he can only stay such a short time when he comes. Whenever he appears, he tells me of one thing or another that he has seen on the previous night, or on that same evening. "Just paint the scenes I describe to you"—this is what he said to me—"and you will have a very pretty picture-book." I have followed his injunction for many evenings. I could make up a new "Thousand and One Nights," in my own way, out of these pictures, but the number might be too great, after all. The pictures I have here given have not been chosen at random, but follow in their proper order, just as they were described to me. Some great gifted painter, or some poet or musician, may make something more of them if he likes; what I have given here are only hasty sketches, hurriedly put upon the paper, with some of my own thoughts interspersed; for the Moon did not come to me every evening—a cloud sometimes hid his face from me.

First Evening

"Last night"—I am quoting the Moon's own words—"last night I was gliding through the cloudless Indian sky. My face was mirrored in the waters of the Ganges, and my beams strove to pierce through the thick intertwining boughs of the bananas, arching beneath me like the tortoise's shell. Forth from the thicket tripped a Hindu maid, light as a gazelle, beautiful as Eve. Airy and ethereal as a vision, and yet sharply defined amid the surrounding shadows, stood this daughter of Hindustan: I could read on her delicate brow the thought that had brought her hither. The thorny creeping plants tore her sandals, but for all that she came rapidly forward. The deer that had come down to the river to quench their thirst, sprang by with a startled bound, for in her hand the maiden bore a lighted lamp. I could see the blood in her delicate fingertips, as she spread them for a screen before the dancing flame. She came down to the stream, and set the lamp upon the water, and let it float away. The flame flickered to and fro, and seemed ready to expire; but still the lamp burned on, and the girl's black sparkling eyes, half-veiled behind their long silken lashes, followed it with a gaze of earnest intensity. She knew that if the lamp continued to burn so long as she could keep it in sight, her betrothed was still alive; but if the lamp was suddenly extinguished, he was dead. And the lamp burned bravely on, and she fell on her knees, and prayed. Near her in the grass lay a speckled snake, but she heeded it not—she thought only of Bramah and of her betrothed. 'He lives!' she shouted joyfully, 'he lives!' And from the mountains the echo came back upon her, 'he lives!'"

Second Evening

"Yesterday," said the Moon to me, "I looked down upon a small courtyard surrounded on all sides by houses. In the courtyard sat a clucking hen with eleven chickens; and a pretty little girl was running and jumping around them. The hen was frightened, and screamed, and spread out her wings over the little brood. Then the girl's father came out and scolded her; and I glided away and thought no more of the matter.

"But this evening, only a few minutes ago, I looked down into the same courtyard. Everything was quiet. But presently the little girl came forth again, crept quietly to the hen-house, pushed back the bolt, and slipped into the apartment of the hen and chickens. They cried out loudly, and came fluttering down from their perches, and ran about in dismay, and the little girl ran after them. I saw it quite plainly, for I looked through a hole in the hen-house wall. I was angry with the wilful child, and felt glad when her father came out and scolded her more violently than yesterday, holding her roughly by the arm: she held down her head, and her blue eyes were full of large tears. 'What are you about here?' he asked. She wept and said, 'I wanted to kiss the hen and beg her pardon for frightening her yesterday; but I was afraid to tell you.'

"And the father kissed the innocent child's forehead, and I kissed her on the mouth and eyes."

Third Evening

"In the narrow street round the corner yonder—it is so narrow that my beams can only glide for a minute along the walls of the house, but in that minute I see enough to learn what the world is made of—in that narrow street I saw a woman. Sixteen years ago that woman was a child, playing in the garden of the old parsonage, in the country. The hedges of rose bush were old, and the flowers were faded. They straggled wild over the paths, and the ragged branches grew up among the boughs of the apple trees; here and there were a few roses still in bloom—not so fair as the queen of flowers generally appears, but still they had colour and scent too. The clergyman's little daughter appeared to me a far lovelier rose, as she sat on her stool under the straggling hedge, hugging and caressing her doll with the battered pasteboard cheeks.

"Ten years afterwards I saw her again. I beheld her in a splendid ballroom: she was the beautiful bride of a rich merchant. I rejoiced at her happiness, and sought her on calm quiet evenings—ah, nobody thinks of my clear eye and my silent glance! Alas! my rose ran wild, like the rose bushes in the garden of the parsonage. There are tragedies in every-day life, and tonight I saw the last act of one.

"She was lying in bed in a house in that narrow street: she was sick unto death, and the cruel landlord came up, and tore away the thin coverlet, her only protection against the cold. 'Get up!' said he; 'your face is enough to frighten one. Get up and dress yourself, give me money, or I'll turn you out into the street! Quick—get up!' She answered, 'Alas! death is gnawing at my heart. Let me rest.' But he forced her to get up and bathe her face, and put a wreath of roses in her hair; and he placed her in a chair at the window, with a candle burning beside her, and went away.

"I looked at her, and she was sitting motionless, with her hands in her lap. The wind caught the open window and shut it with a crash, so that a pane came clattering down in fragments; but still she never moved. The curtain caught fire, and the flames played about her face; and I saw that she was dead. There at the open window sat the dead woman, preaching a sermon against *sin*—my poor faded rose out of the parsonage garden!"

Fourth Evening

"This evening I saw a German play acted," said the Moon. "It was in a little town. A stable had been turned into a theatre; that is to say, the stable had been left standing, and had been turned into private boxes, and all the timber work had been covered with coloured paper. A little iron chandelier hung beneath the ceiling, and that it might be made to disappear into the ceiling, as it does in great theatres, when the *ting-ting* of the prompter's bell is heard, a great inverted tub had been placed just above it.

"'*Ting-ting!*' and the little iron chandelier suddenly rose at least half a yard and disappeared in the tub; and that was the sign that the play was going to begin. A young nobleman and his lady, who happened to be passing through the little town, were present at the performance, and consequently the house was crowded. But under the chandelier was a vacant space like a little crater: not a single soul sat there, for the tallow was dropping, drip, drip! I saw everything, for it was so warm in there that every loophole had been opened. The male and female servants stood outside, peeping through the chinks, although a real policeman was inside, threatening them with a stick. Close by the orchestra could be seen the noble young couple in two old arm-chairs, which were usually occupied by his worship the mayor and his lady; but these latter were today obliged to content themselves with wooden forms, just as if they had been ordinary citizens; and the lady observed quietly to herself, 'One sees, now, that there is rank above rank;' and this incident gave an air of extra festivity to the whole proceedings. The chandelier gave little leaps, the crowd got their knuckles rapped, and I, the Moon, was present at the performance from beginning to end."

Fifth Evening

"Yesterday," began the Moon, "I looked down upon the turmoil of Paris. My eye penetrated into an apartment of the Louvre. An old grandmother, poorly clad—she belonged to the working class—was following one of the under-servants into the great empty throne-room, for this was the apartment she wanted to see—that she was resolved to see; it had cost her many a little sacrifice, and many a coaxing word, to penetrate thus far. She folded her thin hands, and looked round with an air of reverence, as if she had been in a church.

"'Here it was!' she said, 'here!' And she approached the throne, from which hung the rich velvet fringed with gold lace. 'There,' she exclaimed, 'there!' and she knelt and kissed the purple carpet. I think she was actually weeping.

"'But it was not *this very* velvet!' observed the footman, and a smile played about his mouth. 'True, but it was this very place,' replied the woman, 'and it must have looked just like this.' 'It looked so, and yet it did not,' observed the man: 'the windows were beaten in, and the doors were off their hinges, and there was blood upon the floor.' 'But for all that you can say, my grandson died upon the throne of France. Died!' mournfully repeated the old woman. I do not think another word was spoken, and they soon quitted the hall. The evening twilight faded, and my light shone doubly vivid upon the rich velvet that covered the throne of France.

"Now, who do you think this poor woman was? Listen, I will tell you a story.

"It happened, in the Revolution of July, on the evening of the most brilliantly victorious day, when every house was a fortress, every window a breastwork. The people stormed the Tuileries. Even women and children were to be found among the combatants. They penetrated into the apartments and halls of the palace. A poor half-grown boy in a ragged blouse fought among the older insurgents. Mortally wounded with several bayonet thrusts, he sank down. This happened in the throne-room. They laid the bleeding youth upon the throne of France, wrapped the velvet around his wounds, and his blood streamed forth upon the imperial purple. There was a picture! the splendid hall, the fighting groups! A torn flag lay upon the ground, the tricolor was waving above the bayonets, and on the throne lay the poor lad with the pale glorified countenance, his eyes turned towards the sky, his limbs writhing in the death agony, his breast bare, and his poor tattered clothing half-hidden by the rich velvet embroidered with silver lilies. At the boy's cradle a prophecy had been spoken: 'He will die on the throne of France!' The mother's heart dreamt of a second Napoleon.

"My beams have kissed the wreath of *immortelles* on his grave, and this night they kissed the forehead of the old grandame, while in a dream the picture floated before her which thou mayest draw—the poor boy on the throne of France."

Sixth Evening

"I've been in Upsala," said the Moon: "I looked down upon the great plain covered with coarse grass, and upon the barren fields. I mirrored my face in the Fyris river, while the steamboat drove the fish into the rushes. Beneath me floated the waves, throwing long shadows on the so-called graves of Odin, Thor, and Friga. In the scanty turf that covers the hillside names have been cut.[*] There is no monument here, no memorial on which the traveller can have his name carved, no rocky wall on whose surface he can get it painted; so visitors have the turf cut away for that purpose. The naked earth peers through in the form of great letters and names; these form a network over the whole hill. Here is an immortality, which lasts till the fresh turf grows!

"Up on the hill stood a man, a poet. He emptied the mead horn with the broad silver rim, and murmured a name. He begged the winds not to betray him, but I heard the name. I knew it. A count's coronet sparkles above it, and therefore he did not speak it out. I smiled, for I knew that a poet's crown adorns his own name. The nobility of Eleanora d'Este is attached to the name of Tasso. And I also know where the Rose of Beauty blooms!"

Thus spake the Moon, and a cloud came between us. May no cloud separate the poet from the rose!

Seventh Evening

"Along the margin of the shore stretches a forest of firs and beeches, and fresh and fragrant is this wood; hundreds of nightingales visit it every spring. Close beside it is the sea, the ever-changing sea, and between the two is placed the broad high road. One carriage after

---

[*] Travellers on the Continent have frequent opportunities of seeing how universally this custom prevails among travellers. In some places on the Rhine, pots of paint and brushes are offered by the natives to the traveller desirous of "immortalising" himself.

another rolls over it; but I did not follow them, for my eye loves best to rest upon one point. A Hun's Grave* lies there, and the sloe and blackthorn grow luxuriantly among the stones. Here is true poetry in nature.

"And how do you think men appreciate this poetry? I will tell you what I heard there last evening and during the night.

"First, two rich landed proprietors came driving by. 'Those are glorious trees!' said the first. 'Certainly; there are ten loads of firewood in each,' observed the other: 'it will be a hard winter, and last year we got fourteen dollars a load'—and they were gone. 'The road here is wretched,' observed another man who drove past. 'That's the fault of those horrible trees,' replied his neighbour; 'there is no free current of air; the wind can only come from the sea'—and they were gone. The stage coach went rattling past. All the passengers were asleep at this beautiful spot. The postilion blew his horn, but he only thought, 'I can play capitally. It sounds well here. I wonder if those in there like it?'—and the stage coach vanished. Then two young fellows came galloping up on horseback. There's youth and spirit in the blood here! thought I; and, indeed, they looked with a smile at the moss-grown hill and thick forest. 'I should not dislike a walk here with the miller's Christine,' said one—and they flew past.

"The flowers scented the air; every breath of air was hushed: it seemed as if the sea were a part of the sky that stretched above the deep valley. A carriage rolled by. Six people were sitting in it. Four of them were asleep; the fifth was thinking of his new summer coat, which would suit him admirably; the sixth turned to the coachman and asked him if there were anything remarkable connected with yonder heap of stones. 'No,' replied the coachman, 'it's only a heap of stones; but the trees are remarkable.' 'How so?' 'Why, I'll tell you how they are very remarkable. You see, in winter, when the snow lies very deep, and has hidden the whole road so that nothing is to be seen, those trees serve me for a landmark. I steer by them, so as not to drive into the sea; and you see that is why the trees are remarkable.'

---

* Large mounds similar to the "barrows" found in Britain, are thus designated in Germany and the North.

"Now came a painter. He spoke not a word, but his eyes sparkled. He began to whistle. At this the nightingales sang louder than ever. 'Hold your tongues!' he cried testily; and he made accurate notes of all the colours and transitions—blue, and lilac, and dark brown. 'That will make a beautiful picture,' he said. He took it in just as a mirror takes in a view; and as he worked he whistled a march of Rossini. And last of all came a poor girl. She laid aside the burden she carried, and sat down to rest upon the Hun's Grave. Her pale handsome face was bent in a listening attitude towards the forest. Her eyes brightened, she gazed earnestly at the sea and the sky, her hands were folded, and I think she prayed, 'Our Father.' She herself could not understand the feeling that swept through her, but I know that this minute, and the beautiful natural scene, will live within her memory for years, far more vividly and more truly than the painter could portray it with his colours on paper. My rays followed her till the morning dawn kissed her brow."

Eighth Evening

Heavy clouds obscured the sky, and the Moon did not make his appearance at all. I stood in my little room, more lonely than ever, and looked up at the sky where he ought to have shown himself. My thoughts flew far away, up to my great friend, who every evening told me such pretty tales, and showed me pictures. Yes, he has had an experience indeed. He glided over the waters of the Deluge, and smiled on Noah's ark just as he lately glanced down upon me, and brought comfort and promise of a new world that was to spring forth from the old. When the Children of Israel sat weeping by the waters of Babylon, he glanced mournfully upon the willows where hung the silent harps. When Romeo climbed the balcony, and the promise of true love fluttered like a cherub toward heaven, the round Moon hung, half hidden among the dark cypresses, in the lucid air. He saw the captive giant at St. Helena, looking from the lonely rock across the wide ocean, while great thoughts swept through his soul. Ah! what tales the Moon can tell. Human life is like a story to him. Tonight I shall not see thee again, old friend. Tonight I can draw no picture of the memories of thy visit. And, as I looked dreamily towards the clouds, the sky became bright. There was a glancing light, and a beam from the Moon fell upon me. It vanished again, and dark clouds flew past; but still it was a greeting, a friendly good-night offered to me by the Moon.

Ninth Evening

The air was clear again. Several evenings had passed, and the Moon was in the first quarter. Again he gave me an outline for a sketch. Listen to what he told me.

"I have followed the polar bird and the swimming whale to the eastern coast of Greenland. Gaunt ice-covered rocks and dark clouds hung over a valley, where dwarf willows and barberry bushes stood clothed in green. The blooming lychnis exhaled sweet odours.

My light was faint, my face pale as the water lily that, torn from its stem, has been drifting for weeks with the tide. The crown-shaped Northern Light burned fiercely in the sky. Its ring was broad, and from its circumference the rays shot like whirling shafts of fire across the whole sky, flashing in changing radiance from green to red. The inhabitants of that icy region were assembling for dance and festivity; but, accustomed to this glorious spectacle, they scarcely deigned to glance at it. 'Let us leave the souls of the dead to their ball-play with the heads of the walruses,' they thought in their superstition, and they turned their whole attention to the song and dance. In the midst of the circle, and divested of his furry cloak, stood a Greenlander, with a small pipe, and he played and sang a song about catching the seal, and the chorus around chimed in with, '*Eia, Eia, Ah.*' And in their white furs they danced about in the circle, till you might fancy it was a polar bear's ball.

"And now a Court of Judgment was opened. Those Greenlanders who had quarrelled stepped forward, and the offended person chanted forth the faults of his adversary in an extempore song, turning them sharply into ridicule, to the sound of the pipe and the measure of the dance. The defendant replied with satire as keen, while the audience laughed, and gave their verdict. The rocks heaved, the glaciers melted, and great masses of ice and snow came crashing down, shivering to fragments as they fell: it was a glorious Greenland summer night. A hundred paces away, under the open tent of hides, lay a sick man. Life still flowed through his warm blood, but still he was to die—he himself felt it, and all who stood round him knew it also; therefore his wife was already sowing round him the shroud of furs, that she might not afterwards be obliged to touch the dead body. And she asked, 'Wilt thou be buried on the rock, in the firm snow? I will deck the spot with thy *kayak*, and thy arrows, and the *angekokk* shall dance over it. Or wouldst thou rather be buried in the sea?' 'In the sea,' he whispered, and nodded with a mournful smile. 'Yes, it is a pleasant summer tent, the sea,' observed the wife. 'Thousands of seals sport there, the walrus shall lie at thy feet, and the hunt will be safe and merry!' And the yelling children tore the outspread hide from the window-hole, that the dead man might be carried to the ocean, the billowy ocean, that had given him food in life, and that now, in death, was to afford him a place of rest. For his monument, he had the floating, ever-changing icebergs, whereon the seal sleeps, while the storm bird flies round their gleaming summits!"

Tenth Evening

"I knew an old maid," said the Moon. "Every winter she wore a wrapper of yellow satin, and it always remained new, and was the only fashion she followed. In summer she always wore the same straw hat, and I verily believe the very same grey-blue dress.

"She never went out, except across the street to an old female friend; and in later years she did not even take this walk, for the old friend was dead. In her solitude my old maid was always busy at the window, which was adorned in summer with pretty flowers, and in winter with cress, grown upon felt. During the last months I saw her no more at the window, but she was still alive. I knew that, for I had not yet seen her begin the 'long journey,' of which she often spoke with her friend. 'Yes, yes,' she was in the habit of saying, 'when I come to die, I shall take a longer journey than I have made my whole life long. Our family vault is six miles from here. I shall be carried there, and shall sleep there among my family and relatives.' Last night a van stopped at the house. A coffin was carried out, and then I knew that she was dead. They placed straw round the coffin, and the van drove away. There slept the quiet old lady, who had not gone out of her house once for the last year. The van rolled out through the town gate as briskly as if it were going for a pleasant excursion. On the high road the pace was quicker yet. The coachman looked nervously round every now and then—I fancy he half expected to see her sitting on the coffin, in her yellow satin wrapper. And because he was startled, he foolishly lashed his horses, while he held the reins so tightly that the poor beasts were in a foam: they were young and fiery. A hare jumped across the road and startled them, and they fairly ran away. The old sober maiden, who had for years and years moved quietly round and round in a dull circle, was now, in death, rattled over stock and stone on the public highway. The coffin in its covering of straw tumbled out of the van, and was left on the high road, while horses, coachman, and carriage flew past in wild career. The lark rose up carolling from the field, twittering her morning lay over the coffin, and presently perched upon it, picking with her beak at the straw covering, as though she would tear it up. The lark rose up again, singing gaily, and I withdrew behind the red morning clouds."

Eleventh Evening

"I will give you a picture of Pompeii," said the Moon. "I was in the suburb in the Street of Tombs, as they call it, where the fair monuments stand, in the spot where, ages ago, the merry youths, their temples bound with rosy wreaths, danced with the fair sisters of Laïs. Now, the stillness of death reigned around. German mercenaries, in the Neapolitan service, kept guard, played cards, and diced; and a troop of strangers from beyond the mountains came into the town, accompanied by a sentry. They wanted to see the city that had risen from the grave illumined by my beams; and I showed them the wheel-ruts in the streets paved with broad lava slabs; I showed them the names on the doors, and the signs that hung there yet: they saw in the little courtyard the basins of the fountains, ornamented with shells; but no jet of water gushed upwards, no songs sounded forth from the richly-painted chambers, where the bronze dog kept the door.

"It was the City of the Dead; only Vesuvius thundered forth his everlasting hymn, each separate verse of which is called by men an eruption. We went to the temple of Venus, built of snow-white marble, with its high altar in front of the broad steps, and the weeping willows sprouting freshly forth among the pillars. The air was transparent and blue, and black Vesuvius formed the background, with fire ever shooting forth from it, like the stem of the pine tree. Above it stretched the smoky cloud in the silence of the night, like the crown of the pine, but in a blood-red illumination. Among the company was a lady singer, a real and great singer. I have witnessed the homage paid to her in the greatest cities of Europe. When they came to the tragic theatre, they all sat down on the amphitheatre steps, and thus a small part of the house was occupied by an audience, as it had been many centuries ago. The stage still stood unchanged, with its walled side-scenes, and the two arches in the background, through which the beholders saw the same scene that had been exhibited in the old times—a scene painted by nature herself, namely, the mountains between Sorento and Amalfi. The singer gaily mounted the ancient stage, and sang. The place inspired her, and she reminded me of a wild Arab horse, that rushes headlong on with snorting nostrils and flying mane—her song was so light and yet so firm. Anon I thought of the mourning mother beneath the cross at Golgotha, so deep was the expression of pain. And, just as it had done thousands of years ago, the sound of applause and delight now filled the theatre. 'Happy, gifted creature!' all the hearers exclaimed. Five minutes more, and the stage was empty, the company had vanished, and not a sound more was heard—all were gone. But the ruins stood unchanged, as they will stand when centuries shall have gone by, and when none shall know of the momentary applause and of the triumph of the fair songstress; when all will be forgotten and gone, and even for me this hour will be but a dream of the past."

Twelfth Evening

"I looked through the windows of an editor's house," said the Moon. "It was somewhere in Germany. I saw handsome furniture, many books, and a chaos of newspapers. Several young men were present: the editor himself stood at his desk, and two little books, both by young authors, were to be noticed. 'This one has been sent to me,' said he. 'I have not read it yet; what think *you* of the contents?' 'Oh,' said the person addressed—he was a poet himself—'it is good enough; a little broad, certainly; but, you see, the author is still young. The verses might be better, to be sure; the thoughts are sound, though there is certainly a good deal of commonplace among them. But what will you have? You can't be always getting something new. That he'll turn out anything great I don't believe, but you may safely praise him. He is well read, a remarkable Oriental scholar, and has a good judgment. It was he who wrote that nice review of my *Reflections on Domestic Life*. We must be lenient towards the young man.'

"'But he is a complete hack!' objected another of the gentlemen. 'Nothing is worse in poetry than mediocrity, and he certainly does not go beyond this.'

"'Poor fellow,' observed a third, 'and his aunt is so happy about him. It was she, Mr. Editor, who got together so many subscribers for your last translation.'

"'Ah, the good woman! Well, I have noticed the book briefly. Undoubted talent—a welcome offering—a flower in the garden of poetry—prettily brought out—and so on. But this other book—I suppose the author expects me to purchase it? I hear it is praised. He has genius, certainly; don't you think so?'

"'Yes, all the world declares as much,' replied the poet, 'but it has turned out rather wildly. The punctuation of the book, in particular, is very eccentric.'

"'It will be good for him if we pull him to pieces, and anger him a little, otherwise he will get too good an opinion of himself.'

"'But that would be unfair,' objected the fourth. 'Let us not carp at little faults, but rejoice over the real and abundant good that we find here: he surpasses all the rest.'

"'Not so. If he is a true genius, he can bear the sharp voice of censure. There are people enough to praise him. Don't let us quite turn his head.'

"'Decided talent,' wrote the editor, 'with the usual carelessness. That he can write incorrect verses may be seen in page 25, where there are two false quantities. We recommend him to study the ancients, etc.'

"I went away," continued the Moon, "and looked through the windows in the aunt's house. There sat the be-praised poet, the *tame* one; all the guests paid homage to him, and he was happy.

"I sought the other poet out, the *wild* one; him also I found in a great assembly at his patron's, where the tame poet's book was being discussed.

"'I shall read yours also,' said Mæcenas; 'but to speak honestly—you know I never hide my opinion from you—I don't expect much from it, for you are much too wild, too fantastic. But it must be allowed that, as a man, you are highly respectable.'

"A young girl sat in a corner; and she read in a book these words:

"'In the dust lies genius and glory,
 But ev'ry-day talent will *pay*.
It's only the old, old story,
 But the piece is repeated each day.'"

Thirteenth Evening

The Moon said, "Beside the woodland path there are two small farmhouses. The doors are low, and some of the windows are placed quite high, and others close to the ground; and whitethorn and barberry bushes grow around them. The roof of each house is overgrown with moss and with yellow flowers and houseleek. Cabbage and potatoes are the only plants cultivated in the gardens, but out of the hedge there grows a willow tree, and under this willow tree sat a little girl, and she sat with her eyes fixed upon the old oak tree between the two huts.

"It was an old withered stem. It had been sawn off at the top, and a stork had built his nest upon it; and he stood in this nest clapping with his beak. A little boy came and stood by the girl's side: they were brother and sister.

"'What are you looking at?' he asked.

"'I'm watching the stork,' she replied: 'our neighbours told me that he would bring us a little brother or sister today; let us watch to see it come!'

"'The stork brings no such things,' the boy declared, 'you may be sure of that. Our neighbour told me the same thing, but she laughed when she said it, and so I asked her if she could say 'On my honour,' and she could not; and I know by that that the story about the storks is not true, and that they only tell it to us children for fun.'

"'But where do the babies come from, then?' asked the girl.

"'Why, an angel from heaven brings them under his cloak, but no man can see him; and that's why we never know when he brings them.'

"At that moment there was a rustling in the branches of the willow tree, and the children folded their hands and looked at one another: it was certainly the angel coming with the baby. They took each other's hand, and at that moment the door of one of the houses opened, and the neighbour appeared.

"'Come in, you two,' she said. 'See what the stork has brought. It is a little brother.'

"And the children nodded gravely at one another, for they had felt quite sure already that the baby was come."

Fourteenth Evening

"I was gliding over the Lüneburg Heath," the Moon said. "A lonely hut stood by the wayside, a few scanty bushes grew near it, and a nightingale who had lost his way sang sweetly. He died in the coldness of the night: it was his farewell song that I heard.

"The morning dawn came glimmering red. I saw a caravan of emigrant peasant families who were bound to Hamburgh, there to take ship for America, where fancied prosperity would bloom for them. The mothers carried their little children at their backs, the elder ones tottered by their sides, and a poor starved horse tugged at a cart that bore their scanty effects. The cold wind whistled, and therefore the little girl nestled closer to the mother, who, looking up at my decreasing disc, thought of the bitter want at home, and spoke of the heavy taxes they had not been able to raise. The whole caravan thought of the same thing; therefore, the rising dawn seemed to them a message from the sun, of fortune that was to gleam brightly upon them. They heard the dying nightingale sing: it was no false prophet, but a harbinger of fortune. The wind whistled, therefore they did not understand that the nightingale sung, 'Fare away over the sea! Thou hast paid the long passage with all that was thine, and poor and helpless shalt thou enter Canaan. Thou must sell thyself, thy wife, and thy children. But your griefs shall not last long. Behind the broad fragrant leaves lurks the goddess of Death, and her welcome kiss shall breathe fever into thy blood. Fare away, fare away, over the heaving billows.' And the caravan listened well pleased to the song of the nightingale, which seemed to promise good fortune. Day broke through the light clouds; country people went across the heath to church: the black-gowned women with their white head-dresses looked like ghosts that had stepped forth from the church pictures. All around lay a wide dead plain, covered with faded brown heath, and black charred spaces between the white sand hills. The women carried hymn books, and walked into the church. Oh, pray, pray for those who are wandering to find graves beyond the foaming billows."

Fifteenth Evening

"I know a Pulcinella,"* the Moon told me. "The public applaud vociferously directly they see him. Every one of his movements is comic, and is sure to throw the house into convulsions of laughter; and yet there is no art in it all—it is complete nature. When he was yet a little boy, playing about with other boys, he was already Punch. Nature had intended him for it, and had provided him with a hump

---

* The comic or grotesque character of the Italian ballet, from which the English "Punch" takes his origin.

on his back, and another on his breast; but his inward man, his mind, on the contrary, was richly furnished. No one could surpass him in depth of feeling or in readiness of intellect. The theatre was his ideal world. If he had possessed a slender well-shaped figure, he might have been the first tragedian on any stage: the heroic, the great, filled his soul; and yet he had to become a Pulcinella. His very sorrow and melancholy did but increase the comic dryness of his sharply-cut features, and increased the laughter of the audience, who showered plaudits on their favourite. The lovely Columbine was indeed kind and cordial to him; but she preferred to marry the Harlequin. It would have been too ridiculous if beauty and ugliness had in reality paired together.

"When Pulcinella was in very bad spirits, she was the only one who could force a hearty burst of laughter, or even a smile from him: first she would be melancholy with him, then quieter, and at last quite cheerful and happy. 'I know very well what is the matter with you,' she said; 'yes, you're in love!' And he could not help laughing. 'I and Love!' he cried, 'that would have an absurd look. How the public would shout!' 'Certainly, you are in love,' she continued; and added with a comic pathos, 'and I am the person you are in love with.' You see, such a thing may be said when it is quite out of the question—and, indeed, Pulcinella burst out laughing, and gave a leap into the air, and his melancholy was forgotten.

"And yet she had only spoken the truth. He *did* love her, love her adoringly, as he loved what was great and lofty in art. At her wedding he was the merriest among the guests, but in the stillness of night he wept: if the public had seen his distorted face then, they would have applauded rapturously.

"And a few days ago, Columbine died. On the day of the funeral, Harlequin was not required to show himself on the boards, for he was a disconsolate widower. The director had to give a very merry piece, that the public might not too painfully miss the pretty Columbine and the agile Harlequin. Therefore Pulcinella had to be more boisterous and extravagant than ever; and he danced and capered, with despair in his heart; and the audience yelled, and shouted '*bravo, bravissimo!*' Pulcinella was actually called before the curtain. He was pronounced inimitable.

"But last night the hideous little fellow went out of the town, quite alone, to the deserted churchyard. The wreath of flowers on Columbine's grave was already faded, and he sat down there. It was a study for a painter. As he sat with his chin on his hands, his eyes turned up towards me, he looked like a grotesque monument—a Punch on a grave—peculiar and whimsical! If the people could have seen their favourite, they would have cried as usual, '*Bravo, Pulcinella; bravo, bravissimo!*'"

Sixteenth Evening

Hear what the Moon told me. "I have seen the cadet who had just been made an officer put on his handsome uniform for the first time; I have seen the young bride in her wedding dress, and the Prince's girl-wife happy in her gorgeous robes; but never have I seen a felicity equal to that of a little girl of four years old, whom I watched this evening. She had received a new blue dress, and a new pink hat, the splendid attire had just been put on, and all were calling for a candle, for my rays, shining in through the windows of the room, were not bright enough for the occasion, and further illumination was required. There stood the little maid, stiff and upright as a doll, her arms stretched painfully straight out away from the dress, and her fingers apart; and oh, what happiness beamed from her eyes, and from her whole countenance! 'Tomorrow you shall go out in your new clothes,' said her mother; and the little one looked up at her hat, and down at her frock, and smiled brightly. 'Mother,' she cried, 'what will the little dogs think, when they see me in these splendid new things?'"

Seventeenth Evening

"I have spoken to you of Pompeii," said the Moon; "that corpse of a city, exposed in the view of living towns: I know another sight still more strange, and this is not the corpse, but the spectre of a city. Whenever the jetty fountains splash into the marble basins, they seem to me to be telling the story of the floating city. Yes, the spouting water may tell of her, the waves of the sea may sing of her fame! On the surface of the ocean a mist often rests, and that is her widow's veil. The bridegroom of the sea is dead, his palace and his city are his mausoleum! Dost thou know this city? She has never heard the rolling of wheels or the hoof-tread of horses in her streets, through which the fish swim, while the black gondola glides spectrally over the green water. I will show you the place," continued the Moon, "the largest square in it, and you will fancy yourself transported into the city of a fairy tale. The grass grows rank among the broad flagstones, and in the morning twilight thousands of tame pigeons flutter around the solitary lofty tower. On three sides you find yourself surrounded by cloistered walks. In these the silent Turk sits smoking his long pipe, the handsome Greek leans against the pillar and gazes at the upraised trophies and lofty masts, memorials of power that is gone. The flags hang down like mourning scarves. A girl rests there: she has put down her heavy pails filled with water, the yoke with which she has carried them rests on one of her shoulders, and she leans against the mast of victory. That is not a fairy palace you see before you yonder, but a church: the gilded domes and shining orbs flash back my beams; the glorious bronze horses up yonder have made journeys, like the bronze horse in the fairy tale: they have come hither, and gone hence, and have returned again. Do you notice the variegated splendour of the walls and windows? It looks as if Genius had followed the caprices of a child, in the adornment of these singular temples. Do you see the winged lion on the pillar? The gold glitters still, but his wings are tied—the lion is dead, for the king of the sea is dead; the great halls stand desolate, and where gorgeous paintings hung of yore, the naked wall now peers through. The *lazzarone* sleeps under the arcade, whose pavement in old times was to be trodden only by the feet of high nobility. From the deep wells, and perhaps from the prisons by the Bridge of Sighs, rise the accents of woe, as at the time when the tambourine was heard in the gay gondolas, and the golden ring was cast from the *Bucentaur* to Adria, the queen of the seas. Adria! shroud thyself in mists; let the veil of thy widowhood shroud thy form, and clothe in the weeds of woe the mausoleum of thy bridegroom—the marble, spectral Venice."

Eighteenth Evening

"I looked down upon a great theatre," said the Moon. "The house was crowded, for a new actor was to make his first appearance that night. My rays glided over a little window in the wall, and I saw a painted face with the forehead pressed against the panes. It was the hero of the evening. The knightly beard curled crisply about the chin; but there were tears in the man's eyes, for he had been hissed off, and indeed with reason. The poor Incapable! But Incapables cannot be admitted into the empire of Art. He had deep feeling, and loved his art enthusiastically, but the art loved not him. The prompter's bell sounded; '*the hero enters with a determined air*,' so ran the stage direction in his part, and he had to appear before an audience who turned him into ridicule. When the piece was over, I saw a form wrapped in a mantle, creeping down the steps: it was the vanquished knight of the evening. The scene-shifters whispered to one another, and I followed the poor fellow home to his room. To hang one's self is to die a mean death, and poison is not always at hand, I know; but he thought of both. I saw how he looked at his pale face in the glass, with eyes half closed, to see if he should look well as a corpse. A man may be very unhappy, and yet exceedingly affected. He thought of death, of suicide; I believe he pitied himself, for he wept bitterly, and when a man has had his cry out he doesn't kill himself.

"Since that time a year had rolled by. Again a play was to be acted, but in a little theatre, and by a poor strolling company. Again I saw the well-remembered face, with the painted cheeks and the crisp beard. He looked up at me and smiled; and yet he had been hissed off only a minute before—hissed off from a wretched theatre, by a miserable audience. And tonight a shabby hearse rolled out of the town gate. It was a suicide—our painted, despised hero. The driver of the hearse was the only person present, for no one followed except my beams. In a corner of the churchyard the corpse of the suicide was shovelled into the earth, and nettles will soon be growing rankly over his grave, and the sexton will throw thorns and weeds from the other graves upon it."

Nineteenth Evening

"I come from Rome," said the Moon. "In the midst of the city, upon one of the seven hills, lie the ruins of the imperial palace. The wild fig tree grows in the clefts of the wall, and covers the nakedness thereof with its broad grey-green leaves; trampling among heaps of rubbish, the ass treads upon green laurels, and rejoices over the rank thistles. From this spot, whence the eagles of Rome once flew abroad, whence they 'came, saw, and conquered,' our door leads into a little mean house, built of clay between two pillars; the wild vine hangs like a mourning garland over the crooked window. An old woman and her little granddaughter live there: they rule now in the palace of the Cæsars, and show to strangers the remains of its past glories. Of the splendid throne-hall only a naked wall yet stands, and a black cypress throws its dark shadow on the spot where the throne once stood. The dust lies several feet deep on the broken pavement; and the little maiden, now the daughter of the imperial palace, often sits there on her stool when the evening bells ring. The keyhole of the door close by she calls her turret window; through this she can see half Rome, as far as the mighty cupola of St. Peter's.

"On this evening, as usual, stillness reigned around; and in the full beam of my light came the little granddaughter. On her head she carried an earthen pitcher of antique shape filled with water. Her feet were bare, her short frock and her white sleeves were torn. I kissed her pretty round shoulders, her dark eyes, and black shining hair. She mounted the stairs; they were steep, having been made up of rough blocks of broken marble and the capital of a fallen pillar. The coloured lizards slipped away, startled, from before her feet, but she was not frightened at them. Already she lifted her hand to pull the doorbell—a hare's foot fastened to a string formed the bell-handle of the imperial palace. She paused for a moment—of what might she be thinking? Perhaps of the beautiful Christ-child, dressed in gold and silver, which was down below in the chapel, where the silver candlesticks gleamed so bright, and where her little friends sung the hymns in which she also could join? I know not. Presently she moved again—she stumbled; the earthen vessel fell from her head, and broke on the marble steps. She burst into tears. The beautiful daughter of the imperial palace wept over the worthless broken pitcher; with her bare feet she stood there weeping, and dared not pull the string, the bell-rope of the imperial palace!"

Twentieth Evening

It was more than a fortnight since the Moon had shone. Now he stood once more, round and bright, above the clouds, moving slowly onward. Hear what the Moon told me.

"From a town in Fezzan I followed a caravan. On the margin of the sandy desert, in a salt plain, that shone like a frozen lake, and was only covered in spots with light drifting sand, a halt was made. The eldest of the company—the water gourd hung at his girdle, and on his head was a little bag of unleavened bread—drew a square in the sand with his staff, and wrote in it a few words out of the Koran, and then the whole caravan passed over the consecrated spot. A young merchant, a child of the East, as I could tell by his eye and his figure, rode pensively forward on his white snorting steed. Was he thinking, perchance, of his fair young wife? It was only two days ago that the camel, adorned with furs and with costly shawls, had carried her, the beauteous bride, round the walls of the city, while drums and cymbals had sounded, the women sang, and festive shots, of which the bridegroom fired the greatest number, resounded round the camel; and now he was journeying with the caravan across the desert.

"For many nights I followed the train. I saw them rest by the well-side among the stunted palms; they thrust the knife into the breast of the camel that had fallen, and roasted its flesh by the fire. My beams cooled the glowing sands, and showed them the black rocks, dead islands in the immense ocean of sand. No hostile tribes met them in their pathless route, no storms arose, no columns of sand whirled destruction over the journeying caravan. At home the beautiful wife prayed for her husband and her father. 'Are they dead?' she asked of my golden crescent; 'Are they dead?' she cried to my full disc. Now the desert lies behind them. This evening they sit beneath the lofty palm trees, where the crane flutters round them with its long wings, and the pelican watches them from the branches of the mimosa. The luxuriant herbage is trampled down, crushed by the feet of elephants. A troop of negroes are returning from a market in the interior of the land: the women, with copper buttons in their black hair, and decked out in clothes dyed with indigo, drive the heavily-laden oxen, on whose backs slumber the naked black children. A negro leads a young lion which he has bought, by a string. They approach the caravan; the young merchant sits pensive and motionless, thinking of his beautiful wife, dreaming, in the land of the blacks, of his white fragrant lily beyond the desert. He raises his head, and——" But at this moment a cloud passed before the Moon, and then another. I heard nothing more from him this evening.

Twenty-first Evening

"I saw a little girl weeping," said the Moon; "she was weeping over the depravity of the world. She had received a most beautiful doll as a present. Oh, that was a glorious doll, so fair and delicate! She did not seem created for the sorrows of this world. But the brothers of the little girl, those great naughty boys, had set the doll high up in the branches of a tree, and had run away.

"The little girl could not reach up to the doll, and could not help her down, and that is why she was crying. The doll must certainly have been crying too; for she stretched out her arms among the green branches, and looked quite mournful. Yes, these are the troubles of life of which the little girl had often heard tell. Alas, poor doll! it began to grow dark already; and suppose night were to come on completely! Was she to be left sitting there alone on the bough all night long? No, the little maid could not make up her mind to that. 'I'll stay with you,' she said, although she felt anything but happy in her mind. She could almost fancy she distinctly saw little gnomes, with their high-crowned hats, sitting in the bushes; and further back in the long walk, tall spectres appeared to be dancing. They came nearer and nearer, and stretched out their hands towards the tree on which the doll sat; they laughed scornfully, and pointed at her with their fingers. Oh, how frightened the little maid was! 'But if one has not done anything wrong,' she thought, 'nothing evil can harm one. I wonder if I have done anything wrong?' And she considered. 'Oh, yes! I laughed at the poor duck with the red rag on her leg; she limped along so funnily, I could not help laughing; but it's a sin to laugh at animals.' And she looked up at the doll. 'Did you laugh at the duck too?' she asked; and it seemed as if the doll shook her head."

Twenty-second Evening

"I looked down upon Tyrol," said the Moon, "and my beams caused the dark pines to throw long shadows upon the rocks. I looked at the pictures of St. Christopher carrying the Infant Jesus that are painted there upon the walls of the houses, colossal figures reaching from the ground to the roof. St. Florian was represented pouring water on the burning house, and the Lord hung bleeding on the great cross by the wayside. To the present generation these are old pictures, but I saw when they were put up, and marked how one followed the other. On the brow of the mountain yonder is perched, like a swallow's nest, a lonely convent of nuns. Two of the sisters stood up in the tower tolling the bell; they were both young, and therefore their glances flew over the mountain out into the world. A travelling coach passed by below, the postilion wound his horn, and the poor nuns looked after the carriage for a moment with a mournful glance, and a tear gleamed in the eyes of the younger one. And the horn sounded faint and more faintly, and the convent bell drowned its expiring echoes."

Twenty-third Evening

Hear what the Moon told me. "Some years ago, here in Copenhagen, I looked through the window of a mean little room. The father and mother slept, but the little son was not asleep. I saw the flowered cotton curtains of the bed move, and the child peep forth. At first I thought he was looking at the great clock, which was gaily painted in red and green. At the top sat a cuckoo, below hung the heavy leaden weights, and the pendulum with the polished disc of metal went to and fro, and said 'tick, tick.' But no, he was not looking at the clock, but at his mother's spinning wheel, that stood just underneath it. That was the boy's favourite piece of furniture, but he dared not touch it, for if he meddled with it he got a rap on the knuckles. For hours together, when his mother was spinning, he would sit quietly by her side, watching the murmuring spindle and the revolving wheel, and as he sat he thought of many things. Oh, if he might only turn the wheel himself! Father and mother were asleep; he looked at them, and looked at the spinning wheel, and presently a little naked foot peered out of the bed, and then a second foot, and then two little white legs. There he stood. He looked round once more, to see if father and mother were still asleep—yes, they slept; and now he crept *softly, softly*, in his short little nightgown, to the spinning wheel, and began to spin. The thread flew from the wheel, and the wheel whirled faster and faster. I kissed his fair hair and his blue eyes, it was such a pretty picture.

"At that moment the mother awoke. The curtain shook, she looked forth, and fancied she saw a gnome or some other kind of little spectre. 'In Heaven's name!' she cried, and aroused her husband in a frightened way. He opened his eyes, rubbed them with his hands, and looked at the brisk little lad. 'Why, that is Bertel,' said he. And my eye quitted the poor room, for I have so much to see. At the same moment I looked at the halls of the Vatican, where the marble gods are enthroned. I shone upon the group of the Laocoon; the stone seemed to sigh. I pressed a silent kiss on the lips of the Muses, and they seemed to stir and move. But my rays lingered longest about the Nile group with the colossal god. Leaning against the Sphinx, he lies there thoughtful and meditative, as if he were thinking on the rolling centuries; and little love-gods sport with him and with the crocodiles. In the horn of plenty sat with folded arms a little tiny love-god, contemplating the great solemn river-god, a true picture of the boy at the spinning wheel—the features were exactly the same. Charming and life-like stood the little marble form, and yet the wheel of the year has turned more than a thousand times since the time when it sprang forth from the stone. Just as often as the boy in the little room turned the spinning wheel had the great wheel murmured, before the age could again call forth marble gods equal to those he afterwards formed.

"Years have passed since all this happened," the Moon went on to say. "Yesterday I looked upon a bay on the eastern coast of Denmark. Glorious woods are there, and high trees, an old knightly castle with red walls, swans floating in the ponds, and in the background appears, among orchards, a little town with a church. Many boats, the crews all furnished with torches, glided over the silent expanse—but these fires had not been kindled for catching fish, for everything had a festive look. Music sounded, a song was sung, and in one of the boats the man stood erect to whom homage was paid by the rest, a tall sturdy man, wrapped in a cloak. He had blue eyes and long white hair. I knew him, and thought of the Vatican, and of the group of the Nile, and the old marble gods. I thought of the simple little room where little Bertel sat in his night-shirt by the spinning wheel. The wheel of time has turned, and new gods have come forth from the stone. From the boats there arose a shout: 'Hurrah, hurrah for Bertel Thorwaldsen!'"

Twenty-fourth Evening

"I will now give you a picture from Frankfort," said the Moon. "I especially noticed one building there. It was not the house in which Goëthe was born, nor the old Council House, through whose grated windows peered the horns of the oxen that were roasted and given to the people when the emperors were crowned. No, it was a private house, plain in appearance, and painted green. It stood near the old Jews' Street. It was Rothschild's house.

"I looked through the open door. The staircase was brilliantly lighted: servants carrying wax candles in massive silver candlesticks stood there, and bowed low before an old woman, who was being brought downstairs in a litter. The proprietor of the house stood bare-headed, and respectfully imprinted a kiss on the hand of the old woman. She was his mother. She nodded in a friendly manner to him and to the servants, and they carried her into the dark narrow street, into a little house, that was her dwelling. Here her children had been born, from hence the fortune of the family had arisen. If she deserted the despised street and the little house, fortune would also desert her children. That was her firm belief."

The Moon told me no more; his visit this evening was far too short. But I thought of the old woman in the narrow despised street. It would have cost her but a word, and a brilliant house would have arisen for her on the banks of the Thames—a word, and a villa would have been prepared in the Bay of Naples.

"If I deserted the lowly house, where the fortunes of my sons first began to bloom, fortune would desert them!" It was a superstition, but a superstition of such a class, that he who knows the story and has seen this picture, need have only two words placed under the picture to make him understand it; and these two words are: "A mother."

Twenty-fifth Evening

"It was yesterday, in the morning twilight"—these are the words the Moon told me—"in the great city no chimney was yet smoking—and it was just at the chimneys that I was looking. Suddenly a little head emerged from one of them, and then half a body, the arms resting on the rim of the chimney-pot. 'Ya-hip! ya-hip!' cried a voice. It was the little chimney-sweeper, who had for the first time in his life crept through a chimney, and stuck out his head at the top. 'Ya-hip! ya-hip!' Yes, certainly that was a very different thing to creeping about in the dark narrow chimneys! the air blew so fresh, and he could look over the whole city towards the green wood. The sun was just rising. It shone round and great, just in his face, that beamed with triumph, though it was very prettily blacked with soot.

"'The whole town can see me now,' he exclaimed, 'and the moon can see me now, and the sun too. Ya-hip! ya-hip!' And he flourished his broom in triumph."

Twenty-sixth Evening

"Last night I looked down upon a town in China," said the Moon. "My beams irradiated the naked walls that form the streets there. Now and then, certainly, a door is seen; but it is locked, for what does the Chinaman care about the outer world? Close wooden shutters covered the windows behind the walls of the houses; but through the windows of the temple a faint light glimmered. I looked in, and saw the quaint decorations within. From the floor to the ceiling pictures are painted, in the most glaring colours, and richly gilt— pictures representing the deeds of the gods here on earth. In each niche statues are placed, but they are almost entirely hidden by the coloured drapery and the banners that hang down. Before each idol (and they are all made of tin) stood a little altar of holy water, with flowers and burning wax lights on it. Above all the rest stood Fo, the chief deity, clad in a garment of yellow silk, for yellow is here the sacred colour. At the foot of the altar sat a living being, a young priest. He appeared to be praying, but in the midst of his prayer he seemed to fall into deep thought, and this must have been wrong, for his cheeks glowed and he held down his head. Poor Soui-hong! Was he, perhaps, dreaming of working in the little flower garden behind the high street wall? And did that occupation seem more agreeable to him than watching the wax lights in the temple? Or did he wish to sit at the rich feast, wiping his mouth with silver paper between each course? Or was his sin so great that, if he dared utter it, the Celestial Empire would punish it with death? Had his thoughts ventured to fly with the ships of the barbarians, to their homes in far distant England? No, his thoughts did not fly so far, and yet they were sinful, sinful as thoughts born of young hearts, sinful here in the temple, in the presence of Fo and the other holy gods.

"I know whither his thoughts had strayed. At the farther end of the city, on the flat roof paved with porcelain, on which stood the handsome vases covered with painted flowers, sat the beauteous Pu, of the little roguish eyes, of the full lips, and of the tiny feet. The tight shoe pained her, but her heart pained her still more. She lifted her graceful round arm, and her satin dress rustled. Before her stood a glass bowl containing four goldfish. She stirred the bowl carefully with a slender lacquered stick, very slowly, for she, too, was lost in thought. Was she thinking, perchance, how the fishes were richly clothed in gold, how they lived calmly and peacefully in their crystal world, how they were regularly fed, and yet how much happier they might be if they were free? Yes, that she could well understand, the beautiful Pu. Her thoughts wandered away from her home, wandered to the temple, but not for the sake of holy things. Poor Pu! Poor Soui-hong!

"Their earthly thoughts met, but my cold beam lay between the two, like the sword of the cherub."

Twenty-seventh Evening

"The air was calm," said the Moon; "the water was transparent as the purest ether through which I was gliding, and deep below the surface I could see the strange plants that stretched up their long arms towards me like the gigantic trees of the forest. The fishes swam to and fro above their tops. High in the air a flight of wild swans were winging their way, one of which sank lower and lower, with wearied pinions, his eyes following the airy caravan, that melted farther and farther into the distance. With outspread wings he sank slowly, as a soap bubble sinks in the still air, till he touched the water. At length his head lay back between his wings, and silently he lay there, like a white lotus flower upon the quiet lake. And a gentle wind arose, and crisped the quiet surface, which gleamed like the clouds that poured along in great broad waves; and the swan raised his head, and the glowing water splashed like blue fire over his breast and back. The morning dawn illuminated the red clouds, the swan rose strengthened, and flew towards the rising sun, towards the bluish coast whither the caravan had gone; but he flew alone, with a longing in his breast. Lonely he flew over the blue swelling billows."

Twenty-eighth Evening

"I will give you another picture of Sweden," said the Moon. "Among dark pine woods, near the melancholy banks of the Stoxen, lies the old convent church of Wreta. My rays glided through the grating into the roomy vaults, where kings sleep tranquilly in great stone coffins. On the wall, above the grave of each, is placed the emblem of earthly grandeur, a kingly crown; but it is made only of wood, painted and gilt, and is hung on a wooden peg driven into the wall. The worms have gnawed the gilded wood, the spider has spun her web from the crown down to the sand, like a mourning banner, frail and transient as the grief of mortals. How quietly they sleep! I can remember them quite plainly. I still see the bold smile on their lips, that so strongly and plainly expressed joy or grief. When the steamboat winds along like a magic snail over the lakes, a stranger often comes to the church, and visits the burial vault; he asks the names of the kings, and they have a dead and forgotten sound. He glances with a smile at the worm-eaten crowns, and if he happens to be a pious, thoughtful man, something of melancholy mingles with the smile. Slumber on, ye dead ones! The Moon thinks of you, the Moon at night sends down his rays into your silent kingdom, over which hangs the crown of pine wood."

Twenty-ninth Evening

"Close by the high road," said the Moon, "is an inn, and opposite to it is a great wagon-shed, whose straw roof was just being re-thatched. I looked down between the bare rafters and through the open loft into the comfortless space below. The turkey-cock slept on the beam, and the saddle rested in the empty crib. In the middle of the shed stood a travelling carriage; the proprietor was inside, fast asleep, while the horses were being watered. The coachman stretched himself, though I am very sure that he had been most comfortably asleep half the last stage. The door of the servants' room stood open, and the bed looked as if it had been turned over and over; the candle stood on the floor, and had burnt deep down into the socket. The wind blew cold through the shed: it was nearer to the dawn than to midnight. In the wooden frame on the ground slept a wandering family of musicians. The father and mother seemed to be dreaming of the burning liquor that remained in the bottle. The little pale daughter was dreaming too, for her eyes were wet with tears. The harp stood at their heads, and the dog lay stretched at their feet."

Thirtieth Evening

"It was in a little provincial town," the Moon said; "it certainly happened last year, but that has nothing to do with the matter. I saw it quite plainly. Today I read about it in the papers, but there it was not half so clearly expressed. In the taproom of the little inn sat the bear leader, eating his supper; the bear was tied up outside, behind the wood pile—poor Bruin, who did nobody any harm, though he looked grim enough. Up in the garret three little children were playing by the light of my beams; the eldest was perhaps six years old, the youngest certainly not more than two. 'Tramp, tramp'—somebody was coming upstairs: who might it be? The door was thrust open—it was Bruin, the great, shaggy Bruin! He had got tired of waiting down in the courtyard, and had found his way to the stairs. I saw it all," said the Moon. "The children were very much frightened at first at the great shaggy animal; each of them crept into a corner, but he found them all out, and smelt at them, but did them no harm. 'This must be a great dog,' they said, and began to stroke him. He lay down upon the ground, the youngest boy clambered on his back, and bending down a little head of golden curls, played at hiding in the beast's shaggy skin. Presently the eldest boy took his drum, and beat upon it till it rattled again; the bear rose upon his hind legs, and began to dance. It was a charming sight to behold. Each boy now took his gun, and the bear was obliged to have one too, and he held it up quite properly. Here was a capital playmate they had found; and they began marching—one, two; one, two.

"Suddenly some one came to the door, which opened, and the mother of the children appeared. You should have seen her in her dumb terror, with her face as white as chalk, her mouth half open, and her eyes fixed in a horrified stare. But the youngest boy nodded to her in great glee, and called out in his infantile prattle, 'We're playing at soldiers.' And then the bear leader came running up."

Thirty-first Evening

The wind blew stormy and cold, the clouds flew hurriedly past; only for a moment now and then did the Moon become visible. He said, "I looked down from the silent sky upon the driving clouds, and saw the great shadows chasing each other across the earth. I looked upon a prison. A closed carriage stood before it; a prisoner was to be carried away. My rays pierced through the grated window towards the wall: the prisoner was scratching a few lines upon it, as a parting token; but he did not write words, but a melody, the outpouring of his heart. The door was opened, and he was led forth, and fixed his eyes upon my round disc. Clouds passed between us, as if he were not to see my face, nor I his. He stepped into the carriage, the door was closed, the whip cracked, and the horses galloped off into the thick forest, whither my rays were not able to follow him; but as I glanced through the grated window, my rays glided over the notes, his last farewell engraved on the prison wall—where words fail, sounds can often speak. My rays could only light up isolated notes, so the greater part of what was written there will ever remain dark to me. Was it the death-hymn he wrote there? Were these the glad notes of joy? Did he drive away to meet death, or hasten to the embraces of his beloved? The rays of the Moon do not read all that is written by mortals."

Thirty-second Evening

"I love the children," said the Moon, "especially the quite little ones—they are so droll. Sometimes I peep into the room, between the curtain and the window frame, when they are not thinking of me.

It gives me pleasure to see them dressing and undressing. First, the little round naked shoulder comes creeping out of the frock, then the arm; or I see how the stocking is drawn off, and a plump little white leg makes its appearance, and a white little foot that is fit to be kissed, and I kiss it too.

"But about what I was going to tell you. This evening I looked through a window, before which no curtain was drawn, for nobody lives opposite. I saw a whole troop of little ones, all of one family, and among them was a little sister. She is only four years old, but can say her prayers as well as any of the rest. The mother sits by her bed every evening, and hears her say her prayers; and then she has a kiss, and the mother sits by the bed till the little one has gone to sleep, which generally happens as soon as ever she can close her eyes.

"This evening the two elder children were a little boisterous. One of them hopped about on one leg in his long white nightgown, and the other stood on a chair surrounded by the clothes of all the children, and declared he was acting Grecian statues. The third and fourth laid the clean linen carefully in the box, for that is a thing that has to be done; and the mother sat by the bed of the youngest, and announced to all the rest that they were to be quiet, for little sister was going to say her prayers.

"I looked in, over the lamp, into the little maiden's bed, where she lay under the neat white coverlet, her hands folded demurely and her little face quite grave and serious. She was praying the Lord's prayer aloud. But her mother interrupted her in the middle of her prayer. 'How is it,' she asked, 'that when you have prayed for daily bread, you always add something I cannot understand? You must tell me what that is.' The little one lay silent, and looked at her mother in embarrassment. 'What is it you say after *our daily bread*?' 'Dear mother, don't be angry: I only said, *and plenty of butter on it.*'"

The Wicked Prince

Translated by Mrs. H. P. Paull

There lived once upon a time a wicked Prince whose heart and mind were set upon conquering all the countries of the world, and on frightening the people; he devastated their countries with fire and sword, and his soldiers trod down the crops in the fields and destroyed the peasants' huts by fire, so that the flames licked the green leaves off the branches, and the fruit hung dried up on the singed black trees. Many a poor mother fled, her naked baby in her arms, behind the still smoking walls of her cottage; but also there the soldiers followed her, and when they found her, she served as new nourishment to their diabolical enjoyments; demons could not possibly have done worse things than these soldiers! The Prince was of opinion that all this was right, and that it was only the natural course which things ought to take. His power increased day by day, his name was feared by all, and fortune favoured his deeds.

He brought enormous wealth home from the conquered towns, and gradually accumulated in his residence riches which could nowhere be equalled. He erected magnificent palaces, churches, and halls, and all who saw these splendid buildings and great treasures exclaimed admiringly: "What a mighty Prince!" But they did not know what endless misery he had brought upon other countries, nor did they hear the sighs and lamentations which rose up from the débris of the destroyed cities.

The Prince often looked with delight upon his gold and his magnificent edifices, and thought, like the crowd: "What a mighty Prince! But I must have more—much more. No power on earth must equal mine, far less exceed it."

He made war with all his neighbours, and defeated them. The conquered kings were chained up with golden fetters to his chariot when he drove through the streets of his city. These kings had to kneel at his and his courtiers' feet when they sat at table, and live on the morsels which they left. At last the prince had his own statue erected on the public places and fixed on the royal palaces; nay, he even wished it to be placed in the churches, on the altars, but in this the priests opposed him, saying: "Prince, you are mighty indeed, but God's power is much greater than yours; we dare not obey your orders."

"Well," said the Prince. "Then I will conquer God too." And in his haughtiness and foolish presumption he ordered a magnificent ship to be constructed, with which he could sail through the air; it was gorgeously fitted out and of many colours; like the tail of a peacock, it was covered with thousands of eyes, but each eye was the barrel of a gun. The Prince sat in the centre of the ship, and had only to touch a spring in order to make thousands of bullets fly out in all directions, while the guns were at once loaded again. Hundreds of eagles were attached to this ship, and it rose with the swiftness of an arrow up towards the sun. The earth was soon left far below, and looked, with its mountains and woods, like a cornfield where the plough had made furrows which separated green meadows; soon it looked only like a map with indistinct lines upon it; and at last it entirely disappeared in mist and clouds. Higher and higher rose the eagles up into the air; then God sent one of his numberless angels against the ship. The wicked Prince showered thousands of bullets upon him, but they rebounded from his shining wings and fell down like ordinary hailstones. One drop of blood, one single drop, came out of the white feathers of the angel's wings and fell upon the ship in which the Prince sat, burnt into it, and weighed upon it like thousands of hundredweights, dragging it rapidly down to the earth again; the strong wings of the eagles gave way, the wind roared round the Prince's head, and the clouds around—were they formed by the smoke rising up from the burnt cities?—took strange shapes, like crabs many, many miles long, which stretched their claws out after him, and rose up like enormous rocks, from which rolling masses dashed down, and became fire-spitting dragons.

The Prince was lying half-dead in his ship, when it sank at last with a terrible shock into the branches of a large tree in the wood.

"I will conquer God!" said the Prince. "I have sworn it: my will *must* be done!"

And he spent seven years in the construction of wonderful ships to sail through the air, and had darts cast from the hardest steel to break the walls of heaven with. He gathered warriors from all countries, so many that when they were placed side by side they covered the space of several miles. They entered the ships and the Prince was approaching his own, when God sent a swarm of gnats—one swarm of little gnats. They buzzed round the Prince and stung his face and hands; angrily he drew his sword and brandished it, but he only touched the air and did not hit the gnats. Then he ordered his servants to bring costly coverings and wrap him in them, that the gnats might no longer be able to reach him. The servants carried out his orders, but one single gnat had placed itself inside one of the coverings, crept into the Prince's ear and stung him. The place burnt like fire, and the poison entered into his blood. Mad with pain, he tore off the coverings and his clothes too, flinging them far away, and danced about before the eyes of his ferocious soldiers, who now mocked at him, the mad Prince, who wished to make war with God, and was overcome by a single little gnat.

The Sandman

Translated by Mrs. H. P. Paull

There is nobody in the world who knows so many stories as Ole-Luk-Oie, or who can relate them so nicely. In the evening, while the children are seated at the table or in their little chairs, he comes up the stairs very softly, for he walks in his socks, then he opens the doors without the slightest noise, and throws a small quantity of very fine dust in their eyes, just enough to prevent them from keeping them open, and so they do not see him. Then he creeps behind them, and blows softly upon their necks, till their heads begin to droop. But Ole-Luk-Oie does not wish to hurt them, for he is very fond of children, and only wants them to be quiet that he may relate to them pretty stories, and they never are quiet until they are in bed and asleep. As soon as they are asleep, Ole-Luk-Oie seats himself upon the bed. He is nicely dressed; his coat is made of silken stuff; it is impossible to say of what colour, for it changes from green to red, and from red to blue as he turns from side to side. Under each arm he carries an umbrella; one of them, with pictures on the inside, he spreads over the good children, and then they dream the most beautiful stories the whole night. But the other umbrella has no pictures, and this he holds over the naughty children so that they sleep heavily, and wake in the morning without having dreamed at all.

Now we shall hear how Ole-Luk-Oie came every night during a whole week to the little boy named Hjalmar, and what he told him. There were seven stories, as there are seven days in the week.

Monday

"Now pay attention," said Ole-Luk-Oie, in the evening, when Hjalmar was in bed, "and I will decorate the room."

Immediately all the flowers in the flowerpots became large trees, with long branches reaching to the ceiling, and stretching along the walls, so that the whole room was like a greenhouse. All the branches were loaded with flowers, each flower as beautiful and as fragrant as a rose; and, had any one tasted them, he would have found them sweeter even than jam. The fruit glittered like gold, and there were cakes so full of plums that they were nearly bursting. It was incomparably beautiful. At the same time sounded dismal moans from the table-drawer in which lay Hjalmar's school books.

"What can that be now?" said Ole-Luk-Oie, going to the table and pulling out the drawer.

It was a slate, in such distress because of a false number in the sum, that it had almost broken itself to pieces. The pencil pulled and tugged at its string as if it were a little dog that wanted to help, but could not.

And then came a moan from Hjalmar's copy-book. Oh, it was quite terrible to hear! On each leaf stood a row of capital letters, every one having a small letter by its side. This formed a copy; under these were other letters, which Hjalmar had written: they fancied they looked like the copy, but they were mistaken; for they were leaning on one side as if they intended to fall over the pencil-lines.

"See, this is the way you should hold yourselves," said the copy. "Look here, you should slope thus, with a graceful curve."

"Oh, we are very willing to do so, but we cannot," said Hjalmar's letters; "we are so wretchedly made."

"You must be scratched out, then," said Ole-Luk-Oie.

"Oh, no!" they cried, and then they stood up so gracefully it was quite a pleasure to look at them.

"Now we must give up our stories, and exercise these letters," said Ole-Luk-Oie; "One, two—one, two—" So he drilled them till they stood up gracefully, and looked as beautiful as a copy could look. But after Ole-Luk-Oie was gone, and Hjalmar looked at them in the morning, they were as wretched and as awkward as ever.

Tuesday

As soon as Hjalmar was in bed, Ole-Luk-Oie touched, with his little magic wand, all the furniture in the room, which immediately began to chatter, and each article only talked of itself.

Over the chest of drawers hung a large picture in a gilt frame, representing a landscape, with fine old trees, flowers in the grass, and a broad stream, which flowed through the wood, past several castles, far out into the wild ocean. Ole-Luk-Oie touched the picture with his magic wand, and immediately the birds commenced singing, the branches of the trees rustled, and the clouds moved across the sky, casting their shadows on the landscape beneath them. Then Ole-Luk-Oie lifted little Hjalmar up to the frame, and placed his feet in the picture, just on the high grass, and there he stood with the sun shining down upon him through the branches of the trees. He ran to the water, and seated himself in a little boat which lay there, and which was painted red and white. The sails glittered like silver, and six swans, each with a golden circlet round its neck, and a bright blue star on its forehead, drew the boat past the green wood, where the trees talked of robbers and witches, and the flowers of beautiful little elves and fairies, whose histories the butterflies had related to them. Brilliant fish, with scales like silver and gold, swam after the boat, sometimes making a spring and splashing the water round them, while birds, red and blue, small and great, flew after him in two long lines. The gnats danced round them, and the cockchafers cried "Buz, buz." They all wanted to follow Hjalmar, and all had some story to tell him. It was a most pleasant sail. Sometimes the forests were thick and dark, sometimes like a beautiful garden, gay with sunshine and flowers; then he passed great palaces of glass and of marble, and on the balconies stood princesses, whose faces were those of little girls whom Hjalmar knew well, and had often played with. One of them held out her hand, in which was a heart made of sugar, more beautiful than any confectioner ever sold. As Hjalmar sailed by, he caught hold of one side of the sugar heart, and held it fast, and the princess held fast also, so that it broke in two pieces. Hjalmar had one piece, and the princess the other, but Hjalmar's was the largest. At each castle stood little princes acting as sentinels. They presented arms, and had golden swords, and made it rain plums and tin soldiers, so that they must have been real princes.

Hjalmar continued to sail, sometimes through woods, sometimes as it were through large halls, and then by large cities. At last he came to the town where his nurse lived, who had carried him in her arms when he was a very little boy, and had always been kind to him. She nodded and beckoned to him, and then sang the little verses she had herself composed and set to him—

> "How oft my memory turns to thee,
> My own Hjalmar, ever dear!
> When I could watch thy infant glee,
> Or kiss away a pearly tear.
> 'Twas in my arms thy lisping tongue
> First spoke the half-remembered word,
> While o'er thy tottering steps I hung,
> My fond protection to afford.
> Farewell! I pray the Heavenly Power
> To keep thee till thy dying hour."

And all the birds sang the same tune, the flowers danced on their stems, and the old trees nodded as if Ole-Luk-Oie had been telling them stories as well.

Wednesday

How the rain did pour down! Hjalmar could hear it in his sleep;. and when Ole-Luk-Oie opened the window, the water flowed quite up to the window-sill. It had the appearance of a large lake outside, and a beautiful ship lay close to the house.

"Wilt thou sail with me tonight, little Hjalmar?" said Ole-Luk-Oie; "then we shall see foreign countries, and thou shalt return here in the morning."

All in a moment, there stood Hjalmar, in his best clothes, on the deck of the noble ship; and immediately the weather became fine. They sailed through the streets, round by the church, and on every side rolled the wide, great sea. They sailed till the land disappeared, and then they saw a flock of storks, who had left their own country, and were travelling to warmer climates. The storks flew one behind the other, and had already been a long, long time on the wing. One of them seemed so tired that his wings could scarcely carry him. He was the last of the row, and was soon left very far behind. At length he sunk lower and lower, with outstretched wings, flapping them in vain, till his feet touched the rigging of the ship, and he slid from the sails to the deck, and stood before them. Then a sailor-boy caught him, and put him in the hen-house, with the fowls, the ducks, and the turkeys, while the poor stork stood quite bewildered amongst them.

"Just look at that fellow," said the chickens.

Then the turkey-cock puffed himself out as large as he could, and inquired who he was; and the ducks waddled backwards, crying, "Quack, quack."

Then the stork told them all about warm Africa, of the pyramids, and of the ostrich, which, like a wild horse, runs across the desert. But the ducks did not understand what he said, and quacked amongst themselves, "We are all of the same opinion; namely, that he is stupid."

"Yes, to be sure, he is stupid," said the turkey-cock; and gobbled.

Then the stork remained quite silent, and thought of his home in Africa.

"Those are handsome thin legs of yours," said the turkey-cock. "What do they cost a yard?"

"Quack, quack, quack," grinned the ducks; but, the stork pretended not to hear.

"You may as well laugh," said the turkey; "for that remark was rather witty, or perhaps it was above you. Ah, ah, is he not clever? He will be a great amusement to us while he remains here." And then he gobbled, and the ducks quacked, "Gobble, gobble; Quack, quack."

What a terrible uproar they made, while they were having such fun among themselves!

Then Hjalmar went to the hen-house; and, opening the door, called to the stork. Then he hopped out on the deck. He had rested himself now, and he looked happy, and seemed as if he nodded to Hjalmar, as if to thank him. Then he spread his wings, and flew away to warmer countries, while the hens clucked, the ducks quacked, and the turkey-cock turned quite scarlet in the head.

"Tomorrow you shall be made into soup," said Hjalmar to the fowls; and then he awoke, and found himself lying in his little bed.

It was a wonderful journey which Ole-Luk-Oie had made him take this night.

Thursday

"What do you think I have got here?" said Ole-Luk-Oie, "Do not be frightened, and you shall see a little mouse." And then he held out his hand to him, in which lay a lovely little creature. "It has come to invite you to a wedding. Two little mice are going to enter into the marriage state tonight. They reside under the floor of your mother's store-room, and that must be a fine dwelling-place."

"But how can I get through the little mouse-hole in the floor?" asked Hjalmar.

"Leave me to manage that," said Ole-Luk-Oie. "I will soon make you small enough." And then he touched Hjalmar with his magic wand, whereupon he became less and less, until at last he was not longer than a little finger. "Now you can borrow the dress of the tin soldier. I think it will just fit you. It looks well to wear a uniform when you go into company."

"Yes, certainly," said Hjalmar; and in a moment he was dressed as neatly as the neatest of all tin soldiers.

"Will you be so good as to seat yourself in your mamma's thimble," said the little mouse, "that I may have the pleasure of drawing you to the wedding."

"Will you really take so much trouble, young lady?" said Hjalmar. And so in this way he rode to the mouse's wedding.

First they went under the floor, and then passed through a long passage, which was scarcely high enough to allow the thimble to drive under, and the whole passage was lit up with the phosphorescent light of rotten wood.

"Does it not smell delicious?" asked the mouse, as she drew him along. "The wall and the floor have been smeared with bacon-rind; nothing can be nicer."

Very soon they arrived at the bridal hall. On the right stood all the little lady-mice, whispering and giggling, as if they were making game of each other. To the left were the gentlemen-mice, stroking their whiskers with their fore-paws; and in the centre of the hall could be seen the bridal pair, standing side by side, in a hollow cheese-rind, and kissing each other, while all eyes were upon them; for they had already been betrothed, and were soon to be married. More and more friends kept arriving, till the mice were nearly treading each other to death; for the bridal pair now stood in the doorway, and none could pass in or out.

The room had been rubbed over with bacon-rind, like the passage, which was all the refreshment offered to the guests. But for dessert they produced a pea, on which a mouse belonging to the bridal pair had bitten the first letters of their names. This was something quite uncommon. All the mice said it was a very beautiful wedding, and that they had been very agreeably entertained.

After this, Hjalmar returned home. He had certainly been in grand society; but he had been obliged to creep under a room, and to make himself small enough to wear the uniform of a tin soldier.

Friday

"It is incredible how many old people there are who would be glad to have me at night," said Ole-Luk-Oie, "especially those who have done something wrong. 'Good little Ole,' say they to me, 'we cannot close our eyes, and we lie awake the whole night and see all our evil deeds sitting on our beds like little imps, and sprinkling us with hot water. Will you come and drive them away, that we may have a good night's rest?' and then they sigh so deeply and say, 'We would gladly pay you for it. Goodnight, Ole-Luk, the money lies on the window.' But I never do anything for gold." "What shall we do tonight?" asked Hjalmar. "I do not know whether you would care to go to another wedding," he replied, "although it is quite a different affair to the one we saw last night. Your sister's large doll, that is dressed like a man, and is called Herman, intends to marry the doll Bertha. It is also the dolls' birthday, and they will receive many presents."

"Yes, I know that already," said Hjalmar, "my sister always

allows her dolls to keep their birthdays or to have a wedding when they require new clothes; that has happened already a hundred times, I am quite sure."

"Yes, so it may; but tonight is the hundred and first wedding, and when that has taken place it must be the last, therefore this is to be extremely beautiful. Only look."

Hjalmar looked at the table, and there stood the little cardboard doll's house, with lights in all the windows, and drawn up before it were the tin soldiers presenting arms. The bridal pair were seated on the floor, leaning against the leg of the table, looking very thoughtful, and with good reason. Then Ole-Luk-Oie dressed up in grandmother's black gown married them.

As soon as the ceremony was concluded, all the furniture in the room joined in singing a beautiful song, which had been composed by the lead pencil, and which went to the melody of a military tattoo.

> "What merry sounds are on the wind,
> As marriage rites together bind
> A quiet and a loving pair,
> Though formed of kid, yet smooth and fair!
> Hurrah! If they are deaf and blind,
> We'll sing, though weather prove unkind."

And now came the present; but the bridal pair had nothing to eat, for love was to be their food.

"Shall we go to a country house, or travel?" asked the bridegroom.

Then they consulted the swallow who had travelled so far, and the old hen in the yard, who had brought up five broods of chickens.

And the swallow talked to them of warm countries, where the grapes hang in large clusters on the vines, and the air is soft and mild, and about the mountains glowing with colours more beautiful than we can think of.

"But they have no red cabbage like we have," said the hen, "I was once in the country with my chickens for a whole summer, there was a large sand-pit, in which we could walk about and scratch as we liked. Then we got into a garden in which grew red cabbage; oh, how nice it was, I cannot think of anything more delicious."

"But one cabbage stalk is exactly like another," said the swallow; "and here we have often bad weather."

"Yes, but we are accustomed to it," said the hen.

"But it is so cold here, and freezes sometimes."

"Cold weather is good for cabbages," said the hen; "besides we do have it warm here sometimes. Four years ago, we had a summer that lasted more than five weeks, and it was so hot one could scarcely breathe. And then in this country we have no poisonous animals, and we are free from robbers. He must be wicked who does not consider our country the finest of all lands. He ought not to be allowed to live here." And then the hen wept very much and said, "I have also travelled. I once went twelve miles in a coop, and it was not pleasant travelling at all."

"The hen is a sensible woman," said the doll Bertha. "I don't care for travelling over mountains, just to go up and come down again. No, let us go to the sand-pit in front of the gate, and then take a walk in the cabbage garden."

And so they settled it.

Saturday

"Am I to hear any more stories?" asked little Hjalmar, as soon as Ole-Luk-Oie had sent him to sleep.

"We shall have no time this evening," said he, spreading out his prettiest umbrella over the child. "Look at these Chinese," and then the whole umbrella appeared like a large china bowl, with blue trees and pointed bridges, upon which stood little Chinamen nodding their heads. "We must make all the world beautiful for tomorrow morning," said Ole-Luk-Oie, "for it will be a holiday, it is Sunday. I must now go to the church steeple and see if the little sprites who live there have polished the bells, so that they may sound sweetly. Then I must go into the fields and see if the wind has blown the dust from the grass and the leaves, and the most difficult task of all which I have to do, is to take down all the stars and brighten them up. I have to number them first before I put them in my apron, and also to number the places from which I take them, so that they may go back into the right holes, or else they would not remain, and we should have a number of falling stars, for they would all tumble down one after the other."

"Hark ye! Mr. Luk-Oie," said an old portrait which hung on the wall of Hjalmar's bedroom. "Do you know me? I am Hjalmar's great-grandfather. I thank you for telling the boy stories, but you must not confuse his ideas. The stars cannot be taken down from the sky and polished; they are spheres like our earth, which is a good thing for them."

"Thank you, old great-grandfather," said Ole-Luk-Oie. "I thank you; you may be the head of the family, as no doubt you are, but I am older than you. I am an ancient heathen. The old Romans and Greeks named me the Dream-god. I have visited the noblest houses, and continue to do so; still I know how to conduct myself both to high and low, and now you may tell the stories yourself:" and so Ole-Luk-Oie walked off, taking his umbrellas with him.

"Well, well, one is never to give an opinion, I suppose," grumbled the portrait. And it woke Hjalmar.

Sunday

"Good evening," said Ole-Luk-Oie.

Hjalmar nodded, and then sprang out of bed, and turned his great-grandfather's portrait to the wall, so that it might not interrupt them as it had done yesterday. "Now," said he, "you must tell me some stories about five green peas that lived in one pod; or of the chickseed that courted the chickweed; or of the darning needle, who acted so proudly because she fancied herself an embroidery needle."

"You may have too much of a good thing," said Ole-Luk-Oie. "You know that I like best to show you something, so I will show you my brother. He is also called Ole-Luk-Oie but he never visits any one but once, and when he does come, he takes him away on his horse, and tells him stories as they ride along. He knows only two stories. One of these is so wonderfully beautiful, that no one in the world can imagine anything at all like it; but the other is just as ugly and frightful, so that it would be impossible to describe it." Then

Ole-Luk-Oie lifted Hjalmar up to the window. "There now, you can see my brother, the other Ole-Luk-Oie; he is also called Death. You perceive he is not so bad as they represent him in picture books; there he is a skeleton, but now his coat is embroidered with silver, and he wears the splendid uniform of a hussar, and a mantle of black velvet flies behind him, over the horse. Look, how he gallops along." Hjalmar saw that as this Ole-Luk-Oie rode on, he lifted up old and young, and carried them away on his horse. Some he seated in front of him, and some behind, but always inquired first, "How stands the mark-book?"

"Good," they all answered.

"Yes, but let me see for myself," he replied; and they were obliged to give him the books. Then all those who had "Very good," or "Exceedingly good," came in front of the horse, and heard the beautiful story; while those who had "Middling," or "Tolerably good," in their books, were obliged to sit behind, and listen to the frightful tale. They trembled and cried, and wanted to jump down from the horse, but they could not get free, for they seemed fastened to the seat.

"Why, Death is a most splendid Luk-Oie," said Hjalmar. "I am not in the least afraid of him."

"You need have no fear of him," said Ole-Luk-Oie, "if you take care and keep a good conduct book."

"Now I call that very instructive," murmured the great-grandfather's portrait. "It is useful sometimes to express an opinion;" so he was quite satisfied.

These are some of the doings and sayings of Ole-Luk-Oie. I hope he may visit you himself this evening, and relate some more.

The Swineherd

Translated by Mrs. H. P. Paull

Once upon a time lived a poor prince; his kingdom was very small, but it was large enough to enable him to marry, and marry he would. It was rather bold of him that he went and asked the emperor's daughter: "Will you marry me?" but he ventured to do so, for his name was known far and wide, and there were hundreds of princesses who would have gladly accepted him, but would she do so? Now we shall see.

On the grave of the prince's father grew a rose-tree, the most beautiful of its kind. It bloomed only once in five years, and then it had only one single rose upon it, but what a rose! It had such a sweet scent that one instantly forgot all sorrow and grief when one smelt it. He had also a nightingale, which could sing as if every sweet melody was in its throat. This rose and the nightingale he wished to give to the princess; and therefore both were put into big silver cases and sent to her.

The emperor ordered them to be carried into the great hall where the princess was just playing "Visitors are coming" with her ladies-

The Swineherd

in-waiting; when she saw the large cases with the presents therein, she clapped her hands for joy.

"I wish it were a little pussy cat," she said. But then the rose-tree with the beautiful rose was unpacked.

"Oh, how nicely it is made," exclaimed the ladies.

"It is more than nice," said the emperor, "it is charming."

The princess touched it and nearly began to cry.

"For shame, pa," she said, "it is not artificial, it is natural!"

"For shame, it is natural" repeated all her ladies.

"Let us first see what the other case contains before we are angry," said the emperor; then the nightingale was taken out, and it sang so beautifully that no one could possibly say anything unkind about it.

"*Superbe, charmant,*" said the ladies of the court, for they all prattled French, one worse than the other.

"How much the bird reminds me of the musical box of the late lamented empress," said an old courtier, "it has exactly the same tone, the same execution."

"You are right," said the emperor, and began to cry like a little child.

"I hope it is not natural," said the princess.

"Yes, certainly it is natural," replied those who had brought the presents.

"Then let it fly," said the princess, and refused to see the prince.

But the prince was not discouraged. He painted his face, put on common clothes, pulled his cap over his forehead, and came back.

"Good day, emperor," he said, "could you not give me some employment at the court?"

"There are so many," replied the emperor, "who apply for places, that for the present I have no vacancy, but I will remember you. But wait a moment; it just comes into my mind, I require somebody to look after my pigs, for I have a great many."

Thus the prince was appointed imperial swineherd, and as such he lived in a wretchedly small room near the pigsty; there he worked all day long, and when it was night he had made a pretty little pot. There were little bells round the rim, and when the water began to boil in it, the bells began to play the old tune:

"A jolly old sow once lived in a sty,
Three little piggies had she," &c.

But what was more wonderful was that, when one put a finger into the steam rising from the pot, one could at once smell what meals they were preparing on every fire in the whole town. That was indeed much more remarkable than the rose. When the princess with her ladies passed by and heard the tune, she stopped and looked quite pleased, for she also could play it—in fact, it was the only tune she could play, and she played it with one finger.

"That is the tune I know," she exclaimed. "He must be a well-educated swineherd. Go and ask him how much the instrument is."

One of the ladies had to go and ask; but she put on pattens.

"What will you take for your pot?" asked the lady.

"I will have ten kisses from the princess," said the swineherd.

"God forbid," said the lady.

"Well, I cannot sell it for less," replied the swineherd.

"What did he say?" said the princess.

I really cannot tell you," replied the lady.

"You can whisper it into my ear."

"It is very naughty," said the princess, and walked off.

But when she had gone a little distance, the bells rang again so sweetly:

> "A jolly old sow once lived in a sty,
>   Three little piggies had she," &c.

"Ask him," said the princess, "if he will be satisfied with ten kisses from one of my ladies."

"No, thank you," said the swineherd: "ten kisses from the princess, or I keep my pot."

"That is tiresome," said the princess. "But you must stand before me, so that nobody can see it."

The ladies placed themselves in front of her and spread out their dresses, and she gave the swineherd ten kisses and received the pot.

That was a pleasure! Day and night the water in the pot was boiling; there was not a single fire in the whole town of which they did not know what was preparing on it, the chamberlain's as well as the shoemaker's. The ladies danced and clapped their hands for joy.

"We know who will eat soup and pancakes; we know who will eat porridge and cutlets; oh, how interesting!"

"Very interesting, indeed," said the mistress of the household. "But you must not betray me, for I am the emperor's daughter."

"Of course not," they all said.

The swineherd—that is to say, the prince—but they did not know otherwise than that he was a real swineherd—did not waste a single day without doing something; he made a rattle, which, when turned quickly round, played all the waltzes, galops, and polkas known since the creation of the world.

"But that is *superbe*," said the princess passing by. "I have never heard a more beautiful composition. Go down and ask him what the instrument costs; but I shall not kiss him again."

"He will have a hundred kisses from the princess," said the lady, who had gone down to ask him.

"I believe he is mad," said the princess, and walked off, but soon she stopped. "One must encourage art," she said. "I am the emperor's daughter! Tell him I will give him ten kisses, as I did the other day; the remainder one of my ladies can give him.

"But we do not like to kiss him" said the ladies.

"That is nonsense," said the princess; "if I can kiss him, you can also do it. Remember that I give you food and employment." And the lady had to go down once more.

"A hundred kisses from the princess," said the swineherd, "or everybody keeps his own."

"Place yourselves before me," said the princess then. They did as they were bidden, and the princess kissed him.

"I wonder what that crowd near the pigsty means!" said the emperor, who had just come out on his balcony. He rubbed his eyes and put his spectacles on.

"The ladies of the court are up to some mischief, I think. I shall have to go down and see." He pulled up his shoes, for they were down at the heels, and he was very quick about it. When he had come down into the courtyard he walked quite softly, and the ladies were so busily engaged in counting the kisses, that all should be fair, that they did not notice the emperor. He raised himself on tiptoe.

"What does this mean?" he said, when he saw that his daughter was kissing the swineherd, and then hit their heads with his shoe just as the swineherd received the sixty-eighth kiss.

"Go out of my sight," said the emperor, for he was very angry; and both the princess and the swineherd were banished from the empire. There she stood and cried, the swineherd scolded her, and the rain came down in torrents.

"Alas, unfortunate creature that I am!" said the princess, "I wish I had accepted the prince. Oh, how wretched I am!"

The swineherd went behind a tree, wiped his face, threw off his poor attire and stepped forth in his princely garments; he looked so beautiful that the princess could not help bowing to him.

"I have now learnt to despise you," he said. "You refused an honest prince; you did not appreciate the rose and the nightingale; but you did not mind kissing a swineherd for his toys; you have no one but yourself to blame!"

And then he returned into his kingdom and left her behind. She could now sing at her leisure:

>"A jolly old sow once lived in a sty,
>Three little piggies has she," &c.

The Buckwheat

Translated by Mrs. H. P. Paull

Very often, after a violent thunder-storm, a field of buckwheat appears blackened and singed, as if a flame of fire had passed over it. The country people say that this appearance is caused by lightning; but I will tell you what the sparrow says, and the sparrow heard it from an old willow tree which grew near a field of buckwheat, and is there still. It is a large venerable tree, though a little crippled by age. The trunk has been split, and out of the crevice grass and brambles grow. The tree bends forward slightly, and the branches hang quite down to the ground just like green hair. Corn grows in the surrounding fields, not only rye and barley, but oats, pretty oats that, when ripe, look like a number of little golden canary-birds sitting on a bough. The corn has a smiling look and the heaviest and richest ears bend their heads low as if in pious humility. Once there was also a field of buckwheat, and this field was exactly opposite to old willow tree. The buckwheat did not bend like the other grain, but erected its head proudly and stiffly on the stem. "I am as valuable as any other corn," said he, "and I am much handsomer; my flowers are as beautiful as the bloom of the apple blossom, and it is a pleasure to look at us. Do you know of anything prettier than we are, you old willow tree?"

And the willow tree nodded his head, as if he would say, "Indeed I do."

But the buckwheat spread itself out with pride, and said, "Stupid tree; he is so old that grass grows out of his body."

There arose a very terrible storm. All the field-flowers folded their leaves together, or bowed their little heads, while the storm passed over them, but the buckwheat stood erect in its pride. "Bend your head as we do," said the flowers.

"I have no occasion to do so," replied the buckwheat.

"Bend your head as we do," cried the ears of corn; "the angel of the storm is coming; his wings spread from the sky above to the earth beneath. He will strike you down before you can cry for mercy."

"But I will not bend my head," said the buckwheat.

"Close your flowers and bend your leaves," said the old willow tree. "Do not look at the lightning when the cloud bursts; even men cannot do that. In a flash of lightning heaven opens, and we can look in; but the sight will strike even human beings blind. What then must happen to us, who only grow out of the earth, and are so inferior to them, if we venture to do so?"

"Inferior, indeed!" said the buckwheat. "Now I intend to have a peep into heaven." Proudly and boldly he looked up, while the lightning flashed across the sky as if the whole world were in flames.

When the dreadful storm had passed, the flowers and the corn raised their drooping heads in the pure still air, refreshed by the rain, but the buckwheat lay like a weed in the field, burnt to blackness by the lightning. The branches of the old willow tree rustled in the wind, and large water-drops fell from his green leaves as if the old willow were weeping. Then the sparrows asked why he was weeping, when all around him seemed so cheerful. "See," they said, "how the sun shines, and the clouds float in the blue sky. Do you not smell the sweet perfume from flower and bush? Wherefore do you weep, old willow tree?" Then the willow told them of the haughty pride of the buckwheat, and of the punishment which followed in consequence.

This is the story told me by the sparrows one evening when I begged them to relate some tale to me.

The Metal Pig

Translated by Mrs. H. P. Paull

In the city of Florence, not far from the *Piazza del Granduca,* runs a little street called *Porta Rosa.* In this street, just in front of the market-place where vegetables are sold, stands a pig, made of brass and curiously formed. The bright colour has been changed by age to dark green; but clear, fresh water pours from the snout, which shines as if it had been polished, and so indeed it has, for hundreds of poor people and children seize it in their hands as they place their mouths close to the mouth of the animal, to drink. It is quite a picture to see a half-naked boy clasping the well-formed creature by the head, as he presses his rosy lips against its jaws. Every one who visits Florence can very quickly find the place; he has only to ask the first beggar he meets for the Metal Pig, and he will be told where it is.

It was late on a winter evening; the mountains were covered with snow, but the moon shone brightly, and moonlight in Italy is like a dull winter's day in the north; indeed it is better, for clear air seems to raise us above the earth, while in the north a cold, gray, leaden sky appears to press us down to earth, even as the cold damp earth shall one day press on us in the grave. In the garden of the grand duke's palace, under the roof of one of the wings, where a thousand roses bloom in winter, a little ragged boy had been sitting the whole day long; a boy, who might serve as a type of Italy, lovely and smiling, and yet still suffering. He was hungry and thirsty, yet no one gave him anything; and when it became dark, and they were about to close the gardens, the porter turned him out. He stood a long time musing on the bridge which crosses the Arno, and looking at the glittering stars, reflected in the water which flowed between him and the elegant marble bridge Della Trinita. He then walked away towards the Metal Pig, half knelt down, clasped it with his arms, and then put his mouth to the shining snout and drank deep draughts of the fresh water. Close by, lay a few salad-leaves and two chestnuts, which were to serve for his supper. No one was in the street but himself; it belonged only to him, so he boldly seated himself on the pig's back, leaned forward so that his curly head could rest on the head of the animal, and, before he was aware, he fell asleep.

It was midnight. The Metal Pig raised himself gently, and the boy heard him say quite distinctly, "Hold tight, little boy, for I am going to run;" and away he started for a most wonderful ride. First, they arrived at the *Piazza del Granduca*, and the metal horse which bears the duke's statue, neighed aloud. The painted coats-of-arms on the old council-house shone like transparent pictures, and Michael Angelo's David tossed his sling; it was as if everything had life. The metallic groups of figures, among which were Perseus and the Rape of the Sabines, looked like living persons, and cries of terror sounded from them all across the noble square. By the *Palazzo degli Uffizi*, in the arcade, where the nobility assemble for the carnival, the Metal Pig stopped. "Hold fast," said the animal; "hold fast, for I am going up stairs."

The little boy said not a word; he was half pleased and half afraid. They entered a long gallery, where the boy had been before. The walls were resplendent with paintings; here stood statues and busts, all in a clear light as if it were day. But the grandest appeared when the door of a side room opened; the little boy could remember what beautiful things he had seen there, but tonight everything shone in its brightest colours. Here stood the figure of a beautiful woman, as beautifully sculptured as possible by one of the great masters. Her graceful limbs appeared to move; dolphins sprang at her feet, and immortality shone from her eyes. The world called her the Venus de' Medici. By her side were statues, in which the spirit of life breathed in stone; figures of men, one of whom whetted his sword, and was named the Grinder; wrestling gladiators formed another group, the sword had been sharpened for them, and they strove for the goddess of beauty. The boy was dazzled by so much glitter; for the walls were gleaming with bright colours, all appeared living reality.

As they passed from hall to hall, beauty everywhere showed itself; and as the Metal Pig went step by step from one picture to the other, the little boy could see it all plainly. One glory eclipsed another; yet there was one picture that fixed itself on the little boy's memory, more especially because of the happy children it represented, for these the little boy had seen in daylight. Many pass this picture by with indifference, and yet it contains a treasure of poetic feeling; it represents Christ descending into Hades. They are not the lost whom the spectator sees, but the heathen of olden times. The Florentine, Angiolo Bronzino, painted this picture; most beautiful is the expression on the face of the two children, who appear to have full confidence that they shall reach heaven at last. They are embracing each other, and one little one stretches out his hand towards another who stands below him, and points to himself, as if he were saying, "I am going to heaven." The older people stand as if uncertain, yet hopeful, and they bow in humble adoration to the Lord Jesus. On this picture the boy's eyes rested longer than on any other: the Metal Pig stood still before it. A low sigh was heard. Did it come from the picture or from the animal? The boy raised his hands towards the smiling children, and then the Pig ran off with him through the open vestibule.

"Thank you, thank you, you beautiful animal," said the little boy, caressing the Metal Pig as it ran down the steps.

"Thanks to yourself also," replied the Metal Pig; "I have helped you and you have helped me, for it is only when I have an innocent child on my back that I receive the power to run. Yes; as you see, I can even venture under the rays of the lamp, in front of the picture of the Madonna, but I may not enter the church; still from without, and while you are upon my back, I may look in through the open door.

Do not get down yet, for if you do, then I shall be lifeless, as you have seen me in the *Porta Rosa*."

"I will stay with you, my dear creature," said the little boy. So then they went on at a rapid pace through the streets of Florence, till they came to the square before the church of *Santa Croce*. The folding-doors flew open, and light streamed from the altar through the church into the deserted square. A wonderful blaze of light streamed from one of the monuments in the left-side aisle, and a thousand moving stars seemed to form a glory round it; even the coat-of-arms on the tomb-stone shone, and a red ladder on a blue field gleamed like fire. It was the grave of Galileo. The monument is unadorned, but the red ladder is an emblem of art, signifying that the way to glory leads up a shining ladder, on which the prophets of mind rise to heaven, like Elias of old. In the right aisle of the church every statue on the richly carved sarcophagi seemed endowed with life. Here stood Michael Angelo; there Dante, with the laurel wreath round his brow; Alfieri and Machiavelli; for here side by side rest the great men—the pride of Italy. The church itself is very beautiful, even more beautiful than the marble cathedral at Florence, though not so large. It seemed as if the carved vestments stirred, and as if the marble figures they covered raised their heads higher, to gaze upon the brightly coloured glowing altar where the white-robed boys swung the golden censers, amid music and song, while the strong fragrance of incense filled the church, and streamed forth into the square. The boy stretched forth his hands towards the light, and at the same moment the Metal Pig started again so rapidly that he was obliged to cling tightly to him. The wind whistled in his ears, he heard the church door creak on its hinges as it closed, and it seemed to him as if he had lost his senses—then a cold shudder passed over him, and he awoke.

It was morning; the Metal Pig stood in its old place on the *Porta Rosa*, and the boy found he had slipped nearly off its back. Fear and trembling came upon him as he thought of his mother; she had sent him out the day before to get some money, he had not done so, and now he was hungry and thirsty. Once more he clasped the neck of his metal horse, kissed its nose, and nodded farewell to it. Then he wandered away into one of the narrowest streets, where there was scarcely room for a loaded donkey to pass. A great iron-bound door stood ajar; he passed through, and climbed up a brick staircase, with dirty walls and a rope for a balustrade, till he came to an open gallery hung with rags. From here a flight of steps led down to a court, where from a well water was drawn up by iron rollers to the different stories of the house, and where the water-buckets hung side by side. Sometimes the roller and the bucket danced in the air, splashing the water all over the court. Another broken-down staircase led from the gallery, and two Russian sailors running down it almost upset the poor boy. They were coming from their nightly carousal. A woman not very young, with an unpleasant face and a quantity of black hair, followed them. "What have you brought home?" she asked. when she saw the boy.

"Don't be angry," he pleaded; "I received nothing, I have nothing at all;" and he seized his mother's dress and would have kissed it. Then they went into a little room. I need not describe it, but only say that there stood in it an earthen pot with handles, made for holding fire, which in Italy is called a *marito*. This pot she took in her lap, warmed her fingers, and pushed the boy with her elbow.

"Certainly you must have some money," she said. The boy began to cry, and then she struck him with her foot till he cried out louder.

"Will you be quiet? or I'll break your screaming head;" and she swung about the fire-pot which she held in her hand, while the boy crouched to the earth and screamed.

Then a neighbour came in, and she had also a *marito* under her arm. "Felicita," she said, "what are you doing to the child?"

"The child is mine," she answered; "I can murder him if I like, and you too, Giannina." And then she swung about the fire-pot. The other woman lifted up hers to defend herself, and the two pots clashed together so violently that they were dashed to pieces, and fire and ashes flew about the room. The boy rushed out at the sight, sped across the courtyard, and fled from the house. The poor child ran till he was quite out of breath; at last he stopped at the church, the doors of which were opened to him the night before, and went in. Here everything was bright, and the boy knelt down by the first tomb on his right, the grave of Michael Angelo, and sobbed as if his heart would break. People came and went, mass was performed, but no one noticed the boy, excepting an elderly citizen, who stood still and looked at him for a moment, and then went away like the rest.

Hunger and thirst overpowered the child, and he became quite faint and ill. At last he crept into a corner behind the marble monuments, and went to sleep. Towards evening he was awakened by a pull at his sleeve; he started up, and the same old citizen stood before him.

"Are you ill? where do you live? have you been here all day?" were some of the questions asked by the old man. After hearing his answers, the old man took him home to a small house close by, in a back street. They entered a glovemaker's shop, where a woman sat sewing busily. A little white poodle, so closely shaven that his pink skin could plainly be seen, frisked about the room, and gambolled upon the boy.

"Innocent souls are soon intimate," said the woman, as she caressed both the boy and the dog. These good people gave the child food and drink, and said he should stay with them all night, and that the next day the old man, who was called Giuseppe, would go and speak to his mother. A little homely bed was prepared for him, but to him who had so often slept on the hard stones it was a royal couch, and he slept sweetly and dreamed of the splendid pictures and of the Metal Pig. Giuseppe went out the next morning, and the poor child was not glad to see him go, for he knew that the old man was gone to his mother, and that, perhaps, he would have to go back. He wept at the thought, and then he played with the little, lively dog, and kissed it, while the old woman looked kindly at him to encourage him. And what news did Giuseppe bring back? At first the boy could not hear, for he talked a great deal to his wife, and she nodded and stroked the boy's cheek.

Then she said, "He is a good lad, he shall stay with us, he may become a clever glovemaker, like you. Look what delicate fingers he has got; Madonna intended him for a glovemaker." So the boy stayed with them, and the woman herself taught him to sew; and he ate well, and slept well, and became very merry. But at last he began to tease Bellissima, as the little dog was called. This made the woman angry, and she scolded him and threatened him, which made him very unhappy, and he went and sat in his own room full of sad thoughts. This chamber looked upon the street, in which hung skins to dry, and there were thick iron bars across his window. That night he lay awake, thinking of the Metal Pig; indeed, it was always in his thoughts. Suddenly he fancied he heard feet outside going pit-a-pat. He sprung out of bed and went to the window. Could it be the Metal Pig? But there was nothing to be seen; whatever he had heard had passed already. Next morning, their neighbour, the artist, passed by, carrying a paint-box and a large roll of canvas.

"Help the gentleman to carry his box of colours," said the woman to the boy; and he obeyed instantly, took the box, and followed the painter. They walked on till they reached the picture gallery, and mounted the same staircase up which he had ridden that night on the Metal Pig. He remembered all the statues and pictures, the beautiful marble Venus, and again he looked at the Madonna with the Saviour and St. John. They stopped before the picture by Bronzino, in which Christ is represented as standing in the lower world, with the children smiling before Him, in the sweet expectation of entering heaven; and the poor boy smiled, too, for here was his heaven.

"You may go home now," said the painter, while the boy stood watching him, till he had set up his easel.

"May I see you paint?" asked the boy; "may I see you put the picture on this white canvas?"

"I am not going to paint yet," replied the artist; then he brought out a piece of chalk. His hand moved quickly, and his eye measured the great picture; and though nothing appeared but a faint line, the figure of the Saviour was as clearly visible as in the coloured picture.

"Why don't you go?" said the painter. Then the boy wandered home silently, and seated himself on the table, and learned to sew gloves. But all day long his thoughts were in the picture gallery; and so he pricked his fingers and was awkward. But he did not tease Bellissima. When evening came, and the house door stood open, he slipped out. It was a bright, beautiful, starlight evening, but rather cold. Away he went through the already-deserted streets, and soon came to the Metal Pig; he stooped down and kissed its shining nose, and then seated himself on its back.

"You happy creature," he said; "how I have longed for you! we must take a ride tonight."

But the Metal Pig lay motionless, while the fresh stream gushed forth from its mouth. The little boy still sat astride on its back, when he felt something pulling at his clothes. He looked down, and there was Bellissima, little smooth-shaven Bellissima, barking as if she would have said, "Here I am too; why are you sitting there?"

A fiery dragon could not have frightened the little boy so much as did the little dog in this place. "Bellissima in the street, and not *dressed!*" as the old lady called it; "what would be the end of this?"

The dog never went out in winter, unless she was attired in a little lambskin coat which had been made for her; it was fastened round the little dog's neck and body with red ribbons, and was decorated with rosettes and little bells. The dog looked almost like a little kid when she was allowed to go out in winter, and trot after her mistress. And now here she was in the cold, and not dressed. Oh, how would it end? All his fancies were quickly put to flight; yet he kissed the Metal Pig once more, and then took Bellissima in his arms. The poor little thing trembled so with cold, that the boy ran homeward as fast as he could.

"What are you running away with there?" asked two of the police whom he met, and at whom the dog barked. "Where have you stolen that pretty dog?" they asked; and they took it away from him.

"Oh, I have not stolen it; do give it to me back again," cried the boy, despairingly.

"If you have not stolen it, you may say at home that they can send to the watch-house for the dog." Then they told him where the watch-house was, and went away with Bellissima.

Here was a dreadful trouble. The boy did not know whether he had better jump into the Arno, or go home and confess everything. They would certainly kill him, he thought.

"Well, I would gladly be killed," he reasoned; "for then I shall die, and go to heaven:" and so he went home, almost hoping for death.

The door was locked, and he could not reach the knocker. No one was in the street; so he took up a stone, and with it made a tremendous noise at the door.

"Who is there?" asked somebody from within.

"It is I," said he. "Bellissima is gone. Open the door, and then kill me."

Then indeed there was a great panic. Madame was so very fond of Bellissima. She immediately looked at the wall where the dog's dress usually hung; and there was the little lambskin.

"Bellissima in the watch-house!" she cried. "You bad boy! how did you entice her out? Poor little delicate thing, with those rough policemen! and she'll be frozen with cold."

Giuseppe went off at once, while his wife lamented, and the boy wept. Several of the neighbours came in, and amongst them the painter. He took the boy between his knees, and questioned him; and, in broken sentences, he soon heard the whole story, and also about the Metal Pig, and the wonderful ride to the picture-gallery, which was certainly rather incomprehensible. The painter, however, consoled the little fellow, and tried to soften the lady's anger; but she would not be pacified till her husband returned with Bellissima, who had been with the police. Then there was great rejoicing, and the painter caressed the boy, and gave him a number of pictures. Oh, what beautiful pictures these were!—figures with funny heads; and, above all, the Metal Pig was there too. Oh, nothing could be more delightful. By means of a few strokes, it was made to appear on the paper; and even the house that stood behind it had been sketched in. Oh, if he could only draw and paint! He who could do this could conjure all the world before him. The first leisure moment during the next day, the boy got a pencil, and on the back of one of the other drawings he attempted to copy the drawing of the Metal Pig, and he succeeded. Certainly it was rather crooked, rather up and down, one leg thick, and another thin; still it was like the copy, and he was overjoyed at what he had done. The pencil would not go quite as it ought, he had found that out; but the next day he tried again. A second pig was drawn by the side of the first, and this looked a hundred times better; and the third attempt was so good, that everybody might know what it was meant to represent.

And now the glovemaking went on but slowly. The orders given by the shops in the town were not finished quickly; for the Metal Pig had taught the boy that all objects may be drawn upon paper; and Florence is a picture book in itself for any one who chooses to turn over its pages. On the *Piazza dell Trinita* stands a slender pillar, and upon it is the goddess of Justice, blindfolded, with her scales in her hand. She was soon represented on paper, and it was the glovemaker's boy who placed her there. His collection of pictures increased; but as yet they were only copies of lifeless objects, when one day Bellissima came gambolling before him: "Stand still," cried he, "and I will draw you beautifully, to put amongst my collection."

But Bellissima would not stand still, so she must be bound fast in one position. He tied her head and tail; but she barked and jumped, and so pulled and tightened the string, that she was nearly strangled; and just then her mistress walked in.

"You wicked boy! the poor little creature!" was all she could utter.

She pushed the boy from her, thrust him away with her foot, called him a most ungrateful, good-for-nothing, wicked boy, and forbade him to enter the house again. Then she wept, and kissed her little half-strangled Bellissima. At this moment the painter entered the room.

***

In the year 1834 there was an exhibition in the Academy of Arts at Florence. Two pictures, placed side by side, attracted a large number of spectators. The smaller of the two represented a little boy sitting at a table, drawing; before him was a little white poodle, curiously shaven; but as the animal would not stand still, it had been fastened with a string to its head and tail, to keep it in one position. The truthfulness and life in this picture interested every one. The painter was said to be a young Florentine, who had been found in the streets, when a child, by an old glovemaker, who had brought him up. The boy had taught himself to draw: it was also said that a young artist, now famous, had discovered talent in the child just as he was about to be sent away for having tied up madame's favourite little dog, and using it as a model. The glovemaker's boy had also become a great painter, as the picture proved; but the larger picture by its side was a still greater proof of his talent. It represented a handsome boy, clothed in rags, lying asleep, and leaning against the Metal Pig in the street of the *Porta Rosa*. All the spectators knew the spot well. The child's arms were round the neck of the Pig, and he was in a deep sleep. The lamp before the picture of the Madonna threw a strong, effective light on the pale, delicate face of the child. It was a beautiful picture. A large gilt frame surrounded it, and on one corner of the frame a laurel wreath had been hung; but a black band, twined unseen among the green leaves, and a streamer of crape, hung down from it; for within the last few days the young artist had—died.

The Shepherd's Story of the Bond of Friendship

Translated by Mrs. H. P. Paull

The little dwelling in which we lived was of clay, but the door-posts were columns of fluted marble, found near the spot on which it stood. The roof sloped nearly to the ground. It was at this time dark, brown, and ugly, but had originally been formed of blooming olive and laurel branches, brought from beyond the mountains. The house was situated in a narrow gorge, whose rocky walls rose to a perpendicular height, naked and black, while round their summits clouds often hung, looking like white living figures. Not a singing bird was ever heard there, neither did men dance to the sound of the pipe. The spot was one sacred to olden times; even its name recalled a memory of the days when it was called "Delphi." Then the summits of the dark, sacred mountains were covered with snow, and the highest, mount Parnassus, glowed longest in the red evening light. The brook which rolled from it near our house, was also sacred. How well I can remember every spot in that deep, sacred solitude! A fire had been kindled in the midst of the hut, and while the hot ashes lay there red and glowing, the bread was baked in them. At times the snow would be piled so high around our hut as almost to hide it, and then my mother appeared most cheerful. She would hold my head between her hands, and sing the songs she never sang at other times, for the Turks, our masters, would not allow it. She sang—

"On the summit of mount Olympus, in a forest of dwarf firs, lay an old stag. His eyes were heavy with tears, and glittering with colours like dewdrops; and there came by a roebuck, and said, 'What ailest thee, that thou weepest blue and red tears?' And the stag answered, 'The Turk has come to our city; he has wild dogs for the chase, a goodly pack.' 'I will drive them away across the islands!' cried the young roebuck; 'I will drive them away across the islands into the deep sea.' But before evening the roebuck was slain, and before night the hunted stag was dead."

And when my mother sang thus, her eyes would become moist; and on the long eyelashes were tears, but she concealed them and watched the black bread baking in the ashes. Then I would clench my fist, and cry, "We will kill these Turks!" But she repeated the words of the song, "I will drive them across the islands to the deep sea; but before evening came the roebuck was slain, and before the night the hunted stag was dead."

We had been lonely in our hut for several days and nights when my father came home. I knew he would bring me some shells from the gulf of Lepanto, or perhaps a knife with a shining blade. This time he brought, under his sheep-skin cloak, a little child, a little half-naked girl. She was wrapped in a fur; but when this was taken off, and she lay in my mother's lap, three silver coins were found fastened in her dark hair; they were all her possessions. My father told us that the child's parents had been killed by the Turks, and he talked so much about them that I dreamed of Turks all night. He himself had been wounded, and my mother bound up his arm. It was a deep wound, and the thick sheep-skin cloak was stiff with congealed blood. The little maiden was to be my sister. How pretty and bright she looked: even my mother's eyes were not more gentle than hers. Anastasia, as she was called, was to be my sister, because her father had been united to mine by an old custom, which we still follow. They had sworn brotherhood in their youth, and the most beautiful and virtuous maiden in the neighbourhood was chosen to perform the act of consecration upon this bond of friendship. So now this little girl was my sister. She sat in my lap, and I brought her flowers, and feathers from the birds of the mountain. We drank together of the waters of Parnassus, and dwelt for many years beneath the laurel roof of the hut, while, winter after winter, my mother sang her song of the stag who shed red tears. But as yet I did not understand that the sorrows of my own countrymen were mirrored in those tears.

One day there came to our hut Franks, men from a far country, whose dress was different to ours. They had tents and beds with them, carried by horses; and they were accompanied by more than twenty Turks, all armed with swords and muskets. These Franks were friends of the Pacha, and had letters from him, commanding an escort for them. They only came to see our mountain, to ascend Parnassus amid the snow and clouds, and to look at the strange black rocks which raised their steep sides near our hut. They could not find room in the hut, nor endure the smoke that rolled along the ceiling till it found its way out at the low door; so they pitched their tents on a small space outside our dwelling. Roasted lambs and birds were brought forth, and strong, sweet wine, of which the Turks are forbidden to partake.

When they departed, I accompanied them for some distance, carrying my little sister Anastasia, wrapped in a goat-skin, on my back. One of the Frankish gentlemen made me stand in front of a rock, and drew us both as we stood there, so that we looked like one creature. I did not think of it then, but Anastasia and I were really one. She was always sitting on my lap, or riding in the goat-skin on my back; and in my dreams she always appeared to me.

Two nights after this, other men, armed with knives and muskets, came into our tent. They were Albanians, brave men, my mother told me. They only stayed a short time. My sister Anastasia sat on the knee of one of them; and when they were gone, she had not three, but two silver coins in her hair—one had disappeared. They wrapped tobacco in strips of paper, and smoked it; and I remember they were uncertain as to the road they ought to take. But they were obliged to go at last, and my father went with them. Soon after, we heard the sound of firing. The noise continued, and presently soldiers rushed into our hut, and took my mother and myself and Anastasia prisoners. They declared that we had entertained robbers, and that my father had acted as their guide, and therefore we must now go with them. The corpses of the robbers, and my father's corpse, were brought into the hut. I saw my poor dead father, and cried till I fell asleep. When I awoke, I found myself in a prison; but the room was not worse than our own in the hut. They gave me onions and musty wine from a tarred cask; but we were not accustomed to much better fare at home. How long we were kept in prison, I do not know; but many days and nights passed by. We were set free about Easter-time. I carried Anastasia on my back, and we walked very slowly; for my mother was very weak, and it is a long way to the sea, to the Gulf of Lepanto.

On our arrival, we entered a church, in which there were beautiful pictures in golden frames. They were pictures of angels, fair and bright; and yet our little Anastasia looked equally beautiful, as it seemed to me. In the centre of the floor stood a coffin filled with roses. My mother told me it was the Lord Jesus Christ who was represented by these roses. Then the priest announced, "Christ is risen," and all the people greeted each other. Each one carried a burning taper in his hand, and one was given to me, as well as to little Anastasia. The music sounded, and the people left the church hand-in-hand, with joy and gladness. Outside, the women were roasting the paschal lamb. We were invited to partake; and as I sat by the fire, a boy, older than myself, put his arms round my neck, and kissed me, and said, "Christ is risen." And thus it was that for the first time I met Aphtanides.

My mother could make fishermen's nets, for which there was a great demand here in the bay; and we lived a long time by the side of the sea, the beautiful sea, that had a taste like tears, and in its colours reminded me of the stag that wept red tears; for sometimes its waters were red, and sometimes green or blue. Aphtanides knew how to manage our boat, and I often sat in it, with my little Anastasia, while it glided on through the water, swift as a bird flying through the air. Then, when the sun set, how beautifully, deeply blue, would be the tint on the mountains, one rising above the other in the far distance, and the summit of mount Parnassus rising above them all like a glorious crown. Its top glittered in the evening rays like molten gold, and it seemed as if the light came from within it; for long after the sun had sunk beneath the horizon, the mountain-top would glow in the clear, blue sky. The white aquatic birds skimmed the surface of the water in their flight, and all was calm and still as amid the black rocks at Delphi. I lay on my back in the boat, Anastasia leaned against me, while the stars above us glittered more brightly than the lamps in our church. They were the same stars, and in the same position over me as when I used to sit in front of our hut at Delphi, and I had almost begun to fancy I was still there, when suddenly there was a splash in the water—Anastasia had fallen in; but in a moment Aphtanides has sprung in after her, and was now holding her up to me. We dried her clothes as well as we were able, and remained on the water till they were dry; for we did not wish it to be known what a fright we had had, nor the danger which our little adopted sister had incurred, in whose life Aphtanides had now a part.

The summer came, and the burning heat of the sun tinted the leaves of the trees with lines of gold. I thought of our cool mountain-home, and the fresh water that flowed near it; my mother, too, longed for if, and one evening we wandered towards home. How peaceful and silent it was as we walked on through the thick, wild thyme, still fragrant, though the sun had scorched the leaves. Not a single herdsman did we meet, not a solitary hut did we pass; everything appeared lonely and deserted—only a shooting star showed that in the heavens there was yet life. I know not whether the clear, blue atmosphere gleamed with its own light, or if the radiance came from the stars; but we could distinguish quite plainly the outline of the mountains. My mother lighted a fire, and roasted some roots she had brought with her, and I and my little sister slept among the bushes, without fear of the ugly smidraki, from whose throat issues fire, or of the wolf and the jackal; for my mother sat by us, and I considered her presence sufficient protection.

We reached our old home; but the cottage was in ruins, and we had to build a new one. With the aid of some neighbours, chiefly women, the walls were in a few days erected, and very soon covered with a roof of olive-branches. My mother obtained a living by making bottle-cases of bark and skins, and I kept the sheep belonging to the priests, who were sometimes peasants, while I had for my playfellows Anastasia and the turtles.

Once our beloved Aphtanides paid us a visit. He said he had been longing to see us so much; and he remained with us two whole happy days. A month afterwards he came again to wish us goodbye, and brought with him a large fish for my mother. He told us he was going in a ship to Corfu and Patras, and could relate a great many stories, not only about the fishermen who lived near the gulf of Lepanto, but also of kings and heroes who had once possessed Greece, just as the Turks possess it now.

I have seen a bud on a rose bush gradually, in the course of a few weeks, unfold its leaves till it became a rose in all its beauty; and, before I was aware of it, I beheld it blooming in rosy loveliness. The same thing had happened to Anastasia. Unnoticed by me, she had gradually become a beautiful maiden, and I was now also a stout, strong youth. The wolf-skins that covered the bed in which my mother and Anastasia slept, had been taken from wolves which I had myself shot.

Years had gone by when, one evening, Aphtanides came in. He had grown tall and slender as a reed, with strong limbs, and a dark, brown skin. He kissed us all, and had so much to tell of what he had seen of the great ocean, of the fortifications at Malta, and of the marvellous sepulchres of Egypt, that I looked up to him with a kind of veneration. His stories were as strange as the legends of the priests of olden times.

"How much you know!" I exclaimed, "and what wonders you can relate?"

"I think what you once told me, the finest of all," he replied; "you told me of a thing that has never been out of my thoughts—of the good old custom of 'the bond of friendship'—a custom I should like to follow. Brother, let you and I go to church, as your father and Anastasia's father once did. Your sister Anastasia is the most beautiful and most innocent of maidens, and she shall consecrate the deed. No people have such grand old customs as we Greeks."

Anastasia blushed like a young rose, and my mother kissed Aphtanides.

At about two miles from our cottage, where the earth on the hill is sheltered by a few scattered trees, stood the little church, with a silver lamp hanging before the altar. I put on my best clothes, and the white tunic fell in graceful folds over my hips. The red jacket fitted tight and close, the tassel on my Fez cap was of silver, and in my girdle glittered a knife and my pistols. Aphtanides was clad in the blue dress worn by the Greek sailors; on his breast hung a silver medal with the figure of the Virgin Mary, and his scarf was as costly as those worn by rich lords. Every one could see that we were about to perform a solemn ceremony. When we entered the little, unpretending church, the evening sunlight streamed through the open door on the burning lamp, and glittered on the golden picture frames. We knelt down together on the altar steps, and Anastasia drew near and stood beside us. A long, white garment fell in graceful folds over her delicate form, and on her white neck and bosom hung a chain entwined with old and new coins, forming a kind of collar. Her black hair was fastened into a knot, and confined by a headdress formed of gold and silver coins which had been found in an ancient temple. No Greek girl had more beautiful ornaments than these. Her countenance glowed, and her eyes were like two stars. We all three offered a silent prayer, and then she said to us, "Will you be friends in life and in death?"

"Yes," we replied.

"Will you each remember to say, whatever may happen, 'My brother is a part of myself; his secret is my secret, my happiness is his; self-sacrifice, patience, everything belongs to me as they do to him?'"

And we again answered, "Yes." Then she joined out hands and kissed us on the forehead, and we again prayed silently. After this a priest came through a door near the altar, and blessed us all three. Then a song was sung by other holy men behind the altar-screen, and the bond of eternal friendship was confirmed. When we arose, I saw my mother standing by the church door, weeping.

How cheerful everything seemed now in our little cottage by the Delphian springs! On the evening before his departure, Aphtanides sat thoughtfully beside me on the slopes of the mountain. His arm was flung around me, and mine was round his neck. We spoke of the sorrows of Greece, and of the men of the country who could be trusted. Every thought of our souls lay clear before us. Presently

The Shepherd's Story of the Bond of Friendship

I seized his hand: "Aphtanides," I exclaimed, "there is one thing still that you must know—one thing that till now has been a secret between myself and Heaven. My whole soul is filled with love—with a love stronger than the love I bear to my mother and to thee.

"And whom do you love?" asked Aphtanides. And his face and neck grew red as fire.

"I love Anastasia," I replied.

Then his hand trembled in mine, and he became pale as a corpse. I saw it, I understood the cause, and I believe my hand trembled too. I bent towards him, I kissed his forehead, and whispered, "I have never spoken of this to her, and perhaps she does not love me. Brother, think of this; I have seen her daily, she has grown up beside me, and has become a part of my soul."

"And she shall be thine," he exclaimed; "thine! I may not wrong thee, nor will I do so. I also love her, but tomorrow I depart. In a year we will see each other again, but then you will be married; shall it not be so? I have a little gold of my own, it shall be yours. You must and shall take it."

We wandered silently homeward across the mountains. It was late in the evening when we reached my mother's door. Anastasia held the lamp as we entered; my mother was not there. She looked at Aphtanides with a sweet but mournful expression on her face. "Tomorrow you are going to leave us," she said. "I am very sorry."

"Sorry!" he exclaimed, and his voice was troubled with a grief as deep as my own. I could not speak; but he seized her hand and said, "Our brother yonder loves you, and is he not dear to you? His very silence now proves his affection."

Anastasia trembled, and burst into tears. Then I saw no one, thought of none, but her. I threw my arms round her, and pressed my lips to hers. As she flung her arms round my neck, the lamp fell to the ground, and we were in darkness, dark as the heart of poor Aphtanides.

Before daybreak he rose, kissed us all, and said "Farewell," and went away. He had given all his money to my mother for us. Anastasia was betrothed to me, and in a few days afterwards she became my wife.

A Rose from Homer's Grave

Translated by Mrs. H. P. Paull

All the songs of the east speak of the love of the nightingale for the rose in the silent starlight night. The winged songster serenades the fragrant flowers.

Not far from Smyrna, where the merchant drives his loaded camels, proudly arching their long necks as they journey beneath the lofty pines over holy ground, I saw a hedge of roses. The turtle-dove flew among the branches of the tall trees, and as the sunbeams fell upon her wings, they glistened as if they were mother-of-pearl. On the rose bush grew a flower, more beautiful than them all, and to her the nightingale sung of his woes; but the rose remained silent, not even a dewdrop lay like a tear of sympathy on her leaves. At last she bowed her head over a heap of stones, and said, "Here rests the greatest singer in the world; over his tomb will I spread my fragrance, and on it I will let my leaves fall when the storm scatters them. He who sung of Troy became earth, and from that earth I have sprung. I, a rose from the grave of Homer, am too lofty to bloom for a nightingale." Then the nightingale sung himself to death. A camel-

A Rose from Homer's Grave

driver came by, with his loaded camels and his black slaves; his little son found the dead bird, and buried the lovely songster in the grave of the great Homer, while the rose trembled in the wind.

The evening came, and the rose wrapped her leaves more closely round her, and dreamed: and this was her dream.

It was a fair sunshiny day; a crowd of strangers drew near who had undertaken a pilgrimage to the grave of Homer. Among the strangers was a minstrel from the north, the home of the clouds and the brilliant lights of the aurora borealis. He plucked the rose and placed it in a book, and carried it away into a distant part of the world, his fatherland. The rose faded with grief, and lay between the leaves of the book, which he opened in his own home, saying, "Here is a rose from the grave of Homer."

Then the flower awoke from her dream, and trembled in the wind. A drop of dew fell from the leaves upon the singer's grave. The sun rose, and the flower bloomed more beautiful than ever. The day was hot, and she was still in her own warm Asia. Then footsteps approached, strangers, such as the rose had seen in her dream, came by, and among them was a poet from the north; he plucked the rose, pressed a kiss upon her fresh mouth, and carried her away to the home of the clouds and the northern lights. Like a mummy, the flower now rests in his "Iliad," and, as in her dream, she hears him say, as he opens the book, "Here is a rose from the grave of Homer."

The Angel

Translated by Mrs. H. P. Paull

"Whenever a good child dies, an angel of God comes down from heaven, takes the dead child in his arms, spreads out his great white wings, and flies with him over all the places which the child had loved during his life. Then he gathers a large handful of flowers, which he carries up to the Almighty, that they may bloom more brightly in heaven than they do on earth. And the Almighty presses the flowers to His heart, but He kisses the flower that pleases Him best, and it receives a voice, and is able to join the song of the chorus of bliss."

These words were spoken by an angel of God, as he carried a dead child up to heaven, and the child listened as if in a dream. Then they passed over well-known spots, where the little one had often played, and through beautiful gardens full of lovely flowers.

"Which of these shall we take with us to heaven to be transplanted there?" asked the angel.

Close by grew a slender, beautiful, rose bush, but some wicked hand had broken the stem, and the half-opened rosebuds hung faded and withered on the trailing branches.

"Poor rose bush!" said the child, "let us take it with us to heaven, that it may bloom above in God's garden."

The angel took up the rose bush; then he kissed the child, and the little one half opened his eyes. The angel gathered also some beautiful flowers, as well as a few humble buttercups and heart's-ease.

"Now we have flowers enough," said the child; but the angel only nodded, he did not fly upward to heaven.

It was night, and quite still in the great town. Here they remained, and the angel hovered over a small, narrow street, in which lay a large heap of straw, ashes, and sweepings from the houses of people who had removed. There lay fragments of plates, pieces of plaster, rags, old hats, and other rubbish not pleasant to see. Amidst all this confusion, the angel pointed to the pieces of a broken flowerpot, and to a lump of earth which had fallen out of it. The earth had been kept from falling to pieces by the roots of a withered field-flower, which had been thrown amongst the rubbish.

"We will take this with us," said the angel, "I will tell you why as we fly along."

And as they flew the angel related the history.

"Down in that narrow lane, in a low cellar, lived a poor sick boy; he had been afflicted from his childhood, and even in his best days he could just manage to walk up and down the room on crutches once or twice, but no more. During some days in summer, the sunbeams would lie on the floor of the cellar for about half an hour. In this spot the poor sick boy would sit warming himself in the sunshine, and watching the red blood through his delicate fingers as he held them before his face. Then he would say he had been out, yet he knew nothing of the green forest in its spring verdure, till a neighbour's son brought him a green bough from a beech-tree. This he would place over his head, and fancy that he was in the beech-wood while the sun shone, and the birds carolled gaily. One spring day the neighbour's boy brought him some field-flowers, and among them was one to which the root still adhered. This he carefully planted in a flowerpot, and placed in a window-seat near his bed. And the flower had been planted by a fortunate hand, for it grew, put forth fresh shoots, and blossomed every year. It became a splendid flower-garden to the sick boy, and his little treasure upon earth. He watered it, and cherished it, and took care it should have the benefit of every sunbeam that found its way into the cellar, from the earliest morning ray to the evening sunset. The flower entwined itself even in his dreams—for him it bloomed, for him spread its perfume. And it gladdened his eyes, and to the flower he turned, even in death, when the Lord called him. He has been one year with God. During that time the flower has stood in the window, withered and forgotten, till at length cast out among the sweepings into the street, on the day of the lodgers' removal. And this poor flower, withered and faded as it is, we have added to our nosegay, because it gave more real joy than the most beautiful flower in the garden of a Queen."

"But how do you know all this?" asked the child whom the angel was carrying to heaven.

"I know it," said the angel, "because I myself was the poor sick boy who walked upon crutches, and I know my own flower well."

Then the child opened his eyes and looked into the glorious happy face of the angel, and at the same moment they found themselves in that heavenly home where all is happiness and joy. And God pressed the dead child to His heart, and wings were given him so that he could fly with the angel, hand in hand. Then the Almighty pressed all the flowers to His heart; but He kissed the withered field-flower, and it received a voice. Then it joined in the song of the angels, who surrounded the throne, some near, and others in a distant circle, but all equally happy. They all joined in the chorus of praise, both great and small—the good, happy child, and the poor field-flower, that once lay withered and cast away on a heap of rubbish in a narrow, dark street.

The Nightingale

Translated by Mrs. H. P. Paull

In China, you know, the Emperor is a Chinese, and all those about him are Chinamen also. The story I am going to tell you happened a great many years ago, so it is well to hear it now before it is forgotten. The Emperor's palace was the most beautiful in the world. It was built entirely of porcelain, and very costly, but so delicate and brittle that whoever touched it was obliged to be careful. In the garden could be seen the most singular flowers, with pretty silver bells tied to them, which tinkled so that every one who passed could not help noticing the flowers. Indeed, everything in the Emperor's garden was remarkable, and it extended so far that the gardener himself did not know where it ended. Those who travelled beyond its limits knew that there was a noble forest, with lofty trees, sloping down to the deep blue sea, and the great ships sailed under the shadow of its branches. In one of these trees lived a Nightingale, who sang so beautifully that even the poor fishermen, who had so many other things to do, would stop and listen. Sometimes, when they went at night to spread their nets, they would hear her sing, and say, "Oh, is not that beautiful?" But when they returned to their fishing, they forgot the bird until the next night. Then they would hear it again, and exclaim "Oh, how beautiful is the Nightingale's song!"

Travellers from every country in the world came to the city of the Emperor, which they admired very much, as well as the palace and gardens; but when they heard the Nightingale, they all declared it to be the best of all. And the travellers, on their return home, related what they had seen; and learned men wrote books, containing descriptions of the town, the palace, and the gardens; but they did not forget the Nightingale, which was really the greatest wonder. And those who could write poetry composed beautiful verses about the Nightingale, who lived in a forest near the deep sea. The books travelled all over the world, and some of them came into the hands of the Emperor; and he sat in his golden chair, and, as he read, he nodded his approval every moment, for it pleased him to find such a beautiful description of his city, his palace, and his gardens. But when he came to the words, "the Nightingale is the most beautiful of all," he exclaimed, "What is this? I know nothing of any Nightingale. Is there such a bird in my empire? and even in my garden? I have never heard of it. Something, it appears, may be learnt from books."

Then he called one of his lords-in-waiting, who was so high-bred, that when any in an inferior rank to himself spoke to him, or asked him a question, he would answer, "Pooh," which means nothing.

"There is a very wonderful bird mentioned here, called a Nightingale," said the Emperor; "they say it is the best thing in my large kingdom. Why have I not been told of it?"

"I have never heard the name," replied the cavalier; "she has not been presented at court."

"It is my pleasure that she shall appear this evening." said the emperor; the whole world knows what I possess better than I do myself."

"I have never heard of her," said the cavalier; "yet I will endeavor to find her."

But where was the Nightingale to be found? The nobleman went up stairs and down, through halls and passages; yet none of those whom he met had heard of the bird. So he returned to the Emperor, and said that it must be a fable, invented by those who had written the book. "Your Imperial Majesty," said he, "cannot believe everything contained in books; sometimes they are only fiction, or what is called the black art."

"But the book in which I have read this account," said the Emperor, "was sent to me by the great and mighty Emperor of Japan, and therefore it cannot contain a falsehood. I *will* hear the Nightingale, she must be here this evening; she has my highest favour; and if she does not come, the whole court shall be trampled upon after supper is ended."

"Tsing-pe!" cried the lord-in-waiting, and again he ran up and down stairs, through all the halls and corridors; and half the court ran with him, for they did not like the idea of being trampled upon. There was a great inquiry about this wonderful Nightingale, whom all the world knew, but who was unknown to the court.

At last they met with a poor little girl in the kitchen, who said, "Oh, yes, I know the Nightingale quite well; indeed, she can sing. Every evening I have permission to take home to my poor sick mother the scraps from the table; she lives down by the sea-shore, and as I come back I feel tired, and I sit down in the wood to rest, and listen to the Nightingale's song. Then the tears come into my eyes, and it is just as if my mother kissed me."

"Little maiden," said the lord-in-waiting, "I will obtain for you constant employment in the kitchen, and you shall have permission to see the Emperor dine, if you will lead us to the Nightingale; for she is invited for this evening to the palace." So she went into the wood where the Nightingale sang, and half the court followed her. As they went along, a cow began lowing.

"Oh," said a young courtier, "now we have found her; what wonderful power for such a small creature; I have certainly heard it before."

"No, that is only a cow lowing," said the little girl; "we are a long way from the place yet."

Then some frogs began to croak in the marsh.

"Beautiful," said the young courtier again. "Now I hear it, tinkling like little church bells."

"No, those are frogs," said the little maiden; "but I think we shall soon hear her now:" and presently the Nightingale began to sing.

"Hark, hark! there she is," said the girl, "and there she sits," she added, pointing to a little gray bird who was perched on a bough.

"Is it possible?" said the lord-in-waiting, "I never imagined it would be a little, plain, simple thing like that. She has certainly changed colour at seeing so many grand people around her."

"Little Nightingale," cried the girl, raising her voice, "our most gracious Emperor wishes you to sing before him."

"With the greatest pleasure," said the Nightingale, and began to sing most delightfully.

"It sounds like tiny glass bells," said the lord-in-waiting, "and see how her little throat works. It is surprising that we have never heard this before; she will be a great success at court."

"Shall I sing once more before the Emperor?" asked the Nightingale, who thought he was present.

"My excellent little Nightingale," said the courtier, "I have the great pleasure of inviting you to a court festival this evening, where you will gain Imperial favour by your charming song."

"My song sounds best in the green wood," said the bird; but still she came willingly when she heard the Emperor's wish.

The palace was elegantly decorated for the occasion. The walls and floors of porcelain glittered in the light of a thousand lamps. Beautiful flowers, round which little bells were tied, stood in the corridors: what with the running to and fro and the draught, these bells tinkled so loudly that no one could speak to be heard. In the centre of the great hall, a golden perch had been fixed for the Nightingale to sit on. The whole court was present, and the little kitchen-maid had received permission to stand by the door. She was now installed as a real court cook. All were in full dress, and every eye was turned to the little gray bird when the Emperor nodded to her to begin. The Nightingale sang so sweetly that the tears came into the Emperor's eyes, and then rolled down his cheeks, as her song became still more touching and went to every one's heart. The Emperor was so delighted that he declared the Nightingale should have his gold slipper to wear round her neck, but she declined the honour with thanks: she had been sufficiently rewarded already. "I have seen tears in an Emperor's eyes," she said, "that is my richest reward. An Emperor's tears have wonderful power, and are quite sufficient honour for me;" and then she sang again more enchantingly than ever.

"That singing is a lovely gift;" said the ladies of the court to each other; and then they took water in their mouths to make them utter the gurgling sounds of the nightingale when they spoke to any one, so that they might fancy themselves Nightingales. And the footmen and chambermaids also expressed their satisfaction, which is saying a great deal, for they are very difficult to please. In fact the Nightingale's visit was most successful. She was now to remain at court, to have her own cage, with liberty to go out twice a day, and once during the night. Twelve servants were appointed to attend her on these occasions, who each held her by a silken string fastened to her leg. There was certainly not much pleasure in this kind of flying.

The whole city spoke of the wonderful bird, and when two people met, one said "Nightin," and the other said "gale," and they understood what was meant, for nothing else was talked of. Eleven peddlers' children were named after her, but not of them could sing a note.

One day the Emperor received a large packet on which was written "The Nightingale." "Here is no doubt a new book about our celebrated bird," said the Emperor. But instead of a book, it was a work of art contained in a casket, an artificial nightingale made to look like a living one, and covered all over with diamonds, rubies, and sapphires. As soon as the artificial bird was wound up, it could sing like the real one, and could move its tail up and down, which sparkled with silver and gold. Round its neck hung a piece of ribbon, on which was written "The Emperor of Japan's nightingale is poor compared with that of the Emperor of China's."

"This is very beautiful," exclaimed all who saw it, and he who had brought the artificial bird received the title of "Imperial Nightingale-Bringer-in-Chief."

"Now they must sing together," said the court, "and what a duet it will be." But they did not get on well, for the real Nightingale sang in its own natural way, but the artificial bird sang only waltzes.

"That is not a fault," said the music-master, "it is quite perfect to my taste," so then it had to sing alone, and was as successful as the real bird; besides, it was so much prettier to look at, for it sparkled like bracelets and breast-pins. Three and thirty times did it sing the same tunes without being tired; the people would gladly have heard it again, but the emperor said the living Nightingale ought to sing something. But where was she? No one had noticed her when she flew out at the open window, back to her own green woods.

"What strange conduct," said the Emperor, when her flight had been discovered; and all the courtiers blamed her, and said she was a very ungrateful creature.

"But we have the best bird after all," said one, and then they would have the bird sing again, although it was the thirty-fourth time they had listened to the same piece, and even then they had not learnt it, for it was rather difficult. But the music-master praised the bird in the highest degree, and even asserted that it was better than a real Nightingale, not only in its dress and the beautiful diamonds, but also in its musical power. "For you must perceive, my chief lord and Emperor, that with a real Nightingale we can never tell what is going to be sung, but with this bird everything is settled. It can be opened and explained, so that people may understand how the waltzes are formed, and why one note follows upon another."

"This is exactly what we think," they all replied, and then the music-master received permission to exhibit the bird to the people on the following Sunday, and the emperor commanded that they should be present to hear it sing. When they heard it they were like people intoxicated; however it must have been with drinking tea, which is quite a Chinese custom. They all said "Oh!" and held up their forefingers and nodded, but a poor fisherman, who had heard the real Nightingale, said, "it sounds prettily enough, and the melodies are all alike; yet there seems something wanting, I cannot exactly tell what."

And after this the real Nightingale was banished from the empire, and the artificial bird placed on a silk cushion close to the Emperor's bed. The presents of gold and precious stones which had been received with it were round the bird, and it was now advanced to the title of "Little Imperial Toilet Singer," and to the rank of No. 1 on the left hand; for the Emperor considered the left side, on which the heart lies, as the most noble, and the heart of an Emperor is in the same place as that of other people.

The music-master wrote a work, in twenty-five volumes, about the artificial bird, which was very learned and very long, and full of the most difficult Chinese words; yet all the people said they had read it, and understood it, for fear of being thought stupid and having their bodies trampled upon.

So a year passed, and the Emperor, the court, and all the other Chinese knew every little turn in the artificial bird's song; and for that same reason it pleased them better. They could sing with the bird, which they often did. The street-boys sang, "Zi-zi-zi, cluck, cluck, cluck," and the Emperor himself could sing it also. It was really most amusing.

One evening, when the artificial bird was singing its best, and the Emperor lay in bed listening to it, something inside the bird sounded "Whizz." Then a spring cracked. "Whir-r-r" went all the wheels, running round, and then the music stopped. The Emperor immediately sprang out of bed, and called for his physician; but what could *he* do? Then they sent for a watchmaker; and, after a great deal of talking and examination, the bird was put into something like order; but he said that it must be used very carefully, as the barrels were worn, and it would be impossible to put in new ones without injuring the music. Now there was great sorrow, as the bird could only be allowed to play once a year; and even that was dangerous for the works inside it. Then the music-master made a little speech, full of hard words, and declared that the bird was as good as ever; and, of course no one contradicted him.

Five years passed, and then a real grief came upon the land. The Chinese really were fond of their Emperor, and he now lay so ill that he was not expected to live. Already a new Emperor had been chosen and the people who stood in the street asked the lord-in-waiting how the old Emperor was; but he only said, "Pooh!" and shook his head.

Cold and pale lay the Emperor in his royal bed; the whole court thought he was dead, and every one ran away to pay homage to his successor. The chamberlains went out to have a talk on the matter, and the ladies' maids invited company to take coffee. Cloth had been laid down on the halls and passages, so that not a footstep should be heard, and all was silent and still. But the Emperor was not yet dead, although he lay white and stiff on his gorgeous bed, with the long velvet curtains and heavy gold tassels. A window stood open, and the moon shone in upon the Emperor and the artificial bird. The poor Emperor, finding he could scarcely breathe with a strange weight on his chest, opened his eyes, and saw Death sitting there. He had put on the Emperor's golden crown, and held in one hand his sword of state, and in the other his beautiful banner. All around the bed and peeping through the long velvet curtains, were a number of strange heads, some very ugly, and others lovely and gentle-looking. These were the Emperor's good and bad deeds, which stared him in the face now Death sat at his heart.

"Do you remember this?" "Do you recollect that?" they asked one after another, thus bringing to his remembrance circumstances that made the perspiration stand on his brow.

"I know nothing about it," said the Emperor. "Music! music!" he cried; "the large Chinese drum! that I may not hear what they say." But they still went on, and Death nodded like a Chinaman to all they said. "Music! music!" shouted the Emperor. "You little precious golden bird, sing, pray sing! I have given you gold and costly presents; I have even hung my golden slipper round your neck. Sing! sing!" But the bird remained silent. There was no one to wind it up, and therefore it could not sing a note.

Death continued to stare at the emperor with his cold, hollow eyes, and the room was fearfully still. Suddenly there came through the open window the sound of sweet music. Outside, on the bough of a tree, sat the living Nightingale. She had heard of the Emperor's illness, and was therefore come to sing to him of hope and trust. And as she sung, the shadows grew paler and paler; the blood in the Emperor's veins flowed more rapidly, and gave life to his weak limbs; and even Death himself listened, and said, "Go on, little Nightingale, go on."

"Then will you give me the beautiful golden sword and that rich banner? and will you give me the Emperor's crown?" said the bird.

So Death gave up each of these treasures for a song; and the Nightingale continued her singing. She sung of the quiet churchyard, where the white roses grow, where the elder-tree wafts its perfume on the breeze, and the fresh, sweet grass is moistened by the mourners' tears. Then Death longed to go and see his garden, and floated out through the window in the form of a cold, white mist.

"Thanks, thanks, you heavenly little bird. I know you well. I banished you from my kingdom once, and yet you have charmed away the evil faces from my bed, and banished Death from my heart, with your sweet song. How can I reward you?"

"You have already rewarded me," said the Nightingale. "I shall never forget that I drew tears from your eyes the first time I sang to you. These are the jewels that rejoice a singer's heart. But now sleep, and grow strong and well again. I will sing to you again."

And as she sung, the Emperor fell into a sweet sleep; and how mild and refreshing that slumber was! When he awoke, strengthened and restored, the sun shone brightly through the window; but not one of his servants had returned—they all believed he was dead; only the Nightingale still sat beside him, and sang.

"You must always remain with me," said the Emperor. "You shall sing only when it pleases you; and I will break the artificial bird into a thousand pieces."

"No; do not do that," replied the Nightingale; "the bird did very well as long as it could. Keep it here still. I cannot live in the palace, and build my nest; but let me come when I like. I will sit on a bough outside your window, in the evening, and sing to you, so that you may be happy, and have thoughts full of joy. I will sing to you of those who are happy, and those who suffer; of the good and the evil, who are hidden around you. The little singing bird flies far from you and your court to the home of the fisherman and the peasant's cot. I love your heart better than your crown; and yet something holy lingers round that also. I will come, I will sing to you; but you must promise me one thing."

"Everything," said the Emperor, who, having dressed himself in his imperial robes, stood with the hand that held the heavy golden sword pressed to his heart.

"I only ask one thing," she replied; "let no one know that you have a little bird who tells you everything. It will be best to conceal it." So saying, the Nightingale flew away.

The servants now came in to look after the dead Emperor; when, lo! there he stood, and, to their astonishment, said, "Good morning."

The Top and Ball

Translated by Mrs. H. P. Paull

A whipping top and a little ball lay together in a box, among other toys, and the top said to the ball, "Shall we be married, as we live in the same box?"
But the ball, which wore a dress of morocco leather, and thought as much of herself as any other young lady, would not even condescend to reply.

The next day came the little boy to whom the playthings belonged, and he painted the top red and yellow, and drove a brass-headed nail into the middle, so that while the top was spinning round it looked splendid.

"Look at me," said the top to the ball. "What do you say now? Shall we be engaged to each other? We should suit so well; you spring, and I dance. No one could be happier than we should be."

"Indeed! do you think so? Perhaps you do not know that my father and mother were morocco slippers, and that I have a Spanish cork in my body."

"Yes; but I am made of mahogany," said the top. "The major himself turned me. He has a turning lathe of his own, and it is a great amusement to him."

"Can I believe it?" asked the ball.

"May I never be whipped again," said the top, "if I am not telling you the truth."

"You certainly know how to speak for yourself very well," said the ball; "but I cannot accept your proposal. I am almost engaged to a swallow. Every time I fly up in the air, he puts his head out of the nest, and says, 'Will you?' and I have said, 'Yes,' to myself silently, and that is as good as being half engaged; but I will promise never to forget you."

"Much good that will be to me," said the top; and they spoke to each other no more.

Next day the ball was taken out by the boy. The top saw it flying high in the air, like a bird, till it would go quite out of sight. Each time it came back, as it touched the earth, it gave a higher leap than before, either because it longed to fly upwards, or from having a Spanish cork in its body. But the ninth time it rose in the air, it remained away, and did not return. The boy searched everywhere for it, but he searched in vain, for it could not be found; it was gone.

"I know very well where she is," sighed the top; "she is in the swallow's nest, and has married the swallow."

The more the top thought of this, the more he longed for the ball. His love increased the more, just because he could not get her; and that she should have been won by another, was the worst of all. The top still twirled about and hummed, but he continued to think of the ball; and the more he thought of her, the more beautiful she seemed to his fancy.

Thus several years passed by, and his love became quite old. The top, also, was no longer young; but there came a day when he looked handsomer than ever; for he was gilded all over. He was now a golden top, and whirled and danced about till he hummed quite loud, and was something worth looking at; but one day he leaped too high, and then he, also, was gone. They searched everywhere, even in the cellar, but he was nowhere to be found. Where could he be? He had jumped into the dustbin, where all sorts of rubbish were lying: cabbage-stalks, dust, and rain-droppings that had fallen down from the gutter under the roof.

"Now I am in a nice place," said he; "my gilding will soon be washed off here. Oh dear, what a set of rabble I have got amongst!" And then he glanced at a curious round thing like an old apple, which lay near a long, leafless cabbage-stalk. It was, however, not an apple, but an old ball, which had lain for years in the gutter, and was soaked through with water.

"Thank goodness, here comes one of my own class, with whom I can talk," said the ball, examining the gilded top. "I am made of morocco," she said. "I was sewn together by a young lady, and I have a Spanish cork in my body; but no one would think it, to look at me now. I was once engaged to a swallow; but I fell in here from the gutter under the roof, and I have lain here more than five years, and have been thoroughly drenched. Believe me, it is a long time for a young maiden."

The top said nothing, but he thought of his old love; and the more she said, the more clear it became to him that this was the same ball.

The servant then came to clean out the dustbin.

"Ah," she exclaimed, "here is a gilt top." So the top was brought again to notice and honor, but nothing more was heard of the little ball. He spoke not a word about his old love; for that soon died away. When the beloved object has lain for five years in a gutter, and has been drenched through, no one cares to know her again on meeting her in a dustbin.

The Ugly Duckling

Translated by Mrs. H. P. Paull

It was lovely summer weather in the country, and the golden corn, the green oats, and the haystacks piled up in the meadows looked beautiful. The stork walking about on his long red legs chattered in the Egyptian language, which he had learnt from his mother. The corn-fields and meadows were surrounded by large forests, in the midst of which were deep pools. It was, indeed, delightful to walk about in the country. In a sunny spot stood a pleasant old farm-house close by a deep river, and from the house down to the water side grew great burdock leaves, so high, that under the tallest of them a little child could stand upright. The spot was as wild as the centre of a thick wood. In this snug retreat sat a duck on her nest, watching for her young brood to hatch; she was beginning to get tired of her task, for the little ones were a long time coming out of their shells, and she seldom had any visitors. The other Ducks liked much better to swim about in the river than to climb the slippery banks, and sit under a burdock leaf, to have a gossip with her.

At length one shell cracked, and then another, and from each egg came a living creature that lifted its head and cried, "Peep, peep."

"Quack, quack," said the mother, and then they all quacked as well as they could, and looked about them on every side at the large green leaves. Their mother allowed them to look as much as they liked, because green is good for the eyes.

"How large the world is," said the young Ducks, when they found how much more room they now had than while they were inside the egg-shell.

"Do you imagine this is the whole world?" asked the mother; "Wait till you have seen the garden; it stretches far beyond that to the parson's field, but I have never ventured to such a distance. Are you all out?" she continued, rising; "No, I declare, the largest egg lies there still. I wonder how long this is to last, I am quite tired of it;" and she seated herself again on the nest.

"Well, how are you getting on?" asked an old duck, who paid her a visit.

"One egg is not hatched yet," said the Duck, "it will not break. But just look at all the others, are they not the prettiest little ducklings you ever saw? They are the image of their father, who is so unkind, he never comes to see."

"Let me see the egg that will not break," said the Duck; "I have no doubt it is a turkey's egg. I was persuaded to hatch some once, and after all my care and trouble with the young ones, they were afraid of the water. I quacked and clucked, but all to no purpose. I could not get them to venture in. Let me look at the egg. Yes, that is a turkey's egg; take my advice, leave it where it is and teach the other children to swim."

"I think I will sit on it a little while longer," said the Duck; "as I have sat so long already, a few days will be nothing."

"Please yourself," said the old duck, and she went away.

At last the large egg broke, and a young one crept forth crying, "Peep, peep." It was very large and ugly. The Duck stared at it and exclaimed, "It is very large and not at all like the others. I wonder if it really is a turkey. We shall soon find it out, however when we go to the water. It must go in, if I have to push it myself."

On the next day the weather was delightful, and the sun shone brightly on the green burdock leaves, so the Mother Duck took

The Ugly Duckling

her young brood down to the water, and jumped in with a splash. "Quack, quack," cried she, and one after another the little ducklings jumped in. The water closed over their heads, but they came up again in an instant, and swam about quite prettily with their legs paddling under them as easily as possible, and the ugly Duckling was also in the water swimming with them.

"Oh," said the mother, "that is not a turkey; how well he uses his legs, and how upright he holds himself! He is my own child, and he is not so very ugly after all if you look at him properly. Quack, quack! come with me now, I will take you into grand society, and introduce you to the farmyard, but you must keep close to me or you may be trodden upon; and, above all, beware of the cat."

When they reached the farmyard, there was a great disturbance, two families were fighting for an eel's head, which, after all, was carried off by the cat.

"See, children, that is the way of the world," said the Mother Duck, whetting her beak, for she would have liked the eel's head herself. "Come, now, use your legs, and let me see how well you can behave. You must bow your heads prettily to that old Duck yonder; she is the highest born of them all, and has Spanish blood, therefore, she is well off. Don't you see she has a red flag tied to her leg, which is something very grand, and a great honour for a duck; it shows that every one is anxious not to lose her, as she can be recognized both by man and beast. Come, now, don't turn your toes, a well-bred duckling spreads his feet wide apart, just like his father and mother, in this way; now bend your neck, and say 'Quack.'"

The Ducklings did as they were bid, but the other duck stared, and said, "Look, here comes another brood, as if there were not enough of us already! and what a queer looking object one of them is; we don't want him here," and then one flew out and bit him in the neck.

"Let him alone," said the mother; "he is not doing any harm."

"Yes, but he is so big and ugly," said the spiteful Duck "and therefore he must be turned out."

"The others are very pretty children," said the old Duck, with the rag on her leg, "all but that one; I wish his mother could improve him a little."

"That is impossible, your grace," replied the mother; "he is not pretty; but he has a very good disposition, and swims as well or even better than the others. I think he will grow up pretty, and perhaps be smaller; he has remained too long in the egg, and therefore his figure is not properly formed;" and then she stroked his neck and smoothed the feathers, saying, "It is a drake, and therefore not of so much consequence. I think he will grow up strong, and able to take care of himself."

"The other ducklings are graceful enough," said the old Duck. "Now make yourself at home, and if you can find an eel's head, you can bring it to me."

And so they made themselves comfortable.

But the poor Duckling, who had crept out of his shell last of all, and looked so ugly, was bitten and pushed and made fun of, not only by the ducks, but by all the poultry. "He is too big," they all said, and the turkey cock, who had been born into the world with spurs, and fancied himself really an emperor, puffed himself out like a vessel in full sail, and flew at the Duckling, and became quite red in the head with passion, so that the poor little thing did not know where to go, and was quite miserable because he was so ugly and laughed at by the whole farmyard.

So it went on from day to day till it got worse and worse. The poor Duckling was driven about by every one; even his brothers and sisters were unkind to him, and would say, "Ah, you ugly creature, I wish the cat would get you," and his mother said she wished he had never been born. The Ducks pecked him, the chickens beat him, and the girl who fed the poultry kicked him with her feet.

So at last he ran away, frightening the little birds in the hedge as he flew over the palings. "They are afraid of me because I am ugly," he said. So he closed his eyes, and flew still farther, until he came out on a large moor, inhabited by Wild Ducks. Here he remained the whole night, feeling very tired and sorrowful.

In the morning, when the Wild Ducks rose in the air, they stared at their new comrade. "What sort of a Duck are you?" they all said, coming round him. He bowed to them, and was as polite as he could be, but he did not reply to their question.

"You are exceedingly ugly," said the wild ducks, "but that will not matter if you do not want to marry one of our family." Poor thing! he had no thoughts of marriage; all he wanted was permission to lie among the rushes, and drink some of the water on the moor.

After he had been on the moor two days, there came two wild geese, or rather goslings, for they had not been out of the egg long, and were very saucy.

"Listen, friend," said one of them to the duckling, "you are so ugly, that we like you very well. Will you go with us, and become a bird of passage? Not far from here is another moor, in which there are some pretty wild geese, all unmarried. It is a chance for you to get a wife; you may be lucky, ugly as you are."

"Pop, pop," sounded in the air, and the two wild geese fell dead among the rushes, and the water was tinged with blood. "Pop, pop," echoed far and wide in the distance, and whole flocks of wild geese rose up from the rushes. The sound continued from every direction, for the sportsmen surrounded the moor, and some were even seated on branches of trees, overlooking the rushes. The blue smoke from the guns rose like clouds over the dark trees, and as it floated away across the water, a number of sporting dogs bounded in among the rushes, which bent beneath them wherever they went. How they terrified the poor Duckling! He turned away his head to hide it under his wing, and at the same moment a large terrible dog passed quite near him. His jaws were open, his tongue hung from his mouth, and his eyes glared fearfully. He thrust his nose close to the Duckling, showing his sharp teeth, and then, "splash, splash," he went into the water without touching him.

"Oh," sighed the Duckling, "how thankful I am for being so ugly; even a dog will not bite me."

And so he lay quite still, while the shot rattled through the rushes, and gun after gun was fired over him.

It was late in the day before all became quiet, but even then the poor young thing did not dare to move. He waited quietly for several hours, and then, after looking carefully around him, hastened away from the moor as fast as he could. He ran over field and meadow till a storm arose, and he could hardly struggle against it.

Towards evening, he reached a poor little cottage that seemed ready to fall, and only remained standing because it could not decide on which side to fall first. The storm continued so violent, that the Duckling could go no farther; he sat down by the cottage, and then he noticed that the door was not quite closed in consequence of one of the hinges having given way. There was therefore a narrow opening near the bottom large enough for him to slip through, which he did very quietly, and got a shelter for the night.

A woman, a Tom Cat, and a Hen lived in this cottage. The Tom Cat, whom the mistress called, *"My little son,"* was a great favourite; he could raise his back, and purr, and could even throw out sparks from his fur if it were stroked the wrong way. The Hen had very short legs, so she was called *"Chickie short legs."* She laid good eggs, and her mistress loved her as if she had been her own child.

In the morning, the strange visitor was discovered, and the tom cat began to purr, and the hen to cluck.

"What is that noise about?" said the old woman, looking round the room, but her sight was not very good; therefore, when she saw the Duckling she thought it must be a fat duck, that had strayed from home. "Oh what a prize!" she exclaimed, "I hope it is not a drake, for then I shall have some Duck's eggs. I must wait and see."

So the Duckling was allowed to remain on trial for three weeks, but there were no eggs. Now the Tom Cat was the master of the house, and the hen was mistress, and they always said, "We and the world," for they believed themselves to be half the world, and the better half too. The Duckling thought that others might hold a different opinion on the subject, but the hen would not listen to such doubts.

"Can you lay eggs?" she asked.

"No."

"Then have the goodness to hold your tongue."

"Can you raise your back, or purr, or throw out sparks?" said the Tom Cat.

"No."

"Then you have no right to express an opinion when sensible people are speaking."

So the Duckling sat in a corner, feeling very low spirited, till the sunshine and the fresh air came into the room through the open door, and then he began to feel such a great longing for a swim on the water, that he could not help telling the Hen.

"What an absurd idea," said the Hen. "You have nothing else to do, therefore you have foolish fancies. If you could purr or lay eggs, they would pass away."

"But it is so delightful to swim about on the water," said the Duckling, "and so refreshing to feel it close over your head, while you dive down to the bottom."

"Delightful, indeed!" said the Hen, "why you must be crazy! Ask the Cat, he is the cleverest animal I know, ask him how he would like to swim about on the water, or to dive under it, for I will not speak of my own opinion; ask our mistress, the old woman—there is no one in the world more clever than she is. Do you think she would like to swim, or to let the water close over her head?"

"You don't understand me," said the Duckling.

"We don't understand you? Who can understand you, I wonder? Do you consider yourself more clever than the Cat, or the old woman? I will say nothing of myself. Don't imagine such nonsense, child, and thank your good fortune that you have been received here. Are you not in a warm room, and in society from which you may learn something. But you are a chatterer, and your company is not very agreeable. Believe me, I speak only for your own good. I may tell you unpleasant truths, but that is a proof of my friendship. I advise you, therefore, to lay eggs, and learn to purr as quickly as possible."

"I believe I must go out into the world again," said the Duckling.

"Yes, do," said the hen.

So the Duckling left the cottage, and soon found water on which it could swim and dive, but was avoided by all other animals, because of its ugly appearance.

Autumn came, and the leaves in the forest turned to orange and gold. Then, as winter approached, the wind caught them as they fell and whirled them in the cold air. The clouds, heavy with hail and snowflakes, hung low in the sky, and the raven stood on the ferns crying, "Croak, croak." It made one shiver with cold to look at him. All this was very sad for the poor little Duckling.

One evening, just as the sun set amid radiant clouds, there came a large flock of beautiful birds out of the bushes. The Duckling had never seen any like them before. They were swans, and they curved their graceful necks, while their soft plumage shown with dazzling whiteness. They uttered a singular cry, as they spread their glorious wings and flew away from those cold regions to warmer countries across the sea. As they mounted higher and higher in the air, the ugly little Duckling felt quite a strange sensation as he watched them. He whirled himself in the water like a wheel, stretched out his neck towards them, and uttered a cry so strange that it frightened himself. Could he ever forget those beautiful, happy birds; and when at last they were out of his sight, he dived under the water, and rose again almost beside himself with excitement. He knew not the names of these birds, nor where they had flown, but he felt towards them as he had never felt for any other bird in the world. He was not envious of these beautiful creatures, but wished to be as lovely as they. Poor ugly creature, how gladly he would have lived even with the Ducks had they only given him encouragement.

The winter grew colder and colder; he was obliged to swim about on the water to keep it from freezing, but every night the space on which he swam became smaller and smaller. At length it froze so hard that the ice in the water crackled as he moved, and the Duckling had to paddle with his legs as well as he could, to keep the space from closing up. He became exhausted at last, and lay still and helpless, frozen fast in the ice.

Early in the morning, a peasant, who was passing by, saw what had happened. He broke the ice in pieces with his wooden shoe, and carried the Duckling home to his wife. The warmth revived the poor little creature.

But when the children wanted to play with him, the Duckling thought they would do him some harm; so he started up in terror, fluttered into the milk-pan, and splashed the milk about the room. Then the woman clapped her hands, which frightened him still more. He flew first into the butter-cask, then into the meal-tub, and out again. What a condition he was in! The woman screamed, and struck at him with the tongs; the children laughed and screamed, and tumbled over each other, in their efforts to catch him; but luckily he escaped. The door stood open; the poor creature could just manage to slip out among the bushes, and lie down quite exhausted in the newly fallen snow.

It would be very sad, were I to relate all the misery and privations which the poor little Duckling endured during the hard winter; but when it had passed, he found himself lying one morning in a moor, amongst the rushes. He felt the warm sun shining, and heard the lark singing, and saw that all around was beautiful spring.

Then the young bird felt that his wings were strong, as he flapped them against his sides, and rose high into the air. They bore him onwards, until he found himself in a large garden, before he well knew how it had happened. The apple-trees were in full blossom, and the fragrant elders bent their long green branches down to the stream which wound round a smooth lawn. Everything looked beautiful, in the freshness of early spring. From a thicket close by came three beautiful white swans, rustling their feathers, and swimming lightly over the smooth water. The Duckling remembered the lovely birds, and felt more strangely unhappy than ever.

"I will fly to those royal birds," he exclaimed, "and they will kill me, because I am so ugly, and dare to approach them; but it does not matter: better be killed by *them* than pecked by the ducks, beaten by the hens, pushed about by the maiden who feeds the poultry, or starved with hunger in the winter." Then he flew to the water, and swam towards the beautiful swans. The moment they espied the stranger, they rushed to meet him with outstretched wings. "Kill me," said the poor bird; and he bent his head down to the surface of the water, and awaited death. But what did he see in the clear stream below? His own image; no longer a dark, gray bird, ugly and disagreeable to look at, but a graceful and beautiful swan.

To be born in a Duck's nest, in a farmyard, is of no consequence to a bird, if it is hatched from a swan's egg.

He now felt glad at having suffered sorrow and trouble, because it enabled him to enjoy so much better all the pleasure and happiness around him; for the great swans swam round the new-comer, and stroked his neck with their beaks, as a welcome.

Into the garden presently came some little children, and threw bread and cake into the water.

"See," cried the youngest, "there is a new one;" and the rest were delighted, and ran to their father and mother, dancing and clapping their hands, and shouting joyously, "There is another swan come; a new one has arrived." Then they threw more bread and cake into the water, and said, "The new one is the most beautiful of all; he is so young and pretty." And the old swans bowed their heads before him.

Then he felt quite ashamed, and hid his head under his wing; for he did not know what to do, he was so happy, and yet not at all proud. He had been persecuted and despised for his ugliness, and now he heard them say he was the most beautiful of all the birds. Even the elder-tree bent down its bows into the water before him, and the sun shone warm and bright. Then he rustled his feathers, curved his slender neck, and cried joyfully, from the depths of his heart, "I never dreamed of such happiness as this, while I was an ugly Duckling."

The Fir Tree

Translated by Mrs. H. P. Paull

Far down in the forest, where the warm sun and the fresh air made a sweet resting-place, grew a pretty little Fir Tree; and yet it was not happy, it wished so much to be tall like its companions—the pines and firs which grew around it. The sun shone, and the soft air fluttered its leaves, and the little peasant children passed by, prattling merrily, but the Fir Tree heeded them not. Sometimes the children would bring a large basket of raspberries or strawberries, wreathed on a straw, and seat themselves near the Fir Tree, and say, "Is it not a pretty little tree?" which made it feel more unhappy than before. And yet all this while the tree grew a notch or joint taller every year; for by the number of joints in the stem of a Fir Tree we can discover its age. Still, as it grew, it complained, "Oh! how I wish I were as tall as the other trees, then I would spread out my branches on every side, and my top would overlook the wide world. I should have the birds building their nests on my boughs, and when the wind blew, I should bow with stately dignity like my tall companions." The tree was so discontented, that it took no pleasure in the warm sunshine, the birds, or the rosy clouds that floated over it morning and evening. Sometimes, in winter, when the snow lay white and glittering on the ground, a hare would come springing along, and jump right over the little tree; and then how mortified it would feel! Two winters passed, and when the third arrived, the tree had grown so tall that the hare was obliged to run round it. Yet it remained unsatisfied, and would exclaim, "Oh, if I could but keep on growing tall and old! There is nothing else worth caring for in the world!" In the autumn, as usual, the woodcutters came and cut down several of the tallest trees, and the young Fir Tree, which was now grown to its full height, shuddered as the noble trees fell to the earth with a crash. After the branches were lopped off, the trunks looked so slender and bare, that they could scarcely be recognized. Then they were placed upon wagons, and drawn by horses out of the forest. "Where were they going? What would become of them?" The young Fir Tree wished very much to know; so in the spring, when the swallows and the storks came, it asked, "Do you know where those trees were taken? Did you meet them?"

The swallows knew nothing, but the stork, after a little reflection, nodded his head, and said, "Yes, I think I do. I met several new ships when I flew from Egypt, and they had fine masts that smelt like fir. I think these must have been the trees; I assure you they were stately, very stately."

"Oh, how I wish I were tall enough to go on the sea," said the Fir Tree. "What is the sea, and what does it look like?"

"It would take too much time to explain," said the stork, flying quickly away.

"Rejoice in thy youth," said the sunbeam; "rejoice in thy fresh growth, and the young life that is in thee."

And the wind kissed the tree, and the dew watered it with tears; but the Fir Tree regarded them not.

Christmas-time drew near, and many young trees were cut down, some even smaller and younger than the Fir Tree who enjoyed neither rest nor peace with longing to leave its forest home. These young trees, which were chosen for their beauty, kept their branches, and were also laid on wagons and drawn by horses out of the forest.

"Where are they going?" asked the Fir Tree. "They are not taller than I am: indeed, one is much less; and why are the branches not cut off? Where are they going?"

"We know, we know," sang the sparrows; "we have looked in at the windows of the houses in the town, and we know what is done with them. They are dressed up in the most splendid manner. We have seen them standing in the middle of a warm room, and adorned with all sorts of beautiful things—honey cakes, gilded apples, playthings, and many hundreds of wax tapers."

"And then," asked the Fir Tree, trembling through all its branches, "and then what happens?"

"We did not see any more," said the sparrows; "but this was enough for us."

"I wonder whether anything so brilliant will ever happen to me," thought the Fir Tree. "It would be much better than crossing the sea. I long for it almost with pain. Oh! when will Christmas be here? I am now as tall and well grown as those which were taken away last year. Oh! that I were now laid on the wagon, or standing in the warm room, with all that brightness and splendor around me! Something better and more beautiful is to come after, or the trees would not be so decked out. Yes, what follows will be grander and more splendid. What can it be? I am weary with longing. I scarcely know how I feel."

"Rejoice with us," said the air and the sunlight. "Enjoy thine own bright life in the fresh air."

But the tree would not rejoice, though it grew taller every day; and, winter and summer, its dark-green foliage might be seen in the forest, while passers by would say, "What a beautiful tree!"

A short time before Christmas, the discontented Fir Tree was the first to fall. As the axe cut through the stem, and divided the pith, the tree fell with a groan to the earth, conscious of pain and faintness, and forgetting all its anticipations of happiness, in sorrow at leaving its home in the forest. It knew that it should never again see its dear old companions, the trees, nor the little bushes and many-coloured flowers that had grown by its side; perhaps not even the birds. Neither was the journey at all pleasant. The tree first recovered itself while being unpacked in the courtyard of a house, with several other trees; and it heard a man say, "We only want one, and this is the prettiest."

Then came two servants in grand livery, and carried the Fir Tree into a large and beautiful apartment. On the walls hung pictures, and near the great stove stood great china vases, with lions on the lids. There were rocking chairs, silken sofas, large tables, covered with pictures, books, and playthings, worth a great deal of money—at least, the children said so. Then the Fir Tree was placed in a large tub, full of sand; but green baize hung all around it, so that no one could see it was a tub, and it stood on a very handsome carpet. How the Fir Tree trembled! "What was going to happen to him now?" Some young ladies came, and the servants helped them to adorn the tree. On one branch they hung little bags cut out of coloured paper, and each bag was filled with sweetmeats; from other branches hung gilded apples and walnuts, as if they had grown there; and above, and all round, were hundreds of red, blue, and white tapers, which were fastened on the branches. Dolls, exactly like real babies, were placed under the green leaves—the tree had never seen such things before—and at the very top was fastened a glittering star, made of tinsel. Oh, it was very beautiful!

"This evening," they all exclaimed, "how bright it will be!" "Oh, that the evening were come," thought the tree, "and the tapers lighted! then I shall know what else is going to happen. Will the trees of the forest come to see me? I wonder if the sparrows will peep in at the windows as they fly? shall I grow faster here, and keep on all these ornaments summer and winter?" But guessing was of very little use; it made his bark ache, and this pain is as bad for a slender Fir Tree, as headache is for us. At last the tapers were lighted, and then what a glistening blaze of light the tree presented! It trembled so with joy in all its branches, that one of the candles fell among the green leaves and burnt some of them. "Help! help!" exclaimed the young ladies, but there was no danger, for they quickly extinguished the fire. After this, the tree tried not to tremble at all, though the fire frightened him; he was so anxious not to hurt any of the beautiful ornaments, even while their brilliancy dazzled him. And now the folding doors were thrown open, and a troop of children rushed in as if they intended to upset the tree; they were followed more silently by their elders. For a moment the little ones stood silent with astonishment, and then they shouted for joy, till the room rang, and they danced merrily round the tree, while one present after another was taken from it.

"What are they doing? What will happen next?" thought the fir. At last the candles burnt down to the branches and were put out. Then the children received permission to plunder the tree.

Oh, how they rushed upon it, till the branches cracked, and had it not been fastened with the glistening star to the ceiling, it must have been thrown down. The children then danced about with their pretty toys, and no one noticed the tree, except the children's maid who came and peeped among the branches to see if an apple or a fig had been forgotten.

"A story, a story," cried the children, pulling a little fat man towards the tree.

"Now we shall be in the green shade," said the man, as he seated himself under it, "and the tree will have the pleasure of hearing also, but I shall only relate one story; what shall it be? Ivede-Avede, or Humpty Dumpty, who fell down stairs, but soon got up again, and at last married a princess."

"Ivede-Avede," cried some. "Humpty Dumpty," cried others, and there was a fine shouting and crying out. But the Fir Tree remained quite still, and thought to himself, "Shall I have anything to do with all this?" but he had already amused them as much as they wished. Then the old man told them the story of Humpty Dumpty, how he fell down stairs, and was raised up again, and married a princess. And the children clapped their hands and cried, "Tell another, tell another," for they wanted to hear the story of "Ivede-Avede;" but they only had "Humpty Dumpty." After this the Fir Tree became quite silent and thoughtful; never had the birds in the forest told such tales as "Humpty Dumpty," who fell down stairs, and yet married a princess.

"Ah! yes, so it happens in the world," thought the Fir Tree; he believed it all, because it was related by such a nice man. "Ah! well," he thought, "who knows? perhaps I may fall down too, and marry a princess;" and he looked forward joyfully to the next evening, expecting to be again decked out with lights and playthings, gold and fruit. "Tomorrow I will not tremble," thought he; "I will enjoy all my splendor, and I shall hear the story of Humpty Dumpty again, and perhaps Ivede-Avede." And the tree remained quiet and thoughtful all night. In the morning the servants and the housemaid came in. "Now," thought the fir, "all my splendor is going to begin again." But they dragged him out of the room and up stairs to the garret, and threw him on the floor, in a dark corner, where no daylight shone, and there they left him. "What does this mean?" thought the tree, "what am I to do here? I can hear nothing in a place like this," and he had time enough to think, for days and nights passed and no one came near him, and when at last somebody did come, it was only to put away large boxes in a corner. So the tree was completely hidden from sight as if it had never existed. "It is winter now," thought the tree, "the ground is hard and covered with snow, so that people cannot plant me. I shall be sheltered here, I dare say, until spring comes. How thoughtful and kind everybody is to me! Still I wish this place were not so dark, as well as lonely, with not even a little hare to look at. How pleasant it was out in the forest while the snow lay on the ground, when the hare would run by, yes, and jump over me too, although I did not like it then. Oh! it is terrible lonely here."

"Squeak, squeak," said a little mouse, creeping cautiously towards the tree; then came another; and they both sniffed at the Fir Tree and crept between the branches.

"Oh, it is very cold," said the little mouse, "or else we should be so comfortable here, shouldn't we, you old Fir Tree?"

"I am not old," said the Fir Tree, "there are many who are older than I am."

"Where do you come from? and what do you know?" asked the mice, who were full of curiosity. "Have you seen the most beautiful places in the world, and can you tell us all about them? and have you been in the storeroom, where cheeses lie on the shelf, and hams hang from the ceiling? One can run about on tallow candles there, and go in thin and come out fat."

"I know nothing of that place," said the Fir Tree, "but I know the wood where the sun shines and the birds sing." And then the tree told the little mice all about its youth. They had never heard such an account in their lives; and after they had listened to it attentively, they said, "What a number of things you have seen? you must have been very happy."

"Happy!" exclaimed the Fir Tree, and then as he reflected upon what he had been telling them, he said, "Ah, yes! after all those were happy days." But when he went on and related all about Christmas-eve, and how he had been dressed up with cakes and lights, the mice said, "How happy you must have been, you old Fir Tree."

"I am not old at all," replied the tree, "I only came from the forest this winter, I am now checked in my growth."

"What splendid stories you can relate," said the little mice. And the next night four other mice came with them to hear what the tree had to tell. The more he talked the more he remembered, and then he thought to himself, "Those were happy days, but they may come again. Humpty Dumpty fell down stairs, and yet he married the princess; perhaps I may marry a princess too." And the Fir Tree thought of the pretty little birch-tree that grew in the forest, which was to him a real beautiful princess.

"Who is Humpty Dumpty?" asked the little mice. And then the tree related the whole story; he could remember every single word, and the little mice was so delighted with it, that they were ready to jump to the top of the tree. The next night a great many more mice made their appearance, and on Sunday two rats came with them; but they said, it was not a pretty story at all, and the little mice were very sorry, for it made them also think less of it.

"Do you know only one story?" asked the rats.

"Only one," replied the Fir Tree; "I heard it on the happiest evening of my life; but I did not know I was so happy at the time."

"We think it is a very miserable story," said the rats. "Don't you know any story about bacon, or tallow in the storeroom."

"No," replied the tree.

"Many thanks to you then," replied the rats, and they marched off.

The little mice also kept away after this, and the tree sighed, and said, "It was very pleasant when the merry little mice sat round me and listened while I talked. Now that is all passed too. However, I shall consider myself happy when some one comes to take me out of this place." But would this ever happen? Yes; one morning people came to clear out the garret, the boxes were packed away, and the tree was pulled out of the corner, and thrown roughly on the garret floor; then the servant dragged it out upon the staircase where the daylight shone. "Now life is beginning again," said the tree, rejoicing in the sunshine and fresh air. Then it was carried down stairs and taken into the courtyard so quickly, that it forgot to think of itself, and could only look about, there was so much to be seen. The court was close to a garden, where everything looked blooming. Fresh and fragrant roses hung over the little palings. The linden-trees were in blossom; while the swallows flew here and there, crying, "Twit, twit, twit, my mate is coming,"—but it was not the Fir Tree they meant. "Now I shall live," cried the tree, joyfully spreading out its branches; but alas! they were all withered and yellow, and it lay in a corner amongst weeds and nettles. The star of gold paper still stuck in the top of the tree and glittered in the sunshine. In the same courtyard two of the merry children were playing who had danced round the tree at Christmas, and had been so happy. The youngest saw the gilded star, and ran and pulled it off the tree. "Look what is sticking to the ugly old Fir Tree," said the child, treading on the branches till they crackled under his boots. And the tree saw all the fresh bright flowers in the garden, and then looked at itself, and wished it had remained in the dark corner of the garret. It thought of its fresh youth in the forest, of the merry Christmas evening, and of the little mice who had listened to the story of "Humpty Dumpty." "Past! past!" said the old tree; "Oh, had I but enjoyed myself while I could have done so! but now it is too late." Then a lad came and chopped the tree into small pieces, till a large bundle lay in a heap on the ground. The pieces were placed in a fire under the copper, and they quickly blazed up brightly, while the tree sighed so deeply that each sigh was like a pistol-shot. Then the children, who were at play, came and seated themselves in front of the fire, and looked at it and cried, "Pop, pop." But at each "pop," which was a deep sigh, the tree was thinking of a summer day in the forest; and of Christmas evening, and of "Humpty Dumpty," the only story it had ever heard or knew how to relate, till at last it was consumed. The boys still played in the garden, and the youngest wore the golden star on his breast, with which the tree had been adorned during the happiest evening of its existence. Now all was past; the tree's life was past, and the story also—for all stories must come to an end at last.

The Snow Queen

Translated by Mrs. H. P. Paull

Chapter One

Which describes a looking-glass and the broken fragments. You must attend to the commencement of this story, for when we get to the end we shall know more than we do now about a very wicked hobgoblin; he was one of the very worst, for he was a real demon. One day, when he was in a merry mood, he made a looking-glass which had the power of making everything good or beautiful that was reflected in it almost shrink to nothing, while everything that was worthless and bad looked increased in size and worse than ever. The most lovely landscapes appeared like boiled spinach, and the people became hideous, and looked as if they stood on their heads and had no bodies. Their countenances were so distorted that no one could recognize them, and even one freckle on the face appeared to spread over the whole of the nose and mouth. The demon said this was very amusing. When a good or pious thought passed through the mind of any one it was misrepresented in the glass; and then how the demon laughed at his cunning invention. All who went to the demon's school—for he kept a school—talked everywhere of the wonders they had seen, and declared that people could now, for the first time, see what the world and mankind were really like. They carried the glass about everywhere, till at last there was not a land nor a people who had not been looked at through this distorted mirror. They wanted even to fly with it up to heaven to see the angels, but the higher they flew the more slippery the glass became, and they could scarcely hold it, till at last it slipped from their hands, fell to the earth, and was broken into millions of pieces. But now the looking-glass caused more unhappiness than ever, for some of the fragments were not so large as a grain of sand, and they flew about the world into every country. When one of these tiny atoms flew into a person's eye, it stuck there unknown to him, and from that moment he saw everything through a distorted medium, or could see only the worst side of what he looked at, for even the smallest fragment retained the same power which had belonged to the whole mirror. Some few persons even got a fragment of the looking-glass in their hearts, and this was very terrible, for their hearts became cold like a lump of ice. A few of the pieces were so large that they could be used as window-panes; it would have been a sad thing to look at our friends through them. Other pieces were made into spectacles; this was dreadful for those who wore them, for they could see nothing either rightly or justly. At all this the wicked demon laughed till his sides shook—it tickled him so to see the mischief he had done. There were still a number of these little fragments of glass floating about in the air, and now you shall hear what happened with one of them.

Chapter Two
A Little Boy and a Little Girl

In a large town, full of houses and people, there is not room for everybody to have even a little garden, therefore they are obliged to be satisfied with a few flowers in flowerpots. In one of these large towns lived two poor children who had a garden something larger and better than a few flowerpots. They were not brother and sister, but they loved each other almost as much as if they had been. Their parents lived opposite to each other in two garrets, where the roofs of neighbouring houses projected out towards each other and the water-pipe ran between them. In each house was a little window, so that any one could step across the gutter from one window to the other. The parents of these children had each a large wooden box in which they cultivated kitchen herbs for their own use, and a little rose bush in each box, which grew splendidly. Now after a while the parents decided to place these two boxes across the water-pipe, so that they reached from one window to the other and looked like two banks of flowers. Sweet-peas drooped over the boxes, and the rose bushes shot forth long branches, which were trained round the windows and clustered together almost like a triumphal arch of leaves and flowers. The boxes were very high, and the children knew they must not climb upon them, without permission, but they were often, however, allowed to step out together and sit upon their little stools under the rose bushes, or play quietly. In winter all this pleasure came to an end, for the windows were sometimes quite frozen over. But then they would warm copper pennies on the stove, and hold the warm pennies against the frozen pane; there would be very soon a little round hole through which they could peep, and the soft bright eyes of the little boy and girl would beam through the hole at each window as they looked at each other. Their names were Kay and Gerda. In summer they could be together with one jump from the window, but in winter they had to go up and down the long staircase, and out through the snow before they could meet.

"See there are the white bees swarming," said Kay's old grandmother one day when it was snowing.

"Have they a Queen Bee?" asked the little boy, for he knew that the real bees had a queen.

"To be sure they have," said the grandmother. "She is flying there where the swarm is thickest. She is the largest of them all, and never remains on the earth, but flies up to the dark clouds. Often at midnight she flies through the streets of the town, and looks in at the windows, then the ice freezes on the panes into wonderful shapes, that look like flowers and castles."

"Yes, I have seen them," said both the children, and they knew it must be true.

"Can the Snow Queen come in here?" asked the little girl.

"Only let her come," said the boy, "I'll set her on the stove and then she'll melt."

Then the grandmother smoothed his hair and told him some more tales. One evening, when little Kay was at home, half undressed, he climbed on a chair by the window and peeped out through the little hole. A few flakes of snow were falling, and one of them, rather larger than the rest, alighted on the edge of one of the flower boxes. This snowflake grew larger and larger, till at last it became the figure of a woman, dressed in garments of white gauze, which looked like millions of starry snowflakes linked together. She was fair and beautiful, but made of ice—shining and glittering ice. Still she was alive and her eyes sparkled like bright stars, but there was neither peace nor rest in their glance. She nodded towards the window and waved her hand. The little boy was frightened and sprang from the chair; at the same moment it seemed as if a large bird flew by the window. On the following day there was a clear frost, and very soon came the spring. The sun shone; the young green leaves burst forth; the swallows built their nests; windows were opened, and the children sat once more in the garden on the roof, high above all the other rooms. How beautiful the roses blossomed this summer. The little girl had learnt a hymn in which roses were spoken of, and then she thought of their own roses, and she sang the hymn to the little boy, and he sang too:

> "Roses bloom and cease to be,
> But we shall the Christ-child see."

Then the little ones held each other by the hand, and kissed the roses, and looked at the bright sunshine, and spoke to it as if the Christ-child were there. Those were splendid summer days. How beautiful and fresh it was out among the rose bushes, which seemed as if they would never leave off blooming. One day Kay and Gerda sat looking at a book full of pictures of animals and birds, and then just as the clock in the church tower struck twelve, Kay said, "Oh, something has struck my heart!" and soon after, "There is something in my eye."

The little girl put her arm round his neck, and looked into his eye, but she could see nothing.

"I think it is gone," he said. But it was not gone; it was one of those bits of the looking-glass—that magic mirror, of which we have spoken—the ugly glass which made everything great and good appear small and ugly, while all that was wicked and bad became more visible, and every little fault could be plainly seen. Poor little Kay had also received a small grain in his heart, which very quickly turned to a lump of ice. He felt no more pain, but the glass was there still. "Why do you cry?" said he at last; "it makes you look ugly. There is nothing the matter with me now. Oh, see!" he cried suddenly, "that rose is worm-eaten, and this one is quite crooked. After all they are ugly roses, just like the box in which they stand," and then he kicked the boxes with his foot, and pulled off the two roses.

"Kay, what are you doing?" cried the little girl; and then, when he saw how frightened she was, he tore off another rose, and jumped through his own window away from little Gerda.

When she afterwards brought out the picture book, he said, "It was only fit for babies in long clothes," and when grandmother told any stories, he would interrupt her with "but;" or, when he could manage it, he would get behind her chair, put on a pair of spectacles, and imitate her very cleverly, to make people laugh. By-and-by he began to mimic the speech and gait of persons in the street. All that was peculiar or disagreeable in a person he would imitate directly, and people said, "That boy will be very clever; he has a remarkable genius." But it was the piece of glass in his eye, and the coldness in his heart, that made him act like this. He would even tease little Gerda, who loved him with all her heart. His games, too, were quite different; they were not so childish. One winter's day, when it snowed, he brought out a burning-glass, then he held out the tail of his blue coat, and let the snowflakes fall upon it. "Look in this glass, Gerda," said he; and she saw how every flake of snow was magnified, and looked like a beautiful flower or a glittering star. "Is it not clever?" said Kay, "and much more interesting than looking at real flowers. There is not a single fault in it, and the snowflakes are quite perfect till they begin to melt."

Soon after Kay made his appearance in large thick gloves, and with his sledge at his back. He called up stairs to Gerda, "I've got to leave to go into the great square, where the other boys play and ride." And away he went.

In the great square, the boldest among the boys would often tie their sledges to the country people's carts, and go with them a good way. This was capital. But while they were all amusing themselves, and Kay with them, a great sledge came by; it was painted white, and in it sat some one wrapped in a rough white fur, and wearing a white cap. The sledge drove twice round the square, and Kay fastened his own little sledge to it, so that when it went away, he followed with it. It went faster and faster right through the next street, and then the person who drove turned round and nodded pleasantly to Kay, just as if they were acquainted with each other, but whenever Kay wished to loosen his little sledge the driver nodded again, so Kay sat still, and they drove out through the town gate. Then the snow began to fall so heavily that the little boy could not see a hand's breadth before him, but still they drove on; then he suddenly loosened the cord so that the large sled might go on without him, but it was of no use, his little carriage held fast, and away they went like the wind. Then he called out loudly, but nobody heard him, while the snow beat upon him, and the sledge flew onwards. Every now and then it gave a jump as if it were going over hedges and ditches. The boy was frightened, and tried to say a prayer, but he could remember nothing but the multiplication table.

The snowflakes became larger and larger, till they appeared like great white chickens. All at once they sprang on one side, the great sledge stopped, and the person who had driven it rose up. The fur and the cap, which were made entirely of snow, fell off, and he saw a lady, tall and white, it was the Snow Queen.

"We have driven well," said she, "but why do you tremble? Here, Creep into my warm fur." Then she seated him beside her in the sledge, and as she wrapped the fur round him he felt as if he were sinking into a snow drift.

"Are you still cold," she asked, as she kissed him on the forehead. The kiss was colder than ice; it went quite through to his heart, which was already almost a lump of ice; he felt as if he were going to die, but only for a moment; he soon seemed quite well again, and did not notice the cold around him.

"My sledge! don't forget my sledge," was his first thought, and then he looked and saw that it was bound fast to one of the white chickens, which flew behind him with the sledge at its back. The Snow Queen kissed little Kay again, and by this time he had forgotten little Gerda, his grandmother, and all at home.

"Now you must have no more kisses," she said, "or I should kiss you to death."

Kay looked at her, and saw that she was so beautiful, he could not imagine a more lovely and intelligent face; she did not now seem to be made of ice, as when he had seen her through his window, and she had nodded to him. In his eyes she was perfect, and she did not feel at all afraid. He told her he could do mental arithmetic, as far as fractions, and that he knew the number of square miles and the number of inhabitants in the country. And she always smiled so that he thought he did not know enough yet, and she looked round the vast expanse as she flew higher and higher with him upon a black cloud, while the storm blew and howled as if it were singing old songs. They flew over woods and lakes, over sea and land; below them roared the wild wind; the wolves howled and the snow crackled; over them flew the black screaming crows, and above all shone the moon, clear and bright—and so Kay passed through the long winter's night, and by day he slept at the feet of the Snow Queen.

Chapter Three
The Flower Garden of the Woman Who Could Conjure

But how fared little Gerda during Kay's absence? What had become of him, no one knew, nor could any one give the slightest information, excepting the boys, who said that he had tied his sledge to another very large one, which had driven through the street, and out at the town gate. Nobody knew where it went; many tears were shed for him, and little Gerda wept bitterly for a long time. She said she knew he must be dead; that he was drowned in the river which flowed close by the school. Oh, indeed those long winter days were very dreary. But at last spring came, with warm sunshine. "Kay is dead and gone," said little Gerda.

"I don't believe it," said the Sunshine.

"He is dead and gone," she said to the Sparrows.

"We don't believe it," they replied; and at last little Gerda began to doubt it herself. "I will put on my new red shoes," she said one morning, "those that Kay has never seen, and then I will go down to the river, and ask for him." It was quite early when she kissed her old grandmother, who was still asleep; then she put on her red shoes, and went quite alone out of the town gates toward the river. "Is it true that you have taken my little playmate away from me?" said she to the river. "I will give you my red shoes if you will give him back to me." And it seemed as if the waves nodded to her in a strange manner. Then she took off her red shoes, which she liked better than anything else, and threw them both into the river, but they fell near the bank, and the little waves carried them back to the land, just as if the river would not take from her what she loved best, because they could not give her back little Kay. But she thought the shoes had not been thrown out far enough. Then she crept into a boat that lay among the reeds, and threw the shoes again from the farther end of the boat into the water, but it was not fastened. And her movement sent it gliding away from the land. When she saw this she hastened to reach the end of the boat, but before she could so it was more than a yard from the bank, and drifting away faster than ever. Then little Gerda was very much frightened, and began to cry, but no one heard her except the Sparrows, and they could not carry her to land, but they flew along by the shore, and sang, as if to comfort her, "Here we are! Here we are!" The boat floated with the stream; little Gerda sat quite still with only her stockings on her feet; the red shoes floated after her, but she could not reach them because the boat kept so much in advance. The banks on each side of the river were very pretty. There were beautiful flowers, old trees, sloping fields, in which cows and sheep were grazing, but not a man to be seen. Perhaps the river will carry me to little Kay, thought Gerda, and then she became more cheerful, and raised her head, and looked at the beautiful green banks; and so the boat sailed on for hours. At length she came to a large cherry orchard, in which stood a small red house with strange red and blue windows. It had also a thatched roof, and outside were two wooden soldiers, that presented arms to her as she sailed past. Gerda called out to them, for she thought they were alive, but of course they did not answer; and as the boat drifted nearer to the shore, she saw what they really were. Then Gerda called still louder, and there came a very old woman out of the house, leaning on a crutch. She wore a large hat to shade her from the sun, and on it were painted all sorts of pretty flowers. "You poor little child," said the old woman, "how did you manage to come all this distance into the wide world on such a rapid rolling stream?" And then the old woman walked in the water, seized the boat with her crutch, drew it to land, and lifted Gerda out. And Gerda was glad to feel herself on dry ground, although she was rather afraid of the strange old woman. "Come and tell me who you are," said she, "and how came you here."

Then Gerda told her everything, while the old woman shook her head, and said, "Hem-hem;" and when she had finished, Gerda asked if she had not seen little Kay, and the old woman told her he had not passed by that way, but he very likely would come. So she told Gerda not to be sorrowful, but to taste the cherries and look at the flowers; they were better than any picture book, for each of them could tell a story. Then she took Gerda by the hand and led her into the little house, and the old woman closed the door. The windows were very high, and as the panes were red, blue, and yellow, the daylight shone through them in all sorts of singular colours. On the table stood beautiful cherries, and Gerda had permission to eat as many as she would. While she was eating them the old woman combed out her long flaxen ringlets with a golden comb, and the glossy curls hung down on each side of the little round pleasant face, which looked fresh and blooming as a rose. "I have long been wishing for a dear little maiden like you," said the old woman, "and now you must stay with me, and see how happily we shall live together." And while she went on combing little Gerda's hair, she thought less and less about her adopted brother Kay, for the old woman could conjure, although she was not a wicked witch; she conjured only a little for her own amusement, and now, because she wanted to keep Gerda. Therefore she went into the garden, and stretched out her crutch towards all the rose-trees, beautiful though they were; and they immediately sunk into the dark earth, so that no one could tell where they had once stood. The old woman was afraid that if little Gerda saw roses she would think of those at home, and then remember little Kay, and run away. Then she took Gerda into the flower-garden. How fragrant and beautiful it was! Every flower that could be thought of for every season of the year was here in full bloom; no picture book could have more beautiful colours. Gerda jumped for joy, and played till the sun went down behind the tall cherry-trees; then she slept in an elegant bed with red silk pillows, embroidered with coloured violets; and then she dreamed as pleasantly as a Queen on her wedding day. The next day, and for many days after, Gerda played with the flowers in the warm sunshine. She knew every flower, and yet, although there were so many of them, it seemed as if one were missing, but which it was she could not tell. One day, however, as she sat looking at the old woman's hat with the painted flowers on it, she saw that the prettiest of them all was a rose. The old woman had forgotten to take it from her hat when she made all the roses sink into the earth. But it is difficult to keep the thoughts together in everything; one little mistake upsets all our arrangements.

"What, are there no roses here?" cried Gerda; and she ran out into the garden, and examined all the beds, and searched and searched. There was not one to be found. Then she sat down and wept, and her tears fell just on the place where one of the rose-trees had sunk down. The warm tears moistened the earth, and the rose-tree sprouted up at once, as blooming as when it had sunk; and Gerda embraced it and kissed the roses, and thought of the beautiful roses at home, and, with them, of little Kay.

"Oh, how I have been detained!" said the little maiden, "I wanted to seek for little Kay. Do you know where he is?" she asked the Roses; "Do you think he is dead?"

And the roses answered, "No, he is not dead. We have been in the ground where all the dead lie; but Kay is not there."

"Thank you," said little Gerda, and then she went to the other flowers, and looked into their little cups, and asked, "Do you know where little Kay is?" But each flower, as it stood in the sunshine, dreamed only of its own little fairy tale of history. Not one knew anything of Kay. Gerda heard many stories from the flowers, as she asked them one after another about him.

And what, said the Tiger-Lily? "Hark, do you hear the drum?—'turn, turn,'—there are only two notes, always, 'turn, turn.' Listen to the women's song of mourning! Hear the cry of the priest! In her long red robe stands the Hindu widow by the funeral pile. The flames rise around her as she places herself on the dead body of her husband; but the Hindu woman is thinking of the living one in that circle; of him, her son, who lighted those flames. Those shining eyes trouble her heart more painfully than the flames which will soon consume her body to ashes. Can the fire of the heart be extinguished in the flames of the funeral pile?"

"I don't understand that at all," said little Gerda.

"That is my story," said the Tiger-Lily.

What, says the convolvulus? "Near yonder narrow road stands an old knight's castle; thick ivy creeps over the old ruined walls, leaf over leaf, even to the balcony, in which stands a beautiful maiden. She bends over the balustrades, and looks up the road. No rose on its stem is fresher than she; no apple-blossom, wafted by the wind, floats more lightly than she moves. Her rich silk rustles as she bends over and exclaims, 'Will he not come?'

"Is it Kay you mean?" asked Gerda.

"I am only speaking of a story of my dream," replied the flower.

What, said the little snowdrop? "Between two trees a rope is hanging; there is a piece of board upon it; it is a swing. Two pretty little girls, in dresses white as snow, and with long green ribbons fluttering from their hats, are sitting upon it swinging. Their brother who is taller than they are, stands in the swing; he has one arm round the rope, to steady himself; in one hand he holds a little bowl, and in the other a clay pipe; he is blowing bubbles. As the swing goes on, the bubbles fly upward, reflecting the most beautiful varying colours. The last still hangs from the bowl of the pipe, and sways in the wind. On goes the swing; and then a little black dog comes running up. He is almost as light as the bubble, and he raises himself on his hind legs, and wants to be taken into the swing; but it does not stop, and the dog falls; then he barks and gets angry. The children stoop towards him, and the bubble bursts. A swinging plank, a light sparkling foam picture—that is my story."

"It may be all very pretty what you are telling me," said little Gerda, "but you speak so mournfully, and you do not mention little Kay at all."

What do the Hyacinths say? "There were three beautiful sisters, fair and delicate. The dress of one was red, of the second blue, and of the third pure white. Hand in hand they danced in the bright moonlight, by the calm lake; but they were human beings, not fairy elves. The sweet fragrance attracted them, and they disappeared in the wood; here the fragrance became stronger. Three coffins, in which lay the three beautiful maidens, glided from the thickest part of the forest across the lake. The fireflies flew lightly over them, like little floating torches. Do the dancing maidens sleep, or are they dead? The scent of the flower says that they are corpses. The evening bell tolls their knell."

"You make me quite sorrowful," said little Gerda; "your perfume is so strong, you make me think of the dead maidens. Ah! is little Kay really dead then? The roses have been in the earth, and they say no."

"Cling, clang," tolled the Hyacinth Bells. "We are not tolling for little Kay; we do not know him. We sing our song, the only one we know."

Then Gerda went to the Buttercups that were glittering amongst the bright green leaves.

"You are little bright suns," said Gerda; "tell me if you know where I can find my play-fellow."

And the buttercups sparkled gaily, and looked again at Gerda. What song could the Buttercups sing? It was not about Kay.

"The bright warm sun shone on a little court, on the first warm day of spring. His bright beams rested on the white walls of the neighbouring house; and close by bloomed the first yellow flower of the season, glittering like gold in the sun's warm ray. An old woman sat in her arm chair at the house door, and her granddaughter, a poor and pretty servant-maid came to see her for a short visit. When she kissed her grandmother there was gold everywhere: the gold of the heart in that holy kiss; it was a golden morning; there was gold in the beaming sunlight, gold in the leaves of the lowly flower, and on the lips of the maiden. There, that is my story," said the Buttercup.

"My poor old grandmother!" sighed Gerda; "she is longing to see me, and grieving for me as she did for little Kay; but I shall soon go home now, and take little Kay with me. It is no use asking the flowers; they know only their own songs, and can give me no information."

And then she tucked up her little dress, that she might run faster, but the narcissus caught her by the leg as she was jumping over it; so she stopped and looked at the tall yellow flower, and said, "Perhaps you may know something."

Then she stooped down quite close to the flower, and listened; and what did he say?

"I can see myself, I can see myself," said the narcissus. "Oh, how sweet is my perfume! Up in a little room with a bow window, stands a little dancing girl, half undressed; she stands sometimes on one leg, and sometimes on both, and looks as if she would tread the whole world under her feet. She is nothing but a delusion. She is pouring water out of a tea-pot on a piece of stuff which she holds in her hand; it is her bodice. 'Cleanliness is a good thing,' she says. Her white dress hangs on a peg; it has also been washed in the tea-pot, and dried on the roof. She puts it on, and ties a saffron-coloured handkerchief round her neck, which makes the dress look whiter. See how she stretches out her legs, as if she were showing off on a stem. I can see myself, I can see myself."

"What do I care for all that," said Gerda, "you need not tell me such stuff." And then she ran to the other end of the garden. The door was fastened, but she pressed against the rusty latch, and it gave way. The door sprang open, and little Gerda ran out with bare feet into the wide world. She looked back three times, but no one seemed to be following her. At last she could run no longer, so she sat down to rest on a great stone, and when she looked round she saw that the summer was over, and autumn very far advanced. She had known nothing of this in the beautiful garden, where the sun shone and the flowers grew all the year round.

"Oh, how I have wasted my time?" said little Gerda; "it is autumn. I must not rest any longer," and she rose up to go on. But her little feet were wounded and sore, and everything around her looked so cold and bleak. The long willow-leaves were quite yellow. The dew-drops fell like water, leaf after leaf dropped from the trees, the sloe-thorn alone still bore fruit, but the sloes were sour, and set the teeth on edge. Oh, how dark and weary the whole world appeared!

Chapter Four
The Prince and Princess

Gerda was obliged to rest again, and just opposite the place where she sat, she saw a great Crow come hopping across the snow toward her. He stood looking at her for some time, and then he wagged his head and said, "Caw, caw; good day, good day." He pronounced the words as plainly as he could, because he meant to be kind to the little girl; and then he asked her where she was going all alone in the wide world.

The word 'alone' Gerda understood very well, and knew how much it expressed. So then she told the Crow the whole story of her life and adventures, and asked him if he had seen little Kay.

The Crow nodded his head very gravely, and said, "Perhaps I have—it may be."

"No! Do you think you have?" cried little Gerda, and she kissed the Crow, and hugged him almost to death with joy.

"Gently, gently," said the Crow. "I believe I know. I think it may be little Kay; but he has certainly forgotten you by this time for the Princess."

"Does he live with a Princess?" asked Gerda.

"Yes, listen," replied the Crow, "but it is so difficult to speak your language. If you understand the Crows' language then I can explain it better. Do you?"

"No, I have never learnt it," said Gerda, but my grandmother understands it, and used to speak it to me. I wish I had learnt it."

"It does not matter," answered the Crow; "I will explain as well as I can, although it will be very badly done;" and he told her what he had heard. "In this kingdom where we now are," said he, "there lives a Princess, who is so wonderfully clever that she has read all the newspapers in the world, and forgotten them too, although she is so clever. A short time ago, as she was sitting on her throne, which people say is not such an agreeable seat as is often supposed, she began to sing a song which commences in these words:

'Why should I not be married?'

'Why not indeed?' said she, and so she determined to marry if she could find a husband who knew what to say when he was spoken to, and not one who could only look grand, for that was so tiresome. Then she assembled all her court ladies together at the beat of the drum, and when they heard of her intentions they were very much pleased. 'We are so glad to hear it,' said they, 'we were talking about it ourselves the other day.' You may believe that every word I tell you is true," said the Crow, "for I have a tame sweetheart who goes freely about the palace, and she told me all this."

Of course his sweetheart was a Crow, for "birds of a feather flock together," and one Crow always chooses another Crow.

"Newspapers were published immediately, with a border of hearts, and the initials of the Princess among them. They gave notice that every young man who was handsome was free to visit the castle and speak with the Princess; and those who could reply loud enough to be heard when spoken to, were to make themselves quite at home at the palace; but the one who spoke best would be chosen as a husband for the Princess. Yes, yes, you may believe me, it is all as true as I sit here," said the Crow. "The people came in crowds. There was a great deal of crushing and running about, but no one succeeded either on the first or second day. They could all speak very well while they were outside in the streets, but when they entered the palace gates, and saw the guards in silver uniforms, and the footmen in their golden livery on the staircase, and the great halls lighted up, they became quite confused. And when they stood before the throne on which the princess sat, they could do nothing but repeat the last words she had said; and she had no particular wish to hear her own words over again. It was just as if they had all taken something to make them sleepy while they were in the palace, for they did not recover themselves nor speak till they got back again into the street. There was quite a long line of them reaching from the town gate to the palace. I went myself to see them," said the Crow. "They were hungry and thirsty, for at the palace they did not get even a glass

The Snow Queen

of water. Some of the wisest had taken a few slices of bread and butter with them, but they did not share it with their neighbours; they thought if they went in to the Princess looking hungry, there would be a better chance for themselves."

"But Kay! tell me about little Kay!" said Gerda, "was he amongst the crowd?"

"Stop a bit, we are just coming to him. It was on the third day, there came marching cheerfully along to the palace a little personage, without horses or carriage, his eyes sparkling like yours; he had beautiful long hair, but his clothes were very poor."

"That was Kay!" said Gerda joyfully. "Oh, then I have found him;" and she clapped her hands.

"He had a little knapsack on his back," added the Crow.

"No, it must have been his sledge," said Gerda; "for he went away with it."

"It may have been so," said the Crow; "I did not look at it very closely. But I know from my tame sweetheart that he passed through the palace gates, saw the guards in their silver uniform, and the servants in their liveries of gold on the stairs, but he was not in the least embarrassed. 'It must be very tiresome to stand on the stairs,' he said. 'I prefer to go in.' The rooms were blazing with light. Councillors and ambassadors walked about with bare feet, carrying golden vessels; it was enough to make any one feel serious. His boots creaked loudly as he walked, and yet he was not at all uneasy."

"It must be Kay," said Gerda, "I know he had new boots on, I have heard them creak in grandmother's room."

"They really did creak," said the Crow, "yet he went boldly up to the princess herself, who was sitting on a pearl as large as a spinning wheel, and all the ladies of the court were present with their maids, and all the cavaliers with their servants; and each of the maids had another maid to wait upon her, and the cavaliers' servants had their own servants, as well as a page each. They all stood in circles round the princess, and the nearer they stood to the door, the prouder they looked. The servants' pages, who always wore slippers, could hardly be looked at, they held themselves up so proudly by the door."

"It must be quite awful," said little Gerda, "but did Kay win the Princess?"

"If I had not been a crow," said he, "I would have married her myself, although I am engaged. He spoke just as well as I do, when I speak the crows' language, so I heard from my tame sweetheart. He was quite free and agreeable and said he had not come to woo the Princess, but to hear her wisdom; and he was as pleased with her as she was with him."

"Oh, certainly that was Kay," said Gerda, "he was so clever; he could work mental arithmetic and fractions. Oh, will you take me to the palace?"

"It is very easy to ask that," replied the Crow, "but how are we to manage it? However, I will speak about it to my tame sweetheart, and ask her advice; for I must tell you it will be very difficult to gain permission for a little girl like you to enter the palace."

"Oh, yes; but I shall gain permission easily," said Gerda, "for when Kay hears that I am here, he will come out and fetch me in immediately."

"Wait for me here by the palings," said the Crow, wagging his head as he flew away.

It was late in the evening before the Crow returned. "Caw, caw," he said, she sends you greeting, and here is a little roll which she took from the kitchen for you; there is plenty of bread there, and she thinks you must be hungry. It is not possible for you to enter the palace by the front entrance. The guards in silver uniform and the servants in gold livery would not allow it. But do not cry, we will manage to get you in; my sweetheart knows a little back-staircase that leads to the sleeping apartments, and she knows where to find the key."

Then they went into the garden through the great avenue, where the leaves were falling one after another, and they could see the light in the palace being put out in the same manner. And the Crow led little Gerda to the back door, which stood ajar. Oh! how little Gerda's heart beat with anxiety and longing; it was just as if she were going to do something wrong, and yet she only wanted to know where little Kay was. "It must be he," she thought, "with those clear eyes, and that long hair." She could fancy she saw him smiling at her, as he used to at home, when they sat among the roses. He would certainly be glad to see her, and to hear what a long distance she had come for his sake, and to know how sorry they had been at home because he did not come back. Oh what joy and yet fear she felt! They were now on the stairs, and in a small closet at the top a lamp was burning. In the middle of the floor stood the tame Crow, turning her head from side to side, and gazing at Gerda, who curtseyed as her grandmother had taught her to do.

"My betrothed has spoken so very highly of you, my little lady," said the tame Crow, "your life-history, Vita, as it may be called, is very touching. If you will take the lamp I will walk before you. We will go straight along this way, then we shall meet no one."

"It seems to me as if somebody were behind us," said Gerda, as something rushed by her like a shadow on the wall, and then horses with flying manes and thin legs, hunters, ladies and gentlemen on horseback, glided by her, like shadows on the wall.

"They are only dreams," said the Crow, "they are coming to fetch the thoughts of the great people out hunting."

"All the better, for we shall be able to look at them in their beds more safely. I hope that when you rise to honour and favour, you will show a grateful heart."

"You may be quite sure of that," said the Crow from the forest.

They now came into the first hall, the walls of which were hung with rose-coloured satin, embroidered with artificial flowers. Here the dreams again flitted by them but so quickly that Gerda could not distinguish the royal persons. Each hall appeared more splendid than the last, it was enought to bewilder any one. At length they reached a bedroom. The ceiling was like a great palm-tree, with glass leaves of the most costly crystal, and over the centre of the floor two beds, each resembling a lily, hung from a stem of gold. One, in which the Princess lay, was white, the other was red; and in this Gerda had to seek for little Kay. She pushed one of the red leaves aside, and saw a little brown neck. Oh, that must be Kay! She called his name out quite loud, and held the lamp over him. The dreams rushed back into the room on horseback. He woke, and turned his head round, it was not little Kay! The Prince was only like him in the neck, still he was young and pretty. Then the Princess peeped out of her white-lily bed, and asked what was the matter. Then little Gerda wept and told her story, and all that the crows had done to help her.

"You poor child," said the Prince and Princess; then they praised the crows, and said they were not angry for what they had done, but that it must not happen again, and this time they should be rewarded.

"Would you like to have your freedom?" asked the Princess, "or would you prefer to be raised to the position of court crows, with all that is left in the kitchen for yourselves?"

Then both the crows bowed, and begged to have a fixed appointment, for they thought of their old age, and said it would be so comfortable to feel that they had provision for their old days, as they called it. And then the Prince got out of his bed, and gave it up to Gerda—he could do no more; and she lay down. She folded her little hands, and thought, "How good everyone is to me, men and animals too;" then she closed her eyes and fell into a sweet sleep. All the dreams came flying back again to her, and they looked like angels, and one of them drew a little sledge, on which sat Kay, and nodded to her. But all this was only a dream, and vanished as soon as she awoke.

The following day she was dressed from head to foot in silk and velvet, and they invited her to stay at the palace for a few days, and enjoy herself, but she only begged for a pair of boots, and a little carriage, and a horse to draw it, so that she might go into the wide world to seek for Kay. And she obtained, not only boots, but also a muff, and she was neatly dressed; and when she was ready to go, there, at the door, she found a coach made of pure gold, with the coat-of-arms of the Prince and Princess shining upon it like a star, and the coachman, footman, and outriders all wearing golden crowns on their heads. The Prince and Princess themselves helped her into the coach, and wished her success. The forest Crow, who was now married, accompanied her for the first three miles; he sat by Gerda's side, as he could not bear riding backwards. The tame Crow stood in the door-way flapping her wings. She could not go with them, because she had been suffering from headache ever since the new appointment, no doubt from eating too much. The coach was well stored with sweet cakes, and under the seat were fruit and gingerbread nuts. "Farewell, farewell," cried the Prince and Princess, and little Gerda wept, and the Crow wept; and then, after a few miles, the Crow also said "Farewell," and this was the saddest parting. However, he flew to a tree, and stood flapping his black wings as long as he could see the coach, which glittered in the bright sunshine.

Chapter Five
Little Robber-Girl

The coach drove on through a thick forest, where it lighted up the way like a torch, and dazzled the eyes of some robbers, who could not bear to let it pass them unmolested.

"It is gold! It is gold!" cried they, rushing forward, and seizing the horses. Then they struck the little jockeys, the coachman, and the footman dead, and pulled little Gerda out of the carriage.

"She is fat and pretty, and she has been fed with the kernels of nuts," said the old robber-woman, who had a long beard and eyebrows that hung over her eyes. "She is as good as a little lamb; how nice she will taste!" and as she said this, she drew forth a shining knife, that glittered horribly. "Oh!" screamed the old woman the same moment; for her own daughter, who held her back, had bitten her in the ear. She was a wild and naughty girl, and the mother called her an ugly thing, and had not time to kill Gerda.

"She shall play with me," said the little robber-girl; "she shall give me her muff and her pretty dress, and sleep with me in my bed." And then she bit her mother again, and made her spring in the air, and jump about; and all the robbers laughed, and said, "See how she is dancing with her young cub."

"I will have a ride in the coach," said the little robber-girl; and she would have her own way; for she was so self-willed and obstinate.

She and Gerda seated themselves in the coach, and drove away, over stumps and stones, into the depths of the forest. The little robber-girl was about the same size as Gerda, but stronger; she had broader shoulders and a darker skin; her eyes were quite black, and she had a mournful look. She clasped little Gerda round the waist, and said—

"They shall not kill you as long as you don't make us vexed with you. I suppose you are a Princess."

"No," said Gerda; and then she told her all her history, and how fond she was of little Kay.

The robber-girl looked earnestly at her, nodded her head slightly, and said, "They sha'nt kill you, even if I do get angry with you; for I will do it myself." And then she wiped Gerda's eyes, and stuck her own hands in the beautiful muff which was so soft and warm.

The coach stopped in the courtyard of a robber's castle, the walls of which were cracked from top to bottom. Ravens and crows flew in and out of the holes and crevices, while great bulldogs, either of which looked as if it could swallow a man, were jumping about; but they were not allowed to bark. In the large and smoky hall a bright fire was burning on the stone floor. There was no chimney; so the smoke went up to the ceiling, and found a way out for itself. Soup was boiling in a large cauldron, and hares and rabbits were roasting on the spit.

"You shall sleep with me and all my little animals tonight," said the robber-girl, after they had had something to eat and drink. So she took Gerda to a corner of the hall, where some straw and carpets were laid down. Above them, on laths and perches, were more than a hundred pigeons, who all seemed to be asleep, although they moved slightly when the two little girls came near them. "These all belong to me," said the robber-girl; and she seized the nearest to her, held it by the feet, and shook it till it flapped its wings. "Kiss it," cried she, flapping it in Gerda's face. "There sit the wood-pigeons," continued she, pointing to a number of laths and a cage which had been fixed into the walls, near one of the openings. "Both rascals would fly away directly, if they were not closely locked up. And here is my old sweetheart 'Ba;' and she dragged out a reindeer by the horn; he wore a bright copper ring round his neck, and was tied up. "We are obliged to hold him tight too, or else he would run away from us also. I tickle his neck every evening with my sharp knife, which frightens him very much." And then the robber-girl drew a long knife from a chink in the wall, and let it slide gently over the reindeer's neck. The poor animal began to kick, and the little robber-girl laughed, and pulled down Gerda into bed with her.

"Will you have that knife with you while you are asleep?" asked Gerda, looking at it in great fright.

"I always sleep with the knife by me," said the robber-girl. "No one knows what may happen. But now tell me again all about little Kay, and why you went out into the world."

Then Gerda repeated her story over again, while the wood-pigeons in the cage over her cooed, and the other pigeons slept. The little robber-girl put one arm across Gerda's neck, and held the knife in the other, and was soon fast asleep and snoring. But Gerda could not close her eyes at all; she knew not whether she was to live or die. The robbers sat round the fire, singing and drinking, and the old woman stumbled about. It was a terrible sight for a little girl to witness.

Then the Wood-Pigeons said, "Coo, coo; we have seen little Kay. A white fowl carried his sledge, and he sat in the carriage of the Snow Queen, which drove through the wood while we were lying in our nest. She blew upon us, and all the young ones died excepting us two. Coo, coo."

"What are you saying up there?" cried Gerda. "Where was the Snow Queen going? Do you know anything about it?"

"She was most likely travelling to Lapland, where there is always snow and ice. Ask the reindeer that is fastened up there with a rope."

"Yes, there is always snow and ice," said the reindeer; "and it is a glorious place; you can leap and run about freely on the sparkling ice plains. The Snow Queen has her summer tent there, but her strong castle is at the North Pole, on an island called Spitzbergen."

"Oh, Kay, little Kay!" sighed Gerda.

"Lie still," said the robber-girl, "or I shall run my knife into your body."

In the morning Gerda told her all that the Wood-Pigeons had said; and the little robber-girl looked quite serious, and nodded her head, and said, "That is all talk, that is all talk. Do you know where Lapland is?" she asked the Reindeer.

"Who should know better than I do?" said the animal, while his eyes sparkled. "I was born and brought up there, and used to run about the snow-covered plains."

"Now listen," said the robber-girl; "all our men are gone away—only mother is here, and here she will stay; but at noon she always drinks out of a great bottle, and afterwards sleeps for a little while; and then, I'll do something for you." Then she jumped out of bed, clasped her mother round the neck, and pulled her by the beard, crying, "My own little nanny goat, good morning." Then her mother filliped her nose till it was quite red; yet she did it all for love.

When the mother had drunk out of the bottle, and was gone to sleep, the little robber-maiden went to the Reindeer, and said, "I should like very much to tickle your neck a few times more with my knife, for it makes you look so funny; but never mind—I will untie your cord, and set you free, so that you may run away to Lapland; but you must make good use of your legs, and carry this little maiden to the castle of the Snow Queen, where her play-fellow is. You have heard what she told me, for she spoke loud enough, and you were listening."

Then the Reindeer jumped for joy; and the little robber-girl lifted Gerda on his back, and had the forethought to tie her on, and even to give her her own little cushion to sit on.

"Here are your fur boots for you," said she; "for it will be very cold; but I must keep the muff; it is so pretty. However, you shall not be frozen for the want of it; here are my mother's large warm mittens; they will reach up to your elbows. Let me put them on. There, now your hands look just like my mother's."

But Gerda wept for joy.

"I don't like to see you fret," said the little robber-girl; "you ought to look quite happy now; and here are two loaves and a ham, so that you need not starve." These were fastened on the Reindeer, and then the little robber-maiden opened the door, coaxed in all the great dogs, and then cut the string with which the Reindeer was fastened, with her sharp knife, and said, "Now run, but mind you take good care of the little girl." And then Gerda stretched out her hand, with the great mitten on it, towards the little robber-girl, and said, "Farewell," and away flew the reindeer, over stumps and stones, through the great forest, over marshes and plains, as quickly as he could. The wolves howled, and the ravens screamed; while up in the sky quivered red lights like flames of fire. "There are my old northern lights," said the Reindeer; "see how they flash." And he ran on day and night still faster and faster, but the loaves and the ham were all eaten by the time they reached Lapland.

Chapter Six
The Lapland Woman and the Finland Woman

They stopped at a little hut; it was very mean looking; the roof sloped nearly down to the ground, and the door was so low that the family had to creep in on their hands and knees, when they went in and out. There was no one at home but an old Lapland woman, who was cooking fish by the light of a train-oil lamp. The Reindeer told her all about Gerda's story, after having first told his own, which seemed to him the most important, but Gerda was so pinched with the cold that she could not speak. "Oh, you poor things," said the Lapland woman, "you have a long way to go yet. You must travel more than a hundred miles farther, to Finland. The Snow Queen lives there now, and she burns Bengal lights every evening. I will write a few words on a dried stock-fish, for I have no paper, and you can take it from me to the Finland woman who lives there; she can give you better information than I can." So when Gerda was warmed, and had taken something to eat and drink, the woman wrote a few words on the dried fish, and told Gerda to take great care of it. Then she tied her again on the Reindeer, and he set off at full speed. Flash, flash, went the beautiful blue northern lights in the air the whole night long. And at length they reached Finland, and knocked at the chimney of the Finland woman's hut, for it had no door above the ground. They crept in, but it was so terribly hot inside that that woman wore scarcely any clothes; she was small and very dirty looking. She loosened little Gerda's dress, and took off the fur boots and the mittens, or Gerda would have been unable to bear the heat; and then she placed a piece of ice on the Reindeer's head, and read what was written on the dried fish. After she had read it three times, she knew it by heart, so she popped the fish into the soup saucepan, as she knew it was good to eat, and she never wasted anything. The Reindeer told his own story first, and then little Gerda's, and the Finlander twinkled with her clever eyes, but she said nothing. "You are so clever," said the Reindeer; "I know you can tie all the winds of the world with a piece of twine. If a sailor unties one knot, he has a fair wind; when he unties the second, it blows hard; but if the third and fourth are loosened, then comes a storm, which will root up whole forests. Cannot you give this little maiden something which will make her as strong as twelve men, to overcome the Snow Queen?"

"The Power of twelve men!" said the Finland woman; "that would be of very little use." But she went to a shelf and took down and unrolled a large skin, on which were inscribed wonderful characters, and she read till the perspiration ran down from her forehead. But the reindeer begged so hard for little Gerda, and Gerda looked at the Finland woman with such beseeching tearful eyes, that her own eyes began to twinkle again; so she drew the reindeer into a corner, and whispered to him while she laid a fresh piece of ice on his head, "Little Kay is really with the Snow Queen, but he finds everything there so much to his taste and his liking, that he believes it is the finest place in the world; but this is because he has a piece of broken glass in his heart, and a little piece of glass in his eye. These must be taken out, or he will never be a human being again, and the Snow Queen will retain her power over him."

"But can you not give little Gerda something to help her to conquer this power?"

"I can give her no greater power than she has already," said the woman; "don't you see how strong that is? How men and animals are obliged to serve her, and how well she has got through the world, barefooted as she is. She cannot receive any power from me greater than she now has, which consists in her own purity and innocence of heart. If she cannot herself obtain access to the Snow Queen, and remove the glass fragments from little Kay, we can do nothing to help her. Two miles from here the Snow Queen's garden begins; you can carry the little girl so far, and set her down by the large bush which stands in the snow, covered with red berries. Do not stay gossiping, but come back here as quickly as you can." Then the Finland woman lifted little Gerda upon the Reindeer, and he ran away with her as quickly as he could.

"Oh, I have forgotten my boots and my mittens," cried little Gerda, as soon as she felt the cutting cold, but the Reindeer dared not stop, so he ran on till he reached the bush with the red berries; here he set Gerda down, and he kissed her, and the great bright tears trickled over the animal's cheeks; then he left her and ran back as fast as he could.

There stood poor Gerda, without shoes, without gloves, in the midst of cold, dreary, ice-bound Finland. She ran forwards as quickly as she could, when a whole regiment of snowflakes came round her; they did not, however, fall from the sky, which was quite clear and glittering with the Northern Lights. The snowflakes ran along the ground, and the nearer they came to her, the larger they appeared. Gerda remembered how large and beautiful they looked through the burning-glass. But these were really larger, and much more terrible, for they were alive, and were the guards of the Snow Queen, and had the strangest shapes. Some were like great porcupines, others like twisted serpents with their heads stretching out, and some few were like little fat bears with their hair bristled; but all were dazzlingly white, and all were living snowflakes. Then little Gerda repeated the Lord's Prayer, and the cold was so great that she could see her own breath come out of her mouth like steam as she uttered the words. The steam appeared to increase, as she continued her prayer, till it took the shape of little angels who grew larger the moment they touched the earth. They all wore helmets on their heads, and carried spears and shields. Their number continued to increase more and more; and by the time Gerda had finished her prayers, a whole legion stood round her. They thrust their spears into the terrible snowflakes, so that they shivered into a hundred pieces, and little Gerda could go forward with courage and safety. The angels stroked her hands and feet, so that she felt the cold less, and she hastened on to the Snow Queen's castle.

But now we must see what Kay is doing. In truth he thought not of little Gerda, and never supposed she could be standing in the front of the palace.

Chapter Seven
Of the Palace of the Snow Queen and What Happened There at Last

The walls of the palace were formed of drifted snow, and the windows and doors of the cutting winds. There were more than a hundred rooms in it, all as if they had been formed with snow blown together. The largest of them extended for several miles; they were all lighted up by the vivid light of the aurora, and they were so large and empty, so icy cold and glittering! There were no amusements here, not even a little bear's ball, when the storm might have been the music, and the bears could have danced on their hind legs, and shown their good manners. There were no pleasant games of snap-dragon, or touch, or even a gossip over the tea-table, for the young-lady foxes. Empty, vast, and cold were the halls of the Snow Queen. The flickering flame of the Northern Lights could be plainly seen, whether they rose high or low in the heavens, from every part of the castle. In the midst of its empty, endless hall of snow was a frozen lake, broken on its surface into a thousand forms; each piece resembled another, from being in itself perfect as a work of art, and in the centre of this lake sat the Snow Queen, when she was at home. She called the lake "The Mirror of Reason," and said that it was the best, and indeed the only one in the world.

Little Kay was quite blue with cold, indeed almost black, but he did not feel it; for the Snow Queen had kissed away the icy shiverings, and his heart was already a lump of ice. He dragged some sharp, flat pieces of ice to and fro, and placed them together in all kinds of positions, as if he wished to make something out of them; just as we try to form various figures with little tablets of wood which we call "a Chinese puzzle." Kay's fingers were very artistic; it was the icy game of reason at which he played, and in his eyes the figures were very remarkable, and of the highest importance; this opinion was owing to the piece of glass still sticking in his eye. He composed many complete figures, forming different words, but there was one word he never could manage to form, although he wished it very much. It was the word "Eternity." The Snow Queen had said to him, "When you can find out this, you shall be your own master, and I will give you the whole world and a new pair of skates." But he could not accomplish it.

"Now I must hasten away to warmer countries," said the Snow Queen. "I will go and look into the black craters of the tops of the burning mountains, Etna and Vesuvius, as they are called—I shall make them look white, which will be good for them, and for the lemons and the grapes." And away flew the Snow Queen, leaving little Kay quite alone in the great hall which was so many miles in length; so he sat and looked at his pieces of ice, and was thinking so deeply, and sat so still, that any one might have supposed he was frozen.

Just at this moment it happened that little Gerda came through the great door of the castle. Cutting winds were raging around her, but she offered up a prayer and the winds sank down as if they were going to sleep; and she went on till she came to the large empty hall, and caught sight of Kay; she knew him directly; she flew to him and threw her arms round his neck, and held him fast, while she exclaimed, "Kay, dear little Kay, I have found you at last."

But he sat quite still, stiff and cold.

Then little Gerda wept hot tears, which fell on his breast, and penetrated into his heart, and thawed the lump of ice, and washed away the little piece of glass which had stuck there. Then he looked at her, and she sang—

"Roses bloom and cease to be,
But we shall the Christ-child see."

Then Kay burst into tears, and he wept so that the splinter of glass swam out of his eye. Then he recognized Gerda, and said, joyfully, "Gerda, dear little Gerda, where have you been all this time, and where have I been?" And he looked all around him, and said, "How cold it is, and how large and empty it all looks," and he clung to Gerda, and she laughed and wept for joy. It was so pleasing to see them that the pieces of ice even danced about; and when they were tired and went to lie down, they formed themselves into the letters of the word which the Snow Queen had said he must find out before he could be his own master, and have the whole world and a pair of new skates. Then Gerda kissed his cheeks, and they became blooming; and she kissed his eyes, and they shone like her own; she kissed his hands and his feet, and then he became quite healthy and cheerful. The Snow Queen might come home now when she pleased, for there stood his certainty of freedom, in the word she wanted, written in shining letters of ice.

Then they took each other by the hand, and went forth from the great palace of ice. They spoke of the grandmother, and of the roses on the roof, and as they went on the winds were at rest, and the sun burst forth. When they arrived at the bush with red berries, there stood the reindeer waiting for them, and he had brought another young reindeer with him, whose udders were full, and the children drank her warm milk and kissed her on the mouth. Then they carried Kay and Gerda first to the Finland woman, where they warmed themselves thoroughly in the hot room, and she gave them directions about their journey home. Next they went to the Lapland woman, who had made some new clothes for them, and put their sleighs in order. Both the Reindeer ran by their side, and followed them as far as the boundaries of the country, where the first green leaves were budding. And here they took leave of the two Reindeer and the Lapland woman, and all said—Farewell. Then the birds began to twitter, and the forest too was full of green young leaves; and out of it came a beautiful horse, which Gerda remembered, for it was one which had drawn the golden coach. A young girl was riding upon it, with a shining red cap on her head, and pistols in her belt. It was the little robber-maiden, who had got tired of staying at home; she was going first to the north, and if that did not suit her, she meant to try some other part of the world. She knew Gerda directly, and Gerda remembered her: it was a joyful meeting.

"You are a fine fellow to go gadding about in this way," said she to little Kay, "I should like to know whether you deserve that any one should go to the end of the world to find you."

But Gerda patted her cheeks, and asked after the prince and princess.

"They are gone to foreign countries," said the robber-girl.

"And the Crow?" asked Gerda.

"Oh, the Crow is dead," she replied; "his tame sweetheart is now a widow, and wears a bit of black worsted round her leg. She mourns very pitifully, but it is all stuff. But now tell me how you managed to get him back."

Then Gerda and Kay told her all about it.

"Snip, snap, snare! it's all right at last," said the robber-girl.

Then she took both their hands, and promised that if ever she should pass through the town, she would call and pay them a visit. And then she rode away into the wide world. But Gerda and Kay went hand-in-hand towards home; and as they advanced, spring appeared more lovely with its green verdure and its beautiful flowers. Very soon they recognized the large town where they lived, and the tall steeples of the churches, in which the sweet bells were ringing a merry peal as they entered it, and found their way to their grandmother's door. They went upstairs into the little room, where all looked just as it used to do. The old clock was going "tick, tick," and the hands pointed to the time of day, but as they passed through the door into the room they perceived that they were both grown up, and become a man and woman. The roses out on the roof were in full bloom, and peeped in at the window; and there stood the little chairs, on which they had sat when children; and Kay and Gerda seated themselves each on their own chair, and held each other by the hand, while the cold empty grandeur of the Snow Queen's palace vanished from their memories like a painful dream. The grandmother sat in God's bright sunshine, and she read aloud from the Bible, "Except ye become as little children, ye shall in no wise enter into the kingdom of God." And Kay and Gerda looked into each other's eyes, and all at once understood the words of the old song,

"Roses bloom and cease to be,
But we shall the Christ-child see."

And they both sat there, grown up, yet children at heart; and it was summer, warm, beautiful summer.

The Little Elder-Tree Mother

Translated by Mrs. H. P. Paull

There was once a little boy who had caught cold; he had gone out and got wet feet. Nobody had the least idea how it had happened; the weather was quite dry. His mother undressed him, put him to bed, and ordered the teapot to be brought in, that she might make him a good cup of tea from the elder-tree blossoms, which is so warming. At the same time, the kind-hearted old man who lived by himself in the upper storey of the house came in; he led a lonely life, for he had no wife and children; but he loved the children of others very much, and he could tell so many fairy tales and stories, that it was a pleasure to hear him.

"Now, drink your tea," said the mother; "perhaps you will hear a story."

"Yes, if I only knew a fresh one," said the old man, and nodded smilingly. "But how did the little fellow get his wet feet?" he then asked.

"That," replied the mother, "nobody can understand."

"Will you tell me a story?" asked the boy.

"Yes, if you can tell me as nearly as possible how deep is the gutter in the little street where you go to school."

"Just half as high as my top-boots," replied the boy; "but then I must stand in the deepest holes."

"There, now we know where you got your wet feet," said the old man. "I ought to tell you a story, but the worst of it is, I do not know any more."

"You can make one up," said the little boy. "Mother says you can tell a fairy tale about anything you look at or touch."

"That is all very well, but such tales or stories are worth nothing! No, the right ones come by themselves and knock at my forehead saying: 'Here I am.'"

"Will not one knock soon?" asked the boy; and the mother smiled while she put elder-tree blossoms into the teapot and poured boiling water over them. "Pray, tell me a story."

"Yes, if stories came by themselves; they are so proud, they only come when they please.—But wait," he said suddenly, "there is one. Look at the teapot; there is a story in it now."

And the little boy looked at the teapot; the lid rose up gradually, the elder-tree blossoms sprang forth one by one, fresh and white; long boughs came forth; even out of the spout they grew up in all directions, and formed a bush—nay, a large elder tree, which stretched its branches up to the bed and pushed the curtains aside; and there were so many blossoms and such a sweet fragrance! In the midst of the tree sat a kindly-looking old woman with a strange dress; it was as green as the leaves, and trimmed with large white blossoms, so that it was difficult to say whether it was real cloth, or the leaves and blossoms of the elder-tree.

"What is this woman's name?" asked the little boy.

"Well, the Romans and Greeks used to call her a Dryad," said the old man; "but we do not understand that. Out in the sailors' quarter they give her a better name; there she is called Elder-Tree Mother. Now, you must attentively listen to her and look at the beautiful elder-tree.

"Just such a large tree, covered with flowers, stands out there; it grew in the corner of an humble little yard; under this tree sat two old people one afternoon in the beautiful sunshine. He was an old,

old sailor, and she his old wife; they had already great-grandchildren, and were soon to celebrate their golden wedding, but they could not remember the date, and the Elder-Tree Mother was sitting in the tree and looked as pleased as this one here. 'I know very well when the golden wedding is to take place,' she said; but they did not hear it—they were talking of bygone days.

"'Well, do you remember?' said the old sailor, 'when we were quite small and used to run about and play—it was in the very same yard where we now are—we used to put little branches into the ground and make a garden.'

"'Yes,' said the old woman, 'I remember it very well; we used to water the branches, and one of them, an elder-tree branch, took root, and grew and became the large tree under which we are now sitting as old people.'

"'Certainly, you are right,' he said; 'and in yonder corner stood a large water-tub; there I used to sail my boat, which I had cut out myself—it sailed so well; but soon I had to sail somewhere else.'

"'But first we went to school to learn something,' she said, 'and then we were confirmed; we both wept on that day, but in the afternoon we went out hand in hand, and ascended the high round tower and looked out into the wide world right over Copenhagen and the sea; then we walked to Fredericksburg, where the King and the Queen were sailing about in their magnificent boat on the canals.'

"'But soon I had to sail about somewhere else, and for many years I was travelling about far away from home.'

"'And I often cried about you, for I was afraid lest you were drowned and lying at the bottom of the sea. Many a time I got up in the night and looked if the weathercock had turned; it turned often, but you did not return. I remember one day distinctly: the rain was pouring down in torrents; the dust-man had come to the house where I was in service; I went down with the dustbin and stood for a moment in the doorway, and looked at the dreadful weather. Then the postman gave me a letter; it was from you. Heavens! how that letter had travelled about. I tore it open and read it; I cried and laughed at the same time, and was so happy! Therein was written that you were staying in the hot countries, where the coffee grows. These must be marvellous countries. You said a great deal about them, and I read all while the rain was pouring down and I was standing there with the dustbin. Then suddenly some one put his arm round my waist—'

"'Yes, and you gave him a hearty smack on the cheek,' said the old man.

"'I did not know that it was you—you had come as quickly as your letter; and you looked so handsome, and so you do still. You had a large yellow silk handkerchief in your pocket and a shining hat on. You looked so well, and the weather in the street was horrible!'

"'Then we married,' he said. 'Do you remember how we got our first boy, and then Mary, Niels, Peter, John, and Christian?'

'Oh yes; and now they have all grown up, and have become useful members of society, whom everybody cares for.'

"'And their children have had children again,' said the old sailor. 'Yes, these are children's children, and they are strong and healthy. If I am not mistaken, our wedding took place at this season of the year.'

"'Yes, today is your golden wedding-day,' said the little elder-tree mother, stretching her head down between the two old people, who thought that she was their neighbour who was nodding to them; they looked at each other and clasped hands. Soon afterwards the children and grandchildren came, for they knew very well that it was the golden wedding-day; they had already wished them joy and happiness in the morning, but the old people had forgotten it, although they remembered things so well that had passed many, many years ago. The elder-tree smelt strongly, and the setting sun illuminated the faces of the two old people, so that they looked quite rosy; the youngest of the grandchildren danced round them, and cried merrily that there would be a feast in the evening, for they were to have hot potatoes; and the Elder Mother nodded in the tree and cried 'Hooray' with the others."

"But that was no fairy tale," said the little boy who had listened to it.

"You will presently understand it," said the old man who told the story. "Let us ask little Elder-Tree Mother about it."

"That was no fairy tale," said the little Elder-Tree Mother; "but now it comes! Real life furnishes us with subjects for the most wonderful fairy tales; for otherwise my beautiful elder-bush could not have grown forth out of the teapot."

And then she took the little boy out of bed and placed him on her bosom; the elder branches, full of blossoms, closed over them; it was as if they sat in a thick leafy bower which flew with them through the air; it was beautiful beyond all description. The little Elder-Tree Mother had suddenly become a charming young girl, but her dress was still of the same green material, covered with white blossoms, as the elder-tree mother had worn; she had a real elder blossom on her bosom, and a wreath of the same flowers was wound round her curly golden hair; her eyes were so large and so blue that it was wonderful to look at them. She and the boy kissed each other, and then they were of the same age and felt the same joys. They walked hand in hand out of the bower, and now stood at home in a beautiful flower garden. Near the green lawn the father's walking-stick was tied to a post. There was life in this stick for the little ones, for as soon as they seated themselves upon it the polished knob turned into a neighing horse's head, a long black mane was fluttering in the wind, and four strong slender legs grew out. The animal was fiery and spirited; they galloped round the lawn. "Hooray! now we shall ride far away, many miles!" said the boy; "we shall ride to the nobleman's estate where we were last year." And they rode round the lawn again, and the little girl, who, as we know, was no other than the little Elder-Tree Mother, continually cried, "Now we are in the country! Do you see the farmhouse there, with the large baking stove, which projects like a gigantic egg out of the wall into the road? The elder-tree spreads its branches over it, and the cock struts about and scratches for the hens. Look how proud he is! Now we are near the church; it stands on a high hill, under the spreading oak trees; one of them is half dead! Now we are at the smithy, where the fire roars and the half-naked men beat with their hammers so that the sparks fly far and wide. Let's be off to the beautiful farm!" And they passed by everything the little girl, who was sitting behind on the stick, described, and the boy saw it, and yet they only went round the lawn. Then they played in a side-walk, and marked out a little garden on the ground; she took elder-blossoms out of her hair and planted them, and they grew exactly like those the old people planted when they were children, as we have heard before. They walked about hand in hand, just as the old couple had done when they were little, but they did not go to the round tower nor to the Fredericksburg Garden. No; the little girl seized the boy round the waist, and then they flew far into the country. It was spring and it became summer, it was autumn and it became winter, and thousands of pictures reflected themselves in the boy's eyes and heart, and the little girl always sang again, "You will never forget that!" And during their whole flight the elder-tree smelt so sweetly; he noticed the roses and the fresh beeches, but the elder-tree smelt much stronger, for the flowers were fixed on the little girl's bosom, against which the boy often rested his head during the flight.

"It is beautiful here in spring," said the little girl, and they were again in the green beechwood, where the thyme breathed forth sweet fragrance at their feet, and the pink anemones looked lovely in the green moss. "Oh! that it were always spring in the fragrant beechwood!"

"Here it is splendid in summer!" she said, and they passed by old castles of the age of chivalry. The high walls and indented battlements were reflected in the water of the ditches, on which swans were swimming and peering into the old shady avenues. The corn waved in the field like a yellow sea. Red and yellow flowers grew in the ditches, wild hops and convolvuli in full bloom in the hedges. In the evening the moon rose, large and round, and the hayricks in the meadows smelt sweetly. "One can never forget it!"

"Here it is beautiful in autumn!" said the little girl, and the atmosphere seemed twice as high and blue, while the wood shone with crimson, green, and gold. The hounds were running off, flocks of wild fowl flew screaming over the barrows, while the bramble bushes twined round the old stones. The dark-blue sea was covered with white-sailed ships, and in the barns sat old women, girls, and children picking hops into a large tub; the young ones sang songs, and the old people told fairy tales about goblins and sorcerers. It could not be more pleasant anywhere.

"Here it's agreeable in winter!" said the little girl, and all the trees were covered with hoar-frost, so that they looked like white coral. The snow creaked under one's feet, as if one had new boots

The Little Elder-Tree Mother

on. One shooting star after another traversed the sky. In the room the Christmas tree was lit, and there were song and merriment. In the peasant's cottage the violin sounded, and games were played for apple quarters; even the poorest child said, "It is beautiful in winter!"

And indeed it was beautiful! And the little girl showed everything to the boy, and the elder-tree continued to breathe forth sweet perfume, while the red flag with the white cross was streaming in the wind; it was the flag under which the old sailor had served. The boy became a youth; he was to go out into the wide world, far away to the countries where the coffee grows. But at parting the little girl took an elder-blossom from her breast and gave it to him as a keepsake. He placed it in his prayer-book, and when he opened it in distant lands it was always at the place where the flower of remembrance was lying; and the more he looked at it the fresher it became, so that he could almost smell the fragrance of the woods at home. He distinctly saw the little girl, with her bright blue eyes, peeping out from behind the petals, and heard her whispering, "Here it is beautiful in spring, in summer, in autumn, and in winter," and hundreds of pictures passed through his mind.

Thus many years rolled by. He had now become an old man, and was sitting, with his old wife, under an elder-tree in full bloom. They held each other by the hand exactly as the great-grandfather and the great-grandmother had done outside, and, like them, they talked about bygone days and of their golden wedding. The little girl with the blue eyes and elder-blossoms in her hair was sitting high up in the tree, and nodded to them, saying, "Today is the golden wedding!" And then she took two flowers out of her wreath and kissed them. They glittered at first like silver, then like gold, and when she placed them on the heads of the old people each flower became a golden crown. There they both sat like a King and Queen under the sweet-smelling tree, which looked exactly like an elder-tree, and he told his wife the story of the Elder-Tree Mother as it had been told him when he was a little boy. They were both of opinion that the story contained many points like their own, and these similarities they liked best.

"Yes, so it is," said the little girl in the tree. "Some call me Little Elder-Tree Mother; others a Dryad; but my real name is

'Remembrance.' It is I who sit in the tree which grows and grows. I can remember things and tell stories! But let's see if you have still got your flower."

And the old man opened his prayer-book; the elder-blossom was still in it, and as fresh as if it had only just been put in. Remembrance nodded, and the two old people, with the golden crowns on their heads, sat in the glowing evening sun. They closed their eyes and—and—

Well, now the story is ended! The little boy in bed did not know whether he had dreamt it or heard it told; the teapot stood on the table, but no elder-tree was growing out of it, and the old man who had told the story was on the point of leaving the room, and he did go out.

"How beautiful it was!" said the little boy. "Mother, I have been to warm countries!"

"I believe you," said the mother; "if one takes two cups of hot elder-tea it is quite natural that one gets into warm countries!" And she covered him up well, so that he might not take cold. "You have slept soundly while I was arguing with the old man whether it was a story or a fairy tale!"

"And what has become of the little Elder-Tree Mother?" asked the boy.

"She is in the teapot," said the mother; "and there she may remain."

The Elfin Hill

Translated by Mrs. H. P. Paull

A few large Lizards were running nimbly about in the clefts of an old tree; they could understand one another very well, for they spoke the lizard language.

"What a buzzing and a rumbling there is in the elfin hill," said one of the Lizards; "I have not been able to close my eyes for two nights on account of the noise; I might just as well have had the toothache, for that always keeps me awake."

"There is something going on within there," said the other Lizard; "they propped up the top of the hill with four red posts, till cock-crow this morning, so that it is thoroughly aired, and the elfin girls have learnt new dances; there is something."

"I spoke about it to an earth-worm of my acquaintance," said a third Lizard; "the earth-worm had just come from the elfin hill, where he has been groping about in the earth day and night. He has heard a great deal; although he cannot see, poor miserable creature, yet he understands very well how to wriggle and lurk about. They expect friends in the elfin hill, grand company, too; but who they are the earth-worm would not say, or, perhaps, he really did not know. All the will-o'-the-wisps are ordered to be there to hold a torch dance, as it is called. The silver and gold which is plentiful in the hill will be polished and placed out in the moonlight."

"Who can the strangers be?" asked the Lizards; "what can the matter be? Hark, what a buzzing and humming there is!"

Just at this moment the elfin hill opened, and an old elfin maiden, hollow behind,[*] came tripping out; she was the old Elf King's housekeeper, and a distant relative of the family; therefore she wore an amber heart on the middle of her forehead. Her feet moved very fast, "trip, trip;" good Gracious, how she could trip right down to the sea to the night-raven.[†]

"You are invited to the elf hill for this evening," said she; "but will you do me a great favour and undertake the invitations? You ought to do something, for you have no housekeeping to attend to as I have. We are going to have some very grand people, conjurors, who have always something to say; and therefore the old Elf King wishes to make a great display."

"Who is to be invited?" asked the Raven.

"All the world may come to the great ball, even human beings, if they can only talk in their sleep, or do something after our fashion. But for the feast the company must be carefully selected; we can only admit persons of high rank; I have had a dispute myself with the Elf King, as he thought we could not admit ghosts. The merman and his daughter must be invited first, although it may not be agreeable to them to remain so long on dry land, but they shall have a wet stone to sit on, or perhaps something better; so I think they will not refuse this time. We must have all the old demons of the first class, with tails, and the hobgoblins and imps; and then I think we ought not

---

[*] There is a superstition respecting these elfin maiden, that they are only to be looked at in front, and are therefore made hollow, like the inside of a mask.

[†] In former times, when a ghost appeared, the priest condemned it to enter the earth; when it was done, a stake was driven into the spot to which it had been basnished. At midnight a cry was heard, "Let me out!" The stake was then pulled out, and the ex-communicated spirit flew away, in a form of a raven, with a hole in its left wing. This ghost-like bird was called the night-raven.

to leave out the death-horse,* or the grave-pig, or even the church dwarf, although they do belong to the clergy, and are not reckoned among our people; but that is merely their office, they are nearly related to us, and visit us very frequently."

"Croak," said the night-Raven as he flew away with the invitations.

The elfin maidens we're already dancing on the elf hill, and they danced in shawls woven from moonshine and mist, which look very pretty to those who like such things. The large hall within the elf hill was splendidly decorated; the floor had been washed with moonshine, and the walls had been rubbed with magic ointment, so that they glowed like tulip-leaves in the light. In the kitchen were frogs roasting on the spit, and dishes preparing of snail skins, with children's fingers in them, salad of mushroom seed, hemlock, noses and marrow of mice, beer from the marsh woman's brewery, and sparkling salt-petre wine from the grave cellars. These were all substantial food. Rusty nails and church-window glass formed the dessert. The old Elf King had his gold crown polished up with powdered slate-pencil; it was like that used by the first form, and very difficult for an Elf King to obtain. In the bedrooms, curtains were hung up and fastened with the slime of snails; there was, indeed, a buzzing and humming everywhere.

"Now we must fumigate the place with burnt horse-hair and pig's bristles, and then I think I shall have done my part," said the elf man-servant.

"Father, dear," said the youngest daughter, "may I now hear who our high-born visitors are?"

"Well, I suppose I must tell you now," he replied; "two of my daughters must prepare themselves to be married, for the marriages certainly will take place. The old goblin from Norway, who lives in the ancient Dovre mountains, and who possesses many castles built of rock and freestone, besides a gold mine, which is better than all, so it is thought, is coming with his two sons, who are both seeking

---

* It is a popular superstition in Denmark tah a living horse, or a living pig, has been buried under every church that is built. The ghost of the dead horse is supposed to limp upon three legs every night to some house, in which any one was going to die. The ghost of a pig was called a grave-pig.

a wife. The old goblin is a true-hearted, honest, old Norwegian graybeard; cheerful and straightforward. I knew him formerly, when we used to drink together to our good fellowship: he came here once to fetch his wife, she is dead now. She was the daughter of the king of the Chalk-hills at Moen. They say he took his wife from chalk; I shall be delighted to see him again. It is said that the boys are ill-bred, forward lads, but perhaps that is not quite correct, and they will become better as they grow older. Let me see that you know how to teach them good manners."

"And when are they coming?" asked the daughter.

"That depends upon wind and weather," said the Elf King; "they travel economically. They will come when there is the chance of a ship. I wanted them to come over to Sweden, but the old man was not inclined to take my advice. He does not go forward with the times, and that I do not like."

Two Will-o'-the-wisps came jumping in, one quicker than the other, so of course, one arrived first. "They are coming! they are coming!" he cried.

"Give me my crown," said the Elf King, "and let me stand in the moonshine."

The daughters drew on their shawls and bowed down to the ground. There stood the old goblin from the Dovre mountains, with his crown of hardened ice and polished fir-cones. Besides this, he wore a bear-skin, and great, warm boots, while his sons went with their throats bare and wore no braces, for they were strong men.

"Is that a hill?" said the youngest of the boys, pointing to the elf hill, "we should call it a hole in Norway."

"Boys," said the old man, "a hole goes in, and a hill stands out; have you no eyes in your heads?"

Another thing they wondered at was, that they were able without trouble to understand the language.

"Take care," said the old man, "or people will think you have not been well brought up."

Then they entered the elfin hill, where the select and grand company were assembled, and so quickly had they appeared that they seemed to have been blown together. But for each guest the neatest and pleasantest arrangement had been made. The sea folks sat at table in great water-tubs, and they said it was just like being at home. All behaved themselves properly excepting the two young Northern goblins; they put their legs on the table and thought they were all right.

"Feet off the table-cloth!" said the old goblin. They obeyed, but not immediately. Then they tickled the ladies who waited at table, with the fir-cones, which they carried in their pockets. They took off their boots, that they might be more at ease, and gave them to the ladies to hold. But their father, the old Goblin, was very different; he talked pleasantly about the stately Norwegian rocks, and told fine tales of the waterfalls which dashed over them with a clattering noise like thunder or the sound of an organ, spreading their white foam on every side. He told of the salmon that leaps in the rushing waters, while the water-god plays on his golden harp. He spoke of the bright winter nights, when the sledge bells are ringing, and the boys run with burning torches across the smooth ice, which is so transparent that they can see the fishes dart forward beneath their feet. He described everything so clearly, that those who listened could see it all; they could see the saw-mills going, the men-servants and the maidens singing songs, and dancing a Rattling dance—when all at once the old goblin gave the old elfin maiden a kiss, such a tremendous kiss, and yet they were almost strangers to each other.

Then the elfin girls had to dance, first in the usual way, and then with stamping feet, which they performed very well; then followed the artistic and solo dance. Dear me, how they did throw their legs about! No one could tell where the dance begun, or where it ended, nor indeed which were legs and which were arms, for they were all flying about together, like the shavings in a saw-pit! And then they spun round so quickly that the death-horse and the grave-pig became sick and giddy, and were obliged to leave the table.

"Stop!" cried the old goblin, "is that the only house-keeping they can perform? Can they do anything more than dance and throw about their legs, and make a whirlwind?"

"You shall soon see what they can do," said the Elf King. And then he called his youngest daughter to him. She was slender and fair as moonlight, and the most graceful of all the sisters. She took a white chip in her mouth, and vanished instantly; this was her accomplishment. But the old goblin said he should not like his wife to have such an accomplishment, and thought his boys would have the same objection. Another daughter could make a figure like herself follow her, as if she had a shadow, which none of the goblin folk ever had. The third was of quite a different sort; she had learnt in the brew-house of the moor witch how to lard elfin puddings with glow-worms.

"She will make a good housewife," said the old goblin, and then saluted her with his eyes instead of drinking her health; for he did not drink much.

Now came the fourth daughter, with a large harp to play upon; and when she struck the first chord, every one lifted up the left leg (for the goblins are left-legged), and at the second chord they found they must all do just what she wanted.

"That is a dangerous woman," said the old goblin; and the two sons walked out of the hill; they had had enough of it. "And what can the next daughter do?" asked the old goblin.

"I have learnt everything that is Norwegian," said she; "and I will never marry, unless I can go to Norway."

Then her youngest sister whispered to the old Goblin, "That is only because she has heard, in a Norwegian song, that when the world shall decay, the cliffs of Norway will remain standing like monuments; and she wants to get there, that she may be safe; for she is so afraid of sinking."

"Ho! ho!" said the old goblin, "is that what she means? Well, what can the seventh and last do?"

"The sixth comes before the seventh," said the Elf King, for he could reckon; but the sixth would not come forward.

"I can only tell people the truth," said she. "No one cares for me, nor troubles himself about me; and I have enough to do to sew my grave clothes."

So the seventh and last came; and what could she do? Why, she could tell stories, as many as you liked, on any subject.

"Here are my five fingers," said the old goblin; "now tell me a story for each of them."

So she took him by the wrist, and he laughed till he nearly choked; and when she came to the fourth finger, there was a gold ring on it, as if it knew there was to be a betrothal. Then the old Goblin said, "Hold fast what you have: this hand is yours; for I will have you for a wife myself."

Then the elfin girl said that the stories about the ring-finger and little Peter Playman had not yet been told.

"We will hear them in the winter," said the old Goblin, "and also about the fir and the birch-trees, and the ghost stories, and of the tingling frost. You shall tell your tales, for no one over there can do it so well; and we will sit in the stone rooms, where the pine logs are burning, and drink mead out of the golden drinking-horn of the old Norwegian Kings. The water-god has given me two; and when we sit there, Nix comes to pay us a visit, and will sing you all the songs of the mountain shepherdesses. How merry we shall be! The salmon will be leaping in the waterfalls, and dashing against the stone walls, but he will not be able to come in. It is indeed very pleasant to live in old Norway. But where are the lads?"

Where indeed were they? Why, running about the fields, and blowing out the Will-o'-the-wisps, who so good-naturedly came and brought their torches.

"What tricks have you been playing?" said the old goblin. "I have taken a mother for you, and now you may take one of your aunts."

But the youngsters said they would rather make a speech and drink to their good fellowship; they had no wish to marry. Then they made speeches and drank toasts, and tipped their glasses, to show that they were empty. Then they took off their coats, and lay down on the table to sleep; for they made themselves quite at home. But the old goblin danced about the room with his young bride, and exchanged boots with her, which is more fashionable than exchanging rings.

"The cock is crowing," said the old elfin maiden who acted as housekeeper; "now we must close the shutters, that the sun may not scorch us."

Then the hill closed up. But the Lizards continued to run up and down the riven tree; and one said to the other, "Oh, how much I was pleased with the old Goblin!"

"The boys pleased me better," said the Earth-worm. But then the poor miserable creature could not see.

The Red Shoes

Translated by Mrs. H. P. Paull

Once upon a time there was little girl, pretty and dainty. But in summer time she was obliged to go barefooted because she was poor, and in winter she had to wear large wooden shoes, so that her little instep grew quite red.

In the middle of the village lived an old shoemaker's wife; she sat down and made, as well as she could, a pair of little shoes out of some old pieces of red cloth. They were clumsy, but she meant well, for they were intended for the little girl, whose name was Karen.

Karen received the shoes and wore them for the first time on the day of her mother's funeral. They were certainly not suitable for mourning; but she had no others, and so she put her bare feet into them and walked behind the humble coffin.

Just then a large old carriage came by, and in it sat an old lady; she looked at the little girl, and taking pity on her, said to the clergyman, "Look here, if you will give me the little girl, I will take care of her."

Karen believed that this was all on account of the red shoes, but the old lady thought them hideous, and so they were burnt. Karen

The Red Shoes

herself was dressed very neatly and cleanly; she was taught to read and to sew, and people said that she was pretty. But the mirror told her, "You are more than pretty—you are beautiful."

One day the Queen was travelling through that part of the country, and had her little daughter, who was a princess, with her. All the people, amongst them Karen too, streamed towards the castle, where the little princess, in fine white clothes, stood before the window and allowed herself to be stared at. She wore neither a train nor a golden crown, but beautiful red morocco shoes; they were indeed much finer than those which the shoemaker's wife had sewn for little Karen. There is really nothing in the world that can be compared to red shoes!

Karen was now old enough to be confirmed; she received some new clothes, and she was also to have some new shoes. The rich shoemaker in the town took the measure of her little foot in his own room, in which there stood great glass cases full of pretty shoes and white slippers. It all looked very lovely, but the old lady could not see very well, and therefore did not get much pleasure out of it. Amongst the shoes stood a pair of red ones, like those which the princess had worn. How beautiful they were! and the shoemaker said that they had been made for a count's daughter, but that they had not fitted her.

"I suppose they are of shiny leather?" asked the old lady. "They shine so."

"Yes, they do shine," said Karen. They fitted her, and were bought. But the old lady knew nothing of their being red, for she would never have allowed Karen to be confirmed in red shoes, as she was now to be.

Everybody looked at her feet, and the whole of the way from the church door to the choir it seemed to her as if even the ancient figures on the monuments, in their stiff collars and long black robes, had their eyes fixed on her red shoes. It was only of these that she thought when the clergyman laid his hand upon her head and spoke of the holy baptism, of the covenant with God, and told her that she was now to be a grown-up Christian. The organ pealed forth solemnly, and the sweet children's voices mingled with that of their old leader; but Karen thought only of her red shoes. In the afternoon the old lady heard from everybody that Karen had worn red shoes. She said that it was a shocking thing to do, that it was very improper, and that Karen was always to go to church in future in black shoes, even if they were old.

On the following Sunday there was Communion. Karen looked first at the black shoes, then at the red ones—looked at the red ones again, and put them on.

The sun was shining gloriously, so Karen and the old lady went along the footpath through the corn, where it was rather dusty.

At the church door stood an old crippled soldier leaning on a crutch; he had a wonderfully long beard, more red than white, and he bowed down to the ground and asked the old lady whether he might wipe her shoes. Then Karen put out her little foot too. "Dear me, what pretty dancing-shoes!" said the soldier. "Sit fast, when you dance," said he, addressing the shoes, and slapping the soles with his hand.

The old lady gave the soldier some money and then went with Karen into the church.

And all the people inside looked at Karen's red shoes, and all the figures gazed at them; when Karen knelt before the altar and put the golden goblet to her mouth, she thought only of the red shoes. It seemed to her as though they were swimming about in the goblet, and she forgot to sing the psalm, forgot to say the "Lord's Prayer."

Now every one came out of church, and the old lady stepped into her carriage. But just as Karen was lifting up her foot to get in too, the old soldier said: "Dear me, what pretty dancing shoes!" and Karen could not help it, she was obliged to dance a few steps; and when she had once begun, her legs continued to dance. It seemed as if the shoes had got power over them. She danced round the church corner, for she could not stop; the coachman had to run after her and seize her. He lifted her into the carriage, but her feet continued to dance, so that she kicked the good old lady violently. At last they took off her shoes, and her legs were at rest.

At home the shoes were put into the cupboard, but Karen could not help looking at them.

Now the old lady fell ill, and it was said that she would not rise from her bed again. She had to be nursed and waited upon, and this was no one's duty more than Karen's. But there was a grand ball in the town, and Karen was invited. She looked at the red shoes, saying to herself that there was no sin in doing that; she put the red shoes on, thinking there was no harm in that either; and then she went to the ball; and commenced to dance.

But when she wanted to go to the right, the shoes danced to the left, and when she wanted to dance up the room, the shoes danced down the room, down the stairs through the street, and out through the gates of the town. She danced, and was obliged to dance, far out into the dark wood. Suddenly something shone up among the trees, and she believed it was the moon, for it was a face. But it was the old soldier with the red beard; he sat there nodding his head and said: "Dear me, what pretty dancing shoes!"

She was frightened, and wanted to throw the red shoes away; but they stuck fast. She tore off her stockings, but the shoes had grown fast to her feet. She danced and was obliged to go on dancing over field and meadow, in rain and sunshine, by night and by day—but by night it was most horrible.

She danced out into the open churchyard; but the dead there did not dance. They had something better to do than that. She wanted to sit down on the pauper's grave where the bitter fern grows; but for her there was neither peace nor rest. And as she danced past the open church door she saw an angel there in long white robes, with wings reaching from his shoulders down to the earth; his face was stern and grave, and in his hand he held a broad shining sword.

"Dance you shall," said he, "dance in your red shoes till you are pale and cold, till your skin shrivels up and you are a skeleton! Dance you shall, from door to door, and where proud and wicked children live you shall knock, so that they may hear you and fear you! Dance you shall, dance—!"

"Mercy!" cried Karen. But she did not hear what the angel answered, for the shoes carried her through the gate into the fields, along highways and byways, and unceasingly she had to dance.

One morning she danced past a door that she knew well; they were singing a psalm inside, and a coffin was being carried out covered with flowers. Then she knew that she was forsaken by every one and damned by the angel of God.

She danced, and was obliged to go on dancing through the dark night. The shoes bore her away over thorns and stumps till she was all torn and bleeding; she danced away over the heath to a lonely little house. Here, she knew, lived the executioner; and she tapped with her finger at the window and said:

"Come out, come out! I cannot come in, for I must dance."

And the executioner said: "I don't suppose you know who I am. I strike off the heads of the wicked, and I notice that my axe is tingling to do so."

"Don't cut off my head!" said Karen, "for then I could not repent of my sin. But cut off my feet with the red shoes."

And then she confessed all her sin, and the executioner struck off her feet with the red shoes; but the shoes danced away with the little feet across the field into the deep forest.

And he carved her a pair of wooden feet and some crutches, and taught her a psalm which is always sung by sinners; she kissed the hand that guided the axe, and went away over the heath.

"Now, I have suffered enough for the red shoes," she said; "I

The Red Shoes

will go to church, so that people can see me." And she went quickly up to the church-door; but when she came there, the red shoes were dancing before her, and she was frightened, and turned back.

During the whole week she was sad and wept many bitter tears, but when Sunday came again she said: "Now I have suffered and striven enough. I believe I am quite as good as many of those who sit in church and give themselves airs." And so she went boldly on; but she had not got farther than the churchyard gate when she saw the red shoes dancing along before her. Then she became terrified, and turned back and repented right heartily of her sin.

She went to the parsonage, and begged that she might be taken into service there. She would be industrious, she said, and do everything that she could; she did not mind about the wages as long as she had a roof over her, and was with good people. The pastor's wife had pity on her, and took her into service. And she was industrious and thoughtful. She sat quiet and listened when the pastor read aloud from the Bible in the evening. All the children liked her very much, but when they spoke about dress and grandeur and beauty she would shake her head.

On the following Sunday they all went to church, and she was asked whether she wished to go too; but, with tears in her eyes, she looked sadly at her crutches. And then the others went to hear God's Word, but she went alone into her little room; this was only large enough to hold the bed and a chair. Here she sat down with her hymn-book, and as she was reading it with a pious mind, the wind carried the notes of the organ over to her from the church, and in tears she lifted up her face and said: "O God! help me!"

Then the sun shone so brightly, and right before her stood an angel of God in white robes; it was the same one whom she had seen that night at the church-door. He no longer carried the sharp sword, but a beautiful green branch, full of roses; with this he touched the ceiling, which rose up very high, and where he had touched it there shone a golden star. He touched the walls, which opened wide apart, and she saw the organ which was pealing forth; she saw the pictures of the old pastors and their wives, and the congregation sitting in the polished chairs and singing from their hymn-books. The church itself had come to the poor girl in her narrow room, or the room had gone to the church. She sat in the pew with the rest of the pastor's household, and when they had finished the hymn and looked up, they nodded and said, "It was right of you to come, Karen."

"It was mercy," said she.

The organ played and the children's voices in the choir sounded soft and lovely. The bright warm sunshine streamed through the window into the pew where Karen sat, and her heart became so filled with it, so filled with peace and joy, that it broke. Her soul flew on the sunbeams to Heaven, and no one was there who asked after the Red Shoes.

The Jumper

Translated by Mrs. H. P. Paull

The Flea, the Grasshopper, and the Skipjack* once wanted to see which of them could jump highest; and they invited the whole world, and whoever else would come, to see the grand sight. And there the three famous jumpers were met together in the room.

"Yes, I'll give my daughter to him who jumps highest," said the King, "for it would be mean to let these people jump for nothing."

The Flea stepped out first. He had very pretty manners, and bowed in all directions, for he had young ladies' blood in his veins, and was accustomed to consort only with human beings; and that was of great consequence.

Then came the Grasshopper: he was certainly much heavier, but he had a good figure, and wore the green uniform that was born with him. This person, moreover, maintained that he belonged to a very

---

* A children's toy, made from the breastbone of a goose, wax and a stick, which can be made to jump.

old family in the land of Egypt, and that he was highly esteemed there. He had just come from the field, he said, and had been put into a card house three stories high, and all made of picture cards with the figures turned inwards. There were doors and windows in the house, cut in the body of the Queen of Hearts.

"I sing so," he said, "that sixteen native crickets who have chirped from their youth up, and have never yet had a card house of their own, would become thinner than they are with envy if they were to hear me."

Both of them, the Flea and the Grasshopper, took care to announce who they were, and that they considered themselves entitled to marry a Princess.

The Skipjack said nothing, but it was said of him that he thought all the more; and directly the Yard Dog had smelt at him he was ready to assert that the Skipjack was of good family, and formed from the breastbone of an undoubted goose. The old councillor, who had received three medals for holding his tongue, declared that the Skipjack possessed the gift of prophecy; one could tell by his bones whether there would be a severe winter or a mild one; and that's more than one can always tell from the breastbone of the man who writes the almanac.

"I shall not say anything more," said the old King. "I only go on quietly, and always think the best."

Now they were to take their jump. The Flea sprang so high that no one could see him; and then they asserted that he had not jumped at all. That was very mean. The Grasshopper only sprang half as high, but he sprang straight into the King's face, and the King declared that was horribly rude. The Skipjack stood a long time considering; at last people thought that he could not jump at all.

"I only hope he's not become unwell," said the Yard Dog, and then he smelt at him again.

"Tap!" he sprang with a little crooked jump just into the lap of the Princess, who sat on a low golden stool.

Then the King said, "The highest leap was taken by him who jumped up to my daughter; for therein lies the point; but it requires head to achieve that, and the Skipjack has shown that he has a head."

And so he had the Princess.

"I jumped highest, after all," said the Flea. "But it's all the same. Let her have the goose-bone with its lump of wax and bit of stick. I jumped to the highest; but in this world a body is required if one wishes to be seen."

And the Flea went into foreign military service, where it is said he was killed.

The Grasshopper seated himself out in the ditch, and thought and considered how things happened in the world. And he too said, "Body is required! body is required!" And then he sang his own melancholy song, and from that we have gathered this story, which they say is not true, though it's in print.

The Shepherdess and the Chimney-Sweep

Translated by Charles Boner

Have you ever seen a very, very old clothespress, quite black with age, on which all sorts of flourishes and foliage were carved? Just such a one stood in a certain room. It had been handed down as a legacy to the owner from a great great grandmother, and it was carved from top to bottom with roses and tulips; the most curious flourishes were to be seen on it, and between them little stags popped out their heads with zigzag antlers.

But on the top a man at full length was carved. True he was laughable to look at; for he showed his teeth—laughing one could not call it—had goat's legs, little horns on his head, and a long beard. The children in the room always called him General-clothes-press-inspector-head-superintendent-Goat-legs, for this was a name difficult to pronounce, and there are very few who get the title: but to cut him out in wood—that was no trifle. However, there he was. He looked down upon the table and towards the mirror, for there a charming little porcelain Shepherdess was standing. Her shoes were gilded, her gown was tastefully looped up with a red rose, and she had a golden hat and cloak; in short, she was most exquisite.

Close by her stood a little Chimney-Sweep, as black as a coal, although he was made of porcelain too. He was just as clean and pretty as the rest of them; as. to his being a chimney-sweep, that was only what he represented; and the porcelain manufacturer could just as well have made a prince of him as a chimney-sweep, if he had chosen; one was as easy as the other, to a clever workman.

There he stood so prettily with his ladder,* and with a little round face as fair and as rosy as that of the Shepherdess. In reality this was a fault; for a little black he certainly ought to have been. He was quite close to the Shepherdess; both stood where they had been placed; and as soon as they were put there, they had mutually promised each other eternal fidelity; for they suited each other exactly—they were young, they were of the same porcelain, and both equally fragile.

Close to them stood another figure three times as large as they were. It was an old Chinese, that could nod his head. He was made of porcelain too, and said that he was grandfather of the little Shepherdess; but this he could not prove. He asserted, moreover, that he had authority over her, and that was the reason he had nodded his assent to the General-clothes-press-inspectorhead-superintendent-Goat-legs, who paid his addresses to the Shepherdess.

"In him," said the old Chinese, "you will have a husband who, I verily believe, is of mahogany. You will be Mrs. Goatlegs, the wife of a General-clothes-press-inspector-head-superintendent, who has his shelves full of plate, besides what is hidden in secret drawers and recesses."

"I will not go into the dark cupboard," said the little Shepherdess; "I have heard say that he has eleven wives of porcelain in there already."

"Then you may be the twelfth," said the Chinese. "Tonight, as soon as the old clothes-press cracks, as sure as I am a Chinese, we will keep the wedding. And then he nodded his head, and fell asleep.

---

* The flues in Germany are much larger than in the houses in England; so much so indeed, that men only are employed as sweeps. The lower part being very wide, they have short ladders of about eight feet in length to enable them to get up to the narrower part, where they then scramble on in the usual way.— C. B.

But the little Shepherdess wept, and looked at her beloved—at the porcelain Chimney-Sweep.

"I implore you," said she, "fly hence with me into the wide world: for here it is impossible for us to remain."

"I will do all you ask," said the little Chimney-Sweep. "Let us instantly leave this place. I think my trade will enable me to support you."

"If we were only down from the table," said she. "I shall not be happy till we are far from here, and free."

The Shepherdess and the Chimney-Sweep

He consoled her, and showed her how she was to set her little foot on the carved border and on the gilded foliage which twined around the leg of the table, brought his ladder to her assistance, and at last both were on the floor; but when they looked towards the old clothes-press, they observed a great stir. All the carved stags stretched their heads out farther, raised their antlers, and turned round their heads. The General-clothes-press-inspector-head-superintendent gave a jump, arid called to the old Chinese, "They are running away! they are running away!"

At this she grew a little frightened, and jumped quickly over the ridge into a low drawer near the window.

Here lay three or four packs of cards. Which were not complete, and a little puppet-show, which was set up as well as it was possible to do. A play was being performed, and all the ladies, Diamonds as well as Hearts, Clubs and Spades, sat in the front row, and fanned themselves with the tulips they held in their hands, while behind them stood all the knaves ready to wait upon them when they wanted anything. The play was about two persons who could not have each other as they wished, at which the Shepherdess wept, for it was her own history.

"I cannot bear it any longer," said she; "I must get out of the drawer."

But when she had got down on the floor, and looked up to the table, she saw that the old Chinese was awake, and that his whole body was rocking.

"The old Chinese is coming!" cried the little Shepherdess; and down she fell on her porcelain knee, so frightened was she. "A thought has struck me," said the Chimney-Sweep; "let us creep into the great *Pot-pourri* Jar that stands in the corner; there we can lie on roses and lavender, and if he comes after us, throw dust in his eyes."

"'Tis of no use," said she. "Besides, I know that the old Chinese and the Potpourri Jar were once betrothed; and when one has been once on such terms, a little regard always lingers behind. No; for us there is nothing left but to wander forth into the wide world."

"Have you really courage to go forth with me into the wide world?" asked the Chimney-Sweep tenderly. "Have you considered how large it is, and that we can never come back here again?"

"I have thought of all that," said she. And the Sweep gazed fixedly upon and then said, "My way lies up the chimney. Have yon really courage to go with me through the stove, and to creep through all the flues? We shall then get into the main flue, after which I am not at a loss what to do. Up we mount, then, so high that they can never reach us; and at the top is an opening that leads out into the world."

And he led her towards the door of the stove.

"It looks quite black," said she; but still she went with him, and on through all the intricacies of the interior, and through the flues, where a pitchy darkness reigned.

"We are now in the chimney," said he; "and behold, behold, above us is shining the loveliest star!"

It was a real star in the sky that shone straight down upon them, as if to show the way. They climbed and they crept higher and higher. It was a frightful way; but he lifted her up, he held her, and showed her the best places on which to put her little porcelain feet; and thus they reached the top of the chimney, and seated themselves on the edge of it; for they were tired, which is not to be wondered at.

The heaven and all its stars were above them, and all the roofs of the town below them; they could see far around, they had such a splendid view of the world. The poor Shepherdess had never pictured it to herself thus; she leaned her little head on her Sweep, and wept so bitterly that all the gilding of her girdle came off.

"Oh, this is too much!" said she; "I cannot bear it. The world is too large. Oh, were I but again on the little table under the looking-glass! I shall never be happy till I am there again. I have followed you into the wide world; now if you really love me, you may follow me home again."

And the Chimney-Sweep spoke sensibly to her, spoke to her about the old Chinese and the General-clothes-press-inspector-head-superintendent; but she sobbed so violently, and kissed her little Sweep so passionately, that he was obliged to give way, although it was not right to do so.

So now down they climbed again with great difficulty, crept through the flue and into the stove, where they listened behind the door, to discover if anybody was in the room. It was quite still; they peeped out, and there, on the floor, in the middle of the room, lay the old Chinese. He had fallen from the table in trying to follow the fugitives, and was broken in three pieces; his whole back was but a stump, and his head had rolled into a corner, while General-clothes-press-inspector-head-superintendent Goat-legs was standing where he had ever stood, absorbed in thought.

"How dreadful!" said the little Shepherdess. "My old grandfather is dashed to pieces, and we are the cause. I never can survive the accident." And she wrung her little hands in agony.

"He can be mended," said the Chimney-Sweep; "he can easily be mended. Only do not be so hasty. If they glue his back together, and rivet his neck well, he will be as good as new, and will be able to say enough disagreeable things to us for some time to come."

"Do you think so?" said she; and then they clambered up again to the table on which they had stood before.

"You see," said the Sweep, "we might have spared ourselves these disagreeables, after all."

"If we had but mended my old grandfather!" said the Shepherdess. "Does it cost much?"

And mended he was. The family had his back glued, and his neck riveted, so that he was as good as new, except that he could not nod.

"Meseems, you have grown haughty since you were dashed to pieces," said General-clothes-press-inspector-head-superintendent Goat-legs. "However, I think there is not so very much to be proud of. Am I to have her, or am I not?"

Then the Chimney-Sweep and the little Shepherdess looked so touchingly at the old Chinese; they were so afraid he would nod! But he could not, and it was disagreeable to him to tell a stranger that he constantly carried a rivet in his neck. So the little porcelain personages remained together. They blessed the old grandfather's rivet over and over again, and loved each other till they both fell to pieces.

Holger Danske

Translated by Mrs. H. P. Paull

In Denmark there stands an old castle named Kronenburg, close by the Sound of Elsinore, where large ships, both English, Russian, and Prussian, pass by hundreds every day. And they salute the old castle with cannons, "Boom, boom," which is as if they said, "Good day." And the cannons of the old castle answer "Boom," which means "Many thanks." In winter no ships sail by, for the whole Sound is covered with ice as far as the Swedish coast, and has quite the appearance of a high road. The Danish and the Swedish flags wave, and Danes and Swedes say, "Good day," and "Thank you" to each other, not with cannons, but with a friendly shake of the hand; and they exchange white bread and biscuits with each other, because foreign articles taste the best.

But the most beautiful sight of all is the old castle of Kronenburg, where Holger Danske sits in the deep, dark cellar, into which no one goes. He is clad in iron and steel, and rests his head on his strong arm; his long beard hangs down upon the marble table, into which it has become firmly rooted; he sleeps and dreams, but in his dreams he sees everything that happens in Denmark. On each Christmas-eve an angel comes to him and tells him that all he has dreamed is true, and that he may go to sleep again in peace, as Denmark is not yet in any real danger; but should danger ever come, then Holger Danske will rouse himself, and the table will burst asunder as he draws out his beard. Then he will come forth in his strength, and strike a blow that shall sound in all the countries of the world.

An old grandfather sat and told his little grandson all this about Holger Danske, and the boy knew that what his grandfather told him must be true. As the old man related this story, he was carving an image in wood to represent Holger Danske, to be fastened to the prow of a ship; for the old grandfather was a carver in wood, that is, one who carved figures for the heads of ships, according to the names given to them. And now he had carved Holger Danske, who stood there erect and proud, with his long beard, holding in one hand his broad battle-axe, while with the other he leaned on the Danish arms. The old grandfather told the little boy a great deal about Danish men and women who had distinguished themselves in olden times, so that he fancied he knew as much even as Holger Danske himself, who, after all, could only dream; and when the little fellow went to bed, he thought so much about it that he actually pressed his chin against the counterpane, and imagined that he had a long beard which had become rooted to it. But the old grandfather remained sitting at his work and carving away at the last part of it, which was the Danish arms. And when he had finished he looked at the whole figure, and thought of all he had heard and read, and what he had that evening related to his little grandson. Then he nodded his head, wiped his spectacles and put them on, and said, "Ah, yes; Holger Danske will not appear in my lifetime, but the boy who is in bed there may very likely live to see him when the event really comes to pass." And the old grandfather nodded again; and the more he looked at Holger Danske, the more satisfied he felt that he had carved a good image of him. It seemed to glow with the colour of life; the armor glittered like iron and steel. The hearts in the Danish arms grew more and more red; while the lions, with gold crowns on their heads, were leaping up. "That is the most beautiful coat of arms in the world," said the old man. "The lions represent strength; and the hearts, gentleness and love." And as he gazed on the uppermost lion, he thought of King Canute, who chained great England to Denmark's throne; and he looked at the second lion, and thought of Waldemar, who untied Denmark and conquered the Vandals. The third lion reminded him of Margaret, who united Denmark, Sweden, and Norway. But when he gazed at the red hearts, their colours glowed more deeply, even as flames, and his memory followed each in turn. The first led him to a dark, narrow prison, in which sat a prisoner, a beautiful woman, daughter of Christian the Fourth, Eleanor Ulfeld, and the flame became a rose on her bosom, and its blossoms were not more pure than the heart of this noblest and best of all Danish women. "Ah, yes; that is indeed a noble heart in the Danish arms," said the grandfather. and his spirit followed the second flame, which carried him out to sea, where cannons roared and the ships lay shrouded in smoke, and the flaming heart attached itself to the breast of Hvitfeldt in the form of the ribbon of an order, as he blew himself and his ship into the air in order to save the fleet. And the third flame led him to Greenland's wretched huts, where the preacher, Hans Egede, ruled with love in every word and action. The flame was as a star on his breast, and added another heart to the Danish arms. And as the old grandfather's spirit followed the next hovering flame, he knew whither it would lead him. In a peasant woman's humble room stood Frederick the Sixth, writing his name with chalk on the beam. The flame trembled on his breast and in his heart, and it was in the peasant's room that his heart became one for the Danish arms. The old grandfather wiped his eyes, for he had known King Frederick, with his silvery locks and his honest blue eyes, and had lived for him, and he folded his hands and remained for some time silent. Then his daughter came to him and said it was getting late, that he ought to rest for a while, and that the supper was on the table.

"What you have been carving is very beautiful, grandfather," said she. "Holger Danske and the old coat of arms; it seems to me as if I have seen the face somewhere."

"No, that is impossible," replied the old grandfather; "but I have seen it, and I have tried to carve it in wood, as I have retained it in my memory. It was a long time ago, while the English fleet lay in the roads, on the second of April, when we showed that we were true, ancient Danes. I was on board the Denmark, in Steene Bille's squadron; I had a man by my side whom even the cannon balls seemed to fear. He sung old songs in a merry voice, and fired and fought as if he were something more than a man. I still remember his face, but from whence he came, or whither he went, I know not; no one knows. I have often thought it might have been Holger Danske himself, who had swam down to us from Kronenburg to help us in the hour of danger. That was my idea, and there stands his likeness."

The wooden figure threw a gigantic shadow on the wall, and even on part of the ceiling; it seemed as if the real Holger Danske stood behind it, for the shadow moved; but this was no doubt caused by the flame of the lamp not burning steadily. Then the daughter-in-law kissed the old grandfather, and led him to a large arm-chair by the table; and she, and her husband, who was the son of the old man and the father of the little boy who lay in bed, sat down to supper with him. And the old grandfather talked of the Danish lions and the Danish hearts, emblems of strength and gentleness, and explained quite clearly that there is another strength than that which lies in a sword, and he pointed to a shelf where lay a number of old books, and amongst them a collection of Holberg's plays, which are much read and are so clever and amusing that it is easy to fancy we have known the people of those days, who are described in them.

"He knew how to fight also," said the old man; "for he lashed the follies and prejudices of people during his whole life."

Then the grandfather nodded to a place above the looking-glass, where hung an almanac, with a representation of the Round Tower upon it, and said, "Tycho Brahe was another of those who used a sword, but not one to cut into the flesh and bone, but to make the way of the stars of heaven clear, and plain to be understood. And then he whose father belonged to my calling—yes, he, the son of the old image-carver, he whom we ourselves have seen, with his silvery locks and his broad shoulders, whose name is known in all lands;—yes, he was a sculptor, while I am only a carver. Holger Danske can appear in marble, so that people in all countries of the world may hear of the strength of Denmark. Now let us drink the health of Bertel."

But the little boy in bed saw plainly the old castle of Kronenburg, and the Sound of Elsinore, and Holger Danske, far down in the cellar, with his beard rooted to the table, and dreaming of everything that was passing above him.

And Holger Danske did dream of the little humble room in which the image-carver sat; he heard all that had been said, and he nodded in his dream, saying, "Ah, yes, remember me, you Danish people, keep me in your memory, I will come to you in the hour of need."

The bright morning light shone over Kronenburg, and the wind brought the sound of the hunting-horn across from the neighbouring shores. The ships sailed by and saluted the castle with the boom of the cannon, and Kronenburg returned the salute, "Boom, boom." But the roaring cannons did not awake Holger Danske, for they meant only "Good morning," and "Thank you." They must fire in another fashion before he awakes; but wake he will, for there is energy yet in Holger Danske.

The Bell

Translated by Mrs. H. P. Paull

In the narrow streets of a large town people often heard in the evening, when the sun was setting, and his last rays gave a golden tint to the chimney-pots, a strange noise which resembled the sound of a church bell; it only lasted an instant, for it was lost in the continual roar of traffic and hum of voices which rose from the town. "The evening bell is ringing," people used to say; "the sun is setting!" Those who walked outside the town, where the houses were less crowded and interspersed by gardens and little fields, saw the evening sky much better, and heard the sound of the bell much more clearly. It seemed as though the sound came from a church, deep in the calm, fragrant wood, and thither people looked with devout feelings.

A considerable time elapsed: one said to the other, "I really wonder if there is a church out in the wood. The bell has indeed a strange sweet sound! Shall we go there and see what the cause of it is?" The rich drove, the poor walked, but the way seemed to them extraordinarily long, and when they arrived at a number of willow trees on the border of the wood they sat down, looked up into the great branches and thought they were now really in the wood. A confectioner from the town also came out and put up a stall there; then came another confectioner who hung a bell over his stall, which was covered with pitch to protect it from the rain, but the clapper was wanting.

When people came home they used to say that it had been very romantic, and that really means something else than merely taking tea. Three persons declared that they had gone as far as the end of the wood; they had always heard the strange sound, but there it seemed to them as if it came from the town. One of them wrote verses about the bell, and said that it was like the voice of a mother speaking to an intelligent and beloved child; no tune, he said, was sweeter than the sound of the bell.

The Emperor of the country heard of it, and declared that he who would really find out where the sound came from should receive the title of "Bellringer to the World," even if there was no bell at all.

Now many went out into the wood for the sake of this splendid berth; but only one of them came back with some sort of explanation. None of them had gone far enough, nor had he, and yet he said that the sound of the bell came from a large owl in a hollow tree. It was a wisdom owl, which continually knocked its head against the tree, but he was unable to say with certainty whether its head or the hollow trunk of the tree was the cause of the noise.

He was appointed "Bellringer to the World," and wrote every year a short dissertation on the owl, but by this means people did not become any wiser than they had been before.

It was just confirmation-day. The clergyman had delivered a beautiful and touching sermon, the candidates were deeply moved by it; it was indeed a very important day for them; they were all at once transformed from mere children to grown-up people; the childish soul was to fly over, as it were, into a more reasonable being.

The sun shone most brightly; and the sound of the great unknown bell was heard more distinctly than ever. They had a mind to go thither, all except three. One of them wished to go home and try on her ball dress, for this very dress and the ball were the cause of her being confirmed this time, otherwise she would not have been allowed to go. The second, a poor boy, had borrowed a coat and a pair of boots from the son of his landlord to be confirmed in, and he had to return them at a certain time. The third said that he never went into strange places if his parents were not with him; he had always been a good child, and wished to remain so, even after being confirmed, and they ought not to tease him for this; they, however, did it all the same. These three, therefore did not go; the others went on. The sun was shining, the birds were singing, and the confirmed children sang too, holding each other by the hand, for they had no position yet, and they were all equal in the eyes of God. Two of the smallest soon became tired and returned to the town; two little girls sat down and made garlands of flowers, they, therefore, did not go on. When the others arrived at the willow trees, where the confectioner had put up his stall, they said: "Now we are out here; the bell does not in reality exist—it is only something that people imagine!"

Then suddenly the sound of the bell was heard so beautifully and solemnly from the wood that four or five made up their minds to go still further on. The wood was very thickly grown. It was difficult to advance: wood lilies and anemones grew almost too high; flowering convolvuli and brambles were hanging like garlands from tree to tree; while the nightingales were singing and the sunbeams played. That was very beautiful! But the way was unfit for the girls; they would have torn their dresses. Large rocks, covered with moss of various hues, were lying about; the fresh spring water rippled forth with a peculiar sound. "I don't think that can be the bell," said one of the confirmed children, and then he lay down and listened. "We must try to find out if it is!" And there he remained, and let the others walk on.

They came to a hut built of the bark of trees and branches; a large crab-apple tree spread its branches over it, as if it intended to pour all its fruit on the roof, upon which roses were blooming; the long boughs covered the gable, where a little bell was hanging. Was this the one they had heard? All agreed that it must be so, except one who said that the bell was too small and too thin to be heard at such a distance, and that it had quite a different sound to that which had so touched men's hearts.

He who spoke was a King's son, and therefore the others said that such a one always wishes to be cleverer than other people.

Therefore they let him go alone; and as he walked on, the solitude of the wood produced a feeling of reverence in his breast; but still he heard the little bell about which the others rejoiced, and sometimes, when the wind blew in that direction, he could hear the sounds from the confectioner's stall, where the others were singing at tea. But the deep sounds of the bell were much stronger; soon it seemed to him as if an organ played an accompaniment—the sound came from the left, from the side where the heart is. Now something rustled among the bushes, and a little boy stood before the King's son, in wooden shoes and such a short jacket that the sleeves did not reach to his wrists. They knew each other: the boy was the one who had not been able to go with them because he had to take the coat and boots back to his landlord's son. That he had done, and had started again in his wooden shoes and old clothes, for the sound of the bell was too enticing—he felt he must go on.

"We might go together," said the King's son. But the poor boy with the wooden shoes was quite ashamed; he pulled at the short sleeves of his jacket, and said that he was afraid he could not walk so fast; besides, he was of opinion that the bell ought to be sought at the right, for there was all that was grand and magnificent.

"Then we shall not meet," said the King's son, nodding to the poor boy, who went into the deepest part of the wood, where the thorns tore his shabby clothes and scratched his hands, face, and feet until they bled. The King's son also received several good scratches, but the sun was shining on his way, and it is he whom we will now follow, for he was a quick fellow. "I will and must find the bell," he said, "if I have to go to the end of the world."

Ugly monkeys sat high in the branches and clenched their teeth. "Shall we beat him?" they said. "Shall we thrash him? He is a King's son!"

But he walked on undaunted, deeper and deeper into the wood, where the most wonderful flowers were growing; there were standing white star lilies with blood-red stamens, sky-blue tulips shining when the wind moved them; apple-trees covered with apples like large glittering soap bubbles: only think how resplendent these trees were in the sunshine! All around were beautiful green meadows, where hart and hind played in the grass. There grew magnificent oaks and beech-trees; and if the bark was split of any of them, long blades of grass grew out of the clefts; there were also large smooth lakes in the wood, on which the swans were swimming about and flapping their wings. The King's son often stood still and listened; sometimes he thought that the sound of the bell rose up to him out of one of these deep lakes, but soon he found that this was a mistake, and that the bell was ringing still farther in the wood. Then the sun set, the clouds were as red as fire; it became quiet in the wood; he sank down on his knees, sang an evening hymn and said: "I shall never find what I am looking for! Now the sun is setting, and the night, the dark night, is approaching. Yet I may perhaps see the round sun once more before he disappears beneath the horizon. I will climb up these rocks, they are as high as the highest trees!" And then, taking hold of the creepers and roots, he climbed up on the wet stones, where water-snakes were wriggling and the toads, as it were, barked at him: he reached the top before the sun, seen from such a height, had quite set. "Oh, what a splendour!" The sea, the great majestic sea, which was rolling its long waves against the shore, stretched out before him, and the sun was standing like a large bright altar and there where sea and heaven met—all melted together in the most glowing colours; the wood was singing, and his heart too. The whole of nature was one large holy church, in which the trees and hovering clouds formed the pillars, the flowers and grass the woven velvet carpet, and heaven itself was the great cupola; up there the flame colour vanished as soon as the sun disappeared, but millions of stars were lighted; diamond lamps were shining, and the King's son stretched his arms out towards heaven, towards the sea, and towards the wood. Then suddenly the poor boy with the short-sleeved jacket and the wooden shoes appeared; he had arrived just as quickly on the road he had chosen. And they ran towards each other and took one another's hand, in the great cathedral of nature and poesy, and above them sounded the invisible holy bell; happy spirits surrounded them, singing hallelujahs and rejoicing.

Grandmother

Translated by Mrs. H. P. Paull

Grandmother is very old, her face is wrinkled, and her hair is quite white; but her eyes are like two stars, and they have a mild, gentle expression in them when they look at you, which does you good. She wears a dress of heavy, rich silk, with large flowers worked on it; and it rustles when she moves. And then she can tell the most wonderful stories. Grandmother knows a great deal, for she was alive before father and mother—that's quite certain. She has a hymn-book with large silver clasps, in which she often reads; and in the book, between the leaves, lies a rose, quite flat and dry; it is not so pretty as the roses which are standing in the glass, and yet she smiles at it most pleasantly, and tears even come into her eyes. "I wonder why grandmother looks at the withered flower in the old book that way? Do you know?" Why, when grandmother's tears fall upon the rose, and she is looking at it, the rose revives, and fills the room with its fragrance; the walls vanish as in a mist, and all around her is the glorious green wood, where in summer the sunlight streams through thick foliage; and grandmother, why she is young again, a charming maiden, fresh as a rose, with round, rosy cheeks, fair, bright ringlets, and a figure pretty and graceful; but the eyes, those mild, saintly eyes, are the same—they have been left to grandmother. At her side sits a young man, tall and strong; he gives her a rose and she smiles. Grandmother cannot smile like that now. Yes, she is smiling at the memory of that day, and many thoughts and recollections of the past; but the handsome young man is gone, and the rose has withered in the old book, and grandmother is sitting there, again an old woman, looking down upon the withered rose in the book.

Grandmother is dead now. She had been sitting in her armchair, telling us a long, beautiful tale; and when it was finished, she said she was tired, and leaned her head back to sleep awhile. We could hear her gentle breathing as she slept; gradually it became quieter and calmer, and on her countenance beamed happiness and peace. It was as if lighted up with a ray of sunshine. She smiled once more, and then people said she was dead. She was laid in a black coffin, looking mild and beautiful in the white folds of the shrouded linen, though her eyes were closed; but every wrinkle had vanished, her hair looked white and silvery, and around her mouth lingered a sweet smile. We did not feel at all afraid to look at the corpse of her who had been such a dear, good grandmother. The hymn-book, in which the rose still lay, was placed under her head, for so she had wished it; and then they buried grandmother.

On the grave, close by the churchyard wall, they planted a rose-tree; it was soon full of roses, and the nightingale sat among the flowers, and sang over the grave. From the organ in the church sounded the music and the words of the beautiful psalms, which were written in the old book under the head of the dead one.

The moon shone down upon the grave, but the dead was not there; every child could go safely, even at night, and pluck a rose from the tree by the churchyard wall. The dead know more than we do who are living. They know what a terror would come upon us if such a strange thing were to happen, as the appearance of a dead person among us. They are better off than we are; the dead return no more. The earth has been heaped on the coffin, and it is earth only that lies within it. The leaves of the hymn-book are dust; and the rose, with all its recollections, has crumbled to dust also. But over the grave fresh roses bloom, the nightingale sings, and the organ sounds and there still lives a remembrance of old grandmother, with the loving, gentle eyes that always looked young. *Eyes can never die.* Ours will once again behold dear grandmother, young and beautiful as when, for the first time, she kissed the fresh, red rose, that is now dust in the grave.

The Darning-Needle

Translated by Mrs. H. P. Paull

There was once a Darning-Needle who thought herself so fine that she fancied she must be fit for embroidery. "Hold me tight," she would say to the fingers, when they took her up, "don't let me fall; if you do I shall never be found again, I am so very fine."

"That is your opinion, is it?" said the fingers, as they seized her round the body.

"See, I am coming with a train," said the Darning-Needle, drawing a long thread after her; but there was no knot in the thread.

The Fingers then placed the point of the needle against the cook's slipper. There was a crack in the upper leather, which had to be sewn together.

"What coarse work!" said the Darning-Needle, "I shall never get through. I shall break!—I am breaking!" and sure enough she broke. "Did I not say so?" said the Darning-Needle, "I know I am too fine for such work as that."

"This needle is quite useless for sewing now," said the fingers;

The Darning-Needle

but they still held it fast, and the cook dropped some sealing-wax on the needle, and fastened her handkerchief with it in front.

"So now I am a breast-pin," said the Darning-Needle; "I knew very well I should come to honour some day: merit is sure to rise;" and she laughed, quietly to herself, for of course no one ever saw a Darning-Needle laugh. And there she sat as proudly as if she were in a state coach, and looked all around her. "May I be allowed to ask if you are made of gold?" she inquired of her neighbour, a pin; "you have a very pretty appearance, and a curious head, although you are rather small. You must take pains to grow, for it is not every one who has sealing-wax dropped upon him;" and as she spoke, the Darning-Needle drew herself up so proudly that she fell out of the handkerchief right into the sink, which the cook was cleaning. "Now I am going on a journey," said the needle, as she floated away with the dirty water, "I do hope I shall not be lost." But she really was lost in a gutter. "I am too fine for this world," said the Darning-Needle, as she lay in the gutter; "but I know who I am, and that is always some comfort." So the Darning-Needle kept up her proud behavior, and did not lose her good humour. Then there floated over her all sorts of things—chips and straws, and pieces of old newspaper. "See how they sail," said the Darning-Needle; "they do not know what is under them. I am here, and here I shall stick. See, there goes a chip, thinking of nothing in the world but himself— only a chip. There's a straw going by now; how he turns and twists about! Don't be thinking too much of yourself, or you may chance to run against a stone. There swims a piece of newspaper; what is written upon it has been forgotten long ago, and yet it gives itself airs. I sit here patiently and quietly. I know who I am, so I shall not move."

One day something lying close to the Darning-Needle glittered so splendidly that she thought it was a diamond; yet it was only a piece of broken bottle. The Darning-Needle spoke to it, because it sparkled, and represented herself as a breast-pin. "I suppose you are really a diamond?" she said.

"Why yes, something of the kind," he replied; and so each believed the other to be very valuable, and then they began to talk about the world, and the conceited people in it.

"I have been in a lady's work-box," said the Darning-Needle, "and this lady was the cook. She had on each hand five fingers, and anything so conceited as these five fingers I have never seen; and yet they were only employed to take me out of the box and to put me back again."

"Were they not high-born?"

"High-born!" said the Darning-Needle, "no indeed, but so haughty. They were five brothers, all born fingers; they kept very proudly together, though they were of different lengths. The one who stood first in the rank was named the thumb, he was short and thick, and had only one joint in his back, and could therefore make but one bow; but he said that if he were cut off from a man's hand, that man would be unfit for a soldier. Sweet-tooth, his neighbour, dipped himself into sweet or sour, pointed to the sun and moon, and formed the letters when the fingers wrote. Longman, the middle finger, looked over the heads of all the others. Gold-band, the next finger, wore a golden circle round his waist. And little Playman did nothing at all, and seemed proud of it. They were boasters, and boasters they will remain; and therefore I left them."

"And now we sit here and glitter," said the Piece of broken Bottle.

At the same moment more water streamed into the gutter, so that it overflowed, and the Piece of Bottle was carried away.

"So he is promoted," said the Darning-Needle, "while I remain here; I am too fine, but that is my pride, and what do I care?" And so she sat there in her pride, and had many such thoughts as these— "I could almost fancy that I came from a sunbeam, I am so fine. It seems as if the sunbeams were always looking for me under the water. Ah! I am so fine that even my mother cannot find me. Had I still my old eye, which was broken off, I believe I should weep; but no, I would not do that, it is not genteel to cry."

One day a couple of street boys were paddling in the gutter, for they sometimes found old nails, farthings, and other treasures. It was dirty work, but they took great pleasure in it. "Hallo!" cried one, as he pricked himself with the Darning-Needle, "here's a fellow for you."

"I am not a fellow, I am a young lady," said the Darning-Needle; but no one heard her.

The sealing-wax had come off, and she was quite black; but black makes a person look slender, so she thought herself even finer than before.

"Here comes an egg-shell sailing along," said one of the boys; so they stuck the Darning-Needle into the egg-shell.

"White walls, and I am black myself," said the Darning-Needle, "that looks well; now I can be seen, but I hope I shall not be sea-sick, or I shall break again." She was not sea-sick, and she did not break. "It is a good thing against sea-sickness to have a steel stomach, and not to forget one's own importance. Now my sea-sickness has past: delicate people can bear a great deal."

Crack went the egg-shell, as a wagon passed over it. "Good heavens, how it crushes!" said the Darning-Needle. "I shall be sick now. I am breaking!" but she did not break, though the wagon went over her as she lay at full length; and there let her lie.

The Little Match Girl

Translated by Mrs. H. P. Paull

It was terribly cold and nearly dark on the last evening of the old year, and the snow was falling fast. In the cold and the darkness, a poor little girl, with bare head and naked feet, roamed through the streets. It is true she had on a pair of slippers when she left home, but they were not of much use. They were very large, so large, indeed, that they had belonged to her mother, and the poor little creature had lost them in running across the street to avoid two carriages that were rolling along at a terrible rate. One of the slippers she could not find, and a boy seized upon the other and ran away with it, saying that he could use it as a cradle, when he had children of his own. So the little girl went on with her little naked feet, which were quite red and blue with the cold. In an old apron she carried a number of matches, and had a bundle of them in her hands. No one had bought anything of her the whole day, nor had any one given her even a penny. Shivering with cold and hunger, she crept along; poor little child, she looked the picture of misery. The snowflakes fell on her long, fair hair, which hung in curls on her shoulders, but she regarded them not.

Lights were shining from every window, and there was a savory smell of roast goose, for it was New-year's eve—yes, she remembered that. In a corner, between two houses, one of which projected beyond the other, she sank down and huddled herself together. She had drawn her little feet under her, but she could not keep off the cold; and she dared not go home, for she had sold no matches, and could not take home even a penny of money. Her father would certainly beat her; besides, it was almost as cold at home as here, for they had only the roof to cover them, through which the wind howled, although the largest holes had been stopped up with straw and rags. Her little hands were almost frozen with the cold. Ah! perhaps a burning match might be some good, if she could draw it from the bundle and strike it against the wall, just to warm her fingers. She drew one out—"scratch!" how it sputtered as it burnt! It gave a warm, bright light, like a little candle, as she held her hand over it. It was really a wonderful light. It seemed to the little girl that she was sitting by a large iron stove, with polished brass feet and a brass ornament. How the fire burned! and seemed so beautifully warm that the child stretched out her feet as if to warm them, when, lo! the flame of the match went out, the stove vanished, and she had only the remains of the half-burnt match in her hand.

She rubbed another match on the wall. It burst into a flame, and where its light fell upon the wall it became as transparent as a veil, and she could see into the room. The table was covered with a snowy white table-cloth, on which stood a splendid dinner service, and a steaming roast goose, stuffed with apples and dried plums. And what was still more wonderful, the goose jumped down from the dish and waddled across the floor, with a knife and fork in its breast, to the little girl. Then the match went out, and there remained nothing but the thick, damp, cold wall before her.

She lighted another match, and then she found herself sitting under a beautiful Christmas-tree. It was larger and more beautifully decorated than the one which she had seen through the glass door at the rich merchant's. Thousands of tapers were burning upon the green branches, and coloured pictures, like those she had seen in the show-windows, looked down upon it all. The little one stretched out her hand towards them, and the match went out.

The Little Match Girl

The Christmas lights rose higher and higher, till they looked to her like the stars in the sky. Then she saw a star fall, leaving behind it a bright streak of fire. "Some one is dying," thought the little girl, for her old grandmother, the only one who had ever loved her, and who was now dead, had told her that when a star falls, a soul was going up to God.

She again rubbed a match on the wall, and the light shone round her; in the brightness stood her old grandmother, clear and shining, yet mild and loving in her appearance. "Grandmother," cried the little one, "O take me with you; I know you will go away when the match burns out; you will vanish like the warm stove, the roast goose, and the large, glorious Christmas-tree." And she made haste to light the whole bundle of matches, for she wished to keep her grandmother there. And the matches glowed with a light that was brighter than the noon-day, and her grandmother had never appeared so large or so beautiful. She took the little girl in her arms, and they both flew upwards in brightness and joy far above the earth, where there was neither cold nor hunger nor pain, for they were with God.

In the dawn of morning there lay the poor little one, with pale cheeks and smiling mouth, leaning against the wall; she had been frozen to death on the last evening of the year; and the New-year's sun rose and shone upon a little corpse! The child still sat, in the stiffness of death, holding the matches in her hand, one bundle of which was burnt. "She tried to warm herself," said some. No one imagined what beautiful things she had seen, nor into what glory she had entered with her grandmother, on New-year's day.

By the Almshouse Window

Translated by Mrs. H. P. Paull

Near the grass-covered rampart which encircles Copenhagen lies a great red house. Balsams and other flowers greet us from the long rows of windows in the house, whose interior is sufficiently poverty-stricken; and poor and old are the people who inhabit it. The building is the Warton Almshouse.

Look! at the window there leans an old maid. She plucks the withered leaf from the balsam, and looks at the grass-covered rampart, on which many children are playing. What is the old maid thinking of? A whole life drama is unfolding itself before her inward gaze.

"The poor little children, how happy they are—how merrily they play and romp together! What red cheeks and what angels' eyes! but they have no shoes nor stockings. They dance on the green rampart, just on the place where, according to the old story, the ground always sank in, and where a sportive, frolicsome child had been lured by means of flowers, toys and sweetmeats into an open grave ready dug for it, and which was afterwards closed over the child; and from that moment, the old story says, the ground gave way no longer, the mound remained firm and fast, and was quickly covered with the green turf. The little people who now play on that spot know nothing of the old tale, else would they fancy they heard a child crying deep below the earth, and the dewdrops on each blade of grass would be to them tears of woe. Nor do they know anything of the Danish King who here, in the face of the coming foe, took an oath before all his trembling courtiers that he would hold out with the citizens of his capital, and die here in his nest; they know nothing of the men who have fought here, or of the women who from here have drenched with boiling water the enemy, clad in white, and 'biding in the snow to surprise the city.

"No! the poor little ones are playing with light, childish spirits. Play on, play on, thou little maiden! Soon the years will come—yes, those glorious years. The priestly hands have been laid on the candidates for confirmation; hand in hand they walk on the green rampart. Thou hast a white frock on; it has cost thy mother much labour, and yet it is only cut down for thee out of an old larger dress! You will also wear a red shawl; and what if it hang too far down? People will only see how large, how very large it is. You are thinking of your dress, and of the Giver of all good—so glorious is it to wander on the green rampart!

"And the years roll by; they have no lack of dark days, but you have your cheerful young spirit, and you have gained *a friend*—you know not how. You met, oh, how often! You walk together on the rampart in the fresh spring, on the high days and holidays, when all the world come out to walk upon the ramparts, and all the bells of the church steeples seem to be singing a song of praise for the coming spring.

"Scarcely have the violets come forth, but there on the rampart, just opposite the beautiful Castle of Rosenberg, there is a tree bright with the first green buds. Every year this tree sends forth fresh green shoots. Alas! It is not so with the human heart! Dark mists, more in number than those that cover the northern skies, cloud the human heart. Poor child! thy friend's bridal chamber is a black coffin, and thou becomest an old maid. From the almshouse window, behind the balsams, thou shalt look on the merry children at play, and shalt see thine own history renewed."

And that is the life drama that passes before the old maid while she looks out upon the rampart, the green, sunny rampart, where the children, with their red cheeks and bare shoeless feet, are rejoicing merrily, like the other free little birds.

The Old Street Lamp

Translated by Mrs. H. P. Paull

Did you ever hear the story of the old street lamp? It is not remarkably interesting, but for once in a way you may as well listen to it. It was a most respectable old lamp, which had seen many, many years of service, and now was to retire with a pension. It was this evening at its post for the last time, giving light to the street. His feelings were something like those of an old dancer at the theatre, who is dancing for the last time, and knows that on the morrow she will be in her garret, alone and forgotten. The lamp had very great anxiety about the next day, for he knew that he had to appear for the first time at the town hall, to be inspected by the mayor and the council, who were to decide if he were fit for further service or not;—whether the lamp was good enough to be used to light the inhabitants of one of the suburbs, or in the country, at some factory; and if not, it would be sent at once to an iron foundry, to be melted down. In this latter case it might be turned into anything, and he wondered very much whether he would then be able to remember that he had once been a street lamp, and it troubled him exceedingly.

Whatever might happen, one thing seemed certain, that he would be separated from the watchman and his wife, whose family he looked upon as his own. The lamp had first been hung up on that very evening that the watchman, then a robust young man, had entered upon the duties of his office. Ah, well, it was a very long time since one became a lamp and the other a watchman. His wife had a little pride in those days; she seldom condescended to glance at the lamp, excepting when she passed by in the evening, never in the daytime. But in later years, when all these—the watchman, the wife, and the lamp—had grown old, she had attended to it, cleaned it, and supplied it with oil. The old people were thoroughly honest, they had never cheated the lamp of a single drop of the oil provided for it.

This was the lamp's last night in the street, and tomorrow he must go to the town-hall—two very dark things to think of. No wonder he did not burn brightly. Many other thoughts also passed through his mind. How many persons he had lighted on their way, and how much he had seen; as much, very likely, as the mayor and corporation themselves! None of these thoughts were uttered aloud, however; for he was a good, honourable old lamp, who would not willingly do harm to any one, especially to those in authority. As many things were recalled to his mind, the light would flash up with sudden brightness; he had, at such moments, a conviction that he would be remembered. "There was a handsome young man once," thought he; "it is certainly a long while ago, but I remember he had a little note, written on pink paper with a gold edge; the writing was elegant, evidently a lady's hand: twice he read it through, and kissed it, and then looked up at me, with eyes that said quite plainly, 'I am the happiest of men!' Only he and I know what was written on this his first letter from his lady-love. Ah, yes, and there was another pair of eyes that I remember—it is really wonderful how the thoughts jump from one thing to another! A funeral passed through the street; a young and beautiful woman lay on a bier, decked with garlands of flowers, and attended by torches, which quite overpowered my light. All along the street stood the people from the houses, in crowds, ready to join the procession. But when the torches had passed from before me, and I could look round, I saw one person alone, standing, leaning against my post, and weeping. Never shall I forget the sorrowful eyes that looked up at me." These and similar reflections occupied the old street lamp, on this the last time that his light would shine. The sentry, when he is relieved from his post, knows at least who will succeed him, and may whisper a few words to him, but the lamp did not know his successor, or he could have given him a few hints respecting rain, or mist, and could have informed him how far the moon's rays would rest on the pavement, and from which side the wind generally blew, and so on.

On the bridge over the canal stood three persons, who wished to recommend themselves to the lamp, for they thought he could give the office to whomsoever he chose. The first was a herring's head, which could emit light in the darkness. He remarked that it would be a great saving of oil if they placed him on the lamp-post. Number two was a piece of rotten wood, which also shines in the dark. He considered himself descended from an old stem, once the pride of the forest. The third was a glow-worm, and how he found his way there the lamp could not imagine, yet there he was, and could really give light as well as the others. But the rotten wood and the herring's head declared most solemnly, by all they held sacred, that the glow-worm only gave light at certain times, and must not be allowed to compete with themselves. The old lamp assured them that not one of them could give sufficient light to fill the position of a street lamp; but they would believe nothing he said. And when they discovered that he had not the power of naming his successor, they said they were very glad to hear it, for the lamp was too old and worn-out to make a proper choice.

At this moment the wind came rushing round the corner of the street, and through the air-holes of the old lamp. "What is this I hear?" said he; "that you are going away tomorrow? Is this evening the last time we shall meet? Then I must present you with a farewell gift. I will blow into your brain, so that in future you shall not only be able to remember all that you have seen or heard in the past, but your light within shall be so bright, that you shall be able to understand all that is said or done in your presence."

"Oh, that is really a very, very great gift," said the old lamp; "I thank you most heartily. I only hope I shall not be melted down."

"That is not likely to happen yet," said the wind; "and I will also blow a memory into you, so that should you receive other similar presents your old age will pass very pleasantly."

"That is if I am not melted down," said the lamp. "But should I in that case still retain my memory?"

"Do be reasonable, old lamp," said the wind, puffing away.

At this moment the moon burst forth from the clouds. "What will you give the old lamp?" asked the wind.

"I can give nothing," she replied; "I am on the wane, and no lamps have ever given me light while I have frequently shone upon them." And with these words the moon hid herself again behind the clouds, that she might be saved from further importunities. Just then a drop fell upon the lamp, from the roof of the house, but the drop explained that he was a gift from those gray clouds, and perhaps the best of all gifts. "I shall penetrate you so thoroughly," he said, "that you will have the power of becoming rusty, and, if you wish it, to crumble into dust in one night."

But this seemed to the lamp a very shabby present, and the wind thought so too. "Does no one give any more? Will no one give any more?" shouted the breath of the wind, as loud as it could. Then a bright falling star came down, leaving a broad, luminous streak behind it.

"What was that?" cried the herring's head. "Did not a star fall? I really believe it went into the lamp. Certainly, when such high-born personages try for the office, we may as well say 'Goodnight,' and go home."

And so they did, all three, while the old lamp threw a wonderfully strong light all around him.

"This is a glorious gift," said he; "the bright stars have always been a joy to me, and have always shone more brilliantly than I ever could shine, though I have tried with my whole might; and now they have noticed me, a poor old lamp, and have sent me a gift that will enable me to see clearly everything that I remember, as if it still stood before me, and to be seen by all those who love me. And herein lies the truest pleasure, for joy which we cannot share with others is only half enjoyed."

"That sentiment does you honour," said the wind; "but for this purpose wax lights will be necessary. If these are not lighted in you, your particular faculties will not benefit others in the least. The stars have not thought of this; they suppose that you and every other light must be a wax taper: but I must go down now." So he laid himself to rest.

"Wax tapers, indeed!" said the lamp, "I have never yet had these, nor is it likely I ever shall. If I could only be sure of not being melted down!"

The next day. Well, perhaps we had better pass over the next day. The evening had come, and the lamp was resting in a grandfather's chair, and guess where! Why, at the old watchman's house. He had begged, as a favour, that the mayor and corporation would allow him to keep the street lamp, in consideration of his long and faithful service, as he had himself hung it up and lit it on the day he first commenced his duties, four-and-twenty years ago. He looked upon it almost as his own child; he had no children, so the lamp was given to him. There it lay in the great arm-chair near to the warm stove. It seemed almost as if it had grown larger, for it appeared quite to fill the chair. The old people sat at their supper, casting friendly glances at the old lamp, whom they would willingly have admitted to a place at the table. It is quite true that they dwelt in a cellar, two yards deep in the earth, and they had to cross a stone passage to get to their room, but within it was warm and comfortable and strips of list had been nailed round the door. The bed and the little window had curtains, and everything looked clean and neat. On the window seat stood two curious flowerpots which a sailor, named Christian, had brought over from the East or West Indies. They were of clay, and in the form of two elephants, with open backs; they were hollow and filled with earth, and through the open space flowers bloomed. In one grew some very fine chives or leeks; this was the kitchen garden. The other elephant, which contained a beautiful geranium, they called their flower garden. On the wall hung a large coloured print, representing the congress of Vienna, and all the kings and emperors at once. A clock, with heavy weights, hung on the wall and went "tick, tick," steadily enough; yet it was always rather too fast, which, however, the old people said was better than being too slow. They were now eating their supper, while the old street lamp, as we have heard, lay in the grandfather's arm-chair near the stove. It seemed to the lamp as if the whole world had turned round; but after a while the old watchman looked at the lamp, and spoke of what they had both gone through together—in rain and in fog; during the short bright nights of summer, or in the long winter nights, through the drifting snowstorms, when he longed to be at home in the cellar. Then the lamp felt it was all right again. He saw everything that had happened quite clearly, as if it were passing before him. Surely the wind had given him an excellent gift. The old people were very active and industrious, they were never idle for even a single hour. On Sunday afternoons they would bring out some books, generally a book of travels which they were very fond of. The old man would read aloud about Africa, with its great forests and the wild elephants, while his wife would listen attentively, stealing a glance now and then at the clay elephants, which served as flowerpots.

"I can almost imagine I am seeing it all," she said; and then how the lamp wished for a wax taper to be lighted in him, for then the old woman would have seen the smallest detail as clearly as he did himself. The lofty trees, with their thickly entwined branches, the naked negroes on horseback, and whole herds of elephants treading down bamboo thickets with their broad, heavy feet.

"What is the use of all my capabilities," sighed the old lamp, "when I cannot obtain any wax lights; they have only oil and tallow here, and these will not do." One day a great heap of wax-candle ends found their way into the cellar. The larger pieces were burnt, and the smaller ones the old woman kept for waxing her thread. So there were now candles enough, but it never occurred to any one to put a little piece in the lamp.

"Here I am now with my rare powers," thought the lamp, "I have faculties within me, but I cannot share them; they do not know that I could cover these white walls with beautiful tapestry, or change them into noble forests, or, indeed, to anything else they might wish for." The lamp, however, was always kept clean and shining in a corner where it attracted all eyes. Strangers looked upon it as lumber, but the old people did not care for that; they loved the lamp. One day—it was the watchman's birthday—the old woman approached the lamp, smiling to herself, and said, "I will have an illumination today in honour of my old man." And the lamp rattled in his metal frame, for he thought, "Now at last I shall have a light within me," but after all no wax light was placed in the lamp, but oil as usual. The lamp burned through the whole evening, and began to perceive too clearly that the gift of the stars would remain a hidden treasure all his life. Then he had a dream; for, to one with his faculties, dreaming was no difficulty. It appeared to him that the old people were dead, and that he had been taken to the iron foundry to be melted down. It caused him quite as much anxiety as on the day when he had been called upon to appear before the mayor and the council at the town-hall. But though he had been endowed with the power of falling into decay from rust when he pleased, he did not make use of it. He was therefore put into the melting-furnace and changed into as elegant an iron candlestick as you could wish to see, one intended to hold a wax taper. The candlestick was in the form of an angel holding a nosegay, in the centre of which the wax taper was to be placed. It was to stand on a green writing table, in a very pleasant room; many books were scattered about, and splendid paintings hung on the walls. The owner of the room was a poet, and a man of intellect; everything he thought or wrote was pictured around him. Nature showed herself to him sometimes in the dark forests, at others in cheerful meadows where the storks were strutting about, or on the deck of a ship sailing across the foaming sea with the clear, blue sky above, or at night the glittering stars. "What powers I possess!" said the lamp, awaking from his dream; "I could almost wish to be melted down; but no, that must not be while the old people live. They love me for myself alone, they keep me bright, and supply me with oil. I am as well off as the picture of the congress, in which they take so much pleasure." And from that time he felt at rest in himself, and not more so than such an honourable old lamp really deserved to be.

Little Tuk

Translated by Mrs. H. P. Paull

Yes, they called him Little Tuk, but it was not his real name; he had called himself so before he could speak plainly, and he meant it for Charles. It was all very well for those who knew him, but not for strangers.

Little Tuk was left at home to take care of his little sister, Gustava, who was much younger than himself, and he had to learn his lessons at the same time, and the two things could not very well be performed together. The poor boy sat there with his sister on his lap, and sung to her all the songs he knew, and now and then he looked into his geography lesson that lay open before him. By the next morning he had to learn by heart all the towns in Zealand, and all that could be described of them.

His mother came home at last, and took little Gustava in her arms. Then Tuk ran to the window, and read so eagerly that he nearly read his eyes out; for it had become darker and darker every minute, and his mother had no money to buy a light.

"There goes the old washerwoman up the lane," said the mother, as she looked out of the window; "the poor woman can hardly drag herself along, and now she had to drag a pail of water from the well. Be a good boy, Tuk, and run across and help the old woman, won't you?"

So Tuk ran across quickly, and helped her, but when he came back into the room it was quite dark, and there was not a word said about a light, so he was obliged to go to bed on his little truckle bedstead, and there he lay and thought of his geography lesson, and of Zealand, and of all the master had told him. He ought really to have read it over again, but he could not for want of light. So he put the geography book under his pillow, for he had heard that this was a great help towards learning a lesson, but not always to be depended upon. He still lay thinking and thinking, when all at once it seemed as if some one kissed him on his eyes and mouth. He slept and yet he did not sleep; and it appeared as if the old washerwoman looked at him with kind eyes and said, "It would be a great pity if you did not know your lesson tomorrow morning; you helped me, and now I will help you, and Providence will always keep those who help themselves;" and at the same time the book under Tuk's pillow began to move about. "Cluck, cluck, cluck," cried a hen as she crept towards him. "I am a hen from Kjøge,"* and then she told him how many inhabitants the town contained, and about a battle that had been fought there, which really was not worth speaking of.

"Crack, crack," down fell something. It was a wooden bird, the parrot which is used as a target as Præstø.† He said there were as many inhabitants in that town as he had nails in his body. He was very proud, and said, "Thorwalsden lived close to me,‡ and here I am now, quite comfortable."

But now little Tuk was no longer in bed; all in a moment he found himself on horseback. Gallop, gallop, away he went, seated in front of a richly-attired knight, with a waving plume, who held him on the saddle, and so they rode through the wood by the old town of Wordingburg, which was very large and busy. The king's castle was surrounded by lofty towers, and radiant light streamed from all the windows. Within there were songs and dancing; King Waldemar and the young gaily-dressed ladies of the court were dancing together. Morning dawned, and as the sun rose, the whole city and the king's castle sank suddenly down together. One tower after another fell, till at last only one remained standing on the hill where the castle had formerly been.§

---

* Kjøge, a little town in Kjøge Bay. Lifting up children by placing the hands on each side of their heads, is called "showing them Kjøge hens."
† Præstø, a still smaller town.
‡ About a hundred paces from Præstø lies the estate of Nysø, where Thorswaldsen usually resided while in Denmark, and where he executed many memorable works.
§ Wordingburg under King Waldemar was a place of great importance; now it is a very insignificant town: only a lonely tower and the remains of a well show where the castle once stood.

The town now appeared small and poor, and the school-boys read in their books, which they carried under their arms, that it contained two thousand inhabitants; but this was a mere boast, for it did not contain so many.

And again little Tuk lay in his bed, scarcely knowing whether he was dreaming or not, for some one stood by him.

"Tuk! little Tuk!" said a voice. It was a very little person who spoke. He was dressed as a sailor, and looked small enough to be a middy, but he was not one. "I bring you many greetings from Corsøe.[*] It is a rising town, full of life. It has steamships and mail-coaches. In times past they used to call it ugly, but that is no longer true. I lie on the sea-shore," said Corsøe; "I have high roads and pleasure-gardens; I have given birth to a poet who was witty and entertaining, which they are not all. I once wanted to fit out a ship to sail round the world, but I did not accomplish it, though most likely I might have done so. But I am fragrant with perfume, for close to my gates most lovely roses bloom."

Then before the eyes of little Tuk appeared a confusion of colours, red and green; but it cleared off, and he could distinguish a cliff close to the bay, the slopes of which were quite overgrown with verdure, and on its summit stood a fine old church with pointed towers. Springs of water flowed out of the cliff in thick waterspouts, so that there was a continual splashing. Close by sat an old king with a golden crown on his white head. This was King Hroar of the Springs[†] and near the springs stood the town of Roeskilde, as it is called. Then all the kings and queens of Denmark went up the ascent to the old church, hand in hand, with golden

---

[*] Corsøe, on the Great Belt, used to be called the most tiresome town in Denmark before the establishment of steamers. Travellars had to wait for a favourable wind. The title "tiresome" was ingeniously added to the Danish escutcheon by a witticism of Vaudeville Heibergs. The poet Baddesen was born here.

[†] Roeskilde (from Roesquelle, rose-spring, falsely called Rothschild), once the capital of Denmark. The town took its name from King Hroar, and from the numerous springs in the neighbourhood. In its beautiful cathedral most of the kings and queens of Denmark are buried. In Roeskilde the Danish States used to assemble.

crowns on their heads, while the organ played and the fountains sent forth jets of water.

Little Tuk saw and heard it all. "Don't forget the names of these towns," said King Hroar.

All at once everything vanished; but where! It seemed to him like turning over the leaves of a book. And now there stood before him an old peasant woman, who had come from Sorø* where the grass grows in the market-place. She had a green linen apron thrown over her head and shoulders, and it was quite wet, as if it had been raining heavily. "Yes, that it has," said she, and then, just as she was going to tell him a great many pretty stories from Holberg's comedies, and about Waldemar and Absalom, she suddenly shrunk up together, and wagged her head as if she were a frog about to spring. "Croak," she cried; "it is always wet, and as quiet as death in Sorø." Then little Tuk saw she was changed into a frog. "Croak," and again she was an old woman. "One must dress according to the weather," said she. "It is wet, and my town is just like a bottle. By the cork we must go in, and by the cork we must come out again. In olden times I had beautiful fish, and now I have fresh, rosy-cheeked boys in the bottom of the bottle, and they learn wisdom, Hebrew and Greek."

"Croak." How it sounded like the cry of the frogs on the moor, or like the creaking of great boots when some one is marching— always the same tone, so monotonous and wearing, that little Tuk at length fell fast asleep, and then the sound could not annoy him. But even in this sleep came a dream or something like it. His little sister Gustava, with her blue eyes, and fair curly hair, had grown up a beautiful maiden all at once, and without having wings she could fly. And they flew together over Zealand, over green forests and blue lakes.

"Hark, so you hear the cock crow, little Tuk. 'Cock-a-doodle-doo.' The fowls are flying out of Kjøge. You shall have a large farm-yard. You shall never suffer hunger or want. The bird of good omen shall be yours, and you shall become a rich and happy man; your

---

* Sorø, a very quite little town in a beautiful situation, surrounded by forests and lakes. Holberg, the Molière of Denmark, founded a noble academy here. The poets Hanck and Jugeman were professors here. Letztern lives there still.

house shall rise up like King Waldemar's towers, and shall be richly adorned with marble statues, like those at Præstø. Understand me well; your name shall travel with fame round the world like the ship that was to sail from Corsøe, and at Roeskilde—Don't forget the names of the towns, as King Hroar said—you shall speak well and clearly little Tuk, and when at last you lie in your grave you shall sleep peacefully, as—"

"As if I lay in Sorø," said little Tuk awaking. It was bright daylight, and he could not remember his dream, but that was not necessary, for we are not to know what will happen to us in the future. Then he sprang out of bed quickly, and read over his lesson in the book, and knew it all at once quite correctly. The old washerwoman put her head in at the door, and nodded to him quite kindly, and said, "Many thanks, you good child, for your help yesterday. I hope all your beautiful dreams will come true."

Little Tuk did not at all know what he had dreamt, but One above did.

The Shadow

Translated by Mrs. H. P. Paull

In very hot climates, where the heat of the sun has great power, people are usually as brown as mahogany; and in the hottest countries they are negroes, with black skins. A learned man once travelled into one of these warm climates, from the cold regions of the north, and thought he would roam about as he did at home; but he soon had to change his opinion. He found that, like all sensible people, he must remain in the house during the whole day, with every window and door closed, so that it looked as if all in the house were asleep or absent. The houses of the narrow street in which he lived were so lofty that the sun shone upon them from morning till evening, and it became quite unbearable. This learned man from the cold regions was young as well as clever; but it seemed to him as if he were sitting in an oven, and he became quite exhausted and weak, and grew so thin that his Shadow shrivelled up, and became much smaller than it had been at home. The sun took away even what was left of it, and he saw nothing of it till the evening, after sunset. It was really a pleasure, as soon as the lights were brought into the room, to see the Shadow stretch itself against the wall, even to the ceiling, so tall was it; and it really wanted a good stretch to recover its strength. The learned man would sometimes go out into the balcony to stretch himself also; and as soon as the stars came forth in the clear, beautiful sky, he felt revived. People at this hour began to make their appearance in all the balconies in the street; for in warm climates every window has a balcony, in which they can breathe the fresh evening air, which is very necessary, even to those who are used to a heat that makes them as brown as mahogany; so that the street presented a very lively appearance. Here were shoemakers, and tailors, and all sorts of people sitting. In the street beneath, they brought out tables and chairs, lighted candles by hundreds, talked and sang, and were very merry. There were people walking, carriages driving, and mules trotting along, with their bells on the harness, "tingle, tingle," as they went. Then the dead were carried to the grave with the sound of solemn music, and the tolling of the church bells. It was indeed a scene of varied life in the street. One house only, which was just opposite to the one in which the foreign learned man lived, formed a contrast to all this, for it was quite still; and yet somebody dwelt there, for flowers stood in the balcony, blooming beautifully in the hot sun; and this could not have been unless they had been watered carefully. Therefore some one must be in the house to do this. The doors leading to the balcony were half opened in the evening; and although in the front room all was dark, music could be heard from the interior of the house. The foreign learned man considered this music very delightful; but perhaps he fancied it; for everything in these warm countries pleased him, excepting the heat of the sun. The foreign landlord said he did not know who had taken the opposite house—nobody was to be seen there; and as to the music, he thought it seemed very tedious, to him most uncommonly so.

"It is just as if some one was practising a piece that he could not manage; it is always the same piece. He thinks, I suppose, that he will be able to manage it at last; but I do not think so, however long he may play it."

Once the foreigner woke in the night. He slept with the door open which led to the balcony; the wind had raised the curtain before it, and there appeared a wonderful brightness over all in the balcony of the opposite house. The flowers seemed like flames of the most gorgeous colours, and among the flowers stood a beautiful slender maiden. It was to him as if light streamed from her, and dazzled his eyes; but then he had only just opened them, as he awoke from his sleep. With one spring he was out of bed, and crept softly behind the curtain. But she was gone—the brightness had disappeared; the flowers no longer appeared like flames, although still as beautiful as ever. The door stood ajar, and from an inner room sounded music so sweet and so lovely, that it produced the most enchanting thoughts, and acted on the senses with magic power. Who could live there? Where was the real entrance? for, both in the street and in the lane at the side, the whole ground floor was a continuation of shops; and people could not always be passing through them.

One evening the foreigner sat in the balcony. A light was burning in his own room, just behind him. It was quite natural, therefore, that his Shadow should fall on the wall of the opposite house; so that, as he sat amongst the flowers on his balcony, when he moved, his Shadow moved also.

"I think my Shadow is the only living thing to be seen opposite," said the learned man; "see how pleasantly it sits among the flowers. The door is only ajar; the Shadow ought to be clever enough to step in and look about him, and then to come back and tell me what he has seen. You could make yourself useful in this way," said he, jokingly; "be so good as to step in now, will you?" and then he nodded to the Shadow, and the Shadow nodded in return. "Now go, but don't stay away altogether."

Then the foreigner stood up, and the Shadow on the opposite balcony stood up also; the foreigner turned round, the Shadow turned; and if any one had observed, they might have seen it go straight into the half-opened door of the opposite balcony, as the learned man re-entered his own room, and let the curtain fall. The next morning he went out to take his coffee and read the newspapers.

"How is this?" he exclaimed, as he stood in the sunshine. "I have lost my Shadow. So it really did go away yesterday evening, and it has not returned. This is very annoying."

And it certainly did vex him, not so much because the Shadow was gone, but because he knew there was a story of a man without a shadow. All the people at home, in his country, knew this story; and when he returned, and related his own adventures, they would say it was only an imitation; and he had no desire for such things to be said of him. So he decided not to speak of it at all, which was a very sensible determination.

In the evening he went out again on his balcony, taking care to place the light behind him; for he knew that a shadow always wants his master for a screen; but he could not entice him out. He made himself little, and he made himself tall; but there was no shadow, and no shadow came. He said, "Hem, a-hem;" but it was all useless. That was very vexatious; but in warm countries everything grows very quickly; and, after a week had passed, he saw, to his great joy, that a new shadow was growing from his feet, when he walked in the sunshine; so that the root must have remained. After three weeks, he had quite a respectable shadow, which, during his return journey to northern lands, continued to grow, and became at last so large that he might very well have spared half of it. When this learned man arrived at home, he wrote books about the true, the good, and the beautiful, which are to be found in this world; and so days and years passed—many, many years.

One evening, as he sat in his study, a very gentle tap was heard at the door. "Come in," said he; but no one came. He opened the door, and there stood before him a man so remarkably thin that he felt seriously troubled at his appearance. He was, however, very well dressed, and looked like a gentleman. "To whom have I the honour of speaking?" said he.

"Ah, I hoped you would recognize me," said the elegant stranger; "I have gained so much that I have a body of flesh, and clothes to wear. You never expected to see me in such a condition. Do you not recognize your old Shadow? Ah, you never expected that I should return to you again. All has been prosperous with me since I was with you last; I have become rich in every way, and, were I inclined to purchase my freedom from service, I could easily do so." And as he spoke he rattled between his fingers a number of costly trinkets which hung to a thick gold watch-chain he wore round his neck. Diamond rings sparkled on his fingers, and it was all real.

"I cannot recover from my astonishment," said the learned man. "What does all this mean?"

"Something rather unusual," said the Shadow; "but you are yourself an uncommon man, and you know very well that I have followed in your footsteps ever since your childhood. As soon as you found that I have travelled enough to be trusted alone, I went my own way, and I am now in the most brilliant circumstances. But I felt a kind of longing to see you once more before you die, and I wanted to see this place again, for there is always a clinging to the land of one's birth. I know that you have now another shadow; do I owe you anything? If so, have the goodness to say what it is."

"No! Is it really you?" said the learned man. "Well, this is most remarkable; I never supposed it possible that a man's old Shadow could become a human being."

"Just tell me what I owe you," said the Shadow, "for I do not like to be in debt to any man."

"How can you talk in that manner?" said the learned man. "What question of debt can there be between us? You are as free as any one. I rejoice exceedingly to hear of your good fortune. Sit down, old friend, and tell me a little of how it happened, and what you saw in the house opposite to me while we were in those hot climates."

"Yes, I will tell you all about it," said the Shadow, sitting down; "but then you must promise me never to tell in this city, wherever you may meet me, that I have been your Shadow. I am thinking of being married, for I have more than sufficient to support a family."

"Make yourself quite easy," said the learned man; "I will tell no one who you really are. Here is my hand—I promise, and a word is sufficient between man and man."

"Between man and a Shadow," said the Shadow; for he could not help saying so.

It was really most remarkable how very much he had become a man in appearance. He was dressed in a suit of the very finest black cloth, polished boots, and an opera crush hat, which could be folded together so that nothing could be seen but the crown and the rim, besides the trinkets, the gold chain, and the diamond rings already spoken of. The Shadow was, in fact, very well dressed, and this made a man of him. "Now I will relate to you what you wish to know," said the Shadow, placing his foot with the polished leather boot as firmly as possible on the arm of the new shadow of the learned man, which lay at his feet like a poodle dog. This was done, it might be from pride, or perhaps that the new shadow might cling to him, but the prostrate shadow remained quite quiet and at rest, in order that it might listen, for it wanted to know how a shadow could be sent away by its master, and become a man itself. "Do you know," said the Shadow, "that in the house opposite to you lived the most glorious creature in the world? It was poetry. I remained there three weeks, and it was more like three thousand years, for I read all that has ever been written in poetry or prose; and I may say, in truth, that I saw and learnt everything."

"Poetry!" exclaimed the learned man. "Yes, she lives as a hermit in great cities. Poetry! Well, I saw her once for a very short moment, while sleep weighed down my eyelids. She flashed upon me from the balcony like the radiant aurora borealis, surrounded with flowers like flames of fire. Tell me, you were on the balcony that evening; you went through the door, and what did you see?"

"I found myself in an ante-room," said the Shadow. "You still sat opposite to me, looking into the room. There was no light, or at least it seemed in partial darkness, for the door of a whole suite of rooms stood open, and they were brilliantly lighted. The blaze of light would have killed me, had I approached too near the maiden myself, but I was cautious, and took time, which is what every one ought to do."

"And what didst thou see?" asked the learned man.

"I saw everything, as you shall hear. But—it really is not pride on my part, as a free man and possessing the knowledge that I do, besides my position, not to speak of my wealth—I wish you would say you to me instead of thou."

"I beg your pardon," said the learned man; "it is an old habit, which it is difficult to break. You are quite right; I will try to think of it. But now tell me everything that you saw."

"Everything," said the Shadow; "for I saw and know everything."

"What was the appearance of the inner rooms?" asked the scholar. "Was it there like a cool grove, or like a holy temple? Were the chambers like a starry sky seen from the top of a high mountain?"

"It was all that you describe," said the Shadow; "but I did not go quite in—I remained in the twilight of the ante-room—but I was in a very good position—I could see and hear all that was going on in the Court of Poetry."

"But what did you see? Did the gods of ancient times pass through the rooms? Did old heroes fight their battles over again? Were there lovely children at play, who related their dreams?"

"I tell you I have been there, and therefore you may be sure that I saw everything that was to be seen. If you had gone there, you would not have remained a human being, whereas I became one; and at the same moment I became aware of my inner being, my inborn affinity to the nature of poetry. It is true I did not think much about it while I was with you, but you will remember that I was always much larger at sunrise and sunset, and in the moonlight even more visible than yourself, but I did not then understand my inner existence. In the ante-room it was revealed to me. I became a man; I came out in full maturity. But you had left the warm countries. As a man, I felt ashamed to go about without boots or clothes, and that exterior finish by which man is known. So I went my own way; I can tell you, for you will not put it in a book. I hid myself under the cloak of a cake woman, but she little thought who she concealed. It was not till evening that I ventured out. I ran about the streets in the moonlight. I drew myself up to my full height upon the walls, which tickled my back very pleasantly. I ran here and there, looked through the highest windows into the rooms, and over the roofs. I looked in, and saw what nobody else could see, or indeed ought to see; in fact, it is a bad world, and I would not care to be a man, but that men are of some importance. I saw the most miserable things going on between husbands and wives, parents and children—sweet, incomparable children. I have seen what no human being has the power of knowing, although they would all be very glad to know—the evil conduct of their neighbours. Had I written a newspaper, how eagerly it would have been read! Instead of which, I wrote directly to the persons themselves, and great alarm arose in all the town I visited. They had so much fear of me, and yet how dearly they loved me. The professor made me a professor. The tailor gave me new clothes; I am well provided for in that way. The overseer of the mint struck coins for me. The women declared that I was handsome, and so I became the man you now see me. And now I must say adieu. Here is my card. I live on the sunny side of the street, and always stay at home in rainy weather." And the Shadow departed.

"This is all very remarkable," said the learned man.

Years passed, days and years went by, and the Shadow came again. "How are you going on now?" he asked.

"Ah!" said the learned man; "I am writing about the true, the beautiful, and the good; but no one cares to hear anything about it. I am quite in despair, for I take it to heart very much."

"That is what I never do," said the Shadow; "I am growing quite fat and stout, which every one ought to be. You do not understand the world; you will make yourself ill about it; you ought to travel; I am going on a journey in the summer, will you go with me? I should like a travelling companion; will you travel with me as my shadow? It would give me great pleasure, and I will pay all expenses."

"Are you going to travel far?" asked the learned man.

"That is a matter of opinion," replied the Shadow. "At all events, a journey will do you good, and if you will be my shadow, then all your journey shall be paid."

"It appears to me very absurd," said the learned man.

"But it is the way of the world," replied the Shadow, "and always will be." Then he went away.

Everything went wrong with the learned man. Sorrow and trouble pursued him, and what he said about the good, the beautiful, and the true, was of as much value to most people as a nutmeg would be to a cow. At length he fell ill. "You really look like a shadow," people said to him, and then a cold shudder would pass over him, for he had his own thoughts on the subject.

"You really ought to go to some watering-place," said the Shadow on his next visit. "There is no other chance for you. I will take you with me, for the sake of old acquaintance. I will pay the expenses of your journey, and you shall write a description of it to amuse us by the way. I should like to go to a watering-place; my beard does not grow as it ought, which is from weakness, and I must have a beard. Now do be sensible and accept my proposal; we shall travel as intimate friends."

And at last they started together. The Shadow was master now, and the master became the Shadow. They drove together, and rode and walked in company with each other, side by side, or one in front and the other behind, according to the position of the sun. The Shadow always knew when to take the place of honour, but the learned man took no notice of it, for he had a good heart, and was exceedingly mild and friendly.

One day the master said to the Shadow, "We have grown up together from our childhood, and now that we have become travelling companions, shall we not drink to our good fellowship, and say thee and thou to each other?"

"What you say is very straightforward and kindly meant," said the Shadow, who was now really master. "I will be equally kind and straightforward. You are a learned man, and know how wonderful human nature is. There are some men who cannot endure the smell of brown paper; it makes them ill. Others will feel a shuddering sensation to their very marrow, if a nail is scratched on a pane of glass. I myself have a similar kind of feeling when I hear any one say thou to me. I feel crushed by it, as I used to feel in my former position with you. You will perceive that this is a matter of feeling, not pride. I cannot allow you to say thou to me; I will gladly say it to you, and therefore your wish will be half fulfilled." Then the Shadow addressed his former master as thou.

"It is going rather too far," said the latter, "that I am to say you when I speak to him, and he is to say thou to me." However, he was obliged to submit.

They arrived at length at the baths, where there were many strangers, and among them a beautiful princess, whose real disease consisted in being too sharp-sighted, which made every one very uneasy. She saw at once that the new comer was very different to every one else. "They say he is here to make his beard grow," she thought; "but I know the real cause, he is unable to cast a shadow." Then she became very curious on the matter, and one day, while on the promenade, she entered into conversation with the strange gentleman. Being a princess, she was not obliged to stand upon much ceremony, so she said to him without hesitation, "Your illness consists in not being able to cast a shadow."

"Your royal highness must be on the high road to recovery from your illness," said he. "I know your complaint arose from being too sharp-sighted, and in this case it has entirely failed. I happen to have a most unusual shadow. Have you not seen a person who is always at my side? Persons often give their servants finer cloth for their liveries than for their own clothes, and so I have dressed out my shadow like a man; nay, you may observe that I have even given him a shadow of his own; it is rather expensive, but I like to have things about me that are peculiar."

"How is this?" thought the princess; "am I really cured? This must be the best watering-place in existence. Water in our times has certainly wonderful power. But I will not leave this place yet, just as it begins to be amusing. This foreign prince—for he must be a prince—pleases me above all things. I only hope his beard won't grow, or he will leave at once."

In the evening, the princess and the Shadow danced together in the large assembly rooms. She was light, but he was lighter still; she had never seen such a dancer before. She told him from what country she had come, and found he knew it and had been there, but not while she was at home. He had looked into the windows of her father's palace, both the upper and the lower windows; he had seen many things, and could therefore answer the princess, and make allusions which quite astonished her. She thought he must be the cleverest man in all the world, and felt the greatest respect for his knowledge. When she danced with him again she fell in love with him, which the Shadow quickly discovered, for she had with her eyes looked him through and through. They danced once more, and she was nearly telling him, but she had some discretion; she thought of her country, her kingdom, and the number of people over whom she would one day have to rule. "He is a clever man," she thought to herself, "which is a good thing, and he dances admirably, which is also good. But has he well-grounded knowledge? that is an important question, and I must try him." Then she asked him a most difficult question, she herself could not have answered it, and the Shadow made a most unaccountable grimace.

"You cannot answer that," said the princess.

"I learnt something about it in my childhood," he replied; "and believe that even my very shadow, standing over there by the door, could answer it."

"Your shadow," said the princess; "indeed that would be very remarkable."

"I do not say so positively," observed the Shadow; "but I am inclined to believe that he can do so. He has followed me for so many years, and has heard so much from me, that I think it is very likely. But your royal highness must allow me to observe, that he is very proud of being considered a man, and to put him in a good humour, so that he may answer correctly, he must be treated as a man."

"I shall be very pleased to do so," said the princess. So she walked up to the learned man, who stood in the doorway, and spoke to him of the sun, and the moon, of the green forests, and of people near home and far off; and the learned man conversed with her pleasantly and sensibly.

"What a wonderful man he must be, to have such a clever Shadow!" thought she. "If I were to choose him it would be a real blessing to my country and my subjects, and I will do it." So the princess and the Shadow were soon engaged to each other, but no one was to be told a word about it, till she returned to her kingdom.

"No one shall know," said the Shadow; "not even my own shadow;" and he had very particular reasons for saying so.

After a time, the princess returned to the land over which she reigned, and the Shadow accompanied her.

"Listen my friend," said the Shadow to the learned man; "now that I am as fortunate and as powerful as any man can be, I will do something unusually good for you. You shall live in my palace, drive with me in the royal carriage, and have a hundred thousand dollars a year; but you must allow every one to call you a shadow, and never venture to say that you have been a man. And once a year, when I sit in my balcony in the sunshine, you must lie at my feet as becomes a shadow to do; for I must tell you I am going to marry the princess, and our wedding will take place this evening."

"Now, really, this is too ridiculous," said the learned man. "I cannot, and will not, submit to such folly. It would be cheating the whole country, and the princess also. I will disclose everything, and say that I am the man, and that you are only a Shadow dressed up in men's clothes."

"No one would believe you," said the Shadow; "be reasonable, now, or I will call the guards."

"I will go straight to the princess," said the learned man.

"But I shall be there first," replied the Shadow, "and you will be sent to prison." And so it turned out, for the guards readily obeyed him, as they knew he was going to marry the king's daughter.

"You tremble," said the princess, when the Shadow appeared before her. "Has anything happened? You must not be ill today, for this evening our wedding will take place."

"I have gone through the most terrible affair that could possibly happen," said the Shadow; "only imagine, my shadow has gone mad; I suppose such a poor, shallow brain, could not bear much; he fancies that he has become a real man, and that I am his shadow."

"How very terrible," cried the princess; "is he locked up?"

"Oh yes, certainly; for I fear he will never recover."

"Poor shadow!" said the princess; "it is very unfortunate for him; it would really be a good deed to free him from his frail existence; and, indeed, when I think how often people take the part of the lower class against the higher, in these days, it would be policy to put him out of the way quietly."

"It is certainly rather hard upon him, for he was a faithful servant," said the Shadow; and he pretended to sigh.

"Yours is a noble character," said the princess, and bowed herself before him.

In the evening the whole town was illuminated, and cannons fired "boom," and the soldiers presented arms. It was indeed a grand wedding. The princess and the Shadow stepped out on the balcony to show themselves, and to receive one cheer more. But the learned man heard nothing of all these festivities, for he had already been executed.

The Old House

Translated by Mrs. H. P. Paull

A very old house stood once in a street with several that were quite new and clean. The date of its erection had been carved on one of the beams, and surrounded by scrolls formed of tulips and hop-tendrils; by this date it could be seen that the old house was nearly three hundred years old. Verses too were written over the windows in old-fashioned letters, and grotesque faces, curiously carved, grinned at you from under the cornices. One story projected a long way over the other, and under the roof ran a leaden gutter, with a dragon's head at the end. The rain was intended to pour out at the dragon's mouth, but it ran out of his body instead, for there was a hole in the gutter. The other houses in the street were new and well built, with large window panes and smooth walls. Any one could see they had nothing to do with the old house. Perhaps they thought, "How long will that heap of rubbish remain here to be a disgrace to the whole street. The parapet projects so far forward that no one can see out of our windows what is going on in that direction. The stairs are as broad as the staircase of a castle, and as steep as if they led to a church-tower. The iron railing looks like the gate of a cemetery, and there are brass knobs upon it. It is really too ridiculous."

Opposite to the old house were more nice new houses, which had just the same opinion as their neighbours.

At the window of one of them sat a little boy with fresh rosy cheeks, and clear sparkling eyes, who was very fond of the old house, in sunshine or in moonlight. He would sit and look at the wall from which the plaster had in some places fallen off, and fancy all sorts of scenes which had been in former times. How the street must have looked when the houses had all gable roofs, open staircases, and gutters with dragons at the spout. He could even see soldiers walking about with halberds. Certainly it was a very good house to look at for amusement.

An old man lived in it, who wore knee-breeches, a coat with large brass buttons, and a wig, which any one could see was a real wig. Every morning an old man came to clean the rooms, and to wait upon him, otherwise the old man in the knee-breeches would have been quite alone in the house. Sometimes he came to one of the windows and looked out; then the little boy nodded to him, and the old man nodded back again, till they became acquainted, and were friends, although they had never spoken to each other; but that was of no consequence.

The little boy one day heard his parents say, "The old man opposite is very well off, but is terribly lonely." The next Sunday morning the little boy wrapped something in a piece of paper and took it to the door of the old house, and said to the attendant who waited upon the old man, "Will you please give this from me to the gentleman who lives here; I have two tin soldiers, and this is one of them, and he shall have it, because I know he is terribly lonely."

And the old attendant nodded and looked very pleased, and then he carried the tin soldier into the house.

Afterwards he was sent over to ask the little boy if he would not like to pay a visit himself. His parents gave him permission, and so it was that he gained admission to the old house.

The brassy knobs on the railings shone more brightly than ever, as if they had been polished on account of his visit; and on the door were carved trumpeters standing in tulips, and it seemed as if they were blowing with all their might, their cheeks were so puffed out. "Tanta-ra-ra, the little boy is coming; Tanta-ra-ra, the little boy is coming."

Then the door opened. All round the hall hung old portraits of knights in armor, and ladies in silk gowns; and the armor rattled, and the silk dresses rustled. Then came a staircase which went up a long way, and then came down a little way and led to a balcony, which was in a very ruinous state. There were large holes and long cracks, out of which grew grass and leaves, indeed the whole balcony, the courtyard, and the walls were so overgrown with green that they looked like a garden. In the balcony stood flowerpots, on which were heads having asses' ears, but the flowers in them grew just as they pleased. In one pot pinks were growing all over the sides, at least the green leaves were shooting forth stalk and stem, and saying as plainly as they could speak, "The air has fanned me, the sun has kissed me, and I am promised a little flower for next Sunday—really for next Sunday."

Then they entered a room in which the walls were covered with leather, and the leather had golden flowers stamped upon it.

"Gilding will fade in damp weather,
To endure, there is nothing like leather,"

said the walls. Chairs handsomely carved, with elbows on each side, and with very high backs, stood in the room, and as they creaked they seemed to say, "Sit down. Oh dear, how I am creaking. I shall certainly have the gout like the old cupboard. Gout in my back, ugh."

And then the little boy entered the room where the old man sat.

"Thank you for the tin soldier my little friend," said the old man, "and thank you also for coming to see me."

"Thanks, thanks," or "Creak, creak," said all the furniture.

There was so much that the pieces of furniture stood in each other's way to get a sight of the little boy.

On the wall near the centre of the room hung the picture of a beautiful lady, young and gay, dressed in the fashion of the olden times, with powdered hair, and a full, stiff skirt. She said neither "thanks" nor "creak," but she looked down upon the little boy with her mild eyes; and then he said to the old man,

"Where did you get that picture?"

"From the shop opposite," he replied. "Many portraits hang there that none seem to trouble themselves about. The persons they represent have been dead and buried long since. But I knew this lady many years ago, and she has been dead nearly half a century."

Under a glass beneath the picture hung a nosegay of withered flowers, which were no doubt half a century old too, at least they appeared so.

And the pendulum of the old clock went to and fro, and the hands turned round; and as time passed on, everything in the room grew older, but no one seemed to notice it.

"They say at home," said the little boy, "that you are very lonely."

"Oh," replied the old man, "I have pleasant thoughts of all that has passed, recalled by memory; and now you are come to visit me, and that is very pleasant."

Then he took from the book-case, a book full of pictures representing long processions of wonderful coaches, such as are never seen at the present time. Soldiers like the knave of clubs, and citizens with waving banners. The tailors had a flag with a pair of scissors supported by two lions, and on the shoemakers' flag there were not boots, but an eagle with two heads, for the shoemakers must have everything arranged so that they can say, "This is a pair." What a picture book it was; and then the old man went into another room to fetch apples and nuts. It was very pleasant, certainly, to be in that old house.

"I cannot endure it," said the tin soldier, who stood on a shelf, "it is so lonely and dull here. I have been accustomed to live in a family, and I cannot get used to this life. I cannot bear it. The whole day is long enough, but the evening is longer. It is not here like it was in your house opposite, when your father and mother talked so cheerfully together, while you and all the dear children made such a delightful noise. No, it is all lonely in the old man's house. Do you think he gets any kisses? Do you think he ever has friendly looks, or a Christmas tree? He will have nothing now but the grave. Oh, I cannot bear it."

"You must not look only on the sorrowful side," said the little boy; "I think everything in this house is beautiful, and all the old pleasant thoughts come back here to pay visits."

"Ah, but I never see any, and I don't know them," said the tin soldier, "and I cannot bear it."

"You must bear it," said the little boy. Then the old man came back with a pleasant face; and brought with him beautiful preserved fruits, as well as apples and nuts; and the little boy thought no more of the tin soldier. How happy and delighted the little boy was; and after he returned home, and while days and weeks passed, a great deal of nodding took place from one house to the other, and then the little boy went to pay another visit. The carved trumpeters blew "Tanta-ra-ra. There is the little boy. Tanta-ra-ra." The swords and armor on the old knight's pictures rattled. The silk dresses rustled, the leather repeated its rhyme, and the old chairs had the gout in their backs, and cried, "Creak;" it was all exactly like the first time; for in that house, one day and one hour were just like another. "I cannot bear it any longer," said the tin soldier; "I have wept tears of tin, it is so melancholy here. Let me go to the wars, and lose an arm or a leg, that would be some change; I cannot bear it. Now I know what it is to have visits from one's old recollections, and all they bring with them. I have had visits from mine, and you may believe me it is not altogether pleasant. I was very nearly jumping from the shelf. I saw you all in your house opposite, as if you were really present. It was Sunday morning, and you children stood round the table, singing the hymn that you sing every morning. You were standing quietly, with your hands folded, and your father and mother. You were standing quietly, with your hands folded, and your father and mother were looking just as serious, when the door opened, and your little sister Maria, who is not two years old, was brought into the room. You know she always dances when she hears music and singing of any sort; so she began to dance immediately, although she ought not to have done so, but she could not get into the right time because the tune was so slow; so she stood first on one leg and then on the other, and bent her head very low, but it would not suit the music. You all stood looking very grave, although it was very difficult to do so, but I laughed so to myself that I fell down from the table, and got a bruise,

The Old House

which is there still; I know it was not right to laugh. So all this, and everything else that I have seen, keeps running in my head, and these must be the old recollections that bring so many thoughts with them. Tell me whether you still sing on Sundays, and tell me about your little sister Maria, and how my old comrade is, the other tin soldier. Ah, really he must be very happy; I cannot endure this life."

"You are given away," said the little boy; "you must stay. Don't you see that?" Then the old man came in, with a box containing many curious things to show him. Rouge-pots, scent-boxes, and old cards, so large and so richly gilded, that none are ever seen like them in these days. And there were smaller boxes to look at, and the piano was opened, and inside the lid were painted landscapes. But when the old man played, the piano sounded quite out of tune. Then he looked at the picture he had bought at the broker's, and his eyes sparkled brightly as he nodded at it, and said, "Ah, she could sing that tune."

"I will go to the wars! I will go to the wars!" cried the tin soldier as loud as he could, and threw himself down on the floor. Where could he have fallen? The old man searched, and the little boy searched, but he was gone, and could not be found. "I shall find him again," said the old man, but he did not find him. The boards of the floor were open and full of holes. The tin soldier had fallen through a crack between the boards, and lay there now in an open grave. The day went by, and the little boy returned home; the week passed, and many more weeks. It was winter, and the windows were quite frozen, so the little boy was obliged to breathe on the panes, and rub a hole to peep through at the old house. Snow drifts were lying in all the scrolls and on the inscriptions, and the steps were covered with snow as if no one were at home. And indeed nobody was home, for the old man was dead. In the evening, a hearse stopped at the door, and the old man in his coffin was placed in it. He was to be taken to the country to be buried there in his own grave; so they carried him away; no one followed him, for all his friends were dead; and the little boy kissed his hand to the coffin as the hearse moved away with it. A few days after, there was an auction at the old house, and from his window the little boy saw the people carrying away the pictures of old knights and ladies, the flowerpots with the long ears, the old chairs, and the cup-boards. Some were taken one way, some another. Her portrait, which had been bought at the picture dealer's, went back again to his shop, and there it remained, for no one seemed to know her, or to care for the old picture. In the spring; they began to pull the house itself down; people called it complete rubbish. From the street could be seen the room in which the walls were covered with leather, ragged and torn, and the green in the balcony hung straggling over the beams; they pulled it down quickly, for it looked ready to fall, and at last it was cleared away altogether. "What a good riddance," said the neighbours' houses. Very shortly, a fine new house was built farther back from the road; it had lofty windows and smooth walls, but in front, on the spot where the old house really stood, a little garden was planted, and wild vines grew up over the neighbouring walls; in front of the garden were large iron railings and a great gate, which looked very stately. People used to stop and peep through the railings. The sparrows assembled in dozens upon the wild vines, and chattered all together as loud as they could, but not about the old house; none of them could remember it, for many years had passed by, so many indeed, that the little boy was now a man, and a really good man too, and his parents were very proud of him. He was just married, and had come, with his young wife, to reside in the new house with the garden in front of it, and now he stood there by her side while she planted a field flower that she thought very pretty. She was planting it herself with her little hands, and pressing down the earth with her fingers. "Oh dear, what was that?" she exclaimed, as something pricked her. Out of the soft earth something was sticking up. It was—only think!—it was really the tin soldier, the very same which had been lost up in the old man's room, and had been hidden among old wood and rubbish for a long time, till it sunk into the earth, where it must have been for many years. And the young wife wiped the soldier, first with a green leaf, and then with her fine pocket-handkerchief, that smelt of such beautiful perfume. And the tin soldier felt as if he was recovering from a fainting fit. "Let me see him," said the young man, and then he smiled and shook his head, and said, "It can scarcely be the same, but it reminds me of something that happened to one of my tin soldiers when I was a little boy." And then he told his wife about the old house and the old man, and of the tin soldier which he had sent across, because he thought the old man was lonely; and he related the story so clearly that tears came into the eyes of the young wife for the old house and the old man. "It is very likely that this is really the same soldier," said she, and I will take care of him, and always remember what you have told me; but some day you must show me the old man's grave."

"I don't know where it is," he replied; "no one knows. All his friends are dead; no one took care of him, and I was only a little boy."

"Oh, how dreadfully lonely he must have been," said she.

"Yes, terribly lonely," cried the tin soldier; "still it is delightful not to be forgotten."

"Delightful indeed," cried a voice quite near to them; no one but the tin soldier saw that it came from a rag of the leather which hung in tatters; it had lost all its gilding, and looked like wet earth, but it had an opinion, and it spoke it thus:—

"Gilding will fade in damp weather,
To endure, there is nothing like leather."

The Drop of Water

Translated by Mrs. H. P. Paull

Of course you know what is meant by a magnifying glass—one of those round spectacle-glasses that make everything look a hundred times bigger than it is? When any one takes one of these and holds it to his eye, and looks at a drop of water from the pond yonder, he sees above a thousand wonderful creatures that are otherwise never discerned in the water. But there they are, and it is no delusion. It almost looks like a great plateful of spiders jumping about in a crowd. And how fierce they are! They tear off each other's legs. and arms and bodies, before and behind; and yet they are merry and joyful in their way.

Now, there once was an old man whom all the people called Kribble-Krabble, for that was his name. He always wanted the best of everything, and when he could not manage it otherwise, he did it by magic.

There he sat one day, and held his magnifying-glass to his eye, and looked at a drop of water that had been taken out of a puddle by the ditch. But what a kribbling and krabbling was there! All the thousands of little creatures hopped and sprang and tugged at one another, and ate each other up.

"That is horrible!" said old Kribble-Krabble. "Can one not persuade them to live in peace and quietness, so that each one may mind his own business?"

And he thought it over and over, but it would not do, and so he had recourse to magic.

"I must give them colour, that they may be seen more plainly," said he; and he poured something like a little drop of red wine into the drop of water, but it was witches' blood from the lobes of the ear, the finest kind, at ninepence a drop. And now the wonderful little creatures were pink all over. It looked like a whole town of naked wild men.

"What have you there?" asked another old magician, who had no name—and that was the best thing about him.

"Yes, if you can guess what it is," said Kribble-Krabble, "I'll make you a present of it."

But it is not so easy to find out if one does not know.

And the magician who had no name looked through the magnifying-glass.

It looked really like a great town reflected there, in which all the people were running about without clothes. It was terrible! But it was still more terrible to see how one beat and pushed the other, and bit and hacked, and tugged and mauled him. Those at the top were being pulled down, and those at the bottom were struggling upwards.

"Look! look! his leg is longer than mine! Bah! Away with it! There is one who has a little bruise. It hurts him, but it shall hurt him still more."

And they hacked away at him, and they pulled at him, and ate him up, because of the little bruise. And there was one sitting as still as any little maiden, and wishing only for peace and quietness. But now she had to come out, and they tugged at her, and pulled her about, and ate her up.

"That's funny!" said the magician.

"Yes; but what do you think it is?" said Kribble-Krabble. "Can you find that out?"

"Why, one can see that easily enough," said the other. "That's Paris, or some other great city, for they're all alike. It's a great city!"

"It's a drop of puddle water!" said Kribble-Krabble.

The Happy Family

Translated by Mrs. H. P. Paull

The largest green leaf in this country is certainly the burdock-leaf. If you hold it in front of you, it is large enough for an apron; and if you hold it over your head, it is almost as good as an umbrella, it is so wonderfully large. A burdock never grows alone; where it grows, there are many more, and it is a splendid sight; and all this splendor is good for snails. The great white snails, which grand people in olden times used to have made into fricassees; and when they had eaten them, they would say, "O, what a delicious dish!" for these people really thought them good; and these snails lived on burdock-leaves, and for them the burdock was planted.

There was once an old estate where no one now lived to require snails; indeed, the owners had all died out, but the burdock still flourished; it grew over all the beds and walks of the garden—its growth had no check—till it became at last quite a forest of burdocks. Here and there stood an apple or a plum-tree; but for this, nobody would have thought the place had ever been a garden. It was burdock from one end to the other; and here lived the last two surviving snails. They knew not themselves how old they were; but they could remember the time when there were a great many more of them, and that they were descended from a family which came from foreign lands, and that the whole forest had been planted for them and theirs. They had never been away from the garden; but they knew that another place once existed in the world, called the Duke's Palace Castle, in which some of their relations had been boiled till they became black, and were then laid on a silver dish; but what was done afterwards they did not know. Besides, they could not imagine exactly how it felt to be boiled and placed on a silver dish; but no doubt it was something very fine and highly genteel. Neither the cockchafer, nor the toad, nor the earth-worm, whom they questioned about it, would give them the least information; for none of their relations had ever been cooked or served on a silver dish. The old white snails were the most aristocratic race in the world, they knew that. The forest had been planted for them, and the nobleman's castle had been built entirely that they might be cooked and laid on silver dishes.

They lived quite retired and very happily; and as they had no children of their own, they had adopted a little common snail, which they brought up as their own child. The little one would not grow, for he was only a common snail; but the old people, particularly the mother-snail, declared that she could easily see how he grew; and when the father said he could not perceive it, she begged him to feel the little snail's shell, and he did so, and found that the mother was right.

One day it rained very fast. "Listen, what a drumming there is on the burdock-leaves; turn, turn, turn; turn, turn, turn," said the father-snail.

"There come the drops," said the mother; "they are trickling down the stalks. We shall have it very wet here presently. I am very glad we have such good houses, and that the little one has one of his own. There has been really more done for us than for any other creature; it is quite plain that we are the most noble people in the world. We have houses from our birth, and the burdock forest has been planted for us. I should very much like to know how far it extends, and what lies beyond it."

"There can be nothing better than we have here," said the father-snail; "I wish for nothing more."

"Yes, but I do," said the mother; "I should like to be taken to the palace, and boiled, and laid upon a silver dish, as was done to all our ancestors; and you may be sure it must be something very uncommon."

"The nobleman's castle, perhaps, has fallen to decay," said the snail-father, "or the burdock wood may have grown out. You need not be in a hurry; you are always so impatient, and the youngster is getting just the same. He has been three days creeping to the top of that stalk. I feel quite giddy when I look at him."

"You must not scold him," said the mother-snail; "he creeps so very carefully. He will be the joy of our home; and we old folks have nothing else to live for. But have you ever thought where we are to get a wife for him? Do you think that farther out in the wood there may be others of our race?"

"There may be black snails, no doubt," said the old snail; "black snails without houses; but they are so vulgar and conceited too. But we can give the ants a commission; they run here and there, as if they all had so much business to get through. They, most likely, will know of a wife for our youngster."

"I certainly know a most beautiful bride," said one of the ants; "but I fear it would not do, for she is a queen."

"That does not matter," said the old snail; "has she a house?"

"She has a palace," replied the ant, "a most beautiful ant-palace with seven hundred passages."

"Thank-you," said the mother-snail; "but our boy shall not go to live in an ant-hill. If you know of nothing better, we will give the commission to the white gnats; they fly about in rain and sunshine; they know the burdock wood from one end to the other."

"We have a wife for him," said the gnats; "a hundred man-steps from here there is a little snail with a house, sitting on a gooseberry-bush; she is quite alone, and old enough to be married. It is only a hundred man-steps from here."

"Then let her come to him," said the old people. "He has the whole burdock forest; she has only a bush."

So they brought the little lady-snail. She took eight days to perform the journey; but that was just as it ought to be; for it showed her to be one of the right breeding. And then they had a wedding. Six glow-worms gave as much light as they could; but in other respects it was all very quiet; for the old snails could not bear festivities or a crowd. But a beautiful speech was made by the mother-snail. The father could not speak; he was too much overcome. Then they gave the whole burdock forest to the young snails as an inheritance, and repeated what they had so often said, that it was the finest place in the world, and that if they led upright and honourable lives, and their family increased, they and their children might some day be taken to the nobleman's palace, to be boiled black, and laid on a silver dish. And when they had finished speaking, the old couple crept into their houses, and came out no more; for they slept.

The young snail pair now ruled in the forest, and had a numerous progeny. But as the young ones were never boiled or laid in silver dishes, they concluded that the castle had fallen into decay, and that all the people in the world were dead; and as nobody contradicted them, they thought they must be right. And the rain fell upon the burdock-leaves, to play the drum for them, and the sun shone to paint colours on the burdock forest for them, and they were very happy; the whole family were entirely and perfectly happy.

The Story of a Mother

Translated by Mrs. H. P. Paull

A mother sat by her little child; she was very sad, for she feared it would die. It was quite pale, and its little eyes were closed, and sometimes it drew a heavy deep breath, almost like a sigh; and then the mother gazed more sadly than ever on the poor little creature. Some one knocked at the door, and a poor old man walked in. He was wrapped in something that looked like a great horse-cloth; and he required it truly to keep him warm, for it was cold winter; the country everywhere lay covered with snow and ice, and the wind blew so sharply that it cut one's face. The little child had dozed off to sleep for a moment, and the mother, seeing that the old man shivered with the cold, rose and placed a small mug of beer on the stove to warm for him. The old man sat and rocked the cradle; and the mother seated herself on a chair near him, and looked at her sick child who still breathed heavily, and took hold of its little hand.

"You think I shall keep him, do you not?" she said. "Our all-merciful God will surely not take him away from me."

The old man, who was indeed Death himself, nodded his head in a peculiar manner, which might have signified either Yes, or No; and the mother cast down her eyes, while the tears rolled down her cheeks. Then her head became heavy, for she had not closed her eyes for three days and nights, and she slept, but only for a moment. Shivering with cold, she started up and looked round the room. The old man was gone, and her child—it was gone too!—the old man had taken it with him. In the corner of the room the old clock began to strike; "whirr" went the chains, the heavy weight sank to the ground, and the clock stopped; and the poor mother rushed out of the house calling for her child. Out in the snow sat a woman in long black garments, and she said to the mother, "Death has been with you in your room. I saw him hastening away with your little child; he strides faster than the wind, and never brings back what he has taken away."

"Only tell me which way he has gone," said the mother; "tell me the way, I will find him."

"I know the way," said the woman in the black garments; "but before I tell you, you must sing to me all the songs that you have sung to your child; I love these songs, I have heard them before. I am Night, and I saw your tears flow as you sang."

"I will sing them all to you," said the mother; "but do not detain me now. I must overtake him, and find my child."

But Night sat silent and still. Then the mother wept and sang, and wrung her hands. And there were many songs, and yet even more tears; till at length

Night said, "Go to the right, into the dark forest of fir-trees; for I saw Death take that road with your little child."

Within the wood the mother came to cross roads, and she knew not which to take. Just by stood a thorn-bush; it had neither leaf nor flower, for it was the cold winter time, and icicles hung on the branches. "Have you not seen Death go by, with my little child?" she asked.

"Yes," replied the thorn-bush; "but I will not tell you which way he has taken until you have warmed me in your bosom. I am freezing to death here, and turning to ice."

Then she pressed the bramble to her bosom quite close, so that it might be thawed, and the thorns pierced her flesh, and great drops of blood flowed; but the bramble shot forth fresh green leaves, and they became flowers on the cold winter's night, so warm is the heart of a sorrowing mother. Then the bramble-bush told her the path she must take. She came at length to a great lake, on which there was neither ship nor boat to be seen. The lake was not frozen sufficiently for her to pass over on the ice, nor was it open enough for her to wade through; and yet she must cross it, if she wished to find her child. Then she laid herself down to drink up the water of the lake, which was of course impossible for any human being to do; but the bereaved mother thought that perhaps a miracle might take place to help her. "You will never succeed in this," said the lake; "let us make an agreement together which will be better. I love to collect pearls, and your eyes are the purest I have ever seen. If you will weep those eyes away in tears into my waters, then I will take you to the large hothouse where Death dwells and rears flowers and trees, every one of which is a human life."

"Oh, what would I not give to reach my child!" said the weeping mother; and as she still continued to weep, her eyes fell into the depths of the lake, and became two costly pearls.

Then the lake lifted her up, and wafted her across to the opposite shore as if she were on a swing, where stood a wonderful building many miles in length. No one could tell whether it was a mountain covered with forests and full of caves, or whether it had been built. But the poor mother could not see, for she had wept her eyes into the lake. "Where shall I find Death, who went away with my little child?" she asked.

The Story of a Mother

"He has not arrived here yet," said an old gray-haired woman, who was walking about, and watering Death's hothouse. "How have you found your way here? and who helped you?"

"God has helped me," she replied. "He is merciful; will you not be merciful too? Where shall I find my little child?"

"I did not know the child," said the old woman; "and you are blind. Many flowers and trees have faded tonight, and Death will soon come to transplant them. You know already that every human being has a life-tree or a life-flower, just as may be ordained for him. They look like other plants; but they have hearts that beat. Children's hearts also beat: from that you may perhaps be able to recognize your child. But what will you give me, if I tell you what more you will have to do?"

"I have nothing to give," said the afflicted mother; "but I would go to the ends of the earth for you."

"I can give you nothing to do for me there," said the old woman; "but you can give me your long black hair. You know yourself that it is beautiful, and it pleases me. You can take my white hair in exchange, which will be something in return."

"Do you ask nothing more than that?" said she. "I will give it to you with pleasure."

And she gave up her beautiful hair, and received in return the white locks of the old woman. Then they went into Death's vast hothouse, where flowers and trees grew together in wonderful profusion. Blooming hyacinths, under glass bells, and peonies, like strong trees. There grew water-plants, some quite fresh, and others looking sickly, which had water-snakes twining round them, and black crabs clinging to their stems. There stood noble palm-trees, oaks, and plantains, and beneath them bloomed thyme and parsley. Each tree and flower had a name; each represented a human life, and belonged to men still living, some in China, others in Greenland, and in all parts of the world. Some large trees had been planted in little pots, so that they were cramped for room, and seemed about to burst the pot to pieces; while many weak little flowers were growing in rich soil, with moss all around them, carefully tended and cared for. The sorrowing mother bent over the little plants, and heard the human heart beating in each, and recognized the beatings of her child's heart among millions of others.

"That is it," she cried, stretching out her hand towards a little crocus-flower which hung down its sickly head.

"Do not touch the flower," exclaimed the old woman; "but place yourself here; and when Death comes—I expect him every minute—do not let him pull up that plant, but threaten him that if he does you will serve the other flowers in the same manner. This will make him afraid; for he must account to God for each of them. None can be uprooted, unless he receives permission to do so."

There rushed through the hothouse a chill of icy coldness, and the blind mother felt that Death had arrived.

"How did you find your way hither?" asked he; "how could you come here faster than I have?"

"I am a mother," she answered.

And Death stretched out his hand towards the delicate little flower; but she held her hands tightly round it, and held it fast at same time, with the most anxious care, lest she should touch one of the leaves. Then Death breathed upon her hands, and she felt his breath colder than the icy wind, and her hands sank down powerless.

"You cannot prevail against me," said Death.

The Story of a Mother

"But a God of mercy can," said she.

"I only do His will," replied Death. "I am his gardener. I take all His flowers and trees, and transplant them into the gardens of Paradise in an unknown land. How they flourish there, and what that garden resembles, I may not tell you."

"Give me back my child," said the mother, weeping and imploring; and she seized two beautiful flowers in her hands, and cried to Death, "I will tear up all your flowers, for I am in despair."

"Do not touch them," said Death. "You say you are unhappy; and would you make another mother as unhappy as yourself?"

"Another mother!" cried the poor woman, setting the flowers free from her hands.

"There are your eyes," said Death. "I fished them up out of the lake for you. They were shining brightly; but I knew not they were yours. Take them back—they are clearer now than before—and then look into the deep well which is close by here. I will tell you the names of the two flowers which you wished to pull up; and you will see the whole future of the human beings they represent, and what you were about to frustrate and destroy."

Then she looked into the well; and it was a glorious sight to behold how one of them became a blessing to the world, and how much happiness and joy it spread around. But she saw that the life of the other was full of care and poverty, misery and woe.

"Both are the will of God," said Death.

"Which is the unhappy flower, and which is the blessed one?" she said.

"That I may not tell you," said Death; "but thus far you may learn, that one of the two flowers represents your own child. It was the fate of your child that you saw—the future of your own child."

Then the mother screamed aloud with terror, "Which of them belongs to my child? Tell me that. Deliver the unhappy child. Release it from so much misery. Rather take it away. Take it to the kingdom of God. Forget my tears and my entreaties; forget all that I have said or done."

"I do not understand you," said Death. "Will you have your child back? or shall I carry him away to a place that you do not know?"

Then the mother wrung her hands, fell on her knees, and prayed to God, "Grant not my prayers, when they are contrary to Thy will, which at all times must be the best. Oh, hear them not;" and her head sank on her bosom.

Then Death carried away her child to the unknown land.

The Shirt Collar

Translated by Mrs. H. P. Paull

There was once a fine gentleman who possessed among other things a Boot-jack and a Hair-brush; but he had also the finest Shirt Collar in the world, and of this Collar we are about to hear a story. The Collar had become so old that he began to think about getting married; and one day he happened to find himself in the same washing-tub as a Garter. "Upon my word," said the Shirt Collar, "I have never seen anything so slim and delicate, so neat and soft before. May I venture to ask your name?"

"I shall not tell you," replied the Garter.

"Where do you reside when you are at home?" asked the Shirt Collar. But the Garter was naturally shy, and did not know how to answer such a question.

"I presume you are a Girdle," said the Shirt Collar, "a sort of under Girdle. I see that you are useful, as well as ornamental, my little lady."

"You must not speak to me," said the Garter; "I do not think I have given you any encouragement to do so."

"Oh, when any one is as beautiful as you are," said the Shirt Collar, "is not that encouragement enough?"

"Get away; don't come so near me," said the Garter, "you appear to me quite like a man."

"I am a fine gentleman certainly," said the Shirt Collar, "I possess a boot-jack and a hair-brush." This was not true, for these things belonged to his master; but he was a boaster.

"Don't come so near me," said the Garter; "I am not accustomed to it."

"Affectation!" said the Shirt Collar.

Then they were taken out of the wash-tub, starched, and hung over a chair in the sunshine, and then laid on the ironing-board. And now came the glowing iron. "Mistress widow," said the Shirt Collar, "little mistress widow, I feel quite warm. I am changing, I am losing all my creases. You are burning a hole in me. Ugh! I propose to you."

"You old rag," said the flat-iron, driving proudly over the collar, for she fancied herself a steam-engine, which rolls over the railway and draws carriages. "You old rag!" said she.

The edges of the Shirt Collar were a little frayed, so the scissors were brought to cut them smooth. "Oh!" exclaimed the Shirt Collar, "what a first-rate dancer you would make; you can stretch out your leg so well. I never saw anything so charming; I am sure no human being could do the same."

"I should think not," replied the scissors.

"You ought to be a countess," said the Shirt Collar; "but all I possess consists of a fine gentleman, a boot-jack, and a comb. I wish I had an estate for your sake."

"What! is he going to propose to me?" said the Scissors, and she became so angry that she cut too sharply into the Shirt Collar, and it was obliged to be thrown by as useless.

"I shall be obliged to propose to the Hair-brush," thought the Shirt Collar; so he remarked one day, "It is wonderful what beautiful hair you have, my little lady. Have you never thought of being engaged?"

"You might know I should think of it," answered the Hair-brush; "I am engaged to the boot-jack."

"Engaged!" cried the Shirt Collar, "now there is no one left to propose to;" and then he pretended to despise all love-making.

A long time passed, and the Shirt Collar was taken in a bag to the paper-mill. Here was a large company of rags, the fine ones lying by themselves, separated from the coarser, as it ought to be. They had all many things to relate, especially the Shirt Collar, who was a terrible boaster. "I have had an immense number of love affairs," said the Shirt Collar, "no one left me any peace. It is true I was a very fine gentleman; quite stuck up. I had a boot-jack and a brush that I never used. You should have seen me then, when I was turned down. I shall never forget my first love; she was a girdle, so charming, and fine, and soft, and she threw herself into a washing tub for my sake. There was a widow too, who was warmly in love with me, but I left her alone, and she became quite black. The next was a first-rate dancer; she gave me the wound from which I still suffer, she was so passionate. Even my own hair-brush was in love with me, and lost all her hair through neglected love. Yes, I have had great experience of this kind, but my greatest grief was for the Garter—the girdle I meant to say—that jumped into the wash-tub. I have a great deal on my conscience, and it is really time I should be turned into white paper."

And the Shirt Collar came to this at last. All the rags were made into white paper, and the Shirt Collar became the very identical piece of paper which we now see, and on which this story is printed. It happened as a punishment to him, for having boasted so shockingly of things which were not true. And this is a warning to us, to be careful how we act, for we may some day find ourselves in the rag-bag, to be turned into white paper, on which our whole history may be written, even its most secret actions. And it would not be pleasant to have to run about the world in the form of a piece of paper, telling everything we have done, like the boasting Shirt Collar.

The Phœnix Bird

Translated by H. W. Dulcken

In the Garden of Paradise, beneath the Tree of Knowledge, bloomed a rose bush. Here, in the first rose, a bird was born: his flight was like the flashing of light, his plumage was beauteous, and his song ravishing.

But when Eve plucked the fruit of the knowledge of good and evil, when she and Adam were driven from Paradise, there fell from the flaming sword of the cherub a spark into the nest of the bird, which blazed up forthwith. The bird perished in the flames; but from the red egg in the nest there fluttered aloft a new one—the one solitary Phœnix bird. The fable tells us that he dwells in Arabia, and that every year he burns himself to death in his nest; but each time a new Phœnix, the only one in the world, rises up from the red egg.

The bird flutters round us, swift as light, beauteous in colour, charming in song. When a mother sits by her infant's cradle, he stands on the pillow, and, with his wings, forms a glory around the infant's head. He flies through the chamber of content, and brings sunshine into it, and the violets on the humble table smell doubly sweet.

But the Phœnix is not the bird of Arabia alone. He wings his way in the glimmer of the northern lights over the plains of Lapland, and hops among the yellow flowers in the short Greenland summer. Beneath the copper mountains of Fablun, and England's coal mines, he flies, in the shape of a dusty moth, over the hymn-book that rests on the knees of the pious miner. On a lotus leaf he floats down the sacred waters of the Ganges, and the eye of the Hindu maid gleams bright when she beholds him.

The Phœnix bird, dost thou not know him? The Bird of Paradise, the holy swan of song! On the car of Thespis he sat in the guise of a chattering raven, and flapped his black wings, smeared with the lees of wine; over the sounding harp of Iceland swept the swan's red beak; on Shakespeare's shoulder he sat in the guise of Odin's raven, and whispered in the poet's ear "Immortality!" and at the minstrels' feast he fluttered through the halls of the Wartburg.

The Phœnix bird, dost thou not know him? He sang to thee the *Marseillaise*, and thou kissedst the pen that fell from his wing; he came in the radiance of Paradise, and perchance thou didst turn away from him towards the sparrow who sat with tinsel on his wings.

The Bird of Paradise—renewed each century—born in flame, ending in flame! Thy picture, in a golden frame, hangs in the halls of the rich; and thou thyself often fliest around, lonely and disregarded, a myth—"The Phœnix of Arabia."

In Paradise, when thou wert born in the first rose, beneath the Tree of Knowledge, thou receivedst a kiss, and thy right name was given thee—thy name, POETRY.

The Loveliest Rose in the World

Translated by Mrs. H. P. Paull

There lived once a great queen, in whose garden were found at all seasons the most splendid flowers, and from every land in the world. She specially loved roses, and therefore she possessed the most beautiful varieties of this flower, from the wild hedge-rose, with its apple-scented leaves, to the splendid Provence rose. They grew near the shelter of the walls, wound themselves round columns and window-frames, crept along passages and over the ceilings of the halls. They were of every fragrance and colour.

But care and sorrow dwelt within these halls; the queen lay upon a sick bed, and the doctors declared that she must die. "There is still one thing that could save her," said one of the wisest among them. "Bring her the loveliest rose in the world; one which exhibits the purest and brightest love, and if it is brought to her before her eyes close, she will not die."

Then from all parts came those who brought roses that bloomed in every garden, but they were not the right sort. The flower must be one from the garden of love; but which of the roses there showed forth the highest and purest love? The poets sang of this rose, the loveliest in the world, and each named one which he considered worthy of that title; and intelligence of what was required was sent far and wide to every heart that beat with love; to every class, age, and condition.

"No one has yet named the flower," said the wise man. "No one has pointed out the spot where it blooms in all its splendor. It is not a rose from the coffin of Romeo and Juliet, or from the grave of Walburg, though these roses will live in everlasting song. It is not one of the roses which sprouted forth from the blood-stained fame of Winkelreid. The blood which flows from the breast of a hero who dies for his country is sacred, and his memory is sweet, and no rose can be redder than the blood which flows from his veins. Neither is it the magic flower of Science, to obtain which wondrous flower a man devotes many an hour of his fresh young life in sleepless nights, in a lonely chamber."

"I know where it blooms," said a happy mother, who came with her lovely child to the bedside of the queen. "I know where the loveliest rose in the world is. It is seen on the blooming cheeks of my sweet child, when it expresses the pure and holy love of infancy; when refreshed by sleep it opens its eyes, and smiles upon me with childlike affection."

"This is a lovely rose," said the wise man; "but there is one still more lovely."

"Yes, one far more lovely," said one of the women. "I have seen it, and a loftier and purer rose does not bloom. But it was white, like the leaves of a blush-rose. I saw it on the cheeks of the queen. She had taken off her golden crown, and through the long, dreary night, she carried her sick child in her arms. She wept over it, kissed it, and prayed for it as only a mother can pray in that hour of her anguish."

"Holy and wonderful in its might is the white rose of grief, but it is not the one we seek."

"No; the loveliest rose in the world I saw at the Lord's table," said the good old bishop. "I saw it shine as if an angel's face had appeared. A young maiden knelt at the altar, and renewed the vows made at her baptism; and there were white roses and red roses on the blushing cheeks of that young girl. She looked up to heaven with all the purity and love of her young spirit, in all the expression of the highest and purest love."

"May she be blessed!" said the wise man: "but no one has yet named the loveliest rose in the world."

Then there came into the room a child—the queen's little son. Tears stood in his eyes, and glistened on his cheeks; he carried a great book and the binding was of velvet, with silver clasps. "Mother," cried the little boy; "only hear what I have read." And the child seated himself by the bedside, and read from the book of Him who suffered death on the cross to save all men, even who are yet unborn. He read, "Greater love hath no man than this," and as he read a roseate hue spread over the cheeks of the queen, and her eyes became so enlightened and clear, that she saw from the leaves of the book a lovely rose spring forth, a type of Him who shed His blood on the cross.

"I see it," she said. "He who beholds this, the loveliest rose on earth, shall never die."

In a Thousand Years

Translated by W. A. & J. K. Craigie

Yes, in a thousand years people will fly on the wings of steam through the air, over the ocean! The young inhabitants of America will become visitors of old Europe. They will come over to see the monuments and the great cities, which will then be in ruins, just as we in our time make pilgrimages to the mouldering splendours of Southern Asia. In a thousand years they will come!

The Thames, the Danube, and the Rhine still roll their course, Mont Blanc stands firm with its snow-capped summit, and the Northern Lights gleam over the lands of the North; but generation after generation has become dust, whole rows of the mighty of the moment are forgotten, like those who already slumber under the grave-mound on which the rich trader whose ground it is has built a bench, on which he can sit and look out across his waving cornfields.

"To Europe!" cry the young sons of America; "to the land of our ancestors, the glorious land of memories and fancy—to Europe!"

The ship of the air comes. It is crowded with passengers, for the transit is quicker than by sea. The electro-magnetic wire under the ocean has already telegraphed the number of the aerial caravan. Europe is in sight: it is the coast of Ireland that they see, but the passengers are still asleep; they will not be called till they are exactly over England. There they will first step on European shore, in the land of Shakespeare as the educated call it; in the land of politics, the land of machinery, as it is called by others.

Here they stay a whole day. That is all the time the busy race can devote to the whole of England and Scotland. Then the journey is continued through the tunnel under the English Channel, to France, the land of Charlemagne and Napoleon. Molière is named: the learned men talk of a classical and romantic school of remote antiquity: there is rejoicing and shouting for the names of heroes, poets, and men of science, whom our time does not know, but who will be born after our time in Paris, the crater of Europe.

The air steamboat flies over the country whence Columbus went forth, where Cortez was born, and where Calderon sang dramas in sounding verse. Beautiful black-eyed women live still in the blooming valleys, and ancient songs speak of the Cid and the Alhambra.

Then through the air, over the sea, to Italy, where once lay old, everlasting Rome. It has vanished! The Campagna lies desert: a single ruined wall is shown as the remains of St. Peter's, but there is a doubt if this ruin be genuine.

Next to Greece, to sleep a night in the grand hotel at the top of Mount Olympus, to say that they have been there; and the journey is continued to the Bosphorus, to rest there a few hours, and see the place where Byzantium lay; and where the legend tells that the harem stood in the time of the Turks, poor fishermen are now spreading their nets.

Over the remains of mighty cities on the broad Danube, cities which we in our time know not, the travellers pass; but here and there, on the rich sites of those that time shall bring forth, the caravan sometimes descends, and departs thence again.

Down below lies Germany, that was once covered with a close net of railways and canals, the region where Luther spoke, where Goethe sang, and Mozart once held the sceptre of harmony. Great names shone there, in science and in art, names that are unknown to us. One day devoted to seeing Germany, and one for the North, the country of Oersted and Linnæus, and for Norway, the land of the old heroes and the young Normans. Iceland is visited on the journey home: Geyser boils no longer, Hecla is an extinct volcano, but the rocky island is still fixed in the midst of the foaming sea, a continual monument of legend and poetry.

"There is really a great deal to be seen in Europe," says the young American, "and we have seen it in a week, according to the directions of the great traveller" (and here he mentions the name of one of his contemporaries) "in his celebrated work, 'How to See all Europe in a Week.'"

The Swan's Nest

Translated by Mrs. H. P. Paull

Between the Baltic and the North Sea there lies an old swan's nest, wherein swans are born and have been born that shall never die.

In olden times a flock of swans flew over the Alps to the green plains around Milan, where it was delightful to dwell. This flight of swans men called *the Lombards*.

Another flock, with shining plumage and honest eyes, soared southward to Byzantium; the swans established themselves there close by the Emperor's throne, and spread their wings over him as shields to protect him. They received the name of *Varangians*.

On the coast of France there sounded a cry of fear, for the blood-stained swans that came from the North with fire under their wings; and the people prayed, "Heaven deliver us from the wild *Northmen*."

On the fresh sward of England stood the Danish swan by the open seashore, with the crown of three kingdoms on his head; and he stretched out his golden sceptre over the land. The heathens on the

Pomerian coast bent the knee, and the Danish swans came with the banner of the Cross and with the drawn sword.

"That was in the very old times," you say.

In later days two mighty swans have been seen to fly from the nest. A light shone far through the air, far over the lands of the earth; the swan, with the strong beating of his wings, scattered the twilight mists, and the starry sky was seen, and it was as if it came nearer to the earth. That was the swan *Tycho Brahe*.

"Yes, then," you say; "but in our own days?"

We have seen swan after swan soar by in glorious flight. One let his pinions glide over the strings of the golden harp, and it resounded through the North. Norway's mountains seemed to rise higher in the sunlight of former days; there was a rustling among the pine trees and the birches; the gods of the North, the heroes, and the noble women, showed themselves in the dark forest depths.

We have seen a swan beat with his wings upon the marble crag, so that it burst, and the forms of beauty imprisoned in the stone stepped out to the sunny day, and men in the lands round about lifted up their heads to behold these mighty forms.

We have seen a third swan spinning the thread of thought that is fastened from country to country round the world, so that the word may fly with lightning speed from land to land.

And our Lord loves the old swan's nest between the Baltic and the North Sea. And when the mighty birds come soaring through the air to destroy it, even the callow young stand round in a circle on the margin of the nest, and though their breasts may be struck so that their blood flows, they bear it, and strike with their wings and their claws.

Centuries will pass by, swans will fly forth from the nest, men will see them and hear them in the world, before it shall be said in spirit and in truth, "This is the last swan—the last song from the swan's nest."

The Old Grave-Stone

Translated by Mrs. H. P. Paull

In a house, with a large courtyard, in a provincial town, at that time of the year in which people say the evenings are growing longer, a family circle were gathered together at their old home. A lamp burned on the table, although the weather was mild and warm, and the long curtains hung down before the open windows, and without the moon shone brightly in the dark-blue sky.

But they were not talking of the moon, but of a large, old stone that lay below in the courtyard not very far from the kitchen door. The maids often laid the clean copper saucepans and kitchen vessels on this stone, that they might dry in the sun, and the children were fond of playing on it. It was, in fact, an old grave-stone.

"Yes," said the master of the house, "I believe the stone came from the graveyard of the old church of the convent which was pulled down, and the pulpit, the monuments, and the grave-stones sold. My father bought the latter; most of them were cut in two and used for paving-stones, but that one stone was preserved whole, and laid in the courtyard."

The Old Grave-Stone

"Any one can see that it is a grave-stone," said the eldest of the children; "the representation of an hour-glass and part of the figure of an angel can still be traced, but the inscription beneath is quite worn out, excepting the name 'Preben,' and a large 'S' close by it, and a little farther down the name of 'Martha' can be easily read. But nothing more, and even that cannot be seen unless it has been raining, or when we have washed the stone."

"Dear me! how singular. Why that must be the grave-stone of Preben Schwane and his wife."

The old man who said this looked old enough to be the grandfather of all present in the room.

"Yes," he continued, "these people were among the last who were buried in the churchyard of the old convent. They were a very worthy old couple, I can remember them well in the days of my boyhood. Every one knew them, and they were esteemed by all. They were the oldest residents in the town, and people said they possessed a ton of gold, yet they were always very plainly dressed, in the coarsest stuff, but with linen of the purest whiteness. Preben and Martha were a fine old couple, and when they both sat on the bench, at the top of the steep stone steps, in front of their house, with the branches of the linden-tree waving above them, and nodded in a gentle, friendly way to passers by, it really made one feel quite happy. They were very good to the poor; they fed them and clothed them, and in their benevolence there was judgment as well as true Christianity. The old woman died first; that day is still quite vividly before my eyes. I was a little boy, and had accompanied my father to the old man's house. Martha had fallen into the sleep of death just as we arrived there. The corpse lay in a bedroom, near to the one in which we sat, and the old man was in great distress and weeping like a child. He spoke to my father, and to a few neighbours who were there, of how lonely he should feel now she was gone, and how good and true she, his dead wife, had been during the number of years that they had passed through life together, and how they had become acquainted, and learnt to love each other. I was, as I have said, a boy, and only stood by and listened to what the others said; but it filled me with a strange emotion to listen to the old man, and to watch how the colour rose in his cheeks as he spoke of the days of their courtship, of how beautiful she was, and how many little tricks he had been guilty of, that he might meet her. And then he talked of his wedding-day; and his eyes brightened, and he seemed to be carried back, by his words, to that joyful time. And yet there she was, lying in the next room, dead—an old woman, and he was an old man, speaking of the days of hope, long passed away. Ah, well, so it is; then I was but a child, and now I am old, as old as Preben Schwane then was. Time passes away, and all things changed. I can remember quite well the day on which she was buried, and how Old Preben walked close behind the coffin.

"A few years before this time the old couple had had their gravestone prepared, with an inscription and their names, but not the date. In the evening the stone was taken to the churchyard, and laid on the grave. A year later it was taken up, that Old Preben might be laid by the side of his wife. They did not leave behind them wealth, they left behind them far less than people had believed they possessed; what there was went to families distantly related to them, of whom, till then, no one had ever heard. The old house, with its balcony of wickerwork, and the bench at the top of the high steps, under the lime-tree, was considered, by the road-inspectors, too old and rotten to be left standing. Afterwards, when the same fate befell the convent church, and the graveyard was destroyed, the grave-stone of Preben and Martha, like everything else, was sold to whoever would buy it. And so it happened that this stone was not cut in two as many others had been, but now lies in the courtyard below, a scouring block for the maids, and a playground for the children. The paved street now passes over the resting place of Old Preben and his wife; no one thinks of them any more now."

And the old man who had spoken of all this shook his head mournfully, and said, "Forgotten! Ah, yes, everything will be forgotten!" And then the conversation turned on other matters.

But the youngest child in the room, a boy, with large, earnest eyes, mounted upon a chair behind the window curtains, and looked out into the yard, where the moon was pouring a flood of light on the old gravestone—the stone that had always appeared to him so dull and flat, but which lay there now like a great leaf out of a book of history. All that the boy had heard of Old Preben and his wife seemed clearly defined on the stone, and as he gazed on it, and glanced at the clear, bright moon shining in the pure air, it was as if the light of God's countenance beamed over His beautiful world.

"Forgotten! Everything will be forgotten!" still echoed through the room, and in the same moment an invisible spirit whispered to the heart of the boy, "Preserve carefully the seed that has been entrusted to thee, that it may grow and thrive. Guard it well. Through thee, my child, shall the obliterated inscription on the old, weather-beaten grave-stone go forth to future generations in clear, golden characters. The old pair shall again wander through the streets arm-in-arm, or sit with their fresh, healthy cheeks on the bench under the lime-tree, and smile and nod at rich and poor. The seed of this hour shall ripen in the course of years into a beautiful poem. The beautiful and the good are never forgotten, they live always in story or in song."

The Goblin and The Huckster

Translated by H. W. Dulcken

There was once a regular student: he lived in a garret, and nothing at all belonged to him; but there was also once a regular huckster: he lived on the ground floor, and the whole house was his; and the goblin kept with him, for on the huckster's table on Christmas Eve there was always a dish of plum porridge, with a great piece of butter floating in the middle. The huckster could accomplish that; and consequently the goblin stuck to the huckster's shop, and that was very interesting.

One evening the student came through the back door to buy candles and cheese for himself. He had no one to send, and that's why he came himself. He procured what he wanted and paid for it, and the huckster and his wife both nodded a "good evening" to him; and the woman was one who could do more than merely nod—she had an immense power of tongue! And the student nodded too, and then suddenly stood still, reading the sheet of paper in which the cheese had been wrapped. It was a leaf torn out of an old book, a book that ought not to have been torn up, a book that was full of poetry.

The Goblin and The Huckster

"Yonder lies some more of the same sort," said the huckster: "I gave an old woman a little coffee for the books; give me two groschen, and you shall have the remainder."

"Yes," said the student, "give me the book instead of the cheese: I can eat my bread and butter without cheese. It would be a sin to tear the book up entirely. You are a capital man, a practical man, but you understand no more about poetry than does that cask yonder."

Now, that was an insulting speech, especially towards the cask; but the huckster laughed and the student laughed, for it was only said in fun. But the goblin was angry that any one should dare to say such things to a huckster who lived in his own house and sold the best butter.

When it was night, and the shop was closed and all were in bed, the goblin came forth, went into the bedroom, and took away the good lady's tongue; for she did not want that while she was asleep; and whenever he put this tongue upon any object in the room, the said object acquired speech and language, and could express its thoughts and feelings as well as the lady herself could have done; but only one object could use it at a time, and that was a good thing, otherwise they would have interrupted each other.

And the goblin laid the tongue upon the cask in which the old newspapers were lying.

"Is it true," he asked, "that you don't know what poetry means?"

"Of course I know it," replied the cask: "poetry is something that always stands at the foot of a column in the newspapers, and is sometimes cut out. I dare swear I have more of it in me than the student, and I'm only a poor tub compared to the huckster."

Then the goblin put the tongue upon the coffee-mill, and, mercy! how it began to go! And he put it upon the butter-cask, and on the cash-box: they were all of the waste-paper cask's opinion, and the opinion of the majority must be respected.

"Now I shall tell it to the student!" And with these words the goblin went quite quietly up the back stairs to the garret, where the student lived. The student had still a candle burning, and the goblin peeped through the keyhole, and saw that he was reading in the torn book that he had carried up out of the shop downstairs.

But how light it was in his room! Out of the book shot a clear beam, expanding into a thick stem, and into a mighty tree, which grew upward and spread its branches far over the student. Each leaf was fresh, and every blossom was a beautiful female head, some with dark sparkling eyes, others with wonderfully clear blue orbs; every fruit was a gleaming star, and there was a glorious sound of song in the student's room.

Never had the little goblin imagined such splendour, far less had he ever seen or heard anything like it. He stood still on tiptoe, and peeped in till the light went out in the student's garret. Probably the student blew it out, and went to bed; but the little goblin remained standing there nevertheless, for the music still sounded on, soft and beautiful—a splendid cradle song for the student who had lain down to rest.

"This is an incomparable place," said the goblin: "I never expected such a thing! I should like to stay here with the student." And then the little man thought it over—and he was a sensible little man too—but he sighed, "The student has no porridge!" And then he went down again to the huckster's shop: and it was a very good thing that he got down there again at last, for the cask had almost worn out the good woman's tongue, for it had spoken out at one side everything that was contained in it, and was just about turning itself over, to give it out from the other side also, when the goblin came in, and restored the tongue to its owner. But from that time forth the whole shop, from the cash-box down to the firewood, took its tone from the cask, and paid him such respect, and thought so much of him, that when the huckster afterwards read the critical articles on theatricals and art in the newspaper, they were all persuaded the information came from the cask itself.

But the goblin could no longer sit quietly and contentedly listening to all the wisdom down there: so soon as the light glimmered from the garret in the evening he felt as if the rays were strong cables drawing him up, and he was obliged to go and peep through the keyhole; and there a feeling of greatness rolled around him, such as we feel beside the ever-heaving sea when the storm rushes over it, and he burst into tears! He did not know himself why he was weeping, but a peculiar feeling of pleasure mingled with his tears. How wonderfully glorious it must be to sit with the student under the same tree! But that might not be, he was obliged to be content with the view through the keyhole, and to be glad of that. There he stood on the cold landing-place, with the autumn wind blowing down from the loft-hole: it was cold, very cold; but the little mannikin only felt that when the light in the room was extinguished, and the tones in the tree died away. Ha! then he shivered, and crept down again to his warm corner, where it was homely and comfortable.

And when Christmas came, and brought with it the porridge and the great lump of butter, why, then he thought the huckster the better man.

But in the middle of the night the goblin was awaked by a terrible tumult and beating against the window shutters. People rapped noisily without, and the watchman blew his horn, for a great fire had broken out—the whole street was full of smoke and flame. Was it in the house itself, or at a neighbour's? Where was it? Terror seized on all. The huckster's wife was so bewildered that she took her gold earrings out of her ears and put them in her pocket, that at any rate she might save something; the huckster ran for his share-papers; and the maid for her black silk mantilla, for she had found means to purchase one. Each one wanted to save the best thing they had; the goblin wanted to do the same thing, and in a few leaps he was up the stairs, and into the room of the student, who stood quite quietly at the open window, looking at the conflagration that was raging in the house of the neighbour opposite. The goblin seized upon the wonderful book which lay upon the table, popped it into his red cap, and held the cap tight with both hands. The great treasure of the house was saved; and now he ran up and away, quite on to the roof of the house, on to the chimney. There he sat, illuminated by the flames of the burning house opposite, both hands pressed tightly over his cap, in which the treasure lay; and now he knew the real feelings of his heart, and knew to whom it really belonged. But when the fire was extinguished, and the goblin could think calmly again, why, then....

"I must divide myself between the two," he said; "I can't quite give up the huckster, because of the porridge!"

Now, that was spoken quite like a human creature. We all of us visit the huckster for the sake of the porridge.

Under the Willow Tree

Translated by Mrs. H. P. Paull

The region round the little town of Kjøge is very bleak and cold. The town lies on the sea shore, which is always beautiful; but here it might be more beautiful than it is, for on every side the fields are flat, and it is a long way to the forest. But when persons reside in a place and get used to it, they can always find something beautiful in it—something for which they long, even in the most charming spot in the world which is not home. It must be owned that there are in the outskirts of the town some humble gardens on the banks of a little stream that runs on towards the sea, and in summer these gardens look very pretty. Such indeed was the opinion of two little children, whose parents were neighbours, and who played in these gardens, and forced their way from one garden to the other through the gooseberry-bushes that divided them. In one of the gardens grew an elder-tree, and in the other an old willow, under which the children were very fond of playing. They had permission to do so, although the tree stood close by the stream, and they might easily have fallen into the water; but the eye of God watches over the little ones, otherwise they would never be safe. At the same time, these children were very careful not to go too near the water; indeed, the boy was so afraid of it, that in the summer, while the other children were splashing about in the sea, nothing could entice him to join them. They jeered and laughed at him, and he was obliged to bear it all as patiently as he could. Once the neighbour's little girl, Joanna, dreamed that she was sailing in a boat, and the boy—Knud was his name—waded out in the water to join her, and the water came up to his neck, and at last closed over his head, and in a moment he had disappeared. When little Knud heard this dream, it seemed as if he could not bear the mocking and jeering again; how could he dare to go into the water now, after Joanna's dream! He never would do it, for this dream always satisfied him. The parents of these children, who were poor, often sat together while Knud and Joanna played in the gardens or in the road. Along this road—a row of willow trees had been planted to separate it from a ditch on one side of it. They were not very handsome trees, for the tops had been cut off; however, they were intended for use, and not for show. The old willow tree in the garden was much handsomer, and therefore the children were very fond of sitting under it. The town had a large market-place; and at the fair-time there would be whole rows, like streets, of tents and booths containing silks and ribbons, and toys and cakes, and everything that could be wished for. There were crowds of people, and sometimes the weather would be rainy, and splash with moisture the woollen jackets of the peasants; but it did not destroy the beautiful fragrance of the honey cakes and gingerbread with which one booth was filled; and the best of it was, that the man who sold these cakes always lodged during the fair-time with little Knud's parents. So every now and then he had a present of gingerbread, and of course Joanna always had a share. And, more delightful still, the gingerbread seller knew all sorts of things to tell and could even relate stories about his own gingerbread. So one evening he told them a story that made such a deep impression on the children that they never forgot it; and therefore I think we may as well hear it too, for it is not very long.

"Once upon a time," said he, "there lay on my counter two gingerbread cakes, one in the shape of a man wearing a hat, the other of a maiden without a bonnet. Their faces were on the side that was uppermost, for on the other side they looked very different. Most people have a best side to their characters, which they take care to show to the world. On the left, just where the heart is, the gingerbread man had an almond stuck in to represent it, but the maiden was honey cake all over. They were placed on the counter as samples, and after lying there a long time they at last fell in love with each other; but neither of them spoke of it to the other, as they should have done if they expected anything to follow. 'He is a man, he ought to speak the first word,' thought the gingerbread maiden; but she felt quite happy—she was sure that her love was returned. But his thoughts were far more ambitious, as the thoughts of a man often are. He dreamed that he was a real street boy, that he possessed four real pennies, and that he had bought the gingerbread lady, and ate her up. And so they lay on the counter for days and weeks, till they grew hard and dry; but the thoughts of the maiden became ever more tender and womanly. 'Ah well, it is enough for me that I have been able to live on the same counter with him,' said she one day; when suddenly, 'crack,' and she broke in two. 'Ah,' said the gingerbread man to himself, 'if she had only known of my love, she would have kept together a little longer.' And here they both are, and that is their history," said the cake man. "You think the history of their lives and their silent love, which never came to anything, very remarkable; and there they are for you." So saying, he gave Joanna the gingerbread man, who was still quite whole—and to Knud the broken maiden; but the children had been so much impressed by the story, that they had not the heart to eat the lovers up.

The next day they went into the churchyard, and took the two cake figures with them, and sat down under the church wall, which was covered with luxuriant ivy in summer and winter, and looked as if hung with rich tapestry. They stuck up the two gingerbread figures in the sunshine among the green leaves, and then told the story, and all about the silent love which came to nothing, to a group of children. They called it, "love," because the story was so lovely, and the other children had the same opinion. But when they turned to look at the gingerbread pair, the broken maiden was gone! A great boy, out of wickedness, had eaten her up. At first the children cried about it; but afterwards, thinking very probably that the poor lover ought not to be left alone in the world, they ate him up too: but they never forgot the story.

The two children still continued to play together by the elder-tree, and under the willow; and the little maiden sang beautiful songs, with a voice that was as clear as a bell. Knud, on the contrary, had not a note of music in him, but knew the words of the songs, and that of course is something. The people of Kjøge, and even the rich wife of the man who kept the fancy shop, would stand and listen while Joanna was singing, and say, "She has really a very sweet voice."

Those were happy days; but they could not last forever. The neighbours were separated, the mother of the little girl was dead, and her father had thoughts of marrying again and of residing in the capital, where he had been promised a very lucrative appointment as messenger. The neighbours parted with tears, the children wept sadly; but their parents promised that they should write to each other at least once a year.

After this, Knud was bound apprentice to a shoemaker; he was growing a great boy, and could not be allowed to run wild any longer. Besides, he was going to be confirmed. Ah, how happy he would have been on that festal day in Copenhagen with little Joanna; but he still remained at Kjøge, and had never seen the great city, though the town is not five miles from it. But far across the bay, when the sky was clear, the towers of Copenhagen could be seen; and on the day of his confirmation he saw distinctly the golden cross on the principal church glittering in the sun. How often his thoughts were with Joanna! but did she think of him? Yes. About Christmas came a letter from her father to Knud's parents, which stated that they were going on very well in Copenhagen, and mentioning particularly that Joanna's beautiful voice was likely to bring her a brilliant fortune in the future. She was engaged to sing at a concert, and she had already earned money by singing, out of which she sent her dear neighbours at Kjøge a whole dollar, for them to make merry on Christmas eve, and they were to drink her health. She had herself added this in a postscript, and in the same postscript she wrote, "Kind regards to Knud."

The good neighbours wept, although the news was so pleasant; but they wept tears of joy. Knud's thoughts had been daily with

Joanna, and now he knew that she also had thought of him; and the nearer the time came for his apprenticeship to end, the clearer did it appear to him that he loved Joanna, and that she must be his wife; and a smile came on his lips at the thought, and at one time he drew the thread so fast as he worked, and pressed his foot so hard against the knee strap, that he ran the awl into his finger; but what did he care for that? He was determined not to play the dumb lover as both the gingerbread cakes had done; the story was a good lesson to him.

At length he become a journeyman; and then, for the first time, he prepared for a journey to Copenhagen, with his knapsack packed and ready. A master was expecting him there, and he thought of Joanna, and how glad she would be to see him. She was now seventeen, and he nineteen years old. He wanted to buy a gold ring for her in Kjøge, but then he recollected how far more beautiful such things would be in Copenhagen. So he took leave of his parents, and on a rainy day, late in the autumn, wandered forth on foot from the town of his birth. The leaves were falling from the trees; and, by the time he arrived at his new master's in the great metropolis, he was wet through. On the following Sunday he intended to pay his first visit to Joanna's father. When the day came, the new journeyman's clothes were brought out, and a new hat, which he had brought in Kjøge. The hat became him very well, for hitherto he had only worn a cap. He found the house that he sought easily, but had to mount so many stairs that he became quite giddy; it surprised him to find how people lived over one another in this dreadful town.

On entering a room in which everything denoted prosperity, Joanna's father received him very kindly. The new wife was a stranger to him, but she shook hands with him, and offered him coffee.

"Joanna will be very glad to see you," said her father. "You have grown quite a nice young man, you shall see her presently; she is a good child, and is the joy of my heart, and, please God, she will continue to be so; she has her own room now, and pays us rent for it." And the father knocked quite politely at a door, as if he were a stranger, and then they both went in. How pretty everything was in that room! a more beautiful apartment could not be found in the whole town of Kjøge; the Queen herself could scarcely be better accommodated. There were carpets, and rugs, and window curtains hanging to the ground. Pictures and flowers were scattered about. There was a velvet chair, and a looking-glass against the wall, into which a person might be in danger of stepping, for it was as large as a door. All this Knud saw at a glance, and yet, in truth, he saw nothing but Joanna. She was quite grown up, and very different from what Knud had fancied her, and a great deal more beautiful. In all Kjøge there was not a girl like her; and how graceful she looked, although her glance at first was odd, and not familiar; but for a moment only, then she rushed towards him as if she would have kissed him; she did not, however, although she was very near it. Yes, she really was joyful at seeing the friend of her childhood once more, and the tears even stood in her eyes. Then she asked so many questions about Knud's parents, and everything, even to the elder-tree and the willow, which she called "Elder-mother and Willow-father," as if they had been human beings; and so, indeed, they might be, quite as much as the gingerbread cakes. Then she talked about them, and the story of their silent love, and how they lay on the counter together and split in two; and then she laughed heartily; but the blood rushed into Knud's cheeks, and his heart beat quickly. Joanna was not proud at all; he noticed that through her he was invited by her parents to remain the whole evening with them, and she poured out the tea and gave him a cup herself; and afterwards she took a book and read aloud to them, and it seemed to Knud as if the story was all about himself and his love, for it agreed so well with his own thoughts. And then she sang a simple song, which, through her singing, became a true story, and as if she poured forth the feelings of her own heart.

"Oh," he thought, "she knows I am fond of her." The tears he could not restrain rolled down his cheeks, and he was unable to utter a single word; it seemed as if he had been struck dumb.

When he left, she pressed his hand, and said, "You have a kind heart, Knud: remain always as you are now." What an evening of happiness this had been; to sleep after it was impossible, and Knud did not sleep.

At parting, Joanna's father had said, "Now, you won't quite forget us; you must not let the whole winter go by without paying us another visit;" so that Knud felt himself free to go again the following Sunday evening, and so he did. But every evening after working hours—and they worked by candle-light then—he walked out into the town, and through the street in which Joanna lived, to look up at her window. It was almost always lighted up; and one evening he saw the shadow of her face quite plainly on the window blind; that was a glorious evening for him. His master's wife did not like his always going out in the evening, idling, wasting time, as she called it, and she shook her head.

But his master only smiled, and said, "He is a young man, my dear, you know."

"On Sunday I shall see her," said Knud to himself, "and I will tell her that I love her with my whole heart and soul, and that she must be my little wife. I know I am now only a poor journeyman shoemaker, but I will work and strive, and become a master in time. Yes, I will speak to her; nothing comes from silent love. I learnt that from the gingerbread-cake story."

Sunday came, but when Knud arrived, they were all unfortunately invited out to spend the evening, and were obliged to tell him so.

Joanna pressed his hand, and said, "Have you ever been to the theatre? you must go once; I sing there on Wednesday, and if you have time on that day, I will send you a ticket; my father knows where your master lives." How kind this was of her! And on Wednesday, about noon, Knud received a sealed packet with no address, but the ticket was inside; and in the evening Knud went, for the first time in his life, to a theatre. And what did he see? He saw Joanna, and how beautiful and charming she looked! He certainly saw her being married to a stranger, but that was all in the play, and only a pretence; Knud well knew that. She could never have the heart, he thought, to send him a ticket to go and see it, if it had been real. So he looked on, and when all the people applauded and clapped their hands, he shouted "hurrah." He could see that even the king smiled at Joanna, and seemed delighted with her singing. How small Knud felt; but then he loved her so dearly, and thought she loved him, and the man must speak the first word, as the gingerbread maiden had thought. Ah, how much there was for him in that childish story. As soon as Sunday arrived, he went again, and felt as if he were about to enter on holy ground. Joanna was alone to welcome him, nothing could be more fortunate.

"I am so glad you are come," she said. "I was thinking of sending my father for you, but I had a presentiment that you would be here this evening. The fact is, I wanted to tell you that I am going to France. I shall start on Friday. It is necessary for me to go there, if I wish to become a first-rate performer."

Poor Knud! it seemed to him as if the whole room was whirling round with him. His courage failed, and he felt as if his heart would burst. He kept down the tears, but it was easy to see how sorrowful he was.

"You honest, faithful soul," she exclaimed; and the words loosened Knud's tongue, and he told her how truly he had loved her, and that she must be his wife; and as he said this, he saw Joanna change colour, and turn pale. She let his hand fall, and said, earnestly and mournfully, "Knud, do not make yourself and me unhappy. I will always be a good sister to you, one in whom you can trust; but I can never be anything more." And she drew her white hand over his burning forehead, and said, "God gives strength to bear a great deal, if we only strive ourselves to endure."

At this moment her stepmother came into the room, and Joanna said quickly, "Knud is so unhappy, because I am going away;" and it appeared as if they had only been talking of her journey. "Come, be a man" she added, placing her hand on his shoulder; "you are still a child, and you must be good and reasonable, as you were when we were both children, and played together under the willow tree."

Knud listened, but he felt as if the world had slid out of its course. His thoughts were like a loose thread fluttering to and fro in the wind. He stayed, although he could not tell whether she had asked him to do so. But she was kind and gentle to him; she poured out his tea, and sang to him; but the song had not the old tone in it, although it was wonderfully beautiful, and made his heart feel ready to burst. And then he rose to go. He did not offer his hand, but she seized it, and said—

"Will you not shake hands with your sister at parting, my old playfellow?" and she smiled through the tears that were rolling down her cheeks. Again she repeated the word "brother," which was a great consolation certainly; and thus they parted.

She sailed to France, and Knud wandered about the muddy streets of Copenhagen. The other journeymen in the shop asked him why he looked so gloomy, and wanted him to go and amuse himself with them, as he was still a young man. So he went with them to a dancing-room. He saw many handsome girls there, but none like Joanna; and here, where he thought to forget her, she was more life-like before his mind than ever. "God gives us strength to bear much, if we try to do our best," she had said; and as he thought of this, a devout feeling came into his mind, and he folded his hands. Then, as the violins played and the girls danced round the room, he started; for it seemed to him as if he were in a place where he ought not to have brought Joanna, for she was here with him in his heart; and so he went out at once. As he went through the streets at a quick pace, he passed the house where she used to live; it was all dark, empty, and lonely. But the world went on its course, and Knud was obliged to go on too.

Winter came; the water was frozen, and everything seemed buried in a cold grave. But when spring returned, and the first steamer prepared to sail, Knud was seized with a longing to wander forth into the world, but not to France. So he packed his knapsack, and travelled through Germany, going from town to town, but finding neither rest or peace. It was not till he arrived at the glorious old town of Nuremberg that he gained the mastery over himself, and rested his weary feet; and here he remained.

Nuremberg is a wonderful old city, and looks as if it had been cut out of an old picture book. The streets seem to have arranged themselves according to their own fancy, and as if the houses objected to stand in rows or rank and file. Gables, with little towers, ornamented columns, and statues, can be seen even to the city gate; and from the singular-shaped roofs, waterspouts, formed like dragons, or long lean dogs, extend far across to the middle of the street. Here, in the market-place, stood Knud, with his knapsack on his back, close to one of the old fountains which are so beautifully adorned with figures, scriptural and historical, and which spring up between the sparkling jets of water. A pretty servant-maid was just filling her pails, and she gave Knud a refreshing draught; she had a handful of roses, and she gave him one, which appeared to him like a good omen for the future. From a neighbouring church came the sounds of music, and the familiar tones reminded him of the organ at home at Kjøge; so he passed into the great cathedral. The sunshine

Under the Willow Tree

streamed through the painted glass windows, and between two lofty slender pillars. His thoughts became prayerful, and calm peace rested on his soul. He next sought and found a good master in Nuremberg, with whom he stayed and learnt the German language.

The old moat round the town had been converted into a number of little kitchen gardens; but the high walls, with their heavy-looking towers, are still standing. Inside these walls the ropemaker twisted his ropes along a walk built like a gallery, and in the cracks and crevices of the walls elderbushes grow and stretch their green boughs over the small houses which stand below. In one of these houses lived the master for whom Knud worked; and over the little garret window where he sat, the elder-tree waved its branches. Here he dwelt through one summer and winter, but when spring came again, he could endure it no longer. The elder was in blossom, and its fragrance was so homelike, that he fancied himself back again in the gardens of Kjøge. So Knud left his master, and went to work for another who lived farther in the town, where no elder grew. His workshop was quite close to one of the old stone bridges, near to a water-mill, round which the roaring stream rushed and foamed always, yet restrained by the neighbouring houses, whose old, decayed balconies hung over, and seemed ready to fall into the water. Here grew no elder; here was not even a flowerpot, with its little green plant; but just opposite the workshop stood a great willow tree, which seemed to hold fast to the house for fear of being carried away by the water. It stretched its branches over the stream just as those of the willow tree in the garden at Kjøge had spread over the river. Yes, he had indeed gone from Elder-mother to Willow-father. There was a something about the tree here, especially in the moonlight nights, that went direct to his heart; yet it was not in reality the moonlight, but the old tree itself. However, he could not endure it: and why? Ask the willow, ask the blossoming elder! At all events, he bade farewell to Nuremberg and journeyed onwards. He never spoke of Joanna to any one; his sorrow was hidden in his heart. The old childish story of the two cakes had a deep meaning for him. He understood now why the gingerbread man had a bitter almond in his left side; his was the feeling of bitterness, and Joanna, so mild and friendly, was represented by the honey cake maiden. As he thought upon all this, the strap of his knapsack pressed across his chest so that he could hardly breathe; he loosened it, but gained no relief. He saw but half the world around him; the other half he carried with him in his inward thoughts; and this is the condition in which he left Nuremberg. Not till he caught sight of the lofty mountains did the world appear more free to him; his thoughts were attracted to outer objects, and tears came into his eyes. The Alps appeared to him like the wings of earth folded together; unfolded, they would display the variegated pictures of dark woods, foaming waters, spreading clouds, and masses of snow. "At the last day," thought he, "the earth will unfold its great wings, and soar upwards to the skies, there to burst like a soap-bubble in the radiant glance of the Deity. Oh," sighed he, "that the last day were come!"

Silently he wandered on through the country of the Alps, which seemed to him like a fruit garden, covered with soft turf. From the wooden balconies of the houses the young lacemakers nodded as he passed. The summits of the mountains glowed in the red evening sunset, and the green lakes beneath the dark trees reflected the glow. Then he thought of the sea coast by the Bay Kjøge, with a longing in his heart that was, however, without pain. There, where the Rhine rolls onward like a great billow, and dissolves itself into snowflakes, where glistening clouds are ever changing as if here was the place of their creation, while the rainbow flutters about them like a many-coloured ribbon, there did Knud think of the water-mill at Kjøge, with its rushing, foaming waters. Gladly would he have remained in the quiet Rhenish town, but there were too many elders and willow trees.

So he travelled onwards, over a grand, lofty chain of mountains, over rugged—rocky precipices, and along roads that hung on the mountain's side like a swallow's nest. The waters foamed in the depths below him. The clouds lay beneath him. He wandered on, treading upon Alpine roses, thistles, and snow, with the summer sun shining upon him, till at length he bid farewell to the lands of the north. Then he passed on under the shade of blooming chestnut-trees, through vineyards, and fields of Indian corn, till conscious that the mountains were as a wall between him and his early recollections; and he wished it to be so.

Before him lay a large and splendid city, called Milan, and here he found a German master who engaged him as a workman. The master and his wife, in whose workshop he was employed, were an old, pious couple; and the two old people became quite fond of the quiet journeyman, who spoke but little, but worked more, and led a pious, Christian life; and even to himself it seemed as if God had removed the heavy burden from his heart. His greatest pleasure was to climb, now and then, to the roof of the noble church, which was built of white marble. The pointed towers, the decorated and open cloisters, the stately columns, the white statues which smiled upon him from every corner and porch and arch—all, even the church itself, seemed to him to have been formed from the snow of his native land. Above him was the blue sky; below him, the city and the wide-spreading plains of Lombardy; and towards the north, the lofty mountains, covered with perpetual snow. And then he thought of the church of Kjøge, with its red, ivy-clad walls, but he had no longing to go there; here, beyond the mountains, he would die and be buried.

Three years had passed away since he left his home; one year of that time he had dwelt at Milan.

One day his master took him into the town; not to the circus in which riders performed, but to the opera, a large building, itself a sight well worth seeing. The seven tiers of boxes, which reached from the ground to a dizzy height, near the ceiling, were hung with rich, silken curtains; and in them were seated elegantly-dressed ladies, with bouquets of flowers in their hands. The gentlemen were also in full dress, and many of them wore decorations of gold and silver. The place was so brilliantly lighted that it seemed like sunshine, and glorious music rolled through the building. Everything looked more beautiful than in the theatre at Copenhagen, but then Joanna had been there, and—could it be? Yes—it was like magic—she was here also: for, when the curtain rose, there stood Joanna, dressed in silk and gold, and with a golden crown upon her head. She sang, he thought, as only an angel could sing; and then she stepped forward to the front and smiled, as only Joanna could smile, and looked directly at Knud. Poor Knud! he seized his master's hand, and cried out loud, "Joanna," but no one heard him, excepting his master, for the music sounded above everything.

"Yes, yes, it is Joanna," said his master; and he drew forth a printed bill, and pointed to her name, which was there in full. Then it was not a dream. All the audience applauded her, and threw wreaths of flowers at her; and every time she went away they called for her again, so that she was always coming and going. In the street the people crowded round her carriage, and drew it away themselves without the horses. Knud was in the foremost row, and shouted as joyously as the rest; and when the carriage stopped before a brilliantly lighted house, Knud placed himself close to the door of her carriage. It flew open, and she stepped out; the light fell upon her dear face, and he could see that she smiled as she thanked them, and appeared quite overcome. Knud looked straight in her face, and she looked at him, but she did not recognize him. A man, with a glittering star on his breast, gave her his arm, and people said the two were engaged to be married. Then Knud went home and packed up his knapsack; he felt he must return to the home of his childhood, to the elder-tree and the willow. "Ah, under that willow tree!" A man may live a whole life in one single hour.

The old couple begged him to remain, but words were useless. In vain they reminded him that winter was coming, and that the snow had already fallen on the mountains. He said he could easily follow the track of the closely-moving carriages, for which a path must be kept clear, and with nothing but his knapsack on his back, and leaning on his stick, he could step along briskly. So he turned his steps to the mountains, ascended one side and descended the other, still going northward till his strength began to fail, and not a house or village could be seen. The stars shone in the sky above him, and down in the valley lights glittered like stars, as if another sky were beneath him; but his head was dizzy and his feet stumbled, and he felt ill. The lights in the valley grew brighter and brighter, and more numerous, and he could see them moving to and fro, and then he understood that there must be a village in the distance; so he exerted his failing strength to reach it, and at length obtained shelter in a humble lodging. He remained there that night and the whole of the following day, for his body required rest and refreshment, and in the valley there was rain and a thaw. But early in the morning of the third day, a man came with an organ and played one of the melodies of home; and after that Knud could remain there no longer, so he started again on his journey toward the north. He travelled for many days with hasty steps, as if he were trying to reach home before all whom he remembered should die; but he spoke to no one of this longing. No one would have believed or understood this sorrow of his heart, the deepest that can be felt by human nature. Such grief is not for the world; it is not entertaining even to friends, and poor Knud had no friends; he was a stranger, wandering through strange lands to his home in the north.

He was walking one evening through the public roads, the country around him was flatter, with fields and meadows, the air had a frosty feeling. A willow tree grew by the roadside, everything reminded him of home. He felt very tired; so he sat down under the tree, and very soon began to nod, then his eyes closed in sleep. Yet still he seemed conscious that the willow tree was stretching its branches over him; in his dreaming state the tree appeared like a strong, old man—the "Willow-father" himself, who had taken his tired son up in his arms to carry him back to the land of home, to the garden of his childhood, on the bleak open shores of Kjøge. And then he dreamed that it was really the willow tree itself from Kjøge, which had travelled out in the world to seek him, and now had found him and carried him back into the little garden on the banks of the streamlet; and there stood Joanna, in all her splendor, with the golden crown on her head, as he had last seen her, to Welcome him back. And then there appeared before him two remarkable shapes, which looked much more like human beings than when he had seen them in his childhood; they were changed, but he remembered that they were the two gingerbread cakes, the man and the woman, who had shown their best sides to the world and looked so good.

"We thank you," they said to Knud, "for you have loosened our tongues; we have learnt from you that thoughts should be spoken freely, or nothing will come of them; and now something has come of our thoughts, for we are engaged to be married." Then they walked away, hand-in-hand, through the streets of Kjøge, looking very respectable on the best side, which they were quite right to show. They turned their steps to the church, and Knud and Joanna followed them, also walking hand-in-hand; there stood the church, as of old, with its red walls, on which the green ivy grew.

The great church door flew open wide, and as they walked up the broad aisle, soft tones of music sounded from the organ. "Our master first," said the gingerbread pair, making room for Knud and Joanna. As they knelt at the altar, Joanna bent her head over him, and cold, icy tears fell on his face from her eyes. They were indeed tears of ice, for her heart was melting towards him through his strong love, and as her tears fell on his burning cheeks he awoke. He was still sitting under the willow tree in a strange land, on a cold winter evening, with snow and hail falling from the clouds, and beating upon his face.

"That was the most delightful hour of my life," said he, "although it was only a dream. Oh, let me dream again." Then he closed his eyes once more, and slept and dreamed.

Towards morning there was a great fall of snow; the wind drifted it over him, but he still slept on. The villagers came forth to go to church; by the roadside they found a workman seated, but he was dead! frozen to death under a willow tree.

Jack the Dullard

Translated by W. A. & J. K. Craigie

Out in the country lay an old mansion, and in it lived an old proprietor, who had two sons, which two young men thought themselves too clever by half. They wanted to go out and woo the King's daughter; for the maiden in question had publicly announced that she would choose for her husband that one that she thought could best speak for himself.

So these two prepared themselves a full week for the wooing—this was the longest time that could be granted them; but it was enough, for they had previous accomplishments, and these are useful. One of them knew the whole Latin dictionary by heart, and three whole years of the daily paper of the little town, and that either backwards or forwards. The other was deeply read in the corporation laws, and knew by heart what every alderman ought to know; and accordingly he thought he could talk of affairs of state. And he knew one thing more: he, could embroider braces, for he was a tasty, light-fingered fellow.

"I shall win the Princess!" So cried both of them. Therefore their father gave to each a handsome horse. The youth who knew the dictionary and newspaper by heart had a black horse, and he who knew all about the corporation laws received a milk-white steed. Then they rubbed the corners of their mouths with fish-oil, so that they might become very smooth and glib. All the servants stood below in the courtyard, and looked on while they mounted their horses; and just by chance the third son came up. For there were three of them, though nobody counted the third with his brothers, because he was not so learned as they, and indeed he was generally known as "Jack the Dullard".

"Hallo!" said he, "where are you going since you have put on your best clothes?"

"We're going to the King's court, as suitors to the King's daughter. Don't you know the announcement that has been made all through the country?" And they told him all about it.

"My word! I'll be in it too!" cried Jack the Dullard; and his two brothers burst out laughing at him, and rode away.

"Father," said Jack, "I must have a horse too. I do feel so desperately inclined to marry! If she accepts me, she accepts me; and if she won't have me, I'll have her all the same!"

"Don't talk nonsense," said the father. "You shall have no horse from me. You don't know how to speak. Your brothers are very different fellows from you."

"Well," quoth Jack the Dullard, "if I can't have a horse, I'll take the billy-goat, who belongs to me, and he can carry me very well!"

And so he mounted the billy-goat, pressed his heels into its sides, and galloped off along the highway.

"Hei, houp! that was a ride! Here I come!" shouted Jack the Dullard, and he sang till his voice echoed far and wide.

But his brothers rode slowly on in advance of him. They spoke not a word, for they were thinking all about the fine ideas they would have to bring out, and these had to be cleverly prepared beforehand.

"Hallo!" shouted Jack the Dullard. "Here am I! Look what I have found on the high road." And he showed them a dead crow which he had found.

"Dullard!" exclaimed the brothers, "what are you going to do with that?"

"I am going to give it to the Princess."

"Yes, do so," said they; and they laughed, and rode on.

"Hallo, here I am again! Just see what I have found now: you don't find that on the high road every day!"

And the brothers turned round to see what he could have found now.

"Dullard!" they cried, "that is only an old wooden shoe, and the upper part is missing into the bargain; are you going to give that also to the Princess?"

"Most certainly I shall," replied Jack the Dullard; and again the brothers laughed and rode on, and thus they got far in advance of him; but—

"Hallo!" and there was Jack the Dullard again. "It is getting better and better," he cried. "Hurrah! it is quite famous."

"Why, what have you found this time?" inquired the brothers.

"Oh," said Jack the Dullard, "I can hardly tell you. How glad the Princess will be!"

"Bah!" said the brothers; "that is nothing but clay out of the ditch."

"Yes, certainly it is," said Jack the Dullard; "and clay of the finest sort. See, it is so wet, it runs through one's fingers." And he filled his pocket with the clay.

But his brothers galloped on as hard as the harness could stand, and consequently they arrived a full hour earlier at the town gate than could Jack. Now at the gate each suitor was provided with a number, and all were placed in rows, six in each row, and so closely packed together that they could not move their arms; and that was a prudent arrangement, for they would certainly have come to blows, had they been able, merely because one of them stood before the other.

All the inhabitants of the country round about stood in great crowds around the castle, almost under the very windows, to see the Princess receive the suitors; and as each stepped into the hall, his power of speech seemed to desert him. Then the Princess would say, "He is of no use! away with him!"

At last the turn came for that brother who knew the dictionary by heart; but he had absolutely forgotten it; and the boards seemed to re-echo with his footsteps, and the ceiling of the hall was made of looking-glass, so that he saw himself standing on his head; and at the window stood three clerks and a head clerk, and every one of them was writing down every single word that was uttered, so that it might be printed in the newspapers, and sold for a penny at the street corners. It was a terrible ordeal, and they had moreover made such a fire in the stove, that the stove-pipe was quite red hot.

"It is dreadfully hot here!" observed the first brother.

"Yes," replied the Princess, "my father is going to roast young pullets today."

Baa! there he stood. He had not been prepared for a speech of this kind, and had not a word to say, though he intended to say something witty. Baa!

"He is of no use!" said the Princess. "Away with him!"

And he was obliged to go accordingly. And now the second brother came in.

"It is terribly warm here!" he observed.

"Yes, we're roasting pullets today," replied the Princess.

"What—what were you—were you pleased to ob—" stammered he—and all the clerks wrote down, "pleased to ob—"

"He is of no use!" said the Princess. "Away with him!"

Now came the turn of Jack the Dullard. He rode into the hall on his goat.

"Well, it's most desperately hot here."

"Yes, because I'm roasting young pullets," replied the Princess.

"Ah, that's lucky!" exclaimed Jack the Dullard, "then I suppose I can get a crow roasted?"

"With the greatest pleasure," said the Princess. "But have you anything you can roast it in? for I have neither pot nor pan."

"Certainly I have!" said Jack. "Here's a cooking utensil with a tin handle."

And he brought out the old wooden shoe, and put the crow into it.

"Well, that *is* a famous dish!" said the Princess. "But what shall we do for sauce?"

"Oh, I have that in my pocket," said Jack: "I have so much of it that I can afford to throw some away;" and he poured some of the clay out of his pocket.

"I like that!" said the Princess. "You can give an answer, and you have something to say for yourself, and so you shall be my husband. But are you aware that every word we speak is being taken down, and will be published in the paper tomorrow? You will see in every window three clerks and a head clerk; and the old head clerk is the worst of all, for he can't understand anything."

But she only said this to frighten him; and the clerks gave a great shout of delight, and each one spurted a blot out of his pen on to the floor.

"Oh, those are the gentlemen, are they?" said Jack; "then I will give the best I have to the head clerk." And he turned out his pockets, and flung the wet clay full in the head clerk's face.

"That was very cleverly done," observed the Princess. "I could not have done that; but I shall learn in time."

And accordingly Jack the Dullard was made a king, and received a crown and a wife, and sat upon a throne. And this report we have straight from the newspaper of the head clerk—but it is not to be depended upon!

The Last Pearl

Translated by Mrs. H. P. Paull

We are in a rich, happy house, where the master, the servants, the friends of the family are full of joy and felicity. For on this day a son and heir has been born, and mother and child are doing well. The lamp in the bed-chamber had been partly shaded, and the windows were covered with heavy curtains of some costly silken material. The carpet was thick and soft, like a covering of moss. Everything invited to slumber, everything had a charming look of repose; and so the nurse had discovered, for she slept; and well she might sleep, while everything around her told of happiness and blessing. The guardian angel of the house leaned against the head of the bed; while over the child was spread, as it were, a net of shining stars, and each star was a pearl of happiness. All the good stars of life had brought their gifts to the newly born; here sparkled health, wealth, fortune, and love; in short, there seemed to be everything for which man could wish on earth.

"Everything has been bestowed here," said the guardian angel.

"No, not everything," said a voice near him—the voice of the *good angel* of the child; "one fairy has not yet brought her gift, but she will, even if years should elapse, she will bring her gift; it is the *last pearl* that is wanting."

"Wanting!" cried the guardian angel; "nothing must be wanting here; and if it is so, let us fetch it; let us seek the powerful fairy; let us go to her."

"She will come, she will come some day unsought!"

"Her pearl must not be missing; it must be there, that the crown, when worn, may be complete. Where is she to be found? Where does she dwell?" said the guardian angel. "Tell me, and I will procure the pearl."

"Will you do that?" replied the good angel of the child. "Then I will lead you to her directly, wherever she may be. She has no abiding place; she rules in the palace of the emperor, sometimes she enters the peasant's humble cot; she passes no one without leaving a trace of her presence. She brings her gift with her, whether it is a world or a bauble. To this child she must come. You think that to wait for this time would be long and useless. Well, then, let us go for this pearl—the only one lacking amidst all this wealth."

Then hand-in-hand they floated away to the spot where the fairy was now lingering. It was in a large house with dark windows and empty rooms, in which a peculiar stillness reigned. A whole row of windows stood open, so that the rude wind could enter at its pleasure, and the long white curtains waved to and fro in the current of air. In the centre of one of the rooms stood an open coffin, in which lay the body of a woman, still in the bloom of youth and very beautiful. Fresh roses were scattered over her. The delicate folded hands and the noble face glorified in death by the solemn, earnest look, which spoke of an entrance into a better world, were alone visible. Around the coffin stood the husband and children, a whole troop, the youngest in the father's arms. They were come to take a last farewell look of their mother. The husband kissed her hand, which now lay like a withered leaf, but which a short time before had been diligently employed in deeds of love for them all. Tears of sorrow rolled down their cheeks, and fell in heavy drops on the floor, but not a word was spoken. The silence which reigned here expressed a world of grief. With silent steps, still sobbing, they left the room. A burning light remained in the room, and a long, red wick rose far above the flame, which fluttered in the draught of air. Strange men came in and placed the lid of the coffin over the dead, and drove the nails firmly in; while the blows of the hammer resounded through the house, and echoed in the hearts that were bleeding.

"Whither art thou leading me?" asked the guardian angel. "Here dwells no fairy whose pearl could be counted amongst the best gifts of life."

"Yes, she is here; here in this sacred hour," replied the angel, pointing to a corner of the room; and there—where in her life-time, the mother had taken her seat amidst flowers and pictures: in that spot, where she, like the blessed fairy of the house, had welcomed husband, children, and friends, and, like a sunbeam, had spread joy and cheerfulness around her, the centre and heart of them all—there, in that very spot, sat a strange woman, clothed in long, flowing garments, and occupying the place of the dead wife and mother. It was the fairy, and her name was "Sorrow." A hot tear rolled into her lap, and formed itself into a pearl, glowing with all the colours of the rainbow. The angel seized it: the, pearl glittered like a star with seven-fold radiance. The pearl of Sorrow, the last, which must not be wanting, increases the lustre, and explains the meaning of all the other pearls.

"Do you see the shimmer of the rainbow, which unites earth to heaven?" So has there been a bridge built between this world and the next. Through the night of the grave we gaze upwards beyond the stars to the end of all things. Then we glance at the pearl of Sorrow, in which are concealed the wings which shall carry us away to eternal happiness.

A Leaf from the Sky

Translated by H. W. Dulcken

High up yonder, in the thin clear air, flew an angel with a flower from the heavenly garden. As he was kissing the flower, a very little leaf fell down into the soft soil in the midst of the wood, and immediately took root, and sprouted, and sent forth shoots among the other plants.

"A funny kind of slip that," said the plants.

And neither thistle nor stinging-nettle would recognize the stranger.

"That must be a kind of garden plant," said they.

And they sneered; and the plant was despised by them as being a thing out of the garden.

"Where are you coming?" cried the lofty thistles, whose leaves are all armed with thorns.

"You give yourself a good deal of space. That's all nonsense—we are not here to support you!" they grumbled.

And winter came, and snow covered the plant; but the plant imparted to the snowy covering a lustre as if the sun was shining upon it from below as from above. When spring came, the plant appeared as a blooming object, more beautiful than any production of the forest.

And now appeared on the scene the botanical professor, who could show what he was in black and white. He inspected the plant and tested it, but found it was not included in his botanical system; and he could not possibly find out to what class it belonged.

"That must be some subordinate species," he said. "I don't know it. It's not included in any system."

"Not included in any system!" repeated the thistles and the nettles.

The great trees that stood round about saw and heard it; but they said not a word, good or bad, which is the wisest thing to do for people who are stupid.

There came through the forest a poor innocent girl. Her heart was pure, and her understanding was enlarged by faith. Her whole inheritance was an old Bible; but out of its pages a voice said to her, "If people wish to do us evil, remember how it was said of Joseph. They imagined evil in their hearts, but God turned it to good. If we suffer wrong—if we are misunderstood and despised—then we may recall the words of Him who was purity and goodness itself, and who forgave and prayed for those who buffeted Him and nailed Him to the cross." The girl stood still in front of the wonderful plant, whose great leaves exhaled a sweet and refreshing fragrance, and whose flowers glittered like a coloured flame in the sun; and from each flower there came a sound as though it concealed within itself a deep fount of melody that thousands of years could not exhaust. With pious gratitude the girl looked on this beautiful work of the Creator, and bent down one of the branches towards herself to breathe in its sweetness; and a light arose in her soul. It seemed to do her heart good; and gladly would she have plucked a flower, but she could not make up her mind to break one off, for it would soon fade if she did so. Therefore the girl only took a single leaf, and laid it in her Bible at home; and it lay there quite fresh, always green, and never fading.

Among the pages of the Bible it was kept; and, with the Bible, it was laid under the young girl's head when, a few weeks afterwards, she lay in her coffin, with the solemn calm of death on her gentle face, as if the earthly remains bore the impress of the truth that she now stood before her Creator.

But the wonderful plant still bloomed without in the forest. It was almost like a tree to look upon; and all the birds of passage bowed before it.

"That's giving itself foreign airs now," said the thistles and the burdocks; "we never behave like that here."

And the black snails actually spat at the flower.

Then came the swineherd. He was collecting thistles and shrubs, to burn them for the ashes. The wonderful plant was placed bodily in his bundle.

"It shall be made useful," he said; and so said, so done.

But soon afterwards, the king of the country was troubled with a terrible depression of spirits. He was busy and industrious, but that did him no good. They read him deep and learned books, and then they read from the lightest and most superficial that they could find; but it was of no use. Then one of the wise men of the world, to whom they had applied, sent a messenger to tell the king that there was one remedy to give him relief and to cure him. He said:

"In the king's own country there grows in a forest a plant of heavenly origin. Its appearance is thus and thus. It cannot be mistaken."

"I fancy it was taken up in my bundle, and burnt to ashes long ago," said the swineherd; "but I did not know any better."

"You didn't know any better! Ignorance of ignorances!"

And those words the swineherd might well take to himself, for they were meant for him, and for no one else.

Not another leaf was to be found; the only one lay in the coffin of the dead girl, and no one knew anything about that.

And the king himself, in his melancholy, wandered out to the spot in the wood.

"Here is where the plant stood," he said; "it is a sacred place."

And the place was surrounded with a golden railing, and a sentry was posted there.

The botanical professor wrote a long treatise upon the heavenly plant. For this he was gilded all over, and this gilding suited him and his family very well. And indeed that was the most agreeable part of the whole story. But the king remained as low-spirited as before; but that he had always been, at least so the sentry said.

Two Maidens

Translated by H. W. Dulcken

Have you ever seen a maiden? I mean what our paviours call a maiden, a thing with which they ram down the paving-stones in the roads. A maiden of this kind is made altogether of wood, broad below, and girt round with iron rings; at the top she is narrow, and has a stick passed across through her waist; and this stick forms the arms of the maiden.

In the shed stood two maidens of this kind. They had their place among shovels, hand-carts, wheelbarrows, and measuring tapes; and to all this company the news had come that the maidens were no longer to be called "maidens," but "hand-rammers;" which word was the newest and the only correct designation among the paviours for the thing we all know from the old times by the name of "the maiden."

Now, there are among us human creatures certain individuals who are known as "emancipated women;" as, for instance, principals of institutions, dancers who stand professionally on one leg, milliners, and sick nurses; and with this class of emancipated women the two maidens in the shed associated themselves. They were "maidens" among the paviour folk, and determined not to give up this honourable appellation, and let themselves be miscalled rammers.

"Maiden is a human name, but hand-rammer is a *thing*, and we won't be called *things*—that's insulting us."

"My lover would be ready to give up his engagement," said the youngest, who was betrothed to a paviour's hammer; and the hammer is the thing which drives great piles into the earth, like a machine, and therefore does on a large scale what ten maidens effect in a smaller way. "He wants to marry me as a maiden, but whether he would have me, were I a hand-rammer, is a question; so I won't have my name changed."

"And I," said the elder one, "would rather have both my arms broken off."

But the wheelbarrow was of a different opinion; and the wheelbarrow was looked upon as of some consequence, for he considered himself a quarter of a coach, because he went about upon one wheel.

"I must submit to your notice," he said, "that the name 'maiden' is common enough, and not nearly so refined as 'hand-rammer,' or 'stamper,' which latter has also been proposed, and through which you would be introduced into the category of seals; and only think of the great stamp of state, which impresses the royal seal that gives effect to the laws! No, in your case I would surrender my maiden name."

"No, certainly not!" exclaimed the elder. "I am too old for that."

"I presume you have never heard of what is called 'European necessity?'" observed the honest Measuring Tape. "One must be able to adapt oneself to time and circumstances, and if there is a law that the 'maiden' is to be called 'hand-rammer,' why, she must be called 'hand-rammer,' and no pouting will avail, for everything has its measure."

"No; if there must be a change," said the younger, "I should prefer to be called 'Missy,' for that reminds one a little of maidens."

"But I would rather be chopped to chips," said the elder.

At last they all went to work. The maidens rode—that is, they were put in a wheelbarrow, and that was a distinction; but still they were called "hand-rammers." "Mai——!" they said, as they were bumped upon the pavement. "Mai——!" and they were very nearly pronouncing the whole word "maiden;" but they broke off short, and swallowed the last syllable; for after mature deliberation they considered it beneath their dignity to protest. But they always called each other "maiden," and praised the good old days in which everything had been called by its right name, and those who were maidens were called maidens. And they remained as they were; for the hammer really broke off his engagement with the younger one, for nothing would suit him but he must have a maiden for his bride.

Ib and Little Christine

Translated by Mrs. H. P. Paull

In the forest that extends from the banks of the Gudenau, in North Jutland, a long way into the country, and not far from the clear stream, rises a great ridge of land, which stretches through the wood like a wall. Westward of this ridge, and not far from the river, stands a farmhouse, surrounded by such poor land that the sandy soil shows itself between the scanty ears of rye and wheat which grow in it. Some years have passed since the people who lived here cultivated these fields; they kept three sheep, a pig, and two oxen; in fact they maintained themselves very well, they had quite enough to live upon, as people generally have who are content with their lot. They even could have afforded to keep two horses, but it was a saying among the farmers in those parts, "The horse eats himself up;" that is to say, he eats as much as he earns. Jeppe Jans cultivated his fields in summer, and in the winter he made wooden shoes. He also had an assistant, a lad who understood as well as he himself did how to make wooden shoes strong, but light, and in the fashion. They carved shoes and spoons, which paid well; therefore no one could justly call Jeppe Jans and his family poor people. Little Ib, a boy of seven years old and the only child, would sit by, watching the workmen, or cutting a stick, and sometimes his finger instead of the stick. But one day Ib succeeded so well in his carving that he made two pieces of wood look really like two little wooden shoes, and he determined to give them as a present to Little Christina.

"And who was Little Christina?" She was the boatman's daughter, graceful and delicate as the child of a gentleman; had she been dressed differently, no one would have believed that she lived in a hut on the neighbouring heath with her father. He was a widower, and earned his living by carrying firewood in his large boat from the forest to the eel-pond and eel-weir, on the estate of Silkborg, and sometimes even to the distant town of Randers. There was no one under whose care he could leave Little Christina; so she was almost always with him in his boat, or playing in the wood among the blossoming heath, or picking the ripe wild berries. Sometimes, when her father had to go as far as the town, he would take Little Christina, who was a year younger than Ib, across the heath to the cottage of Jeppe Jans, and leave her there. Ib and Christina agreed together in everything; they divided their bread and berries when they were hungry; they

were partners in digging their little gardens; they ran, and crept, and played about everywhere. Once they wandered a long way into the forest, and even ventured together to climb the high ridge. Another time they found a few snipes' eggs in the wood, which was a great event. Ib had never been on the heath where Christina's father lived, nor on the river; but at last came an opportunity. Christina's father invited him to go for a sail in his boat; and the evening before, he accompanied the boatman across the heath to his house. The next morning early, the two children were placed on the top of a high pile of firewood in the boat, and sat eating bread and wild strawberries, while Christina's father and his man drove the boat forward with poles. They floated on swiftly, for the tide was in their favour, passing over lakes, formed by the stream in its course; sometimes they seemed quite enclosed by reeds and water-plants, yet there was always room for them to pass out, although the old trees overhung the water and the old oaks stretched out their bare branches, as if they had turned up their sleeves and wished to show their knotty, naked arms. Old alder-trees, whose roots were loosened from the banks, clung with their fibres to the bottom of the stream, and the tops of the branches above the water looked like little woody islands. The water lilies waved themselves to and fro on the river, everything made the excursion beautiful, and at last they came to the great eel-weir, where the water rushed through the flood-gates; and the children thought this a beautiful sight. In those days there was no factory nor any town house, nothing but the great farm, with its scanty-bearing fields, in which could be seen a few herd of cattle, and one or two farm labourers. The rushing of the water through the sluices, and the scream of the wild ducks, were almost the only signs of active life at Silkborg. After the firewood had been unloaded, Christina's father bought a whole bundle of eels and a sucking-pig, which were all placed in a basket in the stern of the boat. Then they returned again up the stream; and as the wind was favourable, two sails were hoisted, which carried the boat on as well as if two horses had been harnessed to it. As they sailed on, they came by chance to the place where the boatman's assistant lived, at a little distance from the bank of the river. The boat was moored; and the two men, after desiring the children to sit still, both went on shore. they obeyed this order for a very short time, and then forgot it altogether. First they peeped into the basket containing the eels and the sucking-pig; then they must needs pull out the pig and take it in their hands, and feel it, and touch it; and as they both wanted to hold it at the same time, the consequence was that they let it fall into the water, and the pig sailed away with the stream.

Here was a terrible disaster. Ib jumped ashore, and ran a little distance from the boat.

"Oh, take me with you," cried Christina; and she sprang after him. In a few minutes they found themselves deep in a thicket, and could no longer see the boat or the shore. They ran on a little farther, and then Christina fell down, and began to cry.

Ib helped her up, and said, "Never mind; follow me. Yonder is the house." But the house was not yonder; and they wandered still farther, over the dry rustling leaves of the last year, and treading on fallen branches that crackled under their little feet; then they heard a loud, piercing cry, and they stood still to listen. Presently the scream of an eagle sounded through the wood; it was an ugly cry, and it frightened the children; but before them, in the thickest part of the forest, grew the most beautiful blackberries, in wonderful quantities. They looked so inviting that the children could not help stopping; and they remained there so long eating, that their mouths and cheeks became quite black with the juice.

Presently they heard the frightful scream again, and Christina said, "We shall get into trouble about that pig."

"Oh, never mind," said Ib; "we will go home to my father's house. It is here in the wood." So they went on, but the road led

them out of the way; no house could be seen, it grew dark, and the children were afraid. The solemn stillness that reigned around them was now and then broken by the shrill cries of the great horned owl and other birds that they knew nothing of. At last they both lost themselves in the thicket; Christina began to cry, and then Ib cried too; and, after weeping and lamenting for some time, they stretched themselves down on the dry leaves and fell asleep.

The sun was high in the heavens when the two children woke. They felt cold; but not far from their resting-place, on a hill, the sun was shining through the trees. They thought if they went there they

Ib and Little Christine

should be warm, and Ib fancied he should be able to see his father's house from such a high spot. But they were far away from home now, in quite another part of the forest. They clambered to the top of the rising ground, and found themselves on the edge of a declivity, which sloped down to a clear transparent lake. Great quantities of fish could be seen through the clear water, sparkling in the sun's rays; they were quite surprised when they came so suddenly upon such an unexpected sight.

Close to where they stood grew a hazel-bush, covered with beautiful nuts. They soon gathered some, cracked them, and ate the fine young kernels, which were only just ripe. But there was another surprise and fright in store for them. Out of the thicket stepped a tall old woman, her face quite brown, and her hair of a deep shining black; the whites of her eyes glittered like a Moor's; on her back she carried a bundle, and in her hand a knotted stick. She was a gypsy.

The children did not at first understand what she said. She drew out of her pocket three large nuts, in which she told them were hidden the most beautiful and lovely things in the world, for they were wishing nuts. Ib looked at her, and as she spoke so kindly, he took courage, and asked her if she would give him the nuts; and the woman gave them to him, and then gathered some more from the bushes for herself, quite a pocket full. Ib and Christina looked at the wishing nuts with wide open eyes.

"Is there in this nut a carriage, with a pair of horses?" asked Ib.

"Yes, there is a golden carriage, with two golden horses," replied the woman.

"Then give me that nut," said Christina; so Ib gave it to her, and the strange woman tied up the nut for her in her handkerchief.

Ib held up another nut. "Is there, in this nut, a pretty little neckerchief like the one Christina has on her neck?" asked Ib.

"There are ten neckerchiefs in it," she replied, "as well as beautiful dresses, stockings, and a hat and veil."

"Then I will have that one also," said Christina; "and it is a pretty one too. And then Ib gave her the second nut.

The third was a little black thing. "You may keep that one," said Christina; "it is quite as pretty."

"What is in it?" asked Ib.

"The best of all things for you," replied the gypsy. So Ib held the nut very tight.

Then the woman promised to lead the children to the right path, that they might find their way home: and they went forward certainly in quite another direction to the one they meant to take; therefore no one ought to speak against the woman, and say that she wanted to steal the children. In the wild wood-path they met a forester who knew Ib, and, by his help, Ib and Christina reached home, where they found every one had been very anxious about them. They were pardoned and forgiven, although they really had both done wrong, and deserved to get into trouble; first, because they had let the sucking-pig fall into the water; and, secondly, because they had run away. Christina was taken back to her father's house on the heath, and Ib remained in the farm-house on the borders of the wood, near the great land ridge.

The first thing Ib did that evening was to take out of his pocket the little black nut, in which the best thing of all was said to be enclosed. He laid it carefully between the door and the door-post, and then shut the door so that the nut cracked directly. But there was not much kernel to be seen; it was what we should call hollow or worm-eaten, and looked as if it had been filled with tobacco or rich black earth. "It is just what I expected!" exclaimed Ib. "How should there be room in a little nut like this for the best thing of all? Christina will find her two nuts just the same; there will be neither fine clothes or a golden carriage in them."

Winter came; and the new year, and indeed many years passed away; until Ib was old enough to be confirmed, and, therefore, he went during a whole winter to the clergyman of the nearest village to be prepared.

One day, about this time, the boatman paid a visit to Ib's parents, and told them that Christina was going to service, and that she had been remarkably fortunate in obtaining a good place, with most respectable people. "Only think," he said, "She is going to the rich innkeeper's, at the hotel in Herning, many miles west from here. She is to assist the landlady in the housekeeping; and, if afterwards she behaves well and remains to be confirmed, the people will treat her as their own daughter."

So Ib and Christina took leave of each other. People already called them "the betrothed," and at parting the girl showed Ib the two nuts, which she had taken care of ever since the time that they lost themselves in the wood; and she told him also that the little wooden shoes he once carved for her when he was a boy, and gave her as a present, had been carefully kept in a drawer ever since. And so they parted.

After Ib's confirmation, he remained at home with his mother, for he had become a clever shoemaker, and in summer managed the farm for her quite alone. His father had been dead some time, and his mother kept no farm servants. Sometimes, but very seldom, he heard of Christina, through a postilion or eel-seller who was passing. But she was well off with the rich innkeeper; and after being confirmed she wrote a letter to her father, in which was a kind message to Ib and his mother. In this letter, she mentioned that her master and mistress had made her a present of a beautiful new dress, and some nice under-clothes. This was, of course, pleasant news.

One day, in the following spring, there came a knock at the door of the house where Ib's old mother lived; and when they opened it, lo and behold, in stepped the boatman and Christina. She had come to pay them a visit, and to spend the day. A carriage had to come from the Herning hotel to the next village, and she had taken the opportunity to see her friends once more. She looked as elegant as a real lady, and wore a pretty dress, beautifully made on purpose for her. There she stood, in full dress, while Ib wore only his working clothes. He could not utter a word; he could only seize her hand and hold it fast in his own, but he felt too happy and glad to open his lips. Christina, however, was quite at her ease; she talked and talked, and kissed him in the most friendly manner. Even afterwards, when they were left alone, and she asked, "Did you know me again, Ib?" he still stood holding her hand, and said at last, "You are become quite a grand lady, Christina, and I am only a rough working man; but I have often thought of you and of old times." Then they wandered up the great ridge, and looked across the stream to the heath, where the little hills were covered with the flowering broom. Ib said nothing; but before the time came for them to part, it became quite clear to him that Christina must be his wife: had they not even in childhood been called the betrothed? To him it seemed as if they were really engaged to each other, although not a word had been spoken on the subject. They had only a few more hours to remain together, for Christina was obliged to return that evening to the neighbouring village, to be ready for the carriage which was to start the next morning early for Herning. Ib and her father accompanied her to the village. It was a fine moonlight evening; and when they arrived, Ib stood holding Christina's hand in his, as if he could not let her go. His eyes brightened, and the words he uttered came with hesitation from his lips, but from the deepest recesses of his heart: "Christina, if you have not become too grand, and if you can be contented to live in my mother's house as my wife, we will be married some day. But we can wait for a while."

"Oh yes," she replied; "Let us wait a little longer, Ib. I can trust you, for I believe that I do love you. But let me think it over." Then he kissed her lips; and so they parted.

On the way home, Ib told the boatman that he and Christina were as good as engaged to each other; and the boatman found out that he had always expected it would be so, and went home with Ib that evening, and remained the night in the farmhouse; but nothing further was said of the engagement. During the next year, two letters passed between Ib and Christina. They were signed, "Faithful till death;" but at the end of that time, one day the boatman came over to see Ib, with a kind greeting from Christina. He had something else to say, which made him hesitate in a strange manner. At last it came out that Christina, who had grown a very pretty girl, was more lucky than ever. She was courted and admired by every one; but her master's son, who had been home on a visit, was so much pleased with Christina that he wished to marry her. He had a very good situation in an office at Copenhagen, and as she had also taken a liking for him, his parents were not unwilling to consent. But Christina, in her heart, often thought of Ib, and knew how much he thought of her; so she felt inclined to refuse this good fortune, added the boatman. At first Ib said not a word, but he became as white as the wall, and shook his head gently, and then he spoke, "Christina must not refuse this good fortune."

"Then will you write a few words to her?" said the boatman.

Ib sat down to write, but he could not get on at all. The words were not what he wished to say, so he tore up the page. The following morning, however, a letter lay ready to be sent to Christina, and the following is what he wrote:

"The letter written by you to your father I have read, and see from it that you are prosperous in everything, and that still better fortune is in store for you. Ask your own heart, Christina, and think over carefully what awaits you if you take me for your husband, for I possess very little in the world. Do not think of me or of my position; think only of your own welfare. You are bound to me by no promises; and if in your heart you have given me one, I release you from it. May every blessing and happiness be poured out upon you, Christina. Heaven will give me the heart's consolation.

Ever your sincere friend, IB."

This letter was sent, and Christina received it in due time. In the course of the following November, her banns were published in the church on the heath, and also in Copenhagen, where the bridegroom lived. She was taken to Copenhagen under the protection of her future mother-in-law, because the bridegroom could not spare time from his numerous occupations for a journey so far into Jutland. On the journey, Christina met her father at one of the villages through which they passed, and here he took leave of her. Very little was said about the matter to Ib, and he did not refer to it; his mother, however, noticed that he had grown very silent and pensive. Thinking as he did of old times, no wonder the three nuts came into his mind which the gypsy woman had given him when a child, and of the two which he had given to Christina. These wishing nuts, after all, had proved true fortune-tellers. One had contained a gilded carriage and noble horses, and the other beautiful clothes; all of these Christina would now have in her new home at Copenhagen. Her part had come true. And for him the nut had contained only black earth. The gypsy woman had said it was the best for him. Perhaps it was, and this also would be fulfilled. He understood the gypsy woman's meaning now. The black earth—the dark grave—was the best thing for him now.

Again years passed away; not many, but they seemed long years to Ib. The old innkeeper and his wife died one after the other; and the whole of their property, many thousand dollars, was inherited by their son. Christina could have the golden carriage now, and plenty of fine clothes. During the two long years which followed, no letter came from Christina to her father; and when at last her father received one from her, it did not speak of prosperity or happiness. Poor Christina! Neither she nor her husband understood how to economize or save, and the riches brought no blessing with them, because they had not asked for it.

Years passed; and for many summers the heath was covered with bloom; in winter the snow rested upon it, and the rough winds blew across the ridge under which stood Ib's sheltered home. One spring day the sun shone brightly, and he was guiding the plough across his field. The ploughshare struck against something which he fancied was a firestone, and then he saw glittering in the earth a splinter of shining metal which the plough had cut from something

Ib and Little Christine

which gleamed brightly in the furrow. He searched, and found a large golden armlet of superior workmanship, and it was evident that the plough had disturbed a Hun's grave. He searched further, and found more valuable treasures, which Ib showed to the clergyman, who explained their value to him. Then he went to the magistrate, who informed the president of the museum of the discovery, and advised Ib to take the treasures himself to the president.

"You have found in the earth the best thing you could find," said the magistrate.

"The best thing," thought Ib; "the very best thing for me—and found in the earth! Well, if it really is so, then the gypsy woman was right in her prophecy."

So Ib went in the ferry-boat from Aarhus to Copenhagen. To him who had only sailed once or twice on the river near his own home, this seemed like a voyage on the ocean; and at length he arrived at Copenhagen. The value of the gold he had found was paid to him; it was a large sum—six hundred dollars. Then Ib of the heath went out, and wandered about in the great city.

On the evening before the day he had settled to return with the captain of the passage-boat, Ib lost himself in the streets, and took quite a different turning to the one he wished to follow. He wandered on till he found himself in a poor street of the suburb called Christian's Haven. Not a creature could be seen. At last a very little girl came out of one of the wretched-looking houses, and Ib asked her to tell him the way to the street he wanted; she looked up timidly at him, and began to cry bitterly. He asked her what was the matter; but what she said he could not understand. So he went along the street with her; and as they passed under a lamp, the light fell on the little girl's face. A strange sensation came over Ib, as he caught sight of it. The living, breathing embodiment of Little Christina stood before him, just as he remembered her in the days of her childhood. He followed the child to the wretched house, and ascended the narrow, crazy staircase which led to a little garret in the roof. The air in the room was heavy and stifling, no light was burning, and from one corner came sounds of moaning and sighing. It was the mother of the child who lay there on a miserable bed. With the help of a match, Ib struck a light, and approached her.

"Can I be of any service to you?" he asked. "This little girl brought me up here; but I am a stranger in this city. Are there no neighbours or any one whom I can call?"

Then he raised the head of the sick woman, and smoothed her pillow. He started as he did so. It was Christina of the heath! No one had mentioned her name to Ib for years; it would have disturbed his peace of mind, especially as the reports respecting her were not good. The wealth which her husband had inherited from his parents had made him proud and arrogant. He had given up his certain appointment, and travelled for six months in foreign lands, and, on his return, had lived in great style, and got into terrible debt. For a time he had trembled on the high pedestal on which he had placed himself, till at last he toppled over, and ruin came. His numerous merry companions, and the visitors at his table, said it served him right, for he had kept house like a madman. One morning his corpse was found in the canal. The cold hand of death had already touched the heart of Christina. Her youngest child, looked for in the midst of prosperity, had sunk into the grave when only a few weeks old; and at last Christina herself became sick unto death, and lay, forsaken and dying, in a miserable room, amid poverty she might have borne in her younger days, but which was now more painful to her from the luxuries to which she had lately been accustomed. It was her eldest child, also a Little Christina, whom Ib had followed to her home, where she suffered hunger and poverty with her mother.

It makes me unhappy to think that I shall die, and leave this poor child," sighed she. "Oh, what will become of her?" She could say no more.

Then Ib brought out another match, and lighted a piece of candle which he found in the room, and it threw a glimmering light over the wretched dwelling. Ib looked at the little girl, and thought of Christina in her young days. For her sake, could he not love this child, who was a stranger to him? As he thus reflected, the dying woman opened her eyes, and gazed at him. Did she recognize him? He never knew; for not another word escaped her lips.

In the forest by the river Gudenau, not far from the heath, and beneath the ridge of land, stood the little farm, newly painted and whitewashed. The air was heavy and dark; there were no blossoms on the heath; the autumn winds whirled the yellow leaves towards the boatman's hut, in which strangers dwelt; but the little farm stood safely sheltered beneath the tall trees and the high ridge. The turf blazed brightly on the hearth, and within was sunlight, the sparkling light from the sunny eyes of a child; the birdlike tones from the rosy lips ringing like the song of a lark in spring. All was life and joy. Little Christina sat on Ib's knee. Ib was to her both father and mother; her own parents had vanished from her memory, as a dream-picture vanishes alike from childhood and age. Ib's house was well and prettily furnished; for he was a prosperous man now, while the mother of the little girl rested in the churchyard at Copenhagen, where she had died in poverty. Ib had money now—money which had come to him out of the black earth; and he had Christina for his own, after all.

The Thorny Road of Honour

Translated by H. W. Dulcken

An old story yet lives of the "Thorny Road of Honour," of a marksman, who indeed attained to rank and office, but only after a lifelong and weary strife against difficulties. Who has not, in reading this story, thought of his own strife, and of his own numerous "difficulties?" The story is very closely akin to reality; but still it has its harmonious explanation here on earth, while reality often points beyond the confines of life to the regions of eternity. The history of the world is like a magic lantern that displays to us, in light pictures upon the dark ground of the present, how the benefactors of mankind, the martyrs of genius, wandered along the thorny road of honour.

From all periods, and from every country, these shining pictures display themselves to us; each only appears for a few moments, but each represents a whole life, sometimes a whole age, with its conflicts and victories. Let us contemplate here and there one of the company of martyrs—the company which will receive new members until the world itself shall pass away.

The Thorny Road of Honour

We look down upon a crowded amphitheatre. Out of the "Clouds" of Aristophanes, satire and humour are pouring down in streams upon the audience; on the stage Socrates, the most remarkable man in Athens, he who had been the shield and defence of the people against the thirty tyrants, is held up mentally and bodily to ridicule—Socrates, who saved Alcibiades and Xenophon in the turmoil of battle, and whose genius soared far above the gods of the ancients. He himself is present; he has risen from the spectator's bench, and has stepped forward, that the laughing Athenians may well appreciate the likeness between himself and the caricature on the stage: there he stands before them, towering high above them all.

Thou juicy, green, poisonous hemlock, throw thy shadow over Athens—not thou, olive tree of fame!

Seven cities contended for the honour of giving birth to Homer—that is to say, they contended after his death! Let us look at him as he was in his lifetime. He wanders on foot through the cities, and recites his verses for a livelihood; the thought for the morrow turns his hair grey! He, the great seer, is blind, and painfully pursues his way—the sharp thorn tears the mantle of the king of poets. His song yet lives, and through that alone live all the heroes and gods of antiquity.

One picture after another springs up from the east, from the west, far removed from each other in time and place, and yet each one forming a portion of the thorny road of honour, on which the thistle indeed displays a flower, but only to adorn the grave.

The camels pass along under the palm trees; they are richly laden with indigo and other treasures of price, sent by the ruler of the land to him whose songs are the delight of the people, the fame of the country: he whom envy and falsehood have driven into exile has been found, and the caravan approaches the little town in which he has taken refuge. A poor corpse is carried out of the town gate, and the funeral procession causes the caravan to halt. The dead man is he whom they have been sent to seek—Firdusi—who has wandered the thorny road of honour even to the end.

The African, with blunt features, thick lips, and woolly hair, sits on the marble steps of the palace in the capital of Portugal, and begs: he is the submissive slave of Camoens, and but for him, and for the copper coins thrown to him by the passers by, his master, the poet of the "Lusiad," would die of hunger. Now, a costly monument marks the grave of Camoens.

There is a new picture.

Behind the iron grating a man appears, pale as death, with long unkempt beard.

"I have made a discovery," he says, "the greatest that has been made for centuries; and they have kept me locked up here for more than twenty years!"

"Who is the man?"

"A madman," replies the keeper of the madhouse. "What whimsical ideas these lunatics have! He imagines that one can propel things by means of steam. It is Solomon de Cares, the discoverer of the power of steam, whose theory, expressed in dark words, is not understood by Richelieu—and he dies in the madhouse!"

Here stands Columbus, whom the street boys used once to follow and jeer, because he wanted to discover a new world—and he *has* discovered it. Shouts of joy greet him from the breasts of all, and the clash of bells sounds to celebrate his triumphant return; but the clash of the bells of envy soon drowns the others. The discoverer of a world, he who lifted the American gold land from the sea, and gave it to his king—he is rewarded with iron chains. He wishes that these chains may be placed in his coffin, for they witness of the world, and of the way in which a man's contemporaries reward good service.

One picture after another comes crowding on; the thorny path of honour and of fame is over-filled.

Here in dark night sits the man who measured the mountains in the moon; he who forced his way out into the endless space, among stars and planets; he, the mighty man who understood the spirit of nature, and felt the earth moving beneath his feet—Galileo. Blind and deaf he sits—an old man thrust through with the spear of suffering, and amid the torments of neglect, scarcely able to lift his foot—that foot with which, in the anguish of his soul, when men denied the truth, he stamped upon the ground with the exclamation, "*Yet* it moves!"

Here stands a woman of childlike mind, yet full of faith and inspiration; she carries the banner in front of the combating army,

The Thorny Road of Honour

and brings victory and salvation to her fatherland. The sound of shouting arises, and the pile flames up: they are burning the witch, Joan of Arc. Yes, and a future century jeers at the white lily. Voltaire, the satyr of human intellect, writes "*La Pucelle*."

At the *Thing* or assembly at Viborg, the Danish nobles burn the laws of the king—they flame up high, illuminating the period and the lawgiver, and throw a glory into the dark prison tower, where an old man is growing grey and bent. With his finger he marks out a groove in the stone table. It is the popular king who sits there, once the ruler of three kingdoms, the friend of the citizen and the peasant: it is Christian the Second. Enemies wrote his history. Let us remember his improvements of seven and twenty years, if we cannot forget his crime.

A ship sails away, quitting the Danish shores; a man leans against the mast, casting a last glance towards the Island Hueen. It is Tycho Brahé. He raised the name of Denmark to the stars, and was rewarded with injury, loss, and sorrow. He is going to a strange country.

"The vault of heaven is above me everywhere," he says, "and what do I want more?" And away sails the famous Dane, the astronomer, to live honoured and free in a strange land.

"Ay, free, if only from the unbearable sufferings of the body!" comes in a sigh through time, and strikes upon our ear. What a picture! Griffenfeldt, a Danish Prometheus, bound to the rocky island of Munkholm.

We are in America, on the margin of one of the largest rivers; an innumerable crowd has gathered, for it is said that a ship is to sail against wind and weather, bidding defiance to the elements; the man who thinks he can solve the problem is named Robert Fulton. The ship begins its passage, but suddenly it stops. The crowd begins to laugh and whistle and hiss—the very father of the man whistles with the rest.

"Conceit! Foolery!" is the cry. "It has happened just as he deserved: put the crack-brain under lock and key!"

Then suddenly a little nail breaks, which had stopped the machine for a few moments; and now the wheels turn again, the floats break the force of the waters, and the ship continues its course—and the beam of the steam-engine shortens the distance between far lands from hours into minutes.

O human race, canst thou grasp the happiness of such a minute of consciousness, this penetration of the soul by its mission, the moment in which all dejection, and every wound—even those caused by own fault—is changed into health and strength and clearness—when discord is converted to harmony—the minute in which men seem to recognize the manifestation of the heavenly grace in one man, and feel how this one imparts it to all?

Thus the thorny path of honour shows itself as a glory, surrounding the earth with its beams: thrice happy he who is chosen to be a wanderer there, and, without merit of his own, to be placed between the builder of the bridge and the earth, between Providence and the human race!

On mighty wings the spirit of history floats through the ages, and shows—giving courage and comfort, and awakening gentle thoughts—on the dark nightly background, but in gleaming pictures, the thorny path of honour; which does not, like a fairy tale, end in brilliancy and joy here on earth, but stretches out beyond all time, even into eternity!

The Bell Deep

Translated by Mrs. H. P. Paull

"Ding-dong! ding-dong!" It sounds up from the "bell-deep" in the Odense-Au. Every child in the old town of Odense, on the island of Funen, knows the Au, which washes the gardens round about the town, and flows on under the wooden bridges from the dam to the water-mill. In the Au grow the yellow water lilies and brown feathery reeds; the dark velvety flag grows there, high and thick; old and decayed willows, slanting and tottering, hang far out over the stream beside the monk's meadow and by the bleaching ground; but opposite there are gardens upon gardens, each different from the rest, some with pretty flowers and bowers like little dolls' pleasure grounds, often displaying cabbage and other kitchen plants; and here and there the gardens cannot be seen at all, for the great elder trees that spread themselves out by the bank, and hang far out over the streaming waters, which are deeper here and there than an oar can fathom. Opposite the old nunnery is the deepest place, which is called the "bell-deep," and there dwells the old water spirit, the "Au-mann." This spirit sleeps through the day while the sun shines down upon the water; but in starry and moonlit nights he shows himself. He is very old. Grandmother says that she has heard her own grandmother tell of him; he is said to lead a solitary life, and to have nobody with whom he can converse save the great old church Bell. Once the Bell hung in the church tower; but now there is no trace left of the tower or of the church, which was called St. Alban's.

"Ding-dong! ding-dong!" sounded the Bell, when the tower still stood there; and one evening, while the sun was setting, and the Bell was swinging away bravely, it broke loose and came flying down through the air, the brilliant metal shining in the ruddy beam.

"Ding-dong! ding-dong! Now I'll retire to rest!" sang the Bell, and flew down into the Odense-Au, where it is deepest; and that is why the place is called the "bell-deep."

But the Bell got neither rest nor sleep. Down in the Au-mann's haunt it sounds and rings, so that the tones sometimes pierce upward through the waters; and many people maintain that its strains forebode the death of some one; but that is not true, for the Bell is only talking with the Au-mann, who is now no longer alone.

And what is the Bell telling? It is old, very old, as we have already observed; it was there long before grandmother's grandmother was born; and yet it is but a child in comparison with the Au-mann, who is quite an old quiet personage, an oddity, with his hose of eel-skin, and his scaly Jacket with the yellow lilies for buttons, and a wreath of reed in his hair and seaweed in his beard; but he looks very pretty for all that.

What the Bell tells? To repeat it all would require years and days; for year by year it is telling the old stories, sometimes short ones, sometimes long ones, according to its whim; it tells of old times, of the dark hard times, thus:

"In the church of St. Alban, the monk had mounted up into the tower. He was young and handsome, but thoughtful exceedingly. He looked through the loophole out upon the Odense-Au, when the bed of the water was yet broad, and the monks' meadow was still a lake. He looked out over it, and over the rampart, and over the nuns' hill opposite, where the convent lay, and the light gleamed forth from the nun's cell. He had known the nun right well, and he thought of her, and his heart beat quicker as he thought. Ding-dong! ding-dong!"

Yes, this was the story the Bell told.

"Into the tower came also the dapper man-servant of the bishop; and when I, the Bell, who am made of metal, rang hard and loud, and swung to and fro, I might have beaten out his brains. He sat down close under me, and played with two little sticks as if they had been a stringed instrument; and he sang to it. 'Now I may sing it out aloud, though at other times I may not whisper it. I may sing of everything that is kept concealed behind lock and bars. Yonder it is cold and wet. The rats are eating her up alive! Nobody knows of it! Nobody hears of it! Not even now, for the bell is ringing and singing its loud Ding-dong, ding-dong!'

"There was a King in those days. They called him Canute. He bowed himself before bishop and monk; but when he offended the free peasants with heavy taxes and hard words, they seized their weapons and put him to flight like a wild beast. He sought shelter in the church, and shut gate and door behind him. The violent band surrounded the church; I heard tell of it. The crows, ravens and magpies started up in terror at the yelling and shouting that sounded around. They flew into the tower and out again, they looked down upon the throng below, and they also looked into the windows of the church, and screamed out aloud what they saw there. King Canute knelt before the altar in prayer; his brothers Eric and Benedict stood by him as a guard with drawn swords; but the King's servant, the treacherous Blake, betrayed his master. The throng in front of the church knew where they could hit the King, and one of them flung a stone through a pane of glass, and the King lay there dead! The cries and screams of the savage horde and of the birds sounded through the air, and I joined in it also; for I sang 'Ding-dong! ding-dong!'

"The church bell hangs high, and looks far around, and sees the birds around it, and understands their language. The wind roars in upon it through windows and loopholes; and the wind knows everything, for he gets it from the air, which encircles all things, and the church bell understands his tongue, and rings it out into the world, 'Ding-dong! ding-dong!'

"But it was too much for me to hear and to know; I was not able any longer to ring it out. I became so tired, so heavy, that the beam broke, and I flew out into the gleaming Au, where the water is deepest, and where the Au-mann lives, solitary and alone; and year by year I tell him what I have heard and what I know. Ding-dong! ding-dong!"

Thus it sounds complainingly out of the bell-deep in the Odense-Au. That is what grandmother told us.

But the schoolmaster says that there was not any bell that rung down there, for that it could not do so; and that no Au-mann dwelt yonder, for there was no Au-mann at all! And when all the other church bells are sounding sweetly, he says that it is not really the bells that are sounding, but that it is the air itself which sends forth the notes; and grandmother said to us that the Bell itself said it was the air who told it to him, consequently they are agreed on that point, and this much is sure.

"Be cautious, cautious, and take good heed to thyself," they both say.

The air knows everything. It is around us, it is in us, it talks of our thoughts and of our deeds, and it speaks longer of them than does the Bell down in the depths of the Odense-Au where the Au-mann dwells. It rings it out in the vault of heaven, far, far out, forever and ever, till the heaven bells sound "Ding-dong! ding-dong!"

The Bottle Neck

Translated by Mrs. H. P. Paull

Close to the corner of a street, among other abodes of poverty, stood an exceedingly tall, narrow house, which had been so knocked about by time that it seemed out of joint in every direction. This house was inhabited by poor people, but the deepest poverty was apparent in the garret lodging in the gable. In front of the little window, an old bent bird-cage hung in the sunshine, which had not even a proper water-glass, but instead of it the broken neck of a bottle, turned upside down, and a cork stuck in to make it hold the water with which it was filled. An old maid stood at the window; she had hung chickweed over the cage, and the little linnet which it contained hopped from perch to perch and sang and twittered merrily.

"Yes, it's all very well for you to sing," said the bottle neck: that is, he did not really speak the words as we do, for the neck of a bottle cannot speak; but he thought them to himself in his own mind, just as people sometimes talk quietly to themselves.

"Yes, you may sing very well, you have all your limbs uninjured; you should feel what it is like to lose your body, and only have a neck and a mouth left, with a cork stuck in it, as I have: you wouldn't sing then, I know. After all, it is just as well that there are some who can be happy. I have no reason to sing, nor could I sing now if I were ever so happy; but when I was a whole bottle, and they rubbed me with a cork, didn't I sing then? I used to be called a complete lark. I remember when I went out to a picnic with the furrier's family, on the day his daughter was betrothed—it seems as if it only happened yesterday. I have gone through a great deal in my time, when I come to recollect: I have been in the fire and in the water, I have been deep in the earth, and have mounted higher in the air than most other people, and now I am swinging here, outside a bird-cage, in the air and the sunshine. Oh, indeed, it would be worth while to hear my history; but I do not speak it aloud, for a good reason—because I cannot."

Then the bottle neck related his history, which was really rather remarkable; he, in fact, related it to himself, or, at least, thought it in his own mind. The little bird sang his own song merrily; in the street below there was driving and running to and fro, every one thought of his own affairs, or perhaps of nothing at all; but the bottle neck thought deeply. He thought of the blazing furnace in the factory, where he had been blown into life; he remembered how hot it felt when he was placed in the heated oven, the home from which he sprang, and that he had a strong inclination to leap out again directly; but after a while it became cooler, and he found himself very comfortable. He had been placed in a row, with a whole regiment of his brothers and sisters all brought out of the same furnace; some of them had certainly been blown into champagne bottles, and others into beer bottles, which made a little difference between them. In the world it often happens that a beer bottle may contain the most precious wine, and a champagne bottle be filled with blacking, but even in decay it may always be seen whether a man has been well born. Nobility remains noble, as a champagne bottle remains the same, even with blacking in its interior. When the bottles were packed our bottle was packed amongst them; it little expected then to finish its career as a bottle neck, or to be used as a water-glass to a bird's-cage, which is, after all, a place of honour, for it is to be of some use in the world. The bottle did not behold the light of day again, until it was unpacked with the rest in the wine merchant's cellar, and, for the first time, rinsed with water, which caused some very curious sensations. There it lay empty, and without a cork, and it had a peculiar feeling, as if it wanted something it knew not what. At last it was filled with rich and costly wine, a cork was placed in it, and sealed down. Then it was labelled "first quality," as if it had carried off the first prize at an examination; besides, the wine and the bottle were both good, and while we are young is the time for poetry. There were sounds of song within the bottle, of things it could not understand, of green sunny mountains, where the vines grow and where the merry vine-dressers laugh, sing, and are merry. "Ah, how beautiful is life." All these tones of joy and song in the bottle were like the working of a young poet's brain, who often knows not the meaning of the tones which are sounding within him. One morning the bottle found a purchaser in the furrier's apprentice, who was told to bring one of the best bottles of wine. It was placed in the provision basket with ham and cheese and sausages. The sweetest fresh butter and the finest bread were put into the basket by the furrier's daughter herself, for she packed it. She was young and pretty; her brown eyes laughed, and a smile lingered round her mouth as sweet as that in her eyes. She had delicate hands, beautifully white, and her neck was whiter still. It could easily be seen that she was a very lovely girl, and as yet she was not engaged. The provision basket lay in the lap of the young girl as the family drove out to the forest, and the neck of the bottle peeped out from between the folds of the white napkin. There was the red wax on the cork, and the bottle looked straight at the young girl's face, and also at the face of the young sailor who sat near her. He was a young friend, the son of a portrait painter. He had lately passed his examination with honour, as mate, and the next morning he was to sail in his ship to a distant coast. There had been a great deal of talk on this subject while the basket was being packed, and during this conversation the eyes and the mouth of the furrier's daughter did not wear a very joyful expression. The young people wandered away into the green wood, and talked together. What did they talk about? The bottle could not say, for he was in the provision basket. It remained there a long time; but when at last it was brought forth it appeared as if something pleasant had happened, for every one was laughing; the furrier's daughter laughed too, but she said very little, and her cheeks were like two roses. Then her father took the bottle and the corkscrew into his hands. What a strange sensation it was to have the cork drawn for the first time! The bottle could never after that forget the performance of that moment; indeed there was quite a convulsion within him as the cork flew out, and a gurgling sound as the wine was poured forth into the glasses.

"Long life to the betrothed," cried the papa, and every glass was emptied to the dregs, while the young sailor kissed his beautiful bride.

"Happiness and blessing to you both," said the old people-father and mother, and the young man filled the glasses again.

"Safe return, and a wedding this day next year," he cried; and when the glasses were empty he took the bottle, raised it on high, and said, "Thou hast been present here on the happiest day of my life; thou shalt never be used by others!" So saying, he hurled it high in the air.

The furrier's daughter thought she should never see it again, but she was mistaken. It fell among the rushes on the borders of a little woodland lake. The bottle neck remembered well how long it lay there unseen. "I gave them wine, and they gave me muddy water," he had said to himself, "but I suppose it was all well meant." He could no longer see the betrothed couple, nor the cheerful old people; but for a long time he could hear them rejoicing and singing. At length there came by two peasant boys, who peeped in among the reeds and spied out the bottle. Then they took it up and carried it home with them, so that once more it was provided for. At home in their wooden cottage these boys had an elder brother, a sailor, who was about to start on a long voyage. He had been there the day before to say farewell, and his mother was now very busy packing up various things for him to take with him on his voyage. In the evening his father was going to carry the parcel to the town to see his son once more, and take him a farewell greeting from his mother. A small bottle had already been filled with herb tea, mixed with brandy, and wrapped in a parcel; but when the boys came in they brought with them a larger and stronger bottle, which they had found. This bottle would hold so much more than the little one, and they all said the brandy would be so good for complaints of the stomach, especially as it was mixed with medical herbs. The liquid which they now poured into the bottle was not like the red wine with which it had once been filled; these were bitter drops, but they are of great use sometimes-for the stomach. The new large bottle was to go, not the little one: so the bottle once more started on its travels. It was taken on board (for Peter Jensen was one of the crew) the very same ship in which the young mate was to sail. But the mate did not see the bottle: indeed, if he had he would not have known it, or supposed it was the one out of which they had drunk to the felicity of the betrothed and to the prospect of a marriage on his own happy return. Certainly the bottle no longer poured forth wine, but it contained something quite as good; and so it happened that whenever Peter Jensen brought it out, his messmates gave it the name of "the apothecary," for it contained the best medicine to cure the stomach, and he gave it out quite willingly as long as a drop remained. Those were happy days, and the bottle would sing when rubbed with a cork, and it was called a great lark," "Peter Jensen's lark."

Long days and months rolled by, during which the bottle stood empty in a corner, when a storm arose—whether on the passage out or home it could not tell, for it had never been ashore. It was a terrible storm, great waves arose, darkly heaving and tossing the vessel to and fro. The main mast was split asunder, the ship sprang a leak, and the pumps became useless, while all around was black as night. At the last moment, when the ship was sinking, the young mate wrote on a piece of paper, "We are going down: God's will be done." Then he wrote the name of his betrothed, his own name, and that of the ship. Then he put the leaf in an empty bottle that happened to be at hand, corked it down tightly, and threw it into the foaming sea. He knew not that it was the very same bottle from which the goblet of joy and hope had once been filled for him, and now it was tossing on the waves with his last greeting, and a message from the dead. The ship sank, and the crew sank with her; but the bottle flew on like a bird, for it bore within it a loving letter from a loving heart. And as the sun rose and set, the bottle felt as at the time of its first existence, when in the heated glowing stove it had a longing to fly away. It outlived the storms and the calm, it struck against no rocks, was not devoured by sharks, but drifted on for more than a year, sometimes towards the north, sometimes towards the south, just as the current carried it. It was in all other ways its own master, but even of that one may get tired. The written leaf, the last farewell of the bridegroom to his bride, would only bring sorrow when once it reached her hands; but where were those hands, so soft and delicate, which had once spread the table-cloth on the fresh grass in the green wood, on the day of her betrothal? Ah, yes! where was the furrier's daughter? and where was the land which might lie nearest to her home?

The bottle knew not, it travelled onward and onward, and at last all this wandering about became wearisome; at all events it was not its usual occupation. But it had to travel, till at length it reached land—a foreign country. Not a word spoken in this country could the bottle understand; it was a language it had never before heard, and it is a great loss not to be able to understand a language. The bottle was fished out of the water, and examined on all sides. The little letter contained within it was discovered, taken out, and turned and twisted in every direction; but the people could not understand what was written upon it. They could be quite sure that the bottle had been thrown overboard from a vessel, and that something about it was written on this paper: but what was written? that was the question—so the paper was put back into the bottle, and then both were put away in a large cupboard of one of the great houses of the town. Whenever any strangers arrived, the paper was taken out and turned over and over, so that the address, which was only written in pencil, became almost illegible, and at last no one could distinguish any letters on it at all. For a whole year the bottle remained standing in the cupboard, and then it was taken up to the loft, where it soon became covered with dust and cobwebs. Ah! how often then it thought of those better days—of the times when in the fresh, green wood, it had poured forth rich wine; or, while rocked by the swelling waves, it had carried in its bosom a secret, a letter, a last parting sigh. For full twenty years it stood in the loft, and it might have stayed there longer but that the house was going to be rebuilt. The bottle was discovered when the roof was taken off; they talked about it, but the bottle did not understand what they said—a language is not to be learnt by living in a loft, even for twenty years. "If I had been down stairs in the room," thought the bottle, "I might have learnt it." It was

The Bottle Neck

now washed and rinsed, which process was really quite necessary, and afterwards it looked clean and transparent, and felt young again in its old age; but the paper which it had carried so faithfully was destroyed in the washing. They filled the bottle with seeds, though it scarcely knew what had been placed in it. Then they corked it down tightly, and carefully wrapped it up. There not even the light of a torch or lantern could reach it, much less the brightness of the sun or moon. "And yet," thought the bottle, "men go on a journey that they may see as much as possible, and I can see nothing." However, it did something quite as important; it travelled to the place of its destination, and was unpacked.

"What trouble they have taken with that bottle over yonder!" said one, and very likely it is broken after all." But the bottle was not broken, and, better still, it understood every word that was said: this language it had heard at the furnaces and at the wine merchant's; in the forest and on the ship—it was the only good old language it could understand. It had returned home, and the language was as a welcome greeting. For very joy, it felt ready to jump out of people's hands, and scarcely noticed that its cork had been drawn, and its contents emptied out, till it found itself carried to a cellar, to be left there and forgotten. "There's no place like home, even if it's a cellar." It never occurred to him to think that he might lie there for years, he felt so comfortable. For many long years he remained in the cellar, till at last some people came to carry away the bottles, and ours amongst the number.

Out in the garden there was a great festival. Brilliant lamps hung in festoons from tree to tree; and paper lanterns, through which the light shone till they looked like transparent tulips. It was a beautiful evening, and the weather mild and clear. The stars twinkled; and the new moon, in the form of a crescent, was surrounded by the shadowy disc of the whole moon, and looked like a gray globe with a golden rim: it was a beautiful sight for those who had good eyes. The illumination extended even to the most retired of the garden walks, at least not so retired that any one need lose himself there. In the borders were placed bottles, each containing a light, and among them the bottle with which we are acquainted, and whose fate it was, one day, to be only a bottle neck, and to serve as a water-glass to a bird's-cage. Everything here appeared lovely to our bottle, for it was again in the green wood, amid joy and feasting; again it heard music and song, and the noise and murmur of a crowd, especially in that part of the garden where the lamps blazed, and the paper lanterns displayed their brilliant colours. It stood in a distant walk certainly, but a place pleasant for contemplation; and it carried a light; and was at once useful and ornamental. In such an hour it is easy to forget that one has spent twenty years in a loft, and a good thing it is to be able to do so. Close before the bottle passed a single pair, like the bridal pair—the mate and the furrier's daughter—who had so long ago wandered in the wood. It seemed to the bottle as if he were living that time over again. Not only the guests but other people were walking in the garden, who were allowed to witness the splendor and the festivities. Among the latter came an old maid, who seemed to be quite alone in the world. She was thinking, like the bottle, of the green wood, and of a young betrothed pair, who were closely connected with herself; she was thinking of that hour, the happiest of her life, in which she had taken part, when she had herself been one of that betrothed pair; such hours are never to be forgotten, let a maiden be as old as she may. But she did not recognize the bottle, neither did the bottle notice the old maid. And so we often pass each other in the world when we meet, as did these two, even while together in the same town.

The bottle was taken from the garden, and again sent to a wine merchant, where it was once more filled with wine, and sold to an aeronaut, who was to make an ascent in his balloon on the following Sunday. A great crowd assembled to witness the sight; military music had been engaged, and many other preparations made. The bottle saw it all from the basket in which he lay close to a live rabbit. The rabbit was quite excited because he knew that he was to be taken up, and let down again in a parachute. The bottle, however, knew nothing of the "up," or the "down;" he saw only that the balloon was swelling larger and larger till it could swell no more, and began to rise and be restless. Then the ropes which held it were cut through, and the aerial ship rose in the air with the aeronaut and the basket containing the bottle and the rabbit, while the music sounded and all the people shouted "Hurrah."

The Bottle Neck

"This is a wonderful journey up into the air," thought the bottle; "it is a new way of sailing, and here, at least, there is no fear of striking against anything."

Thousands of people gazed at the balloon, and the old maid who was in the garden saw it also; for she stood at the open window of the garret, by which hung the cage containing the linnet, who then had no water-glass, but was obliged to be contented with an old cup. In the window-sill stood a myrtle in a pot, and this had been pushed a little on one side, that it might not fall out; for the old maid was leaning out of the window, that she might see. And she did see distinctly the aeronaut in the balloon, and how he let down the rabbit in the parachute, and then drank to the health of all the spectators in the wine from the bottle. After doing this, he hurled it high into the air. How little she thought that this was the very same bottle which her friend had thrown aloft in her honour, on that happy day of rejoicing, in the green wood, in her youthful days. The bottle had no time to think, when raised so suddenly; and before it was aware, it reached the highest point it had ever attained in its life. Steeples and roofs lay far, far beneath it, and the people looked as tiny as possible. Then it began to descend much more rapidly than the rabbit had done, made somersaults in the air, and felt itself quite young and unfettered, although it was half full of wine. But this did not last long. What a journey it was! All the people could see the bottle; for the sun shone upon it. The balloon was already far away, and very soon the bottle was far away also; for it fell upon a roof, and broke in pieces. But the pieces had got such an impetus in them, that they could not stop themselves. They went jumping and rolling about, till at last they fell into the courtyard, and were broken into still smaller pieces; only the neck of the bottle managed to keep whole, and it was broken off as clean as if it had been cut with a diamond.

"That would make a capital bird's glass," said one of the cellar-men; but none of them had either a bird or a cage, and it was not to be expected they would provide one just because they had found a bottle neck that could be used as a glass. But the old maid who lived in the garret had a bird, and it really might be useful to her; so the bottle neck was provided with a cork, and taken up to her; and, as it often happens in life, the part that had been uppermost was now turned downwards, and it was filled with fresh water. Then they hung it in the cage of the little bird, who sang and twittered more merrily than ever.

"Ah, you have good reason to sing," said the bottle neck, which was looked upon as something very remarkable, because it had been in a balloon; nothing further was known of its history. As it hung there in the bird's-cage, it could hear the noise and murmur of the people in the street below, as well as the conversation of the old maid in the room within. An old friend had just come to visit her, and they talked, not about the bottle neck, but of the myrtle in the window.

"No, you must not spend a dollar for your daughter's bridal bouquet," said the old maid; "you shall have a beautiful little bunch for a nosegay, full of blossoms. Do you see how splendidly the tree has grown? It has been raised from only a little sprig of myrtle that you gave me on the day after my betrothal, and from which I was to make my own bridal bouquet when a year had passed: but that day never came; the eyes were closed which were to have been my light and joy through life. In the depths of the sea my beloved sleeps sweetly; the myrtle has become an old tree, and I am a still older woman. Before the sprig you gave me faded, I took a spray, and planted it in the earth; and now, as you see, it has become a large tree, and a bunch of the blossoms shall at last appear at a wedding festival, in the bouquet of your daughter."

There were tears in the eyes of the old maid, as she spoke of the beloved of her youth, and of their betrothal in the wood. Many thoughts came into her mind; but the thought never came, that quite close to her, in that very window, was a remembrance of those olden times—the neck of the bottle which had, as it were shouted for joy when the cork flew out with a bang on the betrothal day. But the bottle neck did not recognize the old maid; he had not been listening to what she had related, perhaps because he was thinking so much about her.

The Old Bachelor's Nightcap

Translated by H. W. Dulcken

There is a street in Copenhagen that has this strange name—'Hysken Sträde.' Whence comes this name, and what is its meaning? It is said to be German; but injustice has been done to the Germans in this matter, for it would have to be 'Häuschen,' and not 'Hysken.' For here stood, once upon a time, and indeed for a great many years, a few little houses, which were principally nothing more than wooden booths, just as we see now in the market-places at fair-time. They were, perhaps, a little larger, and had windows; but the panes consisted of horn or bladder, for glass was then too expensive to be used in every house. But then we are speaking of a long time ago—so long since, that grandfather and great-grandfather, when they talked about them, used to speak of them as 'the old times'—in fact, it is several centuries ago.

The rich merchants in Bremen and Lubeck carried on trade with Copenhagen. They did not reside in the town themselves, but sent their clerks, who lived in the wooden booths in the Häuschen Street, and sold beer and spices. The German beer was good, and there were many kinds of it, as there were, for instance, Bremen, and Prussinger, and Sous beer, and even Brunswick mumm; and quantities of spices were sold—saffron, and aniseed, and ginger, and especially pepper. Yes, pepper was the chief article here, and so it happened that the German clerks got the nickname 'pepper gentry;' and there was a condition made with them in Lubeck and in Bremen, that they would not marry at Copenhagen, and many of them became very old. They had to care for themselves, and to look after their own comforts, and to put out their own fires—when they had any; and some of them became very solitary old boys, with eccentric ideas and eccentric habits. From them all unmarried men, who have attained a certain age, are called in Denmark 'pepper gentry;' and this must be understood by all who wish to comprehend this history.

The 'pepper gentleman' becomes a butt for ridicule, and is continually told that he ought to put on his nightcap, and draw it down over his eyes, and do nothing but sleep. The boys sing,

> "Cut, cut wood!
> Poor bachelor so good.
> Go, take your nightcap, go to rest,
> For 'tis the nightcap suits you best!"

Yes, that's what they sing about the 'pepperer'—thus they make game of the poor bachelor and his nightcap, and turn it into ridicule, just because they know very little about either. Ah, that kind of nightcap no one should wish to earn! And why not?—We shall hear.

In the old times the 'Housekin Street' was not paved, and the people stumbled out of one hole into another, as in a neglected bye-way; and it was narrow too. The booths leaned side by side, and stood so close together that in the summer time a sail was often stretched from one booth to its opposite neighbour, on which occasion the fragrance of pepper, saffron, and ginger became doubly powerful. Behind the counters young men were seldom seen. The clerks were generally old boys; but they did not look like what we should fancy them, namely, with wig, and nightcap, and plush small-clothes, and with waistcoat and coat buttoned up to the chin. No, grandfather's great-grandfather may look like that, and has been

The 'Old Bachelor's' Nightcap

thus portrayed, but the 'pepper gentry' had no superfluous means, and accordingly did not have their portraits taken; though, indeed, it would be interesting now to have a picture of one of them, as he stood behind the counter or went to church on holy days. His hat was high-crowned and broad-brimmed, and sometimes one of the youngest clerks would mount a feather. The woollen shirt was hidden behind a broad linen collar, the close jacket was buttoned up to the chin, and the cloak hung loose over it; and the trousers were tucked into the broad-toed shoes, for the clerks did not wear stockings. In their girdles they sported a dinner-knife and spoon, and a larger knife was placed there also for the defence of the owner; and this weapon was often very necessary. Just so was Anthony, one of the oldest clerks, clad on high days and holy days, except that, instead of a high-crowned hat, he wore a low bonnet, and under it a knitted cap (a regular nightcap), to which he had grown so accustomed that it was always on his head; and he had two of them—nightcaps, of course. The old fellow was a subject for a painter. He was as thin as a lath, had wrinkles clustering round his eyes and mouth, and long bony fingers, and bushy grey eyebrows: over the left eye hung quite a tuft of hair, and that did not look very handsome, though it made him very noticeable. People knew that he came from Bremen; but that was not his native place, though his master lived there. His own native place was in Thuringia, the town of Eisenach, close by the Wartburg. Old Anthony did not speak much of this, but he thought of it all the more.

The old clerks of the Häuschen Street did not often come together. Each one remained in his booth, which was closed early in the evening; and then it looked dark enough in the street: only a faint glimmer of light forced its way through the little horn-pane in the roof; and in the booth sat, generally on his bed, the old bachelor, his German hymn-book in his hand, singing an evening psalm in a low voice; or he went about in the booth till late into the night, and busied himself about all sorts of things. It was certainly not an amusing life. To be a stranger in a strange land is a bitter lot: nobody cares for you, unless you happen to get in anybody's way.

Often when it was dark night outside, with snow and rain, the place looked very gloomy and lonely. No lamps were to be seen, with the exception of one solitary light hanging before the picture of the Virgin that was fastened against the wall. The plash of the water against the neighbouring rampart at the castle wharf could be plainly heard. Such evenings are long and dreary, unless people devise some employment for themselves. There is not always packing or unpacking to do, nor can the scales be polished or paper bags be made continually; and, failing these, people should devise other employment for themselves. And that is just what old Anthony did; for he used to mend his clothes and put pieces on his boots. When he at last sought his couch, he used from habit to keep his nightcap on. He drew it down a little closer; but soon he would push it up again, to see if the light had been properly extinguished. He would touch it, press the wick together, and then lie down on the other side, and draw his nightcap down again; but then a doubt would come up in him, if every coal in the little fire-pan below had been properly deadened and put out—a tiny spark might have been left burning, and might set fire to something and cause damage. And therefore he rose from his bed, and crept down the ladder, for it could scarcely be called a stair. And when he came to the fire-pan not a spark was to be discovered, and he might just go back again. But often, when he had gone half of the way back, it would occur to him that the shutters might not be securely fastened; yes, then his thin legs must carry him downstairs once more. He was cold, and his teeth chattered in his mouth when he crept back again to bed; for the cold seems to become doubly severe when it knows it cannot stay much longer. He drew up the coverlet closer around him, and pulled down the nightcap lower over his brows, and turned his thoughts away from trade and from the labours of the day. But that did not procure him agreeable entertainment; for now old thoughts came and put up their curtains, and these curtains have sometimes pins in them, with which one pricks oneself, and one cries out "Oh!" and they prick into one's flesh and burn so, that the tears sometimes come into one's eyes; and that often happened to old Anthony—hot tears. The largest pearls streamed forth, and fell on the coverlet or on the floor, and then they sounded as if one of his heart-strings had broken. Sometimes again they seemed to rise up in flame, illuminating a picture of life that never faded out of his heart. If he then dried his eyes with his nightcap, the tear and the picture were indeed crushed, but the source of the tears remained, and welled up afresh from his heart. The pictures did not come up in the order in which the scenes had occurred in reality, for very often the most painful would come together; then again the most joyful would come, but these had the deepest shadows of all.

The beech woods of Denmark are acknowledged to be fine, but the woods of Thuringia arose far more beautiful in the eyes of Anthony. More mighty and more venerable seemed to him the old oaks around the proud knightly castle, where the creeping plants hung down over the stony blocks of the rock; sweeter there bloomed the flowers of the apple tree than in the Danish land. This he remembered very vividly. A glittering tear rolled down over his cheek; and in this tear he could plainly see two children playing—a boy and a girl. The boy had red cheeks, and yellow curling hair, and honest blue eyes. He was the son of the merchant Anthony—it was himself. The little girl had brown eyes and black hair, and had a bright clever look. She was the burgomaster's daughter Molly. The two were playing with an apple. They shook the apple, and heard the pips rattling in it. Then they cut the apple in two, and each of them took a half; they divided even the pips, and ate them all but one, which the little girl proposed that they should lay in the earth.

"Then you shall see," she said, "what will come out. It will be something you don't at all expect. A whole apple tree will come out, but not directly."

And she put the pip in a flowerpot, and both were very busy and eager about it. The boy made a hole in the earth with his finger, and the little girl dropped the pip in it, and they both covered it with earth.

"Now, you must not take it out tomorrow to see if it has struck root," said Molly. "That won't do at all. I did it with my flowers; but only twice. I wanted to see if they were growing—and I didn't know any better then—and the plants withered."

Anthony took away the flowerpot, and every morning, the whole winter through, he looked at it; but nothing was to be seen but the black earth. At length, however, the spring came, and the sun shone warm again; and two little green leaves came up out of the pot.

"Those are for me and Molly," said the boy. "That's beautiful—that's marvellously beautiful!"

Soon a third leaf made its appearance. Whom did that represent? Yes, and there came another, and yet another. Day by day and week by week they grew larger, and the plant began to take the form of a real tree. And all this was now mirrored in a single tear, which was wiped away and disappeared; but it might come again from its source in the heart of old Anthony.

In the neighbourhood of Eisenach a row of stony mountains rises up. One of these mountains is round in outline, and lifts itself above the rest, naked and without tree, bush, or grass. It is called the Venus Mount. In this mountain dwells Lady Venus, one of the deities of the heathen times. She is also called Lady Holle; and every child in and around Eisenach has heard about her. She it was who lured Tannhauser, the noble knight and minstrel, from the circle of the singers of the Wartburg into her mountain.

The 'Old Bachelor's' Nightcap

Little Molly and Anthony often stood by this mountain; and once Molly said:

"You may knock and say, 'Lady Holle, open the door—Tannhauser is here!'"

But Anthony did not dare. Molly, however, did it, though she only said the words "Lady Holle, Lady Holle!" aloud and distinctly; the rest she muttered so indistinctly that Anthony felt convinced she had not really said anything; and yet she looked as bold and saucy as possible—as saucy as when she sometimes came round him with other little girls in the garden, and all wanted to kiss him because he did not like to be kissed and tried to keep them off; and she was the only one who dared to kiss him in spite of his resistance.

"*I* may kiss him!" she would say proudly.

That was her vanity; and Anthony submitted, and thought no more about it.

How charming and how teasing Molly was! It was said that Lady Holle in the mountain was beautiful also, but that her beauty was like that of a tempting fiend. The greatest beauty and grace was possessed by Saint Elizabeth, the patron of the country, the pious Princess of Thuringia, whose good actions have been immortalized in many places in legends and stories. In the chapel her picture was hanging, surrounded by silver lamps; but it was not in the least like Molly.

The apple tree which the two children had planted grew year by year, and became taller and taller—so tall, that it had to be transplanted into the garden, into the fresh air, where the dew fell and the sun shone warm. And the tree developed itself strongly, so that it could resist the winter. And it seemed as if, after the rigour of the cold season was past, it put forth blossoms in spring for very joy. In the autumn it brought two apples—one for Molly and one for Anthony. It could not well have produced less.

The tree had grown apace, and Molly grew like the tree. She was as fresh as an apple-blossom; but Anthony was not long to behold this flower. All things change! Molly›s father left his old home, and Molly went with him, far away. Yes, in our time steam has made the journey they took a matter of a few hours, but then more than a day and a night were necessary to go so far eastward from Eisenach to the furthest border of Thuringia, to the city which is still called Weimar.

And Molly wept, and Anthony wept; but all their tears melted into one, and this tear had the rosy, charming hue of joy. For Molly told him she loved him—loved him more than all the splendours of Weimar.

One, two, three years went by, and during this period two letters were received. One came by a carrier, and a traveller brought the other. The way was long and difficult, and passed through many windings by towns and villages.

Often had Molly and Anthony heard of Tristram and Iseult, and often had the boy applied the story to himself and Molly, though the name Tristram was said to mean 'born in tribulation,' and that did not apply to Anthony, nor would he ever be able to think, like Tristram, "She has forgotten me." But, indeed, Iseult did not forget her faithful knight; and when both were laid to rest in the earth, one on each side of the church, the linden trees grew from their graves over the church roof, and there encountered each other in bloom.

Anthony thought that was beautiful, but mournful; but it could not become mournful between him and Molly: and he whistled a song of the old minne-singer, Walter of the Vogelverde:

> "Under the lindens
> Upon the heath."

And especially that passage appeared charming to him:

> "From the forest, down in the vale,
> Sang her sweet song the nightingale."

This song was often in his mouth, and he sang and whistled it in the moonlight nights, when he rode along the deep hollow way on horseback to get to Weimar and visit Molly. He wished to come unexpectedly, and he came unexpectedly.

He was made welcome with full goblets of wine, with jovial company, fine company, and a pretty room and a good bed were provided for him; and yet his reception was not what he had dreamt and fancied it would be. He could not understand himself—he could not understand the others: but *we* can understand it. One may be admitted into a house and associate with a family without becoming one of them. One may converse together as one would converse in a post-carriage, and know one another as people know each other on a journey, each incommoding the other and wishing that either oneself or the good neighbour were away. Yes, this was the kind of thing Anthony felt.

"I am an honest girl," said Molly; "and I myself will tell you what it is. Much has changed since we were children together—changed inwardly and outwardly. Habit and will have no power over our hearts. Anthony, I should not like to have an enemy in you, now that I shall soon be far away from here. Believe me, I entertain the best wishes for you; but to feel for you what I know now one may feel for a man, has never been the case with me. You must reconcile yourself to this. Farewell, Anthony!"

And Anthony bade her farewell. No tear came into his eye, but he felt that he was no longer Molly's friend. Hot iron and cold iron alike take the skin from our lips, and we have the same feeling when we kiss it: and he kissed himself into hatred as into love.

Within twenty-four hours Anthony was back in Eisenach, though certainly the horse on which he rode was ruined.

"What matter!" he said: "I am ruined too; and I will destroy everything that can remind me of her, or of Lady Holle, or Venus the heathen woman! I will break down the apple tree and tear it up by the roots, so that it shall never bear flower or fruit more!"

But the apple tree was not broken down, though he himself was broken down, and bound on a couch by fever. What was it that raised him up again? A medicine was presented to him which had strength to do this—the bitterest of medicines, that shakes up body and spirit together. Anthony›s father ceased to be the richest of merchants. Heavy days—days of trial—were at the door; misfortune came rolling into the house like great waves of the sea. The father became a poor man. Sorrow and suffering took away his strength. Then Anthony had to think of something else besides nursing his love-sorrows and his anger against Molly. He had to take his father›s place—to give orders, to help, to act energetically, and at last to go out into the world and earn his bread.

Anthony went to Bremen. There he learned what poverty and hard living meant; and these sometimes make the heart hard, and sometimes soften it, even too much.

How different the world was, and how different the people were from what he had supposed them to be in his childhood! What were the minne-singer›s songs to him now?—an echo, a vanishing sound! Yes, that is what he thought sometimes; but again the songs would sound in his soul, and his heart became gentle.

"God's will is best!" he would say then. "It was well that I was not permitted to keep Molly's heart—that she did not remain true to me. What would it have led to now, when fortune has turned away from me? She quitted me before she knew of this loss of prosperity, or had any notion of what awaited me. That was a mercy of Providence towards me. Everything has happened for the best. It was not her fault—and I have been so bitter, and have shown so much rancour towards her!"

And years went by. Anthony›s father was dead, and strangers

lived in the old house. But Anthony was destined to see it again. His rich employer sent him on commercial journeys, and his duty led him into his native town of Eisenach. The old Wartburg stood unchanged on the mountain, with 'the monk and the nun' hewn out in stone. The great oaks gave to the scene the outlines it had possessed in his childish days. The Venus Mount glimmered grey and naked over the valley. He would have been glad to cry, "Lady Holle, Lady Holle, unlock the door, and I shall enter and remain in my native earth!"

That was a sinful thought, and he blessed himself to drive it away. Then a little bird out of the thicket sang clearly, and the old minne-song came into his mind:

"From the forest, down in the vale,
    Sang her sweet song the nightingale."

And here in the town of his childhood, which he thus saw again through tears, much came back into his remembrance. The paternal house stood as in the old times; but the garden was altered, and a field-path led over a portion of the old ground, and the apple tree that he had not broken down stood there, but outside the garden, on the farther side of the path. But the sun threw its rays on the apple tree as in the old days, the dew descended gently upon it as then, and it bore such a burden of fruit that the branches were bent down towards the earth.

"That flourishes!" he said. "The tree can grow!"

Nevertheless, one of the branches of the tree was broken. Mischievous hands had torn it down towards the ground; for now the tree stood by the public way.

"They break its blossoms off without a feeling of thankfulness—they steal its fruit and break the branches. One might say of the tree as has been said of some men—'It was not sung at his cradle that it should come thus.' How brightly its history began, and what has it come to? Forsaken and forgotten—a garden tree by the hedge, in the field, and on the public way! There it stands unprotected, plundered, and broken! It has certainly not died, but in the course of years the number of blossoms will diminish; at last the fruit will cease altogether; and at last—at last all will be over!"

Such were Anthony's thoughts under the tree; such were his thoughts during many a night in the lonely chamber of the wooden house in the distant land—in the Häuschen Street in Copenhagen, whither his rich employer, the Bremen merchant, had sent him, first making it a condition that he should not marry.

"Marry! Ha, ha!" he laughed bitterly to himself.

Winter had set in early; it was freezing hard. Without, a snowstorm was raging, so that every one who could do so remained at home; thus, too, it happened that those who lived opposite to Anthony did not notice that for two days his house had not been unlocked, and that he did not show himself; for who would go out unnecessarily in such weather?

They were grey, gloomy days; and in the house, whose windows were not of glass, twilight only alternated with dark night. Old Anthony had not left his bed during the two days, for he had not the strength to rise; he had for a long time felt in his limbs the hardness of the weather. Forsaken by all, lay the old bachelor, unable to help himself. He could scarcely reach the water-jug that he had placed by his bedside, and the last drop it contained had been consumed. It was not fever, nor sickness, but old age that had struck him down. Up yonder, where his couch was placed, he was overshadowed as it were by continual night. A little spider, which, however, he could not see, busily and cheerfully span its web around him, as if it were weaving a little crape banner that should wave when the old man closed his eyes.

The time was very slow, and long, and dreary. Tears he had none to shed, nor did he feel pain. The thought of Molly never came into his mind. He felt as if the world and its noise concerned him no longer—as if he were lying outside the world, and no one were thinking of him. For a moment he felt a sensation of hunger—of thirst. Yes, he felt them both. But nobody came to tend him—nobody. He thought of those who had once suffered want; of Saint Elizabeth, as she had once wandered on earth; of her, the saint of his home and of his childhood, the noble Duchess of Thuringia, the benevolent lady who had been accustomed to visit the lowliest cottages, bringing to the inmates refreshment and comfort. Her pious deeds shone bright upon his soul. He thought of her as she had come to distribute words of comfort, binding up the wounds of the afflicted, giving meat to the hungry; though her stern husband had chidden her for it. He thought of the legend told of her, how she had been carrying the full basket containing food and wine, when her husband, who watched her footsteps, came forth and asked angrily what she was carrying, whereupon she answered, in fear and trembling, that the basket contained roses which she had plucked in the garden; how he had torn away the white cloth from the basket, and a miracle had been performed for the pious lady; for bread, and wine, and everything in the basket had been transformed into roses!

Thus the saint's memory dwelt in Anthony's quiet mind; thus she stood bodily before his downcast face, before his warehouse in the simple booth in the Danish land. He uncovered his head, and looked into her gentle eyes, and everything around him was beautiful and roseate. Yes, the roses seemed to unfold themselves in fragrance. There came to him a sweet, peculiar odour of apples, and he saw a blooming apple tree, which spread its branches above him—it was the tree which Molly and he had planted together.

And the tree strewed down its fragrant leaves upon him, cooling his burning brow. The leaves fell upon his parched lips, and were like strengthening bread and wine; and they fell upon his breast, and he felt reassured and calm, and inclined to sleep peacefully.

"Now I shall sleep," he whispered to himself. "Sleep is refreshing. Tomorrow I shall be upon my feet again, and strong and well—glorious, wonderful! That apple tree, planted in true affection, now stands before me in heavenly radiance——"

And he slept.

The day afterwards—it was the third day that his shop had remained closed—the snowstorm had ceased, and a neighbour from the opposite house came over towards the booth where dwelt old Anthony, who had not yet shown himself. Anthony lay stretched upon his bed—dead—with his old cap clutched tightly in his two hands! They did not put that cap on his head in his coffin, for he had a new white one.

Where were now the tears that he had wept? What had become of the pearls? They remained in the nightcap—and the true ones do not come out in the wash—they were preserved in the nightcap, and in time forgotten; but the old thoughts and the old dreams still remained in the "bachelor's nightcap." Don't wish for such a cap for yourself. It would make your forehead very hot, would make your pulse beat feverishly, and conjure up dreams which appear like reality. The first who wore that identical cap afterwards felt all that at once, though it was half a century afterwards; and that man was the burgomaster himself, who, with his wife and eleven children, was well and firmly established, and had amassed a very tolerable amount of wealth. He was immediately seized with dreams of unfortunate love, of bankruptcy, and of heavy times.

"Hallo! how the nightcap burns!" he cried out, and tore it from his head.

And a pearl rolled out, and another, and another, and they sounded and glittered.

"This must be gout," said the burgomaster. "Something dazzles my eyes!"

They were tears, shed half a century before by old Anthony from Eisenach.

Every one who afterwards put that nightcap upon his head had visions and dreams which excited him not a little. His own history was changed into that of Anthony, and became a story; in fact, many stories. But some one else may tell *them*. We have told the first. And our last word is—don't wish for "The Old Bachelor's Nightcap."

The Last Dream of the Old Oak Tree: A Christmas Tale

Translated by H. W. Dulcken

In the forest, high up on the steep shore, hard by the open sea coast, stood a very old oak tree. It was exactly three hundred and sixty-five years old, but that long time was not more for the tree than just as many days would be to us men. We wake by day and sleep through the night, and then we have our dreams: it is different with the tree, which keeps awake through three seasons of the year, and does not get its sleep till winter comes. Winter is its time for rest, its night after the long day which is called spring, summer, and autumn.

On many a warm summer day the Ephemera, the fly that lives but for a day, had danced around his crown—had lived, enjoyed, and felt happy; and then rested for a moment in quiet bliss the tiny creature, on one of the great fresh oak leaves; and then the tree always said:

"Poor little thing! Your whole life is but a single day! How very short! It's quite melancholy!"

"Melancholy! Why do you say that?" the Ephemera would then always reply. "It's wonderfully bright, warm, and beautiful all around me, and that makes me rejoice!"

The Last Dream of the Old Oak Tree: A Christmas Tale

"But only one day, and then it's all done!"

"Done!" repeated the Ephemera. "What's the meaning of *done*? Are you *done*, too?"

"No; I shall perhaps live for thousands of your days, and my day is whole seasons long! It's something so long, that you can't at all manage to reckon it out."

"No? then I don't understand you. You say you have thousands of my days; but I have thousands of moments, in which I can be merry and happy. Does all the beauty of this world cease when you die?"

"No," replied the Tree; "it will certainly last much longer—far longer than I can possibly think."

"Well, then, we have the same time, only that we reckon differently."

And the Ephemera danced and floated in the air, and rejoiced in her delicate wings of gauze and velvet, and rejoiced in the balmy breezes laden with the fragrance of meadows and of wild roses and elder-flowers, of the garden hedges, wild thyme, and mint, and daisies; the scent of these was all so strong that the Ephemera was almost intoxicated. The day was long and beautiful, full of joy and of sweet feeling, and when the sun sank low the little fly felt very agreeably tired of all its happiness and enjoyment. The delicate wings would not carry it any more, and quietly and slowly it glided down upon the soft grass blade, nodded its head as well as it could nod, and went quietly to sleep—and was dead.

"Poor little Ephemera!" said the Oak. "That was a terribly short life!"

And on every summer day the same dance was repeated, the same question and answer, and the same sleep. The same thing was repeated through whole generations of ephemera, and all of them felt equally merry and equally happy.

The Oak stood there awake through the spring morning, the noon of summer, and the evening of autumn; and its time of rest, its night, was coming on apace. Winter was approaching.

Already the storms were singing their "good night, good night!" Here fell a leaf, and there fell a leaf.

"We'll rock you, and dandle you! Go to sleep, go to sleep! We sing you to sleep, we shake you to sleep, but it does you good in your old twigs, does it not? They seem to crack for very joy! Sleep sweetly, sleep sweetly! It's your three hundred and sixty-fifth night. Properly speaking, you're only a stripling as yet! Sleep sweetly! The clouds strew down snow, there will be quite a coverlet, warm and protecting, around your feet. Sweet sleep to you, and pleasant dreams!"

And the Oak Tree stood there, denuded of all its leaves, to sleep through the long winter, and to dream many a dream, always about something that had happened to it, just as in the dreams of men.

The great Oak had once been small—indeed, an acorn had been its cradle. According to human computation, it was now in its fourth century. It was the greatest and best tree in the forest; its crown towered far above all the other trees, and could be descried from afar across the sea, so that it served as a landmark to the sailors: the tree had no idea how many eyes were in the habit of seeking it. High up in its green summit the wood-pigeon built her nest, and the cuckoo sat in its boughs, and sang his song; and in autumn, when the leaves looked like thin plates of copper, the birds of passage came and rested there, before they flew away across the sea; but now it was winter, and the tree stood there leafless, so that every one could see how gnarled and crooked the branches were that shot forth from its trunk. Crows and rooks came and took their seat by turns in the boughs, and spoke of the hard times which were beginning, and of the difficulty of getting a living in winter.

It was just at the holy Christmas time, when the tree dreamed its most glorious dream.

The tree had a distinct feeling of the festive time, and fancied he heard the bells ringing from the churches all around; and yet it seemed as if it were a fine summer's day, mild and warm. Fresh and green he spread out his mighty crown; the sunbeams played among the twigs and the leaves; the air was full of the fragrance of herbs and blossoms; gay butterflies chased each other to and fro. The ephemeral insects danced as if all the world were created merely for them to dance and be merry in. All that the tree had experienced for years and years, and that had happened around him, seemed to pass by him again, as in a festive pageant. He saw the knights of ancient days ride by with their noble dames on gallant steeds, with plumes waving in their bonnets and falcons on their wrists. The hunting horn sounded, and the dogs barked. He saw hostile warriors in coloured jerkins and with shining weapons, with spear and halbert, pitching their tents and striking them again. The watch-fires flamed up anew, and men sang and slept under the branches of the tree. He saw loving couples meeting near his trunk, happily, in the moonshine; and they cut the initials of their names in the grey-green bark of his stem. Once—but long years had rolled by since then—citherns and Æolian harps had been hung up on his boughs by merry wanderers, now they hung there again, and once again they sounded in tones of marvellous sweetness. The wood-pigeons cooed, as if they were telling what the tree felt in all this, and the cuckoo called out to tell him how many summer days he had yet to live.

Then it appeared to him as if new life were rippling down into the remotest fibre of his root, and mounting up into his highest branches, to the tops of the leaves. The tree felt that he was stretching and spreading himself, and through his root he felt that there was life and motion even in the ground itself. He felt his strength increase, he grew higher, his stem shot up unceasingly, and he grew more and more, his crown became fuller, and spread out; and in proportion as the tree grew, he felt his happiness increase, and his joyous hope that he should reach even higher—quite up to the warm brilliant sun.

Already had he grown high above the clouds, which floated past beneath his crown like dark troops of passage-birds, or like great white swans. And every leaf of the tree had the gift of sight, as if it had eyes wherewith to see; the stars became visible in broad daylight, great and sparkling; each of them sparkled like a pair of eyes, mild and clear. They recalled to his memory well-known gentle eyes, eyes of children, eyes of lovers who had met beneath his boughs.

It was a marvellous spectacle, and one full of happiness and joy! And yet amid all this happiness the tree felt a longing, a yearning desire that all other trees of the wood beneath him, and all the bushes, and herbs, and flowers, might be able to rise with him, that they too might see this splendour, and experience this joy. The great majestic oak was not quite happy in his happiness, while he had not them all, great and little, about him; and this feeling of yearning trembled through his every twig, through his every leaf, warmly and fervently as through a human heart.

The crown of the tree waved to and fro, as if he sought something in his silent longing, and he looked down. Then he felt the fragrance of thyme, and soon afterwards the more powerful scent of honeysuckle and violets; and he fancied he heard the cuckoo answering him.

Yes, through the clouds the green summits of the forest came peering up, and under himself the Oak saw the other trees, as they grew and raised themselves aloft. Bushes and herbs shot up high, and some tore themselves up bodily by the roots to rise the quicker. The birch was the quickest of all. Like a white streak of lightning, its slender stem shot upwards in a zigzag line, and the branches spread around it like green gauze and like banners; the whole woodland natives, even to the brown plumed rushes, grew up with the rest, and the birds came too, and sang; and on the grass blade that fluttered aloft like a long silken ribbon into the air, sat the grasshopper cleaning his wings with his leg; the May beetles hummed, and the bees murmured, and every bird sang in his appointed manner; all was song and sound of gladness up into the high heaven.

"But the little blue flower by the water-side, where is that?" said the Oak; "and the purple bell-flower and the daisy?" for, you see, the old Oak Tree wanted to have them all about him.

"We are here—we are here!" was shouted and sung in reply.

"But the beautiful thyme of last summer—and in the last year there was certainly a place here covered with lilies of the valley! and the wild apple tree that blossomed so splendidly! and all the glory of the wood that came year by year—if that had only just been born, it might have been here now!"

"We are here, we are here!" replied voices still higher in the air. It seemed as if they had flown on before.

"Why, that is beautiful, indescribably beautiful!" exclaimed the old Oak Tree, rejoicingly. "I have them all around me, great and small; not one has been forgotten! How can so much happiness be imagined? How can it be possible?"

"In heaven, in the better land, it can be imagined, and it is possible!" the reply sounded through the air.

And the old tree, who grew on and on, felt how his roots were tearing themselves free from the ground.

The Last Dream of the Old Oak Tree: A Christmas Tale

"That's right, that's better than all!" said the tree. "Now no fetters hold me! I can fly up now, to the very highest, in glory and in light! And all my beloved ones are with me, great and small—all of them, all!"

That was the dream of the old Oak Tree; and while he dreamt thus a mighty storm came rushing over land and sea—at the holy Christmas tide. The sea rolled great billows towards the shore; there was a cracking and crashing in the tree—his root was torn out of the ground in the very moment while he was dreaming that his root freed itself from the earth. He fell. His three hundred and sixty-five years were now as the single day of the Ephemera.

On the morning of the Christmas festival, when the sun rose, the storm had subsided. From all the churches sounded the festive bells, and from every hearth, even from the smallest hut, arose the smoke in blue clouds, like the smoke from the altars of the druids of old at the feast of thanks offerings. The sea became gradually calm, and on board a great ship in the offing, that had fought successfully with the tempest, all the flags were displayed, as a token of joy suitable to the festive day.

"The tree is down—the old Oak Tree, our landmark on the coast!" said the sailors. "It fell in the storm of last night. Who can replace it? No one can."

This was the funeral oration, short but well meant, that was given to the tree, which lay stretched on the snowy covering on the sea shore; and over its prostrate form sounded the notes of a song from the ship, a carol of the joys of Christmas, and of the redemption of the soul of man by His blood, and of eternal life.

> "Sing, sing aloud, this blessed morn—
> It is fulfilled—and He is born,
> Oh, joy without compare!
> Hallelujah! Hallelujah!"

Thus sounded the old psalm tune, and every one on board the ship felt lifted up in his own way, through the song and the prayer, just as the old tree had felt lifted up in its last, its most beauteous dream in the Christmas night.

The Marsh King's Daughter

Translated by Mrs. H. P. Paull

The storks relate to their little ones a great many stories, and they are all about moors and reed banks, and suited to their age and capacity. The youngest of them are quite satisfied with "Kribble, krabble," or such nonsense, and think it very grand; but the elder ones want something with a deeper meaning, or at least something about their own family.

We are only acquainted with one of the two longest and oldest stories which the storks relate—it is about Moses, who was exposed by his mother on the banks of the Nile, and was found by the king's daughter, who gave him a good education, and he afterwards became a great man; but where he was buried is still unknown.

Every one knows this story, but not the second; very likely because it is quite an inland story. It has been repeated from mouth to mouth, from one stork-mamma to another, for thousands of years; and each has told it better than the last; and now we mean to tell it better than all.

The first stork pair who related it lived at the time it happened, and had their summer residence on the rafters of the Viking's[*] house, which stood near the wild moorlands of Wendsyssell; that is, to speak more correctly, the great moorheath, high up in the north of Jutland, by the Skjagen peak. This wilderness is still an immense wild heath of marshy ground, about which we can read in the "Official Directory." It is said that in olden times the place was a lake, the ground of which had heaved up from beneath, and now the moorland extends for miles in every direction, and is surrounded by damp meadows, trembling, undulating swamps, and marshy ground covered with turf, on which grow bilberry bushes and stunted trees. Mists are almost always hovering over this region, which, seventy years ago, was overrun with wolves. It may well be called the Wild Moor; and one can easily imagine, with such a wild expanse of marsh and lake, how lonely and dreary it must have been a thousand years ago. Many things may be noticed now that existed then. The reeds grow to the same height, and bear the same kind of long, purple-brown leaves, with their feathery tips. There still stands the birch, with its white bark and its delicate, loosely hanging leaves; and with regard to the living beings who frequented this spot, the fly still wears a gauzy dress of the same cut, and the favourite colours of the stork are white, with black and red for stockings. The people, certainly, in those days, wore very different dresses to those they now wear, but if any of them, be he huntsman or squire, master or servant, ventured on the wavering, undulating, marshy ground of the moor, they met with the same fate a thousand years ago as they would now. The wanderer sank, and went down to the Marsh King, as he is named, who rules in the great moorland empire beneath. They also called him "Gunkel

---

[*] Sea Kings, or pirates of the North.

King," but we like the name of "Marsh King" better, and we will give him that name as the storks do. Very little is known of the Marsh King's rule, but that, perhaps, is a good thing.

In the neighbourhood of the moorlands, and not far from the great arm of the North Sea and the Cattegat which is called the Lumfjorden, lay the castle of the Viking, with its water-tight stone cellars, its tower, and its three projecting storeys. On the ridge of the roof the stork had built his nest, and there the stork-mamma sat on her eggs and felt sure her hatching would come to something.

One evening, Stork-papa stayed out rather late, and when he came home he seemed quite busy, bustling, and important. "I have something very dreadful to tell you," said he to the Stork-mamma.

"Keep it to yourself then," she replied. "Remember that I am hatching eggs; it may agitate me, and will affect them."

"You must know it at once," said he. "The daughter of our host in Egypt has arrived here. She has ventured to take this journey, and now she is lost."

"She who sprung from the race of the fairies, is it?" cried the mother stork. "Oh, tell me all about it; you know I cannot bear to be kept waiting at a time when I am hatching eggs."

"Well, you see, mother," he replied, "she believed what the doctors said, and what I have heard you state also, that the moor-flowers which grow about here would heal her sick father; and she has flown to the North in swan's plumage, in company with some other Swan-Princesses, who come to these parts every year to renew their youth. She came, and where is she now!"

"You enter into particulars too much," said the mamma Stork, "and the eggs may take cold; I cannot bear such suspense as this."

"Well," said he, "I have kept watch; and this evening I went among the rushes where I thought the marshy ground would bear me, and while I was there three swans came. Something in their manner of flying seemed to say to me, 'Look carefully now; there is one not all swan, only swan's feathers.' You know, mother, you have the same intuitive feeling that I have; you know whether a thing is right or not immediately."

"Yes, of course," said she; "but tell me about the Princess; I am tired of hearing about the swan's feathers."

"Well, you know that in the middle of the moor there is something like a lake," said the Stork-papa. "You can see the edge of it if you raise yourself a little. Just there, by the reeds and the green banks, lay the trunk of an elder-tree; upon this the three swans stood flapping their wings, and looking about them; one of them threw off her plumage, and I immediately recognized her as one of the Princesses of our home in Egypt. There she sat, without any covering but her long, black hair. I heard her tell the two others to take great care of the swan's plumage, while she dipped down into the water to pluck the flowers which she fancied she saw there. The others nodded, and picked up the feather dress, and took possession of it. I wonder what will become of it? thought I, and she most likely asked herself the same question. If so, she received an answer, a very practical one; for the two swans rose up and flew away with her swan's plumage. 'Dive down now!' they cried; 'thou shalt never more fly in the swan's plumage, thou shalt never again see Egypt; here, on the moor, thou wilt remain.' So saying, they tore the swan's plumage into a thousand pieces, the feathers drifted about like a snow-shower, and then the two deceitful Princesses flew away."

"Why, that is terrible," said the Stork-mamma; "I feel as if I could hardly bear to hear any more, but you must tell me what happened next."

"The Princess wept and lamented aloud; her tears moistened the elder stump, which was really not an elder stump but the Marsh King himself, he who in marshy ground lives and rules. I saw myself how the stump of the tree turned round, and was a tree no more, while long, clammy branches like arms, were extended from it. Then the poor child was terribly frightened, and started up to run away. She hastened to cross the green, slimy ground; but it will not bear any weight, much less hers. She quickly sank, and the elder stump dived immediately after her; in fact, it was he who drew her down. Great black bubbles rose up out of the moor-slime, and with these every trace of the two vanished. And now the princess is buried in the wild marsh, she will never now carry flowers to Egypt to cure her father. It would have broken your heart, mother, had you seen it."

"You ought not to have told me," said she, "at such a time as this; the eggs might suffer. But I think the Princess will soon find help;

some one will rise up to help her. Ah! if it had been you or I, or one of our people, it would have been all over with us."

"I mean to go every day," said he, "to see if anything comes to pass;" and so he did.

A long time went by, but at last he saw a green stalk shooting up out of the deep, marshy ground. As it reached the surface of the marsh, a leaf spread out, and unfolded itself broader and broader, and close to it came forth a bud.

One morning, when the Stork-papa was flying over the stem, he saw that the power of the sun's rays had caused the bud to open, and in the cup of the flower lay a charming child—a little maiden, looking as if she had just come out of a bath. The little one was so like the Egyptian Princess, that the stork, at the first moment, thought it must be the Princess herself, but after a little reflection he decided that it was much more likely to be the daughter of the Princess and the Marsh King; and this explained also her being placed in the cup of a water lily. "But she cannot be left to lie here," thought the stork, "and in my nest there are already so many. But stay, I have thought of something: the wife of the Viking has no children, and how often she has wished for a little one. People always say the stork brings the little ones; I will do so in earnest this time. I shall fly with the child to the Viking's wife; what rejoicing there will be!"

And then the stork lifted the little girl out of the flower-cup, flew to the castle, picked a hole with his beak in the bladder-covered, window, and laid the beautiful child in the bosom of the Viking's wife. Then he flew back quickly to the Stork-mamma and told her what he had seen and done; and the little Storks listened to it all, for they were then quite old enough to do so. "So you see," he continued, "that the Princess is not dead, for she must have sent her little one up here; and now I have found a home for her."

"Ah, I said it would be so from the first," replied the Stork-mamma; "but now think a little of your own family. Our travelling time draws near, and I sometimes feel a little irritation already under the wings. The cuckoos and the nightingale are already gone, and I heard the quails say they should go too as soon as the wind was favourable. Our youngsters will go through all the manoeuvres at the review very well, or I am much mistaken in them."

The Marsh King's Daughter

The Viking's wife was above measure delighted when she awoke the next morning and found the beautiful little child lying in her bosom. She kissed it and caressed it; but it cried terribly, and struck out with its arms and legs, and did not seem to be pleased at all. At last it cried itself to sleep; and as it lay there so still and quiet, it was a most beautiful sight to see. The Viking's wife was so delighted, that body and soul were full of joy. Her heart felt so light within her, that it seemed as if her husband and his soldiers, who were absent, must come home as suddenly and unexpectedly as the little child had done. She and her whole household therefore busied themselves in preparing everything for the reception of her lord. The long, coloured tapestry, on which she and her maidens had worked pictures of their idols, Odin, Thor, and Friga, was hung up. The slaves polished the old shields that served as ornaments; cushions were placed on the seats, and dry wood laid on the fireplaces in the centre of the hall, so that the flames might be fanned up at a moment's notice. The Viking's wife herself assisted in the work, so that at night she felt very tired, and quickly fell into a sound sleep. When she awoke, just before morning, she was terribly alarmed to find that the infant had vanished. She sprang from her couch, lighted a pine-chip, and searched all round the room, when, at last, in that part of the bed where her feet had been, lay, not the child, but a great, ugly frog. She was quite disgusted at this sight, and seized a heavy stick to kill the frog; but the creature looked at her with such strange, mournful eyes, that she was unable to strike the blow. Once more she searched round the room; then she started at hearing the frog utter a low, painful croak. She sprang from the couch and opened the window hastily; at the same moment the sun rose, and threw its beams through the window, till it rested on the couch where the great frog lay. Suddenly it appeared as if the frog's broad mouth contracted, and became small and red. The limbs moved and stretched out and extended themselves till they took a beautiful shape; and behold there was the pretty child lying before her, and the ugly frog was gone. "How is this?" she cried, "have I had a wicked dream? Is it not my own lovely cherub that lies there." Then she kissed it and fondled it; but the child struggled and fought, and bit as if she had been a little wild cat.

The Viking did not return on that day, nor the next; he was, however, on the way home; but the wind, so favourable to the storks, was against him; for it blew towards the south. A wind in favour of one is often against another.

After two or three days had passed, it became clear to the Viking's wife how matters stood with the child; it was under the influence of a powerful sorcerer. By day it was charming in appearance as an angel of light, but with a temper wicked and wild; while at night, in the form of an ugly frog, it was quiet and mournful, with eyes full of sorrow. Here were two natures, changing inwardly and outwardly with the absence and return of sunlight. And so it happened that by day the child, with the actual form of its mother, possessed the fierce disposition of its father; at night, on the contrary, its outward appearance plainly showed its descent on the father's side, while inwardly it had the heart and mind of its mother. Who would be able to loosen this wicked charm which the sorcerer had worked upon it? The wife of the Viking lived in constant pain and sorrow about it. Her heart clung to the little creature, but she could not explain to her husband the circumstances in which it was placed. He was expected to return shortly; and were she to tell him, he would very likely, as was the custom at that time, expose the poor child in the public highway, and let any one take it away who would. The good wife of the Viking could not let that happen, and she therefore resolved that the Viking should never see the child excepting by daylight.

One morning there sounded a rushing of storks' wings over the roof. More than a hundred pair of storks had rested there during the night, to recover themselves after their excursion; and now they soared aloft, and prepared for the journey southward.

"All the husbands are here, and ready!" they cried; "wives and children also!"

"How light we are!" screamed the young Storks in chorus. "Something pleasant seems creeping over us, even down to our toes, as if we were full of live frogs. Ah, how delightful it is to travel into foreign lands!"

"Hold yourselves properly in the line with us," cried papa and mamma. "Do not use your beaks so much; it tries the lungs." And then the Storks flew away.

About the same time sounded the clang of the warriors' trumpets across the heath. The Viking had landed with his men. They were

The Marsh King's Daughter

returning home, richly laden with spoil from the Gallic coast, where the people, as did also the inhabitants of Britain, often cried in alarm, "Deliver us from the wild Northmen."

Life and noisy pleasure came with them into the castle of the Viking on the moorland. A great cask of mead was drawn into the hall, piles of wood blazed, cattle were slain and served up, that they might feast in reality, The priest who offered the sacrifice sprinkled the devoted parishioners with the warm blood; the fire crackled, and the smoke rolled along beneath the roof; the soot fell upon them from the beams; but they were used to all these things. Guests were invited, and received handsome presents. All wrongs and unfaithfulness were forgotten. They drank deeply, and threw in each other's faces the bones that were left, which was looked upon as a sign of good feeling amongst them. A bard, who was a kind of musician as well as warrior, and who had been with the Viking in his expedition, and knew what to sing about, gave them one of his best songs, in which they heard all their warlike deeds praised, and every wonderful action brought forward with honour. Every verse ended with this refrain—

> "Gold and possessions will flee away,
> Friends and foes must die one day;
> Every man on earth must die,
> But a famous name will never die."

And with that they beat upon their shields, and hammered upon the table with knives and bones, in a most outrageous manner.

The Viking's wife sat upon a raised cross seat in the open hall. She wore a silk dress, golden bracelets, and large amber beads. She was in costly attire, and the bard named her in his song, and spoke of the rich treasure of gold which she had brought to her husband. Her husband had already seen the wonderfully beautiful child in the daytime, and was delighted with her beauty; even her wild ways pleased him. He said the little maiden would grow up to be a heroine, with the strong will and determination of a man. She would never wink her eyes, even if, in joke, an expert hand should attempt to cut off her eye-brows with a sharp sword.

The full cask of mead soon became empty, and a fresh one was brought in; for these were people who liked plenty to eat and drink. The old proverb, which every one knows, says that "the cattle know when to leave their pasture, but a foolish man knows not the measure of his own appetite." Yes, they all knew this; but men may know what is right, and yet often do wrong. They also knew "that even the welcome guest becomes wearisome when he sits too long in the house." But there they remained; for pork and mead are good things. And so at the Viking's house they stayed, and enjoyed themselves; and at night the bondmen slept in the ashes, and dipped their fingers in the fat, and licked them. Oh, it was a delightful time!

Once more in the same year the Viking went forth, though the storms of autumn had already commenced to roar. He went with his warriors to the coast of Britain; he said that it was but an excursion of pleasure across the water, so his wife remained at home with the little girl. After a while, it is quite certain the foster-mother began to love the poor frog, with its gentle eyes and its deep sighs, even better than the little beauty who bit and fought with all around her.

The heavy, damp mists of autumn, which destroy the leaves of the wood, had already fallen upon forest and heath. Feathers of plucked birds, as they call the snow, flew about in thick showers, and winter was coming. The sparrows took possession of the stork's nest, and conversed about the absent owners in their own fashion; and they, the Stork pair and all their young ones, where were they staying now? The Storks might have been found in the land of Egypt, where the sun's rays shone forth bright and warm, as it does here at midsummer. Tamarinds and acacias were in full bloom all over the country, the crescent of Mahomet glittered brightly from the cupolas of the mosques, and on the slender pinnacles sat many of the storks, resting after their long journey. Swarms of them took divided possession of the nests—nests which lay close to each other between the venerable columns, and crowded the arches of temples in forgotten cities. The date and the palm lifted themselves as a screen or as a sun-shade over them. The gray pyramids looked like broken shadows in the clear air and the far-off desert, where the ostrich wheels his rapid flight, and the lion, with his subtle eyes, gazes at the marble sphinx which lies half buried in sand. The waters of the Nile had retreated, and the whole bed of the river was covered with frogs, which was a most acceptable prospect for the Stork families. The young Storks thought their eyes deceived them, everything around appeared so beautiful.

"It is always like this here, and this is how we live in our warm country," said the Stork-mamma; and the thought made the young ones almost beside themselves with pleasure.

"Is there anything more to see?" they asked; "are we going farther into the country?"

"There is nothing further for us to see," answered the Stork-mamma. "Beyond this delightful region there are immense forests, where the branches of the trees entwine round each other, while prickly, creeping plants cover the paths, and only an elephant could force a passage for himself with his great feet. The snakes are too large, and the lizards too lively for us to catch. Then there is the desert; if you went there, your eyes would soon be full of sand with the lightest breeze, and if it should blow great guns, you would most likely find yourself in a sand-drift. Here is the best place for you, where there are frogs and locusts; here I shall remain, and so must you." And so they stayed.

The parents sat in the nest on the slender minaret, and rested, yet still were busily employed in cleaning and smoothing their feathers, and in sharpening their beaks against their red stockings; then they would stretch out their necks, salute each other, and gravely raise their heads with the high-polished forehead, and soft, smooth feathers, while their brown eyes shone with intelligence. The female young ones strutted about amid the moist rushes, glancing at the other young storks and making acquaintances, and swallowing a frog at every third step, or tossing a little snake about with their beaks, in a way they considered very becoming, and besides it tasted very good. The young male storks soon began to quarrel; they struck at each other with their wings, and pecked with their beaks till the blood came. And in this manner many of the young ladies and gentlemen were betrothed to each other: it was, of course, what they wanted, and indeed what they lived for. Then they returned to a nest, and there the quarrelling began afresh; for in hot countries people are almost all violent and passionate. But for all that it was pleasant, especially for the old people, who watched them with great joy: all that their young ones did suited them. Every day here there was sunshine, plenty to eat, and nothing to think of but pleasure. But in the rich castle of their Egyptian host, as they called him, pleasure was not to be found. The rich and mighty lord of the castle lay on his couch, in the midst of the great hall, with its many coloured walls looking like the centre of a great tulip; but he was stiff and powerless in all his limbs, and lay stretched out like a mummy. His family and servants stood round him; he was not dead, although he could scarcely be said to live. The healing moor-flower from the North, which was to have been found and brought to him by her who loved him so well, had not arrived. His young and beautiful daughter who, in swan's plumage, had flown over land and seas to the distant north, had never returned. She is dead, so the two swan-maidens had said when they came home; and they made up quite a story about her, and this is what they told—

"We three flew away together through the air," said they: "a hunter caught sight of us, and shot at us with an arrow. The arrow struck our young friend and sister, and slowly singing her farewell song she sank down, a dying swan, into the forest lake. On the shores of the lake, under a spreading birch-tree, we laid her in the cold earth. We had our revenge; we bound fire under the wings of a swallow, who had a nest on the thatched roof of the huntsman. The house took fire, and burst into flames; the hunter was burnt with the house, and the light was reflected over the sea as far as the spreading birch, beneath which we laid her sleeping dust. She will never return to the land of Egypt." And then they both wept. And Stork-papa, who heard the story, snapped with his beak so that it might be heard a long way off.

"Deceit and lies!" cried he; "I should like to run my beak deep into their chests."

"And perhaps break it off," said the mamma Stork, "then what a sight you would be. Think first of yourself, and then of your family; all others are nothing to us."

"Yes, I know," said the Stork-papa; "but tomorrow I can easily place myself on the edge of the open cupola, when the learned and wise men assemble to consult on the state of the sick man; perhaps they may come a little nearer to the truth." And the learned and wise men assembled together, and talked a great deal on every point; but the Stork could make no sense out of anything they said; neither were there any good results from their consultations, either for the sick man, or for his daughter in the marshy heath. When we listen to what people say in this world, we shall hear a great deal; but it is an advantage to know what has been said and done before, when we listen to a conversation. The Stork did, and we know at least as much as he, the Stork.

"Love is a life-giver. The highest love produces the highest life. Only through love can the sick man be cured." This had been said by many, and even the learned men acknowledged that it was a wise saying.

"What a beautiful thought!" exclaimed the papa Stork immediately.

"I don't quite understand it," said the mamma Stork, when her husband repeated it; "however, it is not my fault, but the fault of the thought; whatever it may be, I have something else to think of."

Now the learned men had spoken also of love between this one and that one; of the difference of the love which we have for our neighbour, to the love that exists between parents and children; of the love of the plant for the light, and how the germ springs forth when the sunbeam kisses the ground. All these things were so elaborately and learnedly explained, that it was impossible for Stork-papa to follow it, much less to talk about it. His thoughts on the subject quite weighed him down; he stood the whole of the following day on one leg, with half-shut eyes, thinking deeply. So much learning was quite a heavy weight for him to carry. One thing, however, the papa Stork could understand. Every one, high and low, had from their inmost hearts expressed their opinion that it was a great misfortune for so many thousands of people—the whole country indeed—to have this man so sick, with no hopes of his recovery. And what joy and blessing it would spread around if he could by any means be cured! But where bloomed the flower that could bring him health? They had searched for it everywhere; in learned writings, in the shining stars, in the weather and wind. Inquiries had been made in every by-way that could be thought of, until at last the wise and learned men has asserted, as we have been already told, that "Love, the life-giver, could alone give new life to a father;" and in saying this, they had overdone it, and said more than they understood themselves. They repeated it, and wrote it down as a recipe, "Love is a life-giver." But how could such a recipe be prepared—that was a difficulty they could not overcome. At last it was decided that help could only come from the Princess herself, whose whole soul was wrapped up in her father, especially as a plan had been adopted by her to enable her to obtain a remedy.

More than a year had passed since the Princess had set out at night, when the light of the young moon was soon lost beneath the horizon. She had gone to the marble Sphinx in the desert, shaking the sand from her sandals, and then passed through the long passage, which leads to the centre of one of the great pyramids, where the mighty Kings of antiquity, surrounded with pomp and splendor, lie veiled in the form of mummies. She had been told by the wise men, that if she laid her head on the breast of one of them, from the head she would learn where to find life and recovery for her father. She had performed all this, and in a dream had learnt that she must bring home to her father the lotus flower, which grows in the deep sea, near the moors and heath in the Danish land. The very place and situation had been pointed out to her, and she was told that the flower would restore her father to health and strength. And, therefore, she had gone forth from the land of Egypt, flying over to the open marsh and the wild moor in the plumage of a swan.

The papa and mamma Storks knew all this, and we also know it now. We know, too, that the Marsh King has drawn her down to himself, and that to the loved ones at home she is forever dead. One of the wisest of them said, as the Stork-mamma also said, "That in some way she would, after all, manage to succeed;" and so at last they comforted themselves with this hope, and would wait patiently; in fact, they could do nothing better.

"I should like to get away the swan's feathers from those two treacherous Princesses," said the papa Stork; "then, at least, they would not be able to fly over again to the wild moor, and do more wickedness. I can hide the two suits of feathers over yonder, till we find some use for them."

"But where will you put them?" asked the mamma Stork.

"In our nest on the moor. I and the young ones will carry them by turns during our flight across; and as we return, should they prove too heavy for us, we shall be sure to find plenty of places on the way in which we can conceal them till our next journey. Certainly one suit of swan's feathers would be enough for the Princess, but two are always better. In those northern countries no one can have too many travelling wrappers."

"No one will thank you for it," said Stork-mamma; "but you are master; and, excepting at breeding time, I have nothing to say."

In the Viking's castle on the wild moor, to which the Storks directed their flight in the following spring, the little maiden still remained. They had named her Helga, which was rather too soft a name for a child with a temper like hers, although her form was still beautiful. Every month this temper showed itself in sharper outlines; and in the course of years, while the Storks still made the same journeys in autumn to the hill, and in spring to the moors, the child grew to be almost a woman, and before any one seemed aware of it, she was a wonderfully beautiful maiden of sixteen. The casket was splendid, but the contents were worthless. She was, indeed, wild and savage even in those hard, uncultivated times. It was a pleasure to her to splash about with her white hands in the warm blood of the horse which had been slain for sacrifice. In one of her wild moods she bit off the head of the black cock, which the priest was about to slay for the sacrifice. To her foster-father she said one day, "If thine enemy were to pull down thine house about thy ears, and thou shouldest be sleeping in unconscious security, I would not wake thee; even if I had the power I would never do it, for my ears still tingle with the blow that thou gavest me years ago. I have never forgotten it." But the Viking treated her words as a joke; he was, like every one else, bewitched with her beauty, and knew nothing of the change in the form and temper of Helga at night. Without a saddle, she would sit on a horse as if she were a part of it, while it rushed along at full speed; nor would she spring from its back, even when it quarrelled with other horses and bit them. She would often leap from the high shore into the sea with all her clothes on, and swim to meet the Viking, when his boat was steering home towards the shore. She once cut off a long lock of her beautiful hair, and twisted it into a string for her bow. "If a thing is to be done well," said she, "I must do it myself."

The Viking's wife was, for the time in which she lived, a woman of strong character and will; but, compared to her daughter, she was a gentle, timid woman, and she knew that a wicked sorcerer had the terrible child in his power. It was sometimes as if Helga acted from sheer wickedness; for often when her mother stood on the threshold of the door, or stepped into the yard, she would seat herself on the brink of the well, wave her arms and legs in the air, and suddenly fall right in. Here she was able, from her frog nature, to dip and dive about in the water of the deep well, until at last she would climb forth like a cat, and come back into the hall dripping with water, so that the green leaves that were strewed on the floor were whirled round, and carried away by the streams that flowed from her.

But there was one time of the day which placed a check upon Helga. It was the evening twilight; when this hour arrived she became quiet and thoughtful, and allowed herself to be advised and led; then also a secret feeling seemed to draw her towards her mother. And as usual, when the sun set, and the transformation took place, both in body and mind, inwards and outwards, she would remain quiet and mournful, with her form shrunk together in the shape of a frog. Her body was much larger than those animals ever are, and on this account it was much more hideous in appearance; for she looked like a wretched dwarf, with a frog's head, and webbed fingers. Her eyes had a most piteous expression; she was without a voice, excepting a hollow, croaking sound, like the smothered sobs of a dreaming child.

Then the Viking's wife took her on her lap, and forgot the ugly form, as she looked into the mournful eyes, and often said, "I could wish that thou wouldst always remain my dumb frog child, for thou art too terrible when thou art clothed in a form of beauty." And the Viking woman wrote Runic characters against sorcery and spells of sickness, and threw them over the wretched child; but they did no good.

"One can scarcely believe that she was ever small enough to lie in the cup of the water lily," said the papa Stork; "and now she is grown up, and the image of her Egyptian mother, especially about the eyes. Ah, we shall never see her again; perhaps she has not discovered how to help herself, as you and the wise men said she would. Year after year have I flown across and across the moor, but there was no sign of her being still alive. Yes, and I may as well tell you that you that each year, when I arrived a few days before you to repair the nest, and put everything in its place, I have spent a whole night flying here and there over the marshy lake, as if I had been an owl or a bat, but all to no purpose. The two suit of swan's plumage, which I and the young ones dragged over here from the land of the Nile, are of no use; trouble enough it was to us to bring them here in three journeys, and now they are lying at the bottom of the nest; and if a fire should happen to break out, and the wooden house be burnt down, they would be destroyed."

"And our good nest would be destroyed, too," said the mamma Stork; "but you think less of that than of your plumage stuff and your Moor-Princess. Go and stay with her in the marsh if you like. You are a bad father to your own children, as I have told you already, when I hatched my first brood. I only hope neither we nor our children may have an arrow sent through our wings, owing to that wild girl. Helga does not know in the least what she is about. We have lived in this house longer than she has, she should think of that, and we have never forgotten our duty. We have paid every year our toll of a feather, an egg, and a young one, as it is only right we should do. You don't suppose I can wander about the court-yard, or go everywhere as I used to do in old times. I can do it in Egypt, where I can be a companion of the people, without forgetting myself. But here I cannot go and peep into the pots and kettles as I do there. No, I can only sit up here and feel angry with that girl, the little wretch; and I am angry with you, too; you should have left her lying in the water lily, then no one would have known anything about her."

"You are far better than your conversation," said the papa Stork; "I know you better than you know yourself." And with that he gave a hop, and flapped his wings twice, proudly; then he stretched his neck and flew, or rather soared away, without moving his outspread wings. He went on for some distance, and then he gave a great *flap* with his wings and flew on his course at a rapid rate, his head and neck bending proudly before him, while the sun's rays fell on his glossy plumage.

"He is the handsomest of them all," said the mamma Stork, as she watched him; "but I won't tell him so."

Early in the autumn, the Viking again returned home laden with spoil, and bringing prisoners with him. Among them was a young Christian priest, one of those who contemned the gods of the North. Often lately there had been, both in hall and chamber, a talk of the new faith which was spreading far and wide in the South, and which, through the means of the holy Ansgarius, had already reached as far as Hedeby on the Schlei. Even Helga had heard of this belief in the teachings of One who was named Christ, and who for the love of mankind, and for their redemption, had given up His life. But to her all this had, as it were, gone in one ear and out the other. It seemed that she only understood the meaning of the word "love," when in the form of a miserable frog she crouched together in the corner of the sleeping chamber; but the Viking's wife had listened to the wonderful story, and had felt herself strangely moved by it.

On their return, after this voyage, the men spoke of the beautiful temples built of polished stone, which had been raised for the public worship of this holy love. Some vessels, curiously formed of massive gold, had been brought home among the booty. There was a peculiar fragrance about them all, for they were incense vessels, which had been swung before the altars in the temples by the Christian priests. In the deep stony cellars of the castle, the young Christian priest was immured, and his hands and feet tied together with strips of bark. The Viking's wife considered him as beautiful as Baldur, and his distress raised her pity; but Helga said he ought to have ropes fastened to his heels, and be tied to the tails of wild animals.

"I would let the dogs loose after him" she said; "over the moor and across the heath. Hurrah! that would be a spectacle for the gods, and better still to follow in its course."

But the Viking would not allow him to die such a death as that, especially as he was the disowned and despiser of the high gods. In a few days, he had decided to have him offered as a sacrifice on the blood-stone in the grove. For the first time, a man was to be sacrificed here. Helga begged to be allowed to sprinkle the assembled people with the blood of the priest. She sharpened her glittering knife; and when one of the great, savage dogs, who were running about the Viking's castle in great numbers, sprang towards her, she thrust the knife into his side, merely, as she said, to prove its sharpness.

The Viking's wife looked at the wild, badly disposed girl, with great sorrow; and when night came on, and her daughter's beautiful form and disposition were changed, she spoke in eloquent words to Helga of the sorrow and deep grief that was in her heart. The ugly frog, in its monstrous shape, stood before her, and raised its brown mournful eyes to her face, listening to her words, and seeming to understand them with the intelligence of a human being.

"Never once to my lord and husband has a word passed my lips of what I have to suffer through you; my heart is full of grief about you," said the Viking's wife. "The love of a mother is greater and more powerful than I ever imagined. But love never entered thy heart; it is cold and clammy, like the plants on the moor."

Then the miserable form trembled; it was as if these words had touched an invisible bond between body and soul, for great tears stood in the eyes.

"A bitter time will come for thee at last," continued the Viking's wife; "and it will be terrible for me too. It had been better for thee if thou hadst been left on the high road, with the cold night wind to lull thee to sleep." And the Viking's wife shed bitter tears, and went away in anger and sorrow, passing under the partition of furs, which hung loose over the beam and divided the hall.

The shrivelled frog still sat in the corner alone. Deep silence reigned around. At intervals, a half-stifled sigh was heard from its inmost soul; it was the soul of Helga. It seemed in pain, as if a new life were arising in her heart. Then she took a step forward and listened; then stepped again forward, and seized with her clumsy hands the heavy bar which was laid across the door. Gently, and with much trouble, she pushed back the bar, as silently lifted the latch, and then took up the glimmering lamp which stood in the ante-chamber of the hall. It seemed as if a stronger will than her own gave her strength. She removed the iron bolt from the closed cellar-door, and slipped in to the prisoner. He was slumbering. She touched him with her cold, moist hand, and as he awoke and caught sight of the hideous form, he shuddered as if he beheld a wicked apparition. She drew her knife, cut through the bonds which confined his hands and feet, and beckoned to him to follow her. He uttered some holy names and made the sign of the cross, while the form remained motionless by his side.

"Who art thou?" He asked, "whose outward appearance is that of an animal, while thou willingly performest acts of mercy?"

The frog-figure beckoned to him to follow her, and led him through a long gallery concealed by hanging drapery to the stables, and then pointed to a horse. He mounted upon it, and she sprang up also before him, and held tightly by the animal's mane. The prisoner understood her, and they rode on at a rapid trot, by a road which he would never have found by himself, across the open heath. He forgot her ugly form, and only thought how the mercy and loving-kindness of the Almighty was acting through this hideous apparition. As he offered pious prayers and sang holy songs of praise, she trembled. Was it the effect of prayer and praise that caused this? or, was she shuddering in the cold morning air at the thought of approaching twilight? What were her feelings? She raised herself up, and wanted to stop the horse and spring off, but the Christian priest held her back with all his might, and then sang a pious song, as if this could loosen the wicked charm that had changed her into the semblance of a frog.

And the horse galloped on more wildly than before. The sky painted itself red, the first sunbeam pierced through the clouds, and in the clear flood of sunlight the frog became changed. It was Helga again, young and beautiful, but with a wicked demoniac spirit. He held now a beautiful young woman in his arms, and he was horrified at the sight. He stopped the horse, and sprang from its back. He imagined that some new sorcery was at work. But Helga also leaped from the horse and stood on the ground. The child's short garment reached only to her knee. She snatched the sharp knife from her girdle, and rushed like lightning at the astonished priest. "Let me get at thee!" she cried; "let me get at thee, that I may plunge this knife into thy body. Thou art pale as ashes, thou beardless slave." She pressed in upon him. They struggled with each other in heavy combat, but it was as if an invisible power had been given to the Christian in the struggle. He held her fast, and the old oak under which they stood seemed to help him, for the loosened roots on the ground became entangled in the maiden's feet, and held them fast. Close by rose a bubbling spring, and he sprinkled Helga's face and neck with the water, commanded the unclean spirit to come forth, and pronounced upon her a Christian blessing. But the water of faith has no power unless the well-spring of faith flows within. And yet even here its power was shown; something more than the mere strength of a man opposed itself, through his means, against the evil which struggled within her. His holy action seemed to overpower her. She dropped her arms, glanced at him with pale cheeks and looks of amazement. He appeared to her a mighty magician skilled in secret arts; his language was the darkest magic to her, and the movements of his hands in the air were as the secret signs of a magician's wand. She would not have blinked had he waved over her head a sharp knife or a glittering axe; but she shrunk from him as he signed her with the sign of the cross on her forehead and breast, and sat before him like a tame bird, with her head bowed down. Then he spoke to her, in gentle words, of the deed of love she had performed for him during the night, when she had come to him in the form of an ugly frog, to loosen his bonds, and to lead him forth to life and light; and he told her that she was bound in closer fetters than he had been, and that she could recover also life and light by his means. He would take her to Hedeby* to St. Ansgarius, and there, in that Christian

---

* Now the city of Sleswig.

town, the spell of the sorcerer would be removed. But he would not let her sit before him on the horse, though of her own free will she wished to do so. "Thou must sit behind me, not before me," said he. "Thy magic beauty has a magic power which comes from an evil origin, and I fear it; still I am sure to overcome through my faith in Christ." Then he knelt down, and prayed with pious fervor. It was as if the quiet woodland were a holy church consecrated by his worship. The birds sang as if they were also of this new congregation; and the fragrance of the wild flowers was as the ambrosial perfume of incense; while, above all, sounded the words of Scripture, "A light to them that sit in darkness and in the shadow of death, to guide their feet into the way of peace." And he spoke these words with the deep longing of his whole nature.

Meanwhile, the horse that had carried them in wild career stood quietly by, plucking at the tall bramble-bushes, till the ripe young berries fell down upon Helga's hands, as if inviting her to eat. Patiently she allowed herself to be lifted on the horse, and sat there like a somnambulist—as one who walked in his sleep. The Christian bound two branches together with bark, in the form of a cross, and held it on high as they rode through the forest. The way gradually grew thicker of brushwood, as they rode along, till at last it became a trackless wilderness. Bushes of the wild sloe here and there blocked up the path, so that they had to ride over them. The bubbling spring formed not a stream, but a marsh, round which also they were obliged to guide the horse; still there were strength and refreshment in the cool forest breeze, and no trifling power in the gentle words spoken in faith and Christian love by the young priest, whose inmost heart yearned to lead this poor lost one into the way of light and life. It is said that rain-drops can make a hollow in the hardest stone, and the waves of the sea can smooth and round the rough edges of the rocks; so did the dew of mercy fall upon Helga, softening what was hard, and smoothing what was rough in her character. These effects did not yet appear; she was not herself aware of them; neither does the seed in the lap of earth know, when the refreshing dew and the warm sunbeams fall upon it, that it contains within itself power by which it will flourish and bloom. The song of the mother sinks into the heart of the child, and the little one prattles the words after her, without understanding their meaning; but after a time the thoughts expand, and what has been heard in childhood seems to the mind clear and bright. So now the "Word," which is all-powerful to create, was working in the heart of Helga.

They rode forth from the thick forest, crossed the heath, and again entered a pathless wood. Here, towards evening, they met with robbers.

"Where hast thou stolen that beauteous maiden?" cried the robbers, seizing the horse by the bridle, and dragging the two riders from its back.

The priest had nothing to defend himself with, but the knife he had taken from Helga, and with this he struck out right and left. One of the robbers raised his axe against him; but the young priest sprang on one side, and avoided the blow, which fell with great force on the horse's neck, so that the blood gushed forth, and the animal sunk to the ground. Then Helga seemed suddenly to awake from her long, deep reverie; she threw herself hastily upon the dying animal. The priest placed himself before her, to defend and shelter her; but one of the robbers swung his iron axe against the Christian's head with such force that it was dashed to pieces, the blood and brains were scattered about, and he fell dead upon the ground. Then the robbers seized beautiful Helga by her white arms and slender waist; but at that moment the sun went down, and as its last ray disappeared, she was changed into the form of a frog. A greenish white mouth spread half over her face; her arms became thin and slimy; while broad hands, with webbed fingers, spread themselves out like fans. Then the robbers, in terror, let her go, and she stood among them, a hideous monster; and as is the nature of frogs to do, she hopped up as high as her own size, and disappeared in the thicket. Then the robbers knew that this must be the work of an evil spirit or some secret sorcery, and, in a terrible fright, they ran hastily from the spot.

The full moon had already risen, and was shining in all her radiant splendor over the earth, when from the thicket, in the form of a frog, crept poor Helga. She stood still by the corpse of the Christian priest, and the carcase of the dead horse. She looked at them with eyes that seemed to weep, and from the frog's head came forth a croaking sound, as when a child bursts into tears. She threw herself first upon one, and then upon the other; brought water in her hand, which, from being webbed, was large and hollow, and poured it over them; but they were dead, and dead they would remain. She understood that at last. Soon wild animals would come and tear their dead bodies; but no, that must not happen. Then she dug up the earth, as deep as she was able, that she might prepare a grave for them. She had nothing but a branch of a tree and her two hands, between the fingers of which the webbed skin stretched, and they were torn by the work, while the blood ran down her hands. She saw at last that her work would be useless, more than she could accomplish; so she fetched more water, and washed the face of the dead, and then covered it with fresh green leaves; she also brought large boughs and spread over him, and scattered dried leaves between the branches. Then she brought the heaviest stones that she could carry, and laid them over the dead body, filling up the crevices with moss, till she thought she had fenced in his resting-place strongly enough. The difficult task had employed her the whole night; and as the sun broke forth, there stood the beautiful Helga in all her loveliness, with her bleeding hands, and, for the first time, with tears on her maiden cheeks. It was, in this transformation, as if two natures were striving together within her; her whole frame trembled, and she looked around her as if she had just awoke from a painful dream. She leaned for support against the trunk of a slender tree, and at last climbed to the topmost branches, like a cat, and seated herself firmly upon them. She remained there the whole day, sitting alone, like a frightened squirrel, in the silent solitude of the wood, where the rest and stillness is as the calm of death.

Butterflies fluttered around her, and close by were several ant-hills, each with its hundreds of busy little creatures moving quickly to and fro. In the air, danced myriads of gnats, swarm upon swarm, troops of buzzing flies, ladybirds, dragon-flies with golden wings, and other little winged creatures. The worm crawled forth from the moist ground, and the moles crept out; but, excepting these, all around had the stillness of death: but when people say this, they do not quite understand themselves what they mean. None noticed Helga but a flock of magpies, which flew chattering round the top of the tree on which she sat. These birds hopped close to her on the branches with bold curiosity. A glance from her eyes was a signal to frighten them away, and they were not clever enough to find out who she was; indeed she hardly knew herself.

When the sun was near setting, and the evening's twilight about to commence, the approaching transformation aroused her to fresh exertion. She let herself down gently from the tree, and, as the last sunbeam vanished, she stood again in the wrinkled form of a frog, with the torn, webbed skin on her hands, but her eyes now gleamed with more radiant beauty than they had ever possessed in her most beautiful form of loveliness; they were now pure, mild maidenly eyes that shone forth in the face of a frog. They showed the existence of deep feeling and a human heart, and the beauteous eyes overflowed with tears, weeping precious drops that lightened the heart.

On the raised mound which she had made as a grave for the dead priest, she found the cross made of the branches of a tree, the last work of him who now lay dead and cold beneath it. A sudden thought came to Helga, and she lifted up the cross and planted it upon the grave, between the stones that covered him and the dead horse. The sad recollection brought the tears to her eyes, and in this gentle spirit she traced the same sign in the sand round the grave; and as she formed, with both her hands, the sign of the cross, the web skin fell from them like a torn glove. She washed her hands in the water of the spring, and gazed with astonishment at their delicate whiteness. Again she made the holy sign in the air, between herself and the dead man; her lips trembled, her tongue moved, and the name which she in her ride through the forest had so often heard spoken, rose to her lips, and she uttered the words, "Jesus Christ." Then the frog skin fell from her; she was once more a lovely maiden. Her head bent wearily, her tired limbs required rest, and then she slept.

Her sleep, however, was short. Towards midnight, she awoke; before her stood the dead horse, prancing and full of life, which shone forth from his eyes and from his wounded neck. Close by his side appeared the murdered Christian priest, more beautiful than Baldur, as the Viking's wife had said; but now he came as if in a flame of fire. Such gravity, such stern justice, such a piercing glance shone from his large, gentle eyes, that it seemed to penetrate into every corner of her heart. Beautiful Helga trembled at the look, and her memory returned with a power as if it had been the day of judgment. Every good deed that had been done for her, every loving word that had been said, were vividly before her mind. She understood now that love had kept her here during the day of her trial; while the creature formed of dust and clay, soul and spirit, had wrestled and struggled with evil. She acknowledged that she had only followed the impulses of an evil disposition, that she had done nothing to cure herself; everything had been given her, and all had happened as it were by the ordination of Providence. She bowed herself humbly, confessed her great imperfections in the sight of Him who can read every fault of the heart, and then the priest spoke. "Daughter of the moorland, thou hast come from the swamp and the marshy earth, but from this thou shalt arise. The sunlight shining into thy inmost soul proves the origin from which thou hast really sprung, and has restored the body to its natural form. I am come to thee from the land of the dead, and thou also must pass through the valley to reach the holy mountains where mercy and perfection dwell. I cannot lead thee to Hedeby that thou mayst receive Christian baptism, for first thou must remove the thick veil with which the waters of the moorland are shrouded, and bring forth from its depths the living author of thy being and thy life. Till this is done, thou canst not receive consecration."

Then he lifted her on the horse and gave her a golden censer, similar to those she had already seen at the Viking's house. A sweet perfume arose from it, while the open wound in the forehead of the slain priest, shone with the rays of a diamond. He took the cross from the grave, and held it aloft, and now they rode through the air over the rustling trees, over the hills where warriors lay buried each by his dead war-horse; and the brazen monumental figures rose up and galloped forth, and stationed themselves on the summits of the hills. The golden crescent on their foreheads, fastened with golden knots, glittered in the moonlight, and their mantles floated in the wind. The dragon, that guards buried treasure, lifted his head and gazed after them. The goblins and the satyrs peeped out from beneath the hills, and flitted to and fro in the fields, waving blue, red, and green torches, like the glowing sparks in burning paper. Over woodland and heath, flood and fen, they flew on, till they reached the wild moor, over which they hovered in broad circles. The Christian priest held the cross aloft, and it glittered like gold, while from his lips sounded pious prayers. Beautiful Helga's voice joined with his in the hymns he sung, as a child joins in her mother's song. She swung the censer, and a wonderful fragrance of incense arose from it; so powerful, that the reeds and rushes of the moor burst forth into blossom. Each germ came forth from the deep ground: all that had life raised itself. Blooming water lilies spread themselves forth like a carpet of wrought flowers, and upon them lay a slumbering woman, young and beautiful. Helga fancied that it was her own image she saw reflected in the still water. But it was her mother she beheld, the wife of the Marsh King, the princess from the land of the Nile.

The dead Christian priest desired that the sleeping woman should be lifted on the horse, but the horse sank beneath the load, as if he had been a funeral pall fluttering in the wind. But the sign of the cross made the airy phantom strong, and then the three rode away from the marsh to firm ground.

At the same moment the cock crew in the Viking's castle, and the dream figures dissolved and floated away in the air, but mother and daughter stood opposite to each other.

"Am I looking at my own image in the deep water?" said the mother.

"Is it myself that I see represented on a white shield?" cried the daughter.

Then they came nearer to each other in a fond embrace. The mother's heart beat quickly, and she understood the quickened pulses. "My child!" she exclaimed, "the flower of my heart—my lotus flower of the deep water!" and she embraced her child again and wept, and the tears were as a baptism of new life and love for Helga. "In swan's plumage I came here," said the mother, "and here I threw off my feather dress. Then I sank down through the wavering ground, deep into the marsh beneath, which closed like a wall around me; I found myself after a while in fresher water; still a power drew me down deeper and deeper. I felt the weight of sleep upon my eyelids. Then I slept, and dreams hovered round me. It seemed to me as if I were again in the pyramids of Egypt, and yet the waving elder trunk that had frightened me on the moor stood ever before me. I observed the clefts and wrinkles in the stem; they shone forth in strange colours, and took the form of hieroglyphics. It was the mummy case on which I gazed. At last it burst, and forth stepped the thousand years' old King, the mummy form, black as pitch, black as the shining wood-snail, or the slimy mud of the swamp. Whether it was really the mummy or the Marsh King I know not. He seized me in his arms, and I felt as if I must die. When I recovered myself, I found in my bosom a little bird, flapping its wings, twittering and fluttering. The bird flew away from my bosom, upwards towards the dark, heavy canopy above me, but a long, green band kept it fastened to me. I heard and understood the tenor of its longings. Freedom! Sunlight! To my father! Then I thought of my father, and the sunny land of my birth, my life, and my love. Then I loosened the band, and let the bird fly away to its home—to a father. Since that hour I have ceased to dream; my sleep has been long and heavy, till in this very hour, harmony and fragrance awoke me, and set me free."

The green band which fastened the wings of the bird to the mother's heart, where did it flutter now? whither had it been wafted? The stork only had seen it. The band was the green stalk, the cup of the flower the cradle in which lay the child, that now in blooming beauty had been folded to the mother's heart.

And while the two were resting in each other's arms, the old stork flew round and round them in narrowing circles, till at length he flew away swiftly to his nest, and fetched away the two suits of swan's feathers, which he had preserved there for many years. Then he returned to the mother and daughter, and threw the swan's plumage over them; the feathers immediately closed around them, and they rose up from the earth in the form of two white swans.

"And now we can converse with pleasure," said the Stork-papa; "we can understand one another, although the beaks of birds are so different in shape. It is very fortunate that you came tonight. Tomorrow we should have been gone. The mother, myself and the little ones, we're about to fly to the south. Look at me now: I am an old friend from the Nile, and a mother's heart contains more than her beak. She always said that the Princess would know how to help herself. I and the young ones carried the swan's feathers over here, and I am glad of it now, and how lucky it is that I am here still. When the day dawns we shall start with a great company of other storks.

We'll fly first, and you can follow in our track, so that you cannot miss your way. I and the young ones will have an eye upon you."

"And the lotus-flower which I was to take with me," said the Egyptian Princess, "is flying here by my side, clothed in swan's feathers. The flower of my heart will travel with me; and so the riddle is solved. Now for home! now for home!"

But Helga said she could not leave the Danish land without once more seeing her foster-mother, the loving wife of the Viking. Each pleasing recollection, each kind word, every tear from the heart which her foster-mother had wept for her, rose in her mind, and at that moment she felt as if she loved this mother the best.

"Yes, we must go to the Viking's castle," said the Stork; "mother and the young ones are waiting for me there. How they will open their eyes and flap their wings! My wife, you see, does not say much; she is short and abrupt in her manner; but she means well, for all that. I will flap my wings at once, that they may hear us coming." Then Stork-papa flapped his wings in first-rate style, and he and the swans flew away to the Viking's castle.

In the castle, every one was in a deep sleep. It had been late in the evening before the Viking's wife retired to rest. She was anxious about Helga, who, three days before, had vanished with the Christian priest. Helga must have helped him in his flight, for it was her horse that was missed from the stable; but by what power had all this been accomplished? The Viking's wife thought of it with wonder, thought on the miracles which they said could be performed by those who believed in the Christian faith, and followed its teachings. These passing thoughts formed themselves into a vivid dream, and it seemed to her that she was still lying awake on her couch, while without darkness reigned. A storm arose; she heard the lake dashing and rolling from east and west, like the waves of the North Sea or the Cattegat. The monstrous snake which, it is said, surrounds the earth in the depths of the ocean, was trembling in spasmodic convulsions. The night of the fall of the gods was come, "Ragnorock," as the heathens call the judgment-day, when everything shall pass away, even the high gods themselves. The war trumpet sounded; riding upon the rainbow, came the gods, clad in steel, to fight their last battle on the last battle-field. Before them flew the winged vampires, and the dead warriors closed up the train. The whole firmament was ablaze with the northern lights, and yet the darkness triumphed. It was a terrible hour. And, close to the terrified woman, Helga seemed to be seated on the floor, in the hideous form of a frog, yet trembling, and clinging to her foster-mother, who took her on her lap, and lovingly caressed her, hideous and frog-like as she was. The air was filled with the clashing of arms and the hissing of arrows, as if a storm of hail was descending upon the earth. It seemed to her the hour when earth and sky would burst asunder, and all things be swallowed up in Saturn's fiery lake; but she knew that a new heaven and a new earth would arise, and that corn-fields would wave where now the lake rolled over desolate sands, and the ineffable God reign. Then she saw rising from the region of the dead, Baldur the gentle, the loving, and as the Viking's wife gazed upon him, she recognized his countenance. It was the captive Christian priest. "White Christian!" she exclaimed aloud, and with the words, she pressed a kiss on the forehead of the hideous frog-child. Then the frog-skin fell off, and Helga stood before her in all her beauty, more lovely and gentle-looking, and with eyes beaming with love. She kissed the hands of her foster-mother, blessed her for all her fostering love and care during the days of her trial and misery, for the thoughts she had suggested and awoke in her heart, and for naming the Name which she now repeated. Then beautiful Helga rose as a mighty swan, and spread her wings with the rushing sound of troops of birds of passage flying through the air.

Then the Viking's wife awoke, but she still heard the rushing sound without. She knew it was the time for the storks to depart, and that it must be their wings which she heard. She felt she should like to see them once more, and bid them farewell. She rose from her couch, stepped out on the threshold, and beheld, on the ridge of the roof, a party of storks ranged side by side. Troops of the birds were flying in circles over the castle and the highest trees; but just before her, as she stood on the threshold and close to the well where Helga had so often sat and alarmed her with her wildness, now stood two swans, gazing at her with intelligent eyes. Then she remembered her dream, which still appeared to her as a reality. She thought of Helga in the form of a swan. She thought of a Christian priest, and suddenly a wonderful joy arose in her heart. The swans flapped their wings and arched their necks as if to offer her a greeting, and the Viking's wife spread out her arms towards them, as if she accepted it, and smiled through her tears. She was roused from deep thought by a rustling of wings and snapping of beaks; all the storks arose, and started on their journey towards the South.

"We will not wait for the swans," said the mamma Stork; "if they want to go with us, let them come now; we can't sit here till the plovers start. It is a fine thing after all to travel in families, not like the finches and the partridges. There the male and the female birds fly in separate flocks, which, to speak candidly, I consider very unbecoming."

"What are those swans flapping their wings for?"

"Well, every one flies in his own fashion," said the papa Stork. "The swans fly in an oblique line; the cranes, in the form of a triangle; and the plovers, in a curved line like a snake."

"Don't talk about snakes while we are flying up here," said Stork-mamma. "It puts ideas into the children's heads that can not be realized."

"Are those the high mountains I have heard spoken of?" asked Helga, in the swan's plumage.

"They are storm-clouds driving along beneath us," replied her mother.

"What are yonder white clouds that rise so high?" again inquired Helga.

"Those are mountains covered with perpetual snows, that you see yonder," said her mother. And then they flew across the Alps towards the blue Mediterranean.

"Africa's land! Egyptia's strand!" sang the daughter of the Nile, in her swan's plumage, as from the upper air she caught sight of her native land, a narrow, golden, wavy strip on the shores of the Nile; the other birds espied it also and hastened their flight.

"I can smell the Nile mud and the wet frogs," said the Stork-mamma, "and I begin to feel quite hungry. Yes, now you shall taste something nice, and you will see the marabout bird, and the ibis, and the crane. They all belong to our family, but they are not nearly so handsome as we are. They give themselves great airs, especially the ibis. The Egyptians have spoilt him. They make a mummy of him, and stuff him with spices. I would rather be stuffed with live frogs, and so would you, and so you shall. Better have something in your inside while you are alive, than to be made a parade of after you are dead. That is my opinion, and I am always right."

"The storks are come," was said in the great house on the banks of the Nile, where the lord lay in the hall on his downy cushions, covered with a leopard skin, scarcely alive, yet not dead, waiting and hoping for the lotus-flower from the deep moorland in the far north. Relatives and servants were standing by his couch, when the two beautiful swans who had come with the storks flew into the hall. They threw off their soft white plumage, and two lovely female forms approached the pale, sick old man, and threw back their long hair, and when Helga bent over her grandfather, redness came back to his cheeks, his eyes brightened, and life returned to his benumbed limbs. The old man rose up with health and energy renewed; daughter and grandchild welcomed him as joyfully as if with a morning greeting after a long and troubled dream.

Joy reigned through the whole house, as well as in the Stork's nest; although there the chief cause was really the good food, especially the quantities of frogs, which seemed to spring out of the ground in swarms.

Then the learned men hastened to note down, in flying characters, the story of the two Princesses, and spoke of the arrival of the health-giving flower as a mighty event, which had been a blessing to the house and the land. Meanwhile, the Stork-papa told the story to his family in his own way; but not till they had eaten and were satisfied; otherwise they would have had something else to do than to listen to stories.

"Well," said the Stork-mamma, when she had heard it, "you will be made something of at last; I suppose they can do nothing less."

"What could I be made?" said Stork-papa; "what have I done?— Just nothing."

"You have done more than all the rest," she replied. "But for you and the youngsters the two young Princesses would never have seen Egypt again, and the recovery of the old man would not have been effected. You will become something. They must certainly give you a doctor's hood, and our young ones will inherit it, and their children after them, and so on. You already look like an Egyptian doctor, at least in my eyes."

"I cannot quite remember the words I heard when I listened on the roof," said Stork-papa, while relating the story to his family; "all I know is, that what the wise men said was so complicated and so learned, that they received not only rank, but presents; even the head cook at the great house was honoured with a mark of distinction, most likely for the soup."

"And what did you receive?" said the Stork-mamma. "They certainly ought not to forget the most important person in the affair, as you really are. The learned men have done nothing at all but use their tongues. Surely they will not overlook you."

Late in the night, while the gentle sleep of peace rested on the now happy house, there was still one watcher. It was not Stork-papa, who, although he stood on guard on one leg, could sleep soundly. Helga alone was awake. She leaned over the balcony, gazing at the sparkling stars that shone clearer and brighter in the pure air than they had done in the north, and yet they were the same stars. She thought of the Viking's wife in the wild moorland, of the gentle eyes of her foster-mother, and of the tears she had shed over the poor frog-child that now lived in splendor and starry beauty by the waters of the Nile, with air balmy and sweet as spring. She thought of the love that dwelt in the breast of the heathen woman, love that had been shown to a wretched creature, hateful as a human being, and hideous when in the form of an animal. She looked at the glittering stars, and thought of the radiance that had shone forth on the forehead of the dead man, as she had fled with him over the woodland and moor. Tones were awakened in her memory; words which she had heard him speak as they rode onward, when she was carried, wondering and trembling, through the air; words from the great Fountain of love, the highest love that embraces all the human race. What had not been won and achieved by this love?

Day and night beautiful Helga was absorbed in the contemplation of the great amount of her happiness, and lost herself in the contemplation, like a child who turns hurriedly from the giver to examine the beautiful gifts. She was over-powered with her good fortune, which seemed always increasing, and therefore what might it become in the future? Had she not been brought by a wonderful miracle to all this joy and happiness? And in these thoughts she indulged, until at last she thought no more of the Giver. It was the over-abundance of youthful spirits unfolding its wings for a daring flight. Her eyes sparkled with energy, when suddenly arose a loud noise in the court below, and the daring thought vanished. She looked down, and saw two large ostriches running round quickly in narrow circles; she had never seen these creatures before—great, coarse, clumsy-looking birds with curious wings that looked as if they had been clipped, and the birds themselves had the appearance of having been roughly used. She inquired about them, and for the first time heard the legend which the Egyptians relate respecting the ostrich.

Once, say they, the ostriches were a beautiful and glorious race of birds, with large, strong wings. One evening the other large birds of the forest said to the ostrich, "Brother, shall we fly to the river tomorrow morning to drink, *God willing?*" and the ostrich answered, "I will."

With the break of day, therefore, they commenced their flight;

first rising high in the air, towards the sun, which is the eye of God; still higher and higher the ostrich flew, far above the other birds, proudly approaching the light, trusting in its own strength, and thinking not of the Giver, or saying, *"if God will."* When suddenly the avenging angel drew back the veil from the flaming ocean of sunlight, and in a moment the wings of the proud bird were scorched and shrivelled, and they sunk miserably to the earth. Since that time the ostrich and his race have never been able to rise in the air; they can only fly terror-stricken along the ground, or run round and round in narrow circles. It is a warning to mankind, that in all our thoughts and schemes, and in every action we undertake, we should say, *"if God will."*

Then Helga bowed her head thoughtfully and seriously, and looked at the circling ostrich, as with timid fear and simple pleasure it glanced at its own great shadow on the sunlit walls. And the story of the ostrich sunk deeply into the heart and mind of Helga: a life of happiness, both in the present and in the future, seemed secure for her, and what was yet to come might be the best of all, *God willing.*

Early in the spring, when the storks were again about to journey Northward, beautiful Helga took off her golden bracelets, scratched her name on them, and beckoned to the Stork-father. He came to her, and she placed the golden circlet round his neck, and begged him to deliver it safely to the Viking's wife, so that she might know that her foster-daughter still lived, was happy, and had not forgotten her.

"It is rather heavy to carry," thought Stork-papa, when he had it on his neck; "but gold and honour are not to be flung into the street. The Stork brings good fortune—they'll be obliged to acknowledge that at last."

"You lay gold, and I lay eggs," said Stork-mamma; "with you it is only once in a way, I lay eggs every year But no one appreciates what we do; I call it very mortifying."

"But then we have a consciousness of our own worth, mother," replied Stork-papa.

"What good will that do you?" retorted Stork-mamma; "it will neither bring you a fair wind, nor a good meal."

"The little nightingale, who is singing yonder in the tamarind grove, will soon be going north, too." Helga said she had often heard her singing on the wild moor, so she determined to send a message by her. While flying in the swan's plumage she had learnt the bird language; she had often conversed with the stork and the swallow, and she knew that the nightingale would understand. So she begged the nightingale to fly to the beechwood, on the peninsula of Jutland, where a mound of stone and twigs had been raised to form the grave, and she begged the nightingale to persuade all the other little birds to build their nests round the place, so that evermore should resound over that grave music and song. And the nightingale flew away, and time flew away also.

In the autumn, an eagle, standing upon a pyramid, saw a stately train of richly laden camels, and men attired in armor on foaming Arabian steeds, whose glossy skins shone like silver, their nostrils were pink, and their thick, flowing manes hung almost to their slender legs. A royal Prince of Arabia, handsome as a Prince should be, and accompanied by distinguished guests, was on his way to the stately house, on the roof of which the Storks' empty nests might be seen. They were away now in the far North, but expected to return very soon. And, indeed, they returned on a day that was rich in joy and gladness.

A marriage was being celebrated, in which the beautiful Helga, glittering in silk and jewels, was the bride, and the bridegroom the young Arab Prince. Bride and bridegroom sat at the upper end of the table, between the bride's mother and grandfather. But her gaze was not on the bridegroom, with his manly, sunburnt face, round which curled a black beard, and whose dark fiery eyes were fixed upon her; but away from him, at a twinkling star, that shone down upon her from the sky. Then was heard the sound of rushing wings beating the air. The storks were coming home; and the old Stork pair, although tired with the journey and requiring rest, did not fail to fly down at once to the balustrades of the verandah, for they knew already what feast was being celebrated. They had heard of it on the borders of the land, and also that Helga had caused their figures to be represented on the walls, for they belonged to her history.

"I call that very sensible and pretty," said Stork-papa.

"Yes, but it is very little," said mamma Stork; "they could not possibly have done less."

But, when Helga saw them, she rose and went out into the verandah to stroke the backs of the Storks. The old stork pair bowed their heads, and curved their necks, and even the youngest among the young ones felt honoured by this reception.

Helga continued to gaze upon the glittering star, which seemed to glow brighter and purer in its light; then between herself and the star floated a form, purer than the air, and visible through it. It floated quite near to her, and she saw that it was the dead Christian priest, who also was coming to her wedding feast—coming from the heavenly kingdom.

"The glory and brightness, yonder, outshines all that is known on earth," said he.

Then Helga the fair prayed more gently, and more earnestly, than she had ever prayed in her life before, that she might be permitted to gaze, if only for a single moment, at the glory and brightness of the heavenly kingdom. Then she felt herself lifted up, as it were, above the earth, through a sea of sound and thought; not only around her, but within her, was there light and song, such as words cannot express.

"Now we must return;" he said; "you will be missed."

"Only one more look," she begged; "but one short moment more."

"We must return to earth; the guests will have all departed. Only one more look!—the last!"

Then Helga stood again in the verandah. But the marriage lamps in the festive hall had been all extinguished, and the torches outside had vanished. The storks were gone; not a guest could be seen; no bridegroom—all in those few short moments seemed to have died. Then a great dread fell upon her. She stepped from the verandah through the empty hall into the next chamber, where slept strange warriors. She opened a side door, which once led into her own apartment, but now, as she passed through, she found herself suddenly in a garden which she had never before seen here, the sky blushed red, it was the dawn of morning. Three minutes only in heaven, and a whole night on earth had passed away! Then she saw the storks, and called to them in their own language.

Then Stork-papa turned his head towards here, listened to her words, and drew near. "You speak our language," said he, "what do you wish? Why do you appear—you—a strange woman?"

"It is I—it is Helga! Dost thou not know me? Three minutes ago we were speaking together yonder in the verandah."

"That is a mistake," said the Stork, "you must have dreamed all this."

"No, no," she exclaimed. Then she reminded him of the Viking's castle, of the great lake, and of the journey across the ocean.

Then Stork-papa winked his eyes, and said, "Why that's an old story which happened in the time of my grandfather. There certainly was a Princess of that kind here in Egypt once, who came from the Danish land, but she vanished on the evening of her wedding day, many hundred years ago, and never came back. You may read about it yourself yonder, on a monument in the garden. There you will find swans and storks sculptured, and on the top is a figure of the princess Helga, in marble."

And so it was; Helga understood it all now, and sank on her knees. The sun burst forth in all its glory, and, as in olden times, the form of the frog vanished in his beams, and the beautiful form stood forth in all its loveliness; so now, bathed in light, rose a beautiful form, purer, clearer than air—a ray of brightness—from the Source of light Himself. The body crumbled into dust, and a faded lotus-flower lay on the spot on which Helga had stood.

"Now that is a new ending to the story," said Stork-papa; "I really never expected it would end in this way, but it seems a very good ending."

"And what will the young ones say to it, I wonder?" said Stork-mamma.

"Ah, that is a very important question," replied the Stork.

The Girl who Trod on the Loaf

Translated by H. W. Dulcken

The story of the girl who trod on the loaf, to avoid soiling her shoes, and of the misfortunes that befell this girl, is well known. It has been written, and even printed.

The girl's name was Ingé; she was a poor child, but proud and presumptuous; there was a bad foundation in her, as the saying is. When she was quite a little child, it was her delight to catch flies, and tear off their wings, so as to convert them into creeping things. Grown older, she would take cockchafers and beetles, and spit them on pins. Then she pushed a green leaf or a little scrap of paper towards their feet, and the poor creatures seized it, and held it fast, and turned it over and over, struggling to get free from the pin.

"The cockchafer is reading," Ingé would say. "See how he turns the leaf round and round!"

With years she grew worse rather than better; but she was pretty, and that was her misfortune; otherwise she would have been more sharply reproved than she was.

"Your headstrong will requires something strong to break it!" her own mother often said. "As a little child, you used to trample on my apron; but I fear you will one day trample on my heart."

And that is what she really did.

She was sent into the country, into service in the house of rich people, who kept her as their own child, and dressed her in corresponding style. She looked well, and her presumption increased.

When she had been there about a year, her mistress said to her, "You ought once to visit your parents, Ingé."

And Ingé set out to visit her parents, but it was only to show herself in her native place, and that the people there might see how grand she had become; but when she came to the entrance of the village, and the young husbandmen and maids stood there chatting, and her own mother appeared among them, sitting on a stone to rest, and with a faggot of sticks before her that she had picked up in the wood, then Ingé turned back, for she felt ashamed that she, who was so finely dressed, should have for a mother a ragged woman, who picked up wood in the forest. She did not turn back out of pity for her mother's poverty, she was only angry.

And another half-year went by, and her mistress said again, "You ought to go to your home, and visit your old parents, Ingé. I'll make you a present of a great wheaten loaf that you may give to them; they will certainly be glad to see you again."

And Ingé put on her best clothes, and her new shoes, and drew her skirts around her, and set out, stepping very carefully, that she might be clean and neat about the feet; and there was no harm in that. But when she came to the place where the footway led across the moor, and where there was mud and puddles, she threw the loaf into the mud, and trod upon it to pass over without wetting her feet. But as she stood there with one foot upon the loaf and the other uplifted to step farther, the loaf sank with her, deeper and deeper, till she disappeared altogether, and only a great puddle, from which the bubbles rose, remained where she had been.

And that's the story.

The Girl who Trod on the Loaf

But whither did Ingé go? She sank into the moor ground, and went down to the moor woman, who is always brewing there. The moor woman is cousin to the elf maidens, who are well enough known, of whom songs are sung, and whose pictures are painted; but concerning the moor woman it is only known that when the meadows steam in summer-time it is because she is brewing. Into the moor woman's brewery did Ingé sink down; and no one can endure that place long. A box of mud is a palace compared with the moor woman's brewery. Every barrel there has an odour that almost takes away one's senses; and the barrels stand close to each other; and wherever there is a little opening among them, through which one might push one's way, the passage becomes impracticable from the number of damp toads and fat snakes who sit out their time there. Among this company did Ingé fall; and all the horrible mass of living creeping things was so icy cold, that she shuddered in all her limbs, and became stark and stiff. She continued fastened to the loaf, and the loaf drew her down as an amber button draws a fragment of straw.

The moor woman was at home, and on that day there were visitors in the brewery. These visitors were old Bogey and his grandmother, who came to inspect it; and Bogey's grandmother is a venomous old woman, who is never idle: she never rides out to pay a visit without taking her work with her; and, accordingly, she had brought it on the day in question. She sewed biting-leather to be worked into men's shoes, and which makes them wander about unable to settle anywhere. She wove webs of lies, and strung together hastily-spoken words that had fallen to the ground; and all this was done for the injury and ruin of mankind. Yes, indeed, she knew how to sew, to weave, and to string, this old grandmother!

Catching sight of Ingé, she put up her double eye-glass, and took another look at the girl. "That's a girl who has ability!" she observed, "and I beg you will give me the little one as a memento of my visit here. She'll make a capital statue to stand in my grandson's antechamber."

And Ingé was given up to her, and this is how Ingé came into Bogey's domain. People don't always go there by the direct path, but they can get there by roundabout routes if they have a tendency in that direction.

That was a never-ending antechamber. The visitor became giddy who looked forward, and doubly giddy when he looked back, and saw a whole crowd of people, almost utterly exhausted, waiting till the gate of mercy should be opened to them—they had to wait a long time! Great fat waddling spiders spun webs of a thousand years over their feet, and these webs cut like wire, and bound them like bronze fetters; and, moreover, there was an eternal unrest working in every heart—a miserable unrest. The miser stood there, and had forgotten the key of his strong box, and he knew the key was sticking in the lock. It would take too long to describe the various sorts of torture that were found there together. Ingé felt a terrible pain while she had to stand there as a statue, for she was tied fast to the loaf.

"That's the fruit of wishing to keep one's feet neat and tidy," she said to herself. "Just look how they're all staring at me!" Yes, certainly, the eyes of all were fixed upon her, and their evil thoughts gleamed forth from their eyes, and they spoke to one another, moving their lips, from which no sound whatever came forth: they were very horrible to behold.

"It must be a great pleasure to look at me!" thought Ingé, "and indeed I have a pretty face and fine clothes." And she turned her eyes, for she could not turn her head; her neck was too stiff for that. But she had not considered how her clothes had been soiled in the moor woman's brewhouse. Her garments were covered with mud; a snake had fastened in her hair, and dangled down her back; and out of each fold of her frock a great toad looked forth, croaking like an asthmatic poodle. That was very disconcerting. "But all the rest of them down here look horrible," she observed to herself, and derived consolation from the thought.

The worst of all was the terrible hunger that tormented her. But could she not stoop and break off a piece of the loaf on which she stood? No, her back was too stiff, her hands and arms were benumbed, and her whole body was like a pillar of stone; only she was able to turn her eyes in her head, to turn them quite round so that she could see backwards: it was an ugly sight. And then the flies came up, and crept to and fro over her eyes, and she blinked her eyes, but the flies would not go away, for they could not fly: their wings had been pulled out, so that they were converted into creeping insects: it was horrible torment added to the hunger, for she felt empty, quite, entirely empty. "If this lasts much longer," she said, "I shall not be able to bear it." But she had to bear it, and it lasted on and on.

Then a hot tear fell down upon her head, rolled over her face and neck, down on to the loaf on which she stood; and then another tear rolled down, followed by many more. Who might be weeping for Ingé? Had she not still a mother in the world? The tears of sorrow which a mother weeps for her child always make their way to the child; but they do not relieve it, they only increase its torment. And now to bear this unendurable hunger, and yet not to be able to touch the loaf on which she stood! She felt as if she had been feeding on herself, and had become like a thin, hollow reed that takes in every sound, for she heard everything that was said of her up in the world, and all that she heard was hard and evil. Her mother, indeed, wept much and sorrowed for her, but for all that she said, "A haughty spirit goes before a fall. That was thy ruin, Ingé. Thou hast sorely grieved thy mother."

Her mother and all on earth knew of the sin she had committed; knew that she had trodden upon the loaf, and had sunk and disappeared; for the cowherd had seen it from the hill beside the moor.

"Greatly hast thou grieved thy mother, Ingé," said the mother; "yes, yes, I thought it would be thus."

"Oh that I never had been born!" thought Ingé; "it would have been far better. But what use is my mother's weeping now?"

And she heard how her master and mistress, who had kept and cherished her like kind parents, now said she was a sinful child, and did not value the gifts of God, but trampled them under her feet, and that the gates of mercy would only open slowly to her.

"They should have punished me," thought Ingé, "and have driven out the whims I had in my head."

She heard how a complete song was made about her, a song of the proud girl who trod upon the loaf to keep her shoes clean, and she heard how the song was sung everywhere.

"That I should have to bear so much evil for this!" thought Ingé; "the others ought to be punished, too, for their sins. Yes, then there would be plenty of punishing to do. Ah, how I'm being tortured!" And her heart became harder than her outward form.

"Here in this company one can't even become better," she said, "and I don't want to become better! Look, how they're all staring at me!"

And her heart was full of anger and malice against all men. "Now they've something to talk about at last up yonder. Ah, how I'm being tortured!"

And then she heard how her story was told to the little children, and the little ones called her the godless Ingé, and said she was so naughty and ugly that she must be well punished.

Thus, even the children's mouths spoke hard words of her.

But one day, while grief and hunger gnawed her hollow frame, and she heard her name mentioned and her story told to an innocent child, a little girl, she became aware that the little one burst into tears at the tale of the haughty, vain Ingé.

"But will Ingé never come up here again?" asked the little girl. And the reply was, "She will never come up again."

"But if she were to say she was sorry, and to beg pardon, and say she would never do so again?"

"Yes, then she might come; but she will not beg pardon," was the reply.

"I should be so glad if she would," said the little girl; and she was quite inconsolable. "I'll give my doll and all my playthings if she may only come up. It's too dreadful—poor Ingé!"

And these words penetrated to Ingé's inmost heart, and seemed to do her good. It was the first time any one had said, "Poor Ingé," without adding anything about her faults: a little innocent child was weeping and praying for mercy for her. It made her feel quite strangely, and she herself would gladly have wept, but she could not weep, and that was a torment in itself.

While years were passing above her, for where she was there was no change, she heard herself spoken of more and more seldom. At last, one day a sigh struck on her ear: "Ingé, Ingé, how you have grieved me! I said how it would be!" It was the last sigh of her dying mother.

Occasionally she heard her name spoken by her former employers, and they were pleasant words when the woman said, "Shall I ever see thee again, Ingé? One knows not what may happen."

But Ingé knew right well that her good mistress would never come to the place where she was.

And again time went on—a long, bitter time. Then Ingé heard her name pronounced once more, and saw two bright stars that seemed gleaming above her. They were two gentle eyes closing upon earth. So many years had gone by since the little girl had been inconsolable and wept about "poor Ingé," that the child had become an old woman, who was now to be called home to heaven; and in the last hour of existence, when the events of the whole life stand at once before us, the old woman remembered how as a child she had cried heartily at the story of Ingé.

And the eyes of the old woman closed, and the eye of her soul was opened to look upon the hidden things. She, in whose last thoughts Ingé had been present so vividly, saw how deeply the poor girl had sunk, and burst into tears at the sight; in heaven she stood like a child, and wept for poor Ingé. And her tears and prayers sounded like an echo in the dark empty space that surrounded the tormented captive soul, and the unhoped-for love from above conquered her, for an angel was weeping for her. Why was this vouchsafed to her? The tormented soul seemed to gather in her thoughts every deed she had done on earth, and she, Ingé, trembled and wept such tears as she had never yet wept. She was filled with sorrow about herself: it seemed as though the gate of mercy could never open to her; and while in deep penitence she acknowledged this, a beam, of light shot radiantly down into the depths to her, with a greater force than that of the sunbeam which melts the snow man the boys have built up; and quicker than the snow-flake melts, and becomes a drop of water that falls on the warm lips of a child, the stony form of Ingé was changed to mist, and a little bird soared with the speed of lightning upward into the world of men. But the bird was timid and shy towards all things around; he was ashamed of himself, ashamed to encounter any living thing, and hurriedly sought to conceal himself in a dark hole in an old crumbling wall; there he sat cowering, trembling through his whole frame, and unable to utter a sound, for he had no voice. Long he sat there, before he could rightly see all the beauty around him; for it was beautiful. The air was fresh and mild, the moon cast its mild radiance over the earth; trees and bushes exhaled fragrance, and it was right pleasant where he sat, and his coat of feathers was clean and pure. How all creation seemed to speak of beneficence and love! The bird wanted to sing of the thoughts that stirred in his breast, but he could not; gladly would he have sung as the cuckoo and the nightingale sung in spring-time. But Heaven, that hears the mute song of praise of the worm, could hear the notes of praise which now trembled in the breast of the bird, as David's psalms were heard before they had fashioned themselves into words and song.

For weeks these toneless songs stirred within the bird; at last, the holy Christmas-time approached. The peasant who dwelt near set up a pole by the old wall with, some ears of corn bound to the top, that the birds of heaven might have a good meal, and rejoice in the happy, blessed time.

And on Christmas morning the sun arose and shone upon the ears of corn, which were surrounded by a number of twittering birds. Then out of the hole in the wall streamed forth the voice of another bird, and the bird soared forth from its hiding-place; and in heaven it was well known what bird this was.

It was a hard winter. The ponds were covered with ice, and the beasts of the field and the birds of the air were stinted for food. Our little bird soared away over the high road, and in the ruts of the sledges he found here and there a grain of corn, and at the halting-places some crumbs. Of these he ate only a few, but he called all the other hungry sparrows around him, that they, too, might have some food. He flew into the towns, and looked round about; and wherever a kind hand had strewn bread on the window-sill for the birds, he only ate a single crumb himself, and gave all the rest to the other birds.

In the course of the winter, the bird had collected so many bread crumbs, and given them to the other birds, that they equalled the weight of the loaf on which Ingé had trod to keep her shoes clean; and when the last bread crumb had been found and given, the grey wings of the bird became white, and spread far out.

"Yonder is a sea-swallow, flying away across the water," said the children when they saw the white bird. Now it dived into the sea, and now it rose again into the clear sunlight. It gleamed white; but no one could tell whither it went, though some asserted that it flew straight into the sun.

Ole The Tower-Keeper

Translated by H. W. Dulcken

"In the world it's always going up and down—and now I can't go up any higher!" So said Ole the tower-keeper. "Most people have to try both the ups and the downs; and, rightly considered, we all get to be watchmen at last, and look down upon life from a height."

Such was the speech of Ole, my friend, the old tower-keeper, a strange talkative old fellow, who seemed to speak out everything that came into his head, and who for all that had many a serious thought deep in his heart. Yes, he was the child of respectable people, and there were even some who said that he was the son of a privy councillor, or that he might have been; he had studied too, and had been assistant teacher and deputy clerk; but of what service was all that to him? In those days he lived in the clerk's house, and was to have everything in the house, to be at free quarters, as the saying is; but he was still, so to speak, a fine young gentleman. He wanted to have his boots cleaned with patent blacking, and the clerk could only afford ordinary grease; and upon that point they split—one spoke of stinginess, the other of vanity, and the blacking became the black cause of enmity between them, and at last they parted.

This is what he demanded of the world in general—namely, patent blacking—and he got nothing but grease. Accordingly he at last drew back from all men, and became a hermit; but the church tower is the only place in a great city where hermitage, office, and bread can be found together. So he betook himself up thither, and smoked his pipe as he made his solitary rounds. He looked upward and downward, and had his own thoughts, and told in his way of what he read in books and in himself. I often lent him books, good books; and you may know a man by the company he keeps. He loved neither the English governess-novels, nor the French ones, which he called a mixture of empty wind and raisin-stalks: he wanted biographies and descriptions of the wonders of the world. I visited him at least once a year, generally directly after New Year's-day, and then he always spoke of this and that which the change of the year had put into his head.

I will tell the story of three of these visits, and will reproduce his own words whenever I can remember them.

First Visit

Among the books which I had lately lent Ole, was one which had greatly rejoiced and occupied him. It was a geological book, containing an account of the boulders.

"Yes, they're rare old fellows, those boulders!" he said; "and to think that we should pass them without noticing them! And over the street pavement, the paving-stones, those fragments of the oldest remains of antiquity, one walks without ever thinking about them. I have done the very thing myself. But now I look respectfully at every paving-stone. Many thanks for the book! It has filled me with thought, and has made me long to read more on the subject. The romance of the earth is, after all, the most wonderful of all romances. It's a pity one can't read the first volumes of it, because they're written in a language that we don't understand. One must read in the different strata, in the pebble-stones, for each separate period. Yes, it is a romance, a very wonderful romance, and we all have our place in it. We grope and ferret about, and yet remain where we are, but the ball keeps turning, without emptying the ocean over us; the clod on which we move about, holds, and does not let us through. And then it's a story that has been acting for thousands upon thousands of years, and is still going on. My best thanks for the book about the boulders. Those are fellows indeed! they could tell us something worth hearing, if they only knew how to talk. It's really a pleasure, now and then to become a mere nothing, especially when a man is as highly placed as I am. And then to think that we all, even with patent lacquer, are nothing more than insects of a moment on that ant-hill the earth, though we may be insects with stars and garters, places and offices! One feels quite a novice beside these venerable million-year-old boulders. On New Year's-eve I was reading the book, and had lost myself in it so completely, that I forgot my usual New Year's diversion, namely, the wild hunt to Amack. Ah, you don't know what that is!

"The journey of the witches on broomsticks is well enough known––that journey is taken on St. John's-eve, to the Brocken; but we have a wild journey also, which is national and modern, and that is the journey to Amack on the night of the New Year. All indifferent poets and poetesses, musicians, newspaper writers and artistic notabilities, I mean those who are no good, ride in the New Year's-night through the air to Amack. They sit backwards on their painting brushes or quill pens, for steel pens won't bear them, they're too stiff. As I told you, I see that every New Year's night, and could mention the majority of the riders by name, but I should not like to draw their enmity upon myself, for they don't like people to talk about their ride to Amack on quill pens. I've a kind of niece, who is a fishwife, and who, as she tells me, supplies three respectable newspapers with the terms of abuse and vituperation they use, and she has herself been at Amack as an invited guest; but she was carried out thither, for she does not own a quill pen, nor can she ride. She has told me all about it. Half of what she said is not true, but the other half gives us information enough. When she was out there, the festivities began with a song: each of the guests had written his own song, and each one sung his own song, for he thought that the best, and it was all one, all the same melody. Then those came marching up, in little bands, who are only busy with their mouths. There were ringing bells that sang alternately; and then came the little drummers that beat their tattoo in the family circle; and acquaintance was made with those who write without putting their names, which here means as much as using grease instead of patent blacking; and then there was the beadle with his boy, and the boy was the worst off, for in general he gets no notice taken of him; then too there was the good street-sweeper with his cart, who turns over the dustbin, and calls it 'good, very good, remarkably good.' And in the midst of the pleasure that was afforded by the mere meeting of these folks, there shot up out of the great dirt-heap at Amack a stem, a tree, an immense flower, a great mushroom, a perfect roof, which formed a sort of warehouse for the worthy company, for in it hung everything they had given to the world during the Old Year. Out of the tree poured sparks like flames of fire; these were the ideas and thoughts, borrowed from others, which they had used, and which now got free and rushed away like so many fireworks. They played at 'the stick burns,' and the young poets played at 'heart-burns,' and the witlings played off their jests, and the jests rolled away with a thundering sound, as if empty pots were being shattered against doors. 'It was very amusing!' my niece said; in fact, she said many things that were very malicious but very amusing, but I won't mention them, for a man must be good-natured and not a carping critic. But you will easily perceive that when a man once knows the rights of the journey to Amack, as I know them, it's quite natural that on the New Year's-night one should look out to see the wild chase go by. If in the New Year I miss certain persons who used to be there, I am sure to notice others who are new arrivals: but this year I omitted taking my look at the guests. I bowled away on the boulders, rolled back through millions of years, and saw the stones break loose high up in the North, saw them drifting about on icebergs, long before Noah's ark was constructed, saw them sink down to the bottom of the sea, and reappear with a sand-bank, with that one that peered forth from the flood and said, 'This shall be Zealand!' I saw them become the dwelling-place of birds that are unknown to us, and then become the seat of wild chiefs of whom we know nothing, until with their axes they cut their Runic signs into a few of these stones, which then came into the calendar of time. But as for me, I had gone quite beyond all lapse of time, and had become a cipher and a nothing. Then three or four beautiful falling stars came down, which cleared the air, and gave my thoughts another direction. You know what a falling star is, do you not? The learned men are not at all clear about it. I have my own ideas about shooting stars, as the common people in many parts call them, and my idea is this: How often are silent thanksgivings offered up for one who has done a good and noble action! the thanks are often speechless, but they are not lost for all that. I think these thanks are caught up, and the sunbeams bring the silent, hidden thankfulness over the head of the benefactor; and if it be a whole people that has been expressing its gratitude through a long lapse of time, the thankfulness appears as a nosegay of flowers, and at length falls in the form of a shooting star upon the good man's grave. I am always very much pleased when I see a shooting star, especially in the New Year's-night, and then find out for whom the gift of gratitude was intended. Lately a gleaming star fell in the south-west, as a tribute of thanksgiving to many, many! 'For whom was that star intended?' thought I. It fell, no doubt, on the hill by the Bay of Flensberg, where the Danebrog waves over the graves of Schleppegrell, Läslöes, and their comrades. One star also fell in the midst of the land, fell upon Sorö, a flower on the grave of Holberg, the thanks of the year from a great many—thanks for his charming plays!

"It is a great and pleasant thought to know that a shooting star falls upon our graves; on mine certainly none will fall—no sunbeam brings thanks to me, for here there is nothing worthy of thanks. I shall not get the patent lacquer," said Ole; "for my fate on earth is only grease, after all."

Second Visit

It was New Year's-day, and I went up on the tower. Ole spoke of the toasts that were drunk on the transition from the old year into the new, from one grave into the other, as he said. And he told me a story about the glasses, and this story had a very deep meaning. It was this:

"When on the New Year's-night the clock strikes twelve, the people at the table rise up, with full glasses in their hands, and drain these glasses, and drink success to the New Year. They begin the year with the glass in their hands; that is a good beginning for topers. They begin the New Year by going to bed, and that's a good beginning for drones. Sleep is sure to play a great part in the New Year, and the glass likewise. Do you know what dwells in the glass?" asked Ole. "I will tell you—there dwell in the glass, first, health, and then pleasure, then the most complete sensual delight: and misfortune and the bitterest woe dwell in the glass also. Now suppose we count the glasses—of course I count the different degrees in the glasses for different people.

"You see, the *first glass*, that's the glass of health, and in that the herb of health is found growing; put it up on the beam in the ceiling, and at the end of the year you may be sitting in the arbour of health.

"If you take the *second glass*—from this a little bird soars upwards, twittering in guileless cheerfulness, so that a man may listen to his song and perhaps join in 'Fair is life! no downcast looks! Take courage and march onward!'

"Out of the *third glass* rises a little winged urchin, who cannot certainly be called an angel-child, for there is goblin blood in his veins, and he has the spirit of a goblin; not wishing to hurt or harm you, indeed, but very ready to play off tricks upon you. He'll sit at your ear and whisper merry thoughts to you; he'll creep into your heart and warm you, so that you grow very merry and become a wit, so far as the wits of the others can judge.

"In the *fourth glass* is neither herb, bird, nor urchin: in that glass is the pause drawn by reason, and one may never go beyond that sign.

"Take the *fifth glass*, and you will weep at yourself, you will feel such a deep emotion; or it will affect you in a different way. Out of the glass there will spring with a bang Prince Carnival, nine times and extravagantly merry: he'll draw you away with him, you'll forget your dignity, if you have any, and you'll forget more than you should or ought to forget. All is dance, song, and sound; the masks will carry you away with them, and the daughters of vanity, clad in silk and satin, will come with loose hair and alluring charms: but tear yourself away if you can!

"The *sixth glass*! Yes, in that glass sits a demon, in the form of a little, well-dressed, attractive and very fascinating man, who thoroughly understands you, agrees with you in everything, and becomes quite a second self to you. He has a lantern with him, to give you light as he accompanies you home. There is an old legend about a saint who was allowed to choose one of the seven deadly sins, and who accordingly chose drunkenness, which appeared to him the least, but which led him to commit all the other six. The man's blood is mingled with that of the demon—it is the sixth glass, and with that the germ of all evil shoots up within us; and each one grows up with a strength like that of the grains of mustard seed, and shoots up into a tree, and spreads over the whole world; and most people have no choice but to go into the oven, to be re-cast in a new form.

"That's the history of the glasses," said the tower-keeper Ole, "and it can be told with lacquer or only with grease; but I give it you with both!"

Third Visit

On this occasion I chose the general 'moving-day' for my visit to Ole, for on that day it is anything but agreeable down in the streets in the town; for they are full of sweepings, shreds, and remnants of all sorts, to say nothing of the cast-off bed straw in which one has to wade about. But this time I happened to see two children playing in this wilderness of sweepings. They were playing at "going to bed," for the occasion seemed especially favourable for this sport: they crept under the straw, and drew an old bit of ragged curtain over themselves by way of coverlet. "It was splendid!" they said; but it was a little too strong for me, and besides, I was obliged to mount up on my visit.

"It's moving-day today," he said; "streets and houses are like a dustbin, a large dustbin; but I'm content with a cartload. I may get something good out of that, and I really did get something good out of it, once. Shortly after Christmas I was going up the street; it was rough weather, wet and dirty; the right kind of weather to catch cold in. The dustman was there with his cart, which was full, and looked like a sample of streets on moving-day. At the back of the cart stood a fir tree, quite green still, and with tinsel on its twigs: it had been used on Christmas-eve, and now it was thrown out into the street, and the dustman had stood it up at the back of his cart. It was droll to look at, or you may say it was mournful—all depends on what you think of when you see it; and I thought about it, and thought this and that of many things that were in the cart: or I might have done so, and that comes to the same thing. There was an old lady's glove too: I wonder what that was thinking of? Shall I tell you? The glove was lying there, pointing with its little finger at the tree. 'I'm sorry for the tree,' it thought; 'and I was also at the feast, where the chandeliers glittered. My life was, so to speak, a ball-night: a pressure of the hand, and I burst! My memory keeps dwelling upon that, and I have really nothing else to live for!' This is what the glove thought, or what it might have thought. 'That's a stupid affair with yonder fir tree,' said the potsherds. You see, potsherds think everything is stupid. 'When one is in the dust-cart,' they said, 'one ought not to give one's self airs and wear tinsel. I know that I have been useful in the world, far more useful than such a green stick.' That was a view that might be taken, and I don't think it quite a peculiar one; but for all that the fir tree looked very well: it was like a little poetry in the dust-heap; and truly there is dust enough in the streets on moving-day. The way is difficult and troublesome then, and I feel obliged to run away out of the confusion; or if I am on the tower, I stay there and look down, and it is amusing enough.

"There are the good people below, playing at 'changing houses.' They toil and tug away with their goods and chattels, and the household goblin sits in an old tub and moves with them; all the little griefs of the lodging and the family, and the real cares and sorrows, move with them out of the old dwelling into the new; and what gain is there for them or for us in the whole affair? Yes, there was written long ago the good old maxim: 'Think on the great moving-day of death!' That is a serious thought; I hope it is not disagreeable to you that I should have touched upon it? Death is the most certain messenger after all, in spite of his various occupations. Yes, Death is the omnibus conductor, and he is the passport writer, and he countersigns our service-book, and he is director of the savings bank of life. Do you understand me? All the deeds of our life, the great and the little alike, we put into this savings bank; and when Death calls with his omnibus, and we have to step in, and drive with him into the land of eternity, then on the frontier he gives us our service-book as a pass. As a provision for the journey he takes this or that good deed we have done, and lets it accompany us; and this may be very pleasant or very terrific. Nobody has ever escaped this omnibus journey: there is certainly a talk about one who was not allowed to go—they call him the Wandering Jew: he has to ride behind the omnibus. If he had been allowed to get in, he would have escaped the clutches of the poets.

"Just cast your mind's eye into that great omnibus. The society is mixed, for king and beggar, genius and idiot, sit side by side: they must go without their property and money; they have only the service-book and the gift out of the saving's bank with them. But which of our deeds is selected and given to us? Perhaps quite a little one, one that we have forgotten, but which has been recorded—small as a pea, but the pea can send out a blooming shoot. The poor bumpkin, who sat on a low stool in the corner, and was jeered at and flouted, will perhaps have his worn-out stool given him as a provision; and the stool may become a litter in the land of eternity, and rise up then as a throne, gleaming like gold, and blooming as an arbour. He who always lounged about, and drank the spiced draught of pleasure, that he might forget the wild things he had done here, will have his barrel given to him on the journey, and will have to drink from it as they go on; and the drink is bright and clear, so that the thoughts remain pure, and all good and noble feelings are awakened, and he sees and feels what in life he could not or would not see; and then he has within him the punishment, the *gnawing worm*, which will not die through time incalculable. If on the glasses there stood written '*oblivion*,' on the barrel '*remembrance*' is inscribed.

"When I read a good book, an historical work, I always think at last of the poetry of what I am reading, and of the omnibus of death, and wonder which of the hero's deeds Death took out of the savings bank for him, and what provisions he got on the journey into eternity. There was once a French king—I have forgotten his name, for the names of good people are sometimes forgotten, even by me, but it will come back some day; there was a king who, during a famine, became the benefactor of his people; and the people raised to his memory a monument of snow, with the inscription, 'Quicker than this melts didst thou bring help!' I fancy that Death, looking back upon the monument, gave him a single snowflake as provision, a snowflake that never melts, and this flake floated over his royal head, like a white butterfly, into the land of eternity. Thus too, there was a Louis XI—I have remembered his name, for one remembers what is bad—a trait of him often comes into my thoughts, and I wish one could say the story is not true. He had his lord high constable executed, and he could execute him, right or wrong; but he had the innocent children of the constable, one seven and the other eight years old, placed under the scaffold so that the warm blood of their father spurted over them, and then he had them sent to the Bastille, and shut up in iron cages, where not even a coverlet was given them to protect them from the cold. And King Louis sent the executioner to them every week, and had a tooth pulled out of the head of each, that they might not be too comfortable; and the elder of the boys said, 'My mother would die of grief if she knew that my younger brother had to suffer so cruelly; therefore pull out two of my teeth, and spare him.' The tears came into the hangman's eyes, but the king's will was stronger than the tears; and every week two little teeth were brought to him on a silver plate; he had demanded them, and he had them. I fancy that Death took, these two teeth out of the savings bank of life, and gave them to Louis XI, to carry with him on the great journey into the land of immortality: they fly before him like two flames of fire; they shine and burn, and they bite him, the innocent children's teeth.

"Yes, that's a serious journey, the omnibus ride on the great moving-day! And when is it to be undertaken? That's just the serious part of it. Any day, any how, any minute, the omnibus may draw up. Which of our deeds will Death take out of the savings bank, and give to us as provision? Let us think of the moving-day that is not marked in the calendar."

Anne Lisbeth

Translated by H. W. Dulcken

Anne Lisbeth had a colour like milk and blood; young, fresh, and merry, she looked beautiful, with gleaming white teeth and clear eyes; her footstep was light in the dance, and her mind was lighter still. And what came of it all? Her son was an ugly brat! Yes, he was not pretty; so he was put out to be nursed by the labourer's wife. Anne Lisbeth was taken into the count's castle, and sat there in the splendid room arrayed in silks and velvets; not a breath of wind might blow upon her, and no one was allowed to speak a harsh word to her. No, that might not be; for she was nurse to the count's child, which was delicate and fair as a prince, and beautiful as an angel; and how she loved this child! Her own boy was provided for at the labourer's, where the mouth boiled over more frequently than the pot, and where, in general, no one was at home to take care of the child. Then he would cry; but what nobody knows, that nobody cares for, and he would cry till he was tired, and then he fell asleep; and in sleep one feels neither hunger nor thirst. A capital invention is sleep.

With years, just as weeds shoot up, Anne Lisbeth's child grew, but yet they said his growth was stunted; but he had quite become a member of the family in which he dwelt; they had received money to keep him. Anne Lisbeth was rid of him for good. She had become a town lady, and had a comfortable home of her own; and out of doors she wore a bonnet, when she went out for a walk; but she never walked out to see the labourer—that was too far from the town; and indeed she had nothing to go for; the boy belonged to the labouring people, and she said he could eat his food, and he should do something to earn his food, and consequently he kept Matz's red cow. He could already tend cattle and make himself useful.

The big dog, by the yard gate of the nobleman's mansion, sits proudly in the sunshine on the top of the kennel, and barks at every one who goes by: if it rains he creeps into his house, and there he is warm and dry. Anne Lisbeth's boy sat in the sunshine on the fence of the field, and cut out a pole-pin. In the spring he knew of three strawberry plants that were in blossom, and would certainly bear fruit, and that was his most hopeful thought; but they came to nothing. He sat out in the rain in foul weather, and was wet to the skin, and afterwards the cold wind dried the clothes on his back. When he came to the lordly farmyard he was hustled and cuffed, for the men and maids declared he was horribly ugly; but he was used to that—loved by nobody!

That was how it went with Anne Lisbeth's boy; and how could it go otherwise? It was, once for all, his fate to be beloved by nobody.

Till now a "land crab," the land at last threw him overboard. He went to sea in a wretched vessel, and sat by the helm, while the skipper sat over the grog-can. He was dirty and ugly, half frozen and half starved: one would have thought he had never had enough; and that really was the case.

It was late in autumn, rough, wet, windy weather; the wind cut cold through the thickest clothing, especially at sea; and out to sea went a wretched boat, with only two men on board, or, properly speaking, with only a man and a half, the skipper and his boy. It had only been a kind of twilight all day, and now it became dark; and it was bitter cold. The skipper drank a dram, which was to warm him from within. The bottle was old, and the glass too; it was whole at the top, but the foot was broken off, and therefore it stood upon a little carved block of wood painted blue. "A dram comforts one, and two are better still," thought the skipper. The boy sat at the helm, which he held fast in his hard seamed hands: he was ugly, and his hair was matted, and he looked crippled and stunted; he was the field labourer's boy, though in the church register he was entered as Anne Lisbeth's son.

The wind cut its way through the rigging, and the boat cut through the sea. The sail blew out, filled by the wind, and they drove on in wild career. It was rough and wet around and above, and it might come worse still. Hold! what was that? what struck there? what burst yonder? what seized the boat? It heeled, and lay on its beam ends! Was it a waterspout? Was it a heavy sea coming suddenly down? The boy at the helm cried out aloud, "Heaven help us!" The boat had struck on a great rock standing up from the depths of the sea, and it sank like an old shoe in a puddle; it sank "with man and mouse," as the saying is; and there were mice on board, but only one man and a half, the skipper and the labourer's boy. No one saw it but the swimming seagulls, and the fishes down yonder, and even they did not see it rightly, for they started back in terror when the water rushed into the ship, and it sank. There it lay scarce a fathom below the surface, and those two were provided for, buried and forgotten! Only the glass with the foot of blue wood did not sink; for the wood kept it up; the glass drifted away, to be broken and cast upon the shore—where and when? But, indeed, that is of no consequence. It had served its time, and it had been loved, which Anne Lisbeth's boy had not been. But in heaven no soul will be able to say, "Never loved!"

Anne Lisbeth had lived in the city for many years. She was called Madame, and felt her dignity, when she remembered the old "noble" days in which she had driven in the carriage, and had associated with countesses and baronesses. Her beautiful noble-child was the dearest angel, the kindest heart; he had loved her so much, and she had loved him in return; they had kissed and loved each other, and the boy had been her joy, her second life. Now he was so tall, and was fourteen years old, handsome and clever: she had not seen him since she carried him in her arms; for many years she had not been in the count's palace, for indeed it was quite a journey thither.

"I must once make an effort and go," said Anne Lisbeth. "I must go to my darling, to my sweet count's child. Yes, he certainly must long to see me too, the young count; he thinks of me and loves me as in those days when he flung his angel arms round my neck and cried 'Anne Liz.!' It sounded like music. Yes, I must make an effort and see him again."

She drove across the country in a grazier's cart, and then got out and continued her journey on foot, and thus reached the count's castle. It was great and magnificent as it had always been, and the garden looked the same as ever; but all the people there were strangers to her; not one of them knew Anne Lisbeth, and they did not know of what consequence she had once been there, but she felt sure the countess would let them know it, and her darling boy too. How she longed to see him!

Now, Anne Lisbeth was at her journey's end. She was kept waiting a considerable time, and for those who wait time passes slowly. But before the great people went to table she was called in and accosted very graciously. She was to see her sweet boy after dinner, and then she was to be called in again.

How tall and slender and thin he had grown! But he had still his beautiful eyes, and the angel-sweet mouth! He looked at her, but he said not a word: certainly he did not know her. He turned round, and was about to go away, but she seized his hand and pressed it to her mouth. "Good, good!" said he; and with that he went out of the room—he who filled her every thought—he whom she had loved best, and who was her whole earthly pride. Anne Lisbeth went out of the castle into the open highway, and she felt very mournful; he had been so cold and strange to her, had not a word nor a thought for her, he whom she had once carried day and night, and whom she still carried in her dreams.

A great black raven shot down in front of her on to the high road, and croaked and croaked again. "Ha!" she said, "what bird of ill omen art thou?"

She came past the hut of the labourer; the wife stood at the door, and the two women spoke to one another.

"You look well," said the woman. "You are plump and fat; you're well off."

"Oh, yes," answered Anne Lisbeth.

"The boat went down with them," continued the woman. "Hans skipper and the boy were both drowned. There's an end of them. I always thought the boy would be able to help me out with a few dollars. He'll never cost *you* anything more, Anne Lisbeth."

"So they were drowned?" Anne Lisbeth repeated; and then nothing more was said on the subject.

Anne Lisbeth was very low-spirited because her count-child had shown no disposition to talk with her who loved him so well, and who had journeyed all that way to get a sight of him; and the journey had cost money too, though the pleasure she had derived from it was not great. Still she said not a word about this. She would not relieve her heart by telling the labourer's wife about it, lest the latter should think she did not enjoy her former position at the castle. Then the raven screamed again, and flew past over her once more.

"The black wretch!" said Anne Lisbeth; "he'll end by frightening me today."

She had brought coffee and chicory with her, for she thought it would be a charity towards the poor woman to give them to her to boil a cup of coffee, and then she herself would take a cup too. The woman prepared the coffee, and in the meantime Anne Lisbeth sat down upon a chair and fell asleep. There she dreamed of something she had never dreamed before; singularly enough, she dreamed of her own child that had wept and hungered there in the labourer's hut, had been hustled about in heat and in cold, and was now lying in the depths of the sea, Heaven knows where. She dreamed she was sitting in the hut, where the woman was busy preparing the coffee—she could smell the roasting coffee beans. But suddenly it seemed to her that there stood on the threshold a beautiful young form, as beautiful as the count's child; and this apparition said to her, "The world is passing away! Hold fast to me, for you are my mother after all. You have an angel in heaven. Hold me fast!" And the child-angel stretched out its hand to her; and there was a terrible crash, for the world was going to pieces, and the angel was raising himself above the earth, and holding her by the sleeve so tightly, it seemed to her, that she was lifted up from the ground; but, on the other hand, something heavy hung at her feet and dragged her down, and it seemed to her that hundreds of women clung to her, and cried, "If thou art to be saved, we must be saved too! Hold fast, hold fast!" And then they all hung on to her; but there were too many of them, and—*ritsch, ratsch!*—the sleeve tore, and Anne Lisbeth fell down in horror—and awoke. And indeed she was on the point of falling over, with the chair on which she sat; she was so startled and alarmed that she could not recollect what it was she had dreamed, but she remembered that it had been something dreadful.

The coffee was taken, and they had a chat together; and then Anne Lisbeth went away towards the little town where she was to meet the carrier, and to drive back with him to her own home. But when she came to speak to him, he said he should not be ready to start before the evening of the next day. She began to think about the expense and the length of the way, and when she considered that the route by the sea shore was shorter by two miles than the other, and that the weather was clear and the moon shone, she determined to make her way on foot, and to start at once, that she might be at home by next day.

The sun had set, and the evening bells, tolled in the towers of the village churches, still sounded through the air; but no, it was not the bells, but the cry of the frogs in the marshes. Now they were silent, and all around was still; not a bird was heard, for they were all gone to rest; and even the owl seemed to be at home; deep silence reigned on the margin of the forest and by the sea shore: as Anne Lisbeth walked on she could hear her own footsteps on the sand; there was no sound of waves in the sea; everything out in the deep waters had sunk to silence. All was quiet there, the living and the dead creatures of the sea.

Anne Lisbeth walked on "thinking of nothing at all," as the saying is, or rather, her thoughts wandered; but thoughts had not wandered away from her, for they are never absent from us, they only slumber. But those that have not yet stirred come forth at their time, and begin to stir sometimes in the heart and sometimes in the head, and seem to come upon us as if from above.

It is written that a good deed bears its fruit of blessing, and it is also written that sin is death. Much has been written and much has been said which one does not know or think of in general; and thus it was with Anne Lisbeth. But it may happen that a light arises within one, and that the forgotten things may approach.

All virtues and all vices lie in our hearts. They are in mine and in thine; they lie there like little grains of seed; and then from without comes a ray of sunshine or the touch of an evil hand, or maybe you turn the corner and go to the right or to the left, and that may be decisive; for the little seed-corn perhaps is stirred, and it swells and shoots up, and it bursts, and pours its sap into all your blood, and then your career has commenced. There are tormenting thoughts, which one does not feel when one walks on with slumbering senses, but they are there, fermenting in the heart. Anne Lisbeth walked on thus with her senses half in slumber, but the thoughts were fermenting within her. From one Shrove Tuesday to the next there comes much that weighs upon the heart—the reckoning of a whole year: much is forgotten, sins against Heaven in word and in thought, against our neighbour, and against our own conscience. We don't think of these things, and Anne Lisbeth did not think of them. She had committed no crime against the law of the land, she was very respectable, an honoured and well-placed person, that she knew. And as she walked along by the margin of the sea, what was it she saw lying there? An old hat, a man's hat. Now, where might that have been washed overboard? She came nearer, and stopped to look at the hat. Ha! what was lying yonder? She shuddered; but it was nothing save a heap of sea grass and tangle flung across a long stone; but it looked just like a corpse: it was only sea grass and tangle, and yet she was frightened at it, and as she turned away to walk on much came into her mind that she had heard in her childhood; old superstitions of spectres by the sea shore, of the ghosts of drowned but unburied people whose corpses have been washed up on to the desert shore. The body, she had heard, could do harm to none, but the spirit could pursue the lonely wanderer, and attach itself to him, and demand to be carried to the churchyard that it might rest in consecrated ground. "Hold fast! hold fast!" the spectre would then cry; and while Anne Lisbeth murmured the words to herself, her whole dream suddenly stood before her just as she had dreamed it, when the mothers clung to her and had repeated this word, amid the crash of the world, when her sleeve was torn and she slipped out of the grasp of her child, who wanted to hold her up in that terrible hour. Her child, her own child, which she had never loved, lay now buried in the sea, and might rise up like a spectre from the waters, and cry "Hold fast! carry me to consecrated earth." And as these thoughts passed through her mind, fear gave speed to her feet, so that she walked on faster and faster; fear came upon her like the touch of a cold wet hand that was laid upon her heart, so that she almost fainted; and as she looked out across the sea, all there grew darker and darker; a heavy mist came rolling onward, and clung round bush and tree, twisting them into fantastic shapes. She turned round, and glanced up at the moon, which had risen behind her. It looked like a pale, rayless surface; and a deadly weight appeared to cling to her limbs. "Hold fast!" thought she; and when she turned round a second time and looked at the moon, its white face seemed quite close to her, and the mist hung like a pale garment from her shoulders. "Hold fast! carry me to consecrated earth!" sounded in her ears in strange hollow tones. The sound did not come from frogs or ravens; she saw no sign of any such creatures. "A grave, dig me a grave!" was repeated quite loud. Yes, it was the spectre of her child, the child that lay in the ocean, and whose spirit could have no rest until it was carried to the churchyard, and until a grave had been dug for it in consecrated ground. Thither she would go, and there she would dig; and she went on in the direction of the church, and the weight on her heart seemed to grow lighter, and even to vanish altogether; but when she turned to go home by the shortest way, it returned. "Hold fast! hold fast!" and the words came quite clear, though they were like the croak of a frog or the wail of a bird, "A grave! dig me a grave!"

The mist was cold and damp; her hands and face were cold and damp with horror; a heavy weight again seized her and clung to her, and in her mind a great space opened for thoughts that had never before been there.

Here in the North the beech wood often buds in a single night, and in the morning sunlight it appears in its full glory of youthful green; and thus in a single instant can the consciousness unfold itself of the sin that has been contained in the thoughts, words, and works of our past life. It springs up and unfolds itself in a single second when once the conscience is awakened; and God wakens it when we least expect it. Then we find no excuse for ourselves—the deed is there, and bears witness against us; the thoughts seem to become words, and to sound far out into the world. We are horrified at the thought of what we have carried within us, and have not stifled over what we have sown in our thoughtlessness and pride. The heart hides within itself all the virtues and likewise all the vices, and they grow even in the shallowest ground.

Anne Lisbeth now experienced all the thoughts we have clothed in words. She was overpowered by them, and sank down, and crept along for some distance on the ground. "A grave! dig me a grave!" it sounded again in her ears; and she would gladly have buried herself if in the grave there had been forgetfulness of every deed. It was the first hour of her awakening; full of anguish and horror. Superstition alternately made her shudder with cold and made her blood burn with the heat of fever. Many things of which she had never liked to speak came into her mind. Silent as the cloud shadows in the bright moonshine, a spectral apparition flitted by her: she had heard of it before. Close by her galloped four snorting steeds, with fire spurting from their eyes and nostrils; they dragged a red-hot coach, and within it sat the wicked proprietor who had ruled here a hundred years ago. The legend said that every night at twelve o'clock he drove into his castle yard and out again. There! there! He was not pale as dead men are said to be, but black as a coal. He nodded at Anne Lisbeth and beckoned to her. "Hold fast! hold fast! then you may ride again in a nobleman's carriage, and forget your child!"

She gathered herself up, and hastened to the churchyard; but the black crosses and the black ravens danced before her eyes, and she could not distinguish one from the other. The ravens croaked, as the raven had done that she saw in the daytime, but now she understood what they said. "I am the raven-mother! I am the raven-mother!" each raven croaked, and Anne Lisbeth now understood that the name also applied to her; and she fancied she should be transformed into a black bird, and be obliged to cry what they cried if she did not dig the grave.

And she threw herself on the earth, and with her hands dug a grave in the hard ground, so that the blood ran from her fingers.

"A grave! dig me a grave!" it still sounded; she was fearful that the cock might crow, and the first red streak appear in the east, before she had finished her work, and then she would be lost.

And the cock crowed, and day dawned in the east, and the grave was only half dug. An icy hand passed over her head and face, and down towards her heart. "Only half a grave!" a voice wailed, and fled away. Yes, it fled away over the sea—it was the ocean spectre; and exhausted and overpowered, Anne Lisbeth sunk to the ground, and her senses forsook her.

It was bright day when she came to herself, and two men were raising her up; but she was not lying in the churchyard, but on the sea shore, where she had dug a deep hole in the sand, and cut her hand against a broken glass, whose sharp stem was stuck in a little painted block of wood. Anne Lisbeth was in a fever. Conscience had shuffled the cards of superstition, and had laid out these cards, and she fancied she had only half a soul, and that her child had taken the other half down into the sea. Never would she be able to swing herself aloft to the mercy of Heaven, till she had recovered this other half, which was now held fast in the deep water. Anne Lisbeth got back to her former home, but was no longer the woman she had been: her thoughts were confused like a tangled skein; only one thread, only one thought she had disentangled, namely, that she must carry the spectre of the sea shore to the churchyard, and dig a grave for him, that thus she might win back her soul.

Many a night she was missed from her home; and she was always found on the sea shore, waiting for the spectre. In this way a whole year passed by; and then one night she vanished again, and was not to be found; the whole of the next day was wasted in fruitless search.

Towards evening, when the clerk came into the church to toll the vesper bell, he saw by the altar Anne Lisbeth, who had spent the whole day there. Her physical forces were almost exhausted, but her eyes gleamed brightly, and her cheeks had a rosy flush. The last rays of the sun shone upon her, and gleamed over the altar on the bright buckles of the Bible which lay there, opened at the words of the prophet Joel: "Bend your hearts, and not your garments, and turn unto the Lord!" That was just a chance, the people said; as many things happen by chance.

In the face of Anne Lisbeth, illumined by the sun, peace and rest were to be seen. She said she was happy, for now she had conquered. Last night the spectre of the shore, her own child, had come to her, and had said to her, "Thou hast dug me only half a grave, but thou hast now, for a year and a day, buried me altogether in thy heart, and it is there that a mother can best hide her child!" And then he gave her her lost soul back again, and brought her here into the church.

"Now I am in the house of God," she said, "and in that house we are happy."

And when the sun had set, Anne Lisbeth's soul had risen to that region where there is no more anguish, and Anne Lisbeth's troubles were over.

Children's Prattle

Translated by Mrs. H. P. Paull

At a rich merchant's house there was a children's party, and the children of rich and great people were there. The merchant was a learned man, for his father had sent him to college, and he had passed his examination. His father had been at first only a cattle dealer, but always honest and industrious, so that he had made money, and his son, the merchant, had managed to increase his store. Clever as he was, he had also a heart; but there was less said of his heart than of his money. All descriptions of people visited at the merchant's house, well born, as well as intellectual, and some who possessed neither of these recommendations.

Now it was a children's party, and there was children's prattle, which always is spoken freely from the heart. Among them was a beautiful little girl, who was terribly proud; but this had been taught her by the servants, and not by her parents, who were far too sensible people.

Her father was groom of the Chambers, which is a high office at court, and she knew it. "I am a child of the court," she said; now she might just as well have been a child of the cellar, for no one can help his birth; and then she told the other children that she was well-born, and said that no one who was not well-born could rise in the world. It was no use to read and be industrious, for if a person was not well-born, he could never achieve anything. "And those whose names end with 'sen,'" said she, "can never be anything at all. We must put our arms akimbo, and make the elbow quite pointed, so as to keep these 'sen' people at a great distance." And then she stuck out her pretty little arms, and made the elbows quite pointed, to show how it was to be done; and her little arms were very pretty, for she was a sweet-looking child.

But the little daughter of the merchant became very angry at this speech, for her father's name was Petersen, and she knew that the name ended in 'sen,' and therefore she said as proudly as she could, "But my papa can buy a hundred dollars' worth of bonbons, and give them away to children. Can your papa do that?"

"Yes; and my papa," said the little daughter of the editor of a paper, "my papa can put your papa and everybody's papa into the newspaper. All sorts of people are afraid of him, my mamma says, for he can do as he likes with the paper." And the little maiden looked exceedingly proud, as if she had been a real princess, who may be expected to look proud.

But outside the door, which stood ajar, was a poor boy, peeping through the crack of the door. He was of such a lowly station that he had not been allowed even to enter the room. He had been turning the spit for the cook, and she had given him permission to stand behind the door and peep in at the well-dressed children, who were having such a merry time within; and for him that was a great deal. "Oh, if I could be one of them," thought he, and then he heard what was said about names, which was quite enough to make him more unhappy. His parents at home had not even a penny to spare to buy a newspaper, much less could they write in one; and worse than all, his father's name, and of course his own, ended in 'sen,' and therefore he could never turn out well, which was a very sad thought. But after all, he had been born into the world, and the station of life had been chosen for him, therefore he must be content.

And this is what happened on that evening.

Many years passed, and most of the children became grown-up persons.

There stood a splendid house in the town, filled with all kinds of beautiful and valuable objects. Everybody wished to see it, and people even came in from the country round to be permitted to view the treasures it contained.

Which of the children whose prattle we have described, could call this house his own? One would suppose it very easy to guess. No, no; it is not so very easy. The house belonged to the poor little boy who had stood on that night behind the door. He had really become something great, although his name ended in 'sen,'—for it was Thorwaldsen.

And the three other children—the children of good birth, of money, and of intellectual pride—well, they were respected and honoured in the world, for they had been well provided for by birth and position, and they had no cause to reproach themselves with what they had thought and spoken on that evening long ago, for, after all, it was mere *"children's prattle."*

The Pen and the Inkstand

Translated by Mrs. H. P. Paull

In a poet's room, where his inkstand stood on the table, the remark was once made, "It is wonderful what can be brought out of an inkstand. What will come next? It is indeed wonderful."

"Yes, certainly," said the inkstand to the pen, and to the other articles that stood on the table; "that's what I always say. It is wonderful and extraordinary what a number of things come out of me. It's quite incredible, and I really don't know what is coming next when that man dips his pen into me. One drop out of me is enough for half a page of paper, and what cannot half a page contain? From me, all the works of a poet are produced; all those imaginary characters whom people fancy they have known or met. All the deep feeling, the humour, and the vivid pictures of nature. I myself don't understand how it is, for I am not acquainted with nature, but it is certainly in me. From me have gone forth to the world those wonderful descriptions of troops of charming maidens, and of brave knights on prancing steeds; of the halt and the blind, and I know not what more, for I assure you I never think of these things."

"There you are right," said the pen, "for you don't think at all; if you did, you would see that you can only provide the means. You give the fluid that I may place upon the paper what dwells in me, and what I wish to bring to light. It is the pen that writes: no man doubts that; and, indeed, most people understand as much about poetry as an old inkstand."

"You have had very little experience," replied the inkstand. "You have hardly been in service a week, and are already half worn out. Do you imagine you are a poet? You are only a servant, and before you came I had many like you, some of the goose family, and others of English manufacture. I know a quill pen as well as I know a steel one. I have had both sorts in my service, and I shall have many more when *he* comes—the man who performs the mechanical part—and writes down what he obtains from me. I should like to know what will be the next thing he gets out of me."

"Inkpot!" exclaimed the pen contemptuously.

Late in the evening the poet came home. He had been to a concert, and had been quite enchanted with the admirable performance of a famous violin player whom he had heard there. The performer had produced from his instrument a richness of tone that sometimes sounded like tinkling waterdrops or rolling pearls; sometimes like the birds twittering in chorus, and then rising and swelling in sound like the wind through the fir-trees. The poet felt as if his own heart were weeping, but in tones of melody like the sound of a woman's voice. It seemed not only the strings, but every part of the instrument from which these sounds were produced. It was a wonderful performance and a difficult piece, and yet the bow seemed to glide across the strings so easily that it was as if any one could do it who tried. Even the violin and the bow appeared to perform independently of their master who guided them; it was as if soul and spirit had been breathed into the instrument, so the audience forgot the performer in the beautiful sounds he produced. Not so the poet; he remembered him, and named him, and wrote down his thoughts on the subject. "How foolish it would be for the violin and the bow to boast of their performance, and yet we men often commit that folly. The poet, the artist, the man of science in his laboratory, the general—we all do it; and yet we are only the instruments which the

Almighty uses; to Him alone the honour is due. We have nothing of ourselves of which we should be proud." Yes, this is what the poet wrote down. He wrote it in the form of a parable, and called it "The Master and the Instruments."

"That is what you have got, madam," said the pen to the inkstand, when the two were alone again. "Did you hear him read aloud what I had written down?"

"Yes, what I gave you to write," retorted the inkstand. "That was a cut at you because of your conceit. To think that you could not understand that you were being quizzed. I gave you a cut from within me. Surely I must know my own satire."

"Ink-pitcher!" cried the pen.

"Writing-stick!" retorted the inkstand. And each of them felt satisfied that he had given a good answer. It is pleasing to be convinced that you have settled a matter by your reply; it is something to make you sleep well, and they both slept well upon it. But the poet did not sleep. Thoughts rose up within him like the tones of the violin, falling like pearls, or rushing like the strong wind through the forest. He understood his own heart in these thoughts; they were as a ray from the mind of the Great Master of all minds.

"To *Him* be all the honour."

The Farm-Yard Cock and the Weathercock

Translated by Mrs. H. P. Paull

There were two cocks—one on the dung-hill, the other on the roof. They were both arrogant, but which of the two rendered most service? Tell us your opinion—we'll keep to ours just the same though.

The poultry yard was divided by some planks from another yard in which there was a dung-hill, and on the dung-hill lay and grew a large cucumber which was conscious of being a hot-bed plant.

"One is born to that," said the cucumber to itself. "Not all can be born cucumbers; there must be other things, too. The hens, the ducks, and all the animals in the next yard are creatures too. Now I have a great opinion of the yard cock on the plank; he is certainly of much more importance than the Weathercock who is placed so high and can't even creak, much less crow. The latter has neither hens nor chicks, and only thinks of himself and perspires verdigris. No, the yard cock is really a cock! His step is a dance! His crowing is music, and wherever he goes one knows what a trumpeter is like! If he would only come in here! Even if he ate me up stump, stalk, and all, and I had to dissolve in his body, it would be a happy death," said the cucumber.

In the night there was a terrible storm. The hens, chicks, and even the cock sought shelter; the wind tore down the planks between the two yards with a crash; the tiles came tumbling down, but the Weathercock sat firm. He did not even turn round, for he could not; and yet he was young and freshly cast, but prudent and sedate. He had been born old, and did not at all resemble the birds flying in the air—the sparrows, and the swallows; no, he despised them, these mean little piping birds, these common whistlers. He admitted that the pigeons, large and white and shining like mother-o'-pearl, looked like a kind of Weathercock; but they were fat and stupid, and all their thoughts and endeavours were directed to filling themselves with food, and besides, they were tiresome things to converse with. The birds of passage had also paid the Weathercock a visit and told him of foreign countries, of airy caravans and robber stories that made one's hair stand on end. All this was new and interesting; that is, for the first time, but afterwards, as the Weathercock found out, they repeated themselves and always told the same stories, and that's very tedious, and there was no one with whom one could associate, for one and all were stale and small-minded.

"The world is no good!" he said. "Everything in it is so stupid."

The Weathercock was puffed up, and that quality would have made him interesting in the eyes of the cucumber if it had known it, but it had eyes only for the yard cock, who was now in the yard with it.

The wind had blown the planks, but the storm was over.

"What do you think of *that* crowing?" said the yard cock to the hens and chickens. "It was a little rough—it wanted elegance."

And the hens and chickens came up on the dung-hill, and the cock strutted about like a lord.

"Garden plant!" he said to the cucumber, and in that one word his deep learning showed itself, and it forgot that he was pecking at her and eating it up. "A happy death!"

The hens and the chickens came, for where one runs the others run too; they clucked, and chirped, and looked at the cock, and were proud that he was of their kind.

The Farm-Yard Cock and the Weathercock

"Cock-a-doodle-doo!" he crowed, "the chickens will grow up into great hens at once, if I cry it out in the poultry-yard of the world!"

And hens and chicks clucked and chirped, and the cock announced a great piece of news.

"A cock can lay an egg! And do you know what's in that egg? A basilisk. No one can stand the sight of such a thing; people know that, and now you know it too—you know what is in me, and what a champion of all cocks I am!"

With that the yard cock flapped his wings, made his comb swell up, and crowed again; and they all shuddered, the hens and the little chicks—but they were very proud that one of their number was such a champion of all cocks. They clucked and chirped till the Weathercock heard; he heard it; but he did not stir.

"Everything is very stupid," the Weathercock said to himself. "The yard cock lays no eggs, and I am too lazy to do so; if I liked, I could lay a wind-egg. But the world is not worth even a wind-egg. Everything is so stupid! I don't want to sit here any longer."

With that the Weathercock broke off; but he did not kill the yard cock, although the hens said that had been his intention. And what is the moral? "Better to crow than to be puffed up and break off!"

A Story from the Sand-Dunes

Translated by H. W. Dulcken

This is a story from the sand-dunes or sand-hills of Jutland; though it does not begin in Jutland, the northern peninsula, but far away in the south, in Spain. The ocean is the high road between the nations—transport thyself thither in thought to sunny Spain. There it is warm and beautiful, there the fiery pomegranate blossoms flourish among the dark laurels; from the mountains a cool refreshing wind blows down, upon, and over the orange gardens, over the gorgeous Moorish halls with their golden cupolas and coloured walls: through the streets go children in procession, with candles and with waving flags, and over them, lofty and clear, rises the sky with its gleaming stars. There is a sound of song and of castagnettes, and youths and maidens join in the dance under the blooming acacias, while the mendicant sits upon the hewn marble stone, refreshing himself with the juicy melon, and dreamily enjoying life. The whole is like a glorious dream. And there was a newly married couple who completely gave themselves up to its charm; moreover, they possessed the good things of this life, health and cheerfulness of soul, riches and honour.

A Story from the Sand-Dunes

"We are as happy as it is possible to be," exclaimed the young couple, from the depths of their hearts They had indeed but one step more to mount in the ladder of happiness, in the hope that God would give them a child; a son like them in form and in spirit.

The happy child would be welcomed with rejoicing, would be tended with all care and love, and enjoy every advantage that wealth and ease possessed by an influential family could give.

And the days went by like a glad festival.

"Life is a gracious gift of Providence, an almost inappreciable gift!" said the young wife, "and yet they tell us that fulness of joy is found only in the future life, for ever and ever. I cannot compass the thought."

"And perhaps the thought arises from the arrogance of men," said the husband. "It seems a great pride to believe that we shall live for ever, that we shall be as gods. Were these not the words of the serpent, the origin of falsehood?"

"Surely you do not doubt the future life?" exclaimed the young wife; and it seemed as if one of the first shadows flitted over the sunny heaven of her thoughts.

"Faith promises it, and the priests tells us so!" replied the man; "but amid all my happiness, I feel that it is arrogance to demand a continued happiness, another life after this. Has not so much been given us in this state of existence, that we ought to be, that we *must* be, contented with it?"

"Yes, it has been given to *us*," said the young wife, "but to how many thousands is not this life one scene of hard trial? How many have been thrown into this world, as if only to suffer poverty and shame and sickness and misfortune? If there were no life after this, everything on earth would be too unequally distributed, and the Almighty would not be justice itself."

"Yonder beggar," replied the man, "has his joys which seem to him great, and which rejoice him as much as the king is rejoiced in the splendour of his palace. And then, do you not think that the beast of burden, which suffers blows and hunger, and works itself to death, suffers from its heavy fate? The dumb beast might likewise demand a future life, and declare the decree unjust that does not admit it into a higher place of creation."

"He has said, 'In my Father's house are many mansions,'" replied the young wife: "heaven is immeasurable, as the love of our Maker is immeasurable. Even the dumb beast is His creature; and I firmly believe that no life will be lost, but that each will receive that amount of happiness which he can enjoy, and which is sufficient for him."

"This world is sufficient for me!" said the man, and he threw his arms round his beautiful, amiable wife, and then smoked his cigarette on the open balcony, where the cool air was filled with the fragrance of oranges and pinks. The sound of music and the clatter of castagnettes came up from the road, the stars gleamed above, and two eyes full of affection, the eyes of his wife, looked on him with the undying glance of love.

"Such a moment," he said, "makes it worth while to be born, to fall, and to disappear!" and he smiled. The young wife raised her hand in mild reproach, and the shadow passed away from her world, and they were happy—quite happy.

Everything seemed to work together for them. They advanced in honour, in prosperity, and in joy. There was a change, indeed, but only a change of place; not in enjoyment of life and of happiness. The young man was sent by his sovereign as ambassador to the court of Russia. This was an honourable office, and his birth and his acquirements gave him a title to be thus honoured. He possessed a great fortune, and his wife had brought him wealth equal to his own, for she was the daughter of a rich and respected merchant. One of this merchant's largest and finest ships was to be dispatched during that year to Stockholm, and it was arranged that the dear young people, the daughter and the son-in-law, should travel in it to St. Petersburg. And all the arrangements on board were princely—rich carpets for the feet, and silk and luxury on all sides.

In an old heroic song, "The King's Son of England," it says, "Moreover, he sailed in a gallant ship, and the anchor was gilded with ruddy gold, and each rope was woven through with silk," And this ship involuntarily rose in the mind of him who saw the vessel from Spain, for here was the same pomp, and the same parting thought naturally arose—the thought:

> "God grant that we all in joy
> Once more may meet again."

And the wind blew fairly seaward from the Spanish shore, and the parting was to be but a brief one, for in a few weeks the voyagers would reach their destination; but when they came out upon the high seas, the wind sank, the sea became calm and shining, the stars of heaven gleamed brightly, and they were festive evenings that were spent in the sumptuous cabin.

At length the voyagers began to wish for wind, for a favouring breeze; but the breeze would not blow, or, if it did arise, it was contrary. Thus weeks passed away, two full months; and then at last the fair wind blew—it blew from the south-west. The ship sailed on the high seas between Scotland and Jutland, and the wind increased just as in the old song of "The King's Son of England."

> "And it blew a storm, and the rain came down,
> And they found not land nor shelter,
> And forth they threw their anchor of gold,
> As the wind blew westward, toward Denmark."

This all happened a long, long while ago. King Christian VII then sat on the Danish throne, and he was still a young man. Much has happened since that time, much has changed or has been changed. Sea and moorland have been converted into green meadows, heath has become arable land, and in the shelter of the West Jute huts grow apple trees and rose bushes, though they certainly require to be sought for, as they bend beneath the sharp west wind. In Western Jutland one may go back in thought to the old times, farther back than the days when Christian VII bore rule. As it did then, in Jutland, the brown heath now also extends for miles, with its "Hun's Graves," its aërial spectacles, and its crossing, sandy, uneven roads; westward, where large rivulets run into the bays, extend marshes and meadow land, girdled with lofty sand-hills, which, like a row of Alps, raise their peaked summits towards the sea, only broken by the high clayey ridges, from which the waves year by year bite out huge mouthfuls, so that the impending shores fall down as if by the shock of an earthquake. Thus it is there today, and thus it was many, many years ago, when the happy pair were sailing in the gorgeous ship.

It was in the last days of September, a Sunday, and sunny weather; the chiming of the church bells in the bay of Nissum was wafted along like a chain of sounds. The churches there are erected almost entirely of hewn boulder stones, each like a piece of rock; the North Sea might foam over them, and they would not be overthrown. Most of them are without steeples, and the bells are hung between two beams in the open air. The service was over, and the congregation thronged out into the churchyard, where then, as now, not a tree nor a bush was to be seen; not a single flower had been planted there, nor had a wreath been laid upon the graves. Rough mounds show where the dead had been buried, and rank grass, tossed by the wind, grows thickly over the whole churchyard. Here and there a grave had a monument to show, in the shape of a half-decayed block of wood rudely shaped into the form of a coffin, the said block having been brought from the forest of West Jutland; but the forest of West Jutland is the wild sea itself, where the inhabitants find the hewn beams and planks and fragments which the breakers cast ashore. The wind and the sea fog soon destroy the wood. One of these blocks had been placed by loving hands on a child's grave, and one of the women, who had come out of the church, stepped towards it. She stood still in front of it, and let her glance rest on the discoloured memorial. A few moments afterwards her husband stepped up to her. Neither of them spoke a word, but he took her hand, and they wandered across the brown heath, over moor and meadow, towards the sand-hills; for a long time they thus walked silently side by side.

"That was a good sermon today," the man said at length. "If we had not God to look to, we should have nothing!"

"Yes," observed the woman, "He sends joy and sorrow, and He has a right to send them. Tomorrow our little boy would have been five years old, if we had been allowed to keep him."

"You will gain nothing by fretting, wife," said the man. "The boy is well provided for. He is there whither we pray to go."

And they said nothing more, but went forward to their house among the sand-hills. Suddenly, in front of one of the houses where the sea grass did not keep the sand down with its twining roots, there

A Story from the Sand-Dunes

arose what appeared to be a column of smoke rising into the air. A gust of wind swept in among the hills, whirling the particles of sand high in the air. Another, and the strings of fish hung up to dry flapped and beat violently against the wall of the hut; and then all was still again, and the sun shone down hotly.

Man and wife stepped into the house. They had soon taken off their Sunday clothes, and emerging again, they hurried away over the dunes, which stood there like huge waves of sand suddenly arrested in their course, while the sandweeds and the dunegrass with its bluish stalks spread a changing colour over them. A few neighbours came up, and helped one another to draw the boats higher up on the sand. The wind now blew more sharply than before; it was cutting and cold: and when they went back over the sand-hills, sand and little pointed stones blew into their faces. The waves reared themselves up with their white crowns of foam, and the wind cut off their crests, flinging the foam far around.

The evening came on. In the air was a swelling roar, moaning and complaining like a troop of despairing spirits, that sounded above the hoarse rolling of the sea; for the fisher's little hut was on the very margin. The sand rattled against the window panes, and every now and then came a violent gust of wind, that shook the house to its foundations. It was dark, but towards midnight the moon would rise.

The air became clearer, but the storm swept in all its gigantic force over the perturbed sea. The fisher people had long gone to bed, but in such weather there was no chance of closing an eye. Presently there was a knocking at the window, and the door was opened, and a voice said:

"There's a great ship fast stranded on the outermost reef."

In a moment the fish people had sprung from their couch, and hastily arrayed themselves.

The moon had risen, it was light enough to make the surrounding objects visible, to those who could open their eyes for the blinding clouds of sand. The violence of the wind was terrible; and only by creeping forward between the gusts was it possible to pass among the sand-hills; and now the salt spray flew up from the sea like down, while the ocean foamed like a roaring cataract towards the beach. It required a practised eye to descry the vessel out in the offing. The vessel was a noble brig. The billows now lifted it over the reef, three or four cables' lengths out of the usual channel. It drove towards the land, struck against the second reef, and remained fixed.

To render assistance was impossible; the sea rolled fairly in upon the vessel, making a clean breach over her. Those on shore fancied they heard the cries of help from on board, and could plainly descry the busy useless efforts made by the stranded crew. Now a wave came rolling onward, falling like a rock upon the bowsprit, and tearing it from the brig. The stern was lifted high above the flood. Two people were seen to embrace and plunge together into the sea; in a moment more, and one of the largest waves that rolled towards the sand-hills threw a body upon the shore. It was a woman, and appeared quite dead, said the sailors; but some women thought they discerned signs of life in her, and the stranger was carried across the sand-hills into the fisherman's hut. How beautiful and fair she was! certainly she must be a great lady.

They laid her upon the humble bed that boasted not a yard of linen; but there was a woollen coverlet, and that would keep the occupant warm.

Life returned to her, but she was delirious, and knew nothing of what had happened, or where she was; and it was better so, for everything she loved and valued lay buried in the sea. It was with her ship as with the vessel in the song of "The King's Son of England."

> "Alas, it was a grief to see
> How the gallant ship sank speedily."

Portions of wreck and fragments of wood drifted ashore, and they were all that remained of what had been the ship. The wind still drove howling over the coast. For a few moments the strange lady seemed to rest; but she awoke in pain, and cries of anguish and fear came from her lips. She opened her wonderfully beautiful eyes, and spoke a few words, but none understood her.

And behold, as a reward for the pain and sorrow she had undergone, she held in her arms a new-born child, the child that was to have rested upon a gorgeous couch, surrounded by silken curtains, in the sumptuous home. It was to have been welcomed with joy to a

A Story from the Sand-Dunes

life rich in all the goods of the earth; and now Providence had caused it to be born in this humble retreat, and not even a kiss did it receive from its mother.

The fisher's wife laid the child upon the mother's bosom, and it rested on a heart that beat no more, for she was dead. The child who was to be nursed by wealth and fortune, was cast into the world, washed by the sea among the sand-hills, to partake the fate and heavy days of the poor. And here again comes into our mind the old song of the English king's son, in which mention is made of the customs prevalent at that time, when knights and squires plundered those who had been saved from shipwreck.

The ship had been stranded some distance south of Nissum Bay. The hard, inhuman days in which, as we have stated, the inhabitants of the Jutland shores did evil to the shipwrecked, were long past. Affection and sympathy and self-sacrifice for the unfortunate were to be found, as they are to be found in our own time, in many a brilliant example. The dying mother and the unfortunate child would have found succour and help wherever the wind blew them; but nowhere could they have found more earnest care than in the hut of the poor fisherwife; who had stood but yesterday, with a heavy heart, beside the grave which covered her child, which would have been five years old that day, if God had spared it to her.

No one knew who the dead stranger was, or could even form a conjecture. The pieces of wreck said nothing on the subject.

Into the rich house in Spain no tidings penetrated of the fate of the daughter and the son-in-law. They had not arrived at their destined post, and violent storms had raged during the past weeks. At last the verdict was given, "Foundered at sea—all lost."

But in the sand-hills near Hunsby, in the fisherman's hut, lived a little scion of the rich Spanish family.

Where Heaven sends food for two, a third can manage to make a meal, and in the depths of the sea is many a dish of fish for the hungry.

And they called the boy Jürgen.

"It must certainly be a Jewish child," the people said, "it looks so swarthy."

"It might be an Italian or a Spaniard," observed the clergyman.

But to the fisherwoman these three nations seemed all the same, and she consoled herself with the idea that the child was baptized as a Christian.

The boy throve. The noble blood in his veins was warm, and he became strong on his homely fare. He grew apace in the humble house, and the Danish dialect spoken by the West Jutes became his language. The pomegranate seed from Spanish soil became a hardy plant on the coast of West Jutland. Such may be a man's fate! To this home he clung with the roots of his whole being. He was to have experience of cold and hunger, and the misfortunes and hardships that surrounded the humble; but he tasted also of the poor man's joys.

Childhood has sunny heights for all, whose memory gleams through the whole after life. The boy had many opportunities for pleasure and play. The whole coast, for miles and miles, was full of playthings; for it was a mosaic of pebbles, red as coral, yellow as amber, and others again white and rounded like birds' eggs; and all smoothed and prepared by the sea. Even the bleached fish skeletons, the water plants dried by the wind, seaweed, white, gleaming, and long linen-like bands, waving among the stones, all these seemed made to give pleasure and amusement to the eye and the thoughts; and the boy had an intelligent mind—many and great faculties lay dormant in him. How readily he retained in his mind the stories and songs he heard, and how neat-handed he was! With stones and mussel shells he put together pictures and ships with which one could decorate the room; and he could cut out his thoughts wonderfully on a stick, his foster-mother said, though the boy was still so young and little! His voice sounded sweetly; every melody flowed at once from his lips. Many chords were attained in his heart which might have sounded out into the world, if he had been placed elsewhere than in the fisherman's hut by the North Sea.

One day another ship was stranded there. Among other things, a chest of rare flower bulbs floated ashore. Some were put into the cooking pots, for they were thought to be eatable, and others lay and shrivelled in the sand, but they did not accomplish their purpose, or unfold the richness of colour whose germ was within them. Would it be better with Jürgen? The flower bulbs had soon played their part, but he had still years of apprenticeship before him.

Neither he nor his friends remarked in what a solitary and uniform way one day succeeded another; for there was plenty to do and to see. The sea itself was a great lesson book, unfolding a new leaf every day, such as calm and storm, breakers and waifs. The visits to the church were festal visits. But among the festal visits in the fisherman's house, one was particularly distinguished. It was repeated twice in the year, and was, in fact, the visit of the brother of Jürgen's foster-mother, the eel breeder from Zjaltring, upon the neighbourhood of the "Bow Hill." He used to come in a cart painted red, and filled with eels. The cart was covered and locked like a box, and painted all over with blue and white tulips. It was drawn by two dun oxen, and Jürgen was allowed to guide them.

The eel breeder was a witty fellow, a merry guest, and brought a measure of brandy with him. Every one received a small glassful, or a cupful when there was a scarcity of glasses: even Jürgen had as much as a large thimbleful, that he might digest the fat eel, the eel breeder said, who always told the same story over again, and when his hearers laughed he immediately told it over again to the same audience. As, during his childhood, and even later, Jürgen used many expressions from this story of the eel breeder's, and made use of it in various ways, it is as well that we should listen to it too. Here it is:

"The eels went into the bay; and the mother-eel said to her daughters, who begged leave to go a little way up the bay, 'Don't go too far: the ugly eel spearer might come and snap you all up.' But they went too far; and of eight daughters only three came back to the eel-mother, and these wept and said, 'We only went a little way before the door, and the ugly eel spearer came directly, and stabbed five of our party to death.' 'They'll come again,' said the mother-eel. 'Oh no,' exclaimed the daughters, 'for he skinned them, and cut them in two, and fried them.' 'Oh, they'll come again,' the mother-eel persisted. 'No,' replied the daughters, 'for he ate them up.' 'They'll come again,' repeated the mother-eel. 'But he drank brandy after them,' continued the daughters. 'Ah, then they'll never come back,' said the mother, and she burst out crying, 'It's the brandy that buries the eels.'

"And therefore," said the eel breeder, in conclusion, "it is always right to take brandy after eating eels."

And this story was the tinsel thread, the most humourous recollection of Jürgen's life. *He* likewise wanted to go a little way outside the door, and up the bay—that is to say, out into the world in a ship; and his mother said, like the eel breeder, "There are so many bad people—eel spearers!" But he wished to go a little way past the sand-hills, a little way into the dunes, and he succeeded in doing so. Four merry days, the happiest of his childhood, unrolled themselves, and the whole beauty and splendour of Jutland, all the joy and sunshine of his home, was concentrated in these. He was to go to a festival—though it was certainly a burial feast.

A wealthy relative of the fisherman's family had died. The farm lay deep in the country, eastward, and a point towards the north, as the saying is. Jürgen's foster-parents were to go, and he was to accompany them from the dunes, across heath and moor. They came to the green meadows where the river Skjärn rolls its course, the river of many eels, where mother-eels dwell with their daughters, who are caught and eaten up by wicked people. But men were said sometimes to have acted no better towards their own fellow men; for had not the knight, Sir Bugge, been murdered by wicked people? and though he was well spoken of, had he not wanted to kill the architect, as the legend tells us, who had built for him the castle, with the thick walls and tower, where Jürgen and his parents now stood, and where the river falls into the bay? The wall on the ramparts still remained, and red crumbling fragments lay strewn around. Here it was that Sir Bugge, after the architect had left him, said to one of his men, "Go thou after him, and say, 'Master, the tower shakes.' If he turns round, you are to kill him, and take from him the money I paid him; but if he does not turn round, let him depart in peace." The man obeyed, and the architect never turned round, but called back, "The tower does not shake in the least, but one day there will come a man from the west, in a blue cloak, who will cause it to shake!" And indeed so it chanced, a hundred years later; for the North Sea broke in, and the tower was cast down, but the man who then possessed the castle, Prebjörn Gyldenstjerne, built a new castle higher up, at the end of the meadow, and that stands to this day, and is called Nörre Vosborg.

Past this castle went Jürgen and his foster-parents. They had told him its story during the long winter evenings, and now he saw the lordly castle, with its double moat, and trees, and bushes; the wall, covered with ferns, rose within the moat; but most beautiful of all were the lofty lime trees, which grew up to the highest windows, and filled the air with sweet fragrance. In a corner of the garden towards the north-west stood a great bush full of blossom like winter snow amid the summer's green: it was a juniper bush, the first that Jürgen had seen thus in bloom. He never forgot it, nor the lime tree: the child's soul treasured up these remembrances of beauty and fragrance to gladden the old man.

From Nörre Vosborg, where the juniper blossomed, the way went more easily; for they encountered other guests who were also bound for the burial, and were riding in wagons. Our travellers had to sit all together on a little box at the back of the wagon, but even this was preferable to walking, they thought. So they pursued their journey in the wagon across the rugged heath. The oxen which drew the vehicle slipped every now and then, where a patch of fresh grass appeared amid the heather. The sun shone warm, and it was wonderful to behold how in the far distance something like smoke seemed to be rising; and yet this smoke was clearer than the mist; it was transparent, and looked like rays of light rolling and dancing afar over the heath.

"That is Lokeman driving his sheep," said some one; and this was enough to excite the fancy of Jürgen. It seemed to him as if they were now going to enter fairyland, though everything was still real.

How quiet it was! Far and wide the heath extended around them like a beautiful carpet. The heather bloomed; the juniper bushes and the fresh oak saplings stood up like nosegays from the earth. An inviting place for a frolic, if it were not for the number of poisonous adders of which the travellers spoke, as they did also of the wolves which formerly infested the place, from which circumstance the region was still called the Wolfsborg region. The old man who guided the oxen related how, in the lifetime of his father, the horses had to sustain many a hard fight with the wild beasts that were now extinct; and how he himself, when he went out one morning to bring in the horses, had found one of them standing with its fore-feet on a wolf it had killed, after the savage beast had torn and lacerated the legs of the brave horse.

The journey over the heath and the deep sand was only too quickly accomplished. They stopped before the house of mourning, where they found plenty of guests within and without. Wagon after wagon stood ranged in a row, and horses and oxen went out to crop the scanty pasture. Great sand-hills, like those at home in the North Sea, rose behind the house, and extended far and wide. How had they come here, miles into the interior of the land, and as large and high as those on the coast? The wind had lifted and carried them hither, and to them also a history was attached.

Psalms were sung, and a few of the old people shed tears; beyond this, the guests were cheerful enough, as it appeared to Jürgen, and there was plenty to eat and drink. Eels there were of the fattest, upon which brandy should be poured to bury them, as the eel breeder said; and certainly his maxim was here carried out.

Jürgen went to and fro in the house. On the third day he felt quite at home, like as in the fisherman's hut on the sand-hills where he had passed his early days. Here on the heath there was certainly an unheard-of wealth, for the flowers and blackberries and bilberries were to be found in plenty, so large and sweet, that when they were crushed beneath the tread of the passers by, the heath was coloured with their red juice.

Here was a Hun's Grave, and yonder another. Columns of smoke rose into the still air; it was a heath-fire, he was told, that shone so splendidly in the dark evening.

Now came the fourth day, and the funeral festivities were to conclude, and they were to go back from the land-dunes to the sand-dunes.

"Ours are the best," said the old fisherman, Jürgen's foster-father; "these have no strength."

And they spoke of the way in which the sand-dunes had come into the country, and it seemed all very intelligible. This was the explanation they gave:

A corpse had been found on the coast, and the peasants had buried it in the churchyard; and from that time the sand began to fly, and the sea broke in violently. A wise man in the parish advised them to open the grave and to look if the buried man was not lying sucking his thumb; for if so, he was a man of the sea, and the sea would not rest until it had got him back. So the grave was opened, and he really was found with his thumb in his mouth. So they laid him upon a cart and harnessed two oxen before it; and as if stung by an adder, the oxen ran away with the man of the sea over heath and moorland to the ocean; and then the sand ceased flying inland, but the hills that had been heaped up still remained there. All this Jürgen heard and treasured in his memory from the happiest days of his childhood, the days of the burial feast. How glorious it was to get out into strange regions, and to see strange people! And he was to go farther still. He was not yet fourteen years old when he went out in a ship to see what the world could show him: bad weather, heavy seas, malice, and hard men—these were his experiences, for he became a ship boy. There were cold nights, and bad living, and blows to be endured; then he felt as if his noble Spanish blood boiled within him, and bitter wicked words seethed up to his lips; but it was better to gulp them down, though he felt as the eel must feel when it is flayed and cut up, and put into the frying-pan.

"I shall come again!" said a voice within him. He saw the Spanish coast, the native land of his parents. He even saw the town where they had lived in happiness and prosperity; but he knew nothing of his home or race, and his race knew just as little about him.

The poor ship boy was not allowed to land; but on the last day of their stay he managed to get ashore. There were several purchases to be made, and he was to carry them on board.

There stood Jürgen in his shabby clothes, which looked as if they had been washed in the ditch and dried in the chimney: for the first time he, the inhabitant of the dunes, saw a great city. How lofty the houses seemed, and how full of people were the streets! some pushing this way, some that—a perfect maelstrom of citizens and peasants, monks and soldiers—a calling and shouting, and jingling of bell-harnessed asses and mules, and the church bells chiming between song and sound, hammering and knocking, all going on at once. Every handicraft had its home in the basements of the houses or in the lanes; and the sun shone so hotly, and the air was so close, that one seemed to be in an oven full of beetles, cockchafers, bees, and flies, all humming and murmuring together. Jürgen hardly knew where he was or which way he went. Then he saw just in front of him the mighty portal of the cathedral; the lights were gleaming in the dark aisles, and a fragrance of incense was wafted towards him. Even the poorest beggar ventured up the steps into the temple. The sailor with whom Jürgen went took his way through the church; and Jürgen stood in the sanctuary. Coloured pictures gleamed from their golden ground. On the altar stood the figure of the Virgin with the child Jesus, surrounded by lights and flowers; priests in festive garb were chanting, and choir boys, beautifully attired, swung the silver censer. What splendour, what magnificence did he see here! It streamed through his soul and overpowered him; the church and the faith of his parents surrounded him, and touched a chord in his soul, so that the tears overflowed his eyes.

From the church they went to the market-place. Here a quantity of provisions were given him to carry. The way to the harbour was long, and, tired and overpowered by various emotions, he rested for a few moments before a splendid house, with marble pillars, statues, and broad staircases. Here he rested his burden against the wall. Then a liveried porter came out, lifted up a silver-headed cane, and drove him away—him, the grandson of the house. But no one there knew that, and he just as little as any one. And afterwards he went on board again, and there were hard words and cuffs, little sleep and much work; such were his experiences. They say that it is well to suffer in youth, if age brings something to make up for it.

His time of servitude on shipboard had expired, and the vessel lay once more at Ringkjöbing, in Jutland: he came ashore and went home to the sand-dunes by Hunsby; but his foster-mother had died while he was away on his voyage.

A hard winter followed that summer. Snowstorms swept over land and sea, and there was a difficulty in getting about. How variously things were distributed in the world! here biting cold and snowstorms, while in the Spanish land there was burning sunshine and oppressive heat. And yet, when here at home there came a clear frosty day, and Jürgen saw the swans flying in numbers from the sea towards the land, and across to Vosborg, it appeared to him that people could breathe most freely here; and here too was a splendid summer! In imagination he saw the heath bloom and grow purple with rich juicy berries, and saw the elder trees and the lime trees at Vosborg in blossom. He determined to go there once more.

Spring came on, and the fishery began. Jürgen was an active assistant in this; he had grown in the last year, and was quick at work. He was full of life, he understood how to swim, to tread water, to turn over and tumble in the flood. They often warned him to beware of the troops of dogfish, which could seize the best swimmer, and draw him down, and devour him; but such was not Jürgen's fate.

At the neighbour's on the dune was a boy named Martin, with whom Jürgen was very friendly, and the two took service in the same ship to Norway, and also went together to Holland; and they had never had any quarrel; but a quarrel can easily come, for when a person is hot by nature, he often uses strong gestures, and that is what Jürgen did one day on board when they had a quarrel about nothing at all. They were sitting behind the cabin door, eating out of a delf plate which they had placed between them. Jürgen held his pocket-knife in his hand, and lifted it against Martin, and at the same time became ashy pale in the face, and his eyes had an ugly look. Martin only said,

"Ah! ha! you 're one of that sort, who are fond of using the knife!"

Hardly were the words spoken, when Jürgen's hand sank down. He answered not a syllable, but went on eating, and afterwards walked away to his work. When they were resting again, he stepped up to Martin, and said,

"You may hit me in the face! I have deserved it. But I feel as if I had a pot in me that boiled over."

"There let the thing rest," replied Martin; and after that they were almost doubly as good friends as before; and when afterwards they got back to the dunes and began telling their adventures, this was told among the rest; and Martin said that Jürgen was certainly passionate, but a good fellow for all that.

They were both young and strong, well-grown and stalwart; but Jürgen was the cleverer of the two.

In Norway the peasants go into the mountains, and lead out the cattle there to pasture. On the west coast of Jutland, huts have been erected among the sand-hills; they are built of pieces of wreck, and roofed with turf and heather. There are sleeping-places around the walls, and here the fisher people live and sleep during the early spring. Every fisherman has his female helper, his manager, as she is called, whose business consists in baiting the hooks, preparing the warm beer for the fishermen when they come ashore, and getting their dinners cooked when they come back into the hut tired and hungry. Moreover, the managers bring up the fish from the boat, cut them open, prepare them, and have generally a great deal to do.

Jürgen, his father, and several other fishermen and their managers inhabited the same hut; Martin lived in the next one.

One of the girls, Else by name, had known Jürgen from childhood: they were glad to see each other, and in many things were of the same mind; but in outward appearance they were entirely opposite; for he was brown, whereas she was pale and had flaxen hair, and eyes as blue as the sea in sunshine.

One day as they were walking together, and Jürgen held her hand in his very firmly and warmly, she said to him,

"Jürgen, I have something weighing upon my heart! Let me be your manager, for you are like a brother to me, whereas Martin, who has engaged me—he and I are lovers———but you need not tell that to the rest."

And it seemed to Jürgen as if the loose sand were giving way under his feet. He spoke not a word, but only nodded his head, which signified "yes." More was not required; but suddenly he felt in his heart that he detested Martin; and the longer he considered of this—for he had never thought of Else in this way before—the more did it become clear to him that Martin had stolen from him the only being he loved; and now it was all at once plain to him, that Else was the being in question.

When the sea is somewhat disturbed, and the fishermen come home in their great boat, it is a sight to behold how they cross the reefs. One of the men stands upright in the bow of the boat, and the others watch him, sitting with the oars in their hands. Outside the reef they appear to be rowing not towards the land, but backing out to sea, till the man standing in the boat gives them the sign that the great wave is coming which is to float them across the reef; and accordingly the boat is lifted—lifted high in the air, so that its keel is seen from the shore; and in the next minute the whole boat is hidden from the eye; neither mast nor keel nor people can be seen, as though the sea had devoured them; but in a few moments they emerge like a great sea animal climbing up the waves, and the oars move as if the creature had legs. The second and the third reef are passed in the same manner; and now the fishermen jump into the water; every wave helps them, and pushes the boat well forward, till at length they have drawn it beyond the range of the breakers.

A wrong order given in front of the reef—the slightest hesitation—and the boat must founder.

"Then it would be all over with me, and Martin too!" This thought struck Jürgen while they were out at sea, where his foster-father had been taken alarmingly ill. The fever had seized him. They were only a few oars' strokes from the reef, and Jürgen sprang from his seat, and stood up in the bow.

"Father—let me come!" he said; and his eye glanced towards Martin, and across the waves: but while every oar bent with the exertions of the rowers, as the great wave came towering towards them, he beheld the pale face of his father, and dare not obey the evil impulse that had seized him. The boat came safely across the reef to land, but the evil thought remained in his blood, and roused up every little fibre of bitterness which had remained in his memory since he and Martin had been comrades. But he could not weave the fibres together, nor did he endeavour to do so. He felt that Martin had despoiled him, and this was enough to make him detest his former friend. Several of the fishermen noticed this, but not Martin, who continued obliging and talkative—the latter a little too much.

Jürgen's adopted father had to keep his bed, which became his deathbed, for in the next week he died; and now Jürgen was installed as heir in the little house behind the sand-hills. It was but a little house, certainly, but still it was something, and Martin had nothing of the kind.

"You will not take sea service again, Jürgen?" observed one of the old fishermen. "You will always stay with us, now."

But this was not Jürgen's intention, for he was just thinking of looking about him a little in the world. The eel breeder of Zjaltring had an uncle in Alt-Skage, who was a fisherman, but at the same time a prosperous merchant, who had ships upon the sea; he was said to be a good old man, and it would not be amiss to enter his service. Alt-Skage lies in the extreme north of Jutland, as far removed from the Hunsby dunes as one can travel in that country; and this is just what pleased Jürgen, for he did not want to remain till the wedding of Martin and Else, which was to be celebrated in a few weeks.

The old fisherman asserted that it was foolish now to quit the neighbourhood; for that Jürgen had a home, and Else would probably be inclined to take him rather than Martin.

Jürgen answered so much at random, that it was not easy to understand what he meant; but the old man brought Else to him, and she said, "You have a home now; that ought to be well considered."

And Jürgen thought of many things.

The sea has heavy waves, but there are heavier waves in the human heart. Many thoughts, strong and weak, thronged through Jürgen's brain; and he said to Else,

"If Martin had a house like mine, whom would you rather have?"

"But Martin has no house, and cannot get one."

"But let us suppose he had one."

"Why then I would certainly take Martin, for that's what my heart tells me; but one can't live upon that."

And Jürgen thought of these things all night through. Something was working within him, he could not understand what it was, but he had a thought that was stronger than his love for Else; and so he went to Martin, and what he said and did there was well considered. He let the house to Martin on the most liberal terms, saying that he wished to go to sea again, because it pleased him to do so. And Else kissed him on the mouth when she heard that, for she loved Martin best.

In the early morning Jürgen purposed to start. On the evening before his departure, when it was already growing late, he felt a wish to visit Martin once more; he started, and among the dunes the old fisher met him, who was angry at his going. The old man made jokes about Martin, and declared there must be some magic about that fellow, "of whom all the girls were so fond." Jürgen paid no heed to this speech, but said farewell to the old man, and went on towards the house where Martin dwelt. He heard loud talking within. Martin was not alone, and this made Jürgen waver in his determination, for he did not wish to encounter Else; and on second consideration, he

A Story from the Sand-Dunes

thought it better not to hear Martin thank him again, and therefore turned back.

On the following morning, before break of day, he fastened his knapsack, took his wooden provision box in his hand, and went away among the sand-hills towards the coast path. The way was easier to traverse than the heavy sand road, and moreover shorter; for he intended to go in the first instance to Zjaltring, by Bowberg, where the eel breeder lived, to whom he had promised a visit.

The sea lay pure and blue before him, and mussel shells and sea pebbles, the playthings of his youth, crunched under his feet. While he was thus marching on, his nose suddenly began to bleed: it was a trifling incident, but little things can have great significances. A few large drops of blood fell upon one of his sleeves. He wiped them off and stopped the bleeding, and it seemed to him as if this had cleared and lightened his brain. In the sand the sea-eringa was blooming here and there. He broke off a stalk and stuck it in his hat; he determined to be merry and of good cheer, for he was going into the wide world—"a little way outside the door, in front of the hay," as the young eels had said. "Beware of bad people, who will catch you and flay you, cut you in two, and put you in the frying-pan!" he repeated in his mind, and smiled, for he thought he should find his way through the world—good courage is a strong weapon!

The sun already stood high when he approached the narrow entrance to Nissum Bay. He looked back, and saw a couple of horsemen galloping a long distance behind him, and they were accompanied by other people. But this concerned him nothing.

The ferry was on the opposite side of the bay. Jürgen called to the ferryman; and when the latter came over with the boat, Jürgen stepped in; but before they had gone half-way across, the men whom he had seen riding so hastily behind him, hailed the ferryman, and summoned him to return in the name of the law. Jürgen did not understand the reason of this, but he thought it would be best to turn back, and therefore himself took an oar and returned. The moment the boat touched the shore, the men sprang on board, and, before he was aware, they had bound his hands with a rope.

"Thy wicked deed will cost thee thy life," they said. "It is well that we caught thee."

He was accused of nothing less than murder. Martin had been found dead, with a knife thrust through his neck. One of the fishermen had (late on the previous evening) met Jürgen going towards Martin's house; and this was not the first time Jürgen had raised his knife against Martin—so they knew that he was the murderer. The town in which the prison was built was a long way off, and the wind was contrary for going there; but not half an hour would be required to get across the bay, and a quarter of an hour would bring them from thence to Nörre Vosborg, a great castle with walls and ditches. One of Jürgen's captors was a fisherman, a brother of the keeper of the castle; and he declared it might be managed that Jürgen should for the present be put into the dungeon at Vosborg, where Long Martha the gipsy had been shut up till her execution.

No attention was paid to the defence made by Jürgen; the few drops of blood upon his shirt-sleeve bore heavy witness against him. But Jürgen was conscious of innocence; and as there was no chance of immediately righting himself, he submitted to his fate.

The party landed just at the spot where Sir Bugge's castle had stood and where Jürgen had walked with his foster-parents after the burial feast, during the four happiest days of his childhood. He was led by the old path over the meadow to Vosborg; and again the elder blossomed and the lofty lindens smelt sweet, and it seemed but yesterday that he had left the spot.

In the two wings of the castle a staircase leads down to a spot below the entrance, and from thence there is access to a low vaulted cellar. Here Long Martha had been imprisoned, and hence she had been led away to the scaffold. She had eaten the hearts of five children, and had been under the delusion that if she could obtain two more, she would be able to fly and to make herself invisible. In the midst of the cellar roof was a little narrow air-hole, but no window. The blooming lindens could not waft a breath of comforting fragrance into that abode, where all was dark and mouldy. Only a rough bench stood in the prison; but "a good conscience is a soft pillow," and consequently Jürgen could sleep well.

The thick oaken door was locked, and secured on the outside by an iron bar; but the goblin of superstition can creep through a keyhole into the baron's castle just as into the fisherman's hut; and wherefore should he not creep in here, where Jürgen sat thinking of Long Martha and her evil deeds? Her last thought on the night before her execution had filled this space; and all the magic came into Jürgen's mind which tradition asserted to have been practised there in the old times, when Sir Schwanwedel dwelt there. All this passed through Jürgen's mind, and made him shudder; but a sunbeam—a refreshing thought from without—penetrated his heart even here; it was the remembrance of the blooming elder and the fragrant lime trees.

He was not left there long. They carried him off to the town of Ringkjöbing, where his imprisonment was just as hard.

Those times were not like ours. Hard measure was dealt out to the "common" people; and it was just after the days when farms were converted into knights' estates, on which occasions coachmen and servants were often made magistrates, and had it in their power to sentence a poor man, for a small offence, to lose his property and to corporal punishment. Judges of this kind were still to be found; and in Jutland, far from the capital and from the enlightened well-meaning head of the government, the law was still sometimes very loosely administered; and the smallest grievance that Jürgen had to expect was that his case would be protracted.

Cold and cheerless was his abode—and when would this state of things end? He had innocently sunk into misfortune and sorrow—that was his fate. He had leisure now to ponder on the difference of fortune on earth, and to wonder why this fate had been allotted to him; and he felt sure that the question would be answered in the next life—the existence that awaits us when this is over. This faith had grown strong in him in the poor fisherman's hut; that which had never shone into his father's mind, in all the richness and sunshine of Spain, was vouchsafed as a light of comfort in his poverty and distress—a sign of mercy from God that never deceives.

The spring storms began to blow. The rolling and moaning of the North Sea could be heard for miles inland when the wind was lulled; for then it sounded like the rushing of a thousand wagons over a hard road with a mine beneath. Jürgen, in his prison, heard these sounds, and it was a relief to him. No melody could have appealed so directly to his heart as did these sounds of the sea—the rolling sea, the boundless sea, on which a man can be borne across the world before the wind, carrying his own house with him wherever he is driven, just as the snail carries its home even into a strange land.

How he listened to the deep moaning, and how the thought arose in him—"Free! free! How happy to be free, even without shoes and in ragged clothes!" Sometimes, when such thoughts crossed his mind, the fiery nature rose within him, and he beat the wall with his clenched fists.

Weeks, months, a whole year had gone by, when a vagabond—Niels, the thief, called also the horse couper—was arrested; and now the better times came, and it was seen what wrong Jürgen had endured.

In the neighbourhood of Ringkjöbing, at a beer-house, Niels, the thief, had met Martin on the afternoon before Jürgen's departure from home and before the murder. A few glasses were drunk—not enough to cloud any one's brain, but yet enough to loosen Martin's tongue; and he began to boast, and to say that he had obtained a house, and intended to marry; and when Niels asked where he intended to get the money, Martin shook his pocket proudly, and said,

"The money is there, where it ought to be."

This boast cost him his life; for when he went home, Niels went after him, and thrust a knife through his throat, to rob the murdered man of the expected gold, which did not exist.

This was circumstantially explained; but for us it is enough to know that Jürgen was set at liberty. But what amends did he get for having been imprisoned a whole year, and shut out from all communion with men? They told him he was fortunate in being proved innocent, and that he might go. The burgomaster gave him two dollars for travelling expenses, and many citizens offered him provisions and beer—there were still good men, not all "grind and flay." But the best of all was, that the merchant Brönne of Skjagen, the same into whose service Jürgen intended to go a year since, was just at that time on business in the town of Ringkjöbing. Brönne heard the whole story; and the man had a good heart, and understood what Jürgen must have felt and suffered. He therefore made up his mind to make it up to the poor lad, and convince him that there were still kind folks in the world.

So Jürgen went forth from the prison as if to Paradise, to find freedom, affection, and trust. He was to travel this road now; for no goblet of life is all bitterness: no good man would pour out such measure to his fellow man, and how should He do it, who is love itself?

"Let all that be buried and forgotten," said Brönne the merchant. "Let us draw a thick line through last year; and we will even burn the calendar. And in two days we'll start for dear, friendly, peaceful Skjagen. They call Skjagen an out-of-the-way corner; but it's a good warm chimney-corner, and its windows open towards every part of the world."

That was a journey!—it was like taking fresh breath—out of the cold dungeon air into the warm sunshine! The heath stood blooming in its greatest pride, and the herd-boy sat on the Hun's Grave and blew his pipe, which he had carved for himself out of the sheep's bone. Fata Morgana, the beautiful aërial phenomenon of the desert, showed itself with hanging gardens and swaying forests, and the wonderful cloud phenomenon, called here the "Lokeman driving his flock," was seen likewise.

Up through the land of the Wendels, up towards Skjagen, they went, from whence the men with the long beards (the Longobardi, or Lombards) had emigrated in the days when, in the reign of King Snio, all the children and the old people were to have been killed, till the noble Dame Gambaruk proposed that the young people had better emigrate. All this was known to Jürgen—thus much knowledge he had; and even if he did not know the land of the Lombards beyond the high Alps, he had an idea how it must be there, for in his boyhood he had been in the south, in Spain. He thought of the southern fruits piled up there; of the red pomegranate blossoms; of the humming, murmuring, and toiling in the great beehive of a city he had seen; but, after all, home is best; and Jürgen's home was Denmark.

At length they reached "Wendelskajn," as Skjagen is called in the old Norwegian and Icelandic writings. Then already Old Skjagen, with the western and eastern town, extended for miles, with sand-hills and arable land, as far as the lighthouse near the "Skjagenzweig." Then, as now, the houses were strewn among the wind-raised sand-hills—a desert where the wind sports with the sand, and where the voices of the seamen and the wild swans strike harshly on the ear. In the south-west, a mile from the sea, lies Old Skjagen; and here dwelt merchant Brönne, and here Jürgen was henceforth to dwell. The great house was painted with tar; the smaller buildings had each an overturned boat for a roof; the pig-sty had been put together of pieces of wreck. There was no fence here, for indeed there was nothing to fence in; but long rows of fishes were hung upon lines, one above the other, to dry in the wind. The whole coast was strewn with spoilt herrings; for there were so many of those fish, that a net was scarcely thrown into the sea before they were caught by cartloads; there were so many, that often they were thrown back into the sea, or left to lie on the shore.

The old man's wife and daughter, and his servants too, came rejoicingly to meet him. There was a great pressing of hands, and talking, and questioning. And the daughter, what a lovely face and bright eyes she had!

The interior of the house was roomy and comfortable. Fritters that a king would have looked upon as a dainty dish, were placed on the table; and there was wine from the vineyard of Skjagen—that is, the sea; for there the grapes come ashore ready pressed and prepared in barrels and in bottles.

When the mother and daughter heard who Jürgen was, and how innocently he had suffered, they looked at him in a still more friendly way; and the eyes of the charming Clara were the friendliest of all. Jürgen found a happy home in Old Skjagen. It did his heart good; and his heart had been sorely tried, and had drunk the bitter goblet of love, which softens or hardens according to circumstances. Jürgen's heart was still soft—it was young, and there was still room in it; and therefore it was well that Mistress Clara was going in three weeks in her father's ship to Christiansand, in Norway, to visit an aunt, and to stay there the whole winter.

On the Sunday before her departure they all went to church, to the holy Communion. The church was large and handsome, and had been built centuries before by Scotchmen and Hollanders; it lay at a little distance from the town. It was certainly somewhat ruinous, and the road to it was heavy, through the deep sand; but the people gladly went through the difficulties to get to the house of God, to sing psalms and hear the sermon. The sand had heaped itself up round the walls of the church; but the graves were kept free from it.

A Story from the Sand-Dunes

It was the largest church north of the Limfjord. The Virgin Mary, with the golden crown on her head and the child Jesus in her arms, stood life-like upon the altar; the holy Apostles had been carved in the choir; and on the wall hung portraits of the old burgomasters and councillors of Skjagen; the pulpit was of carved work. The sun shone brightly into the church, and its radiance fell on the polished brass chandelier, and on the little ship that hung from the vaulted roof.

Jürgen felt as if overcome by a holy, childlike feeling, like that which possessed him when, as a boy, he had stood in the splendid Spanish cathedral; but here the feeling was different, for he felt conscious of being one of the congregation.

After the sermon followed the holy Communion. He partook of the bread and wine, and it happened that he knelt beside Mistress Clara; but his thoughts were so fixed upon Heaven and the holy service, that he did not notice his neighbour until he rose from his knees, and then he saw tears rolling down her cheeks.

Two days later she left Skjagen and went to Norway. He stayed behind, and made himself useful in the house and in the business. He went out fishing, and at that time fish were more plentiful and larger than now. Every Sunday when he sat in the church, and his eye rested on the statue of the Virgin on the altar, his glance rested for a time on the spot where Mistress Clara had knelt beside him, and he thought of her, how hearty and kind she had been to him.

And so the autumn and the winter time passed away. There was wealth here, and a real family life; even down to the domestic animals, who were all well kept. The kitchen glittered with copper and tin and white plates, and from the roof hung hams and beef, and winter stores in plenty. All this is still to be seen in many rich farms of the west coast of Jutland: plenty to eat and drink, clean decorated rooms, clever heads, happy tempers, and hospitality prevail there as in an Arab tent.

Never since the famous burial feast had Jürgen spent such a happy time; and yet Mistress Clara was absent, except in the thoughts and memory of all.

In April a ship was to start for Norway, and Jürgen was to sail in it. He was full of life and spirits, and looked so stout and jovial that Dame Brönne declared it did her good to see him.

"And it's a pleasure to see you too, old wife," said the old merchant. "Jürgen has brought life into our winter evenings, and into you too, mother. You look younger this year, and you seem well and bonny. But then you were once the prettiest girl in Wiborg, and that's saying a great deal, for I have always found the Wiborg girls the prettiest of any."

Jürgen said nothing to this, but he thought of a certain maiden of Skjagen; and he sailed to visit that maiden, for the ship steered to Christiansand, in Norway, and a favouring wind bore it rapidly to that town.

One morning merchant Brönne went out to the lighthouse that stands far away from Old Skjagen: the coal fire had long gone out, and the sun was already high when he mounted the tower. The sand-banks extend under the water a whole mile from the shore. Outside these banks many ships were seen that day; and with the help of his telescope the old man thought he descried his own vessel, the "Karen Brönne."

Yes, surely there she was; and the ship was sailing up with Jürgen and Clara on board. The church and the lighthouse appeared to them as a heron and a swan rising from the blue waters. Clara sat on deck, and saw the sand-hills gradually looming forth: if the wind held she might reach her home in about an hour—so near were they to home and its joys—so near were they to death and its terrors. For a plank in the ship gave way, and the water rushed in. The crew flew to the pumps, and attempted to stop the leak. A signal of distress was hoisted; but they were still a full mile from the shore. Fishing boats were in sight, but they were still far distant. The wind blew shoreward, and the tide was in their favour too; but all was insufficient, for the ship sank. Jürgen threw his right arm about Clara, and pressed her close to him.

With what a look she gazed in his face! As he threw himself in God's name into the water with her, she uttered a cry; but still she felt safe, certain that he would not let her sink.

And now, in the hour of terror and danger, Jürgen experienced what the old song told:

> "And written it stood, how the brave king's son
> Embraced the bride his valour had won."

A Story from the Sand-Dunes

How rejoiced he felt that he was a good swimmer! He worked his way onward with his feet and with one hand, while with the other he tightly held the young girl. He rested upon the waves, he trod the water, he practised all the arts he knew, so as to reserve strength enough to reach the shore. He heard how Clara uttered a sigh, and felt a convulsive shudder pass through her, and he pressed her to him closer than ever. Now and then a wave rolled over her; and he was still a few cables' lengths from the land, when help came in the shape of an approaching boat. But under the water—he could see it clearly—stood a white form gazing at him: a wave lifted him up, and the form approached him: he felt a shock, and it grew dark, and everything vanished from his gaze.

On the sand-reef lay the wreck of a ship, the sea washed over it; the white figure-head leant against an anchor, the sharp iron extended just to the surface. Jürgen had come in contact with this, and the tide had driven him against it with double force. He sank down fainting with his load; but the next wave lifted him and the young girl aloft again.

The fishermen grasped them, and lifted them into the boat. The blood streamed down over Jürgen's face; he seemed dead, but he still clutched the girl so tightly that they were obliged to loosen her by force from his grasp. And Clara lay pale and lifeless in the boat, that now made for the shore.

All means were tried to restore Clara to life; but she was dead! For some time he had been swimming onward with a corpse, and had exerted himself to exhaustion for one who was dead.

Jürgen was still breathing. The fishermen carried him into the nearest house upon the sand-hills. A kind of surgeon who lived there, and was at the same time a smith and a general dealer, bound up Jürgen's wounds in a temporary way, till a physician could be got next day from the nearest town.

The brain of the sick man was affected. In delirium he uttered wild cries; but on the third day he lay quiet and exhausted on his couch, and his life seemed to hang by a thread, and the physician said it would be best if this string snapped.

"Let us pray that God may take him to Himself; he will never be a sane man again!"

But life would not depart from him—the thread would not snap; but the thread of memory broke: the thread of all his mental power had been cut through; and, what was most terrible, a body remained—a living healthy body—that wandered about like a spectre.

Jürgen remained in the house of the merchant Brönne.

"He contracted his illness in his endeavour to save our child," said the old man, "and now he is our son."

People called Jürgen imbecile; but that was not the right expression. He was like an instrument, in which the strings are loose and will sound no more; only at times for a few minutes they regained their power, and then they sounded anew: old melodies were heard, snatches of song; pictures unrolled themselves, and then disappeared again in the mist, and once more he sat staring before him, without a thought. We may believe that he did not suffer, but his dark eyes lost their brightness, and looked only like black clouded glass.

"Poor imbecile Jürgen!" said the people.

He it was whose life was to have been so pleasant that it would be "presumption and pride" to expect or believe in a higher existence hereafter. All his great mental faculties had been lost; only hard days, pain, and disappointment had been his lot. He was like a rare plant torn from its native soil, and thrown upon the sand, to wither there. And was the image, fashioned in God's likeness, to have no better destination? Was it to be merely the sport of chance? No. The all-loving God would certainly repay him in the life to come, for what he had suffered and lost here. "The Lord is good to all; and His mercy is over all His works." These words from the Psalms of David, the old pious wife of the merchant repeated in patience and hope, and the prayer of her heart was that Jürgen might soon be summoned to enter into the life eternal.

In the churchyard where the sand blows across the walls, Clara lay buried. It seemed as if Jürgen knew nothing of this—it did not come within the compass of his thoughts, which comprised only fragments of a past time. Every Sunday he went with the old people to church, and sat silent there with vacant gaze. One day, while the Psalms were being sung, he uttered a deep sigh, and his eyes gleamed: they were fixed upon the altar, upon the place where he had knelt with his friend who was dead. He uttered her name, and became pale as death, and tears rolled over his cheeks.

They led him out of the church; and he said to the bystanders that he was well, and had never been ill: he, the heavily afflicted, the waif cast forth upon the world, remembered nothing of his sufferings. And the Lord our Creator is wise and full of loving-kindness—who can doubt it?

In Spain, where the warm breezes blow over the Moorish cupola, among the orange trees and laurels, where song and the sound of castagnettes are always heard, sat in the sumptuous house a childish old man, the richest merchant in the place, while children marched in procession through the streets, with waving flags and lighted tapers. How much of his wealth would the old man not have given to be able to press his children to his heart! his daughter, or her child, that had perhaps never seen the light in this world, far less a Paradise.

"Poor child!"

Yes, poor child—a child still, and yet more than thirty years old; for to that age Jürgen had attained in Old Skjagen.

The drifting sand had covered the graves in the churchyard quite up to the walls of the church; but yet the dead must be buried among their relations and loved ones who had gone before them. Merchant Brönne and his wife now rested here with their children, under the white sand.

It was spring-time, the season of storms. The sand-hills whirled up in clouds, and the sea ran high, and flocks of birds flew like clouds in the storms, shrieking across the dunes; and shipwreck followed shipwreck on the reefs of "Skjagenzweig" from towards the Hunsby dunes. One evening Jürgen was sitting alone in the room. Suddenly his mind seemed to become clearer, and a feeling of unrest came upon him, which in his younger years had often driven him forth upon the heath and the sand-hills.

"Home! home!" he exclaimed. No one heard him. He went out of the house towards the dunes. Sand and stones blew into his face and whirled around him. He went on farther and farther, towards the church: the sand lay high around the walls, half over the windows; but the heap had been shovelled away from the door, and the entrance was free and easy to open; and Jürgen went into the church.

The storm went howling over the town of Skjagen. Within the memory of man the sea had not run so high—a terrible tempest! but Jürgen was in the temple of God, and while black night reigned without, a light arose in his soul, a light that was never to be extinguished; he felt the heavy stone which seemed to weigh upon his head burst asunder. He thought he heard the sound of the organ, but it was the storm and the moaning of the sea. He sat down on one of the seats; and behold, the candles were lighted up one by one; a richness was displayed such as he had only seen in the church in Spain; and all the pictures of the old councillors were endued with life, and stepped forth from the walls against which they had stood for centuries, and seated themselves in the entrance of the church. The gates and doors flew open, and in came all the dead people, festively clad, and sat down to the sound of beautiful music, and filled the seats in the church. Then the psalm tune rolled forth like a sounding sea; and his old foster-parents from the Hunsby dunes were here, and the old merchant Brönne and his wife; and at their side, close to Jürgen, sat their friendly, lovely daughter Clara, who gave her hand to Jürgen, and they both went to the altar, where they had once knelt together, and the priest joined their hands and joined them together for life. Then the sound of music was heard again, wonderful, like a child's voice full of joy and expectation, and it swelled on to an organ's sound, to a tempest of full, noble sounds, lovely and elevating to hear, and yet strong enough to burst the stone tombs.

And the little ship that hung down from the roof of the choir came down, and became wonderfully large and beautiful, with silken sails and golden yards, "and every rope wrought through with silk," as the old song said. The married pair went on board, and the whole congregation with them, for there was room and joyfulness for all. And the walls and arches of the church bloomed like the juniper and the fragrant lime trees, and the leaves and branches waved and distributed coolness; then they bent and parted, and the ship sailed through the midst of them, through the sea, and through the air; and every church taper became a star, and the wind sang a psalm tune, and all sang with the wind:

"In love, to glory—no life shall be lost. Full of blessedness and joy. Hallelujah!"

And these words were the last that Jürgen spoke in this world. The thread snapped that bound the immortal soul, and nothing but a dead body lay in the dark church, around which the storm raged, covering it with loose sand.

The next morning was Sunday, and the congregation and their pastor went forth to the service. The road to church had been heavy; the sand made the way almost impassable; and now, when they at last reached their goal, a great hill of sand was piled up before the entrance, and the church itself was buried. The priest spoke a short prayer, and said that God had closed the door of this house, and the congregation must go and build a new one for Him elsewhere.

So they sang a psalm under the open sky, and went back to their homes.

Jürgen was nowhere to be found in the town of Skjagen, or in the dunes, however much they sought for him. It was thought that the waves, which had rolled far up on the sand, had swept him away.

His body lay buried in a great sepulchre, in the church itself. In the storm the Lord's hand had thrown a handful of earth on his grave; and the heavy mound of sand lay upon it, and lies there to this day.

The whirling sand had covered the high vaulted passages; whitethorn and wild rose-trees grow over the church, over which the wanderer now walks; while the tower, standing forth like a gigantic tombstone over a grave, is to be seen for miles around: no king has a more splendid tombstone. No one disturbs the rest of the dead; no one knew of this, and we are the first who know of this grave—the storm sang the tale to me among the sand-hills.

The Butterfly

Translated by Mrs. H. P. Paull

There was once a butterfly who wished for a bride, and, as may be supposed, he wanted to choose a very pretty one from among the flowers. He glanced, with a very critical eye, at all the flower-beds, and found that the flowers were seated quietly and demurely on their stalks, just as maidens should sit before they are engaged; but there was a great number of them, and it appeared as if his search would become very wearisome. The butterfly did not like to take too much trouble, so he flew off on a visit to the daisies. The French call this flower "Marguerite," and they say that the little daisy can prophesy. Lovers pluck off the leaves, and as they pluck each leaf, they ask a question about their lovers; thus: "Does he or she love me?—Ardently? Distractedly? Very much? A little? Not at all?" and so on. Every one speaks these words in his own language. The butterfly came also to Marguerite to inquire, but he did not pluck off her leaves; he pressed a kiss on each of them, for he thought there was always more to be done by kindness.

The Butterfly

"Darling Marguerite daisy," he said to her, "you are the wisest woman of all the flowers. Pray tell me which of the flowers I shall choose for my wife. Which will be my bride? When I know, I will fly directly to her, and propose."

But Marguerite did not answer him; she was offended that he should call her a woman when she was only a girl; and there is a great difference. He asked her a second time, and then a third; but she remained dumb, and answered not a word. Then he would wait no longer, but flew away, to commence his wooing at once. It was in the early spring, when the crocus and the snowdrop were in full bloom.

"They are very pretty," thought the butterfly; "charming little lasses; but they are rather formal."

Then, as the young lads often do, he looked out for the elder girls. He next flew to the anemones; these were rather sour to his taste. The violet, a little too sentimental. The lime-blossoms, too small, and besides, there was such a large family of them. The apple-blossoms, though they looked like roses, bloomed today, but might fall off tomorrow, with the first wind that blew; and he thought that a marriage with one of them might last too short a time. The pea-blossom pleased him most of all; she was white and red, graceful and slender, and belonged to those domestic maidens who have a pretty appearance, and can yet be useful in the kitchen. He was just about to make her an offer, when, close by the maiden, he saw a pod, with a withered flower hanging at the end.

"Who is that?" he asked.

"That is my sister," replied the pea-blossom.

"Oh, indeed; and you will be like her some day," said he; and he flew away directly, for he felt quite shocked.

A honeysuckle hung forth from the hedge, in full bloom; but there were so many girls like her, with long faces and sallow complexions. No; he did not like her. But which one did he like?

Spring went by, and summer drew towards its close; autumn came; but he had not decided. The flowers now appeared in their most gorgeous robes, but all in vain; they had not the fresh, fragrant air of youth. For the heart asks for fragrance, even when it is no longer young; and there is very little of that to be found in the dahlias or the dry chrysanthemums; therefore the butterfly turned to the mint on the ground. You know, this plant has no blossom; but it is sweetness all over—full of fragrance from head to foot, with the scent of a flower in every leaf.

"I will take her," said the butterfly; and he made her an offer. But the mint stood silent and stiff, as she listened to him. At last she said—

"Friendship, if you please; nothing more. I am old, and you are old, but we may live for each other just the same; as to marrying—no; don't let us appear ridiculous at our age."

And so it happened that the butterfly got no wife at all. He had been too long choosing, which is always a bad plan. And the butterfly became what is called an old bachelor.

It was late in the autumn, with rainy and cloudy weather. The cold wind blew over the bowed backs of the willows, so that they creaked again. It was not the weather for flying about in summer clothes; but fortunately the butterfly was not out in it. He had got a shelter by chance. It was in a room heated by a stove, and as warm as summer. He could exist here, he said, well enough.

"But it is not enough merely to exist," said he, "I need freedom, sunshine, and a little flower for a companion."

Then he flew against the window-pane, and was seen and admired by those in the room, who caught him, and stuck him on a pin, in a box of curiosities. They could not do more for him.

"Now I am perched on a stalk, like the flowers," said the butterfly. "It is not very pleasant, certainly; I should imagine it is something like being married; for here I am stuck fast." And with this thought he consoled himself a little.

"That seems very poor consolation," said one of the plants in the room, that grew in a pot.

"Ah," thought the butterfly, "one can't very well trust these plants in pots; they have too much to do with mankind."

The Bishop of Börglum and His Warriors

Translated by H. W. Dulcken

Our scene is in Northern Jutland, in the so called "wild moor." We hear what is called the "Wester-wow-wow"—the peculiar roar of the North Sea as it breaks against the western coast of Jutland. It rolls and thunders with a sound that penetrates for miles into the land; and we are quite near the roaring. Before us rises a great mound of sand—a mountain we have long seen, and towards which we are wending our way, driving slowly along through the deep sand. On this mountain of sand is a lofty old building—the convent of Börglum. In one of its wings (the larger one) there is still a church. And at this convent we now arrive in the late evening hour; but the weather is clear in the bright June night around us. The eye can range far, far over field and moor to the bay of Aalborg, over heath and meadow, and far across the dark blue sea.

Now we are there, and roll past between barns and other farm buildings; and at the left of the gate we turn aside to the old Castle

Farm, where the lime trees stand in lines along the walls, and, sheltered from the wind and weather, grow so luxuriously that their twigs and leaves almost conceal the windows.

We mount the winding staircase of stone, and march through the long passages under the heavy roof-beams. The wind moans very strangely here, both within and without. It is hardly known how, but people say—yes, people say a great many things when they are frightened or want to frighten others—they say that the old dead choir-men glide silently past us into the church, where mass is sung. They can be heard in the rushing of the storm, and their singing brings up strange thoughts in the hearers—thoughts of the old times into which we are carried back.

On the coast a ship is stranded; and the bishop's warriors are there, and spare not those whom the sea has spared. The sea washes away the blood that has flowed from cloven skulls. The stranded goods belong to the bishop, and there is a store of goods here. The sea casts up tubs and barrels filled with costly wine for the convent cellar; and in the convent is already good store of beer and mead. There is plenty in the kitchen—dead game and poultry, hams and sausages; and fat fish swim in the ponds without.

The Bishop of Börglum is a mighty lord. He has great possessions, but still he longs for more—everything must bow before the mighty Olaf Glob. His rich cousin at Thyland is dead, and his widow is to have the rich inheritance. But how comes it that one relation is always harder towards another than even strangers would be? The widow's husband had possessed all Thyland, with the exception of the Church property. Her son was not at home. In his boyhood he had already started on a journey, for his desire was to see foreign lands and strange people. For years there had been no news of him. Perhaps he had long been laid in the grave, and would never come back to his home to rule where his mother then ruled.

"What has a woman to do with rule?" said the bishop.

He summoned the widow before a court; but what did he gain thereby? The widow had never been disobedient to the law, and was strong in her just rights.

Bishop Olaf, of Börglum, what dost thou purpose? What writest thou on yonder smooth parchment, sealing it with thy seal, and intrusting it to the horsemen and servants, who ride away—far away—to the city of the Pope?

It is the time of falling leaves and of stranded ships, and soon icy winter will come.

Twice had icy winter returned before the bishop welcomed the horsemen and servants back to their home. They came from Rome with a papal decree—a ban, or bull, against the widow who had dared to offend the pious bishop. "Cursed be she, and all that belongs to her. Let her be expelled from the congregation and the Church. Let no man stretch forth a helping hand to her, and let friends and relations avoid her as a plague and a pestilence!"

"What will not bend must break," said the Bishop of Börglum.

And all forsake the widow; but she holds fast to her God. He is her helper and defender.

One servant only—an old maid—remained faithful to her; and, with the old servant, the widow herself followed the plough; and the crop grew, though the land had been cursed by the Pope and the bishop.

"Thou child of hell, I will yet carry out my purpose!" cries the Bishop of Börglum. "Now will I lay the hand of the Pope upon thee, to summon thee before the tribunal that shall condemn thee!"

Then did the widow yoke the two last oxen that remained to her to a wagon, and mounted upon the wagon, with her old servant, and travelled away across the heath out of the Danish land. As a stranger she came into a foreign country, where a strange tongue was spoken and where new customs prevailed. Farther and farther she journeyed, to where green hills rise into mountains, and the vine clothes their sides. Strange merchants drive by her, and they look anxiously after their wagons laden with merchandise. They fear an attack from the armed followers of the robber-knights. The two poor women, in their humble vehicle drawn by two black oxen, travel fearlessly through the dangerous sunken road and through the darksome forest. And now they were in Franconia. And there met them a stalwart knight, with a train of twelve armed followers. He paused, gazed at the strange vehicle, and questioned the women as to the goal of their journey and the place whence they came. Then one of them mentioned Thyland, in Denmark, and spoke of her sorrows—of her woes—which were soon to cease; for so Divine Providence had willed it. For the stranger knight is the widow's son. He seized her hand, he embraced her, and the mother wept. For years she had not been able to weep, but had only bitten her lips till the blood started.

It is the time of falling leaves and of stranded ships, and soon will icy winter come.

The sea rolled wine-tubs to the shore for the bishop's cellar. In the kitchen the deer roasted on the spit before the fire. At Börglum it was warm and cheerful in the heated rooms, while cold winter raged without, when a piece of news was brought to the bishop: "Jens Glob, of Thyland, has come back, and his mother with him." Jens Glob laid a complaint against the bishop, and summoned him before the temporal and the spiritual court.

"That will avail him little," said the bishop. "Best leave off thy efforts, knight Jens."

Again it is the time of falling leaves, of stranded ships—icy winter comes again, and the "white bees" are swarming, and sting the traveller's face till they melt.

"Keen weather today," say the people, as they step in.

Jens Glob stands so deeply wrapped in thought that he singes the skirt of his wide garment.

"Thou Börglum bishop," he exclaims, "I shall subdue thee after all! Under the shield of the Pope, the law cannot reach thee; but Jens Glob shall reach thee!"

Then he writes a letter to his brother-in-law, Olaf Hase, in Sallingland, and prays that knight to meet him on Christmas Eve, at mass, in the church at Widberg. The bishop himself is to read the mass, and consequently will journey from Börglum to Thyland; and this is known to Jens Glob.

Moorland and meadow are covered with ice and snow. The marsh will bear horse and rider, the bishop with his priests, and armed men. They ride the shortest way, through the waving reeds, where the wind moans sadly.

Blow thy brazen trumpet, thou trumpeter clad in foxskin!

it sounds merrily in the clear air. So they ride on over heath and moorland—over what is the garden of Fata Morgana in the hot summer, though now icy, like all the country—towards the church of Widberg.

The wind is blowing his trumpet too—blowing it harder and harder. He blows up a storm—a terrible storm—that increases more and more. Towards the church they ride, as fast as they may through the storm. The church stands firm, but the storm careers on over field and moorland, over land and sea.

Börglum's bishop reaches the church; but Olaf Hase will scarce do so, hard as he may ride. He journeys with his warriors on the farther side of the bay, to help Jens Glob, now that the bishop is to be summoned before the judgment seat of the Highest.

The church is the judgment hall; the altar is the council table. The lights burn clear in the heavy brass candelabra. The storm reads out the accusation and the sentence, roaming in the air over moor and heath, and over the rolling waters. No ferry-boat can sail over the bay in such weather as this.

Olaf Hase makes halt at Ottesworde. There he dismisses his warriors, presents them with their horses and harness, and gives them leave to ride home and greet his wife. He intends to risk his life alone in the roaring waters; but they are to bear witness for him that it is not his fault if Jens Glob stands without reinforcement in the church at Widberg. The faithful warriors will not leave him, but follow him out into the deep waters. Ten of them are carried away; but Olaf Hase and two of the youngest men reach the farther side. They have still four miles to ride.

It is past midnight. It is Christmas. The wind has abated. The church is lighted up; the gleaming radiance shines through the window-frames, and pours out over meadow and heath. The mass has long been finished, silence reigns in the church, and the wax is heard dropping from the candles to the stone pavement. And now Olaf Hase arrives.

In the forecourt Jens Glob greets him kindly, and says,

"I have just made an agreement with the bishop."

"Sayest thou so?" replied Olaf Hase. "Then neither thou nor the bishop shall quit this church alive."

And the sword leaps from the scabbard, and Olaf Hase deals a blow that makes the panel of the church-door, which Jens Glob hastily closes between them, fly in fragments.

"Hold, brother! First hear what the agreement was that I made. I have slain the bishop and his warriors and priests. They will have no word more to say in the matter, nor will I speak again of all the wrong that my mother has endured."

The long wicks of the altar lights glimmer red; but there is a redder gleam upon the pavement, where the bishop lies with cloven skull, and his dead warriors around him, in the quiet of the holy Christmas night.

And four days afterwards the bells toll for a funeral in the convent of Börglum. The murdered bishop and the slain warriors and priests are displayed under a black canopy, surrounded by candelabra decked with crape. There lies the dead man, in the black cloak wrought with silver; the crosier in the powerless hand that was once so mighty. The incense rises in clouds, and the monks chant the funeral hymn. It sounds like a wail—it sounds like a sentence of wrath and condemnation that must be heard far over the land, carried by the wind—sung by the wind—the wail that sometimes is silent, but never dies; for ever again it rises in song, singing even into our own time this legend of the Bishop of Börglum and his hard nephew. It is heard in the dark night by the frightened husbandman, driving by in the heavy sandy road past the convent of Börglum. It is heard by the sleepless listener in the thickly-walled rooms at Börglum. And not only to the ear of superstition is the sighing and the tread of hurrying feet audible in the long echoing passages leading to the convent-door that has long been locked. The door still seems to open, and the lights seem to flame in the brazen candlesticks; the fragrance of incense arises; the church gleams in its ancient splendour; and the monks sing and say the mass over the slain bishop, who lies there in the black silver-embroidered mantle, with the crosier in his powerless hand; and on his pale proud forehead gleams the red wound like fire, and there burn the worldly mind and the wicked thoughts.

Sink down into his grave—into oblivion—ye terrible shapes of the times of old!

Hark to the raging of the angry wind, sounding above the rolling sea. A storm approaches without, calling aloud for human lives. The sea has not put on a new mind with the new time. This night it is a horrible pit to devour up lives, and tomorrow, perhaps, it may be a glassy mirror—even as in the old time that we have buried. Sleep sweetly, if thou canst sleep!

Now it is morning.

The new time flings sunshine into the room. The wind still keeps up mightily. A wreck is announced—as in the old time.

During the night, down yonder by Lökken, the little fishing village with the red-tiled roofs—we can see it up here from the window—a ship has come ashore. It has struck, and is fast imbedded in the sand; but the rocket apparatus has thrown a rope on board, and formed a bridge from the wreck to the mainland; and all on board were saved, and reached the land, and were wrapped in warm blankets; and today they are invited to the farm at the convent of Börglum. In comfortable rooms they encounter hospitality and friendly faces. They are addressed in the language of their country, and the piano sounds for them with melodies of their native land; and before these have died away, and the chord has been struck, the wire of thought, that reaches to the land of the sufferers, announces that they are rescued. Then their anxieties are dispelled; and at even they join in the dance at the feast given in the great hall at Börglum. Waltzes and Styrian dances are given, and Danish popular songs, and melodies of foreign lands in these modern times.

Blessed be thou, new time! Speak thou of summer and of purer gales! Send thy sunbeams gleaming into our hearts and thoughts! On thy glowing canvas let them be painted—the dark legends of the rough hard times that are past!

What the Old Man does is Always Right

Translated by Mrs. H. P. Paull

I will tell you a story that was told me when I was a little boy. Every time I thought of this story, it seemed to me more and more charming; for it is with stories as it is with many people—they become better as they grow older.

I have no doubt that you have been in the country, and seen a very old farmhouse, with a thatched roof, and mosses and small plants growing wild upon it. There is a stork's nest on the ridge of the gable, for we cannot do without the stork. The walls of the house are sloping, and the windows are low, and only one of the latter is made to open. The baking-oven sticks out of the wall like a great knob. An elder-tree hangs over the palings; and beneath its branches, at the foot of the paling, is a pool of water, in which a few ducks are disporting themselves. There is a yard-dog too, who barks at all corners. Just such a farmhouse as this stood in a country lane; and in it dwelt an old couple, a peasant and his wife. Small as their possessions were, they had one article they could not do without, and that was a horse, which contrived to live upon the grass which it found by the side of the high road. The old peasant rode into the town upon this horse, and his neighbours often borrowed it of him, and paid for the loan of it by rendering some service to the old couple. After a time they thought it would be as well to sell the horse, or exchange it for something which might be more useful to them. But what might this *something* be?

"You'll know best, old man," said the wife. "It is fair-day today; so ride into town, and get rid of the horse for money, or make a good exchange; whichever you do will be right to me, so ride to the fair."

And she fastened his neckerchief for him; for she could do that better than he could, and she could also tie it very prettily in a double bow. She also smoothed his hat round and round with the palm of her hand, and gave him a kiss. Then he rode away upon the horse that was to be sold or bartered for something else. Yes, the old man knew what he was about. The sun shone with great heat, and not a cloud was to be seen in the sky. The road was very dusty; for a number of people, all going to the fair, were driving, riding, or walking upon it. There was no shelter anywhere from the hot sunshine. Among the rest a man came trudging along, and driving a cow to the fair. The cow was as beautiful a creature as any cow could be.

"She gives good milk, I am certain," said the peasant to himself. "That would be a very good exchange: the cow for the horse. Hallo there! you with the cow," he said. "I tell you what; I dare say a horse is of more value than a cow; but I don't care for that—a cow will be more useful to me; so, if you like, we'll exchange."

"To be sure I will," said the man.

Accordingly the exchange was made; and as the matter was settled, the peasant might have turned back; for he had done the business he came to do. But, having made up his mind to go to the fair, he determined to do so, if only to have a look at it; so on he went to the town with his cow. Leading the animal, he strode on sturdily, and, after a short time, overtook a man who was driving a sheep. It was a good fat sheep, with a fine fleece on its back.

"I should like to have that fellow," said the peasant to himself. "There is plenty of grass for him by our palings, and in the winter we could keep him in the room with us. Perhaps it would be more profitable to have a sheep than a cow. Shall I exchange?"

The man with the sheep was quite ready, and the bargain was quickly made. And then our peasant continued his way on the high road with his sheep. Soon after this, he overtook another man, who had come into the road from a field, and was carrying a large goose under his arm.

"What a heavy creature you have there!" said the peasant; "it has plenty of feathers and plenty of fat, and would look well tied to a string, or paddling in the water at our place. That would be very useful to my old woman; she could make all sorts of profits out of it. How often she has said, 'If now we only had a goose!' Now here is an opportunity, and, if possible, I will get it for her. Shall we exchange? I will give you my sheep for your goose, and thanks into the bargain."

The other had not the least objection, and accordingly the exchange was made, and our peasant became possessor of the goose. By this time he had arrived very near the town. The crowd on the high road had been gradually increasing, and there was quite a rush of men and cattle. The cattle walked on the path and by the palings, and at the turnpike-gate they even walked into the toll-keeper's potato-field, where one fowl was strutting about with a string tied to its leg, for fear it should take fright at the crowd, and run away and get lost. The tail-feathers of the fowl were very short, and it winked with both its eyes, and looked very cunning, as it said "Cluck, cluck." What were the thoughts of the fowl as it said this I cannot tell you; but directly our good man saw it, he thought, "Why that's the finest fowl I ever saw in my life; it's finer than our parson's brood hen, upon my word. I should like to have that fowl. Fowls can always pick up a few grains that lie about, and almost keep themselves. I think it would be a good exchange if I could get it for my goose. Shall we exchange?" he asked the toll-keeper.

"Exchange," repeated the man; "well, it would not be a bad thing."

And so they made an exchange—the toll-keeper at the turnpike-gate kept the goose, and the peasant carried off the fowl. Now he had really done a great deal of business on his way to the fair, and he was hot and tired. He wanted something to eat, and a glass of ale to refresh himself; so he turned his steps to an inn. He was just about to enter when the ostler came out, and they met at the door. The ostler was carrying a sack. "What have you in that sack?" asked the peasant.

"Rotten apples," answered the ostler; "a whole sackful of them. They will do to feed the pigs with."

"Why that will be terrible waste," he replied; "I should like to take them home to my old woman. Last year the old apple-tree by the grass-plot only bore one apple, and we kept it in the cupboard till it was quite withered and rotten. It was always property, my old woman said; and here she would see a great deal of property—a whole sackful; I should like to show them to her."

"What will you give me for the sackful?" asked the ostler.

"What will I give? Well, I will give you my fowl in exchange."

So he gave up the fowl, and received the apples, which he carried into the inn parlor. He leaned the sack carefully against the stove, and then went to the table. But the stove was hot, and he had not thought of that. Many guests were present—horse dealers, cattle drovers, and two Englishmen. The Englishmen were so rich that their pockets quite bulged out and seemed ready to burst; and they could bet too, as you shall hear. "Hiss-s-s, hiss-s-s." What could that be by the stove? The apples were beginning to roast. "What is that?" asked one.

"Why, do you know"—said our peasant. And then he told them the whole story of the horse, which he had exchanged for a cow, and all the rest of it, down to the apples.

"Well, your old woman will give it you well when you get home," said one of the Englishmen. "Won't there be a noise?"

"What! Give me what?" said the peasant. "Why, she will kiss me, and say, 'what the old man does is always right.'"

"Let us lay a wager on it," said the Englishmen. "We'll wager you a ton of coined gold, a hundred pounds to the hundred-weight."

"No; a bushel will be enough," replied the peasant. "I can only set a bushel of apples against it, and I'll throw myself and my old woman into the bargain; that will pile up the measure, I fancy."

"Done! taken!" and so the bet was made.

Then the landlord's coach came to the door, and the two Englishmen and the peasant got in, and away they drove, and soon arrived and stopped at the peasant's hut. "Good evening, old woman." "Good evening, old man." "I've made the exchange."

"Ah, well, you understand what you're about," said the woman. Then she embraced him, and paid no attention to the strangers, nor did she notice the sack.

"I got a cow in exchange for the horse."

"Thank Heaven," said she. "Now we shall have plenty of milk, and butter, and cheese on the table. That was a capital exchange."

"Yes, but I changed the cow for a sheep."

"Ah, better still!" cried the wife. "You always think of everything; we have just enough pasture for a sheep. Ewe's milk and cheese, woollen jackets and stockings! The cow could not give all these, and her hair only falls off. How you think of everything!"

"But I changed away the sheep for a goose."

"Then we shall have roast goose to eat this year. You dear old man, you are always thinking of something to please me. This is delightful. We can let the goose walk about with a string tied to her leg, so she will be fatter still before we roast her."

"But I gave away the goose for a fowl."

"A fowl! Well, that was a good exchange," replied the woman. "The fowl will lay eggs and hatch them, and we shall have chickens; we shall soon have a poultry-yard. Oh, this is just what I was wishing for."

"Yes, but I exchanged the fowl for a sack of shrivelled apples."

"What! I really must give you a kiss for that!" exclaimed the wife. "My dear, good husband, now I'll tell you something. Do you know, almost as soon as you left me this morning, I began to think of what I could give you nice for supper this evening, and then I thought of fried eggs and bacon, with sweet herbs; I had eggs and bacon, but I wanted the herbs; so I went over to the schoolmaster's: I knew they had plenty of herbs, but the schoolmistress is very mean, although she can smile so sweetly. I begged her to lend me a handful of herbs. 'Lend!' she exclaimed, 'I have nothing to lend; nothing at all grows in our garden, not even a shrivelled apple; I could not even lend you a shrivelled apple, my dear woman. But now I can lend her ten, or a whole sackful, which I'm very glad of; it makes me laugh to think about it;" and then she gave him a hearty kiss.

"Well, I like all this," said both the Englishmen; "always going down the hill, and yet always merry; it's worth the money to see it." So they paid a hundred-weight of gold to the peasant, who, whatever he did, was not scolded but kissed.

Yes, it always pays best when the wife sees and maintains that her husband knows best, and whatever he does is right.

That is a story which I heard when I was a child; and now you have heard it too, and know that "What the old man does is always right."

The Snow Man

Translated by Mrs. H. P. Paull

"It is so delightfully cold," said the Snow Man, "that it makes my whole body crackle. This is just the kind of wind to blow life into one. How that great red thing up there is staring at me!" He meant the sun, who was just setting. "It shall not make me wink. I shall manage to keep the pieces."

He had two triangular pieces of tile in his head, instead of eyes; his mouth was made of an old broken rake, and was, of course, furnished with teeth. He had been brought into existence amidst the joyous shouts of boys, the jingling of sleigh-bells, and the slashing of whips. The sun went down, and the full moon rose, large, round, and clear, shining in the deep blue.

"There it comes again, from the other side," said the Snow Man, who supposed the sun was showing himself once more. "Ah, I have cured him of staring, though; now he may hang up there, and shine, that I may see myself. If I only knew how to manage to move away from this place—I should so like to move. If I could, I would slide along yonder on the ice, as I have seen the boys do; but I don't understand how; I don't even know how to run."

"Away, away," barked the old yard-dog. He was quite hoarse, and could not pronounce "Bow wow" properly. He had once been an indoor dog, and lay by the fire, and he had been hoarse ever since. "The sun will make you run some day. I saw him, last winter, make your predecessor run, and his predecessor before him. Away, away, they all have to go."

"I don't understand you, comrade," said the Snow Man. "Is that thing up yonder to teach me to run? I saw it running itself a little while ago, and now it has come creeping up from the other side.

"You know nothing at all," replied the yard-dog; "but then, you've only lately been patched up. What you see yonder is the moon, and the one before it was the sun. It will come again tomorrow, and most likely teach you to run down into the ditch by the well; for I think the weather is going to change. I can feel such pricks and stabs in my left leg; I am sure there is going to be a change."

"I don't understand him," said the Snow Man to himself; "but I have a feeling that he is talking of something very disagreeable. The one who stared so just now, and whom he calls the sun, is not my friend; I can feel that too."

"Away, away," barked the yard-dog, and then he turned round three times, and crept into his kennel to sleep.

There was really a change in the weather. Towards morning, a thick fog covered the whole country round, and a keen wind arose, so that the cold seemed to freeze one's bones; but when the sun rose, the sight was splendid. Trees and bushes were covered with hoar frost, and looked like a forest of white coral; while on every twig glittered frozen dew-drops. The many delicate forms concealed in summer by luxuriant foliage, were now clearly defined, and looked like glittering lace-work. From every twig glistened a white radiance. The birch, waving in the wind, looked full of life, like trees in summer; and its appearance was wondrously beautiful. And where the sun shone, how everything glittered and sparkled, as if diamond dust had been strewn about; while the snowy carpet of the earth appeared as if covered with diamonds, from which countless lights gleamed, whiter than even the snow itself.

"This is really beautiful," said a young girl, who had come into the garden with a young man; and they both stood still near the Snow Man, and contemplated the glittering scene. "Summer cannot show a more beautiful sight," she exclaimed, while her eyes sparkled.

"And we can't have such a fellow as this in the summer time," replied the young man, pointing to the Snow Man; "he is capital."

The girl laughed, and nodded at the Snow Man, and then tripped away over the snow with her friend. The snow creaked and crackled beneath her feet, as if she had been treading on starch.

"Who are these two?" asked the Snow Man of the yard-dog. "You have been here longer than I have; do you know them?"

"Of course I know them," replied the yard-dog; "she has stroked my back many times, and he has given me a bone of meat. I never bite those two."

"But what are they?" asked the Snow Man.

"They are lovers," he replied; "they will go and live in the same kennel by-and-by, and gnaw at the same bone. Away, away!"

"Are they the same kind of beings as you and I?" asked the Snow Man.

"Well, they belong to the same master," retorted the yard-dog. "Certainly people who were only born yesterday know very little. I can see that in you. I have age and experience. I know every one here in the house, and I know there was once a time when I did not lie out here in the cold, fastened to a chain. Away, away!"

"The cold is delightful," said the Snow Man; "but do tell me tell me; only you must not clank your chain so; for it jars all through me when you do that."

"Away, away!" barked the yard-dog; "I'll tell you; they said I was a pretty little fellow once; then I used to lie in a velvet-covered chair, up at the master's house, and sit in the mistress's lap. They used to kiss my nose, and wipe my paws with an embroidered handkerchief, and I was called 'Ami, dear Ami, sweet Ami.' But after a while I grew too big for them, and they sent me away to the housekeeper's room; so I came to live on the lower story. You can look into the room from where you stand, and see where I was master once; for I was indeed master to the housekeeper. It was certainly a smaller room than those up stairs; but I was more comfortable; for I was not being continually taken hold of and pulled about by the children as I had been. I received quite as good food, or even better. I had my own cushion, and there was a stove—it is the finest thing in the world at this season of the year. I used to go under the stove, and lie down quite beneath it. Ah, I still dream of that stove. Away, away!"

"Does a stove look beautiful?" asked the Snow Man, "is it at all like me?"

"It is just the reverse of you,' said the dog; "it's as black as a crow, and has a long neck and a brass knob; it eats firewood, so that fire spurts out of its mouth. We should keep on one side, or under it, to be comfortable. You can see it through the window, from where you stand.'

Then the Snow Man looked, and saw a bright polished thing with a brazen knob, and fire gleaming from the lower part of it. The Snow Man felt quite a strange sensation come over him; it was very odd, he knew not what it meant, and he could not account for it. But there are people who are not men of snow, who understand what it is. "'And why did you leave her?" asked the Snow Man, for it seemed to him that the stove must be of the female sex. "How could you give up such a comfortable place?"

"I was obliged," replied the yard-dog. "They turned me out of doors, and chained me up here. I had bitten the youngest of my master's sons in the leg, because he kicked away the bone I was gnawing. 'Bone for bone,' I thought; but they were so angry, and from that time I have been fastened with a chain, and lost my bone. Don't you hear how hoarse I am. Away, away! I can't talk any more like other dogs. Away, away, that is the end of it all."

But the Snow Man was no longer listening. He was looking into the housekeeper's room on the lower storey; where the stove stood on its four iron legs, looking about the same size as the Snow Man himself. "What a strange crackling I feel within me," he said. "Shall I ever get in there? It is an innocent wish, and innocent wishes are sure to be fulfilled. I must go in there and lean against her, even if I have to break the window."

"You must never go in there," said the yard-dog, "for if you approach the stove, you'll melt away, away."

"I might as well go," said the Snow Man, "for I think I am breaking up as it is."

During the whole day the Snow Man stood looking in through the window, and in the twilight hour the room became still more inviting, for from the stove came a gentle glow, not like the sun or the moon; no, only the bright light which gleams from a stove when it has been well fed. When the door of the stove was opened, the flames darted out of its mouth; this is customary with all stoves. The light of the flames fell directly on the face and breast of the Snow Man with a ruddy gleam. "I can endure it no longer," said he; "how beautiful it looks when it stretches out its tongue?"

The night was long, but did not appear so to the Snow Man, who stood there enjoying his own reflections, and crackling with the cold. In the morning, the window-panes of the housekeeper's room were covered with ice. They were the most beautiful ice-flowers any Snow Man could desire, but they concealed the stove. These window-panes would not thaw, and he could see nothing of the stove, which he pictured to himself, as if it had been a lovely human being. The snow crackled and the wind whistled around him; it was just the kind of frosty weather a Snow Man might thoroughly enjoy. But he did not enjoy it; how, indeed, could he enjoy anything when he was "stove sick?"

"That is terrible disease for a Snow Man," said the yard-dog; "I have suffered from it myself, but I got over it. Away, away," he barked and then he added, "the weather is going to change." And the weather did change; it began to thaw. As the warmth increased, the Snow Man decreased. He said nothing and made no complaint, which is a sure sign. One morning he broke, and sunk down altogether; and, behold, where he had stood, something like a broomstick remained sticking up in the ground. It was the pole round which the boys had built him up. "Ah, now I understand why he had such a great longing for the stove," said the yard-dog. "Why, there's the shovel that is used for cleaning out the stove, fastened to the pole." The Snow Man had a stove scraper in his body; that was what moved him so. "But it's all over now. Away, away." And soon the winter passed. "Away, away," barked the hoarse yard-dog. But the girls in the house sang,

The Snow Man

"Come from your fragrant home, green thyme;
Stretch your soft branches, willow tree;
The months are bringing the sweet spring-time,
When the lark in the sky sings joyfully.
Come gentle sun, while the cuckoo sings,
And I'll mock his note in my wanderings."

And nobody thought any more of the Snow Man.

In the Duck-Yard

Translated by H. W. Dulcken

A duck arrived from Portugal. Some said she came from Spain, but that's all the same. At any rate she was called the Portuguese, and laid eggs, and was killed and cooked, and that was *her* career. But the ducklings which crept forth from her eggs were afterwards also called Portuguese, and there is something in that. Now, of the whole family there was only one left in the duck-yard, a yard to which the chickens had access likewise, and where the cock strutted about in a very aggressive manner.

"He annoys me with his loud crowing!" observed the Portuguese duck. "But he's a handsome bird, there's no denying that, though he is not a drake. He ought to moderate his voice, but that's an art inseparable from polite education, like that possessed by the little singing birds over in the lime trees in the neighbour's garden. How charmingly they sing! There's something quite pretty in their warbling. I call it Portugal. If I had only such a little singing bird, I'd be a mother to him, kind and good, for that's in my blood, my Portuguese blood!"

And while she was still speaking, a little singing bird came head over heels from the roof into the yard. The cat was behind him, but the bird escaped with a broken wing, and that's how he came tumbling into the yard.

"That's just like the cat; she's a villain!" said the Portuguese duck. "I remember her ways when I had children of my own. That such a creature should be allowed to live, and to wander about upon the roofs! I don't think they do such things in Portugal!"

And she pitied the little singing bird, and the other ducks who were not of Portuguese descent pitied him too.

"Poor little creature!" they said, as one after another came up. "We certainly can't sing," they said, "but we have a sounding board, or something of the kind, within us; we can feel that, though we don't talk of it."

"But I can talk of it," said the Portuguese duck; "and I'll do something for the little fellow, for that's my duty!" And she stepped into the water-trough, and beat her wings upon the water so heartily, that the little singing bird was almost drowned by the bath she got, but the duck meant it kindly. "That's a good deed," she said: "the others may take example by it."

"Piep!" said the little bird; one of his wings was broken, and he found it difficult to shake himself; but he quite understood that the bath was kindly meant. "You are very kind-hearted, madam," he said; but he did not wish for a second bath.

"I have never thought about my heart," continued the Portuguese duck, "but I know this much, that I love all my fellow-creatures except the cat; but nobody can expect me to love her, for she ate up two of my ducklings. But pray make yourself at home, for one can make oneself comfortable. I myself am from a strange country, as you may see from my bearing, and from my feathery dress. My drake is a native of these parts, he's not of my race; but for all that I'm not proud! If any one here in the yard can understand you, I may assert that I am that person."

"She's quite full of Portulak," said a little common duck, who was witty; and all the other common ducks considered the word *Portulak* quite a good joke, for it sounded like Portugal; and they nudged each other and said "Rapp!" It was too witty! And all the other ducks now began to notice the little singing bird.

"The Portuguese has certainly a greater command of language," they said. "For our part, we don't care to fill our beaks with such long words, but our sympathy is just as great. If we don't do anything for you, we march about with you everywhere; and we think that the best thing we can do."

"You have a lovely voice," said one of the oldest. "It must be a great satisfaction to be able to give so much pleasure as you are able to impart. I certainly am no great judge of your song, and consequently I keep my beak shut; and even that is better than talking nonsense to you, as others do."

"Don't plague him so," interposed the Portuguese duck: "he requires rest and nursing. My little singing bird, do you wish me to prepare another bath for you?"

"Oh no! pray let me be dry!" was the little bird's petition.

"The water-cure is the only remedy for me when I am unwell," quoth the Portuguese. "Amusement is beneficial too! The neighbouring fowls will soon come to pay their visit. There are two Cochin Chinese among them. They wear feathers on their legs, are well educated, and have been brought from afar, consequently they stand higher than the others in my regard."

And the fowls came, and the cock came; today he was polite enough to abstain from being rude.

"You are a true singing bird," he said, "and you do as much with your little voice as can possibly be done with it. But one requires a little more shrillness, that every hearer may hear that one is a male."

The two Chinese stood quite enchanted with the appearance of the singing bird. He looked very much rumpled after his bath, so that he seemed to them to have quite the appearance of a little Cochin China fowl. "He's charming," they cried, and began a conversation with him, speaking in whispers, and using the most aristocratic Chinese dialect.

In the Duck-Yard

"We are of your race," they continued. "The ducks, even the Portuguese, are swimming birds, as you cannot fail to have noticed. You do not know us yet; very few know us, or give themselves the trouble to make our acquaintance—not even any of the fowls, though we are born to occupy a higher grade on the ladder than most of the rest. But that does not disturb us: we quietly pursue our path amid the others, whose principles are certainly not ours; for we look at things on the favourable side, and only speak of what is good, though it is difficult sometimes to find something when nothing exists. Except us two and the cock, there's no one in the whole poultry-yard who is at once talented and polite. It cannot even be said of the inhabitants of the duck-yard. We warn you, little singing bird: don't trust that one yonder with the short tail feathers, for she's cunning. The pied one there, with the crooked stripes on her wings, is a strife-seeker, and lets nobody have the last word, though she's always in the wrong. The fat duck yonder speaks evil of every one, and that's against our principles: if we have nothing good to tell, we should hold our beaks. The Portuguese is the only one who has any education, and with whom one can associate, but she is passionate, and talks too much about Portugal."

"I wonder what those two Chinese are always whispering to one another about," whispered one duck to her friend. "They annoy me—we have never spoken to them."

Now the drake came up. He thought the little singing bird was a sparrow.

"Well, I don't understand the difference," he said; "and indeed it's all the same thing. He's only a plaything, and if one has them, why, one has them."

"Don't attach any value to what he says," the Portuguese whispered. "He's very respectable in business matters; and with him business takes precedence of everything. But now I shall lie down for a rest. One owes that to oneself, that one may be nice and fat when one is to be embalmed with apples and plums."

And accordingly she lay down in the sun, and winked with one eye; and she lay very comfortably, and she felt very comfortable, and she slept very comfortably.

The little singing bird busied himself with his broken wing. At last he lay down too, and pressed close to his protectress: the sun shone warm and bright, and he had found a very good place.

But the neighbour's fowls were awake. They went about scratching up the earth; and, to tell the truth, they had paid the visit simply and solely to find food for themselves. The Chinese were the first to leave the duck-yard; and the other fowls soon followed them. The witty little duck said of the Portuguese that the old lady was becoming a ducky dotard. At this the other ducks laughed and cackled aloud. "Ducky dotard," they whispered; "that's too witty!" and then they repeated the former joke about Portulak, and declared that it was vastly amusing. And then they lay down.

They had been lying asleep for some time, when suddenly something was thrown into the yard for them to eat. It came down with such a thwack, that the whole company started up from sleep and clapped their wings. The Portuguese awoke too, and threw herself over on the other side, pressing the little singing bird very hard as she did so.

"Piep!" he cried; "you trod very hard upon me, madam."

"Well, why do you lie in my way?" the duck retorted. "You must not be so touchy. I have nerves of my own, but yet I never called out 'Piep!'

"Don't be angry," said the little bird "the 'piep' came out of my beak unawares."

The Portuguese did not listen to him, but began eating as fast as she could, and made a good meal. When this was ended, and she

In the Duck-Yard

lay down again, the little bird came up, and wanted to be amiable, and sang:

> "Tillee-lilly lee,
> Of the good spring time,
> I'll sing so fine
> As far away I flee."

"Now I want to rest after my dinner," said the Portuguese. "You must conform to the rules of the house while you're here. I want to sleep now."

The little singing bird was quite taken aback, for he had meant it kindly. When Madam afterwards awoke, he stood before her again with a little corn that he had found, and laid it at her feet; but as she had not slept well, she was naturally in a very bad humour.

"Give that to a chicken!" she said, "and don't be always standing in my way."

"Why are you angry with me?" replied the little singing bird. "What have I done?"

"Done!" repeated the Portuguese duck: "your mode of expression is not exactly genteel; a fact to which I must call your attention."

"Yesterday it was sunshine here," said the little bird, "but today it's cloudy and the air is close."

"You don't know much about the weather, I fancy," retorted the Portuguese. "The day is not done yet. Don't stand there looking so stupid."

"But you are looking at me just as the wicked eyes looked when I fell into the yard yesterday."

"Impertinent creature!" exclaimed the Portuguese duck, "would you compare me with the cat, that beast of prey? There's not a drop of malicious blood in me. I've taken your part, and will teach you good manners."

And so saying, she bit off the singing bird's head, and he lay dead on the ground.

"Now, what's the meaning of this?" she said, "could he not bear even that? Then certainly he was not made for this world. I've been like a mother to him I know that, for I've a good heart."

Then the neighbour's cock stuck his head into the yard, and crowed with steam-engine power.

"You'll kill me with your crowing!" she cried. "It's all your fault. He's lost his head, and I am very near losing mine."

"There's not much lying where he fell!" observed the cock.

"Speak of him with respect," retorted the Portuguese duck, "for he had song, manners, and education. He was affectionate and soft, and that's as good in animals, as in your so-called human beings."

And all the ducks came crowding round the little dead singing bird. Ducks have strong passions, whether they feel envy or pity; and as there was nothing here to envy, pity manifested itself, even in the two Chinese.

"We shall never get such a singing bird again; he was almost a Chinese," they whispered, and they wept with a mighty clucking sound, and all the fowls clucked too; but the ducks went about with the redder eyes.

"We've hearts of our own," they said; "nobody can deny that."

"Hearts!" repeated the Portuguese, "yes, that we have, almost as much as in Portugal."

"Let us think of getting something to satisfy our hunger," said the drake, "for that's the most important point. If one of our toys is broken, why, we have plenty more!"

The Ice Maiden

Translated by Mrs. H. P. Paull

I
Little Rudy

We will pay a visit to Switzerland, and wander through that country of mountains, whose steep and rocky sides are overgrown with forest trees. Let us climb to the dazzling snow-fields at their summits, and descend again to the green meadows beneath, through which rivers and brooks rush along as if they could not quickly enough reach the sea and vanish. Fiercely shines the sun over those deep valleys, as well as upon the heavy masses of snow which lie on the mountains.

During the year these accumulations thaw or fall in the rolling avalance, or are piled up in shining glaciers. Two of these glaciers lie in the broad, rocky cliffs, between the Schreckhorn and the Wetterhorn, near the little town of Grindelwald. They are wonderful to behold, and therefore in the summer time strangers come here from all parts of the world to see them. They cross snow-covered mountains, and travel through the deep valleys, or ascend for hours, higher and still higher, the valleys appearing to sink lower and lower as they proceed, and become as small as if seen from an air balloon. Over the lofty summits of these mountains the clouds often hang like a dark veil; while beneath in the valley, where many brown, wooden houses are scattered about, the bright rays of the sun may be shining upon a little brilliant patch of green, making it appear almost transparent. The waters foam and dash along in the valleys beneath; the streams from above trickle and murmur as they fall down the rocky mountain's side, looking like glittering silver bands.

On both sides of the mountain-path stand these little wooden houses; and, as within, there are many children and many mouths to feed, each house has its own little potato garden. These children rush out in swarms, and surround travellers, whether on foot or in carriages. They are all clever at making a bargain. They offer for sale the sweetest little toy-houses, models of the mountain cottages in Switzerland. Whether it be rain or sunshine, these crowds of children are always to be seen with their wares.

About twenty years ago, there might be seen occasionally, standing at a short distance from the other children, a little boy, who was also anxious to sell his curious wares. He had an earnest, expressive countenance, and held the box containing his carved toys tightly with both hands, as if unwilling to part with it. His earnest look, and being also a very little boy, made him noticed by the strangers; so that he often sold the most, without knowing why. An hour's walk farther up the ascent lived his grandfather, who cut and carved the pretty little toy-houses; and in the old man's room stood a large press, full of all sorts of carved things—nut-crackers, knives and forks, boxes with beautifully carved foliage, leaping chamois. It contained everything that could delight the eyes of a child. But the boy, who was named Rudy, looked with still greater pleasure and longing at some old fire-arms which hung upon the rafters, under the ceiling of the room. His grandfather promised him that he should have them some day, but that he must first grow big and strong, and learn how to use them. Small as he was, the goats were placed in his care, and a good goat-keeper should also be a good climber, and such Rudy was;

The Ice Maiden

he sometimes, indeed, climbed higher than the goats, for he was fond of seeking for birds' nests at the top of high trees; he was bold and daring, but was seldom seen to smile, excepting when he stood by the roaring cataract, or heard the descending roll of the avalanche. He never played with the other children, and was not seen with them, unless his grandfather sent him down to sell his curious workmanship. Rudy did not much like trade; he loved to climb the mountains, or to sit by his grandfather and listen to his tales of olden times, or of the people in Meyringen, the place of his birth.

"In the early ages of the world," said the old man, "these people could not be found in Switzerland. They are a colony from the north, where their ancestors still dwell, and are called Swedes."

This was something for Rudy to know, but he learnt more from other sources, particularly from the domestic animals who belonged to the house. One was a large dog, called Ajola, which had belonged to his father; and the other was a tom-cat. This cat stood very high in Rudy's favour, for he had taught him to climb.

"Come out on the roof with me," said the cat; and Rudy quite understood him, for the language of fowls, ducks, cats, and dogs, is as easily understood by a young child as his own native tongue. But it must be at the age when grandfather's stick becomes a neighing horse, with head, legs, and tail. Some children retain these ideas later than others, and they are considered backwards and childish for their age. People say so; but is it so?

"Come out on the roof with me, little Rudy," was the first thing he heard the cat say, and Rudy understood him. "What people say about falling down is all nonsense," continued the cat; "you will not fall, unless you are afraid. Come, now, set one foot here and another there, and feel your way with your fore-feet. Keep your eyes wide open, and move softly, and if you come to a hole jump over it, and cling fast as I do." And this was just what Rudy did. He was often on the sloping roof with the cat, or on the tops of high trees. But, more frequently, higher still on the ridges of the rocks where puss never came.

"Higher, higher!" cried the trees and the bushes, "see to what height we have grown, and how fast we hold, even to the narrow edges of the rocks."

Rudy often reached the top of the mountain before the sunrise, and there inhaled his morning draught of the fresh, invigorating mountain air—God's own gift, which men call the sweet fragrance of plant and herb on the mountain-side, and the mint and wild thyme in the valleys. The overhanging clouds absorb all heaviness from the air, and the winds convey them away over the pine-tree summits. The spirit of fragrance, light and fresh, remained behind, and this was Rudy's morning draught. The sunbeams—those blessing-bringing daughters of the sun—kissed his cheeks. Vertigo might be lurking on the watch, but he dared not approach him. The swallows, who had not less than seven nests in his grandfather's house, flew up to him and his goats, singing, "We and you, you and we." They brought him greetings from his grandfather's house, even from two hens, the only birds of the household; but Rudy was not intimate with them.

Although so young and such a little fellow, Rudy had travelled a great deal. He was born in the canton of Valais, and brought to his grandfather over the mountains. He had walked to Staubbach—a little town that seems to flutter in the air like a silver veil—the glittering, snow-clad mountain Jungfrau. He had also been to the great glaciers; but this is connected with a sad story, for here his mother met her death, and his grandfather used to say that all Rudy's childish merriment was lost from that time. His mother had written in a letter, that before he was a year old he had laughed more than he cried; but after his fall into the snow-covered crevasse, his disposition had completely changed. The grandfather seldom spoke of this, but the fact was generally known. Rudy's father had been a postilion, and the large dog which now lived in his grandfather's cottage had always followed him on his journeys over the Simplon to the lake of Geneva. Rudy's relations, on his father's side, lived in the canton of Valais, in the valley of the Rhone. His uncle was a chamois hunter, and a well-known guide. Rudy was only a year old when his father died, and his mother was anxious to return with her child to her own relations, who lived in the Bernese Oberland. Her father dwelt at a few hours' distance from Grindelwald; he was a carver in wood, and gained so much by it that he had plenty to live upon. She set out homewards in the month of June, carrying her infant in her arms, and, accompanied by two chamois hunters, crossed the Gemmi on her way to Grindelwald. They had already left more than half the journey behind them. They had crossed high ridges, and traversed snow-fields; they could even see her native valley, with its familiar wooden cottages. They had only one more glacier to climb. Some newly fallen snow concealed a cleft which, though it did not extend to the foaming waters in the depths beneath, was still much deeper than the height of a man. The young woman, with the child in her arms, slipped upon it, sank in, and disappeared. Not a shriek, not a groan was heard; nothing but the whining of a little child. More than an hour elapsed before her two companions could obtain from the nearest house ropes and poles to assist in raising them; and it was with much exertion that they at last succeeded in raising from the crevasse what appeared to be two dead bodies. Every means was used to restore them to life. With the child they were successful, but not with the mother; so the old grandfather received his daughter's little son into his house an orphan—a little boy who laughed more than he cried; but it seemed as if laughter had left him in the cold ice-world into which he had fallen, where, as the Swiss peasants say, the souls of the lost are confined till the judgment-day.

The glaciers appear as if a rushing stream had been frozen in its course, and pressed into blocks of green crystal, which, balanced one upon another, form a wondrous palace of crystal for the Ice Maiden—the queen of the glaciers. It is she whose mighty power can crush the traveller to death, and arrest the flowing river in its course.

She is also a child of the air, and with the swiftness of the chamois she can reach the snow-covered mountain tops, where the boldest mountaineer has to cut footsteps in the ice to ascend. She will sail on a frail pine-twig over the raging torrents beneath, and spring lightly from one iceberg to another, with her long, snow-white hair flowing around her, and her dark-green robe glittering like the waters of the deep Swiss lakes. "Mine is the power to seize and crush," she cried. "Once a beautiful boy was stolen from me by man—a boy whom I had kissed, but had not kissed to death. He is again among mankind, and tends the goats on the mountains. He is always climbing higher and higher, far away from all others, but not from me. He is mine; I will send for him." And she gave Vertigo the commission.

It was summer, and the Ice Maiden was melting amidst the green verdure, when Vertigo swung himself up and down. Vertigo has many brothers, quite a troop of them, and the Ice Maiden chose the strongest among them. They exercise their power in different ways, and everywhere. Some sit on the banisters of steep stairs, others on the outer rails of lofty towers, or spring like squirrels along the ridges of the mountains. Others tread the air as a swimmer treads the water, and lure their victims here and there till they fall into the deep abyss. Vertigo and the Ice Maiden clutch at human beings, as the polypus seizes upon all that comes within its reach. And now Vertigo was to seize Rudy.

"Seize him, indeed," cried Vertigo; "I cannot do it. That monster of a cat has taught him her tricks. That child of the human race has a power within him which keeps me at a distance; I cannot possibly reach the boy when he hangs from the branches of trees, over the precipice; or I would gladly tickle his feet, and send him heels over head through the air; but I cannot accomplish it."

"We must accomplish it," said the Ice Maiden; "either you or I must; and I will—I will!"

"No, no!" sounded through the air, like an echo on the mountain church bells chime. It was an answer in song, in the melting tones of a chorus from others of nature's spirits—good and loving spirits, the daughters of the sunbeam. They who place themselves in a circle every evening on the mountain peaks; there they spread out their rose-coloured wings, which, as the sun sinks, become more flaming red, until the lofty Alps seem to burn with fire. Men call this the Alpine glow. After the sun has set, they disappear within the white snow on the mountain-tops, and slumber there till sunrise, when they again come forth. They have great love for flowers, for butterflies, and for mankind; and from among the latter they had chosen little Rudy. "You shall not catch him; you shall not seize him!" they sang.

"Greater and stronger than he have I seized!" said the Ice Maiden.

Then the daughters of the sun sang a song of the traveller, whose cloak had been carried away by the wind. "The wind took the covering, but not the man; it could even seize upon him, but not hold him fast. The children of strength are more powerful, more ethereal, even than we are. They can rise higher than our parent, the sun. They have the magic words that rule the wind and the waves, and compel them to serve and obey; and they can, at last, cast off the heavy, oppressive weight of mortality, and soar upwards." Thus sweetly sounded the bell-like tones of the chorus.

And each morning the sun's rays shone through the one little window of the grandfather's house upon the quiet child. The daughters of the sunbeam kissed him; they wished to thaw, and melt, and obliterate the ice kiss which the queenly maiden of the glaciers had given him as he lay in the lap of his dead mother, in the deep crevasse of ice from which he had been so wonderfully rescued.

II
The Journey to the New Home

Rudy was just eight years old, when his uncle, who lived on the other side of the mountain, wished to have the boy, as he thought he might obtain a better education with him, and learn something more. His grandfather thought the same, so he consented to let him go. Rudy had many to say farewell to, as well as his grandfather. First, there was Ajola, the old dog.

"Your father was the postilion, and I was the postilion's dog," said Ajola. "We have often travelled the same journey together; I knew all the dogs and men on this side of the mountain. It is not my habit to talk much; but now that we have so little time to converse together, I will say something more than usual. I will relate to you a story, which I have reflected upon for a long time. I do not understand it, and very likely you will not, but that is of no consequence. I have, however, learnt from it that in this world things are not equally divided, neither for dogs nor for men. All are not born to lie on the lap and to drink milk: I have never been petted in this way, but I have seen a little dog seated in the place of a gentleman or lady, and travelling inside a post-chaise. The lady, who was his mistress, or of whom he was master, carried a bottle of milk, of which the little dog now and then drank; she also offered him pieces of sugar to crunch. He sniffed at them proudly, but would not eat one, so she ate them herself. I was running along the dirty road by the side of the carriage as hungry as a dog could be, chewing the cud of my own thoughts, which were rather in confusion. But many other things seemed in confusion also. *Why* was not I lying on a lap and travelling in a coach? I could not tell; yet I knew I could not alter my own condition, either by barking or growling."

This was Ajola's farewell speech, and Rudy threw his arms round the dog's neck and kissed his cold nose. Then he took the cat in his arms, but he struggled to get free.

"You are getting too strong for me," he said; "but I will not use my claws against *you*. Clamber away over the mountains; it was I who taught you to climb. Do not fancy you are going to fall, and you will be quite safe." Then the cat jumped down and ran away; he did not wish Rudy to see that there were tears in his eyes.

The hens were hopping about the floor; one of them had no tail; a traveller, who fancied himself a sportsman, had shot off her tail, he had mistaken her for a bird of prey.

"Rudy is going away over the mountains," said one of the hens.

"He is always in such a hurry," said the other; "and I don't like taking leave," so they both hopped out.

But the goats said farewell; they bleated and wanted to go with him, they were so very sorry.

Just at this time two clever guides were going to cross the mountains to the other side of the Gemmi, and Rudy was to go with them on foot. It was a long walk for such a little boy, but he had plenty of strength and invincible courage. The swallows flew with him a little way, singing, "We and you—you and we." The way led across the rushing Lutschine, which falls in numerous streams from the dark clefts of the Grindelwald glaciers. Trunks of fallen trees and blocks of stone form bridges over these streams. After passing a forest of alders, they began to ascend, passing by some blocks of ice that had loosened themselves from the side of the mountain and lay across their path; they had to step over these ice-blocks or walk round them. Rudy crept here and ran there, his eyes sparkling with joy, and he stepped so firmly with his iron-tipped mountain shoe, that he left a mark behind him wherever he placed his foot.

The earth was black where the mountain torrents or the melted ice had poured upon it, but the bluish green, glassy ice sparkled and glittered. They had to go round little pools, like lakes, enclosed between large masses of ice; and, while thus wandering out of their path, they came near an immense stone, which lay balanced on the edge of an icy peak. The stone lost its balance just as they reached it, and rolled over into the abyss beneath, while the noise of its fall was echoed back from every hollow cliff of the glaciers.

They were always going upwards. The glaciers seemed to spread above them like a continued chain of masses of ice, piled up in wild confusion between bare and rugged rocks. Rudy thought for a moment of what had been told him, that he and his mother had once lain buried in one of these cold, heart-chilling fissures; but he soon banished such thoughts, and looked upon the story as fabulous, like many other stories which had been told him. Once or twice, when the men thought the way was rather difficult for such a little boy, they held out their hands to assist him; but he would not accept their assistance, for he stood on the slippery ice as firmly as if he had been a chamois. They came at length to rocky ground; sometimes stepping upon moss-covered stones, sometimes passing beneath stunted fir-trees, and again through green meadows. The landscape was always changing, but ever above them towered the lofty snow-clad mountains, whose names not only Rudy but every other child knew—"The Jungfrau," "The Monk and the Eiger."

Rudy had never been so far away before; he had never trodden on the wide-spreading ocean of snow that lay here with its immovable billows, from which the wind blows off the snowflake now and then, as it cuts the foam from the waves of the sea. The glaciers stand here so close together it might almost be said they are hand-in-hand; and each is a crystal palace for the Ice Maiden, whose power and will it is to seize and imprison the unwary traveller.

The sun shone warmly, and the snow sparkled as if covered with glittering diamonds. Numerous insects, especially butterflies and bees, lay dead in heaps on the snow. They had ventured too high, or the wind had carried them here and left them to die of cold.

Around the Wetterhorn hung a feathery cloud, like a woolbag, and a threatening cloud too, for as it sunk lower it increased in size, and concealed within was a "föhn,"* fearful in its violence should it break loose. This journey, with its varied incidents—the wild paths, the night passed on the mountain, the steep rocky precipices, the hollow clefts, in which the rustling waters from time immemorial had worn away passages for themselves through blocks of stone—all these were firmly impressed on Rudy's memory.

In a forsaken stone building, which stood just beyond the seas of snow, they one night took shelter. Here they found some charcoal and pine branches, so that they soon made a fire. They arranged couches to lie on as well as they could, and then the men seated

---

* A moist wind from the south, which rises on the Swisss mountains and lakes, and fortells a storm.

The Ice Maiden

themselves by the fire, took out their pipes, and began to smoke. They also prepared a warm, spiced drink, of which they partook and Rudy was not forgotten—he had his share. Then they began to talk of those mysterious beings with which the land of the Alps abounds; the hosts of apparitions which come in the night, and carry off the sleepers through the air, to the wonderful floating town of Venice; of the wild herds-man, who drives the black sheep across the meadows. These flocks are never seen, yet the tinkle of their little bells has often been heard, as well as their unearthly bleating. Rudy listened eagerly, but without fear, for he knew not what fear meant; and while he listened, he fancied he could hear the roaring of the spectral herd. It seemed to come nearer and roar louder, till the men heard it also and listened in silence, till, at length, they told Rudy that he must not dare to sleep. It was a "föhn," that violent storm-wind which rushes from the mountain to the valley beneath, and in its fury snaps asunder the trunks of large trees as if they were but slender reeds, and carries the wooden houses from one side of a river to the other as easily as we could move the pieces on a chess-board. After an hour had passed, they told Rudy that it was all over, and he might go to sleep; and, fatigued with his long walk, he readily slept at the word of command.

Very early the following morning they again set out. The sun on this day lighted up for Rudy new mountains, new glaciers, and new snow-fields. They had entered the Canton Valais, and found themselves on the ridge of the hills which can be seen from Grindelwald; but he was still far from his new home. They pointed out to him other clefts, other meadows, other woods and rocky paths, and other houses. Strange men made their appearance before him, and what men! They were misshapen, wretched-looking creatures, with yellow complexions; and on their necks were dark, ugly lumps of flesh, hanging down like bags. They were called *cretins*. They dragged themselves along painfully, and stared at the strangers with vacant eyes. The women looked more dreadful than the men. Poor Rudy! were these the sort of people he should see at his new home?

III
The Uncle

Rudy arrived at last at his uncle's house, and was thankful to find the people like those he had been accustomed to see. There was only one cretin amongst them, a poor idiot boy, one of those unfortunate beings who, in their neglected conditions, go from house to house, and are received and taken care of in different families, for a month or two at a time.

Poor Saperli had just arrived at his uncle's house when Rudy came. The uncle was an experienced hunter; he also followed the trade of a cooper; his wife was a lively little person, with a face like a bird, eyes like those of an eagle, and a long, hairy throat. Everything was new to Rudy—the fashion of the dress, the manners, the employments, and even the language; but the latter his childish ear would soon learn. He saw also that there was more wealth here, when compared with his former home at his grandfather's. The rooms were larger, the walls were adorned with the horns of the chamois, and brightly polished guns. Over the door hung a painting of the Virgin Mary, fresh alpine roses and a burning lamp stood near it. Rudy's uncle was, as we have said, one of the most noted chamois hunters in the whole district, and also one of the best guides. Rudy soon became the pet of the house; but there was another pet, an old hound, blind and lazy, who would never more follow the hunt, well as he had once done so. But his former good qualities were not forgotten, and therefore the animal was kept in the family and treated with every indulgence. Rudy stroked the old hound, but he did not like strangers, and Rudy was as yet a stranger; he did not, however, long remain so, he soon endeared himself to every heart, and became like one of the family.

"We are not very badly off, here in the canton Valais," said his uncle one day; "we have the chamois, they do not die so fast as the wild goats, and it is certainly much better here now than in former times. How highly the old times have been spoken of, but ours is better. The bag has been opened, and a current of air now blows through our once confined valley. Something better always makes its appearance when old, worn-out things fail."

When his uncle became communicative, he would relate stories of his youthful days, and farther back still of the warlike times in which his father had lived. Valais was then, as he expressed it, only a closed-up bag, quite full of sick people, miserable cretins; but the French soldiers came, and they were capital doctors, they soon killed the disease and the sick people, too. The French people knew how to fight in more ways than one, and the girls knew how to conquer too; and when he said this the uncle nodded at his wife, who was a French woman by birth, and laughed. The French could also do battle on the stones. "It was they who cut a road out of the solid rock over the Simplon—such a road, that I need only say to a child of three years old, 'Go down to Italy, you have only to keep in the high road,' and the child will soon arrive in Italy, if he followed my directions."

Then the uncle sang a French song, and cried, "Hurrah! long live Napoleon Buonaparte." This was the first time Rudy had ever heard of France, or of Lyons, that great city on the Rhone where his uncle had once lived. His uncle said that Rudy, in a very few years, would become a clever hunter, he had quite a talent for it; he taught the boy to hold a gun properly, and to load and fire it. In the hunting season he took him to the hills, and made him drink the warm blood of the chamois, which is said to prevent the hunter from becoming giddy; he taught him to know the time when, from the different mountains, the avalanche is likely to fall, namely, at noontide or in the evening, from the effects of the sun's rays; he made him observe the movements of the chamois when he gave a leap, so that he might fall firmly and lightly on his feet. He told him that when on the fissures of the rocks he could find no place for his feet, he must support himself on his elbows, and cling with his legs, and even lean firmly with his back, for this could be done when necessary. He told him also that the chamois are very cunning, they place lookers-out on the watch; but the hunter must be more cunning than they are, and find them out by the scent.

One day, when Rudy went out hunting with his uncle, he hung a coat and hat on an alpine staff, and the chamois mistook it for a man, as they generally do. The mountain path was narrow here; indeed it was scarcely a path at all, only a kind of shelf, close to the yawning abyss. The snow that lay upon it was partially thawed, and the stones crumbled beneath the feet. Every fragment of stone broken off struck the sides of the rock in its fall, till it rolled into the depths beneath, and sunk to rest. Upon this shelf Rudy's uncle laid himself down, and crept forward. At about a hundred paces behind him stood Rudy, upon the highest point of the rock, watching a great vulture hovering in the air; with a single stroke of his wing the bird might easily cast the creeping hunter into the abyss beneath, and make him his prey. Rudy's uncle had eyes for nothing but the chamois, who, with its young kid, had just appeared round the edge of the rock. So Rudy kept his eyes fixed on the bird, he knew well what the great creature wanted; therefore he stood in readiness to discharge his gun at the proper moment. Suddenly the chamois made a spring, and his uncle fired and struck the animal with the deadly bullet; while the young kid rushed away, as if for a long life he had been accustomed to danger and practised flight. The large bird, alarmed at the report of the gun, wheeled off in another direction, and Rudy's uncle was saved from danger, of which he knew nothing till he was told of it by the boy.

While they were both in pleasant mood, wending their way homewards, and the uncle whistling the tune of a song he had learnt in his young days, they suddenly heard a peculiar sound which seemed to come from the top of the mountain. They looked up, and saw above them, on the over-hanging rock, the snow-covering heave and lift itself as a piece of linen stretched on the ground to dry raises itself when the wind creeps under it. Smooth as polished marble slabs, the waves of snow cracked and loosened themselves, and then suddenly, with the rumbling noise of distant thunder, fell like a foaming cataract into the abyss. An avalanche had fallen, not upon Rudy and his uncle, but very near them. Alas, a great deal too near!

"Hold fast, Rudy!" cried his uncle; "hold fast, with all your might."

Then Rudy clung with his arms to the trunk of the nearest tree, while his uncle climbed above him, and held fast by the branches. The avalanche rolled past them at some distance; but the gust of wind that followed, like the storm-wings of the avalanche, snapped asunder the trees and bushes over which it swept, as if they had been but dry rushes, and threw them about in every direction. The tree to which Rudy clung was thus overthrown, and Rudy dashed to the ground. The higher branches were snapped off, and carried away to a great distance; and among these shattered branches lay Rudy's uncle, with his skull fractured. When they found him, his hand was still warm; but it would have been impossible to recognize his face. Rudy stood by, pale and trembling; it was the first shock of his life, the first time he had ever felt fear. Late in the evening he returned home with the fatal news—to that home which was now to be so full of sorrow. His uncle's wife uttered not a word, nor shed a tear, till the corpse was brought in; then her agony burst forth. The poor cretin crept away to his bed, and nothing was seen of him during the whole of the following day. Towards evening, however, he came to Rudy, and said, "Will you write a letter for me? Saperli cannot write; Saperli can only take the letters to the post."

"A letter for you!" said Rudy; "who do you wish to write to?"

"To the Lord Christ," he replied.

"What do you mean?" asked Rudy.

Then the poor idiot, as the cretin was often called, looked at Rudy with a most touching expression in his eyes, clasped his hands, and said, solemnly and devoutly, "Saperli wants to send a letter to Jesus Christ, to pray Him to let Saperli die, and not the master of the house here."

Rudy pressed his hand, and replied, "A letter would not reach Him up above; it would not give him back whom we have lost."

It was not, however, easy for Rudy to convince Saperli of the impossibility of doing what he wished.

"Now you must work for us," said his foster-mother; and Rudy very soon became the entire support of the house.

IV
Babette

Who was the best marksman in the canton Valais? The chamois knew well. "Save yourselves from Rudy," they might well say. And who is the handsomest marksman? "Oh, it is Rudy," said the maidens; but they did not say, "Save yourselves from Rudy." Neither did anxious mothers say so; for he bowed to them as pleasantly as to the young girls. He was so brave and cheerful. His cheeks were brown, his teeth white, and his eyes dark and sparkling. He was now a handsome young man of twenty years. The most icy water could not deter him from swimming; he could twist and turn like a fish. None could climb like he, and he clung as firmly to the edges of the rocks as a limpet. He had strong muscular power, as could be seen when he leapt from rock to rock. He had learnt this first from the cat, and more lately from the chamois. Rudy was considered the best guide over the mountains; every one had great confidence in him. He might have made a great deal of money as guide. His uncle had also taught him the trade of a cooper; but he had no inclination for either; his delight was in chamois-hunting, which also brought him plenty of money. Rudy would be a very good match, as people said, if he would not look above his own station. He was also such a famous partner in dancing, that the girls often dreamt about him, and one and another thought of him even when awake.

"He kissed me in the dance," said Annette, the schoolmaster's daughter, to her dearest friend; but she ought not to have told this, even to her dearest friend. It is not easy to keep such secrets; they are like sand in a sieve; they slip out. It was therefore soon known that Rudy, so brave and so good as he was, had kissed some one while dancing, and yet he had never kissed her who was dearest to him.

"Ah, ah," said an old hunter, "he has kissed Annette, has he? he has begun with A, and I suppose he will kiss through the whole alphabet."

But a kiss in the dance was all the busy tongues could accuse him of. He certainly had kissed Annette, but she was not the flower of his heart.

Down in the valley, near Bex, among the great walnut-trees, by the side of a little rushing mountain-stream, lived a rich miller. His dwelling-house was a large building, three storeys high, with little turrets. The roof was covered with chips, bound together with tin plates, that glittered in sunshine and in the moonlight. The largest of the turrets had a Weathercock, representing an apple pierced by a glittering arrow, in memory of William Tell. The mill was a neat and well-ordered place, that allowed itself to be sketched and written about; but the miller's daughter did not permit any to sketch or write about her. So, at least, Rudy would have said, for her image was pictured in his heart; her eyes shone in it so brightly, that quite a flame had been kindled there; and, like all other fires, it had burst forth so suddenly, that the miller's daughter, the beautiful Babette, was quite unaware of it. Rudy had never spoken a word to her on the subject. The miller was rich, and, on that account, Babette stood very high, and was rather difficult to aspire to. But said Rudy to himself, "Nothing is too high for a man to reach: he must climb with confidence in himself, and he will not fail." He had learnt this lesson in his youthful home.

It happened once that Rudy had some business to settle at Bex. It was a long journey at that time, for the railway had not been opened. From the glaciers of the Rhone, at the foot of the Simplon, between its ever-changing mountain summits, stretches the valley of the canton Valais. Through it runs the noble river of the Rhone, which often overflows its banks, covering fields and highways, and destroying everything in its course. Near the towns of Sion and St. Maurice, the valley takes a turn, and bends like an elbow, and behind St. Maurice becomes so narrow that there is only space enough for the bed of the river and a narrow carriage-road. An old tower stands here, as if it were guardian to the canton Valais, which ends at this point; and from it we can look across the stone bridge to the toll-house on the other side, where the canton Vaud commences. Not far from this spot stands the town of Bex, and at every step can be seen an increase of fruitfulness and verdure. It is like entering a grove of chestnut and walnut-trees. Here and there the cypress and pomegranate blossoms peep forth; and it is almost as warm as an Italian climate. Rudy arrived at Bex, and soon finished the business which had brought him there, and then walked about the town; but not even the miller's boy could be seen, nor any one belonging to the mill, not to mention Babette. This did not please him at all. Evening came on. The air was filled with the perfume of the wild thyme and the blossoms of the lime-trees, and the green woods on the mountains seemed to be covered with a shining veil, blue as the sky. Over everything reigned a stillness, not of sleep or of death, but as if Nature were holding her breath, that her image might be photographed on the blue vault of heaven. Here and there, amidst the trees of the silent valley, stood poles which supported the wires of the electric telegraph. Against one of these poles leaned an object so motionless that it might have been mistaken for the trunk of a tree; but it was Rudy, standing there as still as at that moment was everything around him. He was not asleep, neither was he dead; but just as the various events in the world—matters of momentous importance to individuals—were flying through the telegraph wires, without the quiver of a wire or the slightest tone, so, through the mind of Rudy, thoughts of overwhelming importance were passing, without an outward sign of emotion. The happiness of his future life depended upon the decision of his present reflections. His eyes were fixed on one spot in the distance—a light that twinkled through the foliage from the parlor of the miller's house, where Babette dwelt. Rudy stood so still, that it might have been supposed he was watching for a chamois; but he was in reality like a chamois, who will stand for a moment, looking as if it were chiselled out of the rock, and then, if only a stone rolled by, would suddenly bound forward with a spring, far away from the hunter. And so with Rudy: a sudden roll of his thoughts roused him from his stillness, and made him bound forward with determination to act.

"Never despair!" cried he. "A visit to the mill, to say good evening to the miller, and good evening to little Babette, can do no harm. No one ever fails who has confidence in himself. If I am to be Babette's husband, I must see her some time or other."

Then Rudy laughed joyously, and took courage to go to the mill. He knew what he wanted; he wanted to marry Babette. The clear water of the river rolled over its yellow bed, and willows and lime-trees were reflected in it, as Rudy stepped along the path to the miller's house. But, as the children sing—

"There was no one at home in the house,
Only a kitten at play."

The cat standing on the steps put up its back and cried "mew." But Rudy had no inclination for this sort of conversation; he passed on, and knocked at the door. No one heard him, no one opened the door. "Mew," said the cat again; and had Rudy been still a child, he would have understood this language, and known that the cat wished to tell him there was no one at home. So he was obliged to go to the mill and make inquiries, and there he heard that the miller had gone on a journey to Interlachen, and taken Babette with him, to the great shooting festival, which began that morning, and would continue for eight days, and that people from all the German settlements would be there.

Poor Rudy! we may well say. It was not a fortunate day for his visit to Bex. He had just to return the way he came, through St. Maurice and Sion, to his home in the valley. But he did not despair. When the sun rose the next morning, his good spirits had returned; indeed he had never really lost them. "Babette is at Interlachen," said Rudy to himself, "many days' journey from here. It is certainly a long way for any one who takes the high road, but not so far if he takes a short cut across the mountain, and that just suits a chamois-hunter. I have been that way before, for it leads to the home of my childhood, where, as a little boy, I lived with my grandfather. And there are shooting matches at Interlachen. I will go, and try to stand first in the match. Babette will be there, and I shall be able to make her acquaintance."

Carrying his light knapsack, which contained his Sunday clothes, on his back, and with his musket and his game-bag over his shoulder, Rudy started to take the shortest way across the mountain. Still it was a great distance. The shooting matches were to commence on that day, and to continue for a whole week. He had been told also that the miller and Babette would remain that time with some relatives at Interlachen. So over the Gemmi Rudy climbed bravely, and determined to descend the side of the Grindelwald. Bright and joyous were his feelings as he stepped lightly onwards, inhaling the invigorating mountain air. The valley sunk as he ascended, the circle of the horizon expanded. One snow-capped peak after another rose before him, till the whole of the glittering Alpine range became visible. Rudy knew each ice-clad peak, and he continued his course towards the Schreckhorn, with its white powdered stone finger raised high in the air. At length he had crossed the highest ridges, and before him lay the green pasture lands sloping down towards the valley, which was once his home. The buoyancy of the air made his heart light. Hill and valley were blooming in luxuriant beauty, and his thoughts were youthful dreams, in which old age or death were out of the question. Life, power, and enjoyment were in the future, and he felt free and light as a bird. And the swallows flew round him, as in the days of his childhood, singing "We and you—you and we." All was overflowing with joy. Beneath him lay the meadows, covered with velvety green, with the murmuring river flowing through them, and dotted here and there were small wooden houses. He could see the edges of the glaciers, looking like green glass against the soiled snow, and the deep chasms beneath the loftiest glacier. The church bells were ringing, as if to welcome him to his home with their sweet tones. His heart beat quickly, and for a moment he seemed to have foregotten Babette, so full were his thoughts of old recollections. He was, in imagination, once more wandering on the road where, when a

The Ice Maiden

little boy, he, with other children, came to sell their curiously carved toy houses. Yonder, behind the fir-trees, still stood his grandfather's house, his mother's father, but strangers dwelt in it now. Children came running to him, as he had once done, and wished to sell their wares. One of them offered him an Alpine rose. Rudy took the rose as a good omen, and thought of Babette. He quickly crossed the bridge where the two rivers flow into each other. Here he found a walk overshadowed with large walnut-trees, and their thick foliage formed a pleasant shade. Very soon he perceived in the distance, waving flags, on which glittered a white cross on a red ground—the standard of the Danes as well as of the Swiss—and before him lay Interlachen.

"It is really a splendid town, like none other that I have ever seen," said Rudy to himself. It was indeed a Swiss town in its holiday dress. Not like the many other towns, crowded with heavy stone houses, stiff and foreign looking. No; here it seemed as if the wooden houses on the hills had run into the valley, and placed themselves in rows and ranks by the side of the clear river, which rushes like an arrow in its course. The streets were rather irregular, it is true, but still this added to their picturesque appearance. There was one street which Rudy thought the prettiest of them all; it had been built since he had visited the town when a little boy. It seemed to him as if all the neatest and most curiously carved toy houses which his grandfather once kept in the large cupboard at home, had been brought out and placed in this spot, and that they had increased in size since then, as the old chestnut trees had done. The houses were called hotels; the woodwork on the windows and balconies was curiously carved. The roofs were gaily painted, and before each house was a flower garden, which separated it from the macadamized high road. These houses all stood on the same side of the road, so that the fresh, green meadows, in which were cows grazing, with bells on their necks, were not hidden. The sound of these bells is often heard amidst Alpine scenery. These meadows were encircled by lofty hills, which receded a little in the centre, so that the most beautifully formed of Swiss mountains—the snow-crowned Jungfrau—could be distinctly seen glittering in the distance. A number of elegantly dressed gentlemen and ladies from foreign lands, and crowds of country people from the neighbouring cantons, were assembled in the town. Each marksman wore the number of hits he had made twisted in a garland round his hat. Here were music and singing of all descriptions: hand-organs, trumpets, shouting, and noise. The houses and bridges were adorned with verses and inscriptions. Flags and banners were waving. Shot after shot was fired, which was the best music to Rudy's ears. And amidst all this excitement he quite forgot Babette, on whose account only he had come. The shooters were thronging round the target, and Rudy was soon amongst them. But when he took his turn to fire, he proved himself the best shot, for he always struck the bull's-eye.

"Who may that young stranger be?" was the inquiry on all sides. "He speaks French as it is spoken in the Swiss cantons."

"And makes himself understood very well when he speaks German," said some.

"He lived here, when a child, with his grandfather, in a house on the road to Grindelwald," remarked one of the sportsmen.

And full of life was this young stranger; his eyes sparkled, his glance was steady, and his arm sure, therefore he always hit the mark. Good fortune gives courage, and Rudy was always courageous. He soon had a circle of friends gathered round him. Every one noticed him, and did him homage. Babette had quite vanished from his thoughts, when he was struck on the shoulder by a heavy hand, and a deep voice said to him in French, "You are from the canton Valais."

Rudy turned round, and beheld a man with a ruddy, pleasant face, and a stout figure. It was the rich miller from Bex. His broad, portly person, hid the slender, lovely Babette; but she came forward and glanced at him with her bright, dark eyes. The rich miller was very much flattered at the thought that the young man, who was acknowledged to be the best shot, and was so praised by every one, should be from his own canton. Now was Rudy really fortunate: he had travelled all this way to this place, and those he had forgotten were now come to seek him. When country people go far from home, they often meet with those they know, and improve their acquaintance. Rudy, by his shooting, had gained the first place in the shooting-match, just as the miller at home at Bex stood first, because of his money and his mill. So the two men shook hands, which they had never done before. Babette, too, held out her hand to Rudy frankly, and he pressed it in his, and looked at her so earnestly, that she blushed deeply. The miller talked of the long journey they had travelled, and of the many towns they had seen. It was his opinion that he had really made as great a journey as if he had travelled in a steamship, a railway carriage, or a post-chaise.

"I came by a much shorter way," said Rudy; "I came over the mountains. There is no road so high that a man may not venture upon it."

"Ah, yes; and break your neck," said the miller; "and you look like one who will break his neck some day, you are so daring."

"Oh, nothing ever happens to a man if he has confidence in himself," replied Rudy.

The miller's relations at Interlachen, with whom the miller and Babette were staying, invited Rudy to visit them, when they found he came from the same canton as the miller. It was a most pleasant visit. Good fortune seemed to follow him, as it does those who think and act for themselves, and who remember the proverb, "Nuts are given to us, but they are not cracked for us." And Rudy was treated by the miller's relations almost like one of the family, and glasses of wine were poured out to drink to the welfare of the best shooter. Babette clinked glasses with Rudy, and he returned thanks for the toast. In the evening they all took a delightful walk under the walnut-trees, in front of the stately hotels; there were so many people, and such crowding, that Rudy was obliged to offer his arm to Babette. Then he told her how happy it made him to meet people from the canton Vaud—for Vaud and Valais were neighbouring cantons. He spoke of this pleasure so heartily that Babette could not resist giving his arm a slight squeeze; and so they walked on together, and talked and chatted like old acquaintances. Rudy felt inclined to laugh sometimes at the absurd dress and walk of the foreign ladies; but Babette did not wish to make fun of them, for she knew there must be some good, excellent people amongst them; she, herself, had a godmother, who was a high-born English lady. Eighteen years before, when Babette was christened, this lady was staying at Bex, and she stood godmother for her, and gave her the valuable brooch she now wore in her bosom.

Her godmother had twice written to her, and this year she was expected to visit Interlachen with her two daughters; "but they are old-maids," added Babette, who was only eighteen: "they are nearly thirty." Her sweet little mouth was never still a moment, and all that she said sounded in Rudy's ears as matters of the greatest importance, and at last he told her what he was longing to tell. How often he had been at Bex, how well he knew the mill, and how often he had seen Babette, when most likely she had not noticed him; and lastly, that full of many thoughts which he could not tell her, he had been to the mill on the evening when she and her father has started on their long journey, but not too far for him to find a way to overtake them. He told her all this, and a great deal more; he told her how much he could endure for her; and that it was to see her, and not the shooting-match, which had brought him to Interlachen. Babette became quite silent after hearing all this; it was almost too much, and it troubled her.

And while they thus wandered on, the sun sunk behind the lofty mountains. The Jungfrau stood out in brightness and splendor, as a background to the green woods of the surrounding hills. Every one stood still to look at the beautiful sight, Rudy and Babette among them.

"Nothing can be more beautiful than this," said Babette.

"Nothing!" replied Rudy, looking at Babette.

"Tomorrow I must return home," remarked Rudy a few minutes afterwards.

"Come and visit us at Bex," whispered Babette; "my father will be pleased to see you."

V

On the Way Home

Oh, what a number of things Rudy had to carry over the mountains, when he set out to return home! He had three silver cups, two handsome pistols, and a silver coffee-pot. This latter would be useful when he began housekeeping. But all these were not the heaviest weight he had to bear; something mightier and more important he carried with him in his heart, over the high mountains, as he journeyed homeward.

The weather was dismally dark, and inclined to rain; the clouds hung low, like a mourning veil on the tops of the mountains, and shrouded their glittering peaks. In the woods could be heard the sound of the axe and the heavy fall of the trunks of the trees, as they rolled down the slopes of the mountains. When seen from the heights, the trunks of these trees looked like slender stems; but on a nearer inspection they were found to be large and strong enough for the masts of a ship. The river murmured monotonously, the wind whistled, and the clouds sailed along hurriedly.

Suddenly there appeared, close by Rudy's side, a young maiden; he had not noticed her till she came quite near to him. She was also going to ascend the mountain. The maiden's eyes shone with an unearthly power, which obliged you to look into them; they were strange eyes—clear, deep, and unfathomable.

"Hast thou a lover?" asked Rudy; all his thoughts were naturally on love just then.

"I have none," answered the maiden, with a laugh; it was as if she had not spoken the truth.

"Do not let us go such a long way round," said she. "We must keep to the left; it is much shorter."

"Ah, yes," he replied; "and fall into some crevasse. Do you pretend to be a guide, and not know the road better than that?"

"I know every step of the way," said she; "and my thoughts are collected, while yours are down in the valley yonder. We should think of the Ice Maiden while we are up here; men say she is not kind to their race."

"I fear her not," said Rudy. "She could not keep me when I was a child; I will not give myself up to her now I am a man."

Darkness came on, the rain fell, and then it began to snow, and the whiteness dazzled the eyes.

"Give me your hand," said the maiden; "I will help you to mount." And he felt the touch of her icy fingers.

"*You* help me," cried Rudy; "I do not yet require a woman to help me to climb." And he stepped quickly forwards away from her.

The drifting snow-shower fell like a veil between them, the wind whistled, and behind him he could hear the maiden laughing and singing, and the sound was most strange to hear.

"It certainly must be a spectre or a servant of the Ice Maiden," thought Rudy, who had heard such things talked about when he was a little boy, and had stayed all night on the mountain with the guides.

The snow fell thicker than ever, the clouds lay beneath him; he looked back, there was no one to be seen, but he heard sounds of mocking laughter, which were not those of a human voice.

When Rudy at length reached the highest part of the mountain, where the path led down to the valley of the Rhone, the snow had ceased, and in the clear heavens he saw two bright stars twinkling. They reminded him of Babette and of himself, and of his future happiness, and his heart glowed at the thought.

VI
The Visit to the Mill

What beautiful things you have brought home!" said his old foster-mother; and her strange-looking eagle-eyes sparkled, while she wriggled and twisted her skinny neck more quickly and strangely than ever. "You have brought good luck with you, Rudy. I must give you a kiss, my dear boy."

Rudy allowed himself to be kissed; but it could be seen by his countenance that he only endured the infliction as a homely duty.

"How handsome you are, Rudy!" said the old woman.

"Don't flatter," said Rudy, with a laugh; but still he was pleased.

"I must say once more," said the old woman, "that you are very lucky."

"Well, in that I believe you are right," said he, as he thought of Babette. Never had he felt such a longing for that deep valley as he now had. "They must have returned home by this time," said he to himself, "it is already two days over the time which they fixed upon. I must go to Bex."

So Rudy set out to go to Bex; and when he arrived there, he found the miller and his daughter at home. They received him kindly, and brought him many greetings from their friends at Interlachen.

Babette did not say much. She seemed to have become quite silent; but her eyes spoke, and that was quite enough for Rudy. The miller had generally a great deal to talk about, and seemed to expect that every one should listen to his jokes, and laugh at them; for was not he the rich miller? But now he was more inclined to hear Rudy's adventures while hunting and travelling, and to listen to his descriptions of the difficulties the chamois-hunter has to overcome on the mountain-tops, or of the dangerous snow-drifts which the wind and weather cause to cling to the edges of the rocks, or to lie in the form of a frail bridge over the abyss beneath. The eyes of the brave Rudy sparkled as he described the life of a hunter, or spoke of the cunning of the chamois and their wonderful leaps; also of the powerful fohn and the rolling avalanche. He noticed that the more he described, the more interested the miller became, especially when he spoke of the fierce vulture and of the royal eagle. Not far from Bex, in the canton Valais, was an eagle's nest, more curiously built under a high, over-hanging rock. In this nest was a young eagle; but who would venture to take it? A young Englishman had offered Rudy a whole handful of gold, if he would bring him the young eagle alive.

"There is a limit to everything," was Rudy's reply. "The eagle could not be taken; it would be folly to attempt it."

The wine was passed round freely, and the conversation kept up pleasantly; but the evening seemed too short for Rudy, although it was midnight when he left the miller's house, after this his first visit.

While the lights in the windows of the miller's house still twinkled through the green foliage, out through the open skylight came the parlor-cat on to the roof, and along the water-pipe walked the kitchen-cat to meet her.

"What is the news at the mill?" asked the parlor-cat. "Here in the house there is secret love-making going on, which the father knows nothing about. Rudy and Babette have been treading on each other's paws, under the table, all the evening. They trod on my tail twice, but I did not mew; that would have attracted notice."

"Well, I should have mewed," said the kitchen-cat.

"What might suit the kitchen would not suit the parlor," said the other. "I am quite curious to know what the miller will say when he finds out this engagement."

Yes, indeed; what would the miller say? Rudy himself was anxious to know that; but to wait till the miller heard of it from others was out of the question. Therefore, not many days after this visit, he was riding in the omnibus that runs between the two cantons, Valais and Vaud. These cantons are separated by the Rhone, over which is a bridge that unites them. Rudy, as usual, had plenty of courage, and indulged in pleasant thoughts of the favourable answer he should receive that evening. And when the omnibus returned, Rudy was again seated in it, going homewards; and at the same time the parlor-cat at the miller's house ran out quickly, crying—

"Here, you from the kitchen, what do you think? The miller knows all now. Everything has come to a delightful end. Rudy came here this evening, and he and Babette had much whispering and secret conversation together. They stood in the path near the miller's room. I lay at their feet; but they had no eyes or thoughts for me.

"'I will go to your father at once,' said he; 'it is the most honourable way.'

"'Shall I go with you?' asked Babette; 'it will give you courage.'

"'I have plenty of courage,' said Rudy; 'but if you are with me, he must be friendly, whether he says Yes or No.'

"So they turned to go in, and Rudy trod heavily on my tail; he certainly is very clumsy. I mewed; but neither he nor Babette had any ears for me. They opened the door, and entered together. I was before them, and jumped on the back of a chair. I hardly know what Rudy said; but the miller flew into a rage, and threatened to kick him out of the house. He told him he might go to the mountains, and look after the chamois, but not after our little Babette."

"And what did they say? Did they speak?" asked the kitchen-cat.

"What did they say! why, all that people generally do say when they go a-wooing—'I love her, and she loves me; and when there is milk in the can for one, there is milk in the can for two.'

"'But she is so far above you,' said the miller; 'she has heaps of gold, as you know. You should not attempt to reach her.'

"'There is nothing so high that a man cannot reach, if he will,' answered Rudy; for he is a brave youth.

"'Yet you could not reach the young eagle,' said the miller, laughing. 'Babette is higher than the eagle's nest.'

"'I will have them both,' said Rudy.

"'Very well; I will give her to you when you bring me the young eaglet alive,' said the miller; and he laughed till the tears stood in his eyes. 'But now I thank you for this visit, Rudy; and if you come tomorrow, you will find nobody at home. Goodbye, Rudy.'

"Babette also wished him farewell; but her voice sounded as mournful as the mew of a little kitten that has lost its mother.

"'A promise is a promise between man and man,' said Rudy. 'Do not weep, Babette; I shall bring the young eagle.'

"'You will break your neck, I hope,' said the miller, 'and we shall be relieved from your company.'

"I call that kicking him out of the house," said the parlor-cat. "And now Rudy is gone, and Babette sits and weeps, while the miller sings German songs that he learnt on his journey; but I do not trouble myself on the matter—it would be of no use."

"Yet, for all that, it is a very strange affair," said the kitchen-cat.

VII
The Eagle's Nest

From the mountain-path came a joyous sound of some person whistling, and it betokened good humour and undaunted courage. It was Rudy, going to meet his friend Vesinaud. "You must come and help," said he. "I want to carry off the young eaglet from the top of the rock. We will take young Ragli with us."

"Had you not better first try to take down the moon? That would be quite as easy a task," said Vesinaud. "You seem to be in good spirits."

"Yes, indeed I am. I am thinking of my wedding. But to be serious, I will tell you all about it, and how I am situated."

Then he explained to Vesinaud and Ragli what he wished to do, and why.

"You are a daring fellow," said they; "but it is no use; you will break your neck."

"No one falls, unless he is afraid," said Rudy.

So at midnight they set out, carrying with them poles, ladders, and ropes. The road lay amidst brushwood and underwood, over rolling stones, always upwards higher and higher in the dark night. Waters roared beneath them, or fell in cascades from above. Humid clouds were driving through the air as the hunters reached the precipitous ledge of the rock. It was even darker here, for the sides of the rocks almost met, and the light penetrated only through a small opening at the top. At a little distance from the edge could be heard the sound of the roaring, foaming waters in the yawning abyss beneath them. The three seated themselves on a stone, to await in stillness the dawn of day, when the parent eagle would fly out, as it would be necessary to shoot the old bird before they could think of gaining possession of the young one. Rudy sat motionless, as if he had been part of the stone on which he sat. He held his gun ready to fire, with his eyes fixed steadily on the highest point of the cliff, where the eagle's nest lay concealed beneath the overhanging rock.

The three hunters had a long time to wait. At last they heard a rustling, whirring sound above them, and a large hovering object darkened the air. Two guns were ready to aim at the dark body of the eagle as it rose from the nest. Then a shot was fired; for an instant the bird fluttered its wide-spreading wings, and seemed as if it would fill up the whole of the chasm, and drag down the hunters in its fall. But it was not so; the eagle sunk gradually into the abyss beneath, and the branches of trees and bushes were broken by its weight. Then the hunters roused themselves: three of the longest ladders were brought and bound together; the topmost ring of these ladders would just reach the edge of the rock which hung over the abyss, but no farther. The point beneath which the eagle's nest lay sheltered was much higher, and the sides of the rock were as smooth as a wall. After consulting together, they determined to bind together two more ladders, and to hoist them over the cavity, and so form a communication with the three beneath them, by binding the upper ones to the lower. With great difficulty they contrived to drag the two ladders over the rock, and there they hung for some moments, swaying over the abyss; but no sooner had they fastened them together, than Rudy placed his foot on the lowest step.

The Ice Maiden

It was a bitterly cold morning; clouds of mist were rising from beneath, and Rudy stood on the lower step of the ladder as a fly rests on a piece of swinging straw, which a bird may have dropped from the edge of the nest it was building on some tall factory chimney; but the fly could fly away if the straw were shaken, Rudy could only break his neck. The wind whistled around him, and beneath him the waters of the abyss, swelled by the thawing of the glaciers, those palaces of the Ice Maiden, foamed and roared in their rapid course. When Rudy began to ascend, the ladder trembled like the web of the spider, when it draws out the long, delicate threads; but as soon as he reached the fourth of the ladders, which had been bound together, he felt more confidence—he knew that they had been fastened securely by skilful hands. The fifth ladder, that appeared to reach the nest, was supported by the sides of the rock, yet it swung to and fro, and flapped about like a slender reed, and as if it had been bound by fishing lines. It seemed a most dangerous undertaking to ascend it, but Rudy knew how to climb; he had learnt that from the cat, and he had no fear. He did not observe Vertigo, who stood in the air behind him, trying to lay hold of him with his outstretched polypous arms.

When at length he stood on the topmost step of the ladder, he found that he was still some distance below the nest, and not even able to see into it. Only by using his hands and climbing could he possibly reach it. He tried the strength of the stunted trees, and the thick underwood upon which the nest rested, and of which it was formed, and finding they would support his weight, he grasped them firmly, and swung himself up from the ladder till his head and breast were above the nest, and then what an overpowering stench came from it, for in it lay the putrid remains of lambs, chamois, and birds. Vertigo, although he could not reach him, blew the poisonous vapor in his face, to make him giddy and faint; and beneath, in the dark, yawning deep, on the rushing waters, sat the Ice Maiden, with her long, pale, green hair falling around her, and her death-like eyes fixed upon him, like the two barrels of a gun. "I have thee now," she cried.

In a corner of the eagle's nest sat the young eaglet, a large and powerful bird, though still unable to fly. Rudy fixed his eyes upon it, held on by one hand with all his strength, and with the other threw a noose round the young eagle. The string slipped to its legs. Rudy tightened it, and thus secured the bird alive. Then flinging the sling over his shoulder, so that the creature hung a good way down behind him, he prepared to descend with the help of a rope, and his foot soon touched safely the highest step of the ladder. Then Rudy, remembering his early lesson in climbing, "Hold fast, and do not fear," descended carefully down the ladders, and at last stood safely on the ground with the young living eaglet, where he was received with loud shouts of joy and congratulations.

VIII
What Fresh News the Parlor-Cat Had to Tell

"There is what you asked for," said Rudy, as he entered the miller's house at Bex, and placed on the floor a large basket. He removed the lid as he spoke, and a pair of yellow eyes, encircled by a black ring, stared forth with a wild, fiery glance, that seemed ready to burn and destroy all that came in its way. Its short, strong beak was open, ready to bite, and on its red throat were short feathers, like stubble.

"The young eaglet!" cried the miller.

Babette screamed, and started back, while her eyes wandered from Rudy to the bird in astonishment.

"You are not to be discouraged by difficulties, I see," said the miller.

"And you will keep your word," replied Rudy. "Each has his own characteristic, whether it is honour or courage."

"But how is it you did not break your neck?" asked the miller.

"Because I held fast," answered Rudy; "and I mean to hold fast to Babette."

"You must get her first," said the miller, laughing; and Babette thought this a very good sign.

"We must take the bird out of the basket," said she. "It is getting into a rage; how its eyes glare. How did you manage to conquer it?"

Then Rudy had to describe his adventure, and the miller's eyes opened wide as he listened.

"With your courage and your good fortune you might win three wives," said the miller.

"Oh, thank you," cried Rudy.

"But you have not won Babette yet," said the miller, slapping the young Alpine hunter on the shoulder playfully.

"Have you heard the fresh news at the mill?" asked the parlor-cat of the kitchen-cat. "Rudy has brought us the young eagle, and he is to take Babette in exchange. They kissed each other in the presence of the old man, which is as good as an engagement. He was quite civil about it; drew in his claws, and took his afternoon nap, so that the two were left to sit and wag their tails as much as they pleased. They have so much to talk about that it will not be finished till Christmas." Neither was it finished till Christmas.

The wind whirled the faded, fallen leaves; the snow drifted in the valleys, as well as upon the mountains, and the Ice Maiden sat in the stately palace which, in winter time, she generally occupied. The perpendicular rocks were covered with slippery ice, and where in summer the stream from the rocks had left a watery veil, icicles large and heavy hung from the trees, while the snow-powdered fir-trees were decorated with fantastic garlands of crystal. The Ice Maiden rode on the howling wind across the deep valleys, the country, as far as Bex, was covered with a carpet of snow, so that the Ice Maiden could follow Rudy, and see him, when he visited the mill; and while in the room at the miller's house, where he was accustomed to spend so much of his time with Babette. The wedding was to take place in the following summer, and they heard enough of it, for so many of their friends spoke of the matter.

Then came sunshine to the mill. The beautiful Alpine roses bloomed, and joyous, laughing Babette, was like the early spring, which makes all the birds sing of summer time and bridal days.

"How those two do sit and chatter together," said the parlor-cat; "I have had enough of their mewing."

IX
The Ice Maiden

The walnut and chestnut trees, which extend from the bridge of St. Maurice, by the river Rhone, to the shores of the lake of Geneva, were already covered with the delicate green garlands of early spring, just bursting into bloom, while the Rhone rushed wildly from its source among the green glaciers which form the ice palace of the Ice Maiden. She sometimes allows herself to be carried by the keen wind to the lofty snow-fields, where she stretches herself in the sunshine on the soft snowy-cushions. From thence she throws her far-seeing glance into the deep valley beneath, where human beings are busily moving about like ants on a stone in the sun. "Spirits of strength, as the children of the sun call you," cried the Ice Maiden, "ye are but worms! Let but a snow-ball roll, and you and your houses and your towns are crushed and swept away." And she raised her proud head, and looked around her with eyes that flashed death from their glance. From the valley came a rumbling sound; men were busily at work blasting the rocks to form tunnels, and laying down roads for the railway. "They are playing at work underground, like moles," said she. "They are digging passages beneath the earth, and the noise is like the reports of cannons. I shall throw down my palaces, for the clamor is louder than the roar of thunder." Then there ascended from the valley a thick vapor, which waved itself in the air like a fluttering veil. It rose, as a plume of feathers, from a steam engine, to which, on the lately-opened railway, a string of carriages was linked, carriage to carriage, looking like a winding serpent. The train shot past with the speed of an arrow. "They play at being masters down there, those spirits of strength!" exclaimed the Ice Maiden; "but the powers of nature are still the rulers." And she laughed and sang till her voice sounded through the valley, and people said it was the rolling of an avalanche. But the children of the sun sang in louder strains in praise of the mind of man, which can span the sea as with a yoke, can level mountains, and fill up valleys. It is the power of thought which gives man the mastery over nature.

Just at this moment there came across the snow-field, where the Ice Maiden sat, a party of travellers. They had bound themselves fast to each other, so that they looked like one large body on the slippery plains of ice encircling the deep abyss.

"Worms!" exclaimed the Ice Maiden. "You, the lords of the powers of nature!" And she turned away and looked maliciously at the deep valley where the railway train was rushing by. "There they sit, these thoughts!" she exclaimed. "There they sit in their power over nature's strength. I see them all. One sits proudly apart, like a king; others sit together in a group; yonder, half of them are asleep; and when the steam dragon stops, they will get out and go their way. The thoughts go forth into the world," and she laughed.

"There goes another avalanche," said those in the valley beneath.

"It will not reach us," said two who sat together behind the steam dragon. "Two hearts and one beat," as people say. They were Rudy and Babette, and the miller was with them. "I am like the luggage," said he; "I am here as a necessary appendage."

"There sit those two," said the Ice Maiden. "Many a chamois have I crushed. Millions of Alpine roses have I snapped and broken off; not a root have I spared. I know them all, and their thoughts, those spirits of strength!" and again she laughed.

"There rolls another avalanche," said those in the valley.

X
The Godmother

At Montreux, one of the towns which encircle the northeast part of the lake of Geneva, lived Babette's godmother, the noble English lady, with her daughters and a young relative. They had only lately arrived, yet the miller had paid them a visit, and informed them of Babette's engagement to Rudy. The whole story of their meeting at Interlachen, and his brave adventure with the eaglet, were related to them, and they were all very much interested, and as pleased about Rudy and Babette as the miller himself. The three were invited to come to Montreux; it was but right for Babette to become acquainted with her godmother, who wished to see her very much. A steam-boat started from the town of Villeneuve, at one end of the lake of Geneva, and arrived at Bernex, a little town beyond Montreux, in about half an hour. And in this boat, the miller, with his daughter and Rudy, set out to visit her godmother. They passed the coast which has been so celebrated in song. Here, under the walnut-trees, by the deep blue lake, sat Byron, and wrote his melodious verses about the prisoner confined in the gloomy castle of Chillon. Here, where Clarens, with its weeping-willows, is reflected in the clear water, wandered Rousseau, dreaming of Heloise. The river Rhone glides gently by beneath the lofty snow-capped hills of Savoy, and not far from its mouth lies a little island in the lake, so small that, seen from the shore, it looks like a ship. The surface of the island is rocky; and about a hundred years ago, a lady caused the ground to be covered with earth, in which three acacia-trees were planted, and the whole enclosed with stone walls. The acacia-trees now overshadow every part of the island. Babette was enchanted with the spot; it seemed to her the most beautiful object in the whole voyage, and she thought how much she should like to land there. But the steam-ship passed it by, and did not stop till it reached Bernex. The little party walked slowly from this place to Montreux, passing the sun-lit walls with which the vineyards of the little mountain town of Montreux are surrounded, and peasants' houses, overshadowed by fig-trees, with gardens in which grow the laurel and the cypress.

Halfway up the hill stood the boarding-house in which Babette's godmother resided. She was received most cordially; her godmother was a very friendly woman, with a round, smiling countenance. When a child, her head must have resembled one of Raphael's cherubs; it was still an angelic face, with its white locks of silvery hair. The daughters were tall, elegant, slender maidens.

The young cousin, whom they had brought with them, was dressed in white from head to foot; he had golden hair and golden whiskers, large enough to be divided amongst three gentlemen; and he began immediately to pay the greatest attention to Babette.

Richly bound books, note-paper, and drawings, lay on the large table. The balcony window stood open, and from it could be seen the beautiful wide extended lake, the water so clear and still, that the mountains of Savoy, with their villages, woods, and snow-crowned peaks, were clearly reflected in it.

Rudy, who was usually so lively and brave, did not in the least feel himself at home; he acted as if he were walking on peas, over a slippery floor. How long and wearisome the time appeared; it was like being in a treadmill. And then they went out for a walk, which was very slow and tedious. Two steps forward and one backwards had Rudy to take to keep pace with the others. They walked down to Chillon, and went over the old castle on the rocky island. They saw the implements of torture, the deadly dungeons, the rusty fetters in the rocky walls, the stone benches for those condemned to death, the trap-doors through which the unhappy creatures were hurled upon iron spikes, and impaled alive. They called looking at all these a pleasure. It certainly was the right place to visit. Byron's poetry had made it celebrated in the world. Rudy could only feel that it was a place of execution. He leaned against the stone framework of the window, and gazed down into the deep, blue water, and over to the little island with the three acacias, and wished himself there, away and free from the whole chattering party. But Babette was most unusually lively and good-tempered.

"I have been so amused," she said.

The cousin had found her quite perfect.

"He is a perfect fop," said Rudy; and this was the first time Rudy had said anything that did not please Babette.

The Englishman had made her a present of a little book, in remembrance of their visit to Chillon. It was Byron's poem, "The Prisoner of Chillon," translated into French, so that Babette could read it.

"The book may be very good," said Rudy; "but that finely combed fellow who gave it to you is not worth much."

"He looks something like a flour-sack without any flour," said the miller, laughing at his own wit. Rudy laughed, too, for so had he appeared to him.

XI
The Cousin

When Rudy went a few days after to pay a visit to the mill, he found the young Englishman there. Babette was just thinking of preparing some trout to set before him. She understood well how to garnish the dish with parsley, and make it look quite tempting. Rudy thought all this quite unnecessary. What did the Englishman want there? What was he about? Why should he be entertained, and waited upon by Babette? Rudy was jealous, and that made Babette happy. It amused her to discover all the feelings of his heart; the strong points and weak ones. Love was to her as yet only a pastime, and she played with Rudy's whole heart. At the same time it must be acknowledged that her fortune, her whole life, her inmost thoughts, her best and most noble feelings in this world were all for him. Still the more gloomy he looked, the more her eyes laughed. She could almost have kissed the fair Englishman, with the golden whiskers, if by so doing she could have put Rudy in a rage, and made him run out of the house. That would have proved how much he loved her. All this was not right in Babette, but she was only nineteen years of age, and she did not reflect on what she did, neither did she think that her conduct would appear to the young Englishman as light, and not even becoming the modest and much-loved daughter of the miller.

The Ice Maiden

The mill at Bex stood in the highway, which passed under the snow-clad mountains, and not far from a rapid mountain-stream, whose waters seemed to have been lashed into a foam like soap-suds. This stream, however, did not pass near enough to the mill, and therefore the mill-wheel was turned by a smaller stream which tumbled down the rocks on the opposite side, where it was opposed by a stone mill-dam, and obtained greater strength and speed, till it fell into a large basin, and from thence through a channel to the mill-wheel. This channel sometimes overflowed, and made the path so slippery that any one passing that way might easily fall in, and be carried towards the mill wheel with frightful rapidity. Such a catastrophe nearly happened to the young Englishman. He had dressed himself in white clothes, like a miller's man, and was climbing the path to the miller's house, but he had never been taught to climb, and therefore slipped, and nearly went in head-foremost. He managed, however, to scramble out with wet sleeves and bespattered trousers. Still, wet and splashed with mud, he contrived to reach Babette's window, to which he had been guided by the light that shone from it. Here he climbed the old linden-tree that stood near it, and began to imitate the voice of an owl, the only bird he could venture to mimic. Babette heard the noise, and glanced through the thin window curtain; but when she saw the man in white, and guessed who he was, her little heart beat with terror as well as anger. She quickly put out the light, felt if the fastening of the window was secure, and then left him to howl as long as he liked. How dreadful it would be, thought Babette, if Rudy were here in the house. But Rudy was not in the house. No, it was much worse, he was outside, standing just under the linden-tree. He was speaking loud, angry words. He could fight, and there might be murder! Babette opened the window in alarm, and called Rudy's name; she told him to go away, she did not wish him to remain there.

"You do not wish me to stay," cried he; "then this is an appointment you expected—this good friend whom you prefer to me. Shame on you, Babette!"

"You are detestable!" exclaimed Babette, bursting into tears. "Go away. I hate you."

"I have not deserved this," said Rudy, as he turned away, his cheeks burning, and his heart like fire.

Babette threw herself on the bed, and wept bitterly. "So much as I loved thee, Rudy, and yet thou canst think ill of me."

Thus her anger broke forth; it relieved her, however: otherwise she would have been more deeply grieved; but now she could sleep soundly, as youth only can sleep.

XII
Evil Powers

Rudy left Bex, and took his way home along the mountain path. The air was fresh, but cold; for here amidst the deep snow, the Ice Maiden reigned. He was so high up that the large trees beneath him, with their thick foliage, appeared like garden plants, and the pines and bushes even less. The Alpine roses grew near the snow, which lay in detached stripes, and looked like linen laid out to bleach. A blue gentian grew in his path, and he crushed it with the butt end of his gun. A little higher up, he espied two chamois. Rudy's eyes glistened, and his thoughts flew at once in a different direction; but he was not near enough to take a sure aim. He ascended still higher, to a spot where a few rough blades of grass grew between the blocks of stone and the chamois passed quietly on over the snow-fields. Rudy walked hurriedly, while the clouds of mist gathered round him. Suddenly he found himself on the brink of a precipitous rock. The rain was falling in torrents. He felt a burning thirst, his head was hot, and his limbs trembled with cold. He seized his hunting-flask, but it was empty; he had not thought of filling it before ascending the mountain. He had never been ill in his life, nor ever experienced such sensations as those he now felt. He was so tired that he could scarcely resist lying down at his full length to sleep, although the ground was flooded with the rain. Yet when he tried to rouse himself a little, every object around him danced and trembled before his eyes.

Suddenly he observed in the doorway of a hut newly built under the rock, a young maiden. He did not remember having seen this hut before, yet there it stood; and he thought, at first, that the young maiden was Annette, the schoolmaster's daughter, whom he had once kissed in the dance. The maiden was not Annette; yet it seemed as if he had seen her somewhere before, perhaps near Grindelwald, on the evening of his return home from Interlachen, after the shooting-match.

"How did you come here?" he asked.

"I am at home," she replied; "I am watching my flocks."

"Your flocks!" he exclaimed; "where do they find pasture? There is nothing here but snow and rocks."

"Much you know of what grows here," she replied, laughing. "not far beneath us there is beautiful pasture-land. My goats go there. I tend them carefully; I never miss one. What is once mine remains mine."

"You are bold," said Rudy.

"And so are you," she answered.

"Have you any milk in the house?" he asked; "if so, give me some to drink; my thirst is intolerable."

"I have something better than milk," she replied, "which I will give you. Some travellers who were here yesterday with their guide left behind them a half a flask of wine, such as you have never tasted. They will not come back to fetch it, I know, and I shall not drink it; so you shall have it."

Then the maiden went to fetch the wine, poured some into a wooden cup, and offered it to Rudy.

"How good it is!" said he; "I have never before tasted such warm, invigorating wine." And his eyes sparkled with new life; a glow diffused itself over his frame; it seemed as if every sorrow, every oppression were banished from his mind, and a fresh, free nature were stirring within him. "You are surely Annette, the schoolmaster's daughter," cried he; "will you give me a kiss?"

"Yes, if you will give me that beautiful ring which you wear on your finger."

"My betrothal ring?" he replied.

"Yes, just so," said the maiden, as she poured out some more wine, and held it to his lips. Again he drank, and a living joy streamed through every vein.

"The whole world is mine, why therefore should I grieve?" thought he. "Everything is created for our enjoyment and happiness. The stream of life is a stream of happiness; let us flow on with it to joy and felicity."

Rudy gazed on the young maiden; it was Annette, and yet it was not Annette; still less did he suppose it was the spectral phantom, whom he had met near Grindelwald. The maiden up here on the mountain was fresh as the new fallen snow, blooming as an Alpine rose, and as nimble-footed as a young kid. Still, she was one of Adam's race, like Rudy. He flung his arms round the beautiful being, and gazed into her wonderfully clear eyes—only for a moment; but in that moment words cannot express the effect of his gaze. Was it the spirit of life or of death that overpowered him? Was he rising higher, or sinking lower and lower into the deep, deadly abyss? He knew not; but the walls of ice shone like blue-green glass; innumerable clefts yawned around him, and the water-drops tinkled like the chiming of church bells, and shone clearly as pearls in the light of a pale-blue flame. The Ice Maiden, for she it was, kissed him, and her kiss sent a chill as of ice through his whole frame. A cry of agony escaped from him; he struggled to get free, and tottered from her. For a moment all was dark before his eyes, but when he opened them again it was light, and the Alpine maiden had vanished. The powers of evil had played their game; the sheltering hut was no more to be seen. The water trickled down the naked sides of the rocks, and snow lay thickly all around. Rudy shivered with cold; he was wet through to the skin; and his ring was gone—the betrothal ring that Babette had given him. His gun lay near him in the snow; he took it up and tried to discharge it, but it missed fire. Heavy clouds lay on the mountain clefts, like firm masses of snow. Upon one of these Vertigo sat, lurking after his powerless prey, and from beneath came a sound as if a piece of rock had fallen from the cleft, and was crushing everything that stood in its way or opposed its course.

But, at the miller's, Babette sat alone and wept. Rudy had not been to see her for six days. He who was in the wrong, and who ought to ask her forgiveness; for did she not love him with her whole heart?

XIII
At the Mill

"What strange creatures human beings are," said the parlor-cat to the kitchen-cat; "Babette and Rudy have fallen out with each other. She sits and cries, and he thinks no more about her."

"That does not please me to hear," said the kitchen-cat.

"Nor me either," replied the parlor-cat; "but I do not take it to heart. Babette may fall in love with the red whiskers, if she likes, but he has not been here since he tried to get on the roof."

The powers of evil carry on their game both around us and within us. Rudy knew this, and thought a great deal about it. What was it that had happened to him on the mountain? Was it really a ghostly apparition, or a fever dream? Rudy knew nothing of fever, or any other ailment. But, while he judged Babette, he began to examine his own conduct. He had allowed wild thoughts to chase each other in his heart, and a fierce tornado to break loose. Could he confess to Babette, indeed, every thought which in the hour of temptation might have led him to wrong doing? He had lost her ring, and that very loss had won him back to her. Could she expect him to confess? He felt as if his heart would break while he thought of it, and while so many memories lingered on his mind. He saw her again, as she once stood before him, a laughing, spirited child; many loving words, which she had spoken to him out of the fulness of her love, came like a ray of sunshine into his heart, and soon it was all sunshine as he thought of Babette. But she must also confess she was wrong; that she should do.

He went to the mill—he went to confession. It began with a kiss, and ended with Rudy being considered the offender. It was such a great fault to doubt Babette's truth—it was most abominable of him. Such mistrust, such violence, would cause them both great unhappiness. This certainly was very true, she knew that; and therefore Babette preached him a little sermon, with which she was herself much amused, and during the preaching of which she looked quite lovely. She acknowledged, however, that on one point Rudy was right. Her godmother's nephew was a fop: she intended to burn the book which he had given her, so that not the slightest thing should remain to remind her of him.

"Well, that quarrel is all over," said the kitchen-cat. "Rudy is come back, and they are friends again, which they say is the greatest of all pleasures."

"I heard the rats say one night," said the kitchen-cat, "that the greatest pleasure in the world was to eat tallow candles and to feast on rancid bacon. Which are we to believe, the rats or the lovers?"

"Neither of them," said the parlor-cat; "it is always the safest plan to believe nothing you hear."

The greatest happiness was coming for Rudy and Babette. The happy day, as it is called, that is, their wedding-day, was near at hand. They were not to be married at the church at Bex, nor at the miller's house; Babette's godmother wished the nuptials to be solemnized at Montreux, in the pretty little church in that town. The miller was very anxious that this arrangement should be agreed to. He alone knew what the newly-married couple would receive from Babette's godmother, and he knew also that it was a wedding present well worth a concession. The day was fixed, and they were to travel as far as Villeneuve the evening before, to be in time for the steamer which sailed in the morning for Montreux, and the godmother's daughters were to dress and adorn the bride.

"Here in this house there ought to be a wedding-day kept," said the parlor-cat, "or else I would not give a mew for the whole affair."

"There is going to be great feasting," replied the kitchen-cat. "Ducks and pigeons have been killed, and a whole roebuck hangs on the wall. It makes me lick my lips when I think of it."

"Tomorrow morning they will begin the journey."

Yes, tomorrow! And this evening, for the last time, Rudy and Babette sat in the miller's house as an engaged couple. Outside, the Alps glowed in the evening sunset, the evening bells chimed, and the children of the sunbeam sang, "Whatever happens is best."

XIV
Night Visions

The sun had gone down, and the clouds lay low on the valley of the Rhone. The wind blew from the south across the mountains; it was an African wind, a wind which scattered the clouds for a moment, and then suddenly fell. The broken clouds hung in fantastic forms upon the wood-covered hills by the rapid Rhone. They assumed the shapes of antediluvian animals, of eagles hovering in the air, of frogs leaping over a marsh, and then sunk down upon the rushing stream and appeared to sail upon it, although floating in the air. An uprooted fir-tree was being carried away by the current, and marking out its path by eddying circles on the water. Vertigo and his sisters were dancing upon it, and raising these circles on the foaming river. The moon lighted up the snow on the mountain-tops, shone on the dark woods, and on the drifting clouds those fantastic forms which at night might be taken for spirits of the powers of nature. The mountain-dweller saw them through the panes of his little window. They sailed in hosts before the Ice Maiden as she came out of her palace of ice. Then she seated herself on the trunk of the fir-tree as on a broken skiff, and the water from the glaciers carried her down the river to the open lake.

"The wedding guests are coming," sounded from air and sea. These were the sights and sounds without; within there were visions, for Babette had a wonderful dream. She dreamt that she had been married to Rudy for many years, and that, one day when he was out chamois hunting, and she alone in their dwelling at home, the young Englishman with the golden whiskers sat with her. His eyes were quite eloquent, and his words possessed a magic power; he offered her his hand, and she was obliged to follow him. They went out of the house and stepped downwards, always downwards, and it seemed to Babette as if she had a weight on her heart which continually grew heavier. She felt she was committing a sin against Rudy, a sin against God. Suddenly she found herself forsaken, her clothes torn by the thorns, and her hair gray; she looked upwards in her agony, and there, on the edge of the rock, she espied Rudy. She stretched out her arms to him, but she did not venture to call him or to pray; and had she called him, it would have been useless, for it was not Rudy, only his hunting coat and hat hanging on an alpenstock, as the hunters sometimes arrange them to deceive the chamois. "Oh!" she exclaimed in her agony; "oh, that I had died on the happiest day of my life, my wedding-day. O my God, it would have been a mercy and a blessing had Rudy travelled far away from me, and I had never known him. None know what will happen in the future." And then, in ungodly despair, she cast herself down into the deep rocky gulf. The spell was broken; a cry of terror escaped her, and she awoke.

The dream was over; it had vanished. But she knew she had dreamt something frightful about the young Englishman, yet months had passed since she had seen him or even thought of him. Was he still at Montreux, and should she meet him there on her wedding day? A slight shadow passed over her pretty mouth as she thought of this, and she knit her brows; but the smile soon returned to her lip, and joy sparkled in her eyes, for this was the morning of the day on which she and Rudy were to be married, and the sun was shining brightly. Rudy was already in the parlor when she entered it, and they very soon started for Villeneuve. Both of them were overflowing with happiness, and the miller was in the best of tempers, laughing and merry; he was a good, honest soul, and a kind father.

"Now we are masters of the house," said the parlor-cat.

XV
The Conclusion

It was early in the afternoon, and just at dinner-time, when the three joyous travellers reached Villeneuve. After dinner, the miller placed himself in the arm-chair, smoked his pipe, and had a little nap. The bridal pair went arm-in-arm out through the town and along the high road, at the foot of the wood-covered rocks, and by the deep, blue lake.

The gray walls, and the heavy clumsy-looking towers of the gloomy castle of Chillon, were reflected in the clear flood. The little island, on which grew the three acacias, lay at a short distance, looking like a bouquet rising from the lake. "How delightful it must be to live there," said Babette, who again felt the greatest wish to visit the island; and an opportunity offered to gratify her wish at once, for on the shore lay a boat, and the rope by which it was moored could be very easily loosened. They saw no one near, so they took possession of it without asking permission of any one, and Rudy could row very well. The oars divided the pliant water like the fins of a fish—that water which, with all its yielding softness, is so strong to bear and to carry, so mild and smiling when at rest, and yet so terrible in its destroying power. A white streak of foam followed in the wake of the boat, which, in a few minutes, carried them both to the little island, where they went on shore; but there was only just room enough for two to dance. Rudy swung Babette round two or three times; and then, hand-in-hand, they sat down on a little bench under the drooping acacia-tree, and looked into each other's eyes, while everything around them glowed in the rays of the setting sun.

The fir-tree forests on the mountains were covered with a purple hue like the heather bloom; and where the woods terminated, and the rocks became prominent, they looked almost transparent in the rich crimson glow of the evening sky. The surface of the lake was like a bed of pink rose-leaves.

As the evening advanced, the shadows fell upon the snow-capped mountains of Savoy painting them in colours of deep blue, while their topmost peaks glowed like red lava; and for a moment this light was reflected on the cultivated parts of the mountains, making them appear as if newly risen from the lap of earth, and giving to the snow-crested peak of the Dent du Midi the appearance of the full moon as it rises above the horizon.

Rudy and Babette felt that they had never seen the Alpine glow in such perfection before. "How very beautiful it is, and what happiness to be here!" exclaimed Babette.

"Earth has nothing more to bestow upon me," said Rudy; "an evening like this is worth a whole life. Often have I realized my good fortune, but never more than in this moment. I feel that if my existence were to end now, I should still have lived a happy life. What a glorious world this is; one day ends, and another begins even more beautiful than the last. How infinitely good God is, Babette!"

"I have such complete happiness in my heart," said she.

"Earth has no more to bestow," answered Rudy. And then came the sound of the evening bells, borne upon the breeze over the mountains of Switzerland and Savoy, while still, in the golden splendor of the west, stood the dark blue mountains of Jura.

"God grant you all that is brightest and best!" exclaimed Babette.

"He will," said Rudy. "He will tomorrow. Tomorrow you will be wholly mine, my own sweet wife."

"The boat!" cried Babette, suddenly. The boat in which they were to return had broken loose, and was floating away from the island.

"I will fetch it back," said Rudy; throwing off his coat and boots, he sprang into the lake, and swam with strong efforts towards it.

The dark-blue water, from the glaciers of the mountains, was icy cold and very deep. Rudy gave but one glance into the water beneath; but in that one glance he saw a gold ring rolling, glittering, and sparkling before him. His engaged ring came into his mind; but this was larger, and spread into a glittering circle, in which appeared a clear glacier. Deep chasms yawned around it, the water-drops glittered as if lighted with blue flame, and tinkled like the chiming of church bells. In one moment he saw what would require many words to describe. Young hunters, and young maidens—men and women who had sunk in the deep chasms of the glaciers—stood before him here in lifelike forms, with eyes open and smiles on their lips; and far beneath them could be heard the chiming of the church bells of buried villages, where the villagers knelt beneath the vaulted arches of churches in which ice-blocks formed the organ pipes, and the mountain stream the music.

On the clear, transparent ground sat the Ice Maiden. She raised herself towards Rudy, and kissed his feet; and instantly a cold, deathly chill, like an electric shock, passed through his limbs. Ice or fire! It was impossible to tell, the shock was so instantaneous.

"Mine! mine!" sounded around him, and within him; "I kissed thee when thou wert a little child. I once kissed thee on the mouth, and now I have kissed thee from heel to toe; thou art wholly mine." And then he disappeared in the clear, blue water.

All was still. The church bells were silent; the last tone floated away with the last red glimmer on the evening clouds. "Thou art mine," sounded from the depths below: but from the heights above, from the eternal world, also sounded the words, "Thou art mine!" Happy was he thus to pass from life to life, from earth to heaven. A chord was loosened, and tones of sorrow burst forth. The icy kiss of death had overcome the perishable body; it was but the prelude before life's real drama could begin, the discord which was quickly lost in harmony. Do you think this a sad story? Poor Babette! for her it was unspeakable anguish.

The boat drifted farther and farther away. No one on the opposite shore knew that the betrothed pair had gone over to the little island. The clouds sunk as the evening drew on, and it became dark. Alone, in despair, she waited and trembled. The weather became fearful; flash after flash lighted up the mountains of Jura, Savoy, and Switzerland, while peals of thunder, that lasted for many minutes, rolled over her head. The lightning was so vivid that every single vine stem could be seen for a moment as distinctly as in the sunlight at noon-day; and then all was veiled in darkness. It flashed across the lake in winding, zigzag lines, lighting it up on all sides; while the echoes of the thunder grew louder and stronger. On land, the boats were all carefully drawn up on the beach, every living thing sought shelter, and at length the rain poured down in torrents.

"Where can Rudy and Babette be in this awful weather?" said the miller.

Poor Babette sat with her hands clasped, and her head bowed down, dumb with grief; she had ceased to weep and cry for help.

"In the deep water!" she said to herself; "far down he lies, as if beneath a glacier."

Deep in her heart rested the memory of what Rudy had told her of the death of his mother, and of his own recovery, even after he had been taken up as dead from the cleft in the glacier.

"Ah," she thought, "the Ice Maiden has him at last."

Suddenly there came a flash of lightning, as dazzling as the rays of the sun on the white snow. The lake rose for a moment like a shining glacier; and before Babette stood the pallid, glittering, majestic form of the Ice Maiden, and at her feet lay Rudy's corpse.

"Mine!" she cried, and again all was darkness around the heaving water.

"How cruel," murmured Babette; "why should he die just as the day of happiness drew near? Merciful God, enlighten my understanding, shed light upon my heart; for I cannot comprehend the arrangements of Thy providence, even while I bow to the decree of Thy almighty wisdom and power." And God did enlighten her heart.

A sudden flash of thought, like a ray of mercy, recalled her dream of the preceding night; all was vividly represented before her. She remembered the words and wishes she had then expressed, that what was best for her and for Rudy she might piously submit to.

"Woe is me," she said; "was the germ of sin really in my heart? was my dream a glimpse into the course of my future life, whose thread must be violently broken to rescue me from sin? Oh, miserable creature that I am!"

Thus she sat lamenting in the dark night, while through the deep stillness the last words of Rudy seemed to ring in her ears. "This earth has nothing more to bestow." Words, uttered in the fulness of joy, were again heard amid the depths of sorrow.

Years have passed since this sad event happened. The shores of the peaceful lake still smile in beauty. The vines are full of luscious grapes. Steamboats, with waving flags, pass swiftly by. Pleasure-boats, with their swelling sails, skim lightly over the watery mirror, like white butterflies. The railway is opened beyond Chillon, and goes far into the deep valley of the Rhone. At every station strangers alight with red-bound guide-books in their hands, in which they read of every place worth seeing. They visit Chillon, and observe on the lake the little island with the three acacias, and then read in their guide-book the story of the bridal pair who, in the year 1856, rowed over to it. They read that the two were missing till the next morning, when some people on the shore heard the despairing cries of the bride, and went to her assistance, and by her were told of the bridegroom's fate.

But the guide-book does not speak of Babette's quiet life afterwards with her father, not at the mill—strangers dwell there now—but in a pretty house in a row near the station. On many an evening she sits at her window, and looks out over the chestnut-trees to the snow-capped mountains on which Rudy once roamed. She looks at the Alpine glow in the evening sky, which is caused by the children of the sun retiring to rest on the mountain-tops; and again they breathe their song of the traveller whom the whirlwind could deprive of his cloak but not of his life. There is a rosy tint on the mountain snow, and there are rosy gleams in each heart in which dwells the thought, "God permits nothing to happen, which is not the best for us." But this is not often revealed to all, as it was revealed to Babette in her wonderful dream.

The Snail and the Rose-Tree

Translated by Mrs. H. P. Paull

Round about the garden ran a hedge of hazel-bushes; beyond the hedge were fields and meadows with cows and sheep; but in the middle of the garden stood a Rose-tree in bloom, under which sat a Snail, whose shell contained a great deal—that is, himself.

"Only wait till my time comes," he said; "I shall do more than grow roses, bear nuts, or give milk, like the hazel-bush, the cows and the sheep."

"I expect a great deal from you," said the rose-tree. "May I ask when it will appear?"

"I take my time," said the snail. "*You*'re always in such a hurry. That does not excite expectation."

The following year the snail lay in almost the same spot, in the sunshine under the rose-tree, which was again budding and bearing roses as fresh and beautiful as ever. The snail crept half out of his shell, stretched out his horns, and drew them in again.

"Everything is just as it was last year! No progress at all; the rose-tree sticks to its roses and gets no farther."

The summer and the autumn passed; the rose-tree bore roses and buds till the snow fell and the weather became raw and wet; then it bent down its head, and the snail crept into the ground.

A new year began; the roses made their appearance, and the snail made his too.

"You are an old rose-tree now," said the snail. "You must make haste and die. You have given the world all that you had in you; whether it was of much importance is a question that I have not had time to think about. But this much is clear and plain, that you have not done the least for your inner development, or you would have produced something else. Have you anything to say in defence? You will now soon be nothing but a stick. Do you understand what I say?"

"You frighten me," said the rose-tree. "I have never thought of that."

"No, you have never taken the trouble to think at all. Have you ever given yourself an account why you bloomed, and how your blooming comes about—why just in that way and in no other?"

"No," said the rose-tree. "I bloom in gladness, because I cannot do otherwise. The sun shone and warmed me, and the air refreshed me; I drank the clear dew and the invigorating rain. I breathed and I lived! Out of the earth there arose a power within me, whilst from above I also received strength; I felt an ever-renewed and ever-increasing happiness, and therefore I was obliged to go on blooming. That was my life; I could not do otherwise."

"You have led a very easy life," remarked the snail.

"Certainly. Everything was given me," said the rose-tree. "But still more was given to you. Yours is one of those deep-thinking natures, one of those highly gifted minds that astonishes the world."

"I have not the slightest intention of doing so," said the snail. "The world is nothing to me. What have I to do with the world? I have enough to do with myself, and enough in myself."

"But must we not all here on earth give up our best parts to others, and offer as much as lies in our power? It is true, I have only given roses. But you—you who are so richly endowed—what have you given to the world? What will you give it?"

"What have I given? What am I going to give? I spit at it; it's good for nothing, and does not concern me. For my part, you may go on bearing roses; you cannot do anything else. Let the hazel bush bear nuts, and the cows and sheep give milk; they have each their public. I have mine in myself. I retire within myself and there I stop. The world is nothing to me."

With this the snail withdrew into his house and blocked up the entrance.

"That's very sad," said the rose-tree. "I cannot creep into myself, however much I might wish to do so; I have to go on bearing roses. Then they drop their leaves, which are blown away by the wind. But I once saw how a rose was laid in the mistress's hymn-book, and how one of my roses found a place in the bosom of a young beautiful girl, and how another was kissed by the lips of a child in the glad joy of life. That did me good; it was a real blessing. Those are my recollections, my life."

And the rose-tree went on blooming in innocence, while the snail lay idling in his house—the world was nothing to him.

Years passed by.

The snail had turned to earth in the earth, and the rose-tree too. Even the souvenir rose in the hymn-book was faded, but in the garden there were other rose-trees and other snails. The latter crept into their houses and spat at the world, for it did not concern them.

Shall we read the story all over again? It will be just the same.

The Old Church Bell

Translated by Mrs. H. P. Paull

In the country of Wurtemburg, in Germany, where the acacias grow by the public road, where the apple-trees and the pear-trees in autumn bend to the earth with the weight of the precious fruit, lies the little town of Marbach. As is often the case with many of these towns, it is charmingly situated on the banks of the river Neckar, which rushes rapidly by, passing villages, old knights' castles, and green vineyards, till its waters mingle with those of the stately Rhine. It was late in the autumn; the vine-leaves still hung upon the branches of the vines, but they were already tinted with red and gold; heavy showers fell on the surrounding country, and the cold autumn wind blew sharp and strong. It was not at all pleasant weather for the poor. The days grew shorter and more gloomy, and, dark as it was out of doors in the open air, it was still darker within the small, old-fashioned houses of the village. The gable end of one of these houses faced the street, and with its small, narrow windows, presented a very mean appearance. The family who dwelt in it were also very poor and humble, but they treasured the fear of God in their innermost hearts. And now He was about to send them a child. It was the hour of the mother's sorrow, when there pealed forth from the church tower the sound of festive bells. In that solemn hour the sweet and joyous chiming filled the hearts of those in the humble dwelling with thankfulness and trust; and when, amidst these joyous sounds, a little son was born to them, the words of prayer and praise arose from their overflowing hearts, and their happiness seemed to ring out over town and country in the liquid tones of the church bells' chime. The little one, with its bright eyes and golden hair, had been welcomed joyously on that dark November day. Its parents kissed it lovingly, and the father wrote these words in the Bible, "On the tenth of November, 1759, God sent us a son." And a short time after, when the child had been baptized, the names he had received were added, "John Christopher Frederick."

And what became of the little lad?—the poor boy of the humble town of Marbach? Ah, indeed, there was no one who thought or supposed, not even the old church bell which had been the first to sound and chime for him, that he would be the first to sing the beautiful song of "The Bell." The boy grew apace, and the world advanced with him.

While he was yet a child, his parents removed from Marbach, and went to reside in another town; but their dearest friends remained behind at Marbach, and therefore sometimes the mother and her son would start on a fine day to pay a visit to the little town. The boy was at this time about six years old, and already knew a great many stories out of the Bible, and several religious psalms. While seated in the evening on his little cane-chair, he had often heard his father read from Gellert's fables, and sometimes from Klopstock's grand poem, "The Messiah." He and his sister, two years older than himself, had often wept scalding tears over the story of Him who suffered death on the cross for us all.

On his first visit to Marbach, the town appeared to have changed but very little, and it was not far enough away to be forgotten. The house, with its pointed gable, narrow windows, overhanging walls and stories, projecting one beyond another, looked just the same as in former times. But in the churchyard there were several new graves;

and there also, in the grass, close by the wall, stood the old church bell! It had been taken down from its high position, in consequence of a crack in the metal which prevented it from ever chiming again, and a new bell now occupied its place. The mother and son were walking in the churchyard when they discovered the old bell, and they stood still to look at it. Then the mother reminded her little boy of what a useful bell this had been for many hundred years. It had chimed for weddings and for christenings; it had tolled for funerals, and to give the alarm in case of fire. With every event in the life of man the bell had made its voice heard. His mother also told him how the chiming of that old bell had once filled her heart with joy and confidence, and that in the midst of the sweet tones her child had been given to her. And the boy gazed on the large, old bell with the deepest interest. He bowed his head over it and kissed it, old, thrown away, and cracked as it was, and standing there amidst the grass and nettles. The boy never forgot what his mother told him, and the tones of the old bell reverberated in his heart till he reached manhood. In such sweet remembrance was the old bell cherished by the boy, who grew up in poverty to be tall and slender, with a freckled complexion and hair almost red; but his eyes were clear and blue as the deep sea, and what was his career to be? His career was to be good, and his future life enviable. We find him taking high honours at the military school in the division commanded by the member of a family high in position, and this was an honour, that is to say, good luck. He wore gaiters, stiff collars, and powdered hair, and by this he was recognized; and, indeed, he might be known by the word of command—"March! halt! front!"

The old church bell had long been quite forgotten, and no one imagined it would ever again be sent to the melting furnace to make it as it was before. No one could possibly have foretold this. Equally impossible would it have been to believe that the tones of the old bell still echoed in the heart of the boy from Marbach; or that one day they would ring out loud enough and strong enough to be heard all over the world. They had already been heard in the narrow space behind the school-wall, even above the deafening sounds of "March! halt! front!" They had chimed so loudly in the heart of the youngster, that he had sung them to his companions, and their tones resounded to the very borders of the country. He was not a free scholar in the military school, neither was he provided with clothes or food. But he had his number, and his own peg; for everything here was ordered like clockwork, which we all know is of the greatest utility—people get on so much better together when their position and duties are understood. It is by pressure that a jewel is stamped. The pressure of regularity and discipline here stamped the jewel, which in the future the world so well knew.

In the chief town of the province a great festival was being celebrated. The light streamed forth from thousands of lamps, and the rockets shot upwards towards the sky, filling the air with showers of coloured fiery sparks. A record of this bright display will live in the memory of man, for through it the pupil in the military school was in tears and sorrow. He had dared to attempt to reach foreign territories unnoticed, and must therefore give up fatherland, mother, his dearest friends, all, or sink down into the stream of common life. The old church bell had still some comfort; it stood in the shelter of the church wall in Marbach, once so elevated, now quite forgotten. The wind roared around it, and could have readily related the story of its origin and of its sweet chimes, and the wind could also tell of him to whom he had brought fresh air when, in the woods of a neighbouring country, he had sunk down exhausted with fatigue, with no other worldly possessions than hope for the future, and a written leaf from "Fiesco." The wind could have told that his only protector was an artist, who, by reading each leaf to him, made it plain; and that they amused themselves by playing at nine-pins together. The wind could also describe the pale fugitive, who, for weeks and months, lay in a wretched little road-side inn, where the landlord got drunk and raved, and where the merry-makers had it all their own way. And he, the pale fugitive, sang of the ideal.

For many heavy days and dark nights the heart must suffer to enable it to endure trial and temptation; yet, amidst it all, would the minstrel sing. Dark days and cold nights also passed over the old bell, and it noticed them not; but the bell in the man's heart felt it to be a gloomy time. What would become of this young man, and what would become of the old bell?

The Old Church Bell

The old bell was, after a time, carried away to a greater distance than any one, even the warder in the bell tower, ever imagined; and the bell in the breast of the young man was heard in countries where his feet had never wandered. The tones went forth over the wide ocean to every part of the round world.

We will now follow the career of the old bell. It was, as we have said, carried far away from Marbach and sold as old copper; then sent to Bavaria to be melted down in a furnace. And then what happened?

In the royal city of Bavaria, many years after the bell had been removed from the tower and melted down, some metal was required for a monument in honour of one of the most celebrated characters which a German people or a German land could produce. And now we see how wonderfully things are ordered. Strange things sometimes happen in this world.

In Denmark, in one of those green islands where the foliage of the beechwoods rustles in the wind, and where many Huns' graves may be seen, was another poor boy born. He wore wooden shoes, and when his father worked in a ship-yard, the boy, wrapped up in an old worn-out shawl, carried his dinner to him every day. This poor child was now the pride of his country; for the sculptured marble, the work of his hands, had astonished the world.[*] To him was offered the honour of forming from the clay, a model of the figure of him whose name, "John Christopher Frederick," had been written by his father in the Bible. The bust was cast in bronze, and part of the metal used for this purpose was the old church bell, whose tones had died away from the memory of those at home and elsewhere. The metal, glowing with heat, flowed into the mould, and formed the head and bust of the statue which was unveiled in the square in front of the old castle. The statue represented in living, breathing reality, the form of him who was born in poverty, the boy from Marbach, the pupil of the military school, the fugitive who struggled against poverty and oppression, from the outer world; Germany's great and immortal poet, who sung of Switzerland's deliverer, William Tell, and of the heaven-inspired Maid of Orleans.

---

[*] The Danish sculptor Thorwaldsen.

It was a beautiful sunny day; flags were waving from tower and roof in royal Stuttgart, and the church bells were ringing a joyous peal. One bell was silent; but it was illuminated by the bright sunshine which streamed from the head and bust of the renowned figure, of which it formed a part. On this day, just one hundred years had passed since the day on which the chiming of the old church bell at Marbach had filled the mother's heart with trust and joy—the day on which her child was born in poverty, and in a humble home; the same who, in after-years, became rich, became the noble woman-hearted poet, a blessing to the world—the glorious, the sublime, the immortal bard, John Christoper Frederick Schiller!

The Silver Shilling

Translated by Mrs. H. P. Paull

There was once a shilling, which came forth from the mint springing and shouting, "Hurrah! now I am going out into the wide world." And truly it did go out into the wide world. The children held it with warm hands, the miser with a cold and convulsive grasp, and the old people turned it about, goodness knows how many times, while the young people soon allowed it to roll away from them. The shilling was made of silver, it contained very little copper, and considered itself quite out in the world when it had been circulated for a year in the country in which it had been coined. One day, it really did go out into the world, for it belonged to a gentleman who was about to travel in foreign lands. This gentleman was not aware that the shilling lay at the bottom of his purse when he started, till he one day found it between his fingers. "Why," cried he, "here is a shilling from home; well, it must go on its travels with me now!" and the shilling jumped and rattled for joy, when it was put back again into the purse.

Here it lay among a number of foreign companions, who were

always coming and going, one taking the place of another, but the shilling from home was always put back, and had to remain in the purse, which was certainly a mark of distinction. Many weeks passed, during which the shilling had travelled a long distance in the purse, without in the least knowing where he was. He had found out that the other coins were French and Italian; and one coin said they were in this town, and another said they were in that, but the shilling was unable to make out or imagine what they meant. A man certainly cannot see much of the world if he is tied up in a bag, and this was really the shilling's fate. But one day, as he was lying in the purse, he noticed that it was not quite closed, and so he slipped near to the opening to have a little peep into society. He certainly had not the least idea of what would follow, but he was curious, and curiosity often brings its own punishment. In his eagerness, he came so near the edge of the purse that he slipped out into the pocket of the trousers; and when, in the evening, the purse was taken out, the shilling was left behind in the corner to which it had fallen. As the clothes were being carried into the hall, the shilling fell out on the floor, unheard and unnoticed by any one. The next morning the clothes were taken back to the room, the gentleman put them on, and started on his journey again; but the shilling remained behind on the floor. After a time it was found, and being considered a good coin, was placed with three other coins. "Ah," thought the shilling, "this is pleasant; I shall now see the world, become acquainted with other people, and learn other customs."

"Do you call that a shilling?" said some one the next moment. "That is not a genuine coin of the country—it is false; it is good for nothing."

Now begins the story as it was afterwards related by the shilling himself.

"'False! good for nothing!' said he. That remark went through and through me like a dagger. I knew that I had a true ring, and that mine was a genuine stamp. These people must at all events be wrong, or they could not mean me. But yes, I was the one they called 'false, and good for nothing.'

"'Then I must pay it away in the dark,' said the man who had received me. So I was to be got rid of in the darkness, and be again insulted in broad daylight.

"'False! good for nothing!' Oh, I must contrive to get lost, thought I. And I trembled between the fingers of the people every time they tried to pass me off slyly as a coin of the country. Ah! unhappy shilling that I was! Of what use were my silver, my stamp, and my real value here, where all these qualities were worthless. In the eyes of the world, a man is valued just according to the opinion formed of him. It must be a shocking thing to have a guilty conscience, and to be sneaking about on account of wicked deeds. As for me, innocent as I was, I could not help shuddering before their eyes whenever they brought me out, for I knew I should be thrown back again up the table as a false pretender. At length I was paid away to a poor old woman, who received me as wages for a hard day's work. But she could not again get rid of me; no one would take me. I was to the woman a most unlucky shilling. 'I am positively obliged to pass this shilling to somebody,' said she; 'I cannot, with the best intentions, lay by a bad shilling. The rich baker shall have it—he can bear the loss better than I can. But, after all, it is not a right thing to do.'

"'Ah!' sighed I to myself, 'am I also to be a burden on the conscience of this poor woman? Am I then in my old days so completely changed?' The woman offered me to the rich baker, but he knew the current money too well, and as soon as he received me he threw me almost in the woman's face. She could get no bread for me, and I felt quite grieved to the heart that I should be cause of so much trouble to another, and be treated as a cast-off coin. I who, in my young days, felt so joyful in the certainty of my own value, and knew so well that I bore a genuine stamp. I was as sorrowful now as a poor shilling can be when nobody will have him. The woman took me home again with her, and looking at me very earnestly, she said, 'No, I will not try to deceive any one with thee again. I will bore a hole through thee, that everyone may know that thou art a false and worthless thing; and yet, why should I do that? Very likely thou art a lucky shilling. A thought has just struck me that it is so, and I believe it. Yes, I will make a hole in the shilling,' said she, 'and run a string through it, and then give it to my neighbour's little one to hang round her neck, as a lucky shilling.' So she drilled a hole through me.

"It is really not at all pleasant to have a hole bored through one, but we can submit to a great deal when it is done with a good intention. A string was drawn through the hole, and I became a kind of medal. They hung me round the neck of a little child, and the child laughed at me and kissed me, and I rested for one whole night on the warm, innocent breast of a child.

"In the morning the child's mother took me between her fingers, and had certain thoughts about me, which I very soon found out. First, she looked for a pair of scissors, and cut the string.

"'Lucky shilling!' said she, 'certainly this is what I mean to try.' Then she laid me in vinegar till I became quite green, and after that she filled up the hole with cement, rubbed me a little to brighten me up, and went out in the twilight hour to the lottery collector, to buy herself a ticket, with a shilling that should bring luck. How everything seemed to cause me trouble. The lottery collector pressed me so hard that I thought I should crack. I had been called false, I had been thrown away—that I knew; and there were many shillings and coins with inscriptions and stamps of all kinds lying about. I well knew how proud they were, so I avoided them from very shame. With the collector were several men who seemed to have a great deal to do, so I fell unnoticed into a chest, among several other coins.

"Whether the lottery ticket gained a prize, I know not; but this I know, that in a very few days after, I was recognized as a bad shilling, and laid aside. Everything that happened always seemed to add to my sorrow. Even if a man has a good character, it is of no use for him to deny what is said of him, for he is not considered an impartial judge of himself.

"A year passed, and in this way I had been changed from hand to hand; always abused, always looked at with displeasure, and trusted by no one; but I trusted in myself, and had no confidence in the world. Yes, that was a very dark time.

"At length one day I was passed to a traveller, a foreigner, the very same who had brought me away from home; and he was simple and true-hearted enough to take me for current coin. But would he also attempt to pass me? and should I again hear the outcry, 'False! good-for-nothing!' The traveller examined me attentively, 'I took thee for good coin,' said he; then suddenly a smile spread all over his face. I have never seen such a smile on any other face as on his. 'Now this is singular,' said he, 'it is a coin from my own country; a good, true, shilling from home. Some one has bored a hole through it, and people have no doubt called it false. How curious that it should come into my hands. I will take it home with me to my own house.'

"Joy thrilled through me when I heard this. I had been once more called a good, honest shilling, and I was to go back to my own home, where each and all would recognize me, and know that I was made of good silver, and bore a true, genuine stamp. I should have been glad in my joy to throw out sparks of fire, but it has never at any time been my nature to sparkle. Steel can do so, but not silver. I was wrapped up in fine, white paper, that I might not mix with the other coins and be lost; and on special occasions, when people from my own country happened to be present, I was brought forward and spoken of very kindly. They said I was very interesting, and it was really quite worth while to notice that those who are interesting have often not a single word to say for themselves.

"At length I reached home. All my cares were at an end. Joy again overwhelmed me; for was I not good silver, and had I not a genuine stamp? I had no more insults or disappointments to endure; although, indeed, there was a hole through me, as if I were false; but suspicions are nothing when a man is really true, and every one should persevere in acting honestly, for an will be made right in time. That is my firm belief," said the shilling.

The Snowdrop

Translated by Mrs. H. P. Paull

It was winter-time; the air was cold, the wind was sharp, but within the closed doors it was warm and comfortable, and within the closed door lay the flower; it lay in the bulb under the snow-covered earth.

One day rain fell. The drops penetrated through the snowy covering down into the earth, and touched the flower-bulb, and talked of the bright world above. Soon the Sunbeam pierced its way through the snow to the root, and within the root there was a stirring.

"Come in," said the flower.

"I cannot," said the Sunbeam. "I am not strong enough to unlock the door! When the summer comes I shall be strong!"

"When will it be summer?" asked the Flower, and she repeated this question each time a new sunbeam made its way down to her. But the summer was yet far distant. The snow still lay upon the ground, and there was a coat of ice on the water every night.

"What a long time it takes! what a long time it takes!" said the Flower. "I feel a stirring and striving within me; I must stretch myself, I must unlock the door, I must get out, and must nod a good morning to the summer, and what a happy time that will be!"

And the Flower stirred and stretched itself within the thin rind which the water had softened from without, and the snow and the earth had warmed, and the Sunbeam had knocked at; and it shot forth under the snow with a greenish-white blossom on a green stalk, with narrow thick leaves, which seemed to want to protect it. The snow was cold, but was pierced by the Sunbeam, therefore it was easy to get through it, and now the Sunbeam came with greater strength than before.

"Welcome, welcome!" sang and sounded every ray, and the Flower lifted itself up over the snow into the brighter world. The Sunbeams caressed and kissed it, so that it opened altogether, white as snow, and ornamented with green stripes. It bent its head in joy and humility.

"Beautiful Flower!" said the Sunbeams, "how graceful and delicate you are! You are the first, you are the only one! You are our love! You are the bell that rings out for summer, beautiful summer, over country and town. All the snow will melt; the cold winds will be driven away; we shall rule; all will become green, and then you will have companions, syringas, laburnums, and roses; but you are the first, so graceful, so delicate!"

That was a great pleasure. It seemed as if the air were singing and sounding, as if rays of light were piercing through the leaves and the stalks of the Flower. There it stood, so delicate and so easily broken, and yet so strong in its young beauty; it stood there in its white dress with the green stripes, and made a summer. But there was a long time yet to the summer-time. Clouds hid the sun, and bleak winds were blowing.

"You have come too early," said Wind and Weather. "We have still the power, and you shall feel it, and give it up to us. You should have stayed quietly at home and not have run out to make a display of yourself. Your time is not come yet!"

It was a cutting cold! The days which now come brought not a single sunbeam. It was weather that might break such a little Flower in two with cold. But the Flower had more strength than she herself knew of. She was strong in joy and in faith in the summer, which would be sure to come, which had been announced by her deep longing and confirmed by the warm sunlight; and so she remained standing in confidence in the snow in her white garment, bending her head even while the snowflakes fell thick and heavy, and the icy winds swept over her.

"You'll break!" they said, "and fade, and fade! What did you want out here? Why did you let yourself be tempted? The Sunbeam only made game of you. Now you have what you deserve, you summer gauk."

"Summer gauk!" she repeated in the cold morning hour.

"O summer gauk!" cried some children rejoicingly; "yonder stands one—how beautiful, how beautiful! The first one, the only one!"

These words did the Flower so much good, they seemed to her like warm sunbeams. In her joy the Flower did not even feel when it was broken off. It lay in a child's hand, and was kissed by a child's mouth, and carried into a warm room, and looked on by gentle eyes, and put into water. How strengthening, how invigorating! The Flower thought she had suddenly come upon the summer.

The daughter of the house, a beautiful little girl, was confirmed, and she had a friend who was confirmed, too. He was studying for an examination for an appointment. "He shall be my summer gauk," she said; and she took the delicate Flower and laid it in a piece of scented paper, on which verses were written, beginning with summer gauk and ending with summer gauk. "My friend, be a winter gauk." She had twitted him with the summer. Yes, all this was in the verses, and the paper was folded up like a letter, and the Flower was folded in the letter, too. It was dark around her, dark as in those days when she lay hidden in the bulb. The Flower went forth on her journey, and lay in the post-bag, and was pressed and crushed, which was not at all pleasant; but that soon came to an end.

The journey was over; the letter was opened, and read by the dear friend. How pleased he was! He kissed the letter, and it was laid, with its enclosure of verses, in a box, in which there were many beautiful verses, but all of them without flowers; she was the first, the only one, as the Sunbeams had called her; and it was a pleasant thing to think of that.

She had time enough, moreover, to think about it; she thought of it while the summer passed away, and the long winter went by, and the summer came again, before she appeared once more. But now the young man was not pleased at all. He took hold of the letter very roughly, and threw the verses away, so that the Flower fell on the ground. Flat and faded she certainly was, but why should she be thrown on the ground? Still, it was better to be here than in the fire, where the verses and the paper were being burnt to ashes. What had happened? What happens so often:—the Flower had made a gauk of him, that was a jest; the girl had made a fool of him, that was no jest, she had, during the summer, chosen another friend.

Next morning the sun shone in upon the little flattened Snowdrop, that looked as if it had been painted upon the floor. The servant girl, who was sweeping out the room, picked it up, and laid it in one of the books which were upon the table, in the belief that it must have fallen out while the room was being arranged. Again the flower lay among verses—printed verses—and they are better than written ones—at least, more money has been spent upon them.

And after this years went by. The book stood upon the bookshelf, and then it was taken up and somebody read out of it. It was a good book; verses and songs by the old Danish poet, Ambrosius Stub, which are well worth reading. The man who was now reading the book turned over a page.

"Why, there's a flower!" he said; "a snowdrop, a summer gauk, a poet gauk! That flower must have been put in there with a meaning! Poor Ambrosius Stub! he was a summer fool too, a poet fool; he came too early, before his time, and therefore he had to taste the sharp winds, and wander about as a guest from one noble landed proprietor to another, like a flower in a glass of water, a flower in rhymed verses! Summer fool, winter fool, fun and folly—but the first, the only, the fresh young Danish poet of those days. Yes, thou shalt remain as a token in the book, thou little snowdrop: thou hast been put there with a meaning."

And so the Snowdrop was put back into the book, and felt equally honoured and pleased to know that it was a token in the glorious book of songs, and that he who was the first to sing and to write had been also a snowdrop, had been a summer gauk, and had been looked upon in the winter-time as a fool. The Flower understood this, in her way, as we interpret everything in our way.

That is the story of the Snowdrop.

The Teapot

There was a proud Teapot, proud of being porcelain, proud of its long spout, proud of its broad handle. It had something before and behind—the spout before, the handle behind—and that was what it talked about. But it did not talk of its lid—that was cracked, it was riveted, it had faults; and one does not talk about one's faults—there are plenty of others to do that. The cups, the cream-pot, the sugar-bowl, the whole tea-service would be reminded much more of the lid's weakness, and talk about that, than of the sound handle and the remarkable spout. The Teapot knew it.

"I know you," it said within itself, "I know well enough, too, my fault; and I am well aware that in that very thing is seen my humility, my modesty. We all have faults, but then one also has a talent. The cups get a handle, the sugar-bowl a lid; I get both, and one thing besides in front which they never got—I get a spout, and that makes me a queen on the tea-table. The sugar-bowl and cream-pot are good-looking serving maids; but I am the one who gives, yes, the one high in council. I spread abroad a blessing among thirsty mankind. In my insides the Chinese leaves are worked up in the boiling, tasteless water."

All this said the Teapot in its fresh young life. It stood on the table that was spread for tea, it was lifted by a very delicate hand; but the very delicate hand was awkward, the Teapot fell. The spout snapped off, the handle snapped off; the lid was no worse to speak of—the worst had been spoken of that. The Teapot lay in a swoon on the floor, while the boiling water ran out of it. It was a horrid shame, but the worst was that they jeered at it; they jeered at it, and not at the awkward hand.

"I never shall lose the memory of that!" said the Teapot, when it afterward talked to itself of the course of its life. "I was called an invalid, and placed in a corner, and the day after was given away to a woman who begged victuals. I fell into poverty, and stood dumb both outside and in; but there, as I stood, began my better life. One is one thing and becomes quite another. Earth was placed in me: for a Teapot that is the same as being buried, but in the earth was placed a flower bulb. Who placed it there, who gave it, I know not; given it was, and it took the place of the Chinese leaves and the boiling water, the broken handle and spout. And the bulb lay in the earth, the bulb lay in me, it became my heart, my living heart, such as I never before had. There was life in me, power and might. My pulses beat, the bulb put forth sprouts, it was the springing up of thoughts and feelings; they burst forth in flower. I saw it, I bore it, I forgot myself in its delight. Blessed is it to forget one's self in another. The bulb gave me no thanks, it did not think of me—it was admired and praised. I was so glad at that: how happy must it have been! One day I heard it said that it ought to have a better pot. I was thumped on my back—that was rather hard to bear; but the flower was put in a better pot—and I was thrown away in the yard, where I lie as an old crock. But I have the memory: *that* I can never lose."

"The Will-o'-the-Wisp is in the Town," says the Moor-Woman

Translated by Mrs. H. P. Paull

There was a man who once knew many stories, but they had slipped away from him—so he said. The Story that used to visit him of its own accord no longer came and knocked at his door. And why did it come no longer? It is true enough that for days and years the man had not thought of it, had not expected it to come and knock; and if he had expected it, it would certainly not have come; for without there was war, and within was the care and sorrow that war brings with it.

The stork and the swallows came back from their long journey, for they thought of no danger; and, behold, when they arrived, the nest was burnt, the habitations of men were burnt, the hedges were all in disorder, and everything seemed gone, and the enemy's horses were stamping in the old graves. Those were hard, gloomy times, but they came to an end.

And now they were past and gone—so people said; yet no Story came and knocked at the door, or gave any tidings of its presence.

"I suppose it must be dead, or gone away with many other things," said the man.

But the story never dies. And more than a whole year went by, and he longed—oh, so very much!—for the Story.

"I wonder if the Story will ever come back again and knock?"

And he remembered it so well in all the various forms in which it had come to him, sometimes young and charming, like spring itself, sometimes as a beautiful maiden, with a wreath of thyme in her hair, and a beechen branch in her hand, and with eyes that gleamed like deep woodland lakes in the bright sunshine.

Sometimes it had come to him in the guise of a peddler, and had opened its box and let silver ribbon come fluttering out, with verses and inscriptions of old remembrances.

But it was most charming of all when it came as an old grandmother, with silvery hair, and such large, sensible eyes. She knew so well how to tell about the oldest times, long before the princesses spun with the golden spindles, and the dragons lay outside the castles, guarding them. She told with such an air of truth, that black spots danced before the eyes of all who heard her, and the floor became black with human blood; terrible to see and to hear, and yet so entertaining, because such a long time had passed since it all happened.

"Will it ever knock at my door again?" said the man, and he gazed at the door, so that black spots came before his eyes and upon the floor; he did not know if it was blood, or mourning crape from the dark heavy days.

And as he sat thus, the thought came upon him whether the Story might not have hidden itself, like the princess in the old tale. And he would now go in search of it; if he found it, it would beam in new splendor, lovelier than ever.

"Who knows? Perhaps it has hidden itself in the straw that balances on the margin of the well. Carefully, carefully! Perhaps it lies hidden in a certain flower—that flower in one of the great books on the book-shelf."

And the man went and opened one of the newest books, to gain information on this point; but there was no flower to be found. There he read about Holger Danske; and the man read that the tale had been invented and put together by a monk in France, that it was a romance, "translated into Danish and printed in that language;" that Holger Danske had never really lived, and consequently could never come again, as we have sung, and have been so glad to believe. And William Tell was treated just like Holger Danske. These were all only myths—nothing on which we could depend; and yet it is all written in a very learned book.

"Well, I shall believe what I believe!" said the man. "There grows no plantain where no foot has trod."

And he closed the book and put it back in its place, and went to the fresh flowers at the window. Perhaps the Story might have hidden itself in the red tulips, with the golden yellow edges, or in the fresh rose, or in the beaming camellia. The sunshine lay among the flowers, but no Story.

The flowers which had been here in the dark troublous time had been much more beautiful; but they had been cut off, one after another, to be woven into wreaths and placed in coffins, and the flag had waved over them! Perhaps the Story had been buried with the flowers; but then the flowers would have known of it, and the coffin would have heard it, and every little blade of grass that shot forth would have told of it. The Story never dies.

Perhaps it has been here once, and has knocked; but who had eyes or ears for it in those times? People looked darkly, gloomily, and almost angrily at the sunshine of spring, at the twittering birds, and all the cheerful green; the tongue could not even bear the old merry, popular songs, and they were laid in the coffin with so much that our heart held dear. The Story may have knocked without obtaining a hearing; there was none to bid it welcome, and so it may have gone away.

"I will go forth and seek it. Out in the country! out in the wood! and on the open sea beach!"

Out in the country lies an old manor house, with red walls, pointed gables, and a red flag that floats on the tower. The nightingale sings among the finely-fringed beech-leaves, looking at the blooming apple trees of the garden, and thinking that they bear roses. Here the bees are mightily busy in the summer-time, and hover round their queen with their humming song. The autumn has much to tell of the wild chase, of the leaves of the trees, and of the races of men that are passing away together. The wild swans sing at Christmas-time on the open water, while in the old hall the guests by the fireside gladly listen to songs and to old legends.

Down into the old part of the garden, where the great avenue of wild chestnut trees lures the wanderer to tread its shades, went the man who was in search of the Story; for here the wind had once murmured something to him of "Waldemar Daa and his Daughters." The Dryad in the tree, who was the Story-mother herself, had here told him the "Dream of the Old Oak Tree." Here, in the time of the ancestral mother, had stood clipped hedges, but now only ferns and stinging nettles grew there, hiding the scattered fragments of old sculptured figures; the moss is growing in their eyes, but they can see as well as ever, which was more than the man could do who was in search of the Story, for he could not find that. Where could it be?

The crows flew past him by hundreds across the old trees, and screamed, "Krah! da!—Krah! da!"

And he went out of the garden and over the grass-plot of the yard, into the alder grove; there stood a little six-sided house, with a poultry-yard and a duck-yard. In the middle of the room sat the old woman who had the management of the whole, and who knew accurately about every egg that was laid, and about every chicken that could creep out of an egg. But she was not the Story of which the man was in search; that she could attest with a Christian certificate of baptism and of vaccination that lay in her drawer.

Without, not far from the house, is a hill covered with red-thorn and broom. Here lies an old grave-stone, which was brought here many years ago from the churchyard of the provincial town, a remembrance of one of the most honoured councillors of the place; his wife and his five daughters, all with folded hands and stiff ruffs, stand round him. One could look at them so long, that it had an effect upon the thoughts, and these reacted upon the stones, as if they were telling of old times; at least it had been so with the man who was in search of the Story.

As he came nearer, he noticed a living butterfly sitting on the forehead of the sculptured councillor. The butterfly flapped its wings, and flew a little bit farther, and then returned fatigued to sit upon the grave-stone, as if to point out what grew there. Four-leaved shamrocks grew there; there were seven specimens close to each other. When fortune comes, it comes in a heap. He plucked the shamrocks and put them in his pocket.

"Fortune is as good as red gold, but a new charming story would be better still," thought the man; but he could not find it here.

And the sun went down, round and large; the meadow was covered with vapor. The Moor-woman was at her brewing.

It was evening. He stood alone in his room, and looked out upon the sea, over the meadow, over moor and coast. The moon shone bright, a mist was over the meadow, making it look like a great lake; and, indeed, it was once so, as the legend tells—and in the moonlight the eye realizes these myths.

Then the man thought of what he had been reading in the town, that William Tell and Holger Danske never really lived, but yet live in popular story, like the lake yonder, a living evidence for such myths. Yes, Holger Danske will return again!

As he stood thus and thought, something beat quite strongly against the window. Was it a bird, a bat or an owl? Those are not let in, even when they knock. The window flew open of itself, and an old woman looked in at the man.

"What's your pleasure?" said he. "Who are you? You're looking in at the first floor window. Are you standing on a ladder?"

"You have a four-leaved shamrock in your pocket," she replied. "Indeed, you have seven, and one of them is a six-leaved one."

"Who are you?" asked the man again.

"The Moor-woman," she replied. "The Moor-woman who brews. I was at it. The bung was in the cask, but one of the little moor-imps pulled it out in his mischief, and flung it up into the yard, where it beat against the window; and now the beer's running out of the cask, and that won't do good to anybody."

"Pray tell me some more!" said the man.

"Yes, wait a little," answered the Moor-woman. "I've something else to do just now." And she was gone.

The man was going to shut the window, when the woman already stood before him again.

"Now it's done," she said; "but I shall have half the beer to brew over again tomorrow, if the weather is suitable. Well, what have you to ask me? I've come back, for I always keep my word, and you have seven four-leaved shamrocks in your pocket, and one of them is a six-leaved one. That inspires respect, for that's an order that grows beside the sandy way; but that every one does not find. What have you to ask me? Don't stand there like a ridiculous oaf, for I must go back again directly to my bung and my cask."

And the man asked about the Story, and inquired if the Moor-woman had met it in her journeyings.

"By the big brewing-vat!" exclaimed the woman, "haven't you got stories enough? I really believe that most people have enough of them. Here are other things to take notice of, other things to examine. Even the children have gone beyond that. Give the little boy a cigar, and the little girl a new crinoline; they like that much better. To listen to stories! No, indeed, there are more important things to be done here, and other things to notice!"

"What do you mean by that?" asked the man, "and what do you know of the world? You don't see anything but frogs and Will-o'-the-Wisps!"

"Yes, beware of the Will-o'-the-Wisps," said the Moor-woman, "for they're out—they're let loose—that's what we must talk about! Come to me in the moor, where my presence is necessary, and I will tell you all about it; but you must make haste, and come while your seven four-leaved shamrocks, for which one has six leaves, are still fresh, and the moon stands high!"

And the Moor-woman was gone.

It struck twelve in the town, and before the last stroke had died away, the man was out in the yard, out in the garden, and stood in the meadow. The mist had vanished, and the Moor-woman stopped her brewing.

"You've been a long time coming!" said the Moor-woman. "Witches get forward faster than men, and I'm glad that I belong to the witch folk!"

"What have you to say to me now?" asked the man. "Is it anything about the Story?"

"Can you never get beyond asking about that?" retorted the woman.

"Can you tell me anything about the poetry of the future?" resumed the man.

"Don't get on your stilts," said the crone, "and I'll answer you. You think of nothing but poetry, and only ask about that Story, as if she were the lady of the whole troop. She's the oldest of us all, but she takes precedence of the youngest. I know her well. I've been young, too, and she's no chicken now. I was once quite a pretty elf-maiden, and have danced in my time with the others in the moonlight, and have heard the nightingale, and have gone into the forest and met the Story-maiden, who was always to be found out there, running about. Sometimes she took up her night's lodging in a half-blown tulip, or in a field flower; sometimes she would slip into the church, and wrap herself in the mourning crape that hung down from the candles on the altar."

"You are capitally well-informed," said the man.

"I ought at least to know as much as you," answered the Moor-woman. "Stories and poetry—yes, they're like two yards of the same piece of stuff; they can go and lie down where they like, and one can brew all their prattle, and have it all the better and cheaper. You shall have it from me for nothing. I have a whole cupboard-full of poetry in bottles. It makes essences; and that's the best of it—bitter and sweet herbs. I have everything that people want of poetry, in bottles, so that I can put a little on my handkerchief, on holidays, to smell."

"Why, these are wonderful things that you're telling!" said the man. "You have poetry in bottles?"

"More than you can require," said the woman. "I suppose you know the history of 'the Girl who Trod on the Loaf, so that she might not soil her shoes'? That has been written, and printed too."

"I told that story myself," said the man.

"Yes, then you must know it; and you must know also that the girl sank into the earth directly, to the Moor-woman, just as Old Bogey's grandmother was paying her morning visit to inspect the brewery. She saw the girl gliding down, and asked to have her as a remembrance of her visit, and got her too; while I received a present that's of no use to me—a travelling druggist's shop—a whole cupboard-full of poetry in bottles. Grandmother told me where the cupboard was to be placed, and there it's standing still. Just look! You've your seven four-leaved shamrocks in your pocket, one of which is a six-leaved one, and so you will be able to see it."

And really in the midst of the moor lay something like a great knotted block of alder, and that was the old grandmother's cupboard. The Moor-woman said that this was always open to her and to every one in the land, if they only knew where the cupboard stood. It could be opened either at the front or at the back, and at every side and corner—a perfect work of art, and yet only an old alder stump in appearance. The poets of all lands, and especially those of our own country, had been arranged here; the spirit of them had been extracted, refined, criticised and renovated, and then stored up in bottles. With what may be called great aptitude, if it was not genius the grandmother had taken as it were the flavor of this and of that poet, and had added a little devilry, and then corked up the bottles for use during all future times.

"Pray let me see," said the man.

"Yes, but there are more important things to hear," replied the Moor-woman.

"But now we are at the cupboard!" said the man. And he looked in. "Here are bottles of all sizes. What is in this one? and what in that one yonder?"

"Here is what they call may-balm," replied the woman. "I have not tried it myself. But I have not yet told you the 'more important' thing you were to hear. THE WILL-O'-THE-WISP'S IN THE TOWN! That's of much more consequence than poetry and stories. I ought, indeed, to hold my tongue; but there must be a necessity—a fate—a something that sticks in my throat, and that wants to come out. Take care, you mortals!"

"I don't understand a word of all this!" cried the man.

"Be kind enough to seat yourself on that cupboard," she retorted, "but take care you don't fall through and break the bottles—you know what's inside of them. I must tell of the great event. It occurred no longer ago than the day before yesterday. It did not happen earlier. It has now three hundred and sixty-three days to run about. I suppose you know how many days there are in a year?"

And this is what the Moor-woman told:

"There was a great commotion yesterday out here in the marsh! There was a christening feast! A little Will-o'-the-Wisp was born here—in fact, twelve of them were born all together; and they have permission, if they choose to use it, to go abroad among men, and to move about and command among them, just as if they were born mortals. That was a great event in the marsh, and accordingly all the Will-o'-the-Wisps, male and female, went dancing like little lights across the moor. There are some of them of the dog species, but those are not worth mentioning. I sat there on the cupboard, and had all the twelve little new-born Will-o'-the-Wisps upon my lap. They shone like glow-worms; they already began to hop, and increased in size every moment, so that before a quarter of an hour had elapsed, each of them looked just as large as his father or his uncle. Now, it's an old-established regulation and favour, that when the moon stands just as it did yesterday, and the wind blows just as it blew then, it is allowed and accorded to all Will-o'-the-Wisps—that is, to all those who are born at that minute of time—to become mortals, and individually to exert their power for the space of one year.

"The Will-o'-the-Wisp may run about in the country and through the world, if it is not afraid of falling into the sea, or of being blown out by a heavy storm. It can enter into a person and speak for him, and make all the movements it pleases. The Will-o'-the-Wisp may take whatever form he likes, of man or woman, and can act in their spirit and in their disguise in such a way that he can effect whatever he wishes to do. But he must manage, in the course of the year, to lead three hundred and sixty-five people into a bad way, and in a grand style, too. To lead them away from the right and the truth; and then he reaches the highest point. Such a Will-o'-the-Wisp can attain to the honour of being a runner before the devil's state coach; and then he'll wear clothes of fiery yellow, and breathe forth flames out of his throat. That's enough to make a simple Will-o'-the-Wisp smack his lips. But there's some danger in this, and a great deal of work for a Will-o'-the-Wisp who aspires to play so distinguished a part. If the eyes of the man are opened to what he is, and if the man can then blow him away, it's all over with him, and he must come back into the marsh; or if, before the year is up, the Will-o'-the-Wisp is seized with a longing to see his family, and so returns to it and gives the matter up, it is over with him likewise, and he can no longer burn clear, and soon becomes extinguished, and cannot be lit up again; and when the year has elapsed, and he has not led three hundred and sixty-five people away from the truth and from all that is grand and noble, he is condemned to be imprisoned in decayed wood, and to lie glimmering there, without being able to move; and that's the most terrible punishment that can be inflicted on a lively Will-o'-the-Wisp.

"Now, all this I know, and all this I told to the twelve little Will-o'-the-Wisps whom I had on my lap, and who seemed quite crazy with joy.

"I told them that the safest and most convenient course was to give up the honour, and do nothing at all; but the little flames would not agree to this, and already fancied themselves clad in fiery yellow clothes, breathing flames from their throats.

"'Stay with us,' said some of the older ones.

"'Carry on your sport with mortals,' said the others.

"'The mortals are drying up our meadows; they've taken to draining. What will our successors do?'

"'We want to flame; we will flame—flame!' cried the new-born Will-o'-the-Wisps.

"And thus the affair was settled.

"And now a ball was given, a minute long; it could not well be shorter. The little elf-maidens whirled round three times with the rest, that they might not appear proud, but they preferred dancing with one another.

"And now the sponsors' gifts were presented, and presents were thrown them. These presents flew like pebbles across the sea-water. Each of the elf-maidens gave a little piece of her veil.

"'Take that,' they said, 'and then you'll know the higher dance, the most difficult turns and twists—that is to say, if you should find them necessary. You'll know the proper deportment, and then you can show yourself in the very pick of society.'

"The night raven taught each of the young Will-o'-the-Wisps to say, 'Goo—goo—good,' and to say it in the right place; and that's a great gift which brings its own reward.

"The owl and the stork—but they said it was not worth mentioning, and so we won't mention it.

"*King Waldemar's wild chase* was just then rushing over the moor, and when the great lords heard of the festivities that were going on, they sent a couple of handsome dogs, which hunt on the spoor of the wind, as a present; and these might carry two or three of the Will-o'-the-Wisps. A couple of old Alpas, spirits who occupy themselves with Alp-pressing, were also at the feast; and from these the young Will-o'-the-Wisps learned the art of slipping through every key-hole, as if the door stood open before them. These Alpas offered to carry the youngsters to the town, with which they were well acquainted. They usually rode through the atmosphere on their own back hair, which is fastened into a knot, for they love a hard seat; but now they sat sideways on the wild hunting dogs, took the young Will-o'-the-Wisps in their laps, who wanted to go into the town to mislead and entice mortals, and, whisk! away they were. Now, this is what happened last night. Today the Will-o'-the-Wisps are in the town, and have taken the matter in hand—but where and how? Ah, can you tell me that? Still, I've a lightning conductor in my great toe, and that will always tell me something."

"Why, this is a complete story," exclaimed the man.

"Yes, but it is only the beginning," replied the woman. "Can you tell me how the Will-o'-the-Wisps deport themselves, and how they behave? and in what shapes they have aforetime appeared and led people into crooked paths?"

"I believe," replied the man, "that one could tell quite a romance about the Will-o'-the-Wisps, in twelve parts; or, better still, one might make quite a popular play of them."

"You might write that," said the woman, "but it's best let alone."

"Yes, that's better and more agreeable," the man replied, "for then we shall escape from the newspapers, and not be tied up by them, which is just as uncomfortable as for a Will-o'-the-Wisp to lie in decaying wood, to have to gleam, and not to be able to stir."

"I don't care about it either way," cried the woman. "Let the rest write, those who can, and those who cannot likewise. I'll grant you an old bung from my cask that will open the cupboard where poetry's kept in bottles, and you may take from that whatever may be wanting. But you, my good man, seem to have blotted your hands sufficiently with ink, and to have come to that age of satiety that you need not be running about every year for stories, especially as there are much more important things to be done. You must have understood what is going on?"

"The Will-o'-the-Wisp is in town," said the man. "I've heard it, and I have understood it. But what do you think I ought to do? I should be thrashed if I were to go to the people and say, 'Look, yonder goes a Will-o'-the-Wisp in his best clothes!'"

"They also go in undress," replied the woman. "The Will-o'-the-Wisp can assume all kinds of forms, and appear in every place. He goes into the church, but not for the sake of the service; and perhaps he may enter into one or other of the priests. He speaks in the Parliament, not for the benefit of the country, but only for himself. He's an artist with the colour-pot as well as in the theatre; but when he gets all the power into his own hands, then the pot's empty! I chatter and chatter, but it must come out, what's sticking in my throat, to the disadvantage of my own family. But I must now be the woman that will save a good many people. It is not done with my good will, or for the sake of a medal. I do the most insane things I possibly can, and then I tell a poet about it, and thus the whole town gets to know of it directly."

"The town will not take that to heart," observed the man; "that will not disturb a single person; for they will all think I'm only telling them a story if I say, 'The Will-o'-the-Wisp is in the town, says the Moor-woman. Take care of yourselves!'"

The Windmill

Translated by Mrs. H. P. Paull

A windmill stood upon the hill, proud to look at, and it was proud too.

"I am not proud at all," it said, "but I am very much enlightened without and within. I have sun and moon for my outward use, and for inward use too; and into the bargain I have stearine candles, train oil and lamps, and tallow candles. I may well say that I'm enlightened. I'm a thinking being, and so well constructed that it's quite delightful. I have a good windpipe in my chest, and I have four wings that are placed outside my head, just beneath my hat. The birds have only two wings, and are obliged to carry them on their backs. I am a Dutchman by birth, that may be seen by my figure—a flying Dutchman. They are considered supernatural beings, I know, and yet I am quite natural. I have a gallery round my chest, and house-room beneath it; that's where my thoughts dwell. My strongest thought, who rules and reigns, is called by others 'The Man in the Mill.' He knows what he wants, and is lord over the meal and the bran; but he has his companion, too, and she calls herself 'Mother.' She is the very heart of me. She does not run about stupidly and awkwardly, for she knows what she wants, she knows what she can do, she's as soft as a zephyr and as strong as a storm; she knows how to begin a thing carefully, and to have her own way. She is my soft temper, and the father is my hard one. They are two, and yet one; they each call the other 'My half.' These two have some little boys, young thoughts, that can grow. The little ones keep everything in order. When, lately, in my wisdom, I let the father and the boys examine my throat and the hole in my chest, to see what was going on there—for something in me was out of order, and it's well to examine one's self—the little ones made a tremendous noise. The youngest jumped up into my hat, and shouted so there that it tickled me. The little thoughts may grow—I know that very well; and out in the world thoughts come too, and not only of my kind, for as far as I can see, I cannot discern anything like myself; but the wingless houses, whose throats make no noise, have thoughts too, and these come to my thoughts, and make love to them, as it is called. It's wonderful enough—yes, there are many wonderful things. Something has come over me, or into me— something has changed in the mill-work. It seems as if the one half, the father, had altered, and had received a better temper and a more affectionate helpmate—so young and good, and yet the same, only more gentle and good through the course of time. What was bitter has passed away, and the whole is much more comfortable.

"The days go on, and the days come nearer and nearer to clearness and to joy; and then a day will come when it will be over with me; but not over altogether. I must be pulled down that I may be built up again; I shall cease, but yet shall live on. To become quite a different being, and yet remain the same! That's difficult for me to understand, however enlightened I may be with sun, moon, stearine, train oil, and tallow. My old wood-work and my old brick-work will rise again from the dust!

"I will hope that I may keep my old thoughts, the father in the mill, and the mother, great ones and little ones—the family; for I call them all, great and little, the *company of thoughts*, because I must, and cannot refrain from it.

"And I must also remain 'myself,' with my throat in my chest, my wings on my head, the gallery round my body; else I should not know myself, nor could the others know me, and say, 'There's the mill on the hill, proud to look at, and yet not proud at all.'"

That is what the mill said. Indeed, it said much more, but that is the most important part.

And the days came, and the days went, and yesterday was the last day.

Then the mill caught fire. The flames rose up high, and beat out and in, and bit at the beams and planks, and ate them up. The mill fell, and nothing remained of it but a heap of ashes. The smoke drove across the scene of the conflagration, and the wind carried it away.

Whatever had been alive in the mill remained, and what had been gained by it has nothing to do with this story.

The miller's family—one soul, many thoughts, and yet only one—built a new, a splendid mill, which answered its purpose. It was quite like the old one, and people said, "Why, yonder is the mill on the hill, proud to look at!" But this mill was better arranged, more according to the time than the last, so that progress might be made. The old beams had become worm-eaten and spongy—they lay in dust and ashes. The body of the mill did not rise out of the dust as they had believed it would do. They had taken it literally, and all things are not to be taken literally.

Our Aunt

Translated by Mrs. H. P. Paull

You ought to have known our aunt; she was charming! That is to say, she was not charming at all as the word is usually understood; but she was good and kind, amusing in her way, and was just as any one ought to be whom people are to talk about and to laugh at. She might have been put into a play, and wholly and solely on account of the fact that she only lived for the theatre and for what was done there. She was an honourable matron; but Agent Fabs, whom she used to call "Flabs," declared that our aunt was stage-struck.

"The theatre is my school," said she, "the source of my knowledge. From thence I have resuscitated Biblical history. Now, 'Moses' and 'Joseph in Egypt'—there are operas for you! I get my universal history from the theatre, my geography, and my knowledge of men. Out of the French pieces I get to know life in Paris—slippery, but exceedingly interesting. How I have cried over 'La Famille Roquebourg'—that the man must drink himself to death, so that she may marry the young fellow! Yes, how many tears I have wept in the fifty years I have subscribed to the theatre!"

Our aunt knew every acting play, every bit of scenery, every character, every one who appeared or had appeared. She seemed really only to live during the nine months the theatre was open. Summertime without a summer theatre seemed to be only a time that made her old; while, on the other hand, a theatrical evening that lasted till midnight was a lengthening of her life. She did not say, as other people do, "Now we shall have spring, the stork is here," or, "They've advertised the first strawberries in the papers." She, on the contrary, used to announce the coming of autumn, with "Have you heard they're selling boxes for the theatre? Now the performances will begin."

She used to value a lodging entirely according to its proximity to the theatre. It was a real sorrow to her when she had to leave the little lane behind the playhouse, and move into the great street that lay a little farther off, and live there in a house where she had no opposite neighbours.

"At home," said she, "my windows must be my opera-box. One cannot sit and look into one's self till one's tired; one must see people. But now I live just as if I'd go into the country. If I want to see human beings, I must go into my kitchen, and sit down on the sink, for there only I have opposite neighbours. No; when I lived in my dear little lane, I could look straight down into the ironmonger's shop, and had only three hundred paces to the theatre; and now I've three thousand paces to go, military measurement."

Our aunt was sometimes ill, but however unwell she might feel, she never missed the play. The doctor prescribed one day that she should put her feet in a bran bath, and she followed his advice; but she drove to the theatre all the same, and sat with her feet in bran there. If she had died there, she would have been very glad. Thorwaldsen died in the theatre, and she called that a happy death.

She could not imagine but that in heaven there must be a theatre too. It had not, indeed, been promised us, but we might very well imagine it. The many distinguished actors and actresses who had passed away must surely have a field for their talent.

Our aunt had an electric wire from the theatre to her room. A telegram used to be dispatched to her at coffee-time, and it used to consist of the words, "Herr Sivertsen is at the machinery;" for it was he who gave the signal for drawing the curtain up and down and for changing the scenes.

From him she used to receive a short and concise description of every piece. His opinion of Shakspeare's *Tempest*, was, "Mad nonsense! There's so much to put up, and the first scene begins with 'Water to the front of the wings.'" That is to say, the water had to come forward so far. But when, on the other hand, the same interior scene remained through five acts, he used to pronounce it a sensible, well-written play, a resting play, which performed itself, without putting up scenes.

In earlier times, by which name our aunt used to designate thirty years ago, she and the before-mentioned Herr Sivertsen had been younger. At that time he had already been connected with the machinery, and was, as she said, her benefactor. It used to be the custom in those days that in the evening performances in the only theatre the town possessed, spectators were admitted to the part called the "flies," over the stage, and every machinist had one or two places to give away. Often the flies were quite full of good company; it was said that generals' wives and privy councillors' wives had been up there. It was quite interesting to look down behind the scenes, and to see how the people walked to and fro on the stage when the curtain was down.

Our aunt had been there several times, as well when there was a tragedy as when there was a ballet; for the pieces in which there were the greatest number of characters on the stage were the most interesting to see from the flies. One sat pretty much in the dark up there, and most people took their supper up with them. Once three apples and a great piece of bread and butter and sausage fell down right into the dungeon of Ugolino, where that unhappy man was to be starved to death; and there was great laughter among the audience. The sausage was one of the weightiest reasons why the worthy management refused in future to have any spectators up in the flies.

"But I was there seven-and-thirty times," said our aunt, "and I shall always remember Mr. Sivertsen for that."

On the very last evening when the flies were still open to the public, the "Judgment of Solomon" was performed, as our aunt remembered very well. She had, through the influence of her benefactor, Herr Sivertsen, procured a free admission for the Agent Fabs, although he did not deserve it in the least, for he was always cutting his jokes about the theatre and teasing our aunt; but she had procured him a free admission to the flies, for all that. He wanted to look at this player-stuff from the other side.

"Those were his own words, and they were just like him," said our aunt.

He looked down from above on the 'Judgment of Solomon,' and fell asleep over it. One would have thought that he had come from a dinner where many toasts had been given. He went to sleep, and was locked in. And there he sat through the dark night in the flies, and when he woke, he told a story, but our aunt would not believe it.

"The 'Judgment of Solomon' was over," he said, "and all the people had gone away, up stairs and down stairs; but now the real play began, the after-piece, which was the best of all," said the agent. "Then life came into the affair. It was not the 'Judgment of Solomon' that was performed; no, a real court of judgment was held upon the stage." And Agent Fabs had the impudence to try and make our aunt believe all this. That was the thanks she got for having got him a place in the flies.

What did the agent say? Why, it was curious enough to hear, but there was malice and satire in it.

"It looked dark enough up there," said the agent; "but then the magic business began—a great performance, 'The Judgment in the Theatre.' The box-keepers were at their posts, and every spectator had to show his ghostly pass-book, that it might be decided if he was to be admitted with hands loose or bound, and with or without a muzzle. Grand people who came too late, when the performance had begun, and young people, who could not always watch the time, were tied up outside, and had list slippers put on their feet, with which they were allowed to go in before the beginning of the next act, and they had muzzles too. And then the 'Judgment on the Stage' began."

"All malice, and not a bit of truth in it," said our aunt.

The painter, who wanted to get to Paradise, had to go up a staircase which he had himself painted, but which no man could mount. That was to expiate his sins against perspective. All the plants and buildings, which the property-man had placed, with infinite pains, in countries to which they did not belong, the poor fellow was obliged to put in their right places before cockcrow, if he wanted to get into Paradise. Let Herr Fabs see how he would get in himself; but what he said of the performers, tragedians and comedians, singers and dancers, that was the most rascally of all. Mr. Fabs, indeed!—Flabs! He did not deserve to be admitted at all, and our aunt would not soil her lips with what he said. And he said, did Flabs, that the whole was written down, and it should be printed when he was dead and buried, but not before, for he would not risk having his arms and legs broken.

Once our aunt had been in fear and trembling in her temple of happiness, the theatre. It was on a winter day, one of those days in which one has a couple of hours of daylight, with a gray sky. It was terribly cold and snowy, but aunt must go to the theatre. A little opera and a great ballet were performed, and a prologue and an epilogue into the bargain; and that would last till late at night. Our aunt must needs go; so she borrowed a pair of fur boots of her lodger—boots with fur inside and out, and which reached far up her legs.

She got to the theatre, and to her box; the boots were warm, and she kept them on. Suddenly there was a cry of "Fire!" Smoke was coming from one of the side scenes, and streamed down from the flies, and there was a terrible panic. The people came rushing out, and our aunt was the last in the box, "on the second tier, left-hand side, for from there the scenery looks best," she used to say. "The scenes are always arranged that they look best from the King's side." Aunt wanted to come out, but the people before her, in their fright and heedlessness, slammed the door of the box; and there sat our aunt, and couldn't get out, and couldn't get in; that is to say, she couldn't get into the next box, for the partition was too high for her. She called out, and no one heard her; she looked down into the tier of boxes below her, and it was empty, and low, and looked quite near, and aunt in her terror felt quite young and light. She thought of jumping down, and had got one leg over the partition, the other resting on the bench. There she sat astride, as if on horseback, well wrapped up in her flowered cloak with one leg hanging out—a leg in a tremendous fur boot. That was a sight to behold; and when it was beheld, our aunt was heard too, and was saved from burning, for the theatre was not burned down.

That was the most memorable evening of her life, and she was glad that she could not see herself, for she would have died with confusion.

Her benefactor in the machinery department, Herr Sivertsen, visited her every Sunday, but it was a long time from Sunday to Sunday. In the latter time, therefore, she used to have in a little child "for the scraps;" that is to say, to eat up the remains of the dinner. It was a child employed in the ballet, one that certainly wanted feeding. The little one used to appear, sometimes as an elf, sometimes as a page; the most difficult part she had to play was the lion's hind leg in the "Magic Flute;" but as she grew larger she could represent the fore-feet of the lion. She certainly only got half a guilder for that, whereas the hind legs were paid for with a whole guilder; but then she had to walk bent, and to do without fresh air. "That was all very interesting to hear," said our aunt.

She deserved to live as long as the theatre stood, but she could not last so long; and she did not die in the theatre, but respectably in her bed. Her last words were, moreover, not without meaning. She asked,

"What will the play be tomorrow?"

At her death she left about five hundred dollars. We presume this from the interest, which came to twenty dollars. This our aunt had destined as a legacy for a worthy old spinster who had no friends; it was to be devoted to a yearly subscription for a place in the second tier, on the left side, for the Saturday evening, "for on that evening two pieces were always given," it said in the will; and the only condition laid upon the person who enjoyed the legacy was, that she should think, every Saturday evening, of our aunt, who was lying in her grave.

This was our aunt's religion.

The Toad

Translated by Mrs. H. P. Paull

The well was deep, and therefore the rope had to be a long one; it was heavy work turning the handle when any one had to raise a bucketful of water over the edge of the well. Though the water was clear, the sun never looked down far enough into the well to mirror itself in the waters; but as far as its beams could reach, green things grew forth between the stones in the sides of the well.

Down below dwelt a family of the Toad race. They had, in fact, come head-over-heels down the well, in the person of the old Mother-Toad, who was still alive. The green Frogs, who had been established there a long time, and swam about in the water, called them "well-guests." But the new-comers seemed determined to stay where they were, for they found it very agreeable living "in a dry place," as they called the wet stones.

The Mother-Frog had once been a traveller. She happened to be in the water-bucket when it was drawn up, but the light became too strong for her, and she got a pain in her eyes. Fortunately she scrambled out of the bucket; but she fell into the water with a terrible flop, and had to lie sick for three days with pains in her back. She certainly had not much to tell of the things up above, but she knew this, and all the Frogs knew it, that the well was not all the world. The Mother-Toad might have told this and that, if she had chosen, but she never answered when they asked her anything, and so they left off asking.

"She's thick, and fat and ugly," said the young green Frogs; "and her children will be just as ugly as she is."

"That may be," retorted the mother-Toad, "but one of them has a jewel in his head, or else I have the jewel."

The young frogs listened and stared; and as these words did not please them, they made grimaces and dived down under the water. But the little Toads kicked up their hind legs from mere pride, for each of them thought that he must have the jewel; and then they sat and held their heads quite still. But at length they asked what it was that made them so proud, and what kind of a thing a jewel might be.

"Oh, it is such a splendid and precious thing, that I cannot describe it," said the Mother-Toad. "It's something which one carries about for one's own pleasure, and that makes other people angry. But don't ask me any questions, for I shan't answer you."

"Well, I haven't got the jewel," said the smallest of the Toads; she was as ugly as a toad can be. "Why should I have such a precious thing? And if it makes others angry, it can't give me any pleasure. No, I only wish I could get to the edge of the well, and look out; it must be beautiful up there."

"You'd better stay where you are," said the old Mother-Toad, "for you know everything here, and you can tell what you have. Take care of the bucket, for it will crush you to death; and even if you get into it safely, you may fall out. And it's not every one who falls so cleverly as I did, and gets away with whole legs and whole bones."

"Quack!" said the little Toad; and that's just as if one of us were to say, "Aha!"

She had an immense desire to get to the edge of the well, and to look over; she felt such a longing for the green, up there; and the next morning, when it chanced that the bucket was being drawn up, filled with water, and stopped for a moment just in front of the stone on which the Toad sat, the little creature's heart moved within it, and our Toad jumped into the filled bucket, which presently was drawn to the top, and emptied out.

"Ugh, you beast!" said the farm labourer who emptied the bucket, when he saw the toad. "You're the ugliest thing I've seen for one while." And he made a kick with his wooden shoe at the toad, which just escaped being crushed by managing to scramble into the nettles which grew high by the well's brink. Here she saw stem by stem, but she looked up also; the sun shone through the leaves, which were quite transparent; and she felt as a person would feel who steps suddenly into a great forest, where the sun looks in between the branches and leaves.

"It's much nicer here than down in the well! I should like to stay here my whole life long!" said the little Toad. So she lay there for an hour, yes, for two hours. "I wonder what is to be found up here? As I have come so far, I must try to go still farther." And so she crawled on as fast as she could crawl, and got out upon the highway, where the sun shone upon her, and the dust powdered her all over as she marched across the way.

"I've got to a dry place. now, and no mistake," said the Toad. "It's almost too much of a good thing here; it tickles one so."

She came to the ditch; and forget-me-nots were growing there, and meadow-sweet; and a very little way off was a hedge of whitethorn, and elder bushes grew there, too, and bindweed with white flowers. Gay colours were to be seen here, and a butterfly, too, was flitting by. The Toad thought it was a flower which had broken loose that it might look about better in the world, which was quite a natural thing to do.

"If one could only make such a journey as that!" said the Toad. "Croak! how capital that would be."

Eight days and eight nights she stayed by the well, and experienced no want of provisions. On the ninth day she thought, "Forward! onward!" But what could she find more charming and beautiful? Perhaps a little toad or a few green frogs. During the last night there had been a sound borne on the breeze, as if there were cousins in the neighbourhood.

"It's a glorious thing to live! glorious to get out of the well, and to lie among the stinging-nettles, and to crawl along the dusty road. But onward, onward! that we may find frogs or a little toad. We can't do without that; nature alone is not enough for one." And so she went forward on her journey.

She came out into the open field, to a great pond, round about which grew reeds; and she walked into it.

"It will be too damp for you here," said the Frogs; "but you are very welcome! Are you a he or a she? But it doesn't matter; you are equally welcome."

And she was invited to the concert in the evening—the family concert; great enthusiasm and thin voices; we know the sort of thing. No refreshments were given, only there was plenty to drink, for the whole pond was free.

"Now I shall resume my journey," said the little Toad; for she always felt a longing for something better.

She saw the stars shining, so large and so bright, and she saw the moon gleaming; and then she saw the sun rise, and mount higher and higher.

"Perhaps after all, I am still in a well, only in a larger well. I must get higher yet; I feel a great restlessness and longing." And when the moon became round and full, the poor creature thought, "I wonder if that is the bucket which will be let down, and into which I must step to get higher up? Or is the sun the great bucket? How great it is! how bright it is! It can take up all. I must look out, that I may not miss the opportunity. Oh, how it seems to shine in my head! I don't think the jewel can shine brighter. But I haven't the jewel; not that I cry about that—no, I must go higher up, into splendor and joy! I feel so confident, and yet I am afraid. It's a difficult step to take, and yet it must be taken. Onward, therefore, straight onward!"

She took a few steps, such as a crawling animal may take, and soon found herself on a road beside which people dwelt; but there were flower gardens as well as kitchen gardens. And she sat down to rest by a kitchen garden.

"What a number of different creatures there are that I never knew! and how beautiful and great the world is! But one must look round in it, and not stay in one spot." And then she hopped into the kitchen garden. "How green it is here! how beautiful it is here!"

"I know that," said the Caterpillar, on the leaf, "my leaf is the largest here. It hides half the world from me, but I don't care for the world."

"Cluck, cluck!" And some fowls came. They tripped about in the cabbage garden. The Fowl who marched at the head of them had a long sight, and she spied the Caterpillar on the green leaf, and pecked at it, so that the Caterpillar fell on the ground, where it twisted and writhed.

The Fowl looked at it first with one eye and then with the other, for she did not know what the end of this writhing would be.

"It doesn't do that with a good will," thought the Fowl, and lifted up her head to peck at the Caterpillar.

The Toad was so horrified at this, that she came crawling straight up towards the Fowl.

"Aha, it has allies," quoth the Fowl. "Just look at the crawling thing!" And then the Fowl turned away. "I don't care for the little green morsel; it would only tickle my throat." The other fowls took the same view of it, and they all turned away together.

"I writhed myself free," said the Caterpillar. "What a good thing it is when one has presence of mind! But the hardest thing remains to be done, and that is to get on my leaf again. Where is it?"

And the little Toad came up and expressed her sympathy. She was glad that in her ugliness she had frightened the fowls.

"What do you mean by that?" cried the Caterpillar. "I wriggled myself free from the Fowl. You are very disagreeable to look at. Cannot I be left in peace on my own property? Now I smell cabbage; now I am near my leaf. Nothing is so beautiful as property. But I must go higher up."

"Yes, higher up," said the little Toad; "higher-up! She feels just as I do; but she's not in a good humour today. That's because of the fright. We all want to go higher up." And she looked up as high as ever she could.

The stork sat in his nest on the roof of the farm-house. He clapped with his beak, and the Mother-stork clapped with hers.

"How high up they live!" thought the Toad. "If one could only get as high as that!"

In the farm-house lived two young students; the one was a poet and the other a scientific searcher into the secrets of nature. The one sang and wrote joyously of everything that God had created, and how it was mirrored in his heart. He sang it out clearly, sweetly, richly, in well-sounding verses; while the other investigated created matter itself, and even cut it open where need was. He looked upon God's creation as a great sum in arithmetic—subtracted, multiplied, and tried to know it within and without, and to talk with understanding concerning it; and that was a very sensible thing; and he spoke joyously and cleverly of it. They were good, joyful men, those two,

"There sits a good specimen of a toad," said the naturalist. "I must have that fellow in a bottle of spirits."

"You have two of them already," replied the poet. "Let the thing sit there and enjoy its life."

"But it's so wonderfully ugly," persisted the first.

"Yes, if we could find the jewel in its head," said the poet, "I too should be for cutting it open."

"A jewel!" cried the naturalist. "You seem to know a great deal about natural history."

"But is there not something beautiful in the popular belief that just as the toad is the ugliest of animals, it should often carry the most precious jewel in its head? Is it not just the same thing with men? What a jewel that was that Aesop had, and still more, Socrates!"

The Toad did not hear any more, nor did she understand half of what she had heard. The two friends walked on, and thus she escaped the fate of being bottled up in spirits.

"Those two also were speaking of the jewel," said the Toad to herself. "What a good thing that I have not got it! I might have been in a very disagreeable position."

Now there was a clapping on the roof of the farm-house. Father-Stork was making a speech to his family, and his family was glancing down at the two young men in the kitchen garden.

"Man is the most conceited creature!" said the Stork. "Listen how their jaws are wagging; and for all that they can't clap properly. They boast of their gifts of eloquence and their language! Yes, a fine language truly! Why, it changes in every day's journey we make.

The Toad

One of them doesn't understand another. Now, we can speak our language over the whole earth—up in the North and in Egypt. And then men are not able to fly, moreover. They rush along by means of an invention they call 'railway;' but they often break their necks over it. It makes my beak turn cold when I think of it. The world could get on without men. We could do without them very well, so long as we only keep frogs and earth-worms."

"That was a powerful speech," thought the little Toad. "What a great man that is yonder! and how high he sits! Higher than ever I saw any one sit yet; and how he can swim!" she cried, as the Stork soared away through the air with outspread pinions.

And the Mother-Stork began talking in the nest, and told about Egypt and the waters of the Nile, and the incomparable mud that was to be found in that strange land; and all this sounded new and very charming to the little Toad.

"I must go to Egypt!" said she. "If the Stork or one of his young ones would only take me! I would oblige him in return. Yes, I shall get to Egypt, for I feel so happy! All the longing and all the pleasure that I feel is much better than having a jewel in one's head."

And it was just she who had the jewel. That jewel was the continual striving and desire to go upward—ever upward. It gleamed in her head, gleamed in joy, beamed brightly in her longing.

Then, suddenly, up came the Stork. He had seen the Toad in the grass, and stooped down and seized the little creature anything but gently. The Stork's beak pinched her, and the wind whistled; it was not exactly agreeable, but she was going upward—upward towards Egypt—and she knew it; and that was why her eyes gleamed, and a spark seemed to fly out of them.

"Quunk!—ah!"

The body was dead—the Toad was killed! But the spark that had shot forth from her eyes; what became of that?

The sunbeam took it up; the sunbeam carried the jewel from the head of the toad. Whither?

Ask not the naturalist; rather ask the poet. He will tell it thee under the guise of a fairy tale; and the Caterpillar on the cabbage, and the Stork family belong to the story. Think! the Caterpillar is changed, and turns into a beautiful butterfly; the Stork family flies over mountains and seas, to the distant Africa, and yet finds the shortest way home to the same country—to the same roof. Nay, that is almost too improbable; and yet it is true. You may ask the naturalist, he will confess it is so; and you know it yourself, for you have seen it.

But the jewel in the head of the toad?

Seek it in the sun; see it there if you can.

The brightness is too dazzling there. We have not yet such eyes as can see into the glories which God has created, but we shall receive them by-and-by; and that will be the most beautiful story of all, and we shall all have our share in it.

The Dryad

Translated by W. A. & J. K. Craigie

We are travelling to the Paris Exhibition.
Now we are there! it was a flight, a rush, but quite without witchcraft; we came by steam, in a ship and on a high road.

Our time is the fairy tale time.

We are in the midst of Paris, in a great hotel, all the staircase is decorated with flowers, and soft carpets cover the steps.

Our room is comfortable, the balcony door is standing open to a big square. Down there the spring lives. It has driven to Paris, arriving at the same time as we; it has come in the shape of a big, young chestnut tree, with fine, newly-opened leaves. How it is clothed in all the glory of spring, far beyond all the other trees in the square! One of these has gone out of the number of the living trees, and lies prostrate on the ground, torn up by the roots. There, where it stood, the new chestnut tree shall be planted and grow.

As yet it stands high up in the heavy cart which brought it to Paris this morning from the country, several miles away. There it had stood for years, close beside a mighty oak, under which sat often the kindly old priest, who told stories to the listening children. The young chestnut tree listened with them: the Dryad inside it, who was still a child, could remember the time when the tree was so small that it only reached a little higher than the ferns and long blades of grass. They were then as big as they could be, but the tree grew and increased every year, drank air and sunshine, received dew and rain, and was shaken and lashed by the rough winds: this is necessary for education.

The Dryad rejoiced in her life and experiences, in the sunshine and the song of birds, but happy most of all at the voices of men; she understood their language quite as well as she understood that of animals.

Butterflies, dragon-flies, and common flies—everything that could fly, paid her a visit; they all gossipped together; told about the village, the vineyard, the wood, the old castle with the park, in which were canals and dams; down there in the water, dwelt also living things, which in their own way could also fly from place to place under the water, beings with thought and knowledge; they said nothing, so wise were they.

And the swallow, which had dipped down into the water, told about the lovely goldfish, about the fat bream, the thick tench, and the old, moss-grown carp. The swallow gave a very good description, "but one can see better for oneself," she said; but how should the Dryad ever get to see these beings? She must content herself with being able to look out over the beautiful landscape and see the busy activity of men. That was lovely, but most lovely of all, when the old priest stood here under the oak, and told about France, and about the great deeds of men and women, whose names are named with admiration throughout all times. The Dryad heard of the shepherdess Joan of Arc, of Charlotte Corday; she heard of olden times, of the times of Henry IV, and of Napoleon I, and of greatness and talent, right up to the present day. She heard names, each of which rang in the hearts of the people. France is a worldwide land; a soil of intellect with a crater of freedom.

The village children listened devoutly, and the Dryad not less so; she was a school-child like the others. She saw in the forms of the sailing clouds picture after picture of what she had heard told. The cloudy sky was her picture book.

She felt herself so happy in the lovely France; but had still a feeling that the birds, and every animal which could fly, were much more favoured than she. Even the fly could look about himself, far and wide, much farther than the Dryad's horizon.

France was so extensive and so glorious, but she could only see a little bit of it; like a world, the country stretched out with vineyards, woods, and great towns, and of all of these Paris was the mightiest, and the most brilliant; thither the birds could go, but never she.

Amongst the village children was a little girl, so poor and so ragged, but lovely to look at; she was always laughing and singing, and wreathing red flowers in her black hair.

"Do not go to Paris!" said the old priest. "Poor child! if you go there, it will be your ruin!"

And yet she went.

The Dryad often thought about her, for they had both the same desire and longing for the great city. Spring came, summer, autumn, winter; two or three years passed.

The Dryad's tree bore its first chestnut blossoms, the birds twittered about it in the lovely sunshine. Then there came along the road a grand carriage with a stately lady; she, herself, drove the beautiful prancing horses; a smart little groom sat behind her. The Dryad knew her again, the old priest knew her again, shook his head, and said sorrowfully,

"You did go there! it was your ruin! Poor Marie!"

"She poor!" thought the Dryad. "Why, what a change! she is dressed like a duchess! she became like this in the city of enchantment. Oh, if I were only there in all the splendour and glory! it even throws a light up into the clouds at night, when I look in the direction where I know the city is."

Yes, thither, towards that quarter, the Dryad looked every evening, every night. She saw the glimmering mist on the horizon; she missed it in the bright, moonlight nights; she missed the floating clouds which showed her pictures of the city and of history.

The child grasps at its picture book; the Dryad grasped at the cloud world, her book of thoughts.

The warm summer sky, free from clouds, was for her a blank page, and now for several days she had seen such a sky.

It was the warm summer-time, with sultry days without a breath of air. Every leaf, every flower, lay as in a doze, and men were like that too. Then clouds arose, and that in the quarter where at night the glimmering mist announced, "Here is Paris."

The clouds arose, forming themselves like a whole mountain range, and scudded through the air, out over the whole landscape as far as the Dryad could see.

The clouds lay like enormous purple rocks, layer on layer, high up in the sky. Flashes of lightning darted forth; "they also are servants of God the Lord," the old priest had said. And there came a bluish dazzling flash, a blaze as if the sun itself had burst the purple rocks, and the lightning came down, and splintered the mighty old oak tree to the roots; its crown was rent, its trunk was rent, it fell split asunder as if it spread itself out to embrace the messenger of light. No metal cannon can boom through the air and over the land at the birth of a royal child, as the thunder rumbled here at the death of the old oak tree. The rain streamed down: a refreshing breeze blew, the storm was past, and a Sunday calm fell on everything. The village people gathered round the fallen old oak; the venerable priest spoke words in its praise, and an artist made a sketch of the tree itself as a lasting memorial.

"Everything passes away!" said the Dryad, "passes away like the clouds, and returns no more." The old priest came there no more; the school roof had fallen, and the teachers' chair was gone. The children came no more, but the autumn came, winter came, and the spring came too, and in all the changing seasons the Dryad gazed towards the quarter where every evening and night, far away on the horizon, Paris shone like a shimmering mist. Out from it sped engine after engine, the one train after the other, rushing and roaring, at all hours; in the evening and at midnight, in the morning, and through the whole of the daytime came the trains, and from every one and into every one crowded people from all the countries in the world; a new wonder of the world had called them to Paris. How did this wonder reveal itself?

"A splendid flower of art and industry," they said, "has sprung up on the barren soil of the Field of Mars; a gigantic sunflower, from

The Dryad

whose leaves one can learn geography and statistics, get the learning of a guild-master, be elevated in art and poetry, and learn the size and greatness of different countries."

"A fairy-blossom," said others, "a many-coloured lotus-plant, which spreads its green leaves over the sand, like a velvet carpet, which has sprung forth in the early spring. The summer shall see it in all its glory; the autumn storms will sweep it away; neither root nor leaf shall be left."

Outside the military school stretches the arena of war in times of peace; the field without grass and stalk, a piece of sandy plain cut out of the African desert, where Fata Morgana shows her strange castles in the air and hanging gardens; on the Field of Mars they now stand more brilliant and more wonderful, because genius had made them real.

"The present-day Palace of Aladdin is reared," it was said. Day by day, and hour by hour, it unfolds its rich splendour more and more. Marble and colours adorn its endless halls. "Master Bloodless" here moves his steel and iron limbs in the great machinery-hall. Works of art in metal, in stone, in weaving, proclaim the mental life which is stirring in all the countries of the world. Picture-galleries, masses of flowers, everything that intellect and hand can create in the workshops of the craftsman is here displayed to view. Even relics of ancient days from old castles and peat-mosses have met here.

The overwhelmingly great and varied sight must be reduced and condensed to a toy in order to be reproduced, understood, and seen as a whole.

The Field of Mars, like a great Christmas table, had on it an Aladdin's Palace of industry and art, and round about it were little articles from all countries; every nation found something to remind it of home. Here stood the Egyptian royal palace, here the caravanserai of the desert; the Bedouin coming from his sunny land swung past on his camel; here extended Russian stables with magnificent fiery steeds from the steppes. The little thatched farm-house from Denmark stood with its "Dannebrog" flag beside Gustav Vasa's beautifully carved wooden house from Dalarne in Sweden; American huts; English cottages, French pavilions, kiosks, churches, and theatres lay oddly strewn about, and amidst all that, the fresh green turf, the clear, running water, flowering shrubs, rare trees, glass-houses where one could imagine oneself in a tropical forest; whole rose-gardens, as if brought from Damascus, bloomed under the roof; what colours, what fragrance! Stalactite caves, artificially made, enclosing fresh and salt lakes, gave an exhibition from the kingdom of fish. One stood down on the bottom of the sea among fish and polypi.

All this, they said, the Field of Mars now bears and presents to view, and over this great richly-decked table moves, like a busy swarm of ants, the whole crowd of people, either on foot or drawn in little carriages; all legs cannot stand such an exhausting promenade.

They come here from early morning until late in the evening. Steamer after steamer, full of people, glides down the Seine. The number of carriages is constantly increasing, the crowds of people both on foot and on horseback are increasing, omnibuses and tramcars are stuffed and filled and covered with people—all these streams move to one goal, "The Paris Exhibition!" All the entrances are decorated with the French flag; round about the bazaar-buildings wave the flags of all nations; from the machinery-hall there is a whirring and humming; the bells chime in melody from the towers; the organs play inside the churches; hoarse, snuffling songs from the Oriental cafes mingle with the music. It is like the kingdom of Babel, the language of Babel, a Wonder of the World. It was such indeed—so the reports about it said; who did not hear them? The Dryad knew everything that has been said here about the 'new wonder' in the city of cities.

"Fly, ye birds! fly thither to look, come again and tell!" was the prayer of the Dryad,

The longing swelled to a wish, and became a life's thought; and then one still silent night, when the full moon was shining, there flew out from its disk—the Dryad saw it—a spark, which fell glittering like a meteor; and before the tree, whose branches shook as in a blast of wind, stood a mighty, radiant figure. It spoke in tones so soft and yet as strong as the trump of the Last Day, which kisses to life and calls to judgment.

"Thou shalt enter that place of enchantment, thou shalt there take root, feel the rushing currents, the air and the sunshine there. But thy lifetime shall be shortened, the series of years which awaited thee out here in the open, will shrink there to a small number of seasons. Poor Dryad; it will be thy ruin! thy longing will grow, thy yearning and thy craving will become stronger! The tree itself will become a prison for thee; thou wilt forsake thy dwelling, forsake thy nature, and fly away and mix with human beings, and then thy years will dwindle down to half the lifetime of the ephemeral fly, only a single night; thy life shall be extinguished, the leaves of the tree shall wither and be blown away, to return no more."

Thus it sounded, thus it sang, and the brightness vanished, but not the longing and desire of the Dryad; she trembled with expectation, in a fever of wild anticipation.

"I shall go to the city of cities!" she exultingly cried. "Life begins, gathers like the cloud, and no one knows where it goes."

In the grey dawn, when the moon grew pale and the clouds red, the hour of fulfilment struck, and the promise was redeemed.

People came with spades and poles; they dug round the roots of the tree, deep down, right under it. Then a cart was brought up, drawn by horses, the tree, with the roots and clods of earth hanging to them, was lifted, wrapped in matting which made a warm foot-bag for it, then it was placed on the cart and bound fast. It was to go on a journey to Paris, to grow and remain there in the grandest city of France—the city of cities.

The leaves and branches of the chestnut tree trembled in the first moment of motion; the Dryad trembled in the delight of expectation.

"Away! away!" rang in every pulse-beat, "Away! away!" came the echo in trembling, fluttering words. The Dryad forgot to say 'Farewell' to her native place, to the waving grasses and the innocent daisies, which had looked up to her as to a great lady in our Lord's garden, a young Princess who played the shepherdess out in the country.

The chestnut tree was on the cart, it nodded with its branches "Farewell", or "Away", the Dryad knew not which; she thought and dreamt of the wonderful, new, and yet so familiar scenes which should be unfolded before her. No childish heart in innocent delight, no passion-filled soul, has ever begun its journey to Paris more full of thought than she. "Farewell!" became "Away! away!"

The wheels of the cart went round, the distant became near and was left behind; the country changed, as the clouds change; new vineyards, forests, villages, villas, and gardens sprang up, came in sight, and rolled away again. The chestnut tree moved forward, the Dryad forward with it, engine after engine rushed close past each other and crossed each other; the engines sent out clouds, which formed figures that told of the Paris they came from, and to which the Dryad was bound.

Everything round about knew and must understand whither her way led; she thought that every tree she went past stretched out its branches to her, and begged: "Take me with you! take me with you!" In every tree there was also a Dryad full of longing. What changes! What a journey! It seemed as if houses shot up out of the earth, more and more, closer and closer. Chimneys rose like flowerpots, placed above each other and side by side along the roofs; great inscriptions with letters a yard long, painted figures on the walls from the ground-floor to the cornice shone forth.

"Where does Paris begin, and when shall I be in it?" the Dryad asked herself. The crowds of people increased, the noise and bustle grew greater, carriage followed carriage, men on foot followed men on horse, and all round was shop upon shop, music and song, screaming and talking.

The Dryad in her tree was in the midst of Paris.

The great, heavy cart stopped in a little square, planted with trees, surrounded by high houses, where every window had its balcony. People looked down from there upon the young, fresh chestnut tree which was driven up, and which was now to be planted here, in place of the worn-out, uprooted tree, which lay stretched along the ground. People stood still in the square, and looked at the spring verdure, smiling and delighted; the older trees, still only in bud, greeted her with rustling branches, "Welcome! welcome!" and the fountain which threw its jets of water into the air, letting them splash again into the broad basin, allowed the wind to carry drops over to the newly-arrived tree, as if it would offer it a cup of welcome.

The Dryad felt that its tree was lifted from the cart and placed in its future position. The tree's roots were hidden in the earth, fresh turf was laid over them; blossoming shrubs and pots of flowers were

The Dryad

planted like the tree; here was a whole garden plot right in the middle of the square. The dead, uprooted tree, killed by gas-fumes, kitchen-fumes, and all the plant-killing vapours of a town, was laid on the cart and driven away. The crowd looked on, children and old people sat on benches on the grass, and looked up among the leaves of the newly-planted tree. And we, who tell about it, stood on the balcony, looked down on the young spring verdure just come from the fresh country air, and said, as the old priest would have said: 'Poor Dryad!'

"How happy I am!" said the Dryad, "and yet I cannot quite realize it, nor quite express what I feel; everything is as I expected it! and yet not quite as I expected!"

The houses were so high, and so close: the sun shone properly only upon one wall, and it was pasted over with posters and placards, before which the people stood and made the place crowded. Vehicles went past, light and heavy; omnibuses, those over-filled houses on wheels, rolled along, riders trotted ahead, carts and carriages claimed the right to do the same. The Dryad wondered whether the tall houses, which stood so close, would also flit away, change their shapes like the clouds and glide aside, so that she could see into Paris, and out over it. Notre-Dame must show itself, and the Vendome Column, and the Wonder which had called and was calling so many strangers hither. But the houses did not move.

It was still day, when the lamps were lighted, the gas-rays shone out from the shops and up among the branches of the tree; it was like summer sunshine. The stars came out overhead, the same ones the Dryad had seen in her native place; she thought she felt a breeze from there, so pure and mild. She felt herself elevated and strengthened, and found she had the power of seeing right out through all the leaves of the tree, and had feeling to the farthest tips of the roots. She felt herself in the living human world, looked at with kindly eyes; round about were bustle and music, colours and lights.

From a side street sounded wind-instruments, and the dance-inspiring tunes of the barrel-organ. Yes, to the dance, to the dance! it sounded—to gladness and the pleasure of life.

It was a music that must set men, horses, carriages, trees, and houses dancing, if they could dance. An intoxicating joy arose in the Dryad's breast.

"How delightful and beautiful!" she cried joyfully, "I am in Paris!"

The day which came, the night which followed, and again the next day, offered the same sights, the same stir, the same life, changing and yet always the same,

"Now I know every tree and every flower in the square here! I know every house, balcony and shop here, where I am placed in this little cramped corner which hides the great, mighty town from me. Where are the triumphal arches, the boulevards, and the Wonder of the World? None of all these do I see! I am imprisoned as in a cage amongst the tall houses, which I now know by heart, with their placards, and posters, and sign-boards, all these plaster sweetmeats, which I have no taste for any longer. Where is all that I heard about, know about, longed for, and for the sake of which I wished to come here? What have I grasped, won, or found! I am longing as before, I see a life which I must grasp and live in! I must enter the ranks of the living 1 I must revel there, fly like the birds, see and understand, become wholly human, seize half a day of that in place of years of life in everyday fatigue and tediousness, in which I sicken and droop, and vanish like the mist on the meadow. I must shine like the cloud, shine in the sunlight of life, look out over everything like the cloud, and pass away like it—no one knows whither!"

This was the Dryad's sigh, which lifted itself in prayer.

"Take my lifetime, and give me the half of the Ephemera's life! Free me from my imprisonment, give me human life, human joy for a short space, only this single night, if it must be so, and punish me thus for my presumptuous spirit, my longing for life! Annihilate me; let the fresh, young tree that encloses me then wither and fall, become ashes, and be scattered to the winds."

A rustling passed through the branches of the tree; there came a titillating feeling, a trembling in every leaf, as if fire ran through it or out of it, a blast went through the crown of the tree, and in the midst of it arose a woman's form—the Dryad herself. In the same instant she sat under the gas-illumined, leafy branches, young and beautiful, like poor Marie, to whom it was said, "The great city will be thy ruin!"

The Dryad

The Dryad sat by the foot of the tree, by the door of her house, which she had locked and of which she had thrown away the key. So young, so beautiful! The stars saw her and twinkled. The gas-lamps saw her and beamed and beckoned! How slender she was and yet strong, a child and yet a full-grown maiden. Her clothes were fine as silk, and green as the fresh, newly-unfolded leaves in the crown of the tree; in her nut-brown hair hung a half-blown chestnut blossom; she looked like the goddess of Spring.

Only a short minute she sat motionless and still, then she sprang up, and ran like a gazelle from the place, and disappeared round the corner. She ran, she sprang like the light from a mirror which is carried in the sunshine, the light which with every motion is cast now here and now there; and if one had looked closely, and been able to see what there was to see, how wonderful! At every place where she stopped for a moment, her clothes and her figure were changed according to the character of the place, or the house whose lamp shone upon her.

She reached the Boulevards; a sea of light streamed from the gas in the lamps, shops, and cafes. Young and slender trees stood here in rows; each one hid its Dryad from the beams of the artificial sunlight. The whole of the long, never-ending pavement was like one great assembly-room; tables stood spread with refreshments of all kinds, from champagne and chartreuse down to coffee and beer. There was a display of flowers, of pictures, statues, books, and many-coloured fabrics. From the throng under the tall houses she looked out over the alarming stream under the rows of trees: there rushed a tide of rolling carriages, cabriolets, coaches, omnibuses, and cabs, gentlemen on horseback, and marching regiments—it was risking life and limb to cross over to the opposite side. Now shone a blue light, then the gas-lights were supreme, and suddenly a rocket shot up; whence and whither? Certainly, it was the highway of the great city of the world.

Here sounded soft Italian melodies, there Spanish songs, accompanied by the beating of castanets, but strongest, and swelling above all, sounded the musical-box melodies of the moment, the tickling can-can music, unknown to Orpheus, and never heard by beautiful Helen; even the wheelbarrow must have danced on its one wheel if it could have danced. The Dryad danced, floated, flew, changing in colour like the honey-bird in the sunshine: each house and the world within it gave fresh tints to her. As the gleaming lotus-flower, torn from its root, is borne by the stream on its eddies, she drifted; and wherever she stood, she was again a new shape, therefore no one could follow her, recognize and watch her.

Like cloud-pictures everything flew past her, face after face, but not a single one did she know; she saw no form from her own home. There shone in her thoughts two bright eyes, and she thought of Marie, poor Marie! the happy, ragged child with the red flower in her black hair. She was in the city of the world, rich, and dazzling, as when she drove past the priest's house, the Dryad's tree, and the old oak. She was here, no doubt, in the deafening noise; perhaps she had just got out of that magnificent coach waiting yonder; splendid carriages stood here with laced coachmen, and silk-stockinged footmen. The grand people alighting were all women, richly dressed ladies. They went through the open lattice-door, up the high, broad stairs, which led to a building with white marble columns. Was this perhaps the 'Wonder of the World'? Then certainly Marie was there!

"Sancta Maria!" they sang within; the clouds of incense floated under the lofty painted and gilded arches, where twilight reigned. It was the Church of the Madeleine. Dressed in black, in costly materials made after the latest fashion, ladies of the highest society glided over the polished floor. Coats of arms were on the silver clasps of the prayer-books bound in velvet, and on the fine, strongly-scented handkerchiefs trimmed with costly Brussels lace. Some of the ladies knelt in silent prayer before the altars, others sought the confessionals. The Dryad felt a restlessness, a fear, as if she had entered a place where she ought not to have set foot. Here was the home of silence, the palace of secrets; all was whispered and confided without a sound being heard.

The Dryad saw herself disguised in silk and veil, resembling in form the other rich and high-born ladies; was each of them a child of longing like herself?

There sounded a sigh, so painfully deep; did it come from the confessional corner, or from the breast of the Dryad? She drew her veil closer round her. She breathed the incense and not the fresh air. Here was no place for her longing.

Away! away! in flight without rest! The Ephemera has no rest; its flight is its life!

She was again outside under the blazing gas-lamps by the splendid fountain. "All the streams of water will not be able to wash away the innocent blood which has been shed here." So it has been said.

Foreigners stood here and talked loudly and with animation, as no one dared to do in the High Court of Mystery, from which the Dryad came.

A large stone-slab was turned and lifted up; she did not understand this; she saw an open entrance to the depths of the earth; into this people descended from the starlit sky, from the sunshiny gas-flames, from all the stirring life.

"I am afraid of this!" said one of the women who stood there; "I dare not go down; I don't care either about seeing the sight! Stay with me!"

"And go back home," said the man, "go from Paris without having seen the most remarkable thing, the real wonder of the present time, called into being by the talent and will of a single man!"

"I shall not go down there," was the answer.

"The wonder of the present age," they said. The Dryad heard and understood it; the goal of her greatest longing was reached, and here was the entrance, down in the depths under Paris; she had not thought of this, but when she heard it now, and saw the foreigners going down, she followed them. The spiral staircase was of cast iron, broad and commodious. A lamp gleamed down there, and another one still farther down.

They stood in a labyrinth of endlessly long intersecting halls and arched passages; all the streets and lanes of Paris were to be seen here, as in a dim mirror, the names could be read, every house above had its number here, its root, which struck down under the empty, macadamized footway, which ran along by a broad canal with a stream of rolling mud. Higher up, along the arches, was led the fresh running water, and above all hung, like a net, gas-pipes and telegraph wires. Lamps shone in the distance, like reflected images from the metropolis above. Now and then was heard a noisy rumbling overhead; it was the heavy wagons which drove over the bridges above.

Where was the Dryad?

You have heard of the catacombs: they are but the faintest of outlines compared to this new subterranean world, the wonder of the present day, the drains of Paris. Here stood the Dryad and not out in the world's exhibition on the Field of Mars. She heard exclamations of astonishment, admiration and appreciation.

"From down here," they said, "health and years of life are growing for thousands and thousands up above! Our time is the time of progress with all its blessings."

That was the opinion and the talk of the people, but not of the creatures who lived and dwelt and had been born here, the rats; they squeaked from the rifts in a piece of old wall, so clearly, distinctly and intelligibly to the Dryad.

A big old he-rat, with his tail bitten off, piercingly squeaked his feelings, his discomfort, and his honest opinion, and the family gave him support for every word.

"I am disgusted with this nonsense, this human nonsense, this ignorant talk! Oh yes, it is very fine here now with gas and petroleum! I don't eat that kind of thing! It has become so fine and bright here that one is ashamed of oneself, and does not know why. If we only lived in the time of tallow-candles! it isn't so far back either! That was a romantic time, as they call it!"

"What is that you are talking about?" said the Dryad. "I did not see you before. What are you talking about?"

"The good old days," said the rat, "the happy days of great-grandfather and great-grandmother rats! In those days it was something to come down here. It was a rat's nest different from the whole of Paris! Mother Plague lived down here; she killed people, but never rats. Robbers and smugglers breathed freely down here. Here was the place of refuge for the most interesting personages, who are now only seen in melodramas in the theatre up above. The time of romance is gone in our rat's nest too; we have got fresh air and petroleum down here."

So squeaked the rat! squeaked against the new times in favour of the old days with Mother Plague.

A carriage stood there, a kind of open omnibus with swift, little horses; the party got into it, and rushed along the Boulevard

Sebastopol, the subterranean one: right above stretched the well-known Parisian one full of people.

The carriage disappeared in the dim light; the Dryad also vanished, rose up into the gas-light and the fresh free air; there, and not down in the crossing arches and their suffocating air, could the wonder be found, the Wonder of the World, that which she sought in her short night of life; it must shine stronger than all the gas-lights up here, stronger than the moon which now glided forth. Yes, certainly! and she saw it yonder, it beamed before her, it twinkled and glittered like the star of Venus in the sky.

She saw a shining gate, opening into a little garden, full of light and dancing melodies. Gas-jets shone here as borders round little quiet lakes and pools, where artificial water-plants, cut out of tin-plate bent and painted, glittered in the light, and threw jets of water yard-high out of their chalices. Beautiful weeping-willows, real weeping-willows of the spring-time, drooped their fresh branches like a green transparent yet concealing veil.

Here, amongst the bushes, blazed a bonfire; its red glow shone over small, half-dark, silent arbours, permeated with tones, with a music thrilling to the ear, captivating, alluring, chasing the blood through the veins.

She saw young women, beautiful in festal attire, with trusting smiles, and the light laughing spirit of youth, a "Marie", with a rose in the hair, but without carriage and footmen. How they floated, how they whirled in the wild dance! As if bitten by the Tarantella, they sprang and laughed and smiled, blissfully happy, ready to embrace the whole world.

The Dryad felt herself carried away in the dance. About her slender little foot fitted the silken shoe, chestnut-brown, like the ribbon which floated from her hair over her uncovered shoulders. The green silk garment waved in great folds, but did not conceal the beautifully formed limb with the pretty foot, which seemed as if it wished to describe magic circles in the air. Was she in the enchanted garden of Armida? What was the place called? The name shone outside in gas-jets,

"Mabille"

Sounds of music and clapping of hands, rockets, and murmuring water, popping of champagne corks mingled here. The dance was wildly bacchanalian, and over the whole sailed the moon, with a rather wry face, no doubt. The sky was cloudless, clear and serene; it seemed as if one could see straight into Heaven from "Mabille".

A consuming desire of life thrilled through the Dryad; it was like an opium trance.

Her eyes spoke, her lips spoke, but the words were not heard for the sound of flutes and violins. Her partner whispered words in her ear, they trembled in time to the music of the can-can; she did not understand them—we do not understand them either. He stretched his arms out towards her and about her, and only embraced the transparent, gas-filled air.

The Dryad was carried away by the stream of air, as the wind bears a rose-leaf. On high before her she saw a flame, a flashing light, high up on a tower. The light shone from the goal of her longing, from the red lighthouse on the 'Fata Morgana' of the Field of Mars. She fluttered about the tower; the workmen thought it was a butterfly which they saw dropping down to die in its all too early arrival.

The moon shone, gas-lights and lamps shone in the great halls and in the scattered buildings of all lands, shone over the undulating greensward, and the rocks made by the ingenuity of men, where the waterfall poured down by the strength of "Mr. Bloodless". The depths of the ocean and of the fresh water, the realms of the fishes were opened here; one was at the bottom of the deep pool, one was down in the ocean, in a diving-bell. The water pressed against the thick glass walls above and around. The polypi, fathom-long, flexible, winding, quivering, living arms, clutched, heaved, and grew fast to the bottom of the sea.

A great flounder lay thoughtfully close by, stretched itself out in comfort and ease: the crab crawled like an enormous spider over it, whilst shrimps darted about with a haste, a swiftness, as if they were the moths and butterflies of the sea.

In the fresh water grew water lilies, sedges, and rushes. The goldfishes had placed themselves in rows, like red cows in the field, all with the heads in the same direction, so as to get the current in their mouths. Thick fat tench stared with stupid eyes towards the glass walls; they knew that they were at the Paris Exhibition; they knew that they had made the somewhat difficult journey hither, in barrels filled with water, and had been land-sick on the railway, just as people are sea-sick on the sea. They had come to see the Exhibition, and so they saw it from their own fresh or salt water box, saw the throng of men which moved past from morning to night. All the countries of the world had sent and exhibited their natives, so that the old tench and bream, the nimble perch and the moss-grown carp should see these beings and give their opinions upon the species.

"They are shell-fish!" said a muddy little bleak. "They change their shells two or three times in the day, and make sounds with their mouths—talking, they call it. We don't change, and we make ourselves understood in an easier way; movements with the corners of the mouth, and a stare with the eyes! We have many points of superiority over mankind!"

"They have learnt swimming, though," said a little freshwater fish. "I am from the big lake; men go into the water in the hot season there, but first they put off their shells, and then they swim. The frogs have taught them that, they push with the hind-legs, and paddle with the fore-legs; they can't keep it up long. They would like to imitate us, but they don't get near it. Poor men!"

And the fishes stared; they imagined that the whole crowd of people they had seen in the strong daylight was still moving here; yes, they were convinced that they still saw the same forms which, so to speak, first struck their nerves of apprehension.

A little perch, with beautifully striped skin, and an enviable round back, asserted that the "human mud" was there still; he saw it.

"I also see it; it is so distinct!" said a jaundice-yellow tench. "I see plainly the beautiful well-shaped human figure, 'high-legged lady' or whatever it was they called her; she had our mouth and staring eyes, two balloons behind, and an umbrella let down in front, a great quantity of hanging duck-weed dingling and dangling. She should put it all off, go like us in the guise of nature, and she would look like a respectable tench, as far as human beings can do so!"

"What became of him—he on the string, the male—they dragged?"

"He rode in a bath-chair, sat with paper, pen and ink, and wrote everything down. What was he doing? They called him a reporter."

"He is riding about there still," said a moss-grown maiden carp, with the trials of the world in her throat, so that she was hoarse with it; she had once swallowed a fish-hook, and still swam patiently about with it in her throat.

"A reporter," she said, "that is, speaking plainly and fishily, a kind of cuttlefish among men,"

So the fishes talked in their own manner. But in the midst of the artificial grotto sounded the blows of hammers and the songs of the work-people; they must work at night, so that everything might be finished as soon as possible. They sang in the Dryad's summer night's dream, she herself stood there, ready to fly and vanish.

"They are goldfish!" said she, and nodded to them. "So I have managed to see you after all! I know you! I have known you a long time! The swallow has told me about you in my home country. How pretty you are, how glittering and charming! I could kiss each and all of you! I know the others also! That is certainly the fat tench; that one there, the dainty bream; and here, the old moss-grown carp! I know you! but you don't know me!"

The fish stared and did not understand a single word; they stared out into the dim light. The Dryad was there no longer, she stood out in the open air, where the world's "wonder-blossoms" from the different countries gave out their fragrance, from the land of rye-bread, from the coast of the stock-fish, the empire of russia leather, the river-banks of Eau-de-Cologne, and from the eastern land of the essence of roses.

When, after a ball, we drive home, half-asleep, the tunes we have heard still sound distinctly in our ears; we could sing each and all of them. And as in the eye of a murdered man, the last thing the glance rested on is said to remain photographed on it for a time, so here in the night the bustle and glare of the day was not extinguished. The Dryad felt it and knew that it would roll on in the same way through the coming day. The Dryad stood amongst the fragrant roses, thinking that she recognized them from her home, roses from the park of the castle and from the priest's garden. She also saw the red pomegranate flower here; Marie had worn one like it in her coal-black hair.

Memories from the home of her childhood out in the country flashed through her mind; she drank in the sights round about her with greedy eyes, whilst feverish restlessness possessed her, and carried her through the wonderful halls.

She felt tired, and this tiredness increased. She had a longing to rest upon the soft Eastern cushions and carpets spread around, or to lean against the weeping-willow down by the clear water, and plunge herself into that.

But the Ephemera has no rest. The day was only a few minutes from the end.

Her thoughts trembled, her limbs trembled, she sank down on the grass, by the rippling water.

"Thou springest from the earth with lasting life!" said she; "cool my tongue, give me refreshment!"

"I am not the living fountain!" answered the water. "I flow by machinery!"

"Give me of thy freshness, thou green grass," begged the Dryad. "Give me one of the fragrant flowers!"

"We die when we are broken off!" answered the grass and flowers.

"Kiss me, thou fresh breeze! only one single kiss of life!"

"Soon the sun will kiss the clouds red!" said the wind, "and then wilt thou be amongst the dead, passed away, as all the splendour here will pass away, before the year is gone, and I can again play with the light, loose sand in the square here, and blow the dust along over the ground, dust in the air, dust! all dust!"

The Dryad felt a dread, like that of the woman who in the bath has cut an artery and is bleeding to death, but while bleeding wishes still to live. She raised herself, came some steps forward, and again sank down in front of a little church. The door stood open, candles burned on the altar, and the organ pealed.

What music! such tones the Dryad had never heard, and yet she seemed to hear in them well-known voices. They came from the depths of the heart of the whole creation. She thought she heard the rustling of the old oak tree, she thought she heard the old priest talking about great deeds, and about famous names, and of what God's creatures had power to give as a gift to future times, and must give it in order to win, by that means, eternal life for itself.

The tones of the organ swelled and pealed, and spoke in song: "Thy longing and desire uprooted thee from thy God-given place. It became thy ruin, poor Dryad!"

The organ tones, soft and mild, sounded as if weeping, dying away in tears.

The clouds shone red in the sky. The wind whistled and sang, "Pass away, ye Dead, the sun is rising!"

The first beam fell on the Dryad. Her form shone in changing colours, like the soap-bubble when it breaks, vanishes and becomes a drop, a tear which falls to the ground and disappears.

Poor Dryad! a dew-drop, only a tear, shed, vanished!

The sun shone over the "Fata Morgana" on the Field of Mars, shone over the Great Paris, over the little square with the trees and the splashing fountain, amongst the tall houses, where the chestnut tree stood, but with drooping branches, withered leaves, the tree which only yesterday lifted itself as fresh and full of life as the spring itself. Now it was dead, they said. The Dryad had gone, passed away like the cloud, no one knew whither.

There lay on the ground a withered, broken chestnut flower; the holy water of the Church had no power to call it to life. The foot of man soon trod it down into the dust.

The whole of this actually happened, we saw it ourselves at the Paris Exhibition in 1867, in our own time, in the great, wonderful, time of fairy tale.

The Court Cards

Translated by Mrs. H. P. Paull

How many beautiful things may be cut out of and pasted on paper! Thus a castle was cut out and pasted, so large that it filled a whole table, and it was painted as if it were built of red stones. It had a shining copper roof, it had towers and a draw-bridge, water in the canals just like plate glass, for it was plate-glass, and in the highest tower stood a wooden watchman. He had a trumpet, but he did not blow it.

The whole belonged to a little boy, whose name was William. He raised the draw-bridge himself and let it down again, made his tin soldiers march over it, opened the castle gate and looked into the large and elegant drawing room, where all the court cards of a pack—Hearts, Diamonds, Clubs, and Spades—hung in frames on the walls, like pictures in real drawing rooms. The kings held each a scepter, and wore crowns; the queens wore veils flowing down over their shoulders, and in their hands they held a flower or a fan; the knaves had halberds and nodding plumes.

One evening the little boy peeped through the open castle gate, to catch a glimpse of the court cards in the drawing room, and it seemed to him that the kings saluted him with their scepters, that the Queen of Spades swung the golden tulip which she held in her hand, that the Queen of Hearts lifted her fan, and that all four queens graciously recognized him. He drew a little nearer, in order to see better, and that made him hit his head against the castle so that it shook. Then all the four knaves of Hearts, Diamonds, Clubs, and Spades, raised their halberds, to warn him that he must not try to get in that way.

The little boy understood the hint, and gave a friendly nod; he nodded again, and then said: "Say something!" but the knaves did not say a word. However, the third time be nodded, the Knave of Hearts sprang out of the card, and placed himself in the middle of the floor.

"What is your name?" the knave asked the little boy. "You have clear eyes and good teeth, but your hands are dirty: you do not wash them often enough!"

Now this was rather coarse language, but, of course, not much politeness can be expected from a knave. He is only a common fellow.

"My name is William," said the little boy, "and the castle is mine, and you are my Knave of Hearts!"

"No, I am not. I am my king's and my queen's knave, not yours!" said the Knave of Hearts. "I am not obliged to stay here. I can get down off the card, and out of the frame too, and so can my gracious king and queen, even more easily than I. We can go out into the wide world, but that is such a wearisome march; we have grown tired of it; it is more convenient, more easy, more agreeable, to be sitting in the cards, and just to be ourselves!"

"Have all of you really been human beings once?" asked little William.

"Human beings!" repeated the Knave of Hearts. "Yes, we have; but not so good as we ought to have been! Please now light a little wax candle (I like a red one best, for that is the colour of my king and queen); then I will tell the lord of the castle—I think you said you were the lord of the castle, did you not?—our whole history; but for goodness' sake, don't interrupt me, for if I speak, it must be done without any interruption whatever. I am in a great hurry! Do you see my king, I mean the King of Hearts ? He is the oldest of the four kings there, for he was born first—born with a golden crown and a golden apple. He began to rule at once. His queen was born with a golden fan; that she still has. They both were very agreeably situated, even from infancy. They did not have to go to school, they could play the whole day, build castles, and knock them down, marshal tin soldiers for battle, and play with dolls. When they asked for buttered bread, then there was butter on both sides of the bread, and powdered brown sugar, too, nicely spread over it. It was the good old time, and was called the Golden Age; but they grew tired of it, and so did I. Then the King of Diamonds took the reins of government!"

The knave said nothing more. Little William waited to hear something further, but not a syllable was uttered; so presently he asked—"Well, and then ?"

The Knave of Hearts did not answer; he stood up straight, silent, bold, and stiff, his eyes fixed upon the burning wax candle. Little William nodded; he nodded again, but no reply. Then he turned to the Knave of Diamonds; and when he had nodded to him three times, up he sprang out of the card, in the middle of the floor, and uttered only one single word—

"Wax candle!"

Little William understood what he meant, and immediately lighted a red candle, and placed it before him. Then the Knave of Diamonds presented arms, for that is a token of respect, and said:— "Then the King of Diamonds succeeded to the throne! He was a king with a pane of glass on his breast; also the queen had a pane of glass on her breast, so that people could look right into her. For the rest, they were formed like other human beings, and were so agreeable and so handsome, that a monument was erected in honour of them, which stood for seven years without falling. Properly speaking, it should have stood forever, for so it was intended; but from some unknown reasons, it fell." Then the Knave of Diamonds presented arms, Out of respect for his king, and he looked fixedly on his red wax candle.

But now at once, without any nod or invitation from little William, the Knave of Clubs stepped out, grave and proud, like the stork that struts with such a dignified air over the green meadow. The black clover-leaf in the corner of the card flew like a bird beyond the knave, and then flew back again, and stuck itself where it had been sticking before.

And without waiting for his wax candle, the Knave of Clubs spoke:—

"Not all get butter on both sides of the bread, and brown powdered sugar on that. My king and queen did not get it. They had to go to school, and learn what they had not learnt before. They also had a pane of glass on their breasts, but nobody looked through it, except to see if there was not some.thing wrong with their works inside, in order to find, if possible, some reason for giving them a scolding! I know it; I have served my king and queen all my life-time; I know everything about them, and obey their commands. They bid me say nothing more tonight. keep silent, therefore, and present arms!"

But little William was a kind-hearted boy, so he lighted a candle for this knave also, a shining white one, white like snow. No sooner was the candle lighted, than the Knave of Spades appeared in the middle of the drawing room. He came hurriedly; yet he limped, as if he had a sore leg. Indeed, it had once been broken, and he had had, moreover, many ups and down in his life. He spoke as follows:—

"My brother knaves have each got a candle, and I shall also get one; I know that. But if we poor knaves have so much honour, our kings and queens must have thrice as much. Now, it is proper that my King of Spades and my Queen of Spades should have four candles to gladden them. An additional honour ought to be conferred upon them. Their history and trials are so doleful, that they have very good reason to wear mourning, and to have a grave-digger's spade on their coat of arms. My own fate, poor knave that I am, is deplorable enough. In one game at cards, I have got the nickname of 'Black Peter!' But alas! I have got a still uglier name, which, indeed, it is hardly the thing to mention aloud," and then he whispered, "In another game, I have been nicknamed 'Dirty Mads!' I, who was once the King of Spades' Lord Chamberlain! Is not this a bitter fate? The history of my royal master and queen I will not relate; they don't wish me to do so! Little lord of the castle, as he calls himself, may guess it himself if he chooses, but it is very lamentable—O, no doubt about that! Their circumstances have become very much reduced, and are not likely to change for the better, until we are all riding on the red horse higher than the skies, where there are no haps and mishaps!"

Little William now lighted, as the Knave of Spades had said was proper, three candles for each of the kings, and three for each of the queens; but for the King and Queen of Spades he lighted four candles apiece, and the whole drawing room became as light and transparent as the palace of the richest emperor, and the illustrious kings and queens bowed to each other serenely and graciously. The Queen of Hearts made her golden fan bow; and the Queen of Spades swung her golden tulip in such a way, that a stream of fire issued from it. The royal couples alighted from the cards and frames, and moved in a slow and graceful minuet up and down the floor. They were dancing in the very midst of flames, and the knaves were dancing too.

But alas! the whole drawing room was soon in a blaze; the devouring element roared up through the roof, and all was one crackling and hissing sheet of fire; and in a moment little William's castle itself was enveloped in flames and smoke. The boy became frightened, and ran off, crying to his father and mother—"Fire, fire, fire! my castle is on fire!" He grew pale as ashes, and his little hands trembled like the aspen-leaf. The fire continued sparkling and blazing, but in the midst of this destructive scene, the following words were uttered in a singing tone:—

"Now we are riding on the red horse, higher than the skies! This is the way for kings and queens to go, and this is the way for their knaves to go after them!"

Yes I that was the end of William's castle, and of the court cards. William did not perish in the flames; he is still alive, and he washed his small bands, and said: "I am innocent of the destruction of the castle." And, indeed, it was not his fault that the castle was burnt down.

Good Luck Can Lie in a Pin

Translated by Mrs. H. P. Paull

Now I shall tell a story about good luck. We all know good luck: some see it from year's end to year's end, others only at certain seasons, on a certain day; there are even people who only see it once in their lives, but see it we all do.

Now I need not tell you, for every one knows it, that God sends the little child and lays it in a mother's lap, it may be in the rich castle, and in the well-to-do house, but it may also be in the open field where the cold wind blows. Every one does not know, however, but it is true all the same, that God, when He brings the child, brings also a lucky gift for it: but it is not laid openly by its side; it is laid in some place in the world where one would least expect to find it, and yet it always is found: that is the best of it. It may be laid in an apple; it was so for a learned man who was called Newton: the apple fell, and so he found his good luck. If you do not know the story, then ask some one who knows it to tell it you. I have another story to tell, and that is a story about a pear.

Once upon a time there was a man who was born in poverty,

Good Luck Can Lie in a Pin

had grown up in poverty, and in poverty he had married. He was a turner by trade and made, especially, umbrella handles and rings; but he only lived from hand to mouth. "I never find good luck," he said. This is a story that really happened, and one could name the country and the place where the man lived, but that doesn't matter.

The red, sour rowan-berries grew in richest profusion about his house and garden. In the garden there was also a pear-tree, but it did not bear a single pear, and yet the good luck was laid in that pear-tree, laid in the invisible pears.

One night the wind blew a terrible storm. They told in the newspapers that the big stage-coach was lifted off the road and thrown aside like a rag. It could very well happen then that a great branch was broken off the pear-tree.

The branch was put into the workshop, and the man, as a joke, made a big pear out of it, and then another big one, then a smaller one, and then some very little ones. "The tree must some time or other have pears," the man said, and he gave them to the children to play with.

One of the necessities of life in a wet country is an umbrella. The whole house had only one for common use; if the wind blew too strongly, the umbrella turned inside out; it also snapped two or three times, but the man soon put it right again. The most provoking thing, however, was that the button which held it together when it was down, too often jumped off, or the ring which was round it broke in two.

One day the button flew off; the man searched for it on the floor, and there got hold of one of the smallest of the wooden pears which the children had got to play with. "The button is not to be found," said the man, "but this little thing will serve the same purpose." So he bored a hole in it, pulled a string through it, and the little pear fitted very well into the broken ring. It was assuredly the very best fastener the umbrella had ever had.

Next year when the man was sending umbrella handles to the town, as he regularly did, he also sent some of the little wooden pears, and begged that they might be tried, and so they came to America. There they very soon noticed that the little pears held much better than any other button, and now they demanded of the merchant that all the umbrellas which were sent after that should be fastened with a little pear.

Now, there was something to do! Pears in thousands! Wooden pears on all umbrellas! The man must set to work. He turned and turned. The whole pear-tree was cut up into little pears! It brought in pennies, it brought in shillings!

"My good luck was laid in the pear-tree," said the man.

He now got a big workshop with workmen and boys. He was always in a good humour, and said, "Good luck can lie in a pin!"

I also, who tell the story, say so. People have a saying, "Take a white pin in your mouth and you will be invisible," but it must be the right pin, the one which was given us as a lucky gift by our Lord. I got that, and I also, like the man, can catch chinking gold, gleaming gold, the very best, that kind which shines from children's eyes, the kind that sounds from children's mouths, and from father and mother too. They read the stories, and I stand among them in the middle of the room, but invisible, for I have the white pin in my mouth. If I see that they are delighted with what I tell them, then I also say, "Good luck can lie in a pin!"

Sunshine Stories

Translated by Mrs. H. P. Paull

"Now I am going to tell a story," said the Wind.

"Excuse me," said the Rain, "but now it is my turn—, you have been howling round the corner as hard as ever you could, this long time past."

"Is that your gratitude toward me?" said the Wind. "I who, in honour of you, turn inside out—yes, even break—all the umbrellas, when people won't have anything to do with you."

"I am going to speak!" said the Sunshine. "Silence!"

And the Sunshine said it with such glory and majesty, that the long, weary Wind fell prostrate, and the Rain beat against him, and shook him, and said—"We won't stand it! She always breaks through, that Madam Sunshine; we won't listen to her. What she says is not worth hearing."

But the Sunshine said—"A beautiful swan flew over the rolling, tumbling waves of the ocean. Every one of its feathers shone like gold: one feather drifted down on the great merchant vessel that, with all sail set, was sailing away. The feather dropped on the curly light hair of a young man, whose business it was to have a care for the goods—, supercargo they called him. The bird of Fortune's feather touched his forehead, became a pen in his hand, and brought him such luck, that very soon he became a wealthy merchant—rich enough to have bought for himself spurs of gold; rich enough to change a golden dish into a nobleman's shield; and I shone on it," said the Sunshine.

"The swan flew further, away over the bright green meadow, where the little shepherd-boy, only seven years old, had lain down in the shadow of the old and only tree there was. The swan, in its flight, kissed one of the leaves of the tree. The leaf fell into the boy's hand, and it was changed to three leaves, to ten—yes, to a whole book—and in it he read about all the wonders of nature, about his native language, about faith and knowledge. At night he laid the book under his head, that he might not forget what he had been reading. The wonderful book led him to the school-bench, and thence in search of knowledge. I have read his name among the names of learned men," said the Sunshine.

"The swan flew into the quiet, lonely forest, rested awhile on the dark, deep lake, where the water lilies grow; where the wild apples are to be found on the shore; where the cuckoo and wild pigeon have their homes.

"A poor woman was in the wood, gathering firewood branches that had fallen down, and dry sticks; she carried them in a bundle on her back, and in her arms she held her little child. She saw the golden swan, the bird of Fortune, rise from among the reeds on the shore. What was that that glittered? A golden egg, quite warm yet. She laid it in her bosom, and the warmth remained in it. Surely there was life in the egg! She heard a gentle picking inside of the shell, but mistook the sound, and thought it was her own heart that she heard beating.

"At home, in the poor cottage, she took out the egg; 'tick, tick,' it said, as if it had been a valuable gold watch; but that it was not, only an egg—a real, living egg. The egg cracked and opened, and a dear little baby-swan, all feathered as with purest gold, put out its little head; round its neck it had four rings, and as the poor woman had four boys—three at home, and the little one that she had had with her in the lonely wood—she understood at once that here was a ring for each boy; and just as she thought of that, the little gold-bird took flight. She kissed each ring, made each of the children kiss one of the rings, laid it next to the child's heart, then put it on his finger. I saw it all," said the Sunshine, "and I saw what followed.

"One of the boys was playing in a ditch, and took a lump of clay in his hand, turned and twisted and pressed it between his fingers, till it took shape, and was like Jason, who went in search of and found the golden fleece.

"The second boy ran out on the meadow, where the flowers stood—flowers of all imaginable colours; he gathered a handful, and squeezed them so tight that all the juice spurted into his eyes, and some of it wetted the ring. It cribbled and crawled in his thoughts, and in his hands, and after many a day, and many a year, people in the great city talked of the great painter.

"The third child held the ring so tight in his teeth, that it gave forth sound, an echo of the song in the depth of his heart. Thoughts and feelings rose in beautiful sounds; rose like singing swans; plunged, like swans, into the deep, deep sea. He became a great master, a great composer, of whom every country has the right to say, 'He was mine!'

"And the fourth little one was—yes, he was—the 'ugly duck' of the family; they said he had the pip, and must have pepper and butter, like the little sick chickens, and that he got; but of me he got a warm, sunny kiss," said the Sunshine. "He got ten kisses for one; he was a poet, and was buffeted and kissed, alternately, all his life. But he held what no one could take from him—the Ring of Fortune, from Dame Fortune's golden swan. His thoughts took wings, and flew up and away, like singing butterflies—the emblem of immortality!"

"That was a dreadfully long story," said the Wind.

"And O, how stupid and tiresome!" said the Rain. "Blow on me, please, that I may revive a little."

And the Wind blew, and the Sunshine said, "The swan of Fortune flew over the beautiful bay, where the fishermen had set their nets; the poorest of them wanted to get married, and marry he did. To him the swan brought a piece of amber; amber draws things toward it, and it drew hearts to the house. Amber is the most wonderful incense, and there came a soft perfume, as from a church; there came a sweet breath from out of beautiful nature, that God has made. They were so happy and grateful for their peaceful home, and content even in their poverty. Their life became a real Sunshine story!"

"I think we had better stop now," said the Wind, "the Sunshine has talked long enough, and I am dreadfully bored."

"And I also," said the Rain.

And what do we others, who have heard the story, say?

We say, "Now my story's done."

The Thistle's Experiences

Translated by Mrs. H. P. Paull

Belonging to the lordly manor-house was beautiful, well-kept garden, with rare trees and flowers; the guests of the proprietor declared their admiration of it; the people of the neighbourhood, from town and country, came on Sundays and holidays, and asked permission to see the garden; indeed, whole schools used to pay visits to it.

Outside the garden, by the palings at the road-side, stood a great mighty Thistle, which spread out in many directions from the root, so that it might have been called a thistle bush. Nobody looked at it, except the old Ass which drew the milk-maid's cart. This Ass used to stretch out his neck towards the Thistle, and say, "You are beautiful; I should like to eat you!" But his halter was not long enough to let him reach it and eat it.

There was great company at the manor-house—some very noble people from the capital; young pretty girls, and among them a young lady who came from a long distance. She had come from Scotland, and was of high birth, and was rich in land and in gold—a bride worth winning, said more than one of the young gentlemen; and their lady mothers said the same thing.

The young people amused themselves on the lawn, and played at ball; they wandered among the flowers, and each of the young girls broke off a flower, and fastened it in a young gentleman's buttonhole. But the young Scotch lady looked round, for a long time, in an undecided way. None of the flowers seemed to suit her taste. Then her eye glanced across the paling—outside stood the great thistle bush, with the reddish-blue, sturdy flowers; she saw them, she smiled, and asked the son of the house to pluck one for her.

"It is the flower of Scotland," she said. "It blooms in the scutcheon of my country. Give me yonder flower."

And he brought the fairest blossom, and pricked his fingers as completely as if it had grown on the sharpest rose bush.

She placed the thistle-flower in the buttonhole of the young man, and he felt himself highly honoured. Each of the other young gentlemen would willingly have given his own beautiful flower to have worn this one, presented by the fair hand of the Scottish maiden. And if the son of the house felt himself honoured, what were the feelings of the Thistle bush? It seemed to him as if dew and sunshine were streaming through him.

"I am something more than I knew of," said the Thistle to itself. "I suppose my right place is really inside the palings, and not outside. One is often strangely placed in this world; but now I have at least managed to get one of my people within the pale, and indeed into a buttonhole!"

The Thistle told this event to every blossom that unfolded itself, and not many days had gone by before the Thistle heard, not from men, not from the twittering of the birds, but from the air itself, which stores up the sounds, and carries them far around—out of the most retired walks of the garden, and out of the rooms of the house, in which doors and windows stood open, that the young gentleman who had received the thistle-flower from the hand of the fair Scottish maiden had also now received the heart and hand of the lady in question. They were a handsome pair—it was a good match.

"That match I made up!" said the Thistle; and he thought of the flower he had given for the buttonhole. Every flower that opened heard of this occurrence.

"I shall certainly be transplanted into the garden," thought the Thistle, and perhaps put into a pot, which crowds one in. "That is said to be the greatest of all honours."

And the Thistle pictured this to himself in such a lively manner, that at last he said, with full conviction, "I am to be transplanted into a pot."

Then he promised every little thistle flower which unfolded itself that it also should be put into a pot, and perhaps into a buttonhole, the highest honour that could be attained. But not one of them was put into a pot, much less into a buttonhole. They drank in the sunlight and the air; lived on the sunlight by day, and on the dew by night; bloomed—were visited by bees and hornets, who looked after the honey, the dowry of the flower, and they took the honey, and left the flower where it was.

"The thievish rabble!" said the Thistle. "If I could only stab every one of them! But I cannot."

The flowers hung their heads and faded; but after a time new ones came.

"You come in good time," said the Thistle. "I am expecting every moment to get across the fence."

A few innocent daisies, and a long thin dandelion, stood and listened in deep admiration, and believed everything they heard.

The old Ass of the milk-cart stood at the edge of the field-road, and glanced across at the blooming thistle bush; but his halter was too short, and he could not reach it.

And the Thistle thought so long of the thistle of Scotland, to whose family he said he belonged, that he fancied at last that he had come from Scotland, and that his parents had been put into the national escutcheon. That was a great thought; but, you see, a great thistle has a right to a great thought.

"One is often of so grand a family, that one may not know it," said the Nettle, who grew close by. He had a kind of idea that he might be made into cambric if he were rightly treated.

And the summer went by, and the autumn went by. The leaves fell from the trees, and the few flowers left had deeper colours and less scent. The gardener's boy sang in the garden, across the palings:

> "Up the hill, down the dale we wend,
> That is life, from beginning to end."

The young fir trees in the forest began to long for Christmas, but it was a long time to Christmas yet.

"Here I am standing yet!" said the Thistle. "It is as if nobody thought of me, and yet I managed the match. They were betrothed, and they have had their wedding; it is now a week ago. I won't take a single step-because I can't."

A few more weeks went by. The Thistle stood there with his last single flower large and full. This flower had shot up from near the roots; the wind blew cold over it, and the colours vanished, and the flower grew in size, and looked like a silvered sunflower.

One day the young pair, now man and wife, came into the garden. They went along by the paling, and the young wife looked across it.

"There's the great thistle still growing," she said. "It has no flowers now."

"Oh, yes, the ghost of the last one is there still," said he. And he pointed to the silvery remains of the flower, which looked like a flower themselves.

"It is pretty, certainly," she said. "Such an one must be carved on the frame of our picture."

And the young man had to climb across the palings again, and to break off the calyx of the thistle. It pricked his fingers, but then he had called it a ghost. And this thistle-calyx came into the garden, and into the house, and into the drawing room. There stood a picture— "Young Couple." A thistle-flower was painted in the buttonhole of the bridegroom. They spoke about this, and also about the thistle-flower they brought, the last thistle-flower, now gleaming like silver, whose picture was carved on the frame.

And the breeze carried what was spoken away, far away.

"What one can experience!" said the Thistle Bush. "My first born was put into a buttonhole, and my youngest has been put in a frame. Where shall I go?"

And the Ass stood by the road-side, and looked across at the Thistle.

"Come to me, my nibble darling!" said he. "I can't get across to you."

But the Thistle did not answer. He became more and more thoughtful—kept on thinking and thinking till near Christmas, and then a flower of thought came forth.

"If the children are only good, the parents do not mind standing outside the garden pale."

"That's an honourable thought," said the Sunbeam. "You shall also have a good place."

"In a pot or in a frame?" asked the Thistle.

"In a story," replied the Sunbeam.

The Candles

There was once a large wax light which was very proud of itself. "I was born in wax and made in a mould," it said; "I shine better and burn longer than other lights; my place is in the chandelier or the silver candlestick!"

"That must be delightful!" said the tallow candle. "I am only of tallow, only a dip, but I always console myself by remembering that at any rate, I am something more than a rush light; *that* is only dipped twice, while I am dipped four times to give me my thickness. I am quite satisfied; no doubt it is luckier to be born in wax and not in tallow, but one does not order one's place in the world. *They* get into the glass chandelier in the dining room. I stay in the kitchen, but the kitchen is a good place too; the whole house gets its food from there."

"But there is something more important than food," said the wax candle. "Society! To see people shine and to shine one's self! There will be a ball here this evening. Now you'll see that I and all my family will be sent for at once!"

The Candles

Scarcely had this been said when all the wax candles were sent for, but the tallow candle came along with them too. The lady of the house herself held it in her dainty hand and carried it into the kitchen; there stood a little boy with a basket which was filled with potatoes and apples. All this the good lady gave to the poor boy. "And there's a candle for you as well, my little friend!" said she; "your mother sits and works right through the night; she can make use of it!" The little daughter of the house stood close by and when she heard the words "right through the night," she said with hearty joy; "I shall be up all night, too; we are going to have a ball, and I shall have my large red bows on." How her face beamed! No wax candle can shine like those child-eyes! So the tallow candle was laid beneath the basket-lid and the boy went away with it.

"I wonder where I am going now! thought the candle. "I am on my way to poor people; perhaps I shall get a brass holder, while the wax-candle sits in silver and sees the most elegant people. How delightful it must be to shine before the grand folk. But it is my lot to be tallow, not wax!" And the candle came to the poor people, a widow with three children in a little low room right opposite the rich house. "God bless the good lady for what she gave!" said the mother, "'tis really a lovely light! It may last the whole night." And the candle was lit. "Fut-foi!" it spluttered. "That *was* a nasty-smelling sulphur match she lit me with! That's not the sort of thing they would be likely to offer the wax candle in the rich house over the way!"

There, too, candles were lit, they shone over the street; the carriages rumbled along with the smartly dressed ball guests and the music sounded. "Now they are beginning over there," said the tallow candle, and it thought of the little rich girl's beaming face, more beaming than all the wax lights. "I shall never see *that* sight again!"

Then the smallest of the children of that poor house came in; a little girl. She put her arms round the necks of her brother and sister; she had something very important to tell them, so important that it must be whispered: "This-evening-we-are-going-to-have-only fancy!-we-are-going to-have-*hot potatoes!*" And her face beamed with delight; the candle shone on it; it saw there a joy, a happiness, as great as in the rich house yonder where the little girl had said, "We are going to have a ball this evening, and I shall have my large red bows on!"

"Is it such a great thing to have hot potatoes!" thought the candle; "there's just as much joy among the little ones here as over there!" And it sneezed on the strength of it, that is to say it spluttered, which is as much as a tallow candle *can* do. The table was laid, the potatoes were eaten. Oh, how nice they tasted! It was quite a dinner, and every one got an apple in the bargain, and the smallest child of all said this little verse: "Thou God so good, my thanks to Thee; that thou has given food to me! Amen."

"Wasn't that nicely said, mother?" said the little one right afterward. "Do not be proud!" said the mother, "you should think about the good God who has fed you!"

The little ones were put to bed, were kissed and went straight off to sleep and the mother sat and sewed till late into the night. And the candles shone from the rich house over the way, and the music sounded. The stars twinkled over all the houses, as brightly on the poor as on the rich; there was no difference.

"That was a lovely evening after all!" said the tallow candle. And it thought of the pair of happy children, the one that was light by the wax candle and the one that was lit by the tallow candle!

Danish Popular Legends

Translated by Mrs. H. P. Paull

Denmark is rich in old legends of historical persons, churches, and manors, of hills, of fields, and bottomless moors; sayings from the days of the great plague, from the times of war and peace. The sayings live in books, and on the tongues of the people; they fly far about like a flock of birds, but still are as different from one another as the thrush is from the owl, as the wood-pigeon from the gull. Listen to me, and I will tell you some of them.

It happened one evening in days of yore, when the enemy were pillaging the Danish country, that a battle had been fought and won by the Danes, and many killed and wounded lay on the field of battle. One of these, an enemy, had lost both his legs by a shot. A Danish soldier, standing near by, had just taken out a bottle filled with beer, and was about to put it to his mouth, when the badly wounded man asked him for a drink. As he stopped to hand him the bottle, the enemy discharged his pistol at him, but the shot missed. The soldier drew his bottle back again, drank half of it, and gave the remaining half to his enemy, only saying. "You rascal, now you will only get half of it."

The king afterward hearing of this, granted the soldier and his descendants an armorial bearing of nobility, on which was painted a half-filled bottle, in memory of his deed.

There is a beautiful tradition worth telling about the churchbell of Farum. The parsonage stood close by the church. It was a dark night late in the fall, and the minister was sitting up at a late hour preparing his sabbath sermon, when he heard a slight, strange sound from the large church-bell. No wind was blowing, and the sound was inexplicable to him; he got up, took the keys and went into the church. As he entered the church the sound stopped suddenly, but he heard a faint sigh from above. "Who is there, disturbing the peace of the church?" he asked, in a loud voice. Footsteps were heard from the tower, and he saw in the passage-way a little boy advancing toward him.

"Be not angry!" said the child. "I slipped in here when the Vesper Service was rung; my mother is very sick!" and now the little boy could not say more for the tears that choked him. The minister patted him on the cheek, and encouraged him to be frank, and to tell him all about it.

"They say that my mother—my sweet, good mother—is going to die; but I knew that when one is sick unto death he may recover again and live, if in the middle of the night one dares enter the church, and scrape off a little rust from the large church-bell; that is a safeguard against death. Therefore I came here and hid myself until I heard the clock strike twelve. I was so afraid! I thought of all the dead ones, and of their coming into the church. I dared not look out; I read my Lord's Prayer, and scraped the rust off the bell."

"Come, my good child," said the minister; "our Lord will forsake neither thy mother nor thee." So they went together to the poor cottage, where the sick woman was lying. She slept quietly and soundly. Our Lord granted her life, and his blessings shone over her and her son.

There is a legend about a poor young fellow, Paul Vendelbo, who became a great and honoured man. He was born in Jutland, and had striven and studied so well that he got through the examination as student, but felt a still greater desire to become a soldier and stroll about in foreign countries. One day he walked with two young comrades, who were well off, along the ramparts of Copenhagen, and talked to them of his desire. He stopped suddenly, and looked up at the window of the Professor's house, where a young girl was seated, whose beauty had astonished him and the two others. Perceiving how he blushed, they said in joke, "Go in to her, Paul; and if you can get a voluntary kiss from her at the window, so that we can see it, we will give you money for travelling, that you may go abroad and see if fortune is more favourable for you there than at home."

Paul Vendelbo entered into the house, and knocked at the parlor door.

"My father is not at home," said the young girl.

"Do not be angry with me!" he answered, and the blood rushed up into his checks, "it is not your father I want!" And now he told her frankly and heartily his wish to try the world and acquire an honourable name; he told her of his two friends who were standing in the street, and had promised him money for travelling on the condition that she should voluntarily give him a kiss at the open, honest, and frank face, that her anger disappeared.

"It is not right for you to speak such words to a chaste maid," said she; "but you look so honest, I will not hinder your fortune!" An she led him to the window, and gave him a kiss. His friends kept their promise, and furnished him with money. He went into the service of the Czar, fought in the battle of Pultowa, and acquired nam and honour. Afterward, when Denmark needed him, he returned home, and became a mighty man of the army and of the king's council. One day he entered the Professor's plain room, and it was not just the Professor he wished to see this time either; it was again his daughter, Ingeborg Vinding, who gave him the kiss—the inauguration of his fortune. A fortnight after, Paul Vendelbo Loevenoern (Lioneagle) celebrated his wedding.

The enemy made once a great attack on the Danish island of Funen. One village only was spared; but this was also soon to be sacked and burnt. Two poor people lived in a low-studded house, in the outskirts of the town. It was a dark winter evening; the enemy was expected; and in their anxiety they took the Book of Psalms, and opened it to see if the psalm which they first met with could render them any aid or comfort. They opened the book, and turned to the psalm, "A mighty fortress is our God." Full of confidence, they sang it; and, strengthened in faith, they went to bed and slept well—kept by the Lord's guardianship. When they awoke in the morning it was quite dark in the room, and the daylight could not penetrate; they went to the door, but could not open it. Then they mounted the loft, got the trap-door open, and saw that it was broad daylight; but a heavy drift of snow had in the night fallen upon the whole house and hidden it from the enemies, who in the night-time had pillaged and burnt the town. Then they clasped their hands in thankfulness, and repeated the psalm, "A mighty fortress is our God!" The Lord had guarded them, and raised an intrenchment of snow around them.

From North Seeland there comes a gloomy incident that stirs the thoughts. The church of Roervig is situated far out toward the sand hills by the stormy Kattegat. One evening a large ship dropped anchor out there, and was presumed to be a Russian man-of-war. In the night a knocking was heard at the gate of the parsonage, and several armed and masked persons ordered the minister to put on his ecclesiastical gown and accompany them out to the church. They promised him good pay, but used menaces if he declined to go. He went with them. The church was lighted, unknown people were gathered, and all was in deep silence. Before the altar the bride and bridegroom were waiting, dressed in magnificent clothes, as if they were of high rank, but the bride was pale as a corpse. When the marriage ceremony was finished, a shot was heard, and the bride lay dead before the altar. They took the corpse, and all went away with it. The next morning the ship had weighed anchor. To this day nobody has been able to give any explanation of the event.

The minister who took part in it wrote down the whole event in his Bible, which is handed down in his family. The old church is still standing between the sand hills at the tossing Kattegat, and the story lives in writing and in memory.

I must tell you one more church legend. There lived in Denmark, on the island of Falster, a rich lady of rank, who had no children, and her family was about to die out. So she took a part of her riches, and built a magnificent church. When it was finished, and the altar-candles lighted, she stepped up to the altar-table and prayed on her knees to our Lord, that He would grant her, for her pious gift, a life upon the earth as long as her church was standing. Years went by. Her relations died, her old friends and acquaintances, and all the former servants of the manor were laid in their graves; but she, who made such an evil wish, did not die. Generation upon generation became strange to her, she did not approach anybody, and nobody approached her. She wasted away in a long dotage, and sat abandoned and alone; her senses were blunted, she was like a sleeping, but not like a dead person. Every Christmas Eve the life in her flashed up for a moment, and she got her voice again. Then she would order her people to put her in an oak coffin, and place it in the open burying-place of the church. The minister then would come on the Christmas night to her, in order to recceive her commands. She was laid in the coffin, and it was brought to the church. The minister came, as ordered, every Christmas night, through the choir up to the coffin, raised the cover for the old, wearied lady, who was lying there without rest.

"Is my church still standing?" she asked, with shivering voice; and upon the minister's answer, "It stands still!" she sighed profoundly and sorrowfully, and fell back again. The minister let the cover down, and came again the next Christmas night, and the next again, and still again the following. Now there is no stone of the church left upon another, no traces of the buried dead ones. A large whitethorn grows here on the field, with beautiful flowers every spring, as if it were the sign of the resurrection of life. It is said that it grows on the very spot where the coffin with the noble lady stood, where her dust became dust of earth.

There is an old popular saying that our Lord, when he expelled the fallen angels, let some of them drop down upon the hills, where they live still, and are called "Bjergfolk" (mountain goblins), or "Trolde" (imps). They are always afraid, and flee away when it thunders, which is for them a voice from heaven. Others fell down in the alder moors; they are called "Elverfolk" (alder folks), and among them the women are very handsome to look at, but not to trust; their backs are also hollow, like a dough-trough. Others fell down in old farms and houses; they became dwarfs and "Nisser" (elves). Sometimes they are wont to have intercourse with men, and a great many stories about them are related which are very strang.

Up in Jutland lived in a large hill such a mountain goblin, together with a great many other imps. One of his daughters was married to the smith of the village. The smith was a bad man, and beat his wife. At last she got tired of it, and one day as he was going again to beat her, she took a horse-shoe and broke it over him. She possessed such an immense strength, that she easily could have broken him in pieces too. He thought about it, and did not beat her any more. Yet it was rumored abroad, and her respect among the country-people was lost, and she was known as a "Trold barn" (an imp child). No one in the parish would have any intercourse with her. The mountain goblin got a hint of this; and one Sunday, when the smith and his wife, together with other parishioners, were standing in the church-yard, waiting for the minister, she looked out over the bay, where a fog was rising.

"Now comes father," she said, "and he is angry!" He came, and angry he was.

"Will you throw them to me, or will you rather do the catching?" he asked, and looked with greedy eyes upon the churchpeople.

"The catching!" she said; for she knew well that he would not be so gentle when they fell into his hands. And so the mountain goblin seized one after another, and flung them over the roof of the church, while the daughter, standing on the other side, caught them gently. From that time she got along very well with the parishioners; they were all afraid of the mountain goblin, and many of that kind were scattered about the country. The best they could do was to avoid quarreling with him, and rather turn his acquaintance to their profit. They knew well that the imps had big kettles filled with gold money, and it was certainly worth while to get a handful of it; but for that they had to be cunning and ingenious, like the peasant of whom I am going to tell you; as also of his boy, who was still more cunning.

The peasant had a hill on his field, which he would not leave uncultivated; he ploughed it, but the mountain goblin, who lived in the hill, came out and asked—

"How dare you plough upon my roof?"

"I did not know that it was yours!" said the peasant; "but it is not advantageous for any of us to let such a piece of Land lie uncultivated. Let me plough and sow! and then you reap the first year what is growing over the earth, and I what grows in the earth. Next year we will change." They agreed; and the peasant sowed the first year carrots, and the second corn. The mountain goblin got the top part of the carrots, and the roots of the corn. In this way they lived in harmony together.

But now it happened that there was to be a christening in the house of the peasant. The peasant was much embarrassed, as he could not well omit inviting the mountain goblin, with whom he lived in good accord; but if the imp accepted his invitation, the peasant would fall into bad repute with the minister and the other folk of the parish. Cunning as the peasant ordinarily was, this time he could not find out how to act. He spoke about it to his pig-boy, who was the more cunning of the two.

"I will help you!" said the boy; and taking a large bag, he went out to the hill of the mountain goblin; he knocked, and was let in. Then he said that he came to invite him to the christening. The mountain goblin accepted the invitation, and promised to come.

"I must give a christening-present, I suppose; mustn't I?"

"They usually do," said the boy, and opened the bag. The imp poured money into it.

"Is that sufficient?" The boy lifted the bag.

"Most people give as much!" Then all the money in the large money kettle was poured into the bag.

"Nobody gives more—most less."

"Let me know, now," said the mountain goblin, "the great guests you are expecting."

"Three priests and one bishop," said the boy.

"That is fine; but such gentlemen look only for eating and drinking—they don't care about me. Who else comes!"—"Mother Mary is expected!"—"Hm, hm! but I think there will always be a little place for me behind the stove! Well, and then?"

"Well, then comes 'our Lord.'"—"Hm, hm, hm! that was mighty! but such highly distinguished guests usually come late and go away early. I shall therefore, while they are in, slink away a little. What sort of music shall you have?" "Drum-music!" said the boy; "our Father has ordered heavy thundering, after which we shall dance! drum-music it shall be."

"O, is it not dreadul!" cried the mountain goblin. "Thank your master for the invitation, but I would rather stay at home. Did he not know, then, that thundering and drum are to me, and my whole race, a horror? Once, in my younger days, going out to take a walk, the thunder began to drum, and I got one of the drumsticks over my thigh-bone so that it cracked. I will not have more of that kind of music! Give my thanks and my greetings."

And the boy took the bag on his back, and brought his master the great riches, and the imp's friendly greetings.

We have many legends of this sort, but those we have told ought to be enough for today!

The Great Sea-Serpent

There was a little fish—a salt-water fish—of good family: I don't recall the name—you will have to get that from the learned people. This little fish had eighteen hundred brothers and sisters all just as old as he; they did not know their father and mother, and were obliged to look out for themselves at the very beginning, and swim round, but that was great sport. They had water enough to drink, the entire ocean; they thought nothing about their food, it came when they wanted it. Each did as it pleased, each was to make out its own story—ay, rather none of them thought at all about that. The sun shone down on the water that was light about them, so clear was it. It was a world with the strangest creatures, and some very horrid and big, with great gaping mouths that could gulp down all the eighteen hundred brothers and sisters, but neither did they think of that, for none of them as yet had been swallowed. The small ones swam side by side close together, as herrings and mackerel swim. But as they were swimming their prettiest in the water and thinking of nothing, there sank with prodigious noise, from above, right down through them, a long heavy thing that looked as if it never would come to an end; it stretched out farther and farther, and every one of the little fishes that scampered off was either crushed or got a crack that it could not stand. All the little fishes, and the great ones with them, from the level of the sea to the bottom, were thrown into a panic. The great horrid thing sank deeper and deeper, and grew longer and longer, miles and miles long. The fishes and snails, everything that swims, or creeps, or is driven by the current, saw this fearful thing, this enormous incomprehensible sea-eel which had come down upon them in this fashion.

What was the thing, anyway? ah, we know; it was the great interminable telegraph cable that people were laying between Europe and America.

There was a confusion and commotion amongst all the rightful occupants of the sea where the cable was laid. The flying fishes shot up above the surface as high as they could fling themselves; the blow-fish took a leap an entire gunshot in length over the water, for it can do that; the other fish made for the bottom of the sea, and went down with such haste that they reached it long before the telegraph was seen or known about down there; they poured in on the cod and flounders that lived peaceably at the bottom of the sea and ate their neighbours. One or two of the sea-anemones were so agitated that they threw up their stomachs, but they lived after it just the same, for they can do that. A good many lobsters and crabs got out of their excellent shells, and were obliged to wait for their bones to grow back again.

In all this fright and confusion, the eighteen hundred brethren and sisters became separated, and never agan met, or ever knew each other after that; only some ten of them remain ed still in the same place, and so in a few hours they got over the first fright and began to be curious about the affair. They looked about them, they looked up and they looked down, and down in the depths they fancied they saw the fearful thing that had scared them—yes, had scared all, great and small, lying on the bottom of the sea, as far as their eyes could reach; it was quite thin, but they did not know how thick it might be able to make itself, or how strong it was; it lay very quiet, but then that might be a part of its cunning, they thought.

"Let it lie; it does not come near us!" said the most cautious of the little fishes; but the smallest one of all would not give up trying to find out what the thing could be. It had come down from above, so it was up above that one could best find out about it. So they swam up to the surface. It was perfectly still. They met a dolphin there. The dolphin is a sprightly fellow that can turn somersaults on the water, and it has eyes to see with, so iht must have seen this and known all about it. They asked him, but he had only been thinking about himself and his somersaults, he'd seen nothing, had no answer for them, and only looked high and mighty.

Then they turned to the seal, which was just plunging in; it was more civil, for all that it eats small fish; but today it had had enough. It knew little more than the dolphin.

"Many a night have I lain upon a wet stone and looked far into the country, miles away from here; there are crafty creatures called in their speech men-folk. They plot against us, but usually we slip away from them; that I know well, and the sea-eel too, that you are asking about, he knows it. He has been under their sway, up there on the earth, time out of mind, and it was from there that they were carrying him off on a ship to a distant land. I saw what a trouble they had, Shut they could manage him, because he had become weak on the earth. They laid him in coils and circles. I heard how he ringled and rangled when they laid him down and when he slipped away from them out here. They held on to him with all their might—ever so many hands had hold of him, but he kept slipping away from them down to the bottom; there he is lying now—till further notice, I rather think."

"He is quite thin," said the small fishes.

"They have starved him," said the seal, "but he will soon come to himself, and get his old size and corpulence again. I suppose he is the great sea-serpent that men are so afraid of and talk so much about. I never saw him before, and never believed in a sea-serpent; now I do. I believe he is the sea-serpent," and with that down went the seal.

"How much he knew! how he talked!" said the small fishes; "I never was so wise before; if it only isn't all an untruth."

"We can, anyway, swim down and see for ourselves," said the littlest fish; "on the way we can hear what the others think about it."

"I wouldn't make a stroke with my fins to get at something to know," said the others, and turned away.

"But I would!" said the littlest fellow, and put off down into deep water; but it was a good distance from the place where "the long thing that sank" lay. The little fish looked and hunted on all sides down in tne deep water. Never before had it imagined the world to be so big. The herrings went in great shoals, shining like a mighty ribbon of silver; the mackerel followed after, and looked even finer. There were fishes there of all fashions and marked with every possible colour: jelly-fish, like half-transparent flowers, borne along by the currents. Great plants grew up from the floor of the ocean; grass, fathoms long, and palm-like trees, every leaf tenanted by shining shell-fish.

At last the little fish spied a long dark streak away down, and made his way toward it, but it was neither fish nor cable: it was the gunwale of a sunken vessel, which above and below the deck was broken in two by the force of the sea. The little fish swam into the cabin, where the people who perished when the vessel sank were all washed away, except two: a young woman lay there stretched out, with her little child in her arms. They seemed to be sleeping. The little fish was quite frightened, for it did not know that they never again could waken. Sea-weed hung like a net-work of foliage over the gun—wale above the two beautiful bodies of mother and babe. it was so quiet, so solitary: the little fish scampered away as fast as it could, out where the water was bright and clear, and there were fishes to see. It had not gone far before it met a whale, fearfully big.

"Don't swallow me!" cried the little fish; "I am not even to be tasted, I am so small. and it is a great comfort to me to live."

"What are you doing away down here, where your kind never come?" asked the whale.

So then the little fish told about the astonishingly long eel, or whatever the thing was, that had sunk down from above and produced such a panic amongst all the other creatures in the sea.

"Ho, ho!" said the whale, and he drew in such a rush of water that he was ready to make a prodigious spout when he came to the surface for a breath. "Ho, ho! so that was the thing that tickled me on the back when I was turning round. I thought it was a ship's mast, that I could break up into clothes-pins. But it was not here that it was;

no, a good deal farther out lies the thing. I'll go with you and look for it, for I have nothing else to do;" and so it swam off, and the little fish behind it, not too near, because there was a tearing stream, as it were, in the wake of the whale.

They met a shark and an old saw-fish; they, too, had heard of the famous sea-eel, so long and so thin; they had not seen it, but now they would.

"I'll go with you," said the shark, who was on the same road; "if the great sea-serpent is no thicker than a cable, then I can bite through it in one bite," and he opened his mouth and showed his six rows of teeth—"I can bite dents in a ship's anchor, and certainly can bite off the shank."

"There it is!" said the great whale; "I see him." He thought he saw better than the others. "See how it rises, how it bends and bows and curves!"

But it was not the sea-serpent, but an extraordinarily great eel, ever so many ells long, that drew near.

"Why, I have seen him before!" said the saw-fish. "He never has made a hullabaloo in the sea or frightened any big fish out of his wits." And so they talked to him of the new eel, and asked him if he would go with them on their voyage of discovery.

"If that eel is longer than I am," said the sea-eel, "there will be something disagreeable happening."

"Ay, that there will," said the others; "there are enough of us not to tolerate him!" and so they shot ahead. But then there came right in their way a great monster, bigger than all of them put together; it looked like a floating island, that could not stop itself. It was a venerable whale. Its head was grown over with sea-weed, its back covered with barnacles, and such innumerable oysters and mussels, that its black skin was altogether whitened.

"Come with us, old fellow!" said they. "Here is a new fish come, and we won't stand it."

"I would rather lie where I am lying," said the whale. "Leave me alone; leave me alone. O ah, O ah! I suffer from a dreadful disease! My only relief is to get up toward the surface and get my back up higher; then the great sea-fowl can come and pick at me. That feels so good! only when they do not drive their beaks in too far; sometimes they go in too deep, quite into my blubber. You can see now how a complete skeleton of a fowl is fixed in my back; she struck her claws in too deep, and could not get them out when I went down to the bottom. And now the little fishes have picked at her. See how she looks, and how I look. I am all diseased!"

"That is all imagination!" said the shark. "I am never sick. No fish is ever sick."

"Pardon me," said the whale. "The eel suffers from headache, the carp has the smallpox, and we all have intestinal worms."

"Nonsense!" said the shark, and refused to hear any further, and the others also would rather not; they had something else to attend to.

At last they came to the place where the telegraph cable lay. It has a pretty long bed on the floor of the sea from Europe to America, over sand-banks and sea-mud, rocky ground and weedy places, entire forests of coral. The currents down there, too, change, whirlpools eddy, and fishes swarm in greater masses than the countless flocks of birds that men see when birds of passage take their flight. There is a stir, a splashing there, a humming and rushing; the rushing still haunts a little the great empty conch-shells when we hold them to our ears.

"There lies the fellow!" cried all the great fishes and the little one with them. They saw the cable, the beginning and end of which vanished beyond the reach of their eyes. Sponges and polyps swayed from the ground, rose and fell over it, so that now it was hidden, now came to view. Sea-porcupines, snails, and worms moved over it. Gigantic crabs, that had a complete fringe of creeping things, stalked about it. Dark sea-anemones, or whatever the creature is called that eats with its entire body, lay beside it and smelled of the new creature that had stretched itself on the bottom of the sea. Flounders and codfish turned over in the water so as to get an idea about it from all sides. The star-fish, that always bores down into the mud and can keep its eyes outside, lay and stared to see what was to come of all this bustle.

The telegraph cable lay without stirring, but life and thought were in it. Human thought went through it. "The thing is crafty," said the whale; "it is able to strike me in the stomach, and that is my weak point."

"Let us grope along," said the polyps. "I have long arms and limber fingers; I have been moving by the side of it; now I'll go a little faster," and so it stretched its most flexible, longest arms down to the cable and round about it. "It has no scales!" said the polyps; "it has no skin at all. I do believe it never feeds its own young."

The sea-eel laid itself by the side of the telegraph cable and stretched out as far as it could. "The thing is longer than I am," it said; "but it is not length that does anything; one must have skin, stomach, and flexibility."

The whale dove down deeper than it ever had been. "Art thou fish or art thou plant?" it asked, "or art thou only some piece of work made up above that cannot thrive down here amongst us?"

The telegraph cable did not answer; it has no power for that. Yet thoughts go through it, men's thoughts, that rush in one second miles upon miles from land to land.

"Will you answer, or will you take a crack?" asked the fierce shark, and all the other great fishes asked the same thing.

The cable did not stir, but it had its private thought, and such a one it had a right to have when it was full of thoughts. "Let them only give me a crack! then I shall be hauled up and be myself again; that has happened to others of my race in shallower waters." So it gave no answer; it had something else to attend to; it telegraphed and lay in its lawful place at the bottom of the ocean.

Up above, the sun now went down, as men say. It became like flaming fire, and all the clouds glowed with fiery colour, each more splendid than the other. "Now we shall get the red light," said the polyps, "and can see the thing better, if need be."

"At it! at it!" shouted the shark. "At it! at it!" said the sword-fish and the whale and the eel. They rushed forward, the shark foremost. But just as it was about to grip the wire, the sword-fish, out of pure politeness, ran his saw right into the back of the shark. It was a great mistake, and the shark lost all his strength for biting. There was a hubbub down in the mud. Great fishes and small, sea-anemones and snails rushed at one another, ate each other, mashed and squeezed in. The cable lay quietly and attended to its affairs, and that one ought to do.

The dark night brooded over them, but the ocean s millions upon millions of living creatures lighted it; craw-fish, not so big as a pin-head, gave out light. Some were so small that it took a thousand to make one pin-head, and yet they gave light. It certainly is wonderful, but that's the way it is.

These sea creatures looked at the telegraph wire. "What is that thing?" they asked, "and what isn't it?" Ay, that was the question.

Then there came an old sea-cow. Folks on the earth call its kind a mermaid, or else a merman. This was a she, had a tail and two short arms to splash with, hanging breasts, and sea-weed and sponges on her head, and that was what she was proud of.

"Will you have the society of intelligent people?" said she. "I'm the only one down here that can give it. But I ask in return for it perfectly secure pasturage on the bottom of the sea for me and mine. I am a fish, as you see, and I am also an amphibious animal—with practice. I am the wisest cow in the sea. I know about everything that goes on down here, and all that goes on above. That thing you are pondering over is from above, and whatever plumps down from up there is either dead or comes to be dead and powerless; let it lie there for what it is; it's only some invention of man."

"Now I think there is something more to it," said the little fish.

"Hold your tongue, mackerel!" said the great sea-cow.

"Stickleback!" said the rest, and that was even more insulting.

And the sea-cow explained to them that this terrible thing, which, to be sure, had not given out a single mutter, was only some invention from the dry land. And it delivered a little oration upon the rottenness of men.

"They want to get hold of us." said she. "That's all they live for. They stretch nets for us, and come with bait on a hook to catch us. That thing there is some kind of big string which they think we are going to bite at. They are such stupids! We are not. Only do not touch it, and it will shrivel up and all turn to dust and mud. Everything that comes down from up there is full of cracks and breaks—it's good for nothing."

"Good for nothing!" said all the creatures in the sea, and held fast to the sea-cow's opinion, so as to have an opinion. The little fish had its own thoughts. "That exceedingly long, thin serpent is perhaps the most wonderful fish in the ocean. I have a feeling it is."

"The very most wonderful," say we human folks, and say it with knowledge and assurance. It is the great sea-serpent, long ago the theme of song and story. It was born and nourished and sprang forth from men's cunning and was laid upon the bottom of the sea, stretching from the Eastern to the Western land, bearing messages, quick as light flashes to our earth. It grows in might and in length, grows year by year through all seas, round the world, beneath the stormy waves and the lucid waters, where the skipper looks down as if he sailed through the transparent air, and sees the swarming fish, brilliant fireworks of colour. Down, far down, stretches the serpent, Midgard's snake, that bites its own tail as it encircles the earth. Fish and shell beat upon it with their heads—they understand not the thing—it is from above. Men's thoughts in all languages course through it noiselessly. "The serpent of science for good and evil, Midgard's snake, the most wonderful of all the ocean's wonders, our—GREAT SEA-SERPENT!"

The Gardener and the Manor

Translated by Mrs. H. P. Paull

About one Danish mile from the capital stood an old manor-house, with thick walls, towers, and pointed gable-ends. Here lived, but only in the summer-season, a rich and courtly family. This manor-house was the best and the most beautiful of all the houses they owned. It looked outside as if it had just been cast in a foundry, and within it was comfort itself. The family arms were carved in stone over the door; beautiful roses twined about the arms and the balcony; a grass-plot extended before the house with red-thorn and white-thorn, and many rare flowers grew even outside the conservatory. The manor kept also a very skillful gardener. It was a real pleasure to see the flower-garden, the orchard, and the kitchen-garden. There was still to be seen a portion of the manor's original garden, a few box-tree hedges cut in shape of crowns and pyramids, and behind these two mighty old trees almost always without leaves. One might almost think that a storm or water-spout had scattered great lumps of manure on their branches, but each lump was a bird's-nest. A swarm of rooks and crows from time immemorial had built their nests here. It was a townful of birds, and the birds were the manorial lords here. They did not care for the proprietors, the manor's oldest family branch, nor for the present owner of the manor—these were nothing to them; but they bore with the wandering creatures below them, notwithstanding that once in a while they shot with guns in a way that made the birds' back-bones shiver, and made every bird fly up, crying "Rak, Rak!"

The gardener very often explained to the master the necessity of felling the old trees, as they did not look well, and by taking them away they would probably also get rid of the screaming birds, which would seek another place. But he never could be induced either to give up the trees or the swarm of birds the manor could not spare them, as they were relics of the good old times, that ought always to be kept in remembrance.

"The trees are the birds' heritage by this time!" said the master. "So let them keep them, my good Larsen." Larsen was the gardener's name, but that is of very little consequence in this story. "Haven't you room enough to work in, little Larsen? Have you not the flower-garden, the green-houses, the orchard and the kitchen-garden!" He cared for them, he kept them in order and cultivated them with zeal and ability, and the family knew it; but they did not conceal from him that they often tasted fruits and saw flowers in other houses that surpassed what he had in his garden, and that was a sore trial to the gardener, who always wished to do the best, and really did the best he could. He was good-hearted, and a faithful servant.

The owner sent one day for him, and told him kindly that the day before, at a party given by some friends of rank, they had eaten apples and pears which were so juicy and well-flavored that all the guests had loudly expressed their admiration. To be sure, they were not native fruits, but they ought by all means to be introduced here, and to be acclimatized if possible. They learned that the frtiit was bought of one of the first fruit-dealers in the city, and the gardener was to ride to town and find out about where they came from, and then order some slips for grafting. The gardener was very well acquainted with the dealer, because he was the very person to whom he sold the fruit that grew in the manor-garden, beyond what was needed by the family. So the gardener went to town and asked the fruit-dealer where he had found those apples and pears that were praised so highly.

"They are from your own garden," said the fruit-dealer, and he showed him, both the apples and pears, which he recognized. Now, how happy the gardener felt! He hastened back to his master, and told him that the apples and pears were all from his own garden. But he would not believe it.

"It cannot be possible, Larsen. Can you get a written certificate of that from the fruit-dealer?" And that he could; and brought him a written certificate.

"That is certainly wonderful!" said the family.

And now every day were set on the table great dishes filled with beautiful apples and pears from their own garden; bushels and barrels of these fruits were sent to friends in the city and country, nay, were even sent abroad. It was exceedifigly pleasant; but when they talked with the gardener they said that the last two seasons had been remarkably favourable for fruits, and that fruits had done well all over the country.

Some time passed. The family were at dinner at court. The next day the gardener was sent for. They had eaten melons at the royal table which they found very juicy and well-flavored; they came from his Majesty's green-house. "You must go and see the court-gardener, and let him give you some seeds of those melons."

"But the gardener at the court got his melon-seeds from us," said the gardener, highly delighted.

"But then that man understands how to bring the fruit to a higher perfection," was the answer. "Each particular melon was delicious."

"Well; then, I really may feel proud," said the gardener. "I must tell your lordship that the gardener at the court did not succeed very well with his melons this year, and so, seeing how beautiful ours looked, he tasted them and ordered from me three of them for the castle."

"Larsen, do not pretend to say that those were melons from our garden."

"Really, I dare say as much," said the gardener, who went to the court-gardener and got from him a written certificate to the effect that the melons on the royal. table were from the manor. That was certainly a great surprise to the family, and they did not keep the story to themselves. Melon-seeds were sent far and wide, in the same way as had been done with the slips, which they were now hearing had begun to take, and to bear fruit of an excellent kind. The fruit was named after the manor, and the name was written in English, German, and French.

This was something they never had dreamed of.

"We are afraid that the gardener will come to think too much of himself," said they; but he looked on it in another way: what he wished was to get the reputation of being one of the best gardeners in the country, and to produce every year something exquisite out of all sorts of garden stuff, and that he did. But he often had to hear that the fruits which he first brought, the apples and pears, were after all the best. All other kinds of fruits were inferior to these. The melons, too, were very good, but they belonged to quite another species. His strawberries were very excellent, but by no means better than many others; and when it happened one year that his radishes did not succeed, they only spoke of them, and not of other good things he had made succeed.

It really seemed as if the family felt some relief in saying "It won't turn out well this year, little Larsen!" They seemed quite glad when they could say "It won't turn out well!"

The gardener used always twice a week to bring them fresh flowers, tastefully arranged, and the colours by his arrangements were brought out in stronger light.

"You have good taste, Larsen," said the owner, "but that is a gift from our Lord, not from yourself."

One day the gardener brought a great crystal vase with a floating leaf of a white water lily, upon which was laid, with its long thick stalk descending into the water, a sparkling blue flower as large as a sunflower.

"The sacred lotos of Hindustan!" exclaimed the family. They had never seen such a flower; it was placed every day in the sunshine, and in the evening under artificial light. Every one who saw it found it wonderfully beautiful and rare; and that said the most noble young lady in the country, the wise and kind-hearted princess. The lord of the manor deemed it an honour to present her with the flower, and the princess took it with her to the castle. Now the master of the house went down to the garden to pluck another flower of the same sort, but he could not find any. So he sent for the gardener, and asked him where he kept the blue lotos. "I have been looking for it in vain," said he. "I went into the conservatory, and round about the flower-garden."

"No, it is not there!" said the gardener. "It is nothing else than a common flower from the kitchen-garden, but do you not find it beautiful? It looks as if it was the blue cactus, and yet it is only a kitchen-herb. It is the flower of the artichoke!"

"You should have told us that at the time!" said the master. "We supposed of course that it was a strange and rare flower. You have made us ridiculous in the eyes of the young princess! She saw the flower in our house and thought it beautiful. She did not know the flower, and she is versed in botany, too, but then that has nothing to do with kitchen-herbs. How could you take it into your head, my good Larsen, to put such a flower up in our drawing room? It makes us ridiculous."

And the magnificent blue flower from the kitchen-garden was turned out of the drawing room, which was not at all the place for it. The master made his apology to the princess, telling her that it was only a kitchen-herb which the gardener had taken into his head to exhibit, but that he had been well reprimanded for it.

"That was a pity," said the princess, "for he has really opened our eyes to see the beauty of a flower in a place where we should not have thought of looking for it. Our gardener shall every day, as long as the artichoke is in bloom, bring one of them up into the drawing room."

Then the master told his gardener that he might again bring them a fresh artichoke-flower. "It is, after all, a very nice flower," said he, "and a truly remarkable one." And so the gardener was praised again. "Larsen likes that," said the master; "he is a spoiled child."

In the autumn there came up a great gale, which increased so violently in the night that. several large trees in the outskirts of the wood were torn up by the roots; and to the great grief of the household, but to the gardener's delight, the two big trees blew down, with all their birds' nests on them. In the manor-house they heard during the storm the screaming of rooks and crows, beating their wings against the windows.

The Gardener and the Manor

"Now I suppose you are happy, Larsen," said the master: "the storm has felled the trees, and the birds have gone off to the woods; there is nothing left from the good old days; it is all gone, and we are very sorry for it."

The gardener said nothing, but he thought of what he long had turned over in his mind, how he could make that pretty sunny spot very useful, so that it could become an ornament to the garden and a pride to the family. The great trees which had been blown down had shattered the venerable hedge of box, that was cut into fanciful shapes.

Here he set out a multitude of plants that were not to be seen in other gardens. He made an earthen wall, on which he planted all sorts of native flowers from the fields and woods. What no other gardener had ever thought of planting in the manor-garden he planted, giving each its appropriate soil, and the plants were in sunlight or shadow according as each species required. He cared tenderly for them, and they grew up finely. The juniper-tree from the heaths of Jutland rose in shape and colour like the Italian cypress; the shining, thorny Christ-thorn, as green in the winter's cold as in the summer's sun, was splendid to see. In the foreground grew ferns of various species: some of them looked as if they were children of the palm-tree; others, as if they were parents of the pretty plants called "Venus's golden locks" or "Maiden-hair." Here stood the despised burdock, which is so beautiful in its freshness that it looks well even in a bouquet. The burdock stood in a dry place, but below in the moist soil grew the colt's-foot, also a despised plant, but yet most picturesque, with its tall stem and large leaf. Like a candelabrum with a multitude of branches six feet high, and with flower over against flower, rose the mullein, a mere field plant. Here stood the woodroof and the lily of the valley, the wild calla and the fine three-leaved wood-sorrel. It was a wonder to see all this beauty!

In the front grew in rows very small peartrees from French soil, trained on wires. By plenty of sun and good care they soon bore as juicy fruits as in their own country. Instead of the two old leafless trees was placed a tall flag-staff, where the flag of Dannebrog was displayed; and near by stood another pole, where the hop-tendril in summer or harvest-time wound its fragrant flowers; but in winter-time, after ancient custom, oat-sheaves were fastened to it, that the birds of the air might find here a good meal in the happy Christmas-time.

"Our good Larsen is growing sentimental as he grows old," said the family; "but he is faithful, and quite attached to us."

In one of the illustrated papers there was a picture at New Year's of the old manor, with the flag-staff and the oat-sheaves for the birds of the air, and the paper said that the old manor had preserved that beautiful old custom, and deserved great credit for it.

"They beat the drum for all Larsen's doings," said the family. "He is a lucky fellow, and we may almost be proud of having such a man in our service."

But they were not a bit proud of it. They were very well aware that they were the lords of the manor; they could give Larsen warning, in fact, but they did not. They were good people, and fortunate it is for every Mr. Larsen that there are so many good people like them.

Yes, that is the story of the gardener and the manor. Now you may think a little about it.

The Gate Key

Every key has a history, and there are many kinds of keys—a chamberlain's key, a watch key, Saint Peter's key. We could tell you about all the keys; but now we will only tell about the councilor's gate key.

It had come into being at a locksmith's, but it might well have believed it had been made by a blacksmith, the way the man had worked on it with hammer and file. It was too large for one's trouser pocket, so it had to be put into the overcoat pocket. There it often lay in utter darkness; yet it had its own special hanging place on the wall, beside a childhood silhouette of the Councilor, in which he looked like a dumpling dressed in a frilled shirt.

It is said that every human being acquires in his character and conduct something from the astrological sign under which he has been born, such as the Bull, the Virgin, or Scorpion, as they are called in the almanacs. The Councilor's wife never mentioned the names of any of these; she said that her husband was born under the sign of the "Wheelbarrow," for he always had to be pushed on.

His father had pushed him into an office; his mother had pushed him into matrimony; and his wife had pushed him on to become a councilor; the latter fact, however, she did not mention, being a good, sensible sort of woman who kept quiet in the right place and spoke and pushed in the right place.

He was now along in years—"well proportioned," as he said himself—a well-read man, good-natured, and "key wise" as well, which is something we shall better understand later. He was always in a good humour, loved all mankind, and liked to talk to everybody. If he went into the city, it was difficult to get him home again when his wife was not with him to push him along. He simply had to talk to every acquaintance he met; he had a lot of acquaintances, and this often made him late for dinner. Mrs. Councilor would sit at the window and watch for him. "Here he comes," she would say to the maid; "put the pot on the fire. Now he has stopped to speak to somebody, so take the pot off, or the food will be cooked too much. Now he is finally coming, so put the pot on again!"

But then he wouldn't come, after all. He would stand right under the windows of the house and nod up to her, and if an acquaintance happened to come by then, he could not keep from saying a few words to him; if while he was talking to this one, another one came by, he would take hold of the first by the buttonhole, clasp the other's hand, and shout to a third who wanted to pass by.

This was a heavy trial for the patience of the Councilor's wife. "Councilor! Councilor!" she would shout. "Yes, indeed, that man was born under the sign of the 'Wheelbarrow'; he won't move unless he is being pushed."

He was very fond of visiting bookshops and looking at books and periodicals. He would give his bookseller a small amount of money for the privilege of reading the new books at home, which meant he had permission to cut the leaves of the books along the side but not across the top, for then they could not be sold as new. He was a living newspaper, but a harmless one, and knew everything about engagements, weddings, and funerals, book talk and town talk. Yes, and he even gave out mysterious hints regarding matters no one else knew anything about. This mysterious information came from the gate key.

The Councilor and his wife had lived in their own house since young and newly married, and they'd had that very same gate key since then; but in those days they hadn't yet come to know of its unusual powers, and not until much later had they learned of these.

It was at the time of King Frederick VI. Copenhagen had no gas then; it had only train-oil lamps; it had no Tivoli Gardens, no Casino Theater, no streetcars, and no railways. It had very few public amusements, compared with what it now has. On Sundays one would go for a walk, out beyond the city gates, to the Assistants' Churchyard, read the inscriptions on the graves, sit down in the grass, eat from one's food basket, and drink a glass of schnapps; or one would go to Frederiksberg, where in front of the palace military music was played; and many people would go to see the royal family rowing about in the small, narrow canals of the park, with old King himself steering the boat, and he and the Queen greeting everyone, without distinction of rank. Well-to-do families from the city would come to this place and drink their afternoon tea. They could get hot water at a small farmhouse in the field outside the park, but they had to bring their own tea service along.

One sunny Sunday afternoon the Councilor and his wife went out to the park, the servant girl walking in front with the tea service, a basket of food, and a "sip of Spendrup's Liqueur."

"Bring the gate key," Mrs. Councilor had said, "so we can get in by ourselves when we return; you know, they lock the gate here at nightfall, and the bell cord was broken this morning! It will be late before we get home! After we've been in Frederiksberg Park, we are going to the Casorti's theater at Vesterbro to see the pantomime, Harlequin, Chief of the Thrashers. You see them come down in a cloud; it costs two kroner a person."

And so they went to Frederiksberg, heard the music, saw the royal barges with their waving banners, saw the old King and the white swans. After drinking some very good tea, they hurried away; yet they did not arrive at the theater on time.

The rope-dance act was finished, the dance on stilts was finished, and the pantomime had started; as always, they were too late, and that was the Councilor's fault; every moment on the road, he had stopped to speak to an acquaintance. Within the theater he also found several good friends, and when the performance was over, he and his wife were obliged to accompany a family home at Vesterbro, to enjoy a glass of punch; they would stop for only ten minutes. But this was extended to a whole hour. They talked and talked. Especially entertaining was a Swedish baron, or, perhaps, he was German, for the Councilor hadn't quite caught which—but, on the other hand, the trick with the key that the baron taught him he caught and always remembered. This trick was extraordinarily interesting! He could get the key to answer everything that one asked it, even questions pertaining to the most secret matters. The Councilor's gate key was particularly suitable for performing this trick; its bit was heavy, and this part had to hang downward. The baron let the handle of the key rest on the forefinger of his right hand. There it hung loosely and lightly, and every pulsebeat in his finger could put it into motion and make it swing; and if this failed to happen, the baron understood how unnoticeably to make it turn as he wished. Every turn denoted a letter of the alphabet, and as many letters as desired, from A on through the alphabet, could be indicated by the key. When the first letter of a word was revealed, the key would turn to the opposite side; then the next letter would be sought, and in that manner one got whole words, sentences, and answers to questions. It was all a fake, but at any rate provided amusement; this was the Councilor's first thought, but he did not retain it; he became very engrossed in the key.

"Husband! Husband!" cried Mrs. Councilor. "The Westgate closes at twelve o'clock! We won't get through; we have only a quarter of an hour in which to hurry there."

They had to hurry indeed; several persons who were going into the city soon got ahead of them. They finally approached the outside guardhouse as the clock was striking twelve and the gates were being slammed shut. A number of people were locked out, and among these were the Councilor and his wife, with their servant girl, tea service, and empty food basket. Some stood there greatly frightened, while others were very annoyed, each reacting in his own manner. What could be done? Fortunately, an ordinance had been passed of late that one of the city gates, the Northgate, should not be locked at night, and there pedestrians were allowed to slip through the guardhouse into the city.

The road to the Northgate was by no means short, but the weather was fine, the sky bright with starlight and shooting stars; the frogs were croaking in the ditches and ponds. The party began singing and sang one song after another, but the Councilor did not sing; nor did he look up at the stars or even look at his own feet. He then fell down at the edge of the ditch, the full length of his body alongside it. One might have thought that he had had too much to drink; but it was not the punch, it was the key, that had gone to his head, and kept on turning there. They finally reached the Northgate guardhouse, slipped across the bridge and into the city.

"Now I am happy again," said the Councilor's wife. "Here's our gate."

"But where is the gate key," said the Councilor. It was neither in the back pocket nor in the side pocket.

"Good gracious!" cried the Councilor's wife. "Haven't you got the key? You must have lost it after letting the Baron use it for the key trick. How will we get in now? You know the bell cord was broken this morning, and the watchman doesn't have a key to our home. We are in a hopeless situation!"

The servant girl began to cry. The Councilor was the only one who showed presence of mind.

"We must break in a windowpane at the grocer's downstairs!" he said, "get him up, and then we can get into the building."

He broke one pane; he broke two. "Petersen!" he shouted, as the put the handle of his umbrella in through the windowpanes. Whereupon the grocer's daughter began to scream loudly. The grocer threw open the door of his shop and shouted, "Watchman!" And before he had a chance to see and recognize the Councilor's family and let them in, the watchman blew his whistle, and in the next street another watchman answered and whistled. People appeared in the windows. "Where is the fire? Where is the cause of all the excitement?" they asked, and were still asking such questions even after the Councilor was in his room. There he removed his overcoat—and in it lay the gate key, not in the pocket, but inside the lining; it had slipped through a hole that should not have been in the pocket.

From that night on, the gate key held a unique and great importance, not only when it was taken out in the evening, but also when remaining at home, for in either case the Councilor would show how clever he was by making the key answer questions. He would think of the most likely answer and then pretend to let the key give it. Finally, he himself came to believe in the power of the key.

That was not so of the Pharmacist, however, a young man closely related to the Councilor's wife. The Pharmacist had a good head, a critical mind; he had, as mere schoolboy, sent in critical articles on books and the theater, but without his signature, which is always important. He was what one calls a bel esprit, but he by no means believed in spirits, and, least of all, key spirits.

"Yes, I believe, I believe," he said, "blessed Mr. Councilor, I believe in gate keys and all key spirits as firmly as I believe in that new science which is beginning to become known the table dance and the spirits in old and new furniture. Have you heard about that? I have! I have doubted—you know I am a skeptic—but I have been converted by reading, in a quite reliable foreign paper, a dreadful story. Councilor, can you imagine! I will give you the story as I read it. Two clever children had seen their parents raise the spirits in a large dining-room table. The little ones were alone, and decided they would try, in the same manner, to rub life into an old chest of drawers. Life came, for a spirit was awakened; but it did not tolerate the commands of mere children; it arose, and the chest of drawers creaked; it then shot out the drawers, and with its wooden legs put each of the children in a separate drawer. The chest of drawers then ran off with them, out the open door, down the stairs, into the street, and over to the canal, where it jumped out into the water and drowned both the children. Their little bodies were given Christian burial, but the chest of drawers was taken to the town hall, tried for murder, and burned alive in the market place! I have read this," said the Pharmacist, "in a foreign paper; it is not something I have invented myself. This is the truth, and may the key take me if it isn't! I swear to it—on my oath!"

The Councilor found that such talk was all too much like a coarse joke. The two could never speak agreeably about the key. The Pharmacist was key ignorant.

The Councilor made progress in his key knowledge; the key was his diversion and channel of wisdom.

One evening, as the Councilor was getting ready to go to bed, and was half undressed, there was a knock on the front door. It was the shopkeeper from downstairs who was calling at this late hour; he, too, was half undressed, but he had suddenly had a thought, he said, which he was afraid he would not be able to retain through the night.

"It is my daughter Lotte-Lene I must talk about. She is a beautiful girl, and has been confirmed, and now I would like to see her well provided for."

"But I am not as yet a widower!" said the Councilor, and chuckled, "and I have no son to offer her."

"You must understand me, Councilor," said the man from downstairs. "She can play the piano, and she can sing; you must be able to hear her upstairs. You have no idea of all the things that little girl is able to do; she can talk and entertain people. She is made for the stage, and that is a good course for pretty girls of good families to take; they may even have an opportunity to marry a count, though neither I nor Lotte-Lene are thinking of that. She can indeed sing and play the piano, so the other day I took her up to the singing school. She sang; but she doesn't have a beer bass, as I call it in women, nor does she shriek those very high canary-bird notes which they now demand in singers, and so they advised her strongly against pursuing that career. Well, I thought, if she can't become a singer, she can always become an actress; that only requires the ability to speak. Today I talked about it to the Instructor as they call him. 'Is she well read?' he asked. 'No,' I said, 'not at all.' 'But it is necessary for an actress to be well read!' said he. She still has time for that, was my opinion; and then I went home. She can go to a rental library and read what is to be had there, I thought.

"But then tonight, while I was undressing, it occurred to me—why rent books when one can borrow them? The Councilor has plenty of books; let her read them; there is enough reading here for her, and it could be hers gratis!"

"Lotte-Lene is a nice girl," said the Councilor, "a beautiful girl! She shall have books to read. But has she what one calls grit and spirit—aptitude—genius? And, what is equally important, has she luck with her?"

"She has twice won in the lottery," said the grocer from downstairs. "Once she won a clothes cabinet, and another time six pairs of bed sheets; that I call luck, and that she has!"

"I shall ask the key," said the Councilor. And he placed the key on his right forefinger, and on the grocer's right forefinger as well, and then the key swung and gave out letter after letter.

The key said, "Victory and luck!" And so Lotte-Lene's future was decided.

The Councilor at once gave her two books to read, Dyveke and Knigge's Social Intercourse.

That night marked the beginning of a closer acquaintance between Lotte-Lene and the Councilor and his wife. She would come upstairs to the couple, and the Councilor found her to be a sensible girl; she believed in him and the key. The Councilor's wife saw something childish and innocent in the frankness with which she would at every moment show her great ignorance. The couple was fond of her, he in his way and she in hers, and Lotte-Lene was fond of them.

"It smells so lovely upstairs," Lotte-Lene would say. There was an odor, a fragrance, an apple fragrance, in the hallway, where the Councilor's wife had put away a whole barrel of graystone apples. There was also an incense odor of roses and lavender throughout all the rooms. "There is something refined in that!" Lotte-Lene would say.

Then, too, her eyes were pleased by the many pretty flowers the Councilor's wife always had. Even in the middle of winter, lilacs and cherry-tree slips bloomed here. The leafless twigs were cut off and put into water and in the warm room soon bore leaves and flowers.

"One would have thought that all life was gone from these naked branches, but see how they rise from the dead. It has never occurred to me before," said Lotte-Lene, "how wonderful nature is!"

And the Councilor let her look at his "key book," in which were written strange things the key had said—even about the half of an apple cake that had disappeared from the cupboard on the very evening that the servant girl had had her sweetheart there for a visit. The Councilor had asked his key. "Who has eaten the apple cake, the cat or the sweetheart?" and the key had replied, "The sweetheart." The Councilor had already thought so before asking the key; and the servant girl had confessed, "That cursed key knows everything!"

"Yes, isn't it strange!" said the Councilor. "That key, that key! And about Lotte-Lene it has said, 'Victory and luck.' That we shall see! I swear to it."

"That's wonderful" said Lotte-Lene.

The Councilor's wife was not so confident, but she did not express her doubts when her husband was within hearing distance. She later told Lotte-Lene in confidence that the Councilor, when a young man, had been quite taken with the theater. Had someone pushed him a little in that direction, he surely would have become an actor; his family, however, had pushed him in the opposite direction. But, he had still aspired to the stage, and to further that ambition he had written a play.

"This is a great secret that I am entrusting you with, little Lotte-Lene. The play was not bad; it was accepted at the Royal Theater, and then hissed out, and no one has since heard of it, for which I am glad. I am his wife and know him. Now you want such a career, too. I wish you all that is good, but I don't think that things will work out as predicted; I don't believe in the gate key."

Lotte-Lene believed in it, and in that belief she was united with the Councilor. Within their hearts they had a mutual understanding, in all honour and chastity.

The girl had many qualifications that the Councilor's wife valued. Lotte-Lene knew how to make starch from potatoes, make silk gloves from old silk stockings, and recover her silk dancing shoes, although she could afford to buy all her clothes new. She had, as the grocer said, pennies in the table drawer and credit notes in her money safe. She would make just the wife for the Pharmacist, thought the Councilor's wife, but she did not say so, and of course didn't permit the key to say anything about it. The Pharmacist was going to settle down soon and have his own pharmacy in one of the nearest and largest provincial towns.

Lotte-Lene was continually reading Dyveke and Knigge's Social Intercourse. She kept the two books for two years, and by the end of that time she had learned one, Dyveke, by heart—all the parts, although she wished to play only one, that of Dyveke; she did not, however, want to appear at first in the capital, where there is so much envy, and where they would not have her, anyway. She wanted to start her artistic career, as the Councilor called it, in one of the country's large provincial towns. Now that, strangely enough, turned out to be the same place where the youthful Pharmacist had settled down as the youngest of the town's pharmacists.

The great, long-awaited night came on which Lotte-Lene was to make her debut and have "victory and luck," as the key had said. The Councilor was not there, for he lay in his bed, and his wife was nursing him; he had to have warm napkins and camomile tea; the napkins about his body and the tea in his body.

While the couple was absent from the Dyveke performance, the Pharmacist was there, and wrote a letter about it to his relative, the Councilor's wife.

"Dyveke's ruff was the best thing about it," he wrote. "If I had had the Councilor's gate key in my pocket, I would have pulled it out and used it as a whistle; she deserved it, and the key deserved it, because of its nasty lie about her 'victory and luck.'"

The Councilor read the letter. It was all spitefulness, he said, key hatred, aimed at that innocent girl. And as soon as he was out of bed and was himself again, he sent a short but poisonous note to the Pharmacist, who in turn replied as if he had seen only jest and good humour in the whole epistle. He thanked him for this and for any future contribution to the revelation of the incomparable worth and significance of keys; next he confided to the Councilor that, apart from his activities as an apothecary, he was writing a great key novel in which all the characters were keys and keys alone. A gate key naturally was the central character and—patterned after the Councilor's gate key—was gifted with prophetic vision and second sight; around this all the other keys had to revolve—the old chamberlain's key, experienced in the splendor and festivity of the court; the watch key, small, refined, and distinguished, but worth only a few pennies at the ironmonger's; the key to the church pew, which counted itself among the clergy, and which, from remaining one night in its keyhole in the church, could see ghosts; the larder key, the wine-cellar key, and the coal-cellar key all appeared, and bowed before, and turned around, the gate key. The sunbeams brightened it into silver, and the wind, that spirit of the earth, entered its body and made it whistle!

It was the key of all keys; it was the Councilor's gate key. It was now the key of the heavenly gate itself; it was the papal key; it was infallible!

"Wickedness!" said the Councilor. "Great wickedness!"

He and the Pharmacist never saw each other again—except once, and that was at the funeral of the Councilor's wife.

She was the first to die. There were sorrow an emptiness in the house. Even the slips of cherry which had thrown out fresh roots and flowers seemed to mourn and fade away; they stood forgotten, for she was not there to tend them.

The Councilor and the Pharmacist walked behind her coffin, side by side, as the two nearest relations of the departed. This was not the time, nor were they in the mood, for quarreling. Lotte-Lene tied the mourning crape around the Councilor's hat. She was living in the house again, having long since returned without victory and luck in her career. Yet that still might come; Lotte-Lene had a future before her; the key had said so, and the Councilor had said so.

She went up to him. They talked about the departed and they wept, for Lotte-Lene was tenderhearted; but when they talked about the art, Lotte-Lene felt strong. "Life in the theater is charming," she said, "but there is so much nonsense and envy! I would rather go my own way. Myself first, then art!"

Knigge had told the truth in his chapter about actors; that she was aware of; the key had not told the truth, but she never spoke of this to the Councilor; she was fond of him. Besides, the gate key was his comfort and relief during the whole year of mourning. He gave it questions, and it gave him answers.

And when the year had passed, and he and Lotte-Lene were sitting together one inspiring evening; he asked the key, "Will I marry, and whom will I marry?" No one pushed him, but he pushed the key, and it answered, "Lotte-Lene!"

So it was said, and Lotte-Lene became Mrs. Councilor.

"Victory and luck!"

And these words had been said before—by the gate key.

The Flea and the Professor

Translated by Mrs. H. P. Paull

There was once an aëronaut with whom things went badly; the balloon burst, tumbled the man out, and broke into bits. His boy he had two minutes before sent down with a parachute—that was the boy's luck; he was unhurt and went about with knowledge enough to make him an aëronaut too, but he had no balloon and no means of acquiring one.

But live he must, and so he applied himself to the art of legerdemain and to talking in his stomach; in fact he became a ventriloquist, as they say. He was young, good-looking, and when he got a moustache and had his best clothes on, he could be taken for a nobleman's son. The ladies seemed to think well of him; one young lady even was so taken with his charms and his great dexterity that she went off with him to foreign parts. There he called himself Professor—he could scarcely do less.

His constant thought was how to get himself a balloon and go up into the air with his little wife, but as yet they had no means.

"They'll come yet," said he.

"If only they would," said she.

"We are young folks," said he, "and now I am Professor." She helped him faithfully, sat at the door and sold tickets to the exhibition, and it was a chilly sort of pleasure in winter time. She also helped him in the line of his art. He put his wife in a table-drawer, a large table-drawer; then she crawled into the back part of the drawer, and so was not in the front part—quite an optical illusion to the audience. But one evening when he drew the drawer out, she was also out of sight to him: she was not in the front drawer, not in the back one either, not in the house itself—nowhere to be seen or heard—that was her feat of legerdemain, her entertainment. She never came back again; she was tired of it all, and he grew tired of it, lost his good-humour, could not laugh or make jokes;—and so the people stopped coming, his earnings became scanty, his clothes gave out; and finally he only owned a great flea, which his wife had left him, and so he thought highly of it. And he dressed the flea and taught it to perform, to present arms and to fire a cannon off—but it was a little cannon.

The Professor was proud of the flea, and the flea was proud of himself; he had learned something, and had human blood, and had been besides to the largest cities, had been seen by princes and princesses, had received their high praise, and it was printed in the newspapers and on placards. Plainly it was a very famous flea and could support a Professor and his entire family.

The flea was proud and famous, and yet when he and the Professor travelled they took fourth-class carriages on the railway; they went just as quickly as the first class. They were betrothed to each other; it was a private engagement that would never come out; they never would marry, the flea would remain a bachelor and the Professor a widower. That made it balance.

"Where one has the best luck," said the Professor, "there one ought to go twice." He was a good judge of character, and that is also a science of itself. At last he had travelled over all countries except the wild ones, and so he wanted to go there. They eat Christian men there, to be sure, the Professor knew, but then he was not properly Christian and the flea was not properly a man, so he thought they might venture to travel there and have good success.

They travelled by steamship and by sailing vessel; the flea performed his tricks, and so they got a free passage on the way and arrived at the wild country. Here reigned a little Princess. She was only eight years old, but she was reigning. She had taken away the power from her father and mother, for she had a will, and then she was extraordinarily beautiful—and rude.

Just as soon as the flea had presented arms and fired off the cannon, she was so enraptured with him that she said, "Him or nobody!" She became quite wild with love and was already wild in other ways.

"Sweet, little, sensible child!" said her own father. "If one could only first make a man of him!"

"Leave that to me, old man," said she, and that was not well said by a little Princess when talking with her father, but she was wild. She set the flea on her white hand.

"Now you are a man, reigning with me, but you shall do what I want you to, or else i'll kill you and eat the Professor." The Professor had a great hall to live in. The walls were made of sugar-cane, and he could lick them, but he was not a sweet-tooth. He had a hammock to sleep in. It was as if he were lying in a balloon, such as he had always wished for himself—that was his constant thought.

The flea lived with the Princess, sat upon her delicate hand and upon her white neck. She had taken a hair from her head and made the Professor tie it to the flea's leg, and so she kept him tied to the great red coral drop which she wore in her ear-tip. What a delightful time the Princess had, and the flea too, she thought, but the Professor was not very comfortable. He was a traveler; he liked to drive from town to town, and read about his perseverance and cleverness in teaching a flea to do what men do. But he got out of and into his hammock, lounged about and had good feeding, fresh bird's-eggs, elephant's eyes and roast giraffe. People that eat men do not live entirely on cooked men—no, that is a great delicacy.

"Shoulder of children with sharp sauce," said the Princess's mother, "is the most delicate."

The Professor was tired of it all and would rather go away from the wild land, but he must have his flea with him, for that was his prodigy, and his bread and butter. How was he to get hold of him? That was no easy matter. He strained all his wits, and then he said,

"Now I have it."

"Princess's Father! grant me a favour. May I summon your subjects to present themselves before your Royal Highness? That is what is called a Ceremony in the high and mighty countries of the world.

"Can I, too, learn to do that?" asked the Princess's father.

"That is not quite proper," replied the Professor; "but I shall teach your wild Fathership to fire a cannon off. It goes off with a bang. One sits high up aloft, and then off it goes or down he comes."

"Let me crack it off!" said the Princess's father. But in all the land there was no cannon except the one the flea had brought, and that was so very small.

"I will cast a bigger one!" said the Professor. "Only give me the means. I must have fine silk stuff, needle and thread, rope and cord, together with cordial drops for the balloon, they blow one up so easily and give one the heaves; they are what make the report in the cannons s inside."

"By all means," said the Princess's father, and gave him what he called for. All the court and the entire population came together to see the great cannon cast. The Professor did not summon them before he had the balloon entirely ready to be filled and go up: The flea sat on the Princess's hand and looked on. The balloon was filled, it bulged out and could scarcely be held down, so violent did it become.

"I must have it up in the air before it can be cooled off," said the Professor, and took his seat in the car which hung below. "But I cannot manage and steer it alone. I must have a skillful companion along to help me. There is no one here that can do that except the flea."

"I am not very willing to let him," said the Princess, but still she reached out and handed the flea to the Professor, who placed him on his hand.

"Let go the cords and ropes," he shouted. "Now the balloon's going." They thought he said "the cannon," and so the balloon went higher and higher, up above the clouds, far away from the wild land.

The little Princess, all the family and the people sat and waited—they are waiting still; and if you do not believe it, just take a journey to the wild land; every child there talks about the Professor and the flea, and believes that they are coming back when the cannon is cooled off; but they will not come, they are at home with us, they are in their native country, they travel on the railway, first class, not fourth; they have good success, a great balloon. Nobody asks how they got their balloon or where it came from: they are rich folks now, quite respectable folks, indeed—the flea and the Professor!

The Pea Blossom

Translated by Mrs. H. P. Paull

There were once five peas in one shell, they were green, the shell was green, and so they believed that the whole world must be green also, which was a very natural conclusion. The shell grew, and the peas grew, they accommodated themselves to their position, and sat all in a row. The sun shone without and warmed the shell, and the rain made it clear and transparent; it was mild and agreeable in broad daylight, and dark at night, as it generally is; and the peas as they sat there grew bigger and bigger, and more thoughtful as they mused, for they felt there must be something else for them to do.

"Are we to sit here forever?" asked one; "shall we not become hard by sitting so long? It seems to me there must be something outside, and I feel sure of it."

And as weeks passed by, the peas became yellow, and the shell became yellow.

"All the world is turning yellow, I suppose," said they—and perhaps they were right.

Suddenly they felt a pull at the shell; it was torn off, and held in human hands, then slipped into the pocket of a jacket in company with other full pods.

"Now we shall soon be opened," said one—just what they all wanted.

"I should like to know which of us will travel furthest," said the smallest of the five; "we shall soon see now."

"What is to happen will happen," said the largest pea.

"Crack" went the shell as it burst, and the five peas rolled out into the bright sunshine. There they lay in a child's hand. A little boy was holding them tightly, and said they were fine peas for his peashooter. And immediately he put one in and shot it out.

"Now I am flying out into the wide world," said he; "catch me if you can;" and he was gone in a moment.

"I," said the second, "intend to fly straight to the sun, that is a shell that lets itself be seen, and it will suit me exactly;" and away he went.

"We will go to sleep wherever we find ourselves," said the two next, "we shall still be rolling onwards;" and they did certainly fall on the floor, and roll about before they got into the pea-shooter; but they were put in for all that. "We shall go farther than the others," said they.

"What is to happen will happen," exclaimed the last, as he was shot out of the pea-shooter; and as he spoke he flew up against an old board under a garret-window, and fell into a little crevice, which was almost filled up with moss and soft earth. The moss closed itself round him, and there he lay, a captive indeed, but not unnoticed by God.

"What is to happen will happen," said he to himself.

Within the little garret lived a poor woman, who went out to clean stoves, chop wood into small pieces and perform such-like hard work, for she was strong and industrious. Yet she remained always poor, and at home in the garret lay her only daughter, not quite grown up, and very delicate and weak. For a whole year she had kept her bed, and it seemed as if she could neither live nor die.

"She is going to her little sister," said the woman; "I had but the two children, and it was not an easy thing to support both of them;

but the good God helped me in my work, and took one of them to Himself and provided for her. Now I would gladly keep the other that was left to me, but I suppose they are not to be separated, and my sick girl will very soon go to her sister above." But the sick girl still remained where she was, quietly and patiently she lay all the day long, while her mother was away from home at her work.

Spring came, and one morning early the sun shone brightly through the little window, and threw its rays over the floor of the room. just as the mother was going to her work, the sick girl fixed her gaze on the lowest pane of the window—"Mother," she exclaimed, "what can that little green thing be that peeps in at the window? It is moving in the wind."

The mother stepped to the window and half opened it. "Oh!" she said, "there is actually a little pea which has taken root and is putting out its green leaves. How could it have got into this crack? Well now, here is a little garden for you to amuse yourself with." So the bed of the sick girl was drawn nearer to the window, that she might see the budding plant; and the mother went out to her work.

"Mother, I believe I shall get well," said the sick child in the evening, "the sun has shone in here so brightly and warmly today, and the little pea is thriving so well: I shall get on better, too, and go out into the warm sunshine again."

"God grant it!" said the mother, but she did not believe it would be so. But she propped up with the little stick the green plant which had given her child such pleasant hopes of life, so that it might not be broken by the winds; she tied the piece of string to the window-sill and to the upper part of the frame, so that the pea-tendrils might twine round it when it shot up. And it did shoot up, indeed it might almost be seen to grow from day to day.

"Now really here is a flower coming," said the old woman one morning, and now at last she began to encourage the hope that her sick daughter might really recover. She remembered that for some time the child had spoken more cheerfully, and during the last few days had raised herself in bed in the morning to look with sparkling eyes at her little garden which contained only a single pea-plant. A week after, the invalid sat up for the first time a whole hour, feeling quite happy by the open window in the warm sunshine, while outside grew the little plant, and on it a pink pea-blossom in full bloom. The little maiden bent down and gently kissed the delicate leaves. This day was to her like a festival.

"Our heavenly Father Himself has planted that pea, and made it grow and flourish, to bring joy to you and hope to me, my blessed child," said the happy mother, and she smiled at the flower, as if it had been an angel from God.

But what became of the other peas? Why the one who flew out into the wide world, and said, "Catch me if you can," fell into a gutter on the roof of a house, and ended his travels in the crop of a pigeon. The two lazy ones were carried quite as far, for they also were eaten by pigeons, so they were at least of some use; but the fourth, who wanted to reach the sun, fell into a sink and lay there in the dirty water for days and weeks, till he had swelled to a great size.

"I am getting beautifully fat," said the pea, "I expect I shall burst at last; no pea could do more that that, I think; I am the most remarkable of all the five which were in the shell." And the sink confirmed the opinion.

But the young maiden stood at the open garret window, with sparkling eyes and the rosy hue of health on her cheeks, she folded her thin hands over the pea-blossom, and thanked God for what He had done.

"I," said the sink, "shall stand up for my pea."